# STAR TREK®
## D E S T I N Y

# STAR TREK®
## D E S T I N Y

## DAVID MACK

Based upon STAR TREK and

STAR TREK: THE NEXT GENERATION®
created by Gene Roddenberry

STAR TREK: DEEP SPACE NINE®
created by Rick Berman & Michael Piller

STAR TREK: VOYAGER®
created by Rick Berman & Michael Piller & Jeri Taylor

STAR TREK: ENTERPRISE®
created by Rick Berman & Brannon Braga

### G

GALLERY BOOKS

New York   London   Toronto   Sydney   New Delhi

SF
MAC

Gallery Books
A Division of Simon & Schuster, Inc.
1230 Avenue of the Americas
New York, NY 10020

First Gallery Books trade paperback edition March 2012

GALLERY BOOKS and colophon are registered trademarks of Simon & Schuster, Inc.

For information about special discounts for bulk purchases,
please contact Simon & Schuster Special Sales at
1-866-506-1949 or business@simonandschuster.com.

The Simon & Schuster Speakers Bureau can bring authors to your
live event. For more information or to book an event, contact the
Simon & Schuster Speakers Bureau at 1-866-248-3049 or visit our
website at www.simonspeakers.com.

Manufactured in the United States of America

10  9  8  7  6  5  4  3  2  1

ISBN 978-1-4516-5724-1

*For friends now gone but never forgotten*

# CONTENTS

# BOOK I

# GODS OF NIGHT

# HISTORIAN'S NOTE

The prologue takes place in 2373 (Old Calendar), roughly one week after the events of the *Star Trek: Deep Space Nine* episode "Children of Time." The main narrative of *Gods of Night* takes place in February of 2381, approximately sixteen months after the movie *Star Trek Nemesis*. The flashback portions begin in 2156 and continue through 2168.

*Der Krieg findet immer einen Ausweg.*
(War always finds a way.)

—Bertolt Brecht,
*Mother Courage and Her Children,* sc. 6

# 2373

## PROLOGUE

It was a lifeless husk—its back broken, its skin rent, its mammoth form half buried in the shifting sands of a mountainous dune—and it was even more beautiful than Jadzia Dax remembered.

Her second host, Tobin Dax, had watched the Earth starship *Columbia* NX-02 leave its spacedock more than two hundred years earlier, on what no one then had realized would be its final mission; Tobin had directed the calibration of its starboard warp coils. A pang of sad nostalgia colored Jadzia's thoughts as she stood on the grounded vessel's bow and gazed at its shattered starboard nacelle, which had buckled at its midpoint and lay partially reclaimed by the dry waves of the desert.

Engineers from *Defiant* swarmed over the primary hull of the *Columbia*. They took tricorder readings in between shielding their faces from the scouring lash of a sand-laced sirocco. Behind them lay the delicate peaks of a desolate landscape, a vista of wheat-colored dunes shaped by an unceasing tide of anabatic winds, barren and lonely beneath a blanched sky.

Jadzia counted herself lucky that Captain Sisko had been willing to approve another planetary survey so soon after she had accidentally led them into peril on Gaia, where eight thousand lives had since been erased from history on a lover's capricious whim. Though the crew was eager to return to Deep Space 9 as quickly as possible, Dax's curiosity was always insatiable once aroused, and a flicker of a sensor reading had drawn her to this unnamed, uninhabited planet.

A sudden gust whipped her long, dark ponytail over her shoulder. She swatted it away from her face as she squinted into the blinding crimson flare of the rising suns. Adding to the brightness was a shimmer of light with a humanoid shape, a few meters away from her. The high-pitched drone of the transporter beam was drowned out by a wailing of wind in minor chords.

As the sound and shine faded away, the silhouette of Benjamin Sisko strode toward her across the buckled hull plates.

"Quite a find, Old Man," he said, his mood subdued. Under normal circumstances he would have been elated by a discovery such as this, but the sting of recent events was too fresh and the threat of war too imminent for any of them to take much joy in it. He looked around and then asked, "How're things going?"

"Slowly," Dax said. "Our loadout was for recon, not salvage." She started walking and nodded for him to follow her. "We're seeing some unusual subatomic damage in the hull. Not sure what it means yet. All we know for sure is the *Columbia*'s been here for about two hundred years." They reached the forward edge of the primary hull, where the force of impact had peeled back the metallic skin of the starship to reveal its duranium spaceframe. There *Defiant*'s engineers had installed a broad ramp on a shallow incline, because the ship's original personnel hatches were all choked with centuries of windblown sand.

As they descended into the ship, Sisko asked, "Have you been able to identify any of the crew?" Echoes of their footfalls were muffled, trapped in the hollow beneath the ramp.

"We haven't found any bodies," Dax said, talking over the atonal cries of wind snaking through the *Columbia*'s corridors. "No remains of any kind." Her footsteps scraped across grit-covered deck plates as she led him toward the ship's core.

A dusty haze in the air was penetrated at irregular angles by narrow beams of sunlight that found their way through the dark wreckage. As they moved farther from the sparse light and deeper into the murky shadows of D Deck, Dax thought she saw brief flashes of bluish light, moving behind the bent bulkheads at the edges of her vision. When she turned her head to look for them, however, she found only darkness, and she dismissed the flickers as residual images fooling her retinas as her eyes adapted to the darkness near the ship's core.

"Is it possible," Sisko asked, stepping over the curved obstacle of a collapsed bulkhead brace, "they abandoned ship and settled somewhere on the planet?"

"Maybe," Dax said. "But most of their gear is still on board." She pushed past a tangle of fallen cables and held it aside for Sisko as he followed her. "This desert goes on for nine hundred kilometers in every direction," she continued. "Between you and me, I don't think they'd have gotten very far with just the clothes on their backs."

"That's a good point, but I think it's moot," Sisko said as they rounded a curve into a length of corridor draped with cobwebs, and disturbed a thick brood of small but lethal-looking indigenous arthropods. The ten-legged creatures rapidly scurried into the cracks between the bulkheads and the deck. He and Dax continued walking. "I don't expect to find survivors from a two-hundred-year-old wreck, but I *would* like to know what an old Warp 5 Earth ship is doing in the Gamma Quadrant."

"That makes two of us," Dax said as they turned another corner toward a dead end, where Miles O'Brien hunched beneath a low-hanging tangle of wires and antiquated circuit boards—the remains of a control panel for the *Columbia*'s main computer. "Chief," Dax called out, announcing their approach. "Any luck?"

"Not yet," said the stout engineer. His tightly cut, curly fair hair was matted with sweat and dust. The two officers stepped up behind him as he continued in his gruff Irish brogue, "It's a damned museum piece is what it is. Our tricorders can't talk to it, and I can't find an adapter in *Defiant*'s databases that'll fit these inputs."

Sisko leaned in beside O'Brien, supporting himself with his right hand on the chief's left shoulder. Dax hovered behind O'Brien's right side. The captain stroked his wiry goatee once and said, "Are the memory banks intact?"

O'Brien started to chortle, then caught himself. "Well, they're here," he said. "Whether they work, who knows? I can't even power them up with the parts we have on hand."

Dax asked, "How long will it take to make an adapter?"

"Just for power?" O'Brien said. "Three hours, maybe four. I'd have to do some research to make it work with our EPS grid." He turned away from the Gordian knot of electronics to face Dax and Sisko. "Getting at its data's gonna be the real challenge. Nobody's worked with a core like this in over a century."

"Give me a number, Chief," Sisko said. "How long?"

O'Brien shrugged. "A couple days, at least."

Sisko's jaw tightened, and the worry lines on his brown forehead grew deeper as he expressed his disapproval with a frown. "That's not the answer I was looking for," he said.

"Best I can do," O'Brien said.

With a heavy sigh and a slump of his shoulders, Sisko seemed to surrender to the inevitable. "Fine," he said. "Keep at it, Chief. Let us know if you make any progress."

"Aye, sir," O'Brien said, and he turned back to his work.

Dax and Sisko returned the way they'd come, and they were met at the intersection by Major Kira. The Bajoran woman had been in charge of the search teams looking for the crew's remains. Her rose-colored militia uniform was streaked with dark gray smears of dirt and grime, and a faint speckling of dust clung to her short, close-cropped red hair. "We finished our sweep," she said, her eyes darting nervously back down the corridor. "There's no sign of the crew, or anyone else."

"What about combat damage?" asked Sisko. "Maybe they were boarded and captured."

Kira shook her head quickly. "I don't think so. All the damage I saw fits with a crash-landing. There are no blast effects on the internal bulkheads, no marks from weapons fire. Whatever happened here, it *wasn't* a firefight." Nodding forward toward the route to the exit, she added, "Can we get out of here now?"

"What's wrong, Major?" asked Sisko, whose attention had sharpened in response to Kira's apparent agitation.

The Bajoran woman cast another fearful look down the corridor behind her and frowned as she turned back toward Sisko and Dax. "There's something in here," she said. "I can't explain it, but I can *feel* it." Glaring suspiciously at the overhead, she added, "There's a *borhyas* watching us."

Sisko protested, "A ghost?" As tolerant as he tried to be of Kira's religious convictions, he sometimes grew exasperated with her willingness to embrace superstition. "Are you really telling me you think this ship is haunted?"

"I don't know," Kira said, seemingly frustrated at having to justify her instincts to her friends. "But I heard things, and I felt the hairs on my neck stand up, and I keep seeing blinks of light in the dark—"

Dax cut in, "Blue flashes?"

"Yes!" Kira said, sounding excited by Dax's confirmation.

Sisko shook his head and resumed walking forward. "I've heard enough," he said. "Let's get back to *Defiant*."

Kira and Dax fell into step behind him, and they walked back into the compartment through which they had entered the

*Columbia.* Sisko moved at a quickstep, and Dax had to work to keep pace with him as he headed for the ramp topside.

"Benjamin," Dax said, "I think we need to make a more detailed study of this ship. If I had a little more time, maybe the chief and I could find a way to use *Defiant*'s tractor beams to lift the *Columbia* back to orbit and—" She was cut off by a chirping from Sisko's combadge, followed by Worf's voice.

"*Defiant to Captain Sisko,*" Worf said over the comm.

Sisko answered without breaking stride. "Go ahead."

"*Long-range sensors have detected two Jem'Hadar warships approaching this system,*" Worf said. "*ETA nine minutes.*"

"Sound Yellow Alert and start beaming up the engineers," Sisko said as he climbed the ramp into the blaze of daylight. "Wait for my order to beam up the command team."

"*Acknowledged,*" Worf replied. "*Defiant out.*"

Back atop the crash-deformed hull, Sisko stopped and turned toward Dax. "Sorry, Old Man. The salvage has to wait."

Kira asked, "Should we plant demolitions?" Dax and Sisko reacted with confused expressions, prompting Kira to elaborate, "To prevent the Jem'Hadar from capturing the ship."

"I doubt they'll find much more than we did," Sisko said. "*Columbia*'s over two hundred years old, Major—and technically, it's not even a Federation vessel." He lifted his arm to shade his eyes from the morning suns. "Besides, it's kept its secrets this long. I think we can leave it be."

Dax watched him walk away toward the apex of the primary hull. All around him, in groups of four or five, teams of engineers faded away in luminescent shimmers, transported back to the orbiting *Defiant.* The outline of Sisko's body dissolved in the suns' glare until the captain was just a stick figure in front of a sky of fire. Kira walked beside him on his right, as familiar and comfortable as someone who had always been there.

Sisko's voice emanated from Dax's combadge. "*Command team, stand by to beam up.*"

The broken gray majesty of the *Columbia* lay beneath Dax's feet, an empty tomb harboring secrets untold. It pained her to abandon its mysteries before she'd had time to unravel them . . . but the Dominion was on the move, and war made its own demands.

# 2381

## 1

Captain Ezri Dax stood on the bow of the *Columbia* and made a silent wish that returning to the wreck wouldn't prove to be a mistake, at a time when Starfleet couldn't afford any.

Engineers and science specialists from her crew swarmed over the derelict Warp 5 vessel. Its husk was half interred by the tireless shifting of the desert, much as she had remembered it from her last visit, as Jadzia Dax, more than seven years earlier. The afternoon suns beat down with an almost palpable force, and shimmering waves of heat distortion rippled above the wreck's sand-scoured hull, which coruscated with reflected light. Dax's hands, normally cold like those of other joined Trill, were warm and slick with perspiration.

Lieutenant Gruhn Helkara, Dax's senior science officer on the *Starship Aventine,* ascended the ramp through the rent in the hull and approached her with a smile. It was an expression not often seen on the skinny Zakdorn's droop-ridged face.

"Good news, Captain," he said as soon as he was within polite conversational distance. "The converter's working. Leishman's powering up the *Columbia*'s computer now. I thought you might want to come down and have a look."

"No thanks, Gruhn," Dax said. "I'd prefer to stay topside."

One of the advantages of being a captain was that Ezri no longer had to explain herself to her shipmates if she didn't want to. It spared her the potential embarrassment of admitting that her walk-through of the *Columbia* earlier that day had left her profoundly creeped out. While touring D Deck, she'd been all but certain that she saw the same spectral blue flashes that had lurked along the edges of her vision seven years earlier.

To her silent chagrin, multiple sensor sweeps and tricorder checks had detected nothing out of the ordinary on the *Columbia*. Maybe it had been just her imagination or a trick of the light, but she'd felt the same galvanic tingle on her skin that Kira had described, and she'd been overcome by a desire to get out of the wreck's stygian corridors as quickly as possible.

She'd doubled the security detail on the planet but had said nothing about thinking the ship might be haunted. One of the drawbacks of being a captain was the constant need to maintain a semblance of rationality, and seeing ghosts didn't fit the bill— not one bit.

Helkara squinted at the scorched-white sky and palmed a sheen of sweat from his high forehead, up through his thatch of black hair. "By the gods," he said, breaking their long, awkward silence, "did it actually get *hotter* out here?"

"Yes," Dax said, "it did." She nodded toward the bulge of the ship's bridge module. "Walk with me." The duo strolled up the gentle slope of the *Columbia*'s hull as she continued. "Where are you with the metallurgical analysis?"

"Almost done, sir. You were—" He caught himself. "Sorry. *Jadzia* Dax was right. We've detected molecular distortion in the spaceframe consistent with intense subspatial stress."

Dax was anxious for details. "What was the cause?"

"Hard to be sure," Helkara said.

She frowned. "In other words, you don't know."

"Well, I'm not prepared to make *that* admission yet. I may not have enough data to form a hypothesis, but my tests have ruled out several obvious answers."

"Such as?"

"Extreme warp velocities," Helkara said as they detoured around a large crevasse where two adjacent hull plates had buckled violently inward. "Wormholes. Quantum slipstream vortices. Iconian gateways. Time travel. Oh, and the Q."

She sighed. "Doesn't leave us much to go on."

"No, it doesn't," he said. "But I love a challenge."

Dax could tell that he was struggling not to outpace her. His legs were longer than hers, and he tended to walk briskly. She quickened her step. "Keep at it, Gruhn," she said as they reached the top of the saucer. "Something moved this ship clear across the galaxy. I need to know what it was, and I need to know soon."

"Understood, Captain." Helkara continued aft, toward a gaggle of engineers who were assembling a bulky assortment of machinery that would conduct a more thorough analysis of the *Columbia*'s bizarrely distressed subatomic structures.

Memories drifted through Ezri's thoughts like sand devils over the dunes. Jadzia had detailed the profound oddities that the *Defiant*'s sensors had found in the *Columbia*'s hull, and she had informed Starfleet of her theory that the readings might be a clue to a new kind of subspatial phenomenon. Admiral Howe at Starfleet Research and Development had assured her that her report would be investigated, but when the Dominion War erupted less than two months later, her call for the salvage of the *Columbia* had been sidelined—relegated to a virtual dustbin of defunct projects at Starfleet Command.

And it stayed there, forgotten for almost eight years, until Ezri Dax gave Starfleet a reason to remember it. The salvage of the *Columbia* had just become a priority for the same reason that it had been scuttled: there was a war on. Seven years ago the enemy had been the Dominion. This time it was the Borg.

Five weeks earlier the attacks had begun, bypassing all of the Federation's elaborate perimeter defenses and early warning networks. Without any sign of transwarp activity, wormholes, or gateways, Borg cubes had appeared in the heart of Federation space and launched surprise attacks on several worlds. The *Aventine* had found itself in its first-ever battle, defending the Acamar system from eradication by the Borg. When the fighting was over, more than a third of the ship's crew—including its captain and first officer—had perished, leaving second officer Lieutenant Commander Ezri Dax in command.

One week and three Borg attacks later, Starfleet made Ezri captain of the *Aventine.* By then she'd remembered Jadzia's hypothesis about the *Columbia,* and she reminded Starfleet of her seven-year-old report that a Warp 5 ship had, in the roughly ten years after it had disappeared, somehow journeyed more than seventy-five thousand light-years—a distance that it would have taken the *Columbia* more than three hundred fifty years to traverse under its own power.

Ezri had assured Starfleet Command that solving the mystery of how the *Columbia* had crossed the galaxy without using any of the known propulsion methods could shed some light on how the Borg had begun doing the same thing. It had been a bit of an exaggeration on her part. She couldn't promise that her crew would be able to make a conclusive determination of how the *Columbia* had found its way to this remote, desolate resting place, or that there would be any link whatsoever to the latest series of Borg incursions of Federation space. It had apparently taken the *Columbia* years to get here, while the Borg seemed to be making nearly instantaneous transits from their home territory in the Delta Quadrant. The connection was tenuous at best.

All Dax had was a hunch, and she was following it. If she was right, it would be a brilliant beginning for her first command. If she was wrong, this would probably be her last command.

Her moment of introspection was broken by a soft vibration and a melodious double tone from her combadge. *"Aventine to Captain Dax,"* said her first officer, Commander Sam Bowers.

"Go ahead, Sam," she said.

He sounded tired. *"We just got another priority message from Starfleet Command,"* he said. *"I think you might want to take this one. It's Admiral Nechayev, and she wants a reply."*

*And the axe falls*, Dax brooded. "All right, Sam, beam me up. I'll take it in my ready room."

*"Aye, sir. Stand by for transport."*

Dax turned back to face the bow of the *Columbia* and suppressed the dread she felt at hearing of Nechayev's message. It could be anything: a tactical briefing, new information from Starfleet Research and Development about the *Columbia*, updated specifications for the *Aventine*'s experimental slipstream drive . . . but Dax knew better than to expect good news.

As she felt herself enfolded by the transporter beam, she feared that once again she would have to abandon the *Columbia* before making its secrets her own.

Commander Sam Bowers hadn't been aboard the *Aventine* long enough to know the names of more than a handful of its more than seven hundred fifty personnel, so he was grateful that Ezri had recruited a number of its senior officers from among her former crewmates on Deep Space 9. He had already accepted Dax's invitation to serve as her first officer when he'd learned that Dr. Simon Tarses would be coming aboard with him, as the ship's new chief medical officer, and that Lieutenant Mikaela Leishman would be transferring from *Defiant* to become the *Aventine*'s new chief engineer.

He tried not to dwell on the fact that their predecessors had all recently been killed in fierce battles with the Borg. Better to focus, he decided, on the remarkable opportunity this transfer represented.

The *Aventine* was one of seven new, experimental *Vesta*-class starships. It had been designed as a multimission explorer, and its state-of-the-art weaponry made it one of the few ships in the fleet able to mount even a moderate defense against the Borg. Its sister ships were defending the Federation's core systems—Sol, Vulcan, Andor, and Tellar—while the *Aventine* made its jaunt through the Bajoran wormhole to this uninhabited world in the Gamma Quadrant, for what Bowers couldn't help but think of as a desperate long shot of a mission.

He turned a corner, expecting to find a turbolift, only to arrive at a dead end. *It's not just the crew you don't know,* he chided himself as he turned back and continued looking for the nearest turbolift junction. *Three weeks aboard and you're still getting turned around on the lower decks. Snap out of it, man.*

The sound of muted conversation led Bowers farther down the corridor. A pair of junior officers, a brown-bearded male Tellarite and an auburn-haired human woman, chatted in somber tones in front of a turbolift portal. The Tellarite glanced at Bowers and stopped talking. His companion peeked past him, saw the reason for his silence, and followed suit. Bowers halted behind the duo, who tried to appear casual and relaxed while also avoiding all eye contact with him.

Bowers didn't take it personally. He had seen this kind of behavior before, during the Dominion War. These two officers had served on the *Aventine* during its battle at Acamar five weeks earlier; more than two hundred and fifty of their shipmates had died in that brief engagement. Now, even though Bowers was the new first officer and a seasoned veteran with nearly twenty-five years of experience in Starfleet, in their eyes he was, before all else, merely one of "the replacements."

*Respect has to be earned,* he reminded himself. *Just be patient.* He caught a fleeting sidelong glance by the Tellarite. "Good morning," Bowers said, trying not to sound too chipper.

The Tellarite ensign was dour. "It's afternoon, sir."

*Well, it's a start,* Bowers told himself. Then the turbolift door opened, and he followed the two junior officers inside. The woman called for a numbered deck in the engineering section, and then Bowers said simply, "Bridge." He felt a bit of guilt for inconveniencing them; he and the two engineers were headed in essentially opposite directions, but because of his rank, billet, and destination, the turbolift hurtled directly to the bridge, with the two younger officers along for the ride.

He glanced back at the young woman with a look of sheepish contrition. "Sorry."

"It's okay, sir, it happens," she replied. The same thing had happened to Bowers countless times when he had been a junior officer. It was just one of many petty irritations that everyone had to learn to cope with while living on a starship.

The doors parted with a soft hiss, and Bowers stepped onto the bridge of the *Aventine,* his demeanor one of pure confidence and authority. The beta-shift bridge officers were at their posts. Soft, semimusical feedback tones from their consoles punctuated the low thrumming of the engines through the deck.

Lieutenant Lonnoc Kedair, the ship's chief of security, occupied the center seat at the aft quarter of the bridge. The statuesque Takaran woman stood and relinquished the chair as Bowers approached from her left. "Sir."

He nodded. "I'm ready to relieve you, Lieutenant." A more formal approach to bridge protocol had been one of Bowers's conditions for accepting the job, and Captain Dax had agreed.

"I'm ready to be relieved, sir," Kedair replied, following the old-fashioned protocol for a changing of the watch. She picked up a padd from the arm of the command seat and handed the slim device to Bowers. "Salvage operations for the *Columbia* are proceeding on schedule," she continued. "No contacts in sensor range and all systems nominal, though there have been some reports from the planet's surface that I want to check out."

Bowers looked up from the padd. "What kind of reports?"

A wince creased her scaly face. "The kind that make me think our teams are more fatigued than they're letting on."

He tabbed through a few screens of data on the padd to find the communication logs from the away teams on the planet. "What gives you that impression?"

"A pair of incident reports, filed eleven hours apart, each by a different engineer." She seemed embarrassed to continue. "They claim the wreck of the *Columbia* is haunted, sir."

"Maybe it is," Bowers said with a straight face. "Lord knows I've seen stranger things than that."

Kedair's face turned a darker shade of green. "I don't plan to indulge the crew's belief in the supernatural. I just want to make certain none of our engineers have become delusional."

"Fair enough," Bowers said. He glanced backward over his shoulder. "Is the captain in her ready room?"

"Aye, sir," Kedair said. "She's been on the comm with Admiral Nechayev for the better part of the last half hour."

*That doesn't bode well,* Bowers realized. "Very good," he said to Kedair. "Lieutenant, I relieve you."

"I stand relieved," Kedair said. "Permission to go ashore, sir?"

"Granted. But keep it brief, we might need you back on the watch for gamma shift."

She nodded. "Understood, sir." Then she turned and moved in quick, lanky strides to the turbolift.

No sooner had Bowers settled into the center seat than a double chirrup from the overhead speaker preceded Captain Dax's voice: *"Dax to Commander Bowers. Please report to my ready room."* The channel clicked off. Bowers stood and straightened his tunic before he turned to the beta-shift tactical officer, a Deltan woman who had caught his eye every day since he had come aboard. "Lieutenant Kandel," he said in a dry, professional tone, "you have the conn."

"Aye, sir," Kandel replied. She nodded to a junior officer at the auxiliary tactical station. The young man moved to take over Kandel's post as she crossed the bridge to occupy the center seat. It all transpired with smooth, quiet efficiency.

*Like clockwork,* Bowers mused with satisfaction.

He walked toward Dax's ready room. The portal slid open as he neared, and it closed behind him after he'd entered. Captain Dax stood behind her desk and gazed through a panoramic window of transparent aluminum at the dusky sphere of the planet below.

Though he'd known Dax for years, Bowers still marveled at how young she looked. Ezri was more than a dozen years his junior, and he had to remind himself sometimes that the Dax symbiont living inside her—whose consciousness was united with hers—gave her the resources of several lifetimes, the benefit of hundreds of years of experience.

Since they were alone, Bowers dropped the air of formality that he maintained in front of the crew. "What's goin' on? Is Starfleet pulling the plug on us?"

"They might as well be," Dax said. She sighed and turned to face him. She sounded annoyed. "We have twenty-four hours to finish our salvage and head back to the wormhole. Admiral Jellico wants us to be part of the fleet defending Trill."

"Why the change of plans?"

Dax entered commands into her desktop's virtual interface with a few gentle taps. A holographic projection appeared above the desk. According to the identification tags along its bottom, it was a visual sensor log from the Starfleet vessel *U.S.S. Amargosa*. There wasn't much to see—just a brief, colorful volley of weapons fire with a Borg cube followed by a flash of light, a flurry of gray static, and then nothing.

"The *Amargosa* is one of five ships lost in the last sixteen hours," Dax said. "All in the Onias Sector, and all to the Borg. No one knows if the same Borg cube destroyed all five ships."

"If it was the work of one cube, it might be another scout," Bowers said. "Another test of our defenses."

"And if it wasn't," Ezri said, "then the invasion just started— and we're out here, playing in the dirt." She shook her head in frustration and sat down at her desk. "Either way, we have to break orbit by tomorrow, so we can forget about raising the *Columbia*. We need a new mission profile."

Bowers crossed his arms and ruminated aloud, "Our main objective is to figure out how the *Columbia* got here, and our best chance of doing that is to analyze its computer core. We could beam it up, but then we'd have to re-create its command interfaces here, and that could take days, since it wasn't what we'd planned on. But if Leishman and Helkara's adapters work, we can leave it in situ and download its memory banks by morning."

"And then we can parse the data on our way back," Dax said, finishing his thought. "Not my first choice, but it'll have to do." She looked up at him. "Let's get on it. Before we leave this planet, I want to know what happened to that ship."

In the darkness, there was a hunger.

The need was a silent pain in the blank haze of awareness—a yearning for heat, for life, for solidity.

Mind and presence, the very essence of itself lay trapped in stone, its freedom a dream surrendered and forgotten along with its name and memory.

It was nothing but the unslaked thirst of that moment, unburdened by identity or the obligations of a past. All it knew were paths of least resistance, the push and pull of primal forces, and the icy void at its own core—the all-consuming maw.

For so long there had been nothing but the cold of empty spaces, the weak sustenance of photons. A momentary surge of energy had roused it from a deathly repose and then slipped away, untasted. Now, in a dreamlike blink, it had returned.

At long last it was time.

After aeons of being denied, the hunger would be fed.

# 2156

## 2

"Sensor contacts, bearing one-eight-one, mark seven!"

Captain Erika Hernandez snapped her attention from the line of ships on the main viewer to her alarmed senior tactical officer, Lieutenant Kiona Thayer. "Polarize the hull plating," Hernandez ordered. She was taking no chances. The *Columbia* was a long way from home, escorting a mining convoy home from the Onias Sector, which was the site of the hotly contested intersection of the Romulan Star Empire, the Klingon Empire, and the farthest extremity of Earth-explored space.

A single whoop of the alert klaxon sounded throughout the ship as Hernandez rose from her chair. She took a single step forward, toward the helmsman, Lieutenant Reiko Akagi. "Bring us about," Hernandez said. "Intercept course." She glanced left at her senior communications officer, Ensign Sidra Valerian. "Hail the convoy, tell them to take evasive action."

Thayer looked up from her console. "We can't get a lock on the enemy vessels, Captain. They're jamming our sensors."

"I can't raise the convoy," added Valerian, who turned her desperate stare toward the ships on the viewscreen. Anxiety sharpened her Scottish accent. "Ship-to-ship comms are blocked."

Lieutenant Kalil el-Rashad, the ship's second officer and sciences expert, intensified his efforts at his own console. "I'll try to help you break through it," he said.

"Tactical alert," Hernandez said. She returned to her seat as the turbolift door opened and her first officer, Commander Veronica Fletcher, stepped onto the bridge. The blond New Zealander nodded to Hernandez as she walked past and took over at the unoccupied engineering console directly to Hernandez's right. "Tactical," Hernandez said, "report."

"Signal clearing," Thayer replied. "Six ships, closing at high warp." She looked over her shoulder at the captain. "Romulans."

Valerian made fine adjustments at her panel's controls as she said, "Breaking the scrambler code, Captain. We're intercepting one of their ship-to-ship transmissions." Fear overcame the young woman's training, and her voice wavered as she informed the bridge, "All vessels are being ordered to target us first."

"Arm phase cannons, load torpedoes," Hernandez said. "Number One, tell Major Foyle and his MACOs to lock and load. Helm, all ahead full. Tactical, target the lead Romulan—"

Catastrophic deceleration hurled Hernandez to the deck, pinned her officers to their consoles, and wracked the ship with a groaning crash. Consoles dimmed, and the overhead lights went dark. The throbbing of the engines became a low, falling moan. On the main viewscreen, the long pulls of starlight resolved to a slowly turning starfield, indicating the ship had dropped out of warp and was drifting at sublight.

"Report!" Hernandez shouted as she picked herself up off the deck.

"Command systems aren't responding, Captain," Fletcher said, making futile jabs at her console.

"Valerian," said Hernandez, "patch in the emergency line to engineering, put it on speakers."

A few seconds later, Valerian replied, "Channel open."

"Bridge to engineering," Hernandez said. "Report."

After a few moments of sputtering static on the line, Lieutenant Karl Graylock, the Austrian-born chief engineer, responded, *"Minor damage down here, Captain. Main power's still online, but I don't have any working controls."*

Hernandez sharpened the edge in her voice to mask her deepening concern. "What hit us, Karl?"

*"Nothing from outside,"* Graylock said. *"The last set of readings I saw before we went dark looked like a cascade failure, starting in the communication systems."*

Fletcher cut in, "The intercepted message, Captain. It could've been a Trojan horse, a way to slip a computer virus past our defenses."

"If it was," Hernandez said, "how long to fix it?"

*"We'll have to shut down the whole ship,"* Graylock said. *"Power up the main computer with a portable generator, wipe its command protocols, and restore from the protected backup."*

"I didn't ask for a checklist, Karl, I asked *how long*."

His disgruntled sigh carried clearly over the comm. *"Three, maybe four hours if we—"*

The overhead lights snapped back to full brightness, and every console on the bridge surged back to life. The thrumming of the impulse engines resounded through the bulkheads and deck plates. The bridge officers all checked their consoles.

Fletcher looked more confused than she had before. "We have full power, Captain, but still no command inputs."

Turning in a circle, Hernandez asked, "Is anyone's console responding?" The officers all shook their heads in dismay. Then the resonant pulsing of the engines returned, and the starscape on the main viewer stretched into a tunnel of drifting streaks. "Engineering," Hernandez snapped, "what's going on?"

*"No idea, sir,"* Graylock shouted back, sounding profoundly disturbed by the situation. *"Speed increasing. Warp three . . . warp four . . . warp five, Captain!"*

Thayer recoiled from her console as if it were demonically possessed. "Torpedo launchers powering up, sir!" Staring in horror at the panel, she added, "We're targeting the convoy!"

"Karl, shut down main power!" Hernandez shouted. "Hurry!"

From the helm, Akagi called out, "We're on an intercept course for the convoy, Captain."

Hernandez sensed what was happening, felt it like a cold twist in her gut. It was all unfolding so quickly, and she felt as if she were drugged, too slow to do anything to stop it.

Thayer was pressed against the bulkhead behind her console, mute with shock. Fletcher scrambled over from the engineering station to monitor the tactical console. Her voice trembled with dismay. "Weapons locked, Captain."

Cut off from the ship's command systems, Hernandez didn't have the option of overloading the *Columbia*'s warp reactor—not that it would have changed the outcome of this one-sided slaughter. It would have denied the Romulans the pleasure of using her ship as their weapon, but then there would be nothing to stop them from destroying the convoy anyway.

This was the Romulans' way of rubbing salt in the wound of the *Columbia*'s defeat. The insult added to the injury.

Fletcher's voice was flat and emotionless. "We're firing."

The shrieks of electromagnetically propelled torpedoes leaving the ship reverberated in the deathly silence of the bridge.

On the main viewscreen, images of the defenseless civilian vessels in the convoy were replaced by the spreading red-orange fire blossoms of antimatter-fueled explosions. In less than ten seconds, the entire convoy was destroyed, reduced to a cloud of sparking debris and superheated gases.

Then the lights flickered again and went dark, followed by the bridge consoles. The ship became as quiet as the grave. Hernandez choked back the urge to vomit. Anger and adrenaline left her shaking with impotent fury. Hundreds of men and women had been lost in the convoy, and the last thing they had known before they died was that it was the *Columbia* that killed them.

"I don't get it," Valerian murmured. "We were disabled. The Romulans could've destroyed the convoy. Why use us to do it?"

"Because they could, Sidra," Fletcher said to Valerian. "This is a trial run for how they'll attack the rest of the fleet. We're just the guinea pigs."

Graylock's voice crackled over the intraship emergency comm. *"Engineering to bridge!"*

"Go ahead," Hernandez said.

*"Captain, I think we've got a shot at getting out of this with our skins, but it'll be tight."*

Hernandez forced herself into a semblance of composure and looked around at the rest of the bridge crew. "Stations." Everyone stepped quickly and quietly to their consoles. She returned to her chair. "What's the plan, Karl?"

*"When the Romulans powered us up for the attack on the convoy, they left a residual charge in the warp nacelles. We can trigger a manual release and make a half-second warp jump."*

El-Rashad sounded dubious. "I think they'd notice that."

*"I've got Biggs and Pierce venting plasma through the impulse manifold, and the MACOs are pushing a photonic warhead out of the launch bay. If we detonate the warhead and trigger the jump at exactly the same moment, it should look like we self-destructed."*

"If anyone has a better plan," Hernandez announced, "let's hear it." Silence reigned. "Make it fast, Karl. It won't be long before th—" Explosions hammered the *Columbia*. The deck pitched wildly as sparks fountained from behind bridge panels. A sharp tang of smoke from burnt wiring filled the air. Within seconds, the only light on the bridge came from the irregular

flashes of EPS-powered displays bursting into flames and show-
ering the crew with stinging motes of shattered glass.

Then a bone-jarring concussion launched Hernandez up and
backward through the shadows. She hit the aft bulkhead like
dead weight and felt as if her consciousness had been knocked
free of her body. Sinking into a different, deeper kind of darkness,
she could only hope that the last explosion she'd heard was the
one meant to save the *Columbia* and not one sent to destroy it.

# 2381

## 3

Commander Christine Vale sat in the captain's chair of the *Starship Titan*, stared at the main viewer, and let her thoughts drift in the endless darkness beyond the stars.

A soft murmur of daily routines surrounded her, enveloped her in its familiar cadence of synthetic tones and hushed voices. *Titan* was more than two thousand light-years past the Vela OB2 Association, a dense cluster of new stars that had proved rich in spaceborne life-forms and other wonders. Now the ship was deep into a vast expanse of space that was unmapped and appeared to be unpopulated and untraveled, as well. For the past few weeks, intensive scans for subspace signal traffic had turned up naught but the scratch of cosmic background radiation. This far from the Vela cluster, cosmozoan activity was sparse, and there had been no sign of other starships within a range of twenty-five light-years since leaving the OB2 Association.

Vale saw a certain majesty in that lonely space; it was like a mirror for her soul. Several months earlier, she and a handful of her shipmates had become stranded during a mission to a planet called Orisha. Experiments conducted by the planet's denizens had produced dangerous temporal anomalies that destroyed the *U.S.S. Charon*, a *Luna*-class vessel like *Titan*, and they had almost claimed *Titan*, as well.

Jaza Najem, *Titan*'s senior science officer—and, for a brief time, Vale's lover—had sacrificed himself to protect the ship and its crew; as a result, he had been forced to live out his life in Orisha's past, permanently exiled to history.

It was still hard for Vale to believe that Najem, a man she'd once loved, and who then became her trusted friend, had been dead now for centuries. *He was dead when I met him.*

Months had passed, and her grief still cut like a sword in her side. She had resisted talking with the counselors at first, but she'd consented to a handful of sessions with Dr. Huilan after the captain had made it an order. Not that any of it had done any good. She had been "unwilling to commit to therapy," according to Huilan. Vale chose to think of it in simpler terms: She just didn't want to talk about it.

Shaking off the torpor of her maudlin mood, she got up from the center seat and made a slow tour of the bridge. She took light steps, and the carpeting on the deck muffled her footfalls. A peek over flight controller Aili Lavena's shoulder confirmed that *Titan* was continuing on its last course while Lieutenant Commander Melora Pazlar—who had succeeded Jaza as *Titan*'s senior science officer—continued a detailed star-mapping operation.

A glance at the console of senior operations officer Sariel Rager showed a steady stream of astrocartographic data flooding in and being steadily processed, logged, and filed.

All was quiet at the engineering station, which was manned by Ensign Torvig Bu-kar-nguv, a cybernetically enhanced Choblik. His narrow head was barely visible above the console. The meter-tall biped—to Vale, he resembled a cross between a large, flightless bird and a shorn sheep—used his bionic arms and hands to work the console's controls with delicate precision. At the same time, he made adjustments on the wall panel behind him by means of the bionic manus at the end of his long, agile tail.

Vale quickly lost track of the dozens of systems that Torvig was modifying. "What has you so busy, Ensign?"

The expression on his ovine face switched from one of focused curiosity to petrified innocence. "I'm upgrading the power-distribution efficiency of the internal EPS network."

As usual, the specificity of his answer left Vale very little room to insert any small talk. This time, she decided not to try. "Very well," she said. "Carry on, Ensign."

"Thank you, sir," Torvig replied. His face became a mask of contentment as he resumed working. Vale admired his singularity of focus. He had come aboard the previous year to complete his senior-year work study for Starfleet Academy, and along with fellow cadet Zurin Dakal, had stayed on after his long-distance graduation, as a regular member of *Titan*'s crew.

Ranul Keru, the chief of security, was next on Vale's circuit of the bridge. A bear of a man, the dark-bearded Trill loomed quietly over his console. He looked up and favored Vale with a sly look as she obtrusively leaned over to see what was on his screen. It was a plan for an unannounced security-division drill, a simulated intruder alert. Looking closer, she noted its details with amusement. "A dikironium cloud creature?" She accused him with a raised eyebrow. "That's just mean, Keru."

"It's my job," he said with devilish glee.

"Let me know if any of us survive," she said, moving on.

Commander Tuvok didn't look up as Vale neared the tactical console, but there was something about his demeanor that felt unusual to her. Her curiosity aroused, she stepped behind him and eyed his console readouts. All she saw was a series of long-range sensor reports, all saying the same thing: no contacts. It was the most placid tactical profile she had seen in decades.

She turned to the brown-skinned Vulcan and lowered her voice to a discreet whisper. "Want to show me what you were really working on?"

He didn't say anything at first. Then he responded with a hesitant glance from the corner of his eye, coupled with a tired grimace. He tapped a few commands into his console, and the serene lineup of empty scans was replaced by a complex set of fleet-deployment grids and battle scenarios.

Vale paged through them and asked, "Core system defenses?"

"Yes," Tuvok said, keeping his own voice hushed like hers.

He had prepared dozens of tactical profiles analyzing the recent attacks by the Borg into Federation space. In some of the scenarios, he was assessing strategic and tactical flaws in Starfleet's responses; in others, he had focused on isolating possible breaches in the Federation's perimeter defenses that the Borg might be exploiting.

She singled out one of interest. "Projecting possible next targets?"

"Unfortunately . . . no," Tuvok said.

It took her a moment to infer his meaning. "There have been more attacks."

"Yes," Tuvok said. Then he called up a recent, classified news dispatch from Starfleet Command. "This arrived ten minutes ago. Five ships destroyed by the Borg in the Onias Sector, in separate engagements." Tuvok lowered his eyes. "I did not wish to alarm the crew, so I refrained from announcing its arrival. I had intended to finish my analysis and brief you in writing a few minutes from now, for the sake of discretion."

"Probably for the best," Vale said. Messages from home had become less frequent since *Titan* left the Vela cluster, and the horrifying news of recent weeks had left many of its crew fearful for their families and loved ones in the Federation. She nodded once. "Carry on."

Vale returned to work, but over the relaxed air of her daily routine had been cast a pall of unspoken anxiety. It was the first time since *Titan*'s departure from known space that she wished she could suspend its mission of galactic exploration. Though *Titan* was devoted to peaceful scientific inquiry, it was also a state-of-the-art Federation starship, and its captain was a formidable combatant.

*Starfleet doesn't need another map of another empty sector.* Vale slumped back into the captain's chair. *It needs every ship it can get, on the front line, right now.* But there was no way *Titan*'s crew could be there. It would take them months to get home— and if the Borg threat was as serious as it appeared, *Titan*'s return would come far too late to make any difference. *So let's just keep running into the night,* Vale fumed. *And hope we still have homes to go back to when it's over.* She stared at the viewscreen and struggled to bury her ire and frustration in that cold, endless void beyond the stars.

Xin Ra-Havreii stood on the narrow platform inside the stellar cartography holotank and admired Melora Pazlar from afar. The slender, blond Elaysian woman hovered in the center of the zero-gravity environment, several meters from the end of the platform, manipulating holographic constructs with easy grace.

"You should come up," she said to Ra-Havreii.

He smiled. "I like the view just fine from here."

Pazlar reached out with her left hand, palm open, and selected the floating image of a geology department report that detailed the results of the ship's most recent planetary survey. Bending her arm, she pulled the image toward her, enlarging it in the process. "The new interface is a blast," she said as she paged through the report with small flicks of her fingers.

"I'm glad you like it," Ra-Havreii said. He had designed a sweeping upgrade to the holotank's user interface after Pazlar's promotion to senior science officer. Her uniform had been modified with a complex network of embedded nanosensors, which extended from the soles of her boots to the tips of a pair of tight-fitting black gloves. A clear liquid matrix applied directly to her eyes enabled her to trigger functions inside the holotank with a mere glance. He had transformed this high-tech chamber from a workspace into Pazlar's personal sanctum sanctorum.

She paused in her labors and tossed another flustered grin at the white-haired Efrosian chief engineer. "So, what brings you up from engineering? Worried I'd broken it already?"

"No, I just wanted to see how it works, now that we're out of the test phase," he said. "Trial runs and normal operations can be very different experiences." With a note of melancholy, he added, "A lesson I learned the hard way."

In fact, the reason he was there was that he'd wanted to see her in action. Watching her use the new system was a delight for Ra-Havreii, who envisioned the fetching science officer as a conductor directing a symphony of data and light.

A sweep of her arm whirled the room's rings of data screens in one direction and spun its backdrop of nebulae and stars in another. "Everything's so easy in here," she said. "It makes me hate to leave." In a more conspiratorial tone she added, "Between you and me, I cringe every time the captain calls a staff meeting, because it means putting the armor back on."

Outside the stellar cartography lab, Pazlar, a native of a low-gravity planet, had to wear a custom-made powered exoskeleton in order to walk or stand in *Titan*'s standard one-*g* environment. Her armature worked well enough, but it was cumbersome, and when its power reserves dwindled she was forced to use a mechanized wheelchair instead. Even with those devices, her body was exceptionally fragile, in any environment.

At first, Ra-Havreii had pondered ways to improve Pazlar's ability to move through the ship. Then he'd decided that a more elegant solution would be to bring the ship to her.

"What would you say," he remarked with a dramatic flair, "if I told you that you could go anywhere on the ship, any time you want, without ever putting that pile of metal on again?"

With a languid flourish, she dispelled all her work screens and left herself surrounded by a vista of stars. Crossing her arms with deliberate slowness, she turned in place until she had fixed all her attention on Ra-Havreii. "This, I have to hear."

He waved his hand casually at the galactic panorama. "Am I still welcome in your weightless domain?" She responded with a mock glare that he took as an invitation. In a carefree motion he stepped onto the flat, circular platform at the end of the ramp, and then with a gentle push he launched himself into the zero-gravity area. Having spent years as a starship designer and construction manager, he knew from experience exactly how much force to apply to position himself beside Pazlar. His long white hair and snowy moustache, however, drifted around his face like seaweed buffeted by deep currents.

"Computer," he said, "integrate Ra-Havreii interface modification Melora Four."

*"Modification ready,"* the feminine computer voice said.

He glanced sideways at Pazlar. "I hope you won't think it too forward of me to have named it in your honor."

"I'll let you know when I see what it is," she said.

Ra-Havreii shrugged. "Reasonable. Computer, activate holopresence module. Location: Deck One, conference room." The all-encompassing sphere of outer space was replaced in a gentle, fading transition by a holographic representation of the conference room located behind *Titan*'s main bridge.

The simulacrum was perfect in every detail, down to the scent of the fabric on the chairs and the scratches that Pazlar's armature had made in the table's veneer the last time she had attended a meeting there. Outside its tall windows, warp-distorted stars streaked past.

A subtle change in the environment's gravity enabled Pazlar and Ra-Havreii to stand on the deck rather than float above it.

"Cute trick," Pazlar said.

Ra-Havreii chuckled and held up his index finger. "Wait," he said. "There's more." He tapped his combadge. "Ra-Havreii to Commander Vale."

*"Vale here. Go ahead, Commander."*

"Commander, could I ask you to have one of your bridge personnel step into the Deck One conference room for a moment?"

Vale sounded confused. *"Anyone in particular?"*

"No," Ra-Havreii said. "Whoever can spare a moment."

*"All right,"* Vale said, suspicion coloring her tone. *"Ensign Vennoss is on her way."*

"Thank you, Commander. Ra-Havreii out." He looked at Pazlar

and lifted his thick white eyebrows. "This, I expect, will be the fun part."

A portal that led to a corridor that linked the conference room and the bridge opened with a soft hiss, and Ensign Vennoss, an attractive young Kriosian woman, entered carrying a padd. She stopped short and recoiled in mild surprise from Pazlar.

"Sorry, sir," Vennoss said. "I was expecting to meet Commander Ra-Havreii." Then she eyed Pazlar more closely. "Pardon me if this is none of my business, but don't you normally use a motor-assist armature outside of stellar cartography?"

Pazlar's mute, slack-jawed stare of surprise was an even richer reward than Ra-Havreii had hoped for. He tapped his combadge again. "Ra-Havreii to Ensign Vennoss."

Half a second after he'd finished speaking, his call was repeated from the overhead speaker inside the simulacrum. As Vennoss spoke, he heard her reply both "in person" and echoing from his combadge. "Vennoss here. Go ahead, Commander."

"Lieutenant Commander Pazlar and I are conducting a test of some new holopresence equipment in the stellar cartography lab. Can you bear with us a moment while we make a few adjustments?"

Vennoss gave a single nod. "Yes, sir. My pleasure."

"Thank you." He looked from Vennoss to Pazlar and said in a gentle but prodding way, "Go ahead—talk with her."

It took a second for Pazlar to compose herself, then she straightened her posture to carry herself like a proper officer. "Ensign," she said, and she stopped, apparently uncertain what to say next. Then she continued, "Have there been any new sensor contacts since your last report?"

"No, sir," Vennoss said. "I may have detected a Kerr loop in a nearby star cluster, but I'm still crunching the numbers to confirm it before I put it in the log."

"Ensign," Ra-Havreii said, pausing as he heard his voice emanate from Vennoss's combadge. "Is your analysis on that padd you're carrying?"

The Kriosian blinked. "Yes, sir."

"Would you let Commander Pazlar look at it a moment?"

"Yes, sir," Vennoss said, and she walked up to Pazlar and offered her the padd.

Pazlar stared at it for a second before she accepted it from the ensign. She paged through some of the ensign's facts and figures, and then she handed the padd back to Vennoss. "Thanks, Ensign. I look forward to reading your report."

"Aye, sir."

Ra-Havreii was satisfied with the test. "Thank you, Ensign," he said. "You can return to the bridge now."

Vennoss nodded, gave a small sigh of relief, and exited the way she had come in. As soon as she was gone, Pazlar turned and beamed at Ra-Havreii. "Did you mean what you said? About this being able to go anywhere on the ship?"

"Indeed, I did." He strolled closer to her. "It took weeks," he continued, "but I'm fairly certain the holopresence system is fully integrated in all compartments and on all decks. Your holographic avatar is a completely faithful stand-in for you, and your shipmates' avatars in here should be able to represent them with near-perfect fidelity."

Teasing him every so slightly, she asked, "Near-perfect?"

"Well, all but perfect," he said. "But only to a point."

Perhaps because his reputation had preceded him once again, she asked, "And what, pray tell, might that point be?"

He was standing very near to her, close enough to be captivated by the delicate fragrance of her perfume. "I would say the simulation loses its value at precisely the point where the real thing would be eminently preferable."

She seemed quite amused. "That's a very discreet way of phrasing it."

"Well, yes," he said. "Discretion is a virtue, I'm told." He leaned toward her, a prelude to a kiss—

She pulled away and stepped back. "I'm sorry," she said, avoiding eye contact with him. "I was just kidding around." She turned her back. "I hope I didn't lead you on."

He inhaled to sigh, then held his breath a moment. "No," he said, with as much tact and aplomb as he could muster. "I guess I just got carried away. If there was any error to be found here, it was mine, and I apologize."

"No apology needed," she said, half turning back toward him. "But thank you, anyway."

He bowed his head and showed his open palms next to his legs, a polite gesture of contrition and humility. Inside, however, he felt deeply ashamed. Seeing her empowered and happy had made him forget, just for a moment, that her emotions could be just as fragile as her physique.

Many months had passed since Commander Tuvok, while temporarily under the telepathic influence of a spaceborne entity, had assaulted Pazlar in the ship's main science lab. Not only had he harmed Pazlar physically, breaking some of her bones, he had forced critical information from her memory with a Vulcan mind-meld, a grotesque personal invasion. Since then, she had bravely confronted her fears by working with Tuvok to learn ways of defending herself, in spite of her physical limitations.

But there was no denying that the attack had changed her. She could be warm at times, even jovial—but since the attack she had become more distant, a little bit harder to reach. In a very real sense, she seemed even more isolated than she had before.

Ra-Havreii knew about emotional scars, unforgiven sins, and lingering pain. He still blamed himself for a fatal accident years earlier, in the engine room of *Titan*'s class-prototype ship, the *Luna*. Everyone who had been there, and many others who hadn't, had tried to console him with empty platitudes:

*It wasn't your fault, Xin.*

*There's no way you could have known what would happen.*

*You have to move on.*

He knew better. As the designer of the *Luna* class, it had been his job to know what would happen. It *had* been his fault.

Some wounds, he had learned, could not be left behind. His past stayed with him, haunted him, reminded him always of his limitations. He saw shades of that same pain in Melora.

Efrosians often attuned themselves to one another's emotional needs; it was considered a foundation for intimacy, which in turn strengthened social bonds. So it came as no surprise to Ra-Havreii that Pazlar's profound physical and emotional vulnerabilities had awakened a protective side of his nature. That had, no doubt, been a subconscious factor in his tireless efforts to rebuild the stellar cartography interface and create the holopresence network for her.

He let his gaze linger a moment on her profile. Though he had enjoyed the attention of a wide range of female companions over the years, including a few on *Titan,* such pleasures had always been fleeting. He sometimes suspected that his serial seductions

were really little more than feeble distractions from his suppressed melancholy.

Faced with the emptiness of it all, he breathed a quiet sigh and
watched Melora out of the corner of his eye.

*I should ease up before I make myself fall in love with her.
Besides, what would I do if she fell in love with* me? A shadow of
self-reproach darkened his mood. *Don't be stupid, Xin. You don't
deserve to be that lucky . . . not in this life or the next.*


Deanna Troi had begun tuning out Dr. Ree's voice the moment he
said, "I'm sorry."

He was still talking, but she was only half listening to him
now, as she sank into a black pit of grief and fury. *Not again*, she
raged inside. *I can't go through this again. Not now.*

Will Riker—her *Imzadi*, her husband, her friend—stood beside her and gripped her left hand in both of his as she sat on
the edge of the biobed. She shut her eyes against the cold light of
sickbay while Dr. Ree continued delivering bad news.

"I ran the test several times," he said. "There was no mistake."
He bowed his long, reptilian head and looked at the padd in his
clawed, scaly hand. "The genetic abnormalities are irreparable.
And I fear they will only become worse."

It was so unfair. Burning tears welled in Troi's eyes, and her
throat seized shut on a knot of sorrow and anger. A suffocating
tightness in her chest made it hard to breathe.

Will, sensing that she was unable to speak for herself, asked
the Pahkwa-thanh physician, "Do you know *why* it happened?
Can you tell us if it'll happen again?"

"Not yet," said the dinosaur-like doctor. Troi fixed him with a
sullen glower. It didn't seem to faze him. "I need to make a detailed analysis before I can offer a prognosis."

Troi's empathic senses felt protective indignation pulsing
in waves from her *Imzadi* before he snapped at Dr. Ree, "Why
didn't you do that the *last time*, five months ago?"

"Because a first miscarriage in a humanoid normally isn't
cause for long-term concern," Ree said. "The likelihood of a
miscarriage for a woman who has already had *one* is the same
as for a woman who hasn't. But a *second* event greatly increases

the risk of future complications." Once again he spoke to Troi instead of to Will. "Betazoid women your age often have successful pregnancies, but your half-human ancestry introduces some hormonal factors that muddy the picture a bit. That's why I need to run more tests. With your permission."

Numb, torn between a desire to scream and the impulse to retreat to someplace dark and quiet and simply hide for weeks on end, all Troi could muster in response was a tiny nod of her chin. Then she cast her forlorn gaze at the floor, desperate to be done with this hideous day. The doctor finished entering his notes on the padd, looked up, and said, "Unless you have more questions, we should probably get you prepped."

Will turned his body in a way that interposed his shoulder between Troi and the doctor. "Prepped? For what?"

"To remove the fetus," he said.

Troi covered her abdomen with her right arm, and her response was sharp and instantaneous. "Absolutely not."

A rasp rattled behind Ree's fangs before he said, "Commander, please—I'm recommending this procedure because it's in your best interest medically."

"I don't agree," Troi said, sliding forward off the biobed and onto her feet. She inched closer to Will.

Ree sidestepped to block Will and Troi's path, leaving them cornered between two biobeds. "My dear counselor, forgive me for being blunt, but your fetus will not survive to term. It will die in utero—and unlike your last miscarriage, this one poses a serious risk to your own health, and perhaps your life."

He had made a logical, reasonable argument, but Troi didn't care. Her child, however flawed, was bound to her by slender threads of breath and blood, depended upon her for everything from food to antibodies. So tiny, so defenseless, her fragile scion was an innocent vessel, one in which she and Will had invested all their hopes and dreams. She couldn't bring herself to do what Dr. Ree asked, not even to save herself.

She hardened her resolve. "The answer is no, Doctor."

"As the chief medical officer, I could insist," Ree said. To Will, he added, "As I'm sure you well know, Captain."

Ree's challenge made Will bristle with anger. "My wife said the answer is no, Doctor. I'd advise you to think twice before you try to force the issue." He stretched one arm across Troi's shoulders and nudged her forward toward Ree, who held his ground. Will glared at him. "We're *leaving now,* Doctor."

The hulking Pahkwa-thanh, Troi knew, could easily snap off both their heads with a casual bite of his massive jaws. His frustration and irritation were radiant to Troi's empathic mind, and even more vibrant than her *Imzadi*'s fearless resolve. She expected Ree, as a predator by nature, to relish confrontation. Instead, he turned away and plodded toward his office, his mood a leaden shadow of resentful disappointment.

Will guided her out of sickbay. In the corridor he took her hand, and they walked together in mournful silence toward their quarters. As always, he wore a brave face and played the part of the stoic, but his heartbreak was as palpable to her as her own. She sensed a deeper unease in him, one that he refused to express—a profound inner conflict mixed with fear. There had been undertones of this in his emotions in sickbay, as well. Probing his thoughts, she realized he had strongly disagreed with her decision to refuse Dr. Ree's advice, yet he had backed her choice without hesitation.

As his wife, she was grateful that he had supported her wishes over his own. As a mother, she hated him for being willing to sacrifice their child in her name.

It had been several months since their initial attempt at having a child had ended in tragedy. Her first miscarriage had occurred with no warning, just a surge of pain in the night. Until that moment, they had thought that conception alone would be their greatest hurdle.

They had both been subjected to lengthy, invasive fertility treatments to overcome what Dr. Ree had politely described as "genetic incompatibilities" in their DNA. Several failed attempts at conception had strained her relationship with Will to a degree they'd never endured before, and the hormonal changes she had undergone for the fertility enhancements had weakened her psionic defenses, causing her to project her emotions on others in unexpected and sometimes dangerous ways.

Everything had seemed so much easier when they'd thought that the only things their family-to-be had to fear were "out there," far away and unnamed. Now the greatest threat to their dreams lay within themselves—a flaw, some monstrous defect that had rendered them unfit for the roles they most desired.

Their second attempt at conceiving a child had been an act of hope, a refusal to succumb to despair. Through all of Troi's nights of bitter tears and black moods, Will had never faltered, never given up hope that they would persevere. "I have faith in you," he'd said one night, months earlier. "Faith in us. I have to believe that we'll get through this. I have to believe that."

Until tonight, he had.

Something in Will had changed when Dr. Ree had delivered his diagnosis. She had felt it, an icy resignation in his mind. It lasted only a moment, but it had happened: He'd lost hope.

Lost in her thoughts, she didn't notice that they had been in a turbolift until they stepped out onto the deck where their quarters were located. A few paces into the corridor, she stopped. Will continued for a step until he felt the resistance in her hand, and he turned back, concerned and solicitous. "What's wrong?"

"I don't know," she lied. "I'm just feeling a need to walk for a while. Maybe in the holodeck."

He nodded. "All right. Anywhere you want."

As he started back toward the turbolift, she let go of his hand. "I meant . . . that I'm feeling a need to walk by myself."

His face slackened and paled, and he lowered his chin. "I see," he said in a voice of quiet defeat.

Troi didn't need empathy to know how deeply she had wounded him. All his body language signaled his withdrawal, and his anguish was overwhelming, too intense for her to tune out. She was desperate to comfort him, but her thoughts were awash in her own toxic brew of dark emotions. Twice in less than half a year, their hope of starting a family had turned to ashes, and she didn't know why. She couldn't accept it.

"I'm sorry," she said. "It's just . . . I . . ."

"I understand," he said, and she knew it was true, he did. He was her *Imzadi,* and their emotional bond, normally a comfort, now was an amplifier of their shared grief. It was too much.

"I'm sorry," she said again. Then she walked away, knowing how badly Will wanted to stop her, and hoping that he wouldn't. She hated herself for abandoning him, and she both loved him and hated him for letting her go.

She stepped into a turbolift, and the doors closed behind her. "Holodeck One," she said, and the lift hummed as it accelerated away, circuiting the primary hull.

As the turbolift sped her through the ship, she thought of

her older sister, Kestra, who had drowned at the age of seven, shortly after Troi had been born. Their mother, Lwaxana, had caused herself severe psychological trauma by repressing all her memories of Kestra for decades, until the submerged grief all but destroyed her from within.

At the time, Troi had felt sympathy for her mother, even though she had been horrified that Lwaxana could erase her own child from her memory. Now, faced with her own, imminent second miscarriage, Troi no longer felt revulsion at the thought of her mother's self-inflicted amnesia. She felt envy.

Captain William Riker crossed from the turbolift to his ready room in quick strides, making only fleeting eye contact with his first officer, Christine Vale, who had command of the bridge during beta shift. He made a brief nod as she got up from the center seat. "As you were," Riker said, and he kept walking, trying to raise as minor a wake with his passage as possible. As soon as the ready room's door closed behind him, he slowed his pace and moved in heavy, tired steps to his desk.

Circling behind it to his chair felt like too much effort, so he turned and perched himself on its edge. His head drooped with fatigue. For Deanna's sake he had maintained a façade of placid control, but his emotions felt like a storm battering the empty shores of his psyche. Depression, anger, guilt, and denial followed one another in crushing waves.

Removing himself from Deanna was only an illusion, he knew. The bond he shared with his *Imzadi* transcended distance and physical barriers. Their emotions were so tangible to each other, so present, that when one of them was in the throes of a powerful experience, both of them felt it. Ever since they had first fallen in love, their bond had been so strong that they sometimes were able to communicate telepathically. Such moments were rare, but they had made him feel so connected to her.

And now she felt so distant.

His door chime sounded. He pushed himself up from the desk to a standing posture, turned, and tugged the front of his uniform smooth before he said, "Come in."

The portal slid aside, briefly admitting the ambient sounds of the bridge. Christine Vale stepped inside his ready room and stopped just outside the range of the door's sensor. It shut behind her. Her gaze was level and concerned. "Sir."

"Chris," he said with a forced nonchalance, and he circled behind his desk. "What can I do for you?"

She flashed a weary smile. "I was gonna ask you the same thing." Turning a bit more serious, she asked, "Are you all right? You haven't seemed like yourself for a while now."

He pulled out his chair. "Define 'a while.'"

All traces of jocularity left her tone. "A few months, at least," she said. "Don't get me wrong, you mask it well. But something's changed. You just seem . . . disengaged."

Riker sat down with a tired sigh. "How so?"

"Can we drop the ranks and speak freely, sir?"

Her accusatory tone caught Riker off guard. "Of course," he said. "Always, you know that."

"Will," she said, "what's wrong?"

Instinct impelled him to denial. "Nothing. I'm fine."

"No, Will, you're not." She stepped to his desk and sat down across from him. The concern in her voice grew more pronounced as she continued, "You and I served through some rough times on the *Enterprise,* and I've been your XO for almost a year. And I have *never* seen you act like this. Please talk to me. What's going on?"

He reclined his chair and pulled his hand over his face. It was a reflexive action; he thought he'd done it to massage the fatigue from his head and neck. Only as he prolonged the gesture did he admit to himself that it was a delaying tactic, a way to avoid eye contact and postpone his reply. He hated feeling so exposed, so easily read. Denial was no longer an option, but he still found himself reluctant to confide in her. Finally, he lowered his hand and said, "It's complicated."

"Simplify it," Vale replied.

A heavy breath did nothing to relax him. "I could invoke rank and tell you to leave this alone."

Vale nodded. "Is that what you *want* to do?"

"What, are you a counselor, now?" He swiveled his chair away from her, showing her his profile. "Sometimes, captains have to keep barriers between themselves and their crews."

"And that's fine, up to a point," Vale said. "But right now it seems like your ability to do your job is being impaired by whatever it is you're going through. And seeing as it's my job to make sure this ship and its crew are kept in a state of full readiness, that makes *your* problem *my* problem."

Riker frowned. "I'm still not sure I—"

"Especially since it involves your wife, who's also part of the command staff," Vale added.

He swiveled back to face her, his temper aroused. "How did you know that?"

Vale hesitated before answering, and then she spoke with tact. "Will, I know that you and Deanna had problems conceiving a child. She told me all about it on Orisha. The treatments, the strain it put on the two of you. I noticed you having the same kind of problems then that I'm seeing now. But for a while, the two of you seemed happy, so I'm wondering what's happened."

Denying the obvious was tiring, and he felt his guard slipping; he wondered if it might be a relief to let it down entirely. "You understand," he said, "that what we talk about stays in here. You don't discuss it with anyone—not the crew, not the counselors. . . . *Especially* not the counselors."

"Of course," Vale said.

Riker took another deep breath and let it go slowly as he composed his thoughts and steeled his resolve. "The past few months *have* been hard for me and Deanna," he confided. "You know that we were working with Dr. Ree on fertility treatments—"

"All too well," Vale said, referring to the effect that Troi's empathic projections had had on her personally.

"We thought we'd succeeded," Riker said. He found it difficult to go on. "It hasn't gone as we'd hoped."

As he'd feared, a grim silence fell between himself and Vale, whose expression softened. She leaned forward and folded her hands atop his desk. "How bad is it?"

He couldn't name it. "Bad."

Vale asked in an apprehensive whisper, "A miscarriage?"

Hearing the words spoken in sympathy, rather than in Dr. Ree's cold and clinical rasp, was even more terrible than Riker had imagined. Grief surged upward inside his chest, and he barely nodded his confirmation before tears overflowed his eyes. He covered his mouth for a moment and struggled to contain the sorrow he had been swallowing for so long. "I've been carrying this for months," he said, fighting to talk through halting gasps for air. "Piling one thing on another. Feeling like I'd failed Deanna."

"You didn't fail her," Vale said. "I know you didn't."

"Maybe not, but I feel like I did." He palmed the tears from one cheek and then the other. "She's part Betazoid, so it's hard to know where my desires end and hers begin. It makes me wonder if maybe her wish to have kids was really *mine,* and I led her into this." He got up from his chair, turned away from Vale, and walked to the window behind his desk. "We just found out it's happening again. We're losing another pregnancy. And this time, if she doesn't do something about it . . . it could kill her."

"I'm sure Dr. Ree could—"

"He offered," Riker said. "He almost insisted, actually. Deanna won't have it. She knows she's in danger, and she just won't do it. And instead of arguing with her, I let her refuse treatment and walked her out of sickbay."

Vale's reflection was semitransparent against the backdrop of drifting starlight. "Even so," she said, "that doesn't make any of this your fault."

"It doesn't really matter," Riker said. "It's starting to feel like the damage is done, either way."

He watched Vale's mirror image as she stood and circled behind his desk to stand with him. "What damage?"

"That barrier I was talking about," he said, "the one between me and the crew? It's starting to feel like it's between me and Deanna. We can hear each other's thoughts, but it feels like we don't know how to talk about this." Now he regarded his own ragged reflection in the window. "It's never been easy being such a visible couple on a starship. Even harder now that I'm the captain and this crew is so small, compared to what I was used to on the *Enterprise.*"

"I know what you mean," Vale said. Her own muted grief reminded Riker of the loss of Jaza Najem just months earlier.

"Yeah," Riker said. "I guess you do." He turned to face her. "After the first . . ." The word was so hard for him to say. "After the first miscarriage, I did everything I could to keep Deanna's spirits up. The odds were on our side, Ree told us. But I could tell Deanna wasn't ready to try again, so I waited. I know that losing the baby had to be worse for her. For me it was an idea, but for her it was part of her body—it was *physical*. There's no way I can understand how that *feels* for her."

"But it's good that you know where the difference is," Vale said, trying to reassure him. "That you know *why* her experience is different from yours."

More tears burned Riker's eyes. "But I still don't know how to help her," he admitted. "She's in so much pain, and I feel cut off, and I don't know what to do." Now that he had opened the gates to his grief, he didn't know how to close them again.

Vale pulled him to her, and she closed her arms around him in a sisterly embrace. He hesitated to return the gesture, and then he reluctantly surrendered to it. "It'll be okay, Will," she said, her voice breaking slightly, echoing his sorrow. "You'll be okay, and so will Deanna. You're not alone."

Riker felt embarrassed to have shown such vulnerability to his first officer. *Captain Picard would never have bared his feelings like this,* he thought. He reminded himself that Vale was not just his first officer; she was his friend. Maybe a captain more obsessed with strict protocol and formality would have been stalwart in hiding his feelings, but Riker didn't subscribe to such emotionally stunted ideals of manhood. He didn't believe that expressing emotions made him weak, and he was grateful that he had chosen a first officer who seemed to feel the same way.

As he lingered in Vale's embrace, Riker contemplated the emotional wedge that he felt had been driven between him and Deanna by their recent tragedies. At a time when he most needed comfort, Deanna seemed to recoil from his touch. Her rejection and abandonment of him in the corridor made him all the more grateful now for Vale's compassion.

That was when he began to wonder if perhaps this moment was continuing a shade too long. Vale's head was resting against his chest, her hair color du jour a rich auburn that contrasted with his predominantly black uniform. Riker eased Vale away from him, and as she lifted her face to look at him, he thought he caught a glimpse of a less than platonic emotion in her eyes.

Then they both pushed away from each other and averted their eyes as they composed themselves. "Anyway," Vale said as she backpedaled and smoothed her uniform jacket, "if you need me, or if there's anything I can do to help, just let me know."

"I will," Riker said, and he sat down at his desk and tapped a few keys on his computer's interface. "Thank you, Chris."

"My pleasure, Captain," Vale said, continuing to back away to the other side of Riker's desk. Her hands seemed to be in constant motion—waving, clenching, opening, weaving together at the fingers and flexing. "If there's nothing else?"

"No, thank you," Riker said, pretending to be engrossed in whatever it was on his computer monitor. "Dismissed."

"Aye, sir." She turned and walked quickly out the door, back to duty on the bridge.

Riker watched the door close behind her, and then he ran a hand through his thatch of graying hair. *Did I just imagine that?* he wondered. *Am I wrong, or was that kind of . . . awkward?*

Suddenly, being emotionally unavailable to his crew didn't seem like such a bad idea after all.

"You're obviously looking for someone to blame," said Pral glasch Haaj. "The question is, would you rather it be you or your husband?"

As usual, the Tellarite counselor had chosen to take the most confrontational possible tack in addressing his patient's issues, and Deanna Troi, being a trained counselor and his supervising officer, didn't appreciate it. "This isn't about blame," she said, surprised at how defensive her manner seemed.

"Of course not," he said, his cultured voice tuned to a perfect timbre of derision. "It's just a coincidence, yes?"

The rank insensitivity of his remarks sparked Troi's fury, which she found easier to face than the smothering sorrow of sympathy she'd expected from the ship's other counselor, Dr. Huilan. "We didn't choose this. It's not our fault."

"I see. So it's random chance and not some defect in your respective biologies that's put you on a course for your second miscarriage in half a year."

Troi sprang from the couch, turned her back on the slender Tellarite, and paced toward the far bulkhead of his office. At the wall she turned and began walking back toward him. He watched her with expressionless black eyes, which gave his face a cipherlike quality. "You're just trying to provoke me," she said with a note of resentment.

"Provoke you? Into doing what?"

She stopped and glowered at him. "Now you're trying to make me name my own dysfunction and outline my own needs. Are you this transparent with all your patients?"

"Yes, but most of my patients don't hold doctorates in psychology." He snorted. "Tell me what I'll do next."

"You'll try to shock me by saying something rude."

He shook his head. "I tried that. And I followed it with the echoed remark and the leading question, all of which got me nowhere. So guess what my next trick will be."

It amazed her that even as he was admitting to the failure of his manipulations, he still sounded smug. "I don't know," she confessed. "Reciting old Tellarite parables?"

"No." Haaj reclined and folded his hands behind his head. "Just an honest question: Why are you wasting my time?"

At first, Troi recoiled from the hostility in his voice. Then she replied, "Is this another example of your patented Tellarite argument therapy?"

"I'm serious, Counselor. You're my supervising officer, so I'm expected to show you a certain degree of deference, even in a therapeutic setting—but I don't have time for this. You're clearly not ready for therapy, and you're taking away valuable session time from my patients who are."

She called upon her empathic senses to try and sense whether he was dissembling in order to draw her out. He wore an intense aura of bitter dudgeon. If he was merely pretending to be annoyed with her, he was doing a very convincing job of it, inside and out. "Why do you say I'm not ready for therapy?"

"Are you kidding?" He leaned forward, elbows on his knees. "All you've done since you got here is obstruct the process. You've dissected my method instead of answering my questions, and you'd rather criticize me than examine yourself." He leaned back and folded his hands in his lap. "Therapy only works when the patient is willing to participate."

All his accusations were true, and Troi was ashamed of herself for indulging her appetite for denial. "You're right," she said. "I have been sabotaging the session. I'm sorry."

"Don't apologize to me," he said. "Apologize to Crewman Liryok. This was supposed to be *his* hour."

Troi stared out a window at the wash of starlight streaking

past the ship and felt the subtle vibrations of warp flight in the deck under her feet. "I don't know why I'm having so much trouble surrendering to the process."

"Yes, you do," Haaj said, barely disguising his contempt.

She fixed him with a scathing glare. "No, I don't."

"Do."

He was the most exasperating therapist she'd ever met. "Is this your idea of therapy? Contradiction?"

"You're critiquing me again, Counselor. Why is that?"

She didn't mean to shout, but she did anyway. "I told you, I don't know!"

"And I'm calling you a liar," he said.

The more she felt herself losing control, the calmer he became. There were a thousand things she wanted to yell at him, and they were slamming together inside her mind, a logjam of epithets. Her face and ears felt hot, and her fists clenched while she struggled to put words to her fury.

Then he asked, "What are you feeling right now?" She stared at him, dumbstruck. He continued, "Would you call it rage?"

"Yes," she said, paralyzed by her emotions.

His voice took on a calming tenor. "Breathe, Deanna. Clear your mind, just for a few seconds. Remember your training: What's the difference between anger and rage?"

It was hard for her to pull air into her chest, even harder to hold it there. *I'm hyperventilating,* she realized. With effort, she did as Haaj asked, and then she closed her eyes.

"Ready?" he said. She nodded. He asked, "What's anger?"

"An emotional cue that something is wrong, that we have been injured or mistreated, or that values we consider important are being challenged or disregarded."

He harrumphed. "I imagine you did very well on the essay portions of your exams. . . . Now, tell me what rage is."

"A shame-based expression of anger," she said. "And a reaction to powerlessness."

"Powerlessness," Haaj repeated, tapping his index finger against his upper lip. "Impotence. Helplessness." He wagged his finger at her. "You don't like feeling out of control, do you?"

She crossed her arms over her chest. "I don't know many people who do."

"I do," Haaj said. "There are plenty of folks who like not

having to make decisions or take responsibility. They're happy to go along and believe what they're told, because it's easier than thinking for themselves."

Troi drummed her fingers on her bicep. "And what does that have to do with me?"

"Nothing," the wiry Tellarite said. "It was just a tangent. Those happen sometimes in conversation." Feigning embarrassment, he added, "I'm sorry, I forget. What are we talking about?"

"Control," Troi said, feeling a new tide of rage swell inside her chest.

He clapped his hands. "Ah, yes! Control." He let the words linger between them for a moment before he added, "You've been feeling out of control lately."

She shook her head. "I don't recall saying that."

"But you've certainly been at the mercy of events," Haaj said. "Not much recourse when a tragedy like yours happens."

"No, there isn't."

The Tellarite nodded. "It's too bad Dr. Ree isn't skilled enough to correct the problem."

"It's not his fault," Troi said. "Medicine isn't magic. There's only so much he can do."

"True," Haaj said. "I mean, he can't be expected to compensate for your husband's genetic shortcomings. After all, the captain is, as they say, 'only human.'"

Troi cast a reproachful stare at Haaj. "You're repeating yourself. I already told you it's not about blame."

"Oh, but it most certainly is," he replied. "You're blaming yourself."

She recoiled from his accusation. "I'm not!"

"You're cursing your poisoned womb," Haaj declared, as if it were a piece of gossip everyone else already knew. "To paraphrase Shakespeare, you know the fault lies not in your stars but in yourself."

"There's a difference between an argument and an insult, Doctor," Troi said in her most threatening tone.

Uncowed, he replied, "Do you really expect me to believe you don't blame yourself for back-to-back miscarriages?"

"I don't."

"Then where is all this *shame* coming from?" He continued

as if he was scolding a child. "You said it yourself: You're filled with rage, and rage finds its roots in powerlessness and shame."

Denial had Troi shaking her head as a reflex. "Rage comes from being ashamed of our anger," she said.

"So, you're ashamed of your anger?"

"No!"

"You just said you were! Who are you angry at? Yourself? Your husband? Some higher power that's betrayed your trust?"

His relentless, vicious badgering forced her to turn away, because her fury had become swamped in the rising waters of her grief. Her chest felt crushed, and her throat was as tight as a tourniquet. All her bitter emotions were bleeding into one for which she had no name. She closed her eyes to avoid seeing her dark reflection in the compartment window. Then she heard footfalls behind her, followed by Haaj's voice, somber and soft.

"You're angry at the baby," he said.

It was the sharpest truth that had ever cut her.

Her hands covered her face as deep, funereal bellows of grief roared from some dark chasm inside her. Tears were hot against her face as she doubled over, robbed of her composure by her wailing cries. Haaj's hands found her shoulders and steadied her. He guided her to a chair and eased her into it.

She stared at her tear-moistened palms. "I don't understand it," she said between choking gasps.

"You and William invested this child with your hopes and dreams," Haaj said. "You wanted it to be your future. But now joy has turned to sorrow, and you resent your baby for failing you, when you've already given it so much."

Troi looked up through a blurry veil of tears at Haaj. "But it's so unfair. It's not the baby's fault . . . it's no one's fault."

"You're right," Haaj said. "It's not fair. But when we're wronged, our instinct is to assign blame. Even if it means hurting someone we love—someone who doesn't deserve it."

Dragging her feelings into the open was a hideous sensation and not at all as cathartic as she had hoped. Worse still, it was forcing her to confront other torments and terrors she would have preferred to ignore for a while longer. "Dr. Ree wants me to terminate my pregnancy," she said. "I told him no."

"The good doctor doesn't make such suggestions lightly," Haaj said. "I presume his concern is for your safety?"

Troi shrugged. "So he said."

"And you think he's wrong?"

"No," Troi said. "I know he's probably right. But I can't do it. I won't."

Waggling his index finger, Haaj said, "No, no, Counselor. I'm afraid you need to choose a verb there. Either you *can't* terminate your pregnancy, or you *won't*. 'Can't' implies that you have no choice in the matter, no capacity to make an affirmative decision. 'Won't' suggests a defiant exercise of your free will. So which is it? Can't? Or won't?"

She wrestled with the semantics of his question for several seconds before she answered, "Won't. I won't do it."

"Even though it puts your life in danger?"

A calmness filled her. "It's not important."

Haaj looked deeply worried. "Counselor, are you saying you want to die?"

"No," she said. "I don't."

"But you seem ready to risk your life for a pregnancy that's already failed. Why is that?"

Her calm feeling became an emotional numbness, and in a dull monotone she told him the simple truth: "I don't know."

# 4

The voice of the Borg Collective lurked at the edge of Captain Jean-Luc Picard's awareness, taunting him with inhuman whispers.

It was a susurrus of thoughts—omnipresent, elusive, and inaccessible. Picard had been able to hear them for weeks now, lurking on the periphery of his consciousness, ever since the first wave of unexplained Borg attacks deep inside the protected core systems of the Federation. When he was caught up in the business of command, he could shut them out, but when he tried to relax or sleep, when his mind was idle . . . those were the times when the voice of the Collective smothered him from within. With his eyes closed, he could almost hear the name that continued to stab icy fear into his heart: *Locutus*.

Beverly Crusher's voice pulled him sharply back into the moment. "Look at him, Jean-Luc—isn't he amazing?"

Here-and-now returned in a flood of sensation. He blinked his eyes back into focus on the details. A delicate cup of hot Earl Grey tea in his hand, its subtle aroma soothing his frayed nerves. His wife, Beverly, warm beside him as they sat together on the sofa in their quarters. The murky bluish image on the display of her medical tricorder, which she had thrust in front of him, as if for inspection. He stared at it, awestruck.

*Our son,* he had to remind himself. *That's our son.*

"Words cannot do him justice," Picard said, aglow with a moment of quiet, paternal pride.

Then the soulless voice of the Collective returned and intruded on his moment of reflection to remind him: Pride was irrelevant. Hope was irrelevant. Resistance was futile.

Months earlier, to stop a new Borg queen from rising in the Alpha Quadrant, he'd dared to let himself be transformed once more into Locutus. Hubris had led him to think he could fool the Collective, walk into the largest cube it had ever spawned, and kill its nascent queen with impunity. He had even believed that his mind was strong enough to open itself to the Collective and behold all its secrets at once. Only when it had been too late to turn back had he realized how foolish he'd been.

One mind could not grasp the Collective. It was too great, too complex. It had reminded him of his true stature in the universe: small, weak, fallible, and insignificant.

And now the voice of the Collective thundered in his mind, louder and more intimate than ever before.

His brow grew heavy and furrowed with concern while he gazed down at the sensor image of the child growing inside of Beverly. His jaw tightened, not in anger but in remorse. *You've always known something like this would happen,* he upbraided himself. *You knew it. How could you have been so foolish?*

He had confided in Beverly after the first new wave of Borg attacks. Drowning in the merciless depths of the Collective's devouring group mind, he had needed her strength and passion to anchor him. She'd kept him grounded in all that he loved: her, his life, and their family-to-be.

She turned off the tricorder and set it aside. "You're hearing them again, aren't you?"

Picard nodded. "It's hard not to," he said. "They're always there, just waiting for me to let my guard down."

"Sounds like what I had to do," she said with a teasing edge, trying to cheer him up.

He was smart enough to grab a lifeline when it was offered. He smiled back. "There were definite similarities in strategy."

"Jean-Luc," she said with mock umbrage, "are you saying I wore you down?" She pressed closer against him and stroked his smooth pate. He extended his arm across her shoulders and rested his head against her silky, fiery red hair.

"I'm just saying that I could tell resistance was futile."

"If you call a few pathetic excuses 'resistance,'" she said, obviously enjoying the opportunity to needle him.

It had been nearly three months since the *Enterprise* crew had succeeded in its mission to hunt down and destroy the Borg-assimilated Federation science vessel *U.S.S. Einstein*. At the end of that mission, Beverly had sensed and taken advantage of an opportunity to cajole Picard into the most hopeful undertaking of his life: starting a family with her.

There had been no denying that, on some level, he had wanted this for a long time. The need had been awakened in him nearly ten years earlier, when his older brother, Robert, and young nephew, René, had been killed in a tragic fire at the family's vineyard home in Labarre, France.

Beverly's reason for wanting a family was just as poignant to Picard. Her only child, Wesley—whom she had treasured not only as a son but as the last surviving remnant of her late husband, Jack Crusher—had evolved many years earlier into a Traveler, a wondrous being capable of moving freely through time and space . . . but he also was no longer fully human. The more Wesley had grown into his powers as a Traveler, the less frequently he had returned to visit with Beverly. He had appeared at their hastily arranged, low-key wedding a few months earlier, but there was no telling when he might return—or if he ever would.

After the *Einstein* was destroyed, Picard had thought they'd earned a chance to seize their dream. After all, *Voyager* had destroyed the Borg's transwarp hub to Federation space a few years earlier. The *Enterprise* and her crew had stopped the most fearsome Borg cube ever encountered. And the last rogue Borg element in Federation space seemed to have been eliminated.

For a moment, Picard had dared to hope. He and Beverly had started their family. And less than a month later, as they were still marveling at their newly conceived son, the Borg had begun their blitzkrieg into Federation space.

*You should've known. You've always known.*

There was no going back now. He and Beverly had committed themselves, and they were going to see this through, to whatever end awaited them. Even as they huddled in the dim light of their quarters and shut themselves away from the gathering storm, he knew that this interlude of happy domesticity had never been fated to last. It was doomed to end in tragedy, like every other moment of joy he'd known in his life.

"It's time," he said with a glance at a chrono set on the end table beside him. He extricated himself from her embrace and stood. Then he picked up the tricorder from the sofa and turned it back on, to admire the image of his son again, even if just for a moment. "You're right. He's amazing. In every way."

He switched off the tricorder and set it on a table as Beverly stood beside him. She laid her warm hands on either side of his neck and kissed him tenderly. Resting her forehead against his, she said, "I'll be in sickbay if you need me."

"Meet you back here when it's over."

She nodded somberly, her demeanor calm. They let their hands fall away from each other, and she stayed behind as he left, to avoid the awkward ritual of another farewell in the corridor. Sharpening his mind for battle, he left their quarters at a brisk step and headed for the turbolift, which would bring him to the bridge.

In less than an hour, the *Enterprise* would arrive at the Federation world of Ramatis, near the Klingon border. If Picard and his crew had responded quickly enough to the planet's distress signal, the *Enterprise* might arrive only a few minutes later than the Borg cube that was on its way to the planet.

Picard knew that the time for diplomacy was past.

It was time to go to war.


From his first glimpse of the scorched and glowing northern hemisphere of Ramatis on the *Enterprise*'s main viewer, Worf knew that every living being on the planet's surface was dead—and that the Borg cube in orbit was responsible.

"No life signs on the planet," said Commander Miranda

Kadohata, the ship's second officer. "It's been cooked down to the mantle." She swiveled her seat away from the ops console to add, "The Borg cube is sweeping up all the satellites and defense-platform debris in orbit, probably for raw materials."

Disgust churned up bile in Worf's throat. An enemy that would conquer a world to possess it could be hated and still be respected as an adversary. The Borg, however, had undertaken a campaign of slaughter without even the pretense of assimilating the people of the Federation. Their mission had been defined in stark terms by their actions at Acamar, Barolia, and now this ill-fated world. The Borg agenda was nothing less than genocide.

Captain Picard's voice snapped orders through the grim hush of the bridge. "Helm, intercept course, full impulse." The captain looked at Worf. "Destroy the Borg ship."

"Aye, sir."

Worf moved to stand beside the ship's chief of security and senior tactical officer, Lieutenant Jasminder Choudhury. The lithe, fortyish human woman's unruly mane of raven hair was tied in a tightly bound ponytail much like Worf's own.

"Prepare to execute attack pattern Tango-Red," Worf said. He discreetly pointed out a reading on her console to her. Dropping his voice to a coaching whisper, he added, "Increase the frequency of the transphasic shielding's nutation."

"Aye, sir," Choudhury said with a polite nod as she made the adjustment. She was highly skilled and a quick learner, Worf had observed. When they had first met, he had been concerned that her philosophy regarding security matters—which she shared with her deputy chief, a Betazoid man named Rennan Konya—might be too pacifistic. After seeing them both in action during the mission to stop the Borg-assimilated science vessel *U.S.S. Einstein,* however, Worf no longer had any doubts about their competence, or their ability to wield force when necessary.

As the captain rose from his chair, Worf said, "Arm torpedoes and target the Borg vessel."

He noted with approval how deftly Choudhury found the Borg vessel's known vulnerable points. "Locked," she replied.

Confident that she had no further need of his oversight, he moved to an aft station and configured it to gather damage and casualty reports.

Around the bridge, he saw hunched shoulders and clenched

jaws, people tensed for action in a battle that would require little more than pressing buttons. Kadohata was the exception. Her countenance of mixed Asian and European ancestry was the very portrait of calm, and her British-sounding accent conveyed the same unflappability that Worf had come to expect from the captain. "Borg vessel in firing range in ten seconds," she reported.

The Borg cube loomed like a nightmare on the main viewer.

Worf longed for the raw physicality of the great Klingon battles of old, fought on fields of honor where warriors faced one another with blades to test both prowess and courage. *War was more glorious then. But death remains the same.*

"The Borg cube is arming weapons," Choudhury declared.

Three shots struck the *Enterprise*. Deafening concussions rocked the ship, and consoles along the starboard bulkhead crackled with sparks, belched acrid smoke, and went dark.

Captain Picard glanced at Worf. "Now, Number One."

"Fire at will," Worf said. "Helm, execute attack pattern!"

Streaks like blue fire blazed away from the *Enterprise* and ripped into the towering black grids of dense machinery that served as the outer hull of the Borg cube. Large segments of the Borg ship disintegrated as the torpedoes exploded, and a cobalt-colored conflagration began to consume the cube from within.

Then it returned fire.

The bridge crew was thrown like rag dolls rolling in a drum as the *Enterprise*'s inertial dampers overloaded. Everyone was hurled to port, and they plummeted as the ship kept rolling. In the span of just a few seconds, they struck the consoles along the port bulkhead, tumbled across the overhead, and dropped hard back to the deck as the ship's artificial gravity and inertial compensators reset themselves.

Worf's nose caught the scent of blood, which mingled with smoke and sharpened his focus. He pushed himself up to his hands and knees and looked first to the captain—who was bruised and had suffered a scrape on his forehead, but was not seriously hurt—and then to the main viewer, on which he saw the Borg cube consumed from within by an indigo fury. The cube collapsed into itself. Its core of blue fire turned blinding white . . . and then the ship was just a cloud of carbon dust and superheated gas.

*If we could arm all of Starfleet with these weapons,* Worf imagined, *we could end this war with the Borg on our own terms.*

He finished a cursory review of the damage and casualty reports and moved to the captain's side to help him up.

"Thank you, Mister Worf," the captain said once he was back on his feet. "Damage report."

"Hull breaches on decks twenty-six through twenty-nine, and the ventral shield generators are offline."

Picard nodded once. "Casualties?"

"Several on the lower decks," Worf said. "Mostly blunt-force trauma. No fatalities."

"Good," Picard said. "Are the sensors still operational?"

Worf stole a quick look at Kadohata, who wobbled her hand in a gesture that meant *sort of.* Worf looked at the captain. "Their function is limited."

"Focus our repairs on the sensors. We need them to trace the Borg ship's arrival trajectory."

"Aye, sir."

The captain palmed a sheen of sweat from his forehead and regarded the smoldering planet on the main viewer with a frown. "I'll be in my ready room, Commander. You have the bridge."

The battered and shaken crew remained at their posts and focused on their jobs as Picard left the bridge. Worf could tell that despite their swift victory over the Borg cube, the jarring blow the ship had taken had rattled the nerves of a few of the younger officers. Figuring that the crew would benefit from a bit of encouragement, Worf made a slow tour of the bridge stations and offered quiet, low-key compliments. It did not have the effect he'd hoped for. By the time he reached the tactical station, he noticed sly, questioning looks passing from one junior officer to another.

Choudhury confided to him, "I think you confused them."

He didn't mean to glare at her, it was just a habit. To her credit, she didn't flinch from his withering stare. "I was only trying to improve morale," he said, relaxing his expression.

"*That's* what confused them," she said.

That drew another glare from Worf, which, in turn, provoked a wan smile from Choudhury. *She is teasing me,* Worf realized with amusement. "You also did well."

"Stop," she joked. "You're confusing me."

He exhaled heavily in mock frustration. They stood together for a few moments. She stared at the image of Ramatis on the screen. Worf surveyed the bridge and was about to return to the center seat when Choudhury said, "That was home to nearly a billion people. An entire civilization. And it's gone forever." She looked at Worf. "If the rest of the fleet had transphasic torpedoes, we might be able to stop this from happening again."

"Perhaps," Worf said. "But those decisions are made by the admiralty, and we must respect the chain of command." Choudhury clenched her jaw as if she were struggling not to say something. He found her intensity unusual; she was a tranquil person by nature, and not one to evince strong emotions. "You disagree?"

She returned his inquiring stare with a fiery gaze. "I just wonder sometimes . . . what if the admiralty is wrong?"

"Good question." He left her to brood on that and returned to the center seat to monitor the repair efforts.

In fact, Worf shared Choudhury's sentiments more than he could say. The admiralty, in Worf's opinion, were making a grave error by not distributing the new weapon design, which had been reverse-engineered from prototypes acquired from an alternate future by the late Kathryn Janeway of the *Starship Voyager*. Transphasic warheads were quickly proving to be the best defense against the renewed Borg onslaught. The admiralty, however, remained concerned that the Borg would eventually adapt to this seemingly unstoppable weapon, thereby robbing Starfleet of its last effective defense. Consequently, the *Enterprise* was the only ship in Starfleet that was armed with the warheads. That meant it was up to its crew to find out how the Borg were bypassing the Federation's defenses—and to do so while there was still a Federation left to defend.

With each passing week, the number of Borg attacks had been rising, and Worf had detected a pattern in their targets and frequency. The Borg's invasion was building to what he suspected was some kind of critical mass, and when it was reached, it would be too late to stop it.

Worf glowered at the burning planet on the main viewer. *For a billion people on Ramatis III,* he reminded himself bitterly, *it is* already *too late.*

# 5

Dax entered the *Aventine*'s Deck One conference room to find several of her senior officers waiting for her. She took her seat at the head of the polished, synthetic black granite conference table and nodded to the others.

Bowers sat to her immediate left, and Lieutenant Leishman was seated next to him. Across the table from Leishman was the senior operations officer, Lieutenant Oliana Mirren, a pale and reed-thin woman of Slavic ancestry who wore her dark, curly hair short and closely cropped. Helkara sat between Mirren and Dax. The three humans at the table, Dax noted with quiet amusement, each had a cup of coffee in front of them.

As soon as Dax was settled, she said, "Let's get started."

Helkara leaned forward. "The salvage of the *Columbia*'s logs is under way, Captain. Ensign Riordan is helping its computer talk to ours, and they seem to be getting on splendidly."

Leishman cut in, "I'd just like to commend Ensign Riordan for his work on this project, Captain. If it weren't for the schematics he found in Earth's archives, I doubt we could've made a successful connection to the *Columbia*'s memory banks."

"I'll note it in my log," Dax said. She asked Helkara, "How much of their data have you translated so far?"

The Zakdorn inflated his lower lip while he pondered his answer. It gave him an unflattering resemblance to a Terran bullfrog. "About thirty-five percent, I'd say," he responded at last. "We're dividing our time between downloading the sensor logs and the flight records."

Dax turned her attention toward Mirren. "Have you made any progress in analyzing their data?"

"Some," Mirren said. "By cross-referencing the two sources, we're developing a simulation of the *Columbia*'s crash landing and its approach to the planet. We're starting from the last synchronous data points and working backward from there."

Bowers nodded and then asked, "How far along is the sim?"

"We've locked down roughly the last forty seconds before the *Columbia* impacted the surface," Mirren said. "It looks as if the ship had been on autopilot as it—" A dry crinkling sound stopped her in mid-sentence. She glowered across the table.

Leishman unwrapped a bite-size piece of chocolate, which

Dax suspected was from the chief engineer's jealously guarded personal stash of sweets. Years earlier, on *Defiant,* her colleagues had routinely raided her hidden candy cache, and Dax suspected that history would soon be repeated. Leishman popped the morsel into her mouth and started to chew. She froze as she realized that everyone else was staring at her. Through half-masticated chocolate, she asked in a defensive tone, "What?"

With the ire of an interrupted elementary-school teacher, Mirren replied, "Do you mind?"

"I get low blood sugar," Leishman said with guileless sincerity through cocoa-colored teeth. "Makes me cranky."

Dax quietly savored Sam Bowers's put-upon expression, because she knew from experience that what her XO really wanted to do was laugh. He and Dax both appreciated Leishman's knack for finding out what annoyed high-strung people and then exploiting it for her own clandestine amusement. Apparently, Leishman had decided that Mirren was going to be her latest victim.

Bowers glossed over the interruption. "Mirren, you said the *Columbia*'s autopilot had been engaged?"

"Aye, sir."

"Any idea by whom?"

Mirren shook her head. "Not yet. We're not even sure when it was activated. It might have been online for minutes, or it could've been flying the ship for years."

"All right," Dax said. "We still have twenty-one hours to work on this before we have to pull up stakes. Sam, I want all our resources focused on this. Understood?"

"Yes, sir," Bowers replied.

She planted her palms on the tabletop. "Thank you, everyone. Dismissed." The others stood half a second after Dax, and they moved in a ragged line toward the door to the aft corridor. Leishman fell into step a couple of paces behind Mirren and began whistling a soft and erratic melody. It took only a few seconds for Mirren to look back at Leishman and fume through clenched teeth, "Must you?"

"Sorry," Leishman said. "Helps me think."

As the group exited the conference room, Dax hoped that Mirren developed a sense of humor soon—because if she didn't, she was going to be on the receiving end of Leishman's subtle but deliberate irritations for a long, long time.

\* \* \*

"This place gives me the creeps," said engineering crewman Yott, his voice echoing down the *Columbia*'s empty D Deck corridor.

Chief Celia Komer looked up from the antiquated power-distribution node she was dismantling, brushed a sweaty lock of hair from her face, and scowled teasingly at the fidgety young Bolian man. "Don't tell me you're seeing ghosts, too?"

His eyes darted one way, then another. "Not ghosts," he said. "But something's been following us since we came up from E Deck." A low, reedy moan of wind disturbed the dusting of fine-particle sand they had tracked down from the surface.

Komer sighed. She pointed her palm beacon aft, down one round-ribbed stretch of passageway. Then she turned it forward to light up another before aiming it squarely into Yott's face. "Who's following us? The invisible man?"

"Chief, I'm serious. There's something here."

"Fine." Komer hated to humor superstitious behavior, but it seemed to her that the only way to get Yott back to work would be to take him seriously for a few moments. She set down her coil spanner, stood up, turned, and lifted her tricorder from its holster on her hip. "This'll just take a few seconds," she explained. "I'm running a full-spectrum scan for life-forms and energy readings. Anything special you want me to look for?"

Yott shook his head and continued to shift his gaze every few seconds, as if he expected something to try and ambush him.

"Y'know, you ought to lay off the *raktajino*," Komer said, hoping to lighten the mood. "It makes you jumpy."

To her dismay, Yott seemed immune to humor. "I don't drink *raktajino*," he said. His eyes scanned the ceiling. "Can't you feel it? Like a charge in the air? It smells like ozone."

Komer wondered uncharitably, *How'd this kid ever make it through basic training?* "I'm not reading anything unusual," she said, hoping her matter-of-fact tone would calm him. She pivoted as her scan continued. "No bio signs in this section but us."

"There are things tricorders can't read," Yott said. "Trace elements, exotic energy patterns, extradimensional phenomena—"

"And paranoia," she interrupted. "I can't believe I really have to tell you there's no such thing as—" A flicker of blue light behind a bulkhead caught her eye, and Yott's as well.

He cried out, "You saw that! You saw it!"

Taking a breath to suppress her irritation, she focused the tricorder in the direction of the flash. "Residual energy," she said, her tone one of mild rebuke. "Just a surge in the lines. Makes sense when you think about how much juice we're pumping into this old wreck."

"Not down here," Yott replied, and he lifted his tricorder to show her a schematic on its screen. "The main power relay was severed in the crash, and both the backups are slagged. There's *no power* on this deck." He pointed at the nearby bulkhead. "So where did *that* come from?"

Another groan of hot, dry wind pushed through fractures in the bulkheads. Crackles of noise echoed off the metal interiors of the passageway, growing closer and sharper. Then a light fixture on the overhead stuttered momentarily to life and flared brightly enough to force Komer to shut her eyes. Its afterimage pulsed in myriad hues on her retina.

"Chief!" shouted Yott. He tugged on her sleeve. "Come on!"

Shielding her eyes with her forearm, she backed away from the glare and tapped her combadge. "Komer to—"

Twisted forks of green lightning exploded from the light, in a storm of shining phosphors and searing-hot polymer shards. The synthetic shrapnel overpowered Komer and Yott, peppering their faces with bits of burning debris as the bolts of electricity slammed into their torsos and hurled them hard to the deck.

A steady, high-pitched tone rang in Komer's ears. Spasms wracked her body, but she barely felt them—she was numb from the chest down. Her mouth was dry, and her tongue tasted like copper. As the last of the light's glowing debris fell to the deck and faded away, darkness settled upon her and Yott.

Then a spectral shape formed in the blackness, as pale and silent as a gathering fog. It descended like a heavy liquid sinking into the sea—spreading, dispersing, enveloping the two downed Starfleet personnel on the deck.

For a moment, Komer told herself that she was imagining it, that it was nothing more than a trauma-induced hallucination, another afterimage on her overtaxed retinas.

Then Yott screamed—and as the ghostly motes pierced Komer's body like a million needles of fire, she did, too.

* * *

Lieutenant Lonnoc Kedair strode quickly through the sepulchral darkness of the corridor, toward the cluster of downward-pointed palm-beacon beams. A charnel odor thickened the sultry air.

Four *Aventine* security officers stood with their phaser rifles slung at their sides, facing one another in a circle. Kedair nudged past them and stopped as she saw the two bodies at their feet. Both corpses were contorted in poses of agony and riddled with deep, smoldering cavities. In some places, the two engineers' wounds tunneled clear through their bodies, giving Kedair a view of the deck, which was slick with greasy pools of liquefied biomass.

Kedair turned to Lieutenant Naomi Darrow, the away team's security supervisor. "Who were they?"

"Yott and Komer, sir," Darrow said. "They were collecting evidence for analysis."

Kedair squatted low next to the dead Bolian and examined his wounds more closely. "What killed them?"

"We're not sure," said Darrow. "We picked up some residual energy traces, but nothing that matches any known weapons."

Pointing at a smoking divot in Komer's abdomen, Kedair said, "These look like thermal effects."

"Partly," Darrow said as she pushed a handful of her flaxen hair from her face. "But we think those are secondary. The cause of death looks like molecular disruption."

The security chief shook her head. "I've never seen a disruptor do this. Did you check for biochemical agents?"

"Yes, sir. No biochem signatures of any kind."

It was a genuine mystery—exactly what Kedair hated most.

Everyone on the *Columbia* had heard the bloodcurdling shrieks emanate from the ship's lower decks and echo through its open turbolift shafts, but Kedair was determined to contain and compartmentalize as much information about this incident as she could. She asked Darrow, "Who's been down here?"

Darrow swept the beam of her palm beacon over the other security officers on the scene: Englehorn, T'Prel, and ch'Maras. "Just us," she said.

"Keep it that way," Kedair said. "Have these bodies beamed to sickbay on the *Aventine*. I want Dr. Tarses to start the autopsies immediately."

"Aye, sir," Darrow said.

"And not a word of this to anyone," Kedair said, making eye contact with the four officers in succession. "If anyone asks—"

Englehorn interrupted, "*If?*"

Correcting herself, Kedair continued, "*When* you are asked about what happened, the only thing I want you to say is that there was an incident, and that it's under investigation. Don't mention fatalities, injuries, or anything else. Do not mention Yott or Komer by name. Is that understood?" The four junior officers nodded. "Good. I want you four to secure this deck. Move in pairs and maintain an open channel to the *Aventine*." She looked down at the bodies. "If you encounter anything that might be capable of this, fall back and call for backup. Clear?" Another round of heads bobbing in unison. "Make it happen."

Darrow pointed at the other security officers as she issued their orders. "Englehorn, sweep aft with T'Prel. ch'Maras, forward with me." She looked at Kedair. "Sir, I suggest you beam up to *Aventine* and track our search from there." To the others she added, "Move out."

The four security officers split up and walked away in opposite directions, with one member of each pair monitoring a tricorder's sensor readings while the other kept a phaser rifle leveled and ready. Kedair remained with the bodies as her team continued moving away. Their shadows spread and then vanished beyond circular section bulkheads in the curved corridor. In less than a minute Kedair was alone, her solitary palm beacon casting a harsh blue glow over the dead.

*I was so focused on not fueling their fears that I failed to protect their lives.* Bitter regrets festered in her thoughts. *I should have kept an open mind, no matter what they told me.*

Kedair still didn't believe that the two-hundred-year-old wrecked starship was haunted—but the twisted, horrific corpses in front of her left her no doubt that she, and her away team, were definitely not alone on the *Columbia*.

# 6

Darkness pressed in on Erika Hernandez as she made her slow descent into the frigid abyss of the *Columbia*'s aft turbolift. Her breath misted as it passed over the plastic-sheathed chemical flare clenched in her teeth.

She had underestimated the effort involved in climbing from the bridge portal on A Deck to the entrance of main engineering on D Deck. The blue glow of the flare was fading slowly after having burned for more than an hour. It was still bright enough to let her see the rungs under her hands, but her feet probed the cold blackness for each new, unseen foothold.

Above her, and attached to her by a safety line that was secured on the bridge, was Lieutenant Vincenzo Yacavino, the second-in-command of the ship's MACO detachment. At the request of Commander Fletcher—who, like most first officers, was quite protective of her captain—he had climbed up from the MACOs' berthing area on C Deck to escort Hernandez safely belowdecks. A necklace of variously colored emergency flares was strung around his neck. He called down to her, "Are you all right, *signora*?"

"Mm-hmm," Hernandez mumble-hummed past the flare in her teeth. Then, a few meters below, she saw flickers of light.

She quickened her pace and reached the open turbolift portal of D Deck. Using handholds and a narrow lip of metal that protruded from the shaft bulkhead beside the opening, she eased her way off the ladder and onto the catwalk at the forward end of main engineering. As soon as Yacavino had joined her on the platform, she unfastened the safety line that he had looped in a crisscross pattern around her torso. She would rather have borrowed one of the MACOs' tactical harnesses, which were designed and reinforced for rappelling, but most of the spares had been lost in the same blast that had crippled her ship.

Almost every available emergency light on the *Columbia* had been brought to bear in its engineering compartment, but because most of the lights were focused on specific areas of interest, the majority of the deck remained steeped in smoky shadows. An acrid pall of scorched metal put a sharp tang in the air.

Karl Graylock, the chief engineer, stood with warp-drive specialist Daria Pierce at a control console on the elevated platform behind the warp reactor. The surface panel of the console had been removed, exposing half-melted circuit boards and blackened wiring. On the lower deck, more than a dozen engineers removed heavy plates from the reactor housing, decoupled enormous plasma relays, and sifted through a dusty pile of crystal shards and debris.

No one paid much attention to Hernandez as she walked down the stairs from the catwalk and continued toward Graylock.

"Try cross-circuiting to A," he said to Pierce as he made a minor adjustment to something inside the console. He watched Pierce make a few changes of her own. They both stared intently into the mangled workings of the console, then shook their heads in shared frustration. "Nothing," Graylock said, his shoulders sagging in defeat.

"Karl," Hernandez said. Normally, he snapped-to at the sound of her voice. This time he sat back against the railing opposite the control panel and looked down at the captain with a weary expression. "*Ja*, Captain?"

"Good news," she said with faint optimism. "Looks like your plan worked. If the Romulans had figured it out, we'd probably all be dead by now."

Graylock's dour frown was steady. "Is that your idea of cheering us up, Captain? Because if it is, you suck at it."

"I take it things aren't going well down here?"

"You could say that," Graylock replied. He climbed down from the platform and led Hernandez on a slow stroll down the length of the reactor. "The warp drive is irreparable," he said. "All that's left of the crystal matrix is dust and splinters. At least half the coils in each nacelle are ruptured, maybe more. And the ventral plasma relays were all severed in the last explosion."

Hernandez glanced inside the reactor through a gap left by a detached pylon conduit. She could see for herself that Graylock wasn't exaggerating. The damage was extensive.

"So what are we looking at? Do we need the *Enterprise* to bring us a whole new warp drive?"

The stocky chief engineer turned and folded his arms over his chest. "*Ja,* that would help." He leaned back against the oblong reactor housing. "And if you can think of a way to ask them, or anyone else, I will be most impressed, Captain."

It took her a moment to deduce his implication. "Subspace communications?"

"*Kaput,*" he said. "The virus corrupted our software and firmware, and the explosion that covered our escape destroyed both our shuttlepods and the transceiver array. We can send and receive light-speed signals, if you don't mind waiting the rest of your life for a reply."

"Wonderful," Hernandez muttered. "Isn't there something we can raid for parts to fix the subspace antenna?"

Graylock gestured vaguely around the compartment. "We don't have enough working parts to keep the lights on, and you want me to reinvent subspace radio?"

Hernandez sighed. "Since you brought it up, when *can* we expect to have the lights back?"

"It depends." He looked back at his engineers, who were tinkering with an assortment of broken or deformed components that looked more like scrap metal bound for reclamation than like the essential components of a starship's warp propulsion system. "If we can all stay awake, maybe ten hours."

"Make it six," Hernandez said. "I want the turbolifts running before alpha shift goes to their racks."

"*Jawohl,* Captain," Graylock said with a nod. "I'll keep Commander Fletcher informed of our efforts."

She returned his nod. "Carry on."

None of the engineers looked up from their tasks as she walked back to the catwalk staircase and rejoined Lieutenant Yacavino at the open portal to the turbolift shaft. "Time to head back up to A Deck," she said to the fit, dark-haired MACO. "Let's get ready to climb." He picked up the safety line and started paying out slack to wrap around her. As he reached behind her back to loop the end of the tether around her thigh, she gave him a teasing scowl. "And watch your hands this time, Mister. I want to keep our relationship professional."

\* \* \*

Commander Veronica Fletcher waited until the door of the captain's ready room closed before she said, "It's worse than we thought."

Captain Hernandez pushed her chair back from the small desk tucked into the corner of the compartment. She crossed her legs and nodded to another chair. "Have a seat."

Fletcher pulled out the chair and sat down. She handed a small clipboard to Hernandez. "We lost more than half the crew in the attack, and most of the MACOs were killed setting off the diversionary blast."

"Damn it," Hernandez whispered. "Where'd the jump take us?"

"Kalil plotted our position against the known shipping lanes," she explained as the captain looked over the second page of the brief report. "We're well outside normal sensor range. And with the convoy gone, there probably won't be much friendly traffic out here for a while."

"If ever," Hernandez said.

The captain's downbeat manner troubled Fletcher. "Being a bit pessimistic, aren't you?"

Worry lines deepened on Hernandez's brow. "If yesterday's events are any guide, this entire sector is likely to be under enemy control soon." Her countenance darkened. "This was only the beginning—the first salvo in a war with the Romulans."

"You don't know that," Fletcher said. "It might have been an isolated skirmish, or—"

"They ambushed us," Hernandez interrupted. "They came in numbers, and they turned our own weapons on the convoy. This was planned. They've been preparing for a long time, and now they're making their move—and we're stuck out here, with no way home and no way to send a warning." She launched herself from her chair and then halted, a coiled spring with nowhere to go. Turning away to look out the compartment's single, small viewport, she added with simmering frustration, "The goddamn war's actually starting, and we're stuck on the sidelines."

Fletcher sighed. "So, what are we supposed to do?"

Several seconds passed while Fletcher waited for the captain's answer. The exposed overhead conduits, normally alive with a low buzzing, were silent, exacerbating Fletcher's sense of the ship's predicament. Finally, Hernandez turned away from the window and back toward her first officer. "We survive," she said. "If the war has begun, Earth won't have any ships to spare on a search-and-rescue mission this far from home. Whatever else happens, we have to assume we're on our own now."

Fletcher wasn't ready yet to embrace the worst-case scenario. She asked, "What if Earth *does* send a rescue ship? Our best bet of being found would be to return to our original course, at any speed."

"That's also our best chance of being found by the enemy," Hernandez said. "They knew our route well enough to hit us with almost no warning. Using the same route to limp home strikes me as a bad idea." She covered her eyes and massaged her temples with one hand. "Besides, without the transceiver array, we're mute. Even if someone came looking for us, we can't respond to their hails. At anything less than close range, we might be mistaken for an alien ship that doesn't want to make contact."

The captain stepped past Fletcher and crossed the cramped room to another short desktop wedged into the opposite corner. She poked through a jumble of papers and bound volumes on the shelf above it, then pulled down and opened a large book. "Have a look at this," she said to Fletcher, who got up and joined the captain at the other desk. Hernandez continued, "This is from our last mapping run before we met the convoy."

Studying the dense cluster of symbols and coordinates on the map, Fletcher was unable to anticipate the captain's plan. "What are we looking for?"

"The basics," Hernandez said. "A nice Minshara-class planet where we can stock up on food and water. Preferably, one with enough expertise to help us make some repair parts for the warp drive." She planted her finger on an unnamed star system that so far had merited no more than a brief footnote in the galactic catalog. "That's what I'm talking about. Nitrogen-oxygen atmosphere, liquid water, and subspace signal emissions."

Fletcher shook her head. "Shaky readings, sir. And at that range? They could have been caused by a sensor malfunction."

"All right," Hernandez countered. "How do you explain the high-energy particles flooding out of that system?"

"It could be anything," Fletcher said. "That star's pretty dense. For all we know, we might be picking up signals from a system behind it, due to gravitational lensing."

The captain looked unconvinced. "I don't think so," she said. "If we were seeing a lensed signal, there'd be other distortions. These readings may be scarce, but they're clear. There's a planet there with the resources we need, and it's the closest safe harbor in the sector."

"We don't know that it's safe, and 'close' is a relative term," Fletcher said. "It's eleven-point-four light-years away. How are we supposed to get there without the warp drive?"

Hernandez shut the book with a heavy slap. "We still have impulse engines, and I mean to use them."

As the captain put the book back on the shelf, Fletcher was compelled to ask, "Are you serious? Even at full impulse—"

"Forget full impulse," Hernandez cut in. "I want the main impulse system in overdrive. We need to get as close to lightspeed as we can without hitting it."

Fletcher was aghast. "You're talking about time-dilation effects," she said.

"Yes, I am," Hernandez said. She returned to her desk in the other corner. "Don't give me that look. Think about it for a second, and you'll see why we have to do this."

The captain's urgent tone made her point clear to Fletcher. "To ration our provisions," she said, and the captain nodded in confirmation. The *Columbia* had been fueled and supplied for a two-year deployment before leaving Earth. Without warp drive, interstellar travel to a world capable of restocking the ship's stores and repairing its damaged systems might take years or even decades. "What fraction of c are we talking about?"

"Within one-ten-thousandth," Hernandez said.

After a quick round of mental calculations, Fletcher said, "So, a time-dilation ratio of about seventy-to-one?"

"Give or take," Hernandez replied.

"So why not just make a run for home?"

Hernandez raised her eyebrows in a gentle expression of mock surprise. "Because 'home' is over eighty light-years away. I'd rather not waste the better part of a century getting there. If I'm right, we can find what we need to fix the warp drive in that star system and get home while at least a few people we know are still alive."

The prospect of twelve years being transformed by the laws of relativity into a short-lived purgatory disturbed Fletcher, but the notions of starving to death in deep space or returning home as a centenarian troubled her even more. "I'll get Graylock to work on the impulse drive," Fletcher said. "It'll take a few hours to remove the safeties before we can overdrive the coils past one-quarter c."

The captain nodded. "Tell him to beef up the main deflector, too. At the speeds we're talking about, the mass and kinetic energy of oncoming particles'll be pretty intense."

"And once we hit relativistic speeds, our sensors'll be blind to just about everything," Fletcher said. "We'll also become a serious X-ray source."

Hernandez smiled. "I prefer to think of it as becoming our own interstellar emergency flare."

Fletcher chortled. "We'd just better hope we don't get noticed by the Romulans or the Klingons."

"They'd probably mistake us for some kind of primitive colony ship," Hernandez said. "Maybe we'll get lucky and be taken prisoner aboard a ship that actually has a working warp drive. Now, if you want something to worry about, try the hard radiation from blueshifting."

Fletcher nodded. "We'd better have Dr. Metzger start us all on radiation-treatment protocols. And I'll have Thayer restrict access to the outer compartments."

"Good thinking," said Hernandez.

"Then the only things we still need are a deck of cards and some good books. If you like, I can loan you the first six *Captain Proton* novels."

"Thank you, Number One," said Hernandez, who no longer seemed to be paying attention. She sounded unusually somber.

"Are you sure you're all right, Captain?"

A rueful grimace twisted the captain's mouth. "I'm fine," she said. "It just bugs me that the time when Earth needs us most is the one time we can't be there." She turned her gaze out the viewport. "All we can do is hope that when we finally bring our ship home, there's still a home worth bringing it to."

Stephen Foyle pivoted from one foot to the other while he dribbled the basketball from hand to hand, turning his body to keep his opponent at bay. Sweat dripped from above his hairline, tracing winding paths out of his gray brush cut and down his face. A thick sheen of perspiration on his arms and legs caught the glare of the overhead lights in the ship's gymnasium.

Gage Pembleton taunted him in a tone of crisp superiority. "What are you waiting for, Major? An invitation?"

"Patience, First Sergeant," Foyle said. He lurched forward, and Pembleton matched his stride. Then Foyle passed the ball backward between his own legs, spun, and slipped behind Pembleton's back for a drive at the basket. By the time the younger, brown-skinned man had caught up to Foyle, the major had made a graceful layup, banking the ball off the backboard.

The orange ball hushed through the net, and Pembleton caught it off the bounce. "Not bad," he said. He tossed the ball with a single bounce at Foyle. "But it's still eleven-eight."

Foyle checked the ball and passed it back. "For now."

A musky scent of deodorant overpowered by exertion trailed Pembleton as he dribbled the ball back to the top of the key to start his possession. "What time is it?"

"Getting tired?"

"No, I want you to sing me 'Happy Birthday' at 1340 hours."

"That's not funny," Foyle said, irked to be reminded of Captain Hernandez's decision to send them all on a slow-time cruise into oblivion. He imagined that he could feel an hour slipping away with every minute, days vanishing into every hour.

At the center-court circle, Pembleton turned and waited for Foyle to strike a defensive pose. The lanky Canadian started dribbling and pivoted to show Foyle his back. "I'll spot you three points if you can take the ball before I score," he said in his drawl of a baritone. "Give you a chance to tie it up."

Foyle grinned. "Don't go getting—"

Pembleton was off the deck, spinning in midair, hefting the ball high over his head with his long, wiry arms and massive hands. Foyle sprang to block the shot, hands flailing, but the ball was gone, sailing on a long and poetic arc into the basket. It slapped through the net, bounced twice off the deck, and rolled behind the end line as Foyle watched with a tired frown.

"Thirteen-eight," Pembleton said. As the major opened his mouth to protest, the sergeant pointed at their feet and added, "Behind the line, two points."

"Now you're just showing off," Foyle said. They walked

downcourt together to retrieve the ball. The major's nostrils filled with the funky stench of his sweat-soaked tank top and sodden socks, and his thighs and calves felt as if they were tying themselves in knots and turning to wood. He palmed the excess perspiration from his face and dried his hands on his cotton athletic trunks. Then he squatted to pick up the ball and was unable to stop himself from exhaling a pained grunt. "I think I need a time-out," he said.

"No time-outs in one-on-one," Pembleton taunted. Unfazed by Foyle's bitter glare, he added, "Your rules."

Foyle tucked the ball under his left arm and walked toward the benches at the sideline. "Don't make me pull rank."

"It's your game, Major. I just play in it."

Pembleton followed him to the bench and sat down on the other side of a stack of soft, white towels. He kept his back straight and his head up, and his breaths were long and slow.

Foyle slumped as soon as he was seated, and he reached under the bench for his squeeze bottle of water. The major lifted the nozzle to his lips and clamped his hand tight, filling his mouth with a stream of cool liquid. He downed a third of the bottle in half a minute. "I can't believe she's doing this," he said after catching his breath.

The sergeant maintained an attentive silence. He picked up a towel and dried his shaved head as Foyle continued.

"There has to be some way to get a signal back to Earth. We could've cannibalized something to fix the transceiver array and sent a Mayday to Starfleet—or even to Vulcan, if we had to." He took another swig of water. "Instead, she's got us sitting out the war. Didn't even ask me before she put us all on the slow boat to nowhere."

Pembleton chided him, "She didn't *ask* you? Tell me, Major, when did the ship become a democracy? Do I get a vote, too?"

"You know what I mean, Pembleton," Foyle said, weary and frustrated. "It's the same old story. She thinks just because we're MACOs, we don't need to know. Hell, even the illusion of being consulted would be nice once in a while."

"So, if she had let you speak your mind, and then did the same thing anyway, you'd be fine with that?"

The question forced Foyle to stop and think for a moment. "No," he admitted, "I wouldn't. I mean, what if this planet we're going to can't help us? What then? Should we just keep making these near-light trips while the galaxy changes around us at warp speed? It's just so damned stupid. There has to be a better answer than wasting twelve years of our lives."

"It's not our lives she's wasting," Pembleton said. "It's everyone else's. I was supposed to be home in time to see my oldest start school. He'll be in college by the time we drop back to normal spaceflight. I feel like I've missed his *whole life.*" He dried his arms and then tossed away the towel. "For us," he continued, "this'll just be a couple of boring months. But for my wife and my boys . . . I might as well be dead."

That same thought haunted Foyle, as well. They were five days into their journey, and he knew that home on Earth, his wife, Valerie, was likely marking the anniversary of the last time she had seen him or heard his voice. The *Columbia* and its crew had been missing in action for more than a year in Earth time.

*She won't have given up on me yet,* he assured himself. *But she won't wait forever. Sooner or later, she'll go on with her life, without me. I might get home while she's still alive, but it won't matter, because my life will be gone. Our life.*

"There's still time for a change of plan," Foyle said. He watched Pembleton to measure his reaction. "If we drop the ship back to quarter impulse, we can focus on repairing the transceiver, maybe get a message home before everybody we know gives up on us."

"Nice idea. But if that was a possibility, I have to think we'd be doing it already."

"Maybe," Foyle said. "But what if it's just that Graylock needs to take orders from someone who knows how to motivate him?" He glanced at Pembleton.

The sergeant kept his expression a cipher. For as long as Foyle had served with him, Pembleton had been a master at encrypting his feelings. "It might take a pretty big shakeup in the command structure to cause a change like that," the sergeant said. His eyes betrayed nothing as he returned Foyle's stare. "Permission to speak freely, sir?"

"Granted."

"Considering the amount of damage to the ship, and the skill we've seen Graylock use to keep it running, I'm inclined to believe him when he says the transceiver can't be fixed. And if the captain thinks this is our best shot, I'd say trust her."

Foyle responded with a slow nod. "So, you don't think a change in strategy or leadership would be in our best interest?"

"Under these circumstances? No."

Something about the tenor of that answer prompted Foyle to press on. "And if, at some future juncture, our circumstances were to change . . . ?"

Pembleton shrugged and replied with an ominous nonchalance, "Well . . . that's a different question."

# 2381

## 7

Melora Pazlar felt as if she were the stillness at the center of everything. Floating in the womblike zero *g* of *Titan*'s stellar cartography lab, she was surrounded by a holographic sphere of stars, a virtual front-row seat to the universe.

Aloft and held in place by tractor beams so gentle that even her fragile senses couldn't feel them, she turned in slow degrees. She manipulated images of science-department reports and sensor analyses that were superimposed over the holographic backdrop, rearranging them with fluid arcs of her arms and subtle turns of her wrist. It was like a silent ballet.

She marveled at Ra-Havreii's handiwork. *He really is a genius,* she thought with admiration and delight. Then she remembered their almost-kiss and her reflexive retreat. She had pondered it for the past several hours while she worked, and she still didn't know why she had rebuffed him. The Efrosian was handsome and charming, and had a whispered reputation among the ship's female humanoids as a considerate companion. He had everything going for him, and he clearly was more than a little interested in her, and she knew that a few years earlier she might have welcomed him eagerly.

Now, however, she couldn't imagine letting his lips touch hers without a shiver traveling down her spine. The idea of his hands on her flesh made her pull her arms to her sides, and her entire body tensed and began to fold in on itself.

Bending forward, she propelled herself into a slow tumble around her center of gravity. She forced her arms wide, as if to take the stars and nebulae into her delicate embrace, and she cleared her mind while drawing deep breaths. Tuvok had taught her well how to master her emotions and calm her mind. He had even imparted some wisdom in the area of self-defense, by emphasizing styles and techniques based on evasion. She had become an expert at slipping away from people.

A soft but insistent synthetic tone beeped in quick triple pulses, breaking her moment of reflection. The sound made bright echoes against the unseen surfaces of the holotank. Pazlar used bend-and-stretch gestures to arrest her forward rolling. It took a few seconds for her to become still once again. All the while, the computer's alert continued chirping at her. When at last she was steady, she stretched out her arm and waved her hand in a semicircle to halt the shrill signal. "Computer, report."

*"Anomalous energy signature detected,"* replied the feminine voice of the ship's computer.

Pazlar tried not to get her hopes up. *Titan*'s crew had charted many unusual energy signatures in this region, and few had proved worthy of even a cursory follow-up. "Elaborate."

*"Concentrated pulses of triquantum waves with a subspatial distortion factor of four-point-six teracochranes."*

This was something new. "Have we identified the source?"

*"Affirmative. Bearing 335.46, mark 291.14, distance eighteen-point-two light-years."*

"Show me what we have about the pulses' point of origin," Pazlar said. "Provide a false-spectrum display of the pulses' trajectories and superimpose over my starmap interface. Prepare secondary data displays." More focused now, Pazlar began her fluid choreography of data screens as she called them into existence. "Particle analysis of the wave pulses." Down and to the left. "Cross-reference with past energy emissions from this sector." Right and up diagonally.

The luminosity of her holographic environment became blinding as several beams of laser-intense white light radiated in all directions from what looked like an empty point in deep space. Pazlar squinted against the glare. "Computer, tone it down a bit, please." The beams faded to a dim blue, and she was grateful that Ra-Havreii's user interface had been programmed with a sophisticated grasp of idioms in several languages.

There was nowhere in the holotank that Pazlar could position herself without being intersected by multiple beams. "Computer, estimate the power level of these bursts."

*"Unable to comply. Power levels have exceeded the limits of our sensor capacity. Severe subspatial distortion is interfering with scans of the origin point."*

Now Pazlar was worried. Subspatial distortion? At that power level? Not good. She pulled the empty sector-grid chart to the front of her array of screens. "Pazlar to Lieutenant Rager."

*Titan's* senior operations officer answered over the comm, *"Go ahead."*

"Sariel," Pazlar said, "I need a priority reassignment of the main sensor array." She felt a low-power force field give her tactile feedback as she entered commands on her holographic interface. "I'm sending over a grid reference, and I need to see every last bit of it in maximum detail as soon as possible."

Rager was apologetic. *"Melora, I can't do that. Some of the scans we're running were ordered by Commander Tuvok. If you want to cancel his assignments, you'll need approval from the XO."* A computer feedback tone was audible over the channel. *"Hang on, I just got your file."* A few moments later, Rager muttered, *"You sent me a blank grid reference? You want me to drop everything to point the main array at nothing?"*

"I don't think it's nothing," Pazlar said. "Something at those coordinates is sending out high-energy bursts in every direction. More to the point, it's something *we can't see.*" She sent over her readings of the wave pulses and waited until she heard the chime of its arrival through the open channel.

*"All right,"* Rager said. *"That is interesting. I can bump a couple of the research projects and let you have the gravi—"*

"Sariel," Pazlar snapped, "look at the energy profile for the pulses! Now look at the ambient readings in the center of that grid reference. Are you looking?"

Anger put an edge on Rager's voice. *"Yes, but I don't . . ."* She paused for a few seconds. Then she answered with understanding and alarm, *"Triquantum waves."*

"Also known as a telltale sign of transwarp conduits."

*"The array's all yours."*


"Spell it out for me," Riker said to Pazlar, whose holographic avatar sat at the conference table with the rest of *Titan's* senior bridge officers. "How close are these pulses to Borg transwarp signatures?"

"Similar, but not identical," Pazlar said. "Their energy levels are greater than anything we've ever seen the Borg use, but their subspatial distortions share a number of properties with transwarp conduits. They might be related."

Keru leaned forward to look at Riker. "I agree, Captain. It's possible the Borg have developed a new form of transwarp to replace the network they lost."

Riker was troubled by Keru's speculation, but at the same time he was grateful to have something to work on. It was just after 2300 hours, nearly the end of beta shift, his normal time for retiring to bed with Deanna. This situation would give him a reason to stay awake a few more hours and let her go to sleep first, before he returned to their quarters. He looked at Lieutenant Rager. "Do we know what's generating these pulses?"

The brown-skinned woman shook her head. "No, sir. We've made the most detailed scans we can from this distance, and so far we haven't seen anything at the pulses' origin point. But we have come up with a few anomalies."

"Naturally," Keru quipped. "Never a shortage of those."

After shooting a glare at the chief of security, Rager continued, "Most of our scans showed the sector as empty, except for a pretty harsh radiation field. But when we mapped the currents of cosmic particles passing through the sector, we found this." She entered a command on her padd, and a computer-generated animation appeared on the conference room's wall-mounted viewscreen. It showed countless overlapping streams bending around a central point. "Even though we can't read any sign of space-time curvature in that area, particles moving through it have their directions and velocities altered as if they'd run into something big."

Intrigued and worried in equal measure, Riker asked, "Big like a Borg transwarp hub?"

"No," Pazlar said. "Big like a star system."

"All right," Riker said. "I remember seeing a planetary cloaking device during my first year on the *Enterprise*. It's not hard to imagine someone taking it to the next step."

"The question, then," Keru said, "is who that someone is."

Rager keyed in more commands on her padd and changed the animation on the viewscreen to show the trajectories of several of the energy pulses. "It's worth noting," she said, "that a few of these bursts appear to be targeted at Federation space. The energy signatures taper off after about twenty light-years from their point of origin, so if they are the leading ends of transwarp conduits, there's no telling where they let out."

Riker looked at his first officer, who had been unusually quiet so far during the meeting. "Chris? What do you think?"

Vale addressed her reply to Pazlar. "Sounds like you might have stumbled onto a Borg installation," she said. "This might be how they've been bypassing our perimeter defenses."

"Hang on," Rager said. "Don't you think we might be jumping to conclusions here? She only said there are *similarities* to Borg transwarp frequencies."

Tuvok added, "I concur with Lieutenant Rager. There is no evidence that the Borg have ever ventured into this region of the Beta Quadrant. Furthermore, if we are dealing with a cloaked star system, such an undertaking would, presumably, take a great deal of time to accomplish. Because we are within eighteen light-years of the pulses' source, the cloaking would have to have occurred at least eighteen years ago, or else light from the star would still be visible to us."

Pazlar's avatar perked up. "That's right," she said. "I need to check something." She picked up her padd—which was part of her projected holopresence—and worked quickly while the conversation continued around her.

"You both make good points," Vale said to Rager and Tuvok. "However, the fact that energy bursts are being directed from here toward the Federation, at the same time that the Borg are slipping through our defenses, is highly suspect. Even if the Borg didn't *create* the thing sending the pulses, they might have discovered it and found a way to exploit it."

Keru added, "Or maybe *it* is using *them* against *us*."

"Also a possibility," Vale said. Turning to Tuvok, she added, "Either way, if there is a link between this phenomenon and the Borg, it'll be our job to stop it."

"To borrow a human expression," Tuvok said, "'easier said than done.' If the Borg have established a stronghold in a cloaked star system, there will be no way to estimate their numbers until it is too late to turn back. We might well find ourselves severely outnumbered."

Keru nodded and looked at Vale. "He's right. It's not like we can call for reinforcements out here."

"I've got something interesting," Pazlar interrupted. She relayed her padd's information to the wall viewscreen. "I cross-referenced the star charts we got from the Pa'haquel and the

Vomnin to see if they'd ever noted a star at these coordinates. They have." She got up and walked to the monitor to point out details as she talked. "In fact, we noted it ourselves, in a wide-area mapping survey several months ago, before we entered its 'dark zone.' It was a main-sequence star, high metallicity. Its gravitational signature indicated several planets in orbit. About eight hundred years ago, it started fading, and its gravitational signature changed in a way that suggests it lost its planets. Approximately seven hundred years ago, it went dark. So, today, to anyone within seven hundred light-years, it's as good as invisible."

Riker asked with real curiosity, "What happened to it? Did it go supernova? Collapse into a black hole?"

"No, sir," Pazlar said. "It just . . . went dark."

Keru deadpanned, "Gee, that's not ominous." He turned to Riker. "If they don't want to be seen, maybe we don't, either."

"Agreed," Riker said. "Tuvok, do what you can to reduce our sensor profile. Rager, deploy subspace radio boosters at shorter intervals, in case we need to get a signal back to Starfleet in a hurry. Keru, get your security teams ready to make an assault on the Borg, and be ready to repel boarders. Pazlar, keep analyzing the energy pulses, and report any new findings." As he pushed his chair back from the table, he said to Vale, "Commander, put us on an intercept course for the source of those pulses, maximum warp." Riker stood and made a quick exit, followed by the other officers.

They moved as a unit down a short passage to the bridge. There, Riker settled wearily into his chair as Vale ordered the course change. The pitch of the engines' whine climbed rapidly as *Titan* accelerated to its maximum rated warp speed. On the main viewscreen, the stars were no longer just streaks or even blurs so much as snap-flashes of light racing past, forming a tunnel of light around the *Luna*-class starship.

Vale finished making her circuit of the bridge and placed herself just behind Riker's left shoulder. "I just had a worrying thought," she said in a confidential tone. "It seems to me that someone who'd turn their star system invisible probably won't be thrilled to receive visitors."

"Good point," Riker said. "Take the ship to Yellow Alert."

* * *

Ranul Keru took two steps inside the auxiliary engineering lab and realized he was surrounded.

Machines of alien grace were grouped together in what seemed to Keru like a haphazard fashion, leaning against one another, clumped in tight clusters, or set front to back in ragged lines along the lab's bulkheads. The odors of chemical solvents and superheated metal assaulted Keru's nostrils, and he stepped carefully through the maze of incomplete inventions.

He followed his ears. Despite the blanketing hum of whirring generators, hissing ventilators, and purring servos, he still discerned the irregular tapping and scraping of a tinkerer at work. On the other side of an incomplete frame snaked with wires and patched with isolinear arrays, he caught the flash of a phased-pulse welding iron. When the red-ringed indigo afterimage faded from his retina and he could see again, he spied his friend Torvig eyeing a misshapen gadget on the bench.

"Hi, Vig," Keru said, making a small wave of greeting. "I buzzed a couple of times but got no answer, so I let myself in."

The Choblik engineer rolled his head to one side, an oddly endearing affectation that Keru had learned was used by Torvig's people as a gesture of trust—an unspoken show of faith that the new arrival would not go for one's jugular. "It's good to see you, Ranul," Torvig said. He trotted in bouncing steps toward Keru, his prehensile tail undulating behind him to help preserve his balance. When the squat, cervine young officer was closer to the burly Trill security chief, he craned his head back to make eye contact. "Is there something I can make for you?"

Keru smiled, being careful not to bare his teeth. "Maybe," he said. "You seem busy enough, though. What're you working on?"

"Prototypes and scale models," Torvig said. He gestured with one of his silvery bionic arms toward his workbench. "Let me show you." He flounced like an excited child back to his U-shaped work area, and Keru followed him.

Long, mechanical arms studded with tools and utilities reached down from the ceiling, where they swiveled from ball joints. A few curious devices hovered or tumbled in place, like tools abandoned in zero gravity. One side of the dark gray work surface was littered with dust, metal shavings, stray isolinear rods, optronic cables, and hundreds of sparkling bits of debris. Heat lingered in the air, a testament to interrupted efforts.

Standing upright at the end of Torvig's work area was a narrow, rectangular slab more than two meters tall, half a meter wide, and barely four millimeters thick; it was black and cast a mirror-quality reflection. "I've been working on this for many weeks," Torvig said, aglow with pride. "What do you think?"

Keru was at a loss for words. He wasn't certain if the slab was meant to represent an engineering achievement or an artistic one. Not wanting to offend Torvig, he finally settled on a neutral and factually incontrovertible declaration. "Shiny."

"Yes, it resists biological and synthetic residues even better than I had hoped," Torvig boasted. He directed an expectant stare at Keru. "Go ahead. Try it."

Again, Keru had no idea how to respond. He looked at Torvig, whose stare did not waver. *All right,* Keru told himself, *he asked you to try it out. That implies it does something. It's functional. Just look for an "on" switch or something.*

He leaned close to the black slab, eyed it with unblinking intensity, and traced its edges with his vision, desperate to suss out some clue to its purpose. Then he caught his reflection on its flat surface, and he paused to wince at the new gray hairs that had crept into his dark beard. Torvig's voice was close behind him. "You don't know what it is, do you?"

"Sure I do," Keru lied—and then he remembered how proud Torvig was of the slab's resistance to biological residues. "I was just admiring your workmanship, was all." He reached out and lightly touched it with one calloused fingertip.

The slab came alive with color and motion. Information scrolled across its surface just below Keru's eye line, and images and schematics arranged themselves in convenient blocks beneath a command interface with links to every officer and noncom he supervised. He was so impressed at the streamlined efficiency of it that it took him a moment to notice that all of the written elements of the interface had been rendered in his native language—and not merely the dominant version of Trill, but his own local dialect. "That's amazing," Keru said. "It's like it was made just for me." Suspicious, he asked, "You didn't make this just for me, did you?"

"No, of course not," Torvig said. He nuzzled the slab with his snout, and the entire interface changed, muting its colors, reconfiguring its iconography and even the audible qualities of its feedback tones into something completely unfamiliar to Keru. "I made this for everybody," Torvig continued. "It can recognize the biometric signature of every *Titan* crew member and present the data and options they are most likely to need at any given moment. When one is on duty it displays work-related options. During one's off-hours, it becomes more personal, recreational." The Choblik snagged a small remote control from the workbench with the bionic hand at the end of his tail. "Best of all," he added, "it's even configured for our shipmates who prefer to see in other spectra than visible light, and it has ultrasonic as well as subsonic modes." Torvig entered a few commands on his control device, and Keru felt a few fleeting pulses of heat from the slab, which was otherwise blank and silent.

Keru recalled an incident from several months earlier, when Torvig—then a midshipman cadet—had decided to research the mysterious humanoid phenomenon of "gut feelings" by secretly infesting his crewmates' replicated meals with nanoprobes.

"Vig, if I ask you how you obtained the biometric profiles of everyone on the ship, do you have reason to suspect I'll be unhappy about your answer?"

"I believe it to be a distinct possibility," Torvig said.

The Trill sighed. "Then I won't ask." He nodded his approval at the slab. "Amazing work, by the way."

"Thank you. I have an appointment to show it to Commander Ra-Havreii tomorrow afternoon. I'm asking his permission to install them throughout the ship."

"Good luck," Keru said.

Torvig deactivated the black panel, put the control device back on his workbench, and puttered around a moment, imposing a bit of order on the chaos, before he turned back toward Keru. "You said there might be something I could build for you."

"Well, not exactly," Keru said. He felt awkward about his true motive for the visit. "I'm more interested in having you work with one of my security teams. We might have a dangerous away mission ahead of us, and I know you're good at finding ways to help people work together more effectively."

The young ensign's interest took on a keener edge. "What manner of challenge do you expect to face?"

That question brought Keru into territory he would have preferred never to discuss again. "The Borg," he said.

Torvig's enthusiasm dimmed in one surprised blink of his enormous, round eyes. "I see."

It was a delicate subject between them. When they had first started serving together on *Titan,* Keru had found himself more than a little unnerved by Torvig's cybernetic enhancements. They had reminded him of the biomechanical fusions of the Borg, who years earlier had claimed the life of his lover, Sean.

As a result, for his first few months of shared service with Torvig, Keru had treated the young Choblik unjustly, singling him out for harsher discipline and stricter oversight than he had deserved. Only after Counselor Haaj had forced Keru to start confronting his own prejudices had he been able to put his fears aside and start treating Torvig fairly.

After Torvig graduated from Starfleet Academy and received his field commission to ensign, he and Keru had—to Keru's surprise—started becoming friends. This, however, was the first time Keru had ever come to ask Torvig for a favor.

"I think your expertise with cybernetics will be useful in helping us learn to defend ourselves against the Borg," Keru said, "but I want to make it clear that I'm *not* asking you to do this simply because you have bionic enhancements. I've learned over the years that brains are often a lot more valuable than brawn in a dangerous situation. I want you on my away team because you're a great engineer—a great *problem-solver.*"

Torvig extended his neck as tall as it could go, and he tilted his head left and then right. Strong emotions made his voice tremble. "'A great problem-solver,'" he said. "That's one of the highest compliments my kind ever bestow upon one another."

"It's got some cachet among my people, too," Keru said.

The Choblik offered one bionic hand to Keru, who took it in a friendly clasp. "You honor me," Torvig said. "Thank you."

"Don't thank me, Vig," Keru said with regret as he released Torvig's hand. "Because if I'm right, we're going to war—and I just put you on the front line."

# 8

Though the *Enterprise* was alone in orbit above a dead planet, its bridge buzzed with activity.

Captain Picard sat in his chair, at the center of the elevated aft level. He was surrounded by the muted chatter of voices over the comms, hushed replies from his senior command officers, and the mechanical clatter of a damage-control team replacing a number of blown-out companels. Worf moved among the bridge's many stations and supervised the crew's intelligence-gathering efforts, while Commander Kadohata directed several simultaneous repair projects from the operations console.

In his hand, Picard held a padd that displayed the most recent dispatches from Starfleet Command. Most of the news from Earth consisted of updated fleet deployment profiles. During normal peacetime conditions, Starfleet might have several dozen ships temporarily out of service for maintenance or upgrades. In addition, up to ten percent of the fleet in service was expected to be assigned to deep-space exploration at any given time.

Over the past four weeks, every ship in Starfleet had been recalled to Federation space and deployed into defensive battle fleets. The only exceptions were a handful of vessels that were simply not fit for service, and a few dozen, including *Titan* and some of her *Luna*-class sister ships, that were too far away to return in less than two months. The situation had become so desperate that even large civilian vessels were being armed and pressed into service to defend some of the more remote worlds.

Picard shook his head and wondered, *How much more of this can Starfleet take?* The losses were mounting more quickly than reinforcements could be mustered. If the steady stream of Borg incursions wasn't halted soon, within a matter of weeks rapid attrition would leave the Federation defenseless.

He looked up as Worf and Lieutenant Choudhury approached his chair. "Yes, Commander?"

Worf looked at the security chief and then at the captain. "Lieutenant Choudhury has a theory," he said.

Hopeful, Picard asked Choudhury, "About the Borg ship's entry point into Federation space?"

Choudhury pursed her lips slightly. "No, sir," she said, straightening her posture. "We haven't been able to track its prior movements beyond half a light-year outside the system."

"I see," Picard said, masking his disappointment. "Then what does your theory concern?"

He noticed Worf casting a sidelong glance at her before she said, "I think I know where the next Borg attack will be, sir."

That commanded Picard's full attention. "Explain."

Worf spoke first. "We have detected new Borg signals and energy signatures in this sector."

"And I think there's a Borg ship closing in on Korvat," Choudhury said. "If we go now at maximum warp, there's a chance we could get there ahead of the Borg." Her eyes fell for a moment on the main viewer, which still showed the burned-black northern hemisphere of Ramatis.

Her use of the singular pronoun—"*I think*"—gave the captain pause. He looked to his first officer. "Do you concur with Lieutenant Choudhury, Mister Worf?"

The Klingon shifted uncomfortably for a few seconds, and then he said in his most diplomatic baritone, "I agree that it is possible Korvat is the next target."

"Possible?" Looking back and forth between Choudhury and Worf, Picard said, "Do I detect a lack of consensus?"

More cryptic looks passed between the two officers. Then Worf replied, "We agree that there is another Borg ship in the sector, and that we should destroy it."

"But you have reservations regarding the lieutenant's analysis," said Picard, who was trying to get to the heart of the matter with as much tact as possible.

Choudhury was soft-spoken in her response. "Commander Worf's doubts are reasonable, sir," she said. "My conclusion that the Borg are headed to Korvat is more a hunch than a deduction—but I still recommend that we break orbit, set course for Korvat, and proceed there at maximum warp."

"Based on what, Lieutenant?"

She spoke with quiet confidence. "Based on the facts that Korvat is just as likely to be the target as three other worlds in this sector, and, of the four possible targets, it's the only one we can reach ahead of the Borg. If I'm wrong, and one of the other worlds is the next target, we won't reach them in time anyway. And if I'm right, we might be able to give Korvat a fighting chance to survive."

The security chief returned Picard's gaze with steady surety. The captain looked at Worf, who in turn looked at Choudhury and deadpanned, "When you put it that way . . ."

Picard nodded. "Very well." He raised his voice to be heard across the bridge. "Helm, break orbit and set course for Korvat, maximum warp. Commander Kadohata, send a warning ahead to the *Gibraltar* and the *Leonov*. Let them know we'll join them at Korvat as soon as we're able."

"Aye, sir," Kadohata said from the ops console.

"Mister Worf," Picard said. "Step up our damage-control efforts. I need the ship ready for combat when we reach Korvat." The Klingon first officer nodded his acknowledgment of the order and moved away to carry it out.

On the main viewer, the curve of the planet sank below the screen's bottom edge, leaving nothing but the star-flecked vista of the Milky Way. "We've cleared orbit, Captain," reported the conn officer, Lieutenant Gary Weinrib.

Pointing forward with an outstretched hand, Picard set his ship in motion with a word. "Engage."

*"Absolutely not, Captain,"* said Admiral Alynna Nechayev over the subspace comm, her angular features and silver-blond hair framed by the edges of the desktop monitor in Picard's ready room. *"The risk is too great, and you know it."*

Picard found it difficult to remain calm when he knew the stakes were so dire. "I think the potential benefits outweigh those risks, Admiral. If my officers' analysis is correct, and a Borg cube is on course to attack Korvat, our best chance of defending the planet is to give the new torpedo designs to the ships that are already there."

Nechayev shook her head. *"We've reviewed your analysis, Jean-Luc. It's inconclusive, at best. The cube you've detected could be en route to any of a number of targets. The only reason your ship is en route to Korvat is because it's the only potential target you can reach in time to make a difference."*

"That's true, Admiral," Picard said. "But if you're wrong—if Korvat is the target, and the Borg attack it before we can arrive—you'll be committing two Federation starships to a futile battle, and condemning millions of people on that planet to death. And my instincts tell me that my chief of security is correct—Korvat *is* the target."

*"I'm not dismissing your instincts, Jean-Luc, especially not when it comes to the Borg. But this isn't a matter of second-guessing your tactics in the field. Beyond the possibility that the Borg might adapt to transphasic weapons if we overuse them,*

*transmitting that data over a subspace channel creates an unacceptable risk of its interception by the Borg. What if they break our encryption protocols, assimilate the transphasic torpedo, and turn it against us?"*

She was right, and that only added to his frustration. "I acknowledge the risk," he said, "but an entire world and millions of lives hang in the balance."

*"No, Jean-Luc,"* replied Nechayev. *"Hundreds of worlds are at stake, along with nearly a trillion lives. And I can't let you jeopardize all of them on a gamble to save one that might not even be under attack."*

"What if we can confirm that Korvat is the next target?"

He heard the regret in her voice as she said, *"The answer would still have to be no."*

Picard sank into a quiet despair. "Has it come to this? Are we prepared to sacrifice entire worlds because we're not willing to risk our own safety for theirs? Shall we let simple arithmetic dictate who should live and who should die?"

Remorse stole the certainty from Nechayev's eyes and left her with a grim and weary mien. *"You see the battlefield, Jean-Luc. I have to see the war."*

Lieutenant Rennan Konya felt the tension in the air.

Commanders Kadohata and La Forge flanked a wall-mounted companel in the chief engineer's office, adjacent to main engineering. Konya and Dr. Crusher stood opposite them. Coursing between them all was a palpable aura of anxiety that emanated from everyone in the office, including Konya himself.

He suspected that only he could detect the tangible quality of the group's shared concern, thanks to his carefully trained Betazoid empathic talent. By the standards of his own people, he was a weak telepath, one whose limited gift was unequal to the profound task of making reciprocal contact with the higher minds of others. Instead, he'd focused on teaching himself to read a more primitive region of people's minds—the motor cortex. Its signals were simpler to interpret and far more accessible.

In hand-to-hand combat it gave him an almost imperceptible advantage: He could feel what opponents intended to do a split second before they did it. It also had distinctly pleasant uses in more personal situations, but sometimes it worked a bit like empathy, to tell him when people were fearful or anxious. This was one of those times.

"We need something new," said Kadohata, who had summoned the others to this midnight brainstorming session. "Our best weapon against the Borg was neutralized when they captured our multivector pathogen at Barolia, and Starfleet's worried that the Borg will adapt to the transphasic torpedoes if we use them too often." She lifted her chin in a half nod at a star system diagram on the companel's screen. "If Choudhury's right, we'll be seeing the Borg again in less than an hour. So think fast."

Crusher shrugged. "Unless we can get a sample of the new 'royal jelly' the Borg are using to gestate their queens, I'm not sure I can update the androgen formula."

Kadohata asked, "What kind of changes could the Borg have made to block the formula from working?"

"Protein resequencing, or maybe new antigens," Crusher said. "Even a targeted biofilter would be enough to screen out the formula."

La Forge cut in, "Then there's still the 'Royal Protocol' to deal with." He turned his synthetic eyes from Kadohata to Konya as he explained. "The Borg don't have to grow new queens from scratch—they can just reprogram existing female drones with the operating system for one."

He looked back at Kadohata as she noted, "That's where your nanobot sabotage came into play."

"Right," La Forge said. The chief engineer's face showed no anger, but Konya could feel the man's ire coiling inside him. "It was designed not to give the Borg time to adapt once it was deployed. But it sounds like they acquired an unreleased specimen and reverse-engineered it."

The unrelenting negativity was raising Kadohata's pulse and blood pressure. She asked La Forge, "Isn't there any other way to disrupt their link?"

"Maybe," said the chief engineer. "But I have no idea how to go about looking for it. We have no access to the Collective, no living Borg drones to experiment on, and no time to do the research. Plus, last time—" Words seemed to catch in his throat, and Konya felt La Forge's profound discomfort as the man made himself finish his sentence. "Last time I had Data to help me."

Konya had never met Data, but like most people in Starfleet he had heard more than a few tall tales about the android. The last such story had not had a happy ending: Data had sacrificed himself to save Captain Picard's life and destroy a ship-based thalaron weapon that had boasted enough power to exterminate entire planets with a single shot. Judging from La Forge's pained expression, Konya surmised that Data and the chief engineer had been close friends as well as colleagues.

"Mister Konya," Kadohata said, commanding his attention. "For now, transphasic torpedoes still work against the Borg. Do you know what makes these warheads tick?"

"Sort of," Konya said. "They're based on creating dissonant feedback pulses in an asymmetrically phased subspace compression wave." As he had expected, his answer provoked nods from La Forge and Kadohata and a confused stare from Crusher. For the doctor's benefit, he added, "Essentially, the torpedo spreads out the energy of the wave among multiple subspace phase states. When the Borg modulate their defenses against one or more phases of the compression pulse, they make themselves vulnerable to the remaining pulses. And the phase shifts vary randomly, so the Borg can't anticipate the transphasic state of one torpedo based on the previous one." Crusher nodded.

For the first time since the meeting had started, Kadohata sounded hopeful. "How else can we apply that theory?"

"I've started working on creating a transphasic mode for our shield generators," Konya said. "If I'm right, they should make it very hard for the Borg to score direct hits on us. But we still have to be careful—it won't take them long to change over to wide-dispersal firing patterns. And the downside of these protocols is power drain. Running them'll cut our maximum warp speed down to nine-point-one, and there's a risk we could burn out the shield emitters in a prolonged battle."

Crusher asked, "How about the phasers? Could we rig them to fire a transphasic pulse?"

"Sure," Konya said, "if you feel like blowing up all our emitter crystals." Putting aside his sarcasm, he continued, "An iron-60 crystal matrix might be able to handle it, but not at power levels high enough to be effective. The essential problem is that phasers are designed to synchronize energy streams, and transphasic weapons rely on unsynching them."

"Apples and oranges, then," Crusher said.

"More like apples and trout," La Forge replied.

Kadohata keyed in some notes on her padd. "Konya, can you have the transphasic shields working before we reach Korvat?"

"Yes," he said. He looked at La Forge and added, "I'll need some help from you and your team in engineering, though."

"You've got it," La Forge said. "Send down the specs and we'll make it happen."

The second officer finished tapping on her padd. "Keep me posted on your progress. I'd like to have at least one bit of good news for the captain before we go into combat." She looked around at the other officers and nodded. "Thanks, everyone."

Crusher was the first person out of La Forge's office, followed by Konya and Kadohata, who walked together to the same turbolift. His psionic sense of the second officer's physical state made him aware of her myriad minor aches and pains.

As the two of them stepped into the turbolift, he tried to sound sympathetic as he said, "Stressed out, huh?"

"A little," Kadohata said, her London-like accent enhancing her gift for understatement. "I never look forward to giving the captain bad news, but that's all we seem to have lately."

He nodded. "You carry most of your stress in your lower back," he said. "It must get uncomfortable."

"Yes," she said with a suspicious glance. "It does."

"If you'd like to relieve some of that tension, I could—"

"I'm married, Lieutenant. Happily. With three children."

Konya blinked, amused by her reaction. "That's nice. I was going to say that I could recommend some excellent massage-spa programs in the holodeck that would help. . . . Sir."

"Oh," Kadohata said. Keeping her eyes on the turbolift doors, she added, "Thanks." After a moment, she added, "Sorry."

Konya felt Kadohata's pulse quicken and her temperature rise. But even without his empathic senses, he would have been hard-pressed not to notice her intense blush response. *Red is a good color on her,* he decided.


Worf carried his *bat'leth* and walked at a quick step through the corridor, eager to reach the holodeck. The *Enterprise* was still at least two hours from Korvat and ready for action; now it was time for him to clear his thoughts and sharpen his focus, and for him that meant sixty minutes of exertion in his most intense "calisthenics" holoprogram, which La Forge had facetiously nicknamed "Nausicaans with Knives."

A female Bajoran ensign cast a wary look at the weapon in Worf's hand as he passed by her. The Klingon honor blade, which had become a familiar sight to many of Worf's shipmates on the *Enterprise*-D, continued to draw bemused stares from his new comrades. It had only added to his already fearsome reputation.

He arrived at the holodeck portal and reached over to activate his calisthenics routine. To his surprise, there was already a program running, one that he didn't recognize. It wasn't marked as private, and the portal wasn't locked, so he tapped a control on the companel to open the doors.

Magnetic seals released with a soft, rising hum. Then a quasi-hydraulic hiss of escaping air accompanied a muted rumbling of servomotors as the doors parted, revealing a majestic vista of jagged stone, ethereal mist, and azure sky.

Jasminder Choudhury stood on the mountaintop ledge with her back to Worf. She raised her arms in a fluid motion from her sides until her palms met high above her head. Her rib cage retracted as she exhaled and lowered her arms. Then she finished the traditional yoga breathing exercise by bringing her hands back together, palm to palm, in front of her chest.

Worf stepped into the serene-looking holographic simulation and caught the scent of alpine sage in the cool, thin air. Behind him, the holodeck doors closed with an obtrusive whine and an echoing thud, and then they vanished into the panorama of mountain peaks jutting up through a slow-rolling sea of clouds.

Choudhury inhaled and lifted her arms again, and she seemed to take no notice of Worf's arrival. As her palms met above her head, he cleared his throat with a resonant grunt of annoyance.

She continued her exercise until she had completed another slow exhalation, and her hands were once again pressed together in front of her. Then she let her arms drop to her sides as she turned and cast an untroubled smile in Worf's direction. "Yes, Commander?"

"What are you doing here?"

The trim, tall woman looked amused. "Yoga."

He furrowed his brow at her flippant answer. "I reserved this hour for my private use."

"I thought you'd reserved Holodeck Two," she said.

"No, I reserved *this* holodeck." As he studied her face, he became convinced that she was not surprised by this apparent and unusual scheduling mistake. "This was not an error, was it?"

Choudhury shook her head. "I don't know what you—"

"I have served with you long enough to know that you are methodical, organized, and precise. You would not use another person's reserved holodeck time by mistake." He stepped closer to her, his demeanor one of overt challenge. "Why are you here?"

Even as he loomed over her, she maintained her enigmatic, close-lipped smile. "All right," she said. "You've caught me. I was hoping to catch you alone, and your exercise hour seemed like the best time."

"The best time for what?"

"To learn about your training regimen," she said as a gust of wind fluttered her loose, brightly colored silk exercise clothes. "I hope you won't think it's out of line for me to say so, but you're one of the most *stoic* Klingons I've ever met."

"Stoic?" He reflected on the boundless reservoir of angst with which his life had afflicted him. "Hardly."

She responded with a reproving tilt of her head. "Compared to most Klingons I've met, you're a man made of stone. I know it's rude to describe someone based on racial stereotypes, but there have been times, when we've been working together, that you've seemed almost . . . well, Vulcan."

Her comment reminded Worf of his mind-meld with the famed Ambassador Spock, many years earlier, during a mission to stop the ancient telepathic tyrant known as Malkus. The meld had been a profound experience, one that had imparted lasting effects of which he had been unaware at the time. Lingering traces of Vulcan stoicism now infused some of his mannerisms, and snippets of Vulcan sayings sometimes infiltrated his discourse. He had, until this moment, thought that he and Captain Picard—who also had melded with Spock, on a separate occasion—were the only ones who would ever notice his echoes of those affectations.

Choudhury interrupted his moment of reflection. "I'm sorry if I offended you just now," she said.

"Not at all, Lieutenant," Worf said. "It is an *interesting* observation." He eyed her with curiosity. "Is this what you hope to learn more about by emulating my training regimen?"

With a coquettish shrug of one shoulder, she replied, "It's *one* thing I'd like to learn about you."

Intrigued by her forthright manner, he asked, "What *other* aspects of my life do you find of interest?"

"Permission to speak freely, sir?"

"Granted."

She stepped forward into his personal space. "You're one of the most intriguing people I've ever met, Worf, and I'd like to learn whatever you're willing to teach me."

"Are you certain that you are ready?"

"I'm a quick learner."

He liked her attitude.

"Computer," he said. "New program: Worf Calisthenics Number Four." The mountaintop yoga retreat dissolved and was replaced by the interior of a Klingon martial-arts school. A cold stone-tile floor appeared under their feet, and walls of thick, dark wooden beams surrounded them. The ceiling rose high overhead, but, compared to the open dome of sky in the previous simulation, it felt oddly close. Red and black banners emblazoned with the Klingon trefoil were draped high on the walls, above racks loaded with a variety of bladed Klingon weapons. Above Worf and Choudhury was a balcony level, from which a master could observe training drills for new students.

"Let me teach you *Mok'bara*," Worf said.

# 9

Dr. Simon Tarses had seen some gruesome spectacles during his nearly fifteen years in Starfleet, but the pair of crispy-molten corpses that had been beamed into his sickbay from the *Columbia* qualified as one of the most unique and horrifying.

After completing the preliminary autopsies, he had decided to beam down from the *Aventine* with a mixed team of medical investigators and security specialists, all of whom, including himself, had some measure of training in forensics.

He and the rest of the group emerged from the coruscating haze of the transporter beam inside an oppressively dark section of a passageway on D Deck of the *Columbia*. Before he or the members of his team could activate their palm beacons, a blue light snapped on in front of them. Its beam was aimed into his eyes, half blinding him.

As he raised his arm for shade, he pierced the darkness and saw the dour, squamous frown of Lieutenant Kedair. "I told the captain no one should come down here," Kedair said.

"She didn't agree," Tarses replied as the other members of his team activated their own lights, filling their section of the passage with pale blue light and overlapping shadows. "I have orders to collect evidence. Lead the way, please."

Kedair scowled as she turned and led the group through the curved passageway. The *Columbia* was a small ship compared to some on which Tarses had served, and it was a short walk to the scene of the mysterious homicides. They were still a few sections away when the odors of putrefaction started to become overwhelming. Tarses suppressed his gag reflex—a skill he had learned while dissecting cadavers in medical school.

Then they arrived at the scene of the two deaths, and it was every bit as horrible as Tarses had imagined it would be when he'd seen the corpses. With the bodies removed from the passageway, all that remained were isolated pools of congealed fatty liquids and stains of scorched blood, all surrounding humanoid-shaped patches of clean metal deck plating.

"Have at it," Kedair said, and she stepped away and tapped her combadge. "Kedair to Darrow. Regroup at location alpha, we have visitors."

*"Acknowledged,"* said a female voice via Kedair's combadge.

Tarses squatted beside the pockmarked puddle of boiled flesh and half-disintegrated synthetic fabrics. He lifted his tricorder and activated a series of preprogrammed scans. "All right, folks," he said. "Let's work quickly, before the good lieutenant here has an apoplexy worrying about us."

"I don't worry, Doctor," Kedair said. "I anticipate undesirable events and outcomes, and try to prevent them."

"Well, you should take it easy," Tarses said. "At this rate, you'll *anticipate* yourself to death."

The security chief rolled her eyes and walked away. Tarses turned his attention to the results of his tricorder's molecular scan. Around him, the forensic specialists worked at a brisk pace, keeping their conversations to a minimum. Some were removing core samples from the deck or bulkheads; one was gathering scrapings of charred tissue or swabs of still-tacky lique-fied biomass. One of the security specialists was creating a holographic documentation of the passageway section.

A crunching squish of a footstep near Tarses turned his head, and he saw one of Kedair's security officers, a human woman, making an awkward passage of the narrow gap between him and a Benzite ballistics expert. Tarses berated her, "Do you mind?" When she looked down with a confused expression at the crouching chief medical officer, he added with a frantic wave at her feet, "You're standing in my blood!"

She backpedaled until she was clear of the forensic team, and then she took up a sentry position a few meters away.

Tarses continued working and fighting the urge to retch. Ignoring the rotten-perfume odor of burned skin and fat did not make it go away, but Tarses clung to the fading hope that his nose might soon acclimate to the sickly stench so he could concentrate solely on his work.

Outside the cocoon of light in which Tarses and his team worked, a dim sparkle formed in the impenetrable darkness. That faint glimmer multiplied with a sonorous rush. Sound and light blossomed a few sections down the passageway, and a humanoid figure took shape inside the transporter beam's prismatic halo.

Captain Dax emerged from the fading glow and found herself illuminated by a half-dozen palm beacons. Lifting her hands in front of her face, she said, "As you were. Please." The beams were redirected, leaving her in a penumbra of reflected light.

Kedair slipped past the forensic team and moved to meet the captain as she approached. Tarses flipped his tricorder closed and followed Kedair. Together they intercepted Dax, who raised her chin toward the forensic team. "What've we got?"

"Still no definite cause of death," Tarses said.

Before Tarses could elaborate, Kedair said, "We've ruled out friendly fire, and my team has kept this deck secured since the bodies were found. Except for the doctor and his forensic team, no one's been down here."

Tarses was quick to add, "My preliminary autopsies found evidence of neuroelectric damage in both subjects' brain tissues, and their bodies exhibit molecular dissociation on all levels, from the epidermis to the marrow."

Dax looked to Kedair and asked, "What can kill like that?"

"The caustic effects are similar to damage inflicted by the Horta," the Takaran woman said.

"Except that the caustic injuries were highly localized," Tarses pointed out, "and instead of fusing synthetic and organic matter on the corpses, it dissolved them without mixing them."

Kedair narrowed her eyes and clenched her jaw. "Which is what made me think of a Denebian predator called a *teblor*," she said with ill-masked irritation.

"Interesting," Tarses said, deriving more than a touch of schadenfreude from poking holes in Kedair's guesses. "But the *teblor* doesn't possess anything like a neuroelectric attack. And if memory serves, it lives and hunts in environments with a peak temperature of no more than two degrees Celsius."

Crossing her arms, Kedair said, "Yes, I admit, it's a bit warm for a *teblor* on this rock with no name. Of course, an Altairan cave-fisher—"

"Would leave a trail of easily followed slime back to its watery lair, neither of which seems to exist within a thousand kilometers of here," Tarses said.

"Doctor," said Dax, "instead of telling me what the killer isn't, can you offer any insight about what it might be?"

It was Kedair's turn to gloat as Tarses admitted, "Not at the moment, Captain."

"We're running out of time down here," Dax said. "Starfleet Command wants us out of orbit in just over fifteen hours. I've asked for an extension because of what happened to Yott and Komer, but I wouldn't count on it." To Kedair she continued, "Send nonsecurity personnel back to the *Aventine* and run a hard-target search of every compartment, locker, crawl space, nook, and cranny on this ship. If whatever killed our people is still here, I want it found."

"We could use some extra sensor capability," Kedair said.

Dax nodded. "I'll have Leishman free up whatever you need." She looked at Tarses. "Has your team collected enough evidence for analysis?"

"Enough for a start," Tarses said. "But I'd really like to widen the search to see if—"

"Denied," Dax said. "I need you on the ship, analyzing the data we have in hand."

Disappointed, Tarses replied, "Aye, sir. I just hope we haven't missed anything."

"Time is short, Doctor," said Dax. "And the perfect is the enemy of the good. Make do with what we've got—and do it fast."

Its hunger was all.

Radiant shells of organic matter glowed in the empty spaces that surrounded it. They appeared and vanished in bright curtains of energy, in columns of fire shot down from someplace far above this crude prison of thwarted desire. They skated the surface of the gravity well, clutching blinding sparks.

Temptations, one and all.

Streams of data moved faster than light, traveling between the shells and the sky and their own glowing stones. There were fewer of the shells now, and they continued to diminish in numbers.

Panic pushed the hunger in pursuit of a cluster of shells. So little of its strength remained that even gravity, nature's most feeble instrument, threatened to overcome it and drag it down to its final dissipation in the silicon sea.

It risked everything to pierce the new stone: every iota of will, every drop of fear. Annihilation or escape—either would be better than limbo.

All that mattered now was the sky.

# 2168

## 10

The flight of the *Columbia* had lasted sixty-three days, and it had lasted just over twelve years.

The high-frequency overdrive whine of the impulse engines fell rapidly as a pinpoint of light on the bridge's main viewer brightened and grew larger. Captain Hernandez gripped the armrests of her chair as her ship shimmied around her, its inertial dampers struggling to compensate for the extreme stresses of rapid deceleration from relativistic velocity.

Lieutenant Brynn Mealia, the gamma-shift helmsman, declared in a soft Irish lilt, "Thirty seconds to orbit."

"Katrin," Hernandez said to Ensign Gunnarsdóttir, the bridge engineering officer, "can we shore up the dampers?"

Gunnarsdóttir started flipping switches and adjusting dials on her console. "Patching in emergency battery power, Captain."

Seconds later the ship's passage became smoother, and Hernandez used the moments to lament the years that she had let pass by her ship, her crew, and herself. For weeks she had been imagining Earth spinning in a blur, its billions of people playing out the dramas of their lives while the crew of the *Columbia* pushed themselves beyond the normal boundaries of space-time—cheating it, evading it, living in the past while the rest of the galaxy moved on without them. She had heard the grumblings of her crew grow increasingly bitter as the weeks had dragged past, and just a few days—months?—earlier she had heard one of the ship's MACO troopers jokingly refer to the *Columbia* as "the *Flying Dutchman*."

"Slowing to full impulse," Mealia said. "Three-quarters impulse . . . half . . . one-quarter impulse, Captain."

A lush blue-green sphere dominated the viewscreen. It looked like a pristine, uncolonized world, with no traces of habitation. Hernandez looked over her shoulder at Lieutenant el-Rashad, who was monitoring a sensor control station. "You're sure the energy readings from the planet are artificial?"

The thin, serious-looking second officer lifted his eyes from his console and said, "Positive, Captain." Thumbing a few switches, he added, "I can't lock in on the sources, but I can narrow it down and switch to a visual scan. Magnification to five hundred." On the viewscreen, at the edge of a greenish swath of richly forested planetary surface, she beheld what looked like a scintillating jewel.

Hernandez stood from her chair and studied the image on the screen. "Is that a city?"

"If not, it's the strangest rock formation I've ever seen," said Commander Fletcher, who was watching from beside the weapons console with Lieutenant Thayer. The first officer had a quizzical look on her face as she stared at the viewscreen. "Kalil, are we reading any life-forms at those coordinates?"

El-Rashad looked surprised by the question. "We're not reading anything at those coordinates, Commander. There's some kind of scattering field blocking our scans of the city."

Hernandez looked back at her bridge officers. "Thayer, can you compensate for that?"

Thayer poked at her console. "Negative, Captain." She patched in a new image on the main viewer: another brilliant speck on the surface. "We're seeing dozens of cities, spread around the planet. They're all extremely similar in mass and configuration . . . but we can't get precise readings, because they're all protected by scattering fields with an average radius of two hundred kilometers."

Every new report deepened Hernandez's curiosity, and for a moment the heartbreak of a dozen lost years was forgotten. "What about the other planets in the system?"

"Uninhabited, Captain," said el-Rashad. "No evidence of colonization or exploration."

Thinking ahead, Hernandez asked, "How's the air down there?"

"Breathable," said el-Rashad. "Maybe a bit on the thick side for most of us."

Hernandez pondered the top-down image of the city on the viewscreen for a moment longer, captivated by its symmetry and its mystery. Then she returned to her chair and sat down.

"Kiona, can you detect any sign of patrol ships in this system, or defensive batteries on the planet?"

"Nothing of the kind, Captain," Thayer replied.

The captain was intrigued. She wondered aloud in Fletcher's direction, "Odd, don't you think? This close to both Romulan and Klingon space, and the planet has no obvious defenses."

"Just because they aren't obvious doesn't mean they don't exist," Fletcher said.

"True," Hernandez said. She looked to the communications officer. "Sidra, can we hail them on a regular radio frequency?"

Ensign Valerian shook her head. "I've been trying for a couple of minutes now. No response so far." She looked up from her console and added with a note of seemingly misplaced optimism, "It's possible there's no one down there."

Thayer replied, "Then why are all the scattering fields still active?"

"Good question, Lieutenant," Hernandez said. "And it begs another one: Can we find a way through them?"

El-Rashad checked his readings, tossed a few switches, and said, "If we were on the surface, we could walk through. They block signals, but they aren't harmful."

"Captain," Thayer cut in. "One of the scattering fields is contracting." She used an override switch to change the image on the main viewer. "A city near the equator seems to be reducing its field radius in response to our scans."

The captain was on her feet. "Current radius?"

"Still shrinking," Thayer said. "Thirty kilometers. Twenty." She adjusted some settings and added, "Holding at fifteen kilometers, sir."

Fletcher flashed a crooked smile at Hernandez. "Walking distance. If you ask me, that looks like an invitation."

"Agreed," Hernandez said. "Assemble a landing party and fire up the transporter, Commander. We're going down there."

Less than an hour after he had beamed down into the heart of a tropical rainforest along the planet's sun-baked equator, Major Foyle's camouflage fatigues were soaked with sweat.

His second-in-command, Lieutenant Yacavino, and his senior noncom, Sergeant Pembleton, who had beamed down with him, also had become drenched in their own perspiration. Like the major, they were victims of the hot, soupy air in the densely over-grown tropical forest. Privates Crichlow, Mazzetti, and Steinhauer had beamed down ten minutes behind them, after chief engineer Graylock had reset the *Columbia*'s temperamental transporter, and their uniforms were beginning to cling to them, as well.

The six MACOs had deployed in pairs, with each of the deci-mated company's leaders escorted by a private. Pembleton was on point, along with Mazzetti. Foyle and Crichlow stayed several meters behind them, on their left flank, moving parallel with Yacavino and Steinhauer, who were on Pembleton's right flank. For this mission they had traded in their standard gray-ice cam-ouflage for dark-green forest patterns.

Foyle stepped over tangled vines and thick fallen branches while gazing down the barrel of his phase rifle, which he braced against his shoulder. A bright, sawing tinnitus of insect noise enveloped him, and shafts of intense light slashed through the sultry afternoon mists drifting down from the jungle's canopy. Thorned plants tugged at his fatigues, and underfoot the ground gave way to mud.

Something snapped in the underbrush ahead of Pembleton, who raised his fist to halt the team. Then he opened his hand and lowered it, palm down. Foyle and the others kneeled slowly, all but disappearing into the thick, waist-high fronds and ferns. Crichlow kept his rifle steady with one hand; with the other, the gawky Englishman pulled his hand scanner from his equipment belt and thumbed it open to its "on" position. A few quick inputs by Crichlow set the device for silent operation, and he began a slow sweep of the area around the landing party.

A flash of fur and motion. The creature was tiny, smaller than a squirrel, and it was very fast as it skittered up the trunk of a tree that put Earth's most magnificent redwoods to shame. Foyle watched the little beast skitter away into the leaves, and then he looked at Crichlow, who nodded in confirmation. Satisfied, the major looked ahead to Pembleton and twirled his raised index finger twice, then pointed forward. The sergeant acknowledged the order, stood, lifted his weapon, and advanced through a nar-row pass into a shadowy thicket, followed closely by Mazzetti. Foyle and the rest of his team moved forward as well, continuing on their patrol of the beam-in site's outer perimeter.

It was easy to get disoriented in a forest such as this; Foyle had seen it happen even to experienced soldiers. He had recommended to Pembleton that he use a hand scanner to verify that he was maintaining a consistent five-hundred-meter radius from the beam-in site, a clearing that at this distance was not the least bit visible through the claustrophobic press of trees, lichen, and hanging vines. Pembleton had refused the suggestion, preferring to trust his own instincts.

As much as Foyle had faith in his sergeant, he believed even more strongly in taking precautions. Consequently, he had Steinhauer monitoring their position with a hand scanner; if Pembleton wandered more than twenty meters outside of the radius, it was Steinhauer's job to alert Foyle. They had been walking for nearly an hour, covering almost three and a half kilometers of linear distance, and Steinhauer had not yet found any cause to speak up. *So far, so good,* mused Foyle.

He squinted as he passed through a shaft of bright light that had speared its way through the ceiling of boughs to the lush vegetation at his feet. Much of the forest remained shrouded in viridian twilight. He and his men waded the shallow green underbrush, scouting for natural hazards and predators that might lie between the rest of the landing party and the massive urban center the flight crew had detected, approximately fifteen-point-two kilometers to the west.

Ahead of the major, Pembleton and Mazzetti stood at the base of a colossal tree and waved the other two pairs toward them. As soon as the six men had regrouped, Pembleton pointed at a pair of crossed sticks stuck in the ground beside a gnarled, meter-tall root. Foyle recognized the twigs instantly; the sergeant had planted them there to mark the starting point of their perimeter patrol. "Full circle," Pembleton said. "Perimeter's clear, Major. Site secure for beam-in."

"Very good," Foyle said. "Take us back to the clearing. We'll set up a tight perimeter there and signal the ship."

"Yes, Major," replied Pembleton, who made a quick survey of the area to get his bearings and led the landing party through a sea of green leaves with nothing resembling a trail.

The hike back to the clearing was slow going, and not only because of the heat, the humidity, the uphill terrain, and the need to circumnavigate massive arboreal obstacles. More than two months of combating radiation effects caused by the *Columbia*'s near-light journey had taken a heavy toll on the crew, in the form of chronic mild radiation sickness and severe fatigue.

*A climb like this never would've bothered me before,* Foyle ruminated. *I guess it's true what my grandfather used to say: "It's not the years, it's the mileage."*

Minutes later, as the MACOs emerged from the tree line and entered the forest glade, Foyle pulled his communicator from his equipment belt and flipped it open. "Foyle to *Columbia*."

Hernandez answered, *"This is* Columbia. *Go ahead, Major."*

"Site secure," he said. "You can beam down when ready."

*"Glad to hear it. Any last-minute advice?"*

"Yes," he said. "Make sure everyone packs a full canteen."

The twelve-person landing party moved single file through the humbling grandeur of the primeval forest, which was composed of trees wider in circumference and taller than any that Hernandez had ever seen before. The forest canopy was an unbroken ceiling of green nearly two hundred meters overhead, thick enough to block all but hints of the planet's searing daylight.

Hernandez was the second person in the formation. Pembleton walked ahead of her, serving as the point man on the long march to the alien city. Behind her was her first officer, Fletcher. Then followed Major Foyle, Private Crichlow, chief engineer Graylock, Lieutenant Thayer, Private Mazzetti, Lieutenant Valerian, Dr. Johanna Metzger, Private Steinhauer, and the MACOs' second-in-command, Lieutenant Yacavino.

Rivulets of sweat trickled between Hernandez's shoulder blades and down her spine under her uniform as she looked back at Fletcher. "How old do you think these trees are?"

Fletcher retrieved a hand scanner from her belt and made a quick sweep of the forest. The soft whirring sound of the device made Pembleton look back and scowl at them, though he apparently respected the privileges of rank too much to say anything. Then Fletcher closed the scanner and said, "Some of them might be as old as fourteen thousand years. There are carbon deposits from old forest fires that probably cleared away a lot of smaller, competing trees several millennia ago."

"It's a botanist's dream," Hernandez said. "But I can't figure out why the forest floor is so overgrown when it gets barely any light. What's feeding all this greenery?"

"Maybe they don't rely on photosynthesis," Fletcher said. "Or maybe they have a symbiotic relationship with the trees."

From the back of the line, Ensign Valerian asked with rhetorical sarcasm, "Are we there yet?"

"People," Foyle interjected, "it'd be safer for all of us if we didn't talk."

Dr. Metzger replied, "Safe from what? There's no sign anyone even knows we're here."

The stern-faced MACO commander directed his answer to the group. "When in doubt, *always* assume you're being watched."

"Just do as he says, folks," Hernandez said. "Keeping us alive till we make contact is the major's job. Let him do it."

She ignored the unintelligible grumbles from Valerian and Metzger and resumed her focus on Pembleton's back. He had stressed to her the importance not only of following his path, but of making the effort to step exactly where he'd stepped, both for her safety and to help conceal the landing party's numbers in case they were tracked. The same instructions had been passed to all her personnel, and so everyone concentrated on the monotony of walking in someone else's footprints.

After a sweltering and—in Hernandez's opinion—interminable stretch of hiking, Sergeant Pembleton stopped and raised his fist, halting the group. It was their first break since the march had begun. He waved everyone to a relaxed crouch. While the group settled and sank into the concealing fronds, Pembleton leaned his phase rifle against a tree trunk. Then he removed his hard-shell backpack, opened it, and took out a canteen. He took a drink and passed it to Hernandez. "One swallow," he said, "then pass it to the next person."

She looked at the wet ring around the mouth of the canteen. "Why can't I just drink from my own?"

"Only two kinds of canteen are quiet on a march," he said. "Full ones and empty ones. If you take just a few swigs from one, it'll swish while you walk, or give you away when you're trying to hide. But if we all drink from one canteen until it's empty, that won't happen."

Unable to fault his reasoning, she took a mouthful of water

from the canteen and passed it to Fletcher, who helped herself to a drink. Person by person, it was handed back along the line.

Fletcher wiped a sheen of perspiration from her brow and said in a low voice to Hernandez, "Y'know what I'm gonna do when we get home? Buy a vineyard in Napa Valley."

That was certainly news to Hernandez. "A vineyard? Really?"

"Yeah," said the vivacious New Zealander. "I bet I can drink enough wine to make myself rich."

Still suspicious, Hernandez asked, "How can you afford to buy a winery? Last time we were on leave, you couldn't afford to pick up a round of drinks."

"Well," Fletcher said with a shrug, "I figure I've got twelve years of back pay coming to me when we get home. And since a Romulan ambush put us in this mess, I figure I'm entitled to twelve years of combat bonuses, too."

Hernandez chuckled. "I knew if anyone could find the silver lining to this mess, it'd be you."

Foyle tapped Fletcher's shoulder. When she turned her head toward him, he handed her the now-empty canteen. She passed it forward to Hernandez, who returned it to Pembleton.

He tucked the canteen inside his pack. Then he closed the pack and put it back on. As he stood and grabbed his rifle, he said, "Everybody up. We're moving out."

"Sergeant," Hernandez said, "what's our ETA to the city?"

"About six hours, if we can keep this pace. It'll be hard in this heat."

Fletcher said over the captain's shoulder, "Maybe we should wait for nightfall. Might be cooler then."

"It'll also be pitch-dark in this forest," Pembleton said. "That won't hurt our ability to navigate, but it will make us more vulnerable to predators. The best thing we can do is keep going until we at least get clear of the trees."

"And how long will that take?" asked Hernandez.

"Four hours and forty minutes," Pembleton said. "That'll put us at the edge of the grasslands that lead to the city."

"All right, then," Hernandez said. "Let's get going."

Pembleton adjusted his grip on his rifle and advanced through the waist-high waving greenery that dominated the relatively narrow gaps between the giant trees. Hernandez fell in behind him, watching the ground for signs of where he had placed his feet with each step. The muted shuffle of people walking seemed to be swallowed up by the steady drone of insect noise and the soft scratching of wind-rustled foliage.

Every few minutes, Hernandez stole a look backward to make certain the entire landing party was still accounted for, even though it was Lieutenant Yacavino's job, as the rear guard, to make certain no one went missing. After a while, she stopped looking back and kept herself focused on their destination.

The hours dragged on, seemingly multiplied by the heat and Hernandez's exhaustion. At her request, Pembleton increased the frequency of their stops, to once per hour. Each break consumed another canteen of water, and on the fourth stop they rested a bit longer and picked at their cold rations. After lunch ended, the landing party segregated by gender, and each person sought out some small measure of privacy in the thick undergrowth.

As the landing party regrouped, Hernandez looked around and realized that the trees in this part of the forest, while still larger than anything on Earth, were smaller than those they had left behind, and they were spaced a bit more generously. Looking ahead in the direction they had been traveling, she could almost see some faint glow of white daylight in the distance.

The sharp, crisp sound of finger snaps turned her head and silenced the murmuring of the group. Private Steinhauer had his hand scanner out and open, and as the other MACOs looked at him, he made short chopping movements with his hand in several directions around the landing party. Hernandez followed his gestures and was barely able to notice unusual flutters in the thick greenery, like ripples in water.

In slow, steady motions, Major Foyle and the other MACOs raised and braced their rifles. Sergeant Pembleton motioned the rest of the landing party to get down. Then he selected a target and put himself between it and Hernandez. Around the rest of the landing party, the MACOs formed a tight circle.

"Set for stun," Hernandez reminded everyone in a whisper. "Remember this is a first-contact mission."

The MACOs checked their rifles' settings and nodded to Foyle, who said in a low monotone, "Weapons free."

The forest erupted with bright flashes of phased energy and echoed with the screeching of rifles discharging in three-shot bursts. Piercing shrieks added to the cacophony as the soldiers' shots found their marks. Enormous, semi-transparent creatures that reminded Hernandez of millipedes reared up out of the fronds, their antennae twitching and their multisegmented bodies wriggling from multiple hits by the phase rifles. Within seconds, all the creatures were in retreat.

Foyle shouted, "Cease fire!" The staccato roar of rifle fire stopped, leaving only its distant echoes reverberating in the cavernous spaces of the forest.

Hernandez noticed only then that she had drawn her own phase pistol without realizing it. She tucked the weapon back in its holster on her belt. Then she looked around and saw the other flight-crew officers doing the same thing.

Foyle and his men lowered their rifles and nodded at one another as they watched the *Columbia* personnel holster their sidearms. "Thank you for the backup," the major said, "but we have it under control."

"*Gracias,* Major," Hernandez said.

"*De nada,* Captain," Foyle said. He waved to Pembleton, who gave him his attention. "Sergeant, I want a defensive formation until we clear the forest."

"Yes, sir," Pembleton said. "Mazzetti, Crichlow—each of you take a flank. Steinhauer, join Yacavino on rear guard. Major, will you join me on point?"

"Absolutely," Foyle said, stepping past Fletcher and Hernandez. When he reached the front, he turned back and said to the landing party, "We're less than an hour from clearing the forest. I'd like to pick up the pace and get this over with. Anyone who doesn't think they can handle it, speak up now." No one said anything. "All right. Double-time. Let's move out!"

The jogging pace was twice as difficult to sustain as Hernandez had expected, but she was determined not to set an example of frailty. Inhaling the muggy air was a labor, and within ten minutes her chest hurt with each heaving breath. Her black bangs were matted to her forehead by sweat, and knifing pains between her ribs felt as if they penetrated into her lungs. Exertion left the muscles in her calves and thighs coiled and burning, and each running step sent jolts of impact trauma through her knees. Only the widening slivers of light through the trees kept her stride from faltering.

She noticed Fletcher striding alongside her, her longer legs making it easy for her to overtake the captain. Fletcher asked with vexing good humor, "Hangin' in there, Captain?"

Lacking the air to respond, Hernandez shot a venomous glare at her XO and kept loping along behind Foyle and Pembleton.

After almost twenty minutes of jogging, the tree line was within sight. A dark wall of Brobdingnagian trunks rose like columns in front of a curtain of pale illumination. Hernandez found it hard to let her eyes adjust; she stared at the light until she could make out the details. A narrow, vertical slice of landscape emerged from behind a veil of shimmering haze: green land below, a crimson shine on the horizon, and a cloud-streaked sky above. But then the forest became a black mass around her, and she was unable to see where she was going.

She blinked and cast her eyes toward her feet, so that her eyes could readjust to the shadowy realm beneath the arboreal giants. The landscape beyond the tree line was washed away once more in a radiant, white flood. As the landing party neared the forest's edge, the ferns and fronds that choked the ground became taller, and the spaces between them narrower and harder to traverse. Within moments, the lush green foliage towered over their heads, aglow with the intense light that slanted almost horizontally into the forest near its perimeter.

Pembleton slowed to a walking pace and called back to the others, "Regroup and stay close till we get clear of this stuff."

The heat from above grew stronger, and the light became much brighter. Filtered through the tall plants, it bathed the landing party in an emerald glow.

Then they broke through the wall of green into daylight.

Slack-jawed and silent, the landing party fanned out in a long line and stared at the vista before them.

Rolling knolls covered in knee-high flaxen grasses and brightly hued wildflowers punctuated the otherwise gradual downward slope of the landscape. The crescent border of the forest stretched north and south for hundreds of kilometers, disappearing into the misty distance. Flatlands stretched west toward the horizon, in front of which rose a jagged mountain range backed by a seemingly endless bank of storm clouds.

Rising from the center of the golden plain was a massive city unlike any that Hernandez had ever seen. Metallic white and shaped like a broad bowl filled with fragile towers, it looked as if it were perfectly symmetrical, but her eyes couldn't discern all the minuscule details of its architecture from this distance. Its surfaces gleamed with reflected light.

"No air traffic," Fletcher said. She took her hand scanner from her belt and activated it. After making a few adjustments, she added, "And we're inside the scattering field, so scanners are drawing a blank."

Hernandez eyed the landscape around the metropolis. "No roads," she said. "It's like this place has no history."

Major Foyle asked, "What are you talking about?"

"A city this big doesn't just spring up from nowhere," Hernandez explained. "Urban centers are hubs for commerce, industry, and travel. Even in a society long past the age of ground travel, you'd expect to find evidence of old roads leading to a city this size."

"Not to mention infrastructure," Fletcher said. "I'm not seeing any signs of civil engineering outside the city. No water or sewage-removal systems, no power grids, no comm lines."

"I'm sure this is all fascinating, Captain," said Major Foyle, "but I just need to know one thing right now: Are we going forward, or going back?"

Hernandez nodded at the city. "Forward, Major. We have to see if anybody's home."

"Then we'd better get going," Foyle said, pointing at the kilometers-long shadow of the city that was angled in their direction. "We're losing the light."

Hernandez looked up at the blinding orange orb of the sun, which was making slow progress toward the horizon. "Move out," she said, and she started walking to lead the way.

Her officers fell in as a group behind her, while Foyle silently directed his MACOs with hand signals to spread out in a triangle-shaped formation around the *Columbia* team.

Though the alien city was still nearly three kilometers away, it loomed large above the wild spaces of the plains, an intricate jewel standing like a citadel of order and authority amid the undefiled chaos of nature. Hernandez's admiration of the city's austere beauty was enhanced by its contrast with the storm-bruised dome of sky in the distance.

Fletcher seemed wary of the majestic white metropolis as she asked Hernandez, "What'll we do if it's deserted?"

"Plant a flag," Hernandez said, only half joking.

Still leery, Fletcher said, "And if it's *not* deserted?"

"We'll start with 'hello' and see how it goes from there."

"Some plan," Fletcher quipped. "Showing up on their front porch empty-handed. Maybe we should've brought a gift."

Hernandez played along. "Like what?"

"I dunno," Fletcher said. "A nice casserole, maybe. Or a basket of muffins. Everybody likes a basket of muffins."

"I'll put that on the first-contact checklist from now on," Hernandez said. "Phase pistol, universal translator, first-aid kit, and a basket of muffins."

Fletcher shrugged. "Couldn't hurt."

The slight downhill grade made the hike to the city an easy one, and the group picked up speed as they continued.

Hernandez sighed and muttered, "Damn you, Fletcher." When she saw her first officer's aghast reaction, she added, "Now I can't stop thinking about blueberry muffins. Thanks a lot."

"My work here is done," Fletcher said.

It was half an hour before anyone spoke again.

As the landing party crested the last knoll between them and the city, they saw that the metropolis didn't rest at ground level. The center of its convex underside hovered several dozen meters above the planet, and its outer edges were hundreds of meters off the ground. It was like standing beneath a giant, levitating bowl of dark metal. Hernandez saw no obvious means of reaching its surface.

Pembleton craned his neck and stared up at the city's edge. "Well, that's just great."

Fletcher said to Hernandez, "We could walk under it. There might be an entrance somewhere along its bottom."

Karl Graylock, who hadn't said a word since beaming down several hours earlier, peered through a pair of magnifying binoculars and shook his head. "*Nein*," he said. "The ventral surface has no apertures. Going under the city is a waste of time, Captain."

Hernandez saw Ensign Valerian fiddling with the settings of her communicator. "Sidra. Anything?"

Valerian shook her head. "Sorry, Captain. No signals on the standard channels. I'm scanning a wider range now, but all I'm getting is background radiation."

Lieutenant Thayer folded her arms and stared upward at the unreachable city. Hernandez stepped beside the tactical officer and asked, "Ideas, Kiona?"

Thayer look dismayed. "Short of throwing rocks at their windows, no."

Foyle interjected, "My men and I could fire a few shots, get their attention."

"I don't think that's a good idea," Hernandez said.

The major shrugged. "Then I have nothing."

Hernandez stared up at the majestic structure looming above them, and she watched it dim as the planet's massive, tangerine-hued star sank behind the mountain range in the west. She sighed heavily. "Well," she said, "that's just great."

Then she saw it.

Hernandez backed away from the city's edge, her gaze still directed upward as she said, "We've got company."

The rest of the landing party backpedaled alongside her as they turned their eyes to the rim of the megalopolis, hundreds of meters above. A vaguely humanoid shape, its limbs barely discernible in the twilight, stepped off the city's edge and descended as if borne aloft on the breeze. Its feet and head seemed large, ponderous, and not at all delicate, even from a distance. The landing party regrouped in a semicircle around Hernandez, who stepped forward to meet the being that floated with steady grace to the ground in front of them.

Only in the broadest possible sense would Hernandez have described the creature as humanoid. It had a torso, two arms, two legs, one head, and a face, but any resemblance to a human ended there.

Its skull was bulbous and quite large, and had two valvelike protuberances high up along the back. Two almond-shaped, upswept, lidless eyes of silver-flecked sea-green were set wide apart on the alien's face, which looked as if it had been stretched until the nose flattened and disappeared, leaving only a taut, lipless mouth curled into a permanent frown. It had no chin to speak of; its face continued to its chest in an unbroken slope of loose, leathery skin folds.

Segmented, tubular growths emerged beneath the base of the being's skull and hugged its shoulders as they curved down into its chest and blended into its mottled hide. Overlapping ridges concealed its shoulders, upper arms, and elbows, like interlocking plates in a suit of well-made armor.

As it took a cautious step in their direction, Hernandez froze, and the landing party tensed silently behind her.

Seeing the creature in motion had emphasized how different its physical proportions were to their own. Its arms were freakishly long by human standards, and its legs seemed impossibly thin to support its weight, even though its chest was birdlike. Its wide, long feet had two enormous forward toes of equal length on either side of a deep curve, and a clawlike third toe near the heel, along the instep.

Loose strips of violet fabric hung over its ungainly body, wrapped around its bony thighs, and were draped between its legs to just above its ankles. Underneath the fabric was a fitted piece of armor that covered the being's torso. A circular plate attached to the back of the armor rose up behind its shoulders and framed its head in a manner that for Hernandez evoked the images of haloed saints on stained-glass windows.

It gestured at the landscape with three delicate-looking, undulating tendrils at the end of its arm. "Welcome to Erigol," it said, in a voice with a deep male timbre. "I am Inyx, the chief scientist of Axion."

"Hello, Inyx," Hernandez said. "I'm Captain Erika Hernandez of the Earth vessel *Columbia*." She pivoted and nodded at the landing party. "These are members of my crew."

Inyx turned his head slowly one way and then the other, gently twisting the rough, mottled waddles of green-and-purple skin between his face and chest. "You have come seeking aid."

"Yes," Hernandez said. "Our ship—"

"—was damaged in a conflict," Inyx said. "We observed the incident, and we noted your approach."

Hernandez traded confused glances with Fletcher and Foyle before she replied to Inyx, "You've been watching us travel here for over twelve years?"

"Yes," Inyx said. "Do you wish to enter Axion?"

His casual response to her question and the matter-of-fact manner in which he had proffered his invitation left Hernandez feeling conversationally off balance. "Yes, we would," she said finally. "It's why we're here."

"An ingress is being extended," Inyx said. He lifted one arm and waggled one of his ribbonlike digits upward. Hernandez and her team looked up and saw that a cylindrical shaft had sprung from the ostensibly unbroken shell of the city's underside and was quickly extending toward the surface near them. It touched the ground without a sound or vibration, despite its apparent mass. Inyx walked toward it. Hernandez hesitated for a moment before she followed him. Foyle and Fletcher flanked her as the landing party fell in behind them.

A pinpoint formed on the column's silvery-white metallic surface and opened like an iris, into an aperture wide enough for the landing party to pass through three across. The interior of the cylinder glowed with amber light. Inyx stepped inside first and then moved to the left of the entrance to facilitate the others' passage. As soon as everyone had stepped in and was clear of its threshold, the aperture spiraled shut.

Hernandez stood beside Inyx and stared at his unexpressive face. She felt an awkward need to make small talk. "Our species is known as human," she said.

"We know," Inyx replied. "You are one of many species in this part of the galaxy who have recently developed starflight capabilities—an occurrence of dubious virtue."

Masking her concern over the possible meanings of his remark, she asked, "What are your people called?"

"Caeliar. For simplicity's sake, you may use it in its noun form as a singular or as a plural, and also as an adjective."

Overhead, the top of the cylinder retracted, revealing the late evening sky. Then the walls of the cylinder fell away, and Hernandez saw that she, Inyx, and the landing party stood on the far perimeter of a magnificent city.

Below the ramparts, wide thoroughfares of moving walkways were flanked by lofty towers that looked like sketches of steel and glass. Great vertical columns rose side by side hundreds of meters above the city, their edifices decorated with intricate, repeated designs, and all of them linked by tenuous filaments, as if they had been wrought from platinum and gossamer.

"It's beautiful," Fletcher said over Hernandez's shoulder.

"This is Axion," Inyx said. "Our capital city."

Under their feet, the elevator disk that had lifted them from the surface detached from Axion's foundation and drifted upward. Then, without any sense of acceleration, it sped forward into the city, which filled its enormous, concave foundation. Canyons of gleaming metal and unearthly light blurred past. The disk transited a circular tunnel through the base of a skyscraper, then shot out beneath a network of airy, open walkways that bridged the yawning space between two clusters of buildings. Swaths of the metropolis were lush with vegetation, some of it wild, some of it artfully landscaped. Lights sparkled to life in the spires as the night at last took hold over the city.

As the hoverdisk carried the landing party deeper into Axion, Hernandez asked Inyx, "Where are we going?"

"To your accommodations," Inyx said.

"I guess I could use a rest, after the day we've had," Hernandez said. A look at her landing party garnered no objections. Looking back at Inyx, she continued, "When can we talk to someone about getting help fixing our ship?"

"Your ship will not be repaired," Inyx said.

The landing party's expressions of wonderment at the city's beauties were replaced by surprised and indignant glowers. Hernandez felt her own features harden with anger, then she forced herself to relax and remain diplomatic. "We wouldn't expect you to perform any labor, of course. You obviously have remarkable manufacturing capabilities. If your people could just help us fabricate some spare parts—"

"Perhaps I was not clear," Inyx interrupted. "We will not aid you in the restoration of your vessel."

Hernandez's temper began to get the best of her. "Could you at least send a subspace signal back to Earth so another ship can come out here and get us?"

"We have that capability," Inyx said. "But we will do no such thing. Multiple warnings were sent over subspace radio to your vessel during its approach and were not heeded."

Fletcher adopted a defensive tone. "Our subspace array is damaged," she said as the hoverdisk blurred through another tunnel. "We can't send or receive any signals via subspace."

"Yes," Inyx said. "We realized that when we conducted a more intensive scan of your vessel. It was the only reason we allowed you to proceed without interference."

The breeze that accompanied their flight felt good to

Hernandez after the heat of the day, but she was too upset to appreciate it. "What are you saying? That if our comms had worked, you'd have destroyed us?"

"No," Inyx said. "Most likely we would have shifted you to another galaxy, one relatively devoid of sentient forms but still capable of sustaining your lives." As the disk glided around a long, shallow curve, he continued, "For many of your millennia, we have lived in seclusion. In recent centuries, as the local forms began traveling the stars, we masked our power signatures and obstructed scans of our world, to preserve our privacy. Clearly, however, our efforts have been ineffective."

Major Foyle snapped, "So you were going to fling us into another galaxy?" He tried to step toward Inyx and was restrained by Hernandez's hand on his chest as he continued, "Why not just send us back to Earth?"

"Preventing you from coming here would only have aroused your interest," Inyx said. "Your curiosity would have compelled your inevitable return, and others would have followed. We could not permit this. Allowing you to depart now that you have been here would pose the same threat. For this reason, we cannot allow you to transmit any signals back to your people."

Seething, Foyle asked, "Then why don't you just kill us?"

"We will not destroy sentient life," Inyx said. "But we will protect our privacy. Only the fact that you could not reveal your discovery of our world enabled me to petition the Quorum for leniency on your behalf."

The hoverdisk stopped in front of a tower and made a vertical ascent at a dizzying speed. A touch of vertigo left Hernandez unsteady on her feet, and Fletcher and Foyle each gripped one of her arms for a moment to steady her. Then the disk edged forward and docked at a rooftop garden that led to a sprawling interior space of open floors, skylights, and walls of windows offering panoramic views.

Inyx stepped off the disk and ushered the landing party into the penthouse suite with a wave of his disconcertingly long arm and rippling fingers. "I hope that you find your new accommodations satisfactory," he said. "We have interfaced with your ship's computer to acquaint ourselves with your nutritional requirements and other biological needs. This space has been configured accordingly."

"Nicest jail cell I've ever seen," Fletcher said.

"Do not think of yourselves as prisoners," counseled Inyx.

Hernandez fixed him with an icy stare. "What are we, then?"

"Honored guests," Inyx said. "With restrictions."

She had to know. "And my ship?"

"It will not be harmed," Inyx said. "But, like yourselves, it can never again leave Erigol."

# 2381

## 11

"The Borg cube is approaching Korvat," Lieutenant Choudhury announced to the rest of the *Enterprise*'s bridge crew.

Picard felt the tangible malevolence of the Collective in his gut, and he heard its soulless voice whispering at the gate of his thoughts as his ship hurtled at high warp toward another hostile encounter. "Time to intercept?"

From the tactical station, Choudhury said, "Six minutes."

*Against the Borg,* Picard knew, *six minutes can be an eternity.* "Status of the planet's defenses?"

Kadohata answered as she reviewed data on the operations console. "Orbital platforms charging, surface batteries online. *Gibraltar* and *Leonov* are moving to engage."

Watching the relayed tactical data scroll across his left-side command screen, Picard feared for the two Federation starships defending Korvat. Even though the *Gibraltar* was a *Sovereign*-class vessel like the *Enterprise,* and the *Alexey Leonov* was a hardy *Defiant*-class escort, neither was armed with transphasic torpedoes. Without that advantage, their part in the coming battle might prove tragically short-lived.

To Picard's right, Worf shifted with visible discomfort in the first officer's chair. The Klingon had always preferred to be on his feet during times of battle. Now, however, his place was here, beside Picard, coordinating the command of the ship's vast resources and hundreds of personnel.

"Number One, what's our status?"

Worf didn't need to look at his console as he answered. "Shield modifications active, Captain. All weapons ready."

"Take us to battle stations," Picard said.

"Aye, sir," Worf said, and he acted without delay. He triggered the Red Alert klaxon, which wailed once shipwide. Then he opened a shipwide comm channel. "Attention all decks, this is the XO. All hands to battle stations. This is not an exercise.

Bridge out." He closed the channel and continued issuing orders in rapid succession around the bridge—raising shields, arming weapons, and preemptively deploying damage-control teams.

In the midst of his crew's preparations for combat, Picard was paralyzed in his chair, his face slack, his thoughts erased like scratches on a beach washed smooth by a rising tide. Control, composure, and focus all vanished as the voice of the Collective spoke to him, its malice and contempt undiluted by the gulf of empty space it had bridged to touch his mind. All its hatred for him was expressed in a single word, one that always made him recoil in disgust, as if from an unspeakable obscenity.

*Locutus.*

The memory from which he could never hide. The atrocity he could never forget. It had been fifteen years since the Borg had first assimilated him and appointed him to speak on their behalf to humanity and the Federation. For a brief time he had been their unwilling intermediary, their instrument of conquest and intimidation. They had stolen his knowledge and experience and used them against his friends and fellow Starfleet officers; as a result, thirty-nine starships were destroyed and more than eleven thousand people were slaughtered at Wolf 359.

Picard's former first officer, Will Riker, along with the senior officers of the *Enterprise*-D, had liberated him less than a day after he had been taken. The physical wounds of his brief assimilation had healed soon thereafter, but the true scars of that horrible violation had lingered ever since, like a shadow on his psyche—a shadow with a name. *Locutus.*

It revolted him to hear the Collective in the privacy of his thoughts; he despised it as much for what it had done to him as for what it was. There was no shutting it out, no matter how hard he tried. Some part of that horrid, soul-devouring nightmare had left its imprint in his memory, its mark upon his essential nature, and now it could compel Picard's attention whenever it so desired.

One voice stood apart from the hive mind: the Queen. Once she had tried to seduce him. Now her voice was dark with spite.

*The hour for humanity's assimilation is past, Locutus. The time has come for you and your kind to be exterminated.*

He refused to respond to her in thought or deed. Instead, he took advantage of his momentary intimacy with the Collective to eavesdrop on its secrets, to use its intrusions to his own advantage against his old adversary. It seemed fitting to him that, in keeping with the Borg's culture of interdependency, his perpetual weak spot should be its Achilles' heel, as well. Eight years earlier, during the Battle of Sector 001, he had sussed out a vulnerability in the design of the Borg's ubiquitous cube-shaped vessels. To stop a gigantic Borg cube months earlier, he had risked letting himself become Locutus once again, to restore his link to the Collective and gain access to its secrets.

He hoped to uncover another such tactical advantage now, in the crucial moments before the battle.

A dark revelation unfolded in his mind's eye.

The Collective's agenda—in its alacrity, aggression, and scope—surpassed his worst fears. Aghast, he retreated from the vision, into the redoubt of his own thoughts. Denial was the natural response, but he knew better than to indulge it; there were no lies within the Collective, only certainties.

A gentle shaking dispelled the susurrating group voice of the Collective from his thoughts, and he blinked once to reorient himself. He was still seated in his chair on the bridge; Worf leaned down beside him, with one large hand on Picard's shoulder. He asked, "Are you all right, Captain?"

"No," Picard said, his emotions numbed from contact with the Collective. He stood, took a step forward, and said in a low voice, "We've underestimated them." Then he turned to face Worf and Lieutenant Choudhury. "We've made a terrible mistake."

Choudhury looked taken aback by the captain's words. "Well," she said with a glance at the image of Korvat on the main viewer, "at least we were right about their next target."

Picard felt his countenance harden with anger and regret. "No," he said. "We weren't." He faced the main viewscreen and continued, "Korvat isn't *the* target, it's *a* target—one of five the Borg are about to attack in unison. Commander Kadohata: Send code-one alerts to Khitomer and Starbases 234, 157, and 343."

"Aye, sir," Kadohata replied, her hands already translating his order into action on her console.

"Captain," Worf said. "There might still be time to send the new torpedo designs to the starbases."

"We can't," Picard said, his frustration churning bile into his throat. "Admiral Nechayev's orders were quite specific." His hands curled into fists. "All we can do is fight the battle in front of us."

Dropping his voice, Worf protested, "Sir, if the starbases try to fight the Borg without transphasic torpedoes—"

"It's too late," Picard said, as another flash from the Collective assaulted him with images of carnage. "It's begun."

"They're locking weapons again, Commander! What do we do?"

Smoke and fumes filled the bridge of the *U.S.S. Ranger*. Voices crying out for orders or for help buffeted the ship's first officer, Commander Jennifer Nero, as she knelt beside the fallen Captain Pachal and searched in vain for his pulse.

Another blast from the Borg cube rocked the *Nebula*-class starship hard to port, hurling Nero's crewmates toward the bulkhead and sprawling her atop the burned and bloodstained body of the captain. She pushed herself off him and struggled to her feet. "Schultheiss, th'Fairoh, get back to your posts!"

As the shaken human woman and timorous Andorian *thaan* scrambled back to their seats at the ops and conn consoles, Nero moved to take the center seat. She sat down and swept stray wisps of her red hair back behind her ears. "Ankiel," she said, looking over at the sinewy, crew-cut tactical officer, "where are the *Constant* and the *Arimathea*?"

"Coming up behind the Borg," replied Ankiel, whose eyes stayed on his console. "They're firing." He shook his head. "No effect. The Borg's shields are adapting too fast."

"Let's see if we can adapt faster," Nero said. "Bridge to main engineering."

*"Braden here,"* answered the chief engineer over the comm.

Nero crossed her fingers. "Is the captain's plan ready?"

*"Almost,"* Braden said. *"One minute till we arm the MPI."*

Unable to remain seated, Nero got up and strode forward. "Th'Fairoh, overtake the Borg cube. Schultheiss, transfer weapons power to the warp drive. Ankiel, stand by to activate the MPI on my command."

The MPI—molecular phase inverter—wasn't a device that had seen much use on the *Ranger*. On the rare occasions when it had been put into service, it had been used to restore phase-shifted matter to the normal space-time continuum. Typically, objects were knocked a few millicochranes out of phase by transporter mishaps or by exposure to severely miscalibrated warp fields. It had taken the imagination and rare technological expertise of the *Ranger*'s now-slain commanding officer, Peter Pachal, to conceive of a new use for this obscure piece of technology: They would employ it to turn their ship into an unstoppable missile with catastrophic destructive potential.

In the end, it would be all about timing—intercepting the Borg cube before it got too close to Khitomer, and activating the MPI late enough in the attack that the Borg wouldn't have time to adapt to the tactic and counteract it.

Ankiel called out, "The *Constant*'s been hit!"

Nero watched the main viewer as lifeboats ejected from the *Akira*-class vessel like spores from a dandelion. A fiery conflagration erupted from the ship's aft section and broke the ship into wreckage before consuming it in a blinding flash. The explosion was vast, and in seconds it swallowed the loose cloud of lifeboats, none of which emerged from its burning embrace. Then the firestorm passed below the bottom edge of the viewer, left behind as the *Ranger* continued its desperate pursuit of the Borg ship speeding toward Khitomer.

Between the *Ranger* and the Borg was the *Arimathea*, which continued to harry the Borg with woefully ineffective phaser fire and steady photon-torpedo barrages.

"Schultheiss," Nero said, "tell the *Arimathea* to break off before they—" She was cut off by the sight of emerald-hued beams from the Borg vessel crisscrossing the *Centaur*-class cruiser and obliterating it in a flash that would spread its wreckage across millions of cubic kilometers as its warp field collapsed.

Grim silence fell over the *Ranger*'s bridge crew. *It's up to us, now,* Nero realized. "Bridge to engineering, report."

*"Arming the MPI now,"* Braden said. *"Make sure we keep her steady—we'll be getting a pretty big boost in speed once we slip out of phase."*

"Noted," said Nero. "Schultheiss, stand by to trigger the MPI. Mister Ankiel, arm all quantum warheads and release the log buoy. Th'Fairoh, lay in a ramming trajectory for the Borg cube and prepare to increase speed to maximum warp."

"Trigger ready," Schultheiss replied. "At helm's command."

From the tactical console, Ankiel said simply, "Armed." Nero forced herself not to dwell on the fact that the *Ranger*'s sizable inventory of quantum torpedo warheads had been linked to the ship's antimatter fuel pods. If the captain's plan worked, and they slipped inside the Borg's defense screens long enough to detonate the warheads—and themselves—even the Borg's amazing regenerative abilities would be unable to withstand total, instantaneous subatomic annihilation.

She was about to give the order to proceed with the final attack when she eyed the conn and saw that the intercept course had not been locked in. "Th'Fairoh," she said, "lay in the course. It's time."

The wiry young Andorian sat with his blue hands side by side in his lap and stared at his console. He made slow, almost imperceptible swivels of his head, side to side, the movement so fluid that it didn't impart the slightest quiver to his antennae. "No," he muttered, his voice below a whisper.

Nero spoke in sharper tones this time. "Mister th'Fairoh, I gave you an order. Lock in the course and prepare to engage."

Her directive made his head tremble in nervous microturns, and his hands curled closed, with his fingernails biting into his palms. "No," he repeated. "I can't." He looked up at her, his countenance fearful and his eyes wide. "This is pointless! Don't you get it? It's a lost cause. We can't beat them! They'll just keep coming, over and over. Why throw our lives away? What good will stopping one Borg ship do?" Growing more hysterical, he continued, "We don't even know if this plan'll work! The captain's already dead, we've lost a third of the crew, and Khitomer's not even a Federation planet! What are we still doing here? We have to break off, we have to run—"

The Andorian *thaan* scrambled up from his seat. Nero yelled, "Stay at your post!" It didn't stop him. She stepped forward to restrain him, to force him back into his chair at the conn, but she underestimated the strength advantage that panic had given him. He tried to push past her, and it was a struggle to hold him back. "Dammit, th'Fairoh! Sit dow—" His fist caught her in the chin and knocked her backward onto the deck.

The angry screech of a phaser was loud enough to be painful in the confines of the bridge. Nero watched as the blazing orange beam slammed into th'Fairoh's torso and held him paralyzed, twitching in front of the energy stream like a puppet on a taut wire. Then the beam ceased, and the Andorian collapsed face-first to the deck.

A few meters away, Ankiel stood with his arm outstretched and his sidearm still aimed at the unconscious flight controller. Seconds later he seemed satisfied that th'Fairoh would not be getting up any time soon. He holstered his weapon. "Looks like you'll have to do the honors, Commander," he said.

Nero grabbed the seat of the conn officer's chair and pulled herself up into it. A deep, throbbing pain blossomed in her jaw, and she tasted the salty-metallic tang of blood between her loosened molars. Rather than spit it onto the deck of the bridge, she forced herself to swallow it. Then she coughed once to clear her throat and eyed the controls in front of her.

Entering the first few commands was easy. "Patching in all power," she said, talking herself through the steps to reduce it to the level of mere process and avoid thinking about what it meant. "Intercept trajectory plotted," she said. Making her fingers key in the next action was more difficult. She felt herself resisting the inevitable. Through will alone she entered the order and announced, "Course locked."

Then she froze, her hands hovering above the console.

She stared at the main viewscreen. On it was the image of the Borg cube, accelerating away from them, opening the gap on its way to the historic planet of Khitomer, where the Federation and the Klingon Empire had taken their first, uncertain steps toward détente and, ultimately, alliance. But Khitomer was not merely a political landmark; that lush world was home to a thriving Klingon colony of more than half a million people, all of whom would now live or die based on what the crew of the *Starship Ranger* did next.

Schultheiss leaned over from the ops console toward Nero. "Commander," she said without raising her voice, "we have to attack in the next twenty seconds, or we won't be able to stop the Borg without causing serious casualties on the planet."

Nero felt tears welling in her eyes as she faced the terrible finality of their situation. She looked around at the other bridge officers, all of whom were looking at her, waiting for the signal to proceed. Her voice faltered slightly as she asked, "Everyone ready?" Heads nodded in unison. She smiled sadly. "It's been an honor serving with you all." Turning back to face the main viewer, she poised her finger above the blinking control pad that would trigger the MPI and accelerate the ship to its rendezvous with the Borg. She paused just long enough to say to Schultheiss, "Thanks, Christine."

"My pleasure," Schultheiss said.

One deep breath in, one last breath out. *I only have to be brave for a moment*, Nero told herself. She triggered the MPI.

A moment later, it was over.


Governor Talgar stood on the balcony outside his office and watched the sky of Khitomer. Age and political duty had robbed him of the chance to take up arms and meet the Borg in honorable combat, but he refused to be shepherded like some weakling into the secure bunker beneath the administrative complex. When death came for him, he wanted to meet it with a smile.

The colony's regiment of soldiers were defending all the checkpoints that led inside the walled section of Khitomer City, and manning the surface-to-space artillery units, for whatever good it might do. Talgar had no illusions about the Borg's ability to eradicate his colony and the world on which it stood. Their preparations for war were little more than a formality.

His aide, a tall Defense Force lieutenant named Nazh, lurked just inside the doorway behind him. The younger Klingon's anxiety was palpable and irritating to Talgar, who had long resented being forced to employ the *petaQ* simply because Nazh was a kinsman of a member of the High Council. Talgar turned and growled at him, "Did you bring it?"

"Yes, sir," Nazh said.

"Then give it to me, *yIntagh*," Talgar said, reaching out his hand. Nazh pushed a carved-onyx goblet into his grasp, and Talgar lifted it to his lips and guzzled three bitter mouthfuls of *warnog,* until all that remained in the cup were dregs.

The sky was a blank slate, blue-gray like gunmetal, clear under the noonday sun, unblemished by clouds or air traffic. It seemed so serene, but Talgar knew that a deathblow was coming, a killing stroke that would fall without preamble. The Borg were not noble, and they neither had nor lacked honor; what they were was decisive and swift. The governor appreciated his enemy's ruthless efficiency for what it was: a weapon.

Inside his office, a shrill buzzing emanated from his desk. He grimaced at the disruption and said to Nazh, "Get that."

His lieutenant walked in quick strides to the desk, silenced the alert, and worked for a few moments at the desktop console. Then he looked up and declared, "Governor, it's from Colonel Nokar. He says you should see this."

Talgar grumbled incoherently out of frustration, turned, and walked back inside to his desk. He brusquely pushed Nazh aside and eyed the data and images on his wide desktop display. Despite having been informed hours earlier by the High Command that there were no Defense Force vessels close enough to reach his world before the Borg attacked, he clung to the hope that a *Vor'cha*-class attack cruiser or two might have defied the Council or the limitations of their own engines to join the fight at the last minute.

Instead, he saw a trio of Federation starships engaged in a futile, running battle with the Borg cube, which did not deviate from its course even as it pummeled their shields and blasted rents in their hulls. Over an audio channel, he heard Colonel Nokar remark with his typical snideness, *"Looks like Starfleet's in the mood to lose a few more ships today."*

Nazh let out a sardonic *harrumph* and said, "At least *they* think Khitomer's worth fighting for."

The governor punched the impudent lieutenant and sent him sprawling backward over a guest chair. "No one asked you." He turned his attention back to his desktop, in time to see the first of the three Starfleet vessels disintegrate under a steady barrage from the black cube. Several seconds later, the second of the three vessels was sliced into fiery debris by the Borg, and the third began to fall steadily behind.

"A valiant effort, friends," Talgar muttered to the diminishing image of the last Starfleet ship as he watched the image of the enemy vessel grow larger. He expected the Federation cruiser to abandon its hopeless pursuit in a few moments, since there appeared to be no way for it to overtake the cube, and no means for it to fight the cube if it did.

Then the Starfleet vessel, which the colony's sensors had just identified as the *U.S.S. Ranger*, accelerated instantly to a velocity that was almost off the scale. The sensors tried to keep up with it, but all that Talgar saw on his display was a jumble of conflicting data—and then the Borg cube vanished in a blaze of white light. His display went dark, but from outside his office came a blinding flare at least twice as bright as Khitomer's sun. It faded away within seconds, but a tingle of heat lingered in the air.

Talgar poked at the unresponsive desktop interface for a moment before he glared at Nazh and said, "Get Colonel Nokar on the comm, now."

Nazh, for once, didn't complain or procrastinate. He powered down the interface and triggered its restart sequence. It took nearly half a minute before the system was working again and a comm channel had been opened to the underground command bunker, from which Nokar had been directing his pointless, surface-based defense campaign.

"Colonel," Talgar said, "report!"

"*We're still analyzing the Starfleet ship's attack,*" Nokar said. "*It looks like they shifted their vessel just far enough out of phase to breach the Borg's shields before sacrificing their ship in a suicide attack.*"

Wary of being too optimistic, Talgar asked in a neutral manner, "Status of the Borg vessel?"

"*Destroyed, Governor,*" Nokar said. "*Vaporized.*"

Talgar marveled at the news. "*Qapla',*" he said, as a salute to the fallen heroes of the *Ranger*. Then, to Nokar, he added, "Where be your gibes now, eh, Colonel? A thousand times I've heard you mock our allies, and now you get to keep drawing breath because of them." He wasn't surprised that Nokar had no riposte for that, and as he cut the channel he imagined a sullen expression darkening the colonel's weathered, angular face.

Turning to Nazh, Talgar said, "The Empire hasn't seen an act of courage like that since Narendra, and it's time the High Council heard about it. Open a channel to Chancellor Martok."

Decades of diplomatic service had taught Talgar to make the most of opportunities when they presented themselves. For years, the chancellor's foes on the High Council had been impeding his efforts to forge a tighter bond with the Federation. Their most recent obstructions had entailed diverting Defense Force ships and resources to avoid aiding the Federation in its renewed conflict with the Borg. Calling the escalating struggle "an internal Federation matter," a bloc of councillors, led by Kopek, had begun undermining Martok's influence and authority in matters of imperial defense. But that was about to change.

An image flickered and then settled on the governor's desktop display—it was the stern, one-eyed visage of Chancellor Martok himself. *"What do you want, Talgar?"*

"The Borg have come to Khitomer, old friend," Talgar said, "and our allies have defended us with their lives." Over the subspace channel, he sent Martok the colony's sensor data of the three Starfleet ships' battle and the *Ranger*'s decisive victory over the Borg cube. As he observed the chancellor's reaction to the news, he knew that his assumption had been correct: This was the ammunition Martok had been waiting for to sway the Council.

In his guttural rasp of a baritone, Martok asked rhetorically, *"You know what this means, don't you?"*

"Yes, my lord," Talgar said. "It means this is the hour when men of honor go to war."

The command center of Starbase 234 was collapsing in on itself, and all that Admiral Owen Paris could think about was finding a working comm terminal.

Fire-control teams scrambled past the admiral on both sides as he stumbled over the wreckage strewn across the floor. Flames danced in the shadows between buckled walls, and a cloud of oily smoke gathered overhead, obscuring the ceiling.

Paris grabbed a lieutenant whose black uniform was trimmed at the collar in mustard yellow. "Is your console working?"

Grime and blood coated the woman's face, which contorted in frustration as she replied, "No, sir." She freed herself from his grasp with a rough twist and continued on her way.

He tightened his left fist around the data chip he'd carried from his office and staggered forward, through the mayhem of firefighters shouting instructions over the tumult of tactical officers issuing battle orders. A thunderclap of detonation rocked the station with the force of an earthquake.

Someone called out above the din, "Shields failing!" Then another bone-jarring blast knocked Admiral Paris off his feet and reminded him that even a bunker of cast rodinium was no match for the weapons of the Borg. He landed hard atop a mound of twisted metal and shattered companel fragments that tore through his uniform and lacerated his forearms and knees.

With only his right hand free, he found it difficult to push himself back to his feet. Then a pair of delicate but strong hands locked around his bicep and pulled him upright.

He turned his head and saw the base's chief of security, Commander Sandra Rhodes, nod toward a short stairway to the command center's lower level. "This way, sir," said the lithe brunette. "I've got a channel ready for you." A resounding boom seemed to tremble the foundations of the planet, and more chunks of debris fell from above, crashing to the deck all around them. One close call coated them in dust. Rhodes stayed by Paris's side as she pressed one hand into his back to keep him moving forward.

Scrambling down the steps, Paris cursed himself for leaving something so vital until it was long past too late. He'd made his share of mistakes in life—not least among them the Tezwa debacle, in which he'd actually conspired with other Starfleet officers to unseat a sitting Federation president—and he'd borne his guilt and his regrets in silence. But there was one burden he could not bear to take with him to the grave.

The lights stuttered and went out, plunging the underground chamber into darkness. Only the pale, faltering glow of a few duty consoles remained lit, beacons in the night. From behind, Rhodes's insistent but gentle pressure guided him forward.

His ankle caught on something sharp and hard, and he tripped. By instinct he reached out to break his fall—

The data chip fell from his hand and plinked brightly across the rubble-covered floor, its tiny sound the only clue to where it had landed. Scuttling back and forth on all fours, he began to hyperventilate. Owen Paris, the model of stoicism, was on the verge of tears, his chest heaving with panicked breaths.

"I dropped it," he called out to Rhodes. "God help me, Sandy, I dropped it!"

He swirled his hands over the stinging shards of shattered polymer on the ground as he searched in blind desperation for the chip. His palms grew sticky with caked dust and his own blood. From close by he heard Rhodes shout to the firefighters, "We need some light over here! Now!"

Sharp cracks heralded the ignition of several bright violet emergency flares in various directions around him. Some were held by members of the base's command team, some by engineers struggling to contain the fires. A few of them worked their way toward Paris, who continued rooting through the debris until the scarlet glow cast everything into harsh monochrome shadows and highlights. Then a glint of light caught the data chip's edge, and he snatched it from the dust.

A deafening concussion was followed by the roar of an implosion that brought down half the command center's ceiling. More than a dozen Starfleet personnel vanished beneath the cascade of broken metal and pulverized rock.

*No time to lose now,* Paris admonished himself, and he left Rhodes behind as he lurched and barreled ahead toward the still-illuminated console. With his last steps he fell against it, and he fumbled the data chip in his bloody fingers for a few seconds until he inserted it into the proper port on the panel.

As he began entering the transmission sequence, another station nearby exploded. Shrapnel from the blast raked his face and body, and a dull thud of impact on the side of his neck was the last thing he felt before he landed, numb, on the deck.

*Stupid old man,* he chastised himself. *Slow and stupid.*

Rhodes was at his side a moment later, looking frightened for the first time that Paris had seen since his transfer to Starbase 234 four months earlier. "It's a neck injury, sir," she said. "Don't try to move." Over her shoulder, she cried out, "Medic! The admiral's down! I need a medic over here!"

Paris's voice was a dry whisper of pain. "Sandy," he rasped, fearful that she might not hear him over the crackling of flames and the settling of debris. He said again, "Sandy."

She leaned down and said, "Don't talk, sir. Moving your jaw might do more damage in your neck." She was trying to sound unemotional, but in his opinion she was doing a lousy job of it.

"Listen to me, Sandy," Paris said. "It's important."

"All right," she said, steeling herself.

He tried to swallow before he spoke, but his mouth was dry and tasted of dirt. "Message on the data chip," he said, his voice growing reedier with each word. "Send it. Hurry."

It was to her credit, he thought, that she chose not to argue with him. Instead, she clambered over to the console and wiped off the fresh blanket of soot and crystalline dust. After a glance at the settings he had already keyed in, she shook her head. "Encryption protocols are down without the main computer."

"Doesn't matter," Paris said. "Send it."

This time she resisted. "Sir, if we send a signal in the clear to Starfleet Command, the Borg—"

"No," Paris protested, marshaling the last of his strength to make sure she understood. "Not . . . to Starfleet. . . . To my boy."

Rhodes's teary eyes reflected Paris's sorrows as she replied, "Aye, sir." She worked at the failing console for several seconds, and then she returned to Paris's side, kneeled beside him, and took his hand. "It's done, sir."

"Thank you, Sandy," Paris said, the last vestiges of his iron-clad composure deserting him as his strength faded. "I needed him to know," he confessed, ". . . that I'm sorry."

She cupped her hand under his cheek. "I'm sure he knows."

"Maybe. But I had to say it. . . . I had to *say* it."

As a final eruption of stone and fire engulfed the command center, Owen Paris was grateful that he'd been spared the indignity of tears.


Picard felt like the calm at the center of a hurricane. He had plunged his ship and crew into battle with a single order: *Destroy the Borg cube.* Telling his officers *what* to do was his role; telling them *how* to do it, he left to Worf.

"Helm, lay in attack pattern Sierra-Blue," Worf said over the steady comm chatter of tactical reports from *Gibraltar* and *Leonov.* The two vessels were already engaged in a losing battle against the Borg cube that had entered Korvat's orbit and begun bombarding the surface. Worf continued, "Lieutenant Choudhury, arm transphasic torpedoes."

"Armed," Choudhury replied, entering commands with fast, quick touches on her console. "Twenty seconds to firing range."

Picard stared at the magnified image of Korvat on the main viewscreen. The planet's orbital defense platforms had all been reduced to tumbling clouds of glowing-hot junk. Crimson blooms of fire erupted on the planet's surface. From ops, Kadohata reported, "The planet's surface defenses have been neutralized."

Picard flashed back for a moment to the scenes of devastation he'd witnessed on Tezwa less than two years earlier. Then the damage had been inflicted by Klingons using photon torpedoes; he shuddered to imagine what horrors the Borg had just wrought.

*If only we'd been here a few minutes sooner,* he cursed silently as the situation unfolded around him.

"The Borg are locking weapons on the planet's capital," Choudhury said. Then she added with surprise, "The *Gibraltar*'s maneuvering into their firing solution!"

Everyone on the *Enterprise*'s bridge turned their eyes to the main viewscreen as the other *Sovereign*-class ship positioned itself between the Borg cube and its target, rolling to present as broad a barrier as possible. A searing beam of sickly green energy from the cube slammed into the *Gibraltar* just behind its deflector dish. The *Gibraltar*'s shields collapsed, and the green energy beam ripped into its underside. Fissures spiderwebbed across its exterior, spread through its elliptical saucer section, and buckled the pylons of its warp nacelles. Vermillion flames and jets of superheated gas erupted from broad cracks in its hull. Picard winced as if he were watching his own ship fall beneath a mortal blow.

Then a flash of white light filled the screen, and when it faded seconds later, the *Gibraltar* was gone.

"We're in firing range," Choudhury said. "Locking weapons."

"Fire at will," Worf said.

On the screen, a quartet of brilliant blue projectiles raced toward the Borg cube as it fired again at Korvat's capital city. The *Alexey Leonov* tried to emulate the *Gibraltar*'s self-sacrifice, only to be picked off by a dense fusillade from the Borg cube. Another blinding flare whited-out the main viewer.

All four of the *Enterprise*'s transphasic torpedoes found their target. Even as they broke the Borg cube into pieces and consumed them in blue fire, the Borg got off one last shot—a massive pulse of emerald-hued energy that arrowed down through Korvat's atmosphere and laid waste to its capital.

Two fire clouds blossomed like obscene flowers on the screen in front of Picard, who for the second time in one day bore witness to a burning world and its dispersing black halo of collateral damage.

Worf left his chair and prowled from station to station. "Commander Kadohata, scan the planet's surface for survivors."

The svelte second officer tapped at her console and sighed. Her dry, Port Shangri-la accent leached the emotion from her voice as she reported, "Isolated life signs in a number of highland regions and on a few antarctic islands." She filtered the data on her screens. "I'm reading roughly twenty-nine thousand people left alive on the surface, sir." Picard appreciated her artful omission, her choice to emphasize the number of survivors rather than confirm the deaths of more than ten million people. Then she continued, "Toxins in the atmosphere and water are spreading rapidly. If the survivors aren't evacuated in the next seventy-two hours, they'll receive lethal doses of theta radiation."

"Lieutenant Choudhury," Worf said, "send Starfleet Command a priority request for evacuation transports."

Kadohata turned from her station to look at Worf. "Shouldn't we start rescuing them ourselves?"

"We do not have room for that many refugees," Worf said. "We also have nowhere to relocate them to."

The slim human woman looked back and forth in frustration between Worf and the captain. "So we're just going to leave those people there?"

Picard replied, "We have other mission priorities, Commander." He looked away from Kadohata's accusing stare and said to Choudhury, "Any reports from the other four targets?"

"Starbase 234 was destroyed," she said, "but it looks like they took the Borg down with them. Khitomer's safe—thanks to a kamikaze attack by the *Ranger*." Glancing at her console, she added, "The battles at Starbases 157 and 343 are still in progress." She frowned. "Starbase 157 is sending a Mayday, sir."

Against his better judgment, Picard said, "On speaker."

Crackles of static, wails of feedback noise . . . and then panicked shouts over the cries of the dying and the erratic percussion of explosions. *". . . phasers overloaded . . ."* More static. *". . . hit them with everything we've got . . . still coming . . ."* A scratch of deep-space background radiation noise. *". . . all power . . . can't break our shields . . ."* A screech and a high-frequency tone pitched in and out on a long oscillation. *". . . coming right at us! They're on a ramming trajectory!"*

A long, loud burst of noise was followed by silence.

"They're gone," Choudhury said, her eyes downcast as she closed the channel.

An incoming signal chirruped on Kadohata's console. She reviewed it in a glance and reported, "Priority message from the *Excalibur*, sir. They're signaling all-clear at Starbase 343."

Choudhury looked perplexed at the news. "How'd they stop the Borg without using transphasic torpedoes?"

"With a miracle, Lieutenant," Picard said with dry humor. "That's Captain Calhoun's ship. I've learned to expect the impossible from him and his crew." He shook his head as he thought of the hotheaded young Xenexian man he'd coaxed into Starfleet all those years ago—and the unorthodox, nigh-infamous starship commander he'd become.

From an auxiliary console, the *Enterprise*'s half-Vulcan, half-human contact specialist and relief flight controller T'Ryssa Chen heaved a tired sigh. "I'm just glad it's over."

Her comment rankled Picard. "Glad *what's* over, Lieutenant?"

The young woman recoiled from Picard's curt response, as usual favoring the human half of her ancestry over the Vulcan. Her reply was hesitant and uncertain. "The invasion. The Borg cubes were destroyed."

Picard knew that he had to make the situation clear to Chen, and to anyone else who might have made the same, misguided assumption about the outcome of the battle they'd just fought.

"This isn't over," he said to her. "It's only begun." He got up from his chair and made a slow turn as he continued. "The Borg have been planning this invasion for years, and it won't end as easily as this. They're going to keep coming—hammering us every day, week after week, for as long as it takes . . . until we, or they, are gone."

His officers watched him with grim, resolute expressions as he revealed what he'd learned in his latest brush with the Collective. "This is a clash of civilizations," he explained, "and it will end when one of us falls."

# 12

Tuvok found the zero-gravity environment of *Titan*'s stellar cartography lab inconvenient but manageable, though he had to suppress a deep, subtle tinge of envy at Lieutenant Commander Pazlar's graceful ease of motion.

*Envy.* The presence of such a petty emotion shamed him, despite being known to no one but himself. Over the years his control of his emotions had been degraded by one incident after another. It had started years earlier, with a mind meld to his *Voyager* crewmate Lon Suder, a Betazoid man who also had been a violent sociopath. In his effort to stabilize the homicidal Suder, Tuvok had almost unhinged himself.

Other traumas—including a period of brutal incarceration on Romulus before he'd joined the crew of *Titan*—had exacerbated Tuvok's difficulties. Most recently, Tuvok's mind had been telepathically hijacked into the service of space-dwelling life-forms known to Starfleet by the nickname "star jellies." While in their control, he had assaulted Pazlar and compromised the ship's security. Under the care of Counselor Troi, he had begun learning Betazoid techniques for channeling and controlling his emotions, but he remained wary of his feelings and the damage that they could do when he failed to master them.

"I have the next set of projections ready," Pazlar said. The delicate Elaysian reached out, her arms wide, and pulled the holographic image of the galaxy closer, compressing its scale with a balletic drawing together of her palms until they were centimeters apart. She and Tuvok towered like cosmic giants in the midst of the spiral majesty of the Milky Way, which girdled their torsos in a broad band. "That's the source of the signals," she said, pointing out a blinking red pinpoint half a meter in front of them. "And here's a model of the signals' trajectories." She waved dozens of pale-blue beams into existence, all of them emanating in a tight, fan-shaped cluster from the pinpoint and reaching toward Federation space.

"Highlight the segments of those trajectories that fall within Federation space," Tuvok said.

Pazlar sighed. "Sure, since you asked so nicely." She entered the command into the holographic interface, which left an odd pattern of blue lines cutting through a tiny, red-tinted region demarcating Federation territory. "There's no way to tell where any of them terminate," she said as Tuvok patched his padd into the computer and began noting major UFP star systems along the beams' paths. "For all we know, they're looking at another galaxy and we just happen to be in their way."

"That is a possibility," Tuvok said. "However, unless we investigate it, we cannot know for certain." A list of star systems appeared on the screen of his padd. He skimmed it and said to Pazlar, "Please enlarge the map of the Federation."

The simulation zoomed in on the red patch and expanded it until it surrounded them and all but filled the hololab. At that magnification, the angles between the various beams became far more subtle. "There must be dozens of populated systems within a light-year of each pulse," Pazlar said.

"Eighty-three, to be precise," Tuvok said, correcting her careless approximation. "However, I propose that we can limit our search to a specific region." He transmitted a set of data to the computer, and it appeared in the simulation as a dense cluster of yellow dots in a corner of the three-dimensional map. "Magnify, please." He waited until Pazlar had enlarged that isolated region, and then continued, "The recent Borg incursions into Federation space have all occurred along the border between the Klingon Empire and the Federation, from Acamar to Ramatis." Pointing at the lone bold, blue streak that cut through the image, he added, "If these energy pulses are being used by the Borg, then this would likely be their conduit."

"I don't see any populated star systems near it," she said. "But if its terminus opens in interstellar space, that might explain why Starfleet hasn't been able to locate it."

"Possibly," Tuvok said. He paused as he traced the beam's path through the cloudy stain of the Azure Nebula. A tiny detail snared his attention. Pointing at the nebula's center, he said, "Magnify again, please." Pazlar reached out and cupped the nebula in both hands, then she spread her hands and arms apart, instantly ballooning the gaseous cluster to dozens of times its previous size. The narrow beam of blue light cut straight through an astrocartographic marker. "Most curious," Tuvok said.

"That's one way of putting it," Pazlar said, eyeing the image with surprise and wonder. "It passes right through that supernova remnant." She chuckled. "If the Borg are using that beam as some kind of subspace passage, that remnant's the end of the line. Even in subspace, if they hit that, they'd be dead."

"Indeed," Tuvok said. "And if that is their entry point into Federation space, the radiation from the remnant and the nebula would provide them with excellent cover from the region's sensor network." He arched one eyebrow in satisfaction. "We should inform the captain immediately."

Pazlar mumbled, "Mm-hm," and she began entering a new series of commands into the hololab's interface.

Tuvok watched her for a moment, expecting her to explain her sudden burst of activity and inspiration. After several seconds, he concluded that the intensely focused and independent-minded science officer was not going to volunteer such information. He would have to ask her for it.

"What are you doing?"

"Setting up new parameters for the simulation," she said, still keying in commands. "Seeing that beam run smack into the supernova remnant got me thinking: We cast the net too wide."

"Explain," Tuvok said.

She made some minor adjustments via the interface as she answered him. "Well, instead of looking for all the systems that fall within a certain range of the beams, why not just look for the ones that actually intersect? In other words, ignore the near misses and just look for the direct hits. It's bound to yield fewer results, and if what we saw in the nebula's any indicator, they might be a lot more relevant."

"An interesting hypothesis. How long will it take to run the new simulation if you include all known galactic points?"

"Another hour," she said, "but I think it'll be worth it."

"Very well," he said. "Computer," Tuvok said, "platform." He felt the gentle tug of a tractor beam nudge him toward the circular platform below him and Pazlar. He could have navigated his way out of the zero-*g* environment with minimal difficulty, but because of his lack of recent experience with free fall, the effort might have taken him a few minutes, and he was eager to meet with the captain and continue his work. Allowing the computer to facilitate his exit from stellar cartography was both logical and expedient.

His feet touched down on the platform, and the tractor beam gradually released him into the low-gravity zone. He looked up at Pazlar, who hovered several meters above him. "Notify me when the results are ready for analysis," he said. "I will continue my research in science lab one after I've informed the captain of our discovery."

"Aye, sir," Pazlar said. Then she returned to her work, and Tuvok walked toward the exit. As the hatch to the corridor opened, he stole a look back at Pazlar, floating free in her faux heavens, manipulating millions of ersatz stars with waves of her hands, blissfully submerged in her labors.

As he departed into the corridor, Tuvok struggled once again to extinguish that same troubling spark of envy.

Dr. Shenti Yisec Eres Ree paced on taloned feet, awaiting his patient's arrival in sickbay. Delivering bad news had never been a pleasant experience for him, and he had found it was often best done as soon as possible and with little or no preamble. All the same, he despised the task. He had considered letting the matter lie until morning, rather than forcing himself to remain awake well into his regular sleep period. Then he had seen the report, realized its importance, and issued his urgent summons.

Caught up in his tests and his analysis, he had missed the scheduled hour for the crew's carnivores to dine in the mess hall. Hunger burned in his gut, so intensely that he could almost taste the raw meat and the fresh marrow he craved. Despite the lateness of the hour, he knew that he could still use the mess hall and eat as he liked, but he would miss the camaraderie of his fellow flesh-eaters. The omnivores and herbivores on *Titan* had grown accustomed to witnessing the bloody feeding spectacle of carnivores playing with their food, though the majority of them remained discomfited by the idea of sitting in proximity to it while consuming their own meals.

*Too bad,* Ree decided. *They'll just have to deal with it. A little bit of splatter never hurt anyone.*

The door sighed open and Counselor Troi walked in, attired in civilian clothes. She was bleary-eyed from being woken up, and she appeared anxious, clenching her right hand into a fist and cupping it in her left hand. "You said it was urgent?"

"Yes, Counselor," Ree said. He turned and led her toward his private office. "Please come in and sit down."

She shook her head. "I'd rather stand."

"As you prefer." He continued inside his office and waited until she was inside before he closed the door for privacy. As it closed, it shifted from transparent to translucent, along with the windows that looked out on sickbay. "I've finished my tests. I'm sorry to say the news isn't good."

Laying a hand on her belly, she asked, "You know why this is happening?"

He bobbed his long, therapodian head in a rough imitation of a nod. "I do." He reached over to his desk and scooped up a data padd with his long, clawed fingers. "According to your medical history, sixteen years ago, on Stardate 42073, you became pregnant after contact with an unidentified alien being composed of energy. Hours later, you gave birth to a son."

"Ian," she said.

"Yes." Reviewing her file, he continued, "The boy matured at a remarkable rate—approximately eight years in a single day. At the same time, a sample of plasma plague supposedly in stasis started to grow, its development accelerated by a field of Eichner radiation—the source of which was your son, Ian."

Troi covered her mouth as if to hold back a cry of alarm. Her eyes were shining with tears, and her voice was a throaty gasp through her fingers. "No, please don't tell me . . ."

"I'm sorry, Counselor," Ree said. "But you should know all the facts." He handed her the padd. She took it in one shaking hand and stared at it while he continued. "Research conducted a few years ago at the Vulcan Science Academy showed that sustained exposure to Eichner radiation can cause erratic mutations in mitochondrial DNA. For the purpose of their study, 'sustained' exposure was defined as anything longer than four hours. You gestated Ian for more than thirty-six hours."

She covered her face with her hands. "No," she said through a keening cry. Struggling for control, she said, "Dr. Pulaski said there were no complications. She said all my readings were as if I'd never been pregnant."

Ree bowed his head a moment. "Her exam was as accurate as it could have been," he said, looking up. "But she relied on hormonal data and basic cellular analysis. The damage occurred on a much deeper and more subtle level."

The counselor's stance became unsteady, so Ree took her gently by the shoulders and eased her into a chair beside his desk. She was all but imploding in front of him.

"Forgive me," he said. "There's more." The data padd started to fall from her hand, and he plucked it gingerly from her grasp. "The Eichner radiation caused subtle, random genetic defects in all of your unreleased ova."

Troi peeked out from behind her hands. "But you can fix that, can't you? Reconstruct the genetic sequence . . .?"

Where a human might have sighed, Ree stifled a low, rasping

growl. "No, I can't," he said. "If it were a single, uniform mutation, I might have been able to extract an ovum, resequence its
chromosomes, fertilize it in vitro, and reimplant it. But that's not
what has happened here." He keyed up a screen of visual guides
on the padd to illustrate his point. "The damage to your ovaries
hasn't resulted merely in corrupted genetic information. It's also
led to lost information. It would have been extremely difficult to
resequence a mutated ova without a healthy specimen as a tem-
plate. I wouldn't know where to begin filling in the blanks of an
incomplete chromosome."

The half-Betazoid woman bowed her head into her hands
and wept. All that Ree could do was sit in silence and let her
cry. Though he found the parasitic nature of mammalian pregnancy to be unnerving, he understood the profound sense of
connection that it created between female mammals and their
young. *This would be so much easier if she were a Pahkwa-
thanh,* he thought sadly. Among his kind, when an egg failed to
hatch, its mother would break it open and devour both young
and yolk, to conserve resources and provide for the next offspring. *So much simpler than stillbirth,* he reasoned. *Not to
mention cathartic.*

After a few minutes, Troi ceased her lamentations and calmed
herself. Wiping tears from her reddened eyes, she asked, "What's
my prognosis, then, Doctor?"

"That depends on the actions you take. Are you asking for my
recommendation?"

"Yes, I am."

He scrolled to the final page of information on the padd and
handed it back to Troi. "As your physician, I advise you to terminate your pregnancy immediately. The fetus is not viable, and
if it's not removed, I predict its growth will rupture your uterine
wall and cause a potentially fatal hemorrhage."

"When?"

"I'm not certain. It could be tomorrow, or next month."

Troi's expression was grave and distant. "What are the odds of
this happening with my next pregnancy?"

Medical ethics compelled him to tell her the truth. "Almost
certain," he said. "My medical opinion is that the odds of you
and Captain Riker having a healthy offspring are negligible, and
I would recommend you cease trying. Since the damage to your

ova cannot be repaired . . ." He hesitated, and was sorry that he'd let the first half of the sentence leave his tongue. He felt as if he had failed her, though he knew that he had done everything he could.

"What?" prompted Troi. "Since it can't be repaired . . . what?"

Ree turned away a moment, then decided to finish what he'd started. "I'd recommend a radical hysterectomy, Counselor. To prevent further failed pregnancies, and to protect you from the risk of future oncological complications."

She looked stunned, as if he had just hammered her with a whack of his long, muscular tail. He waited for her to say something. Instead she turned her face away from him and blinked slowly a couple of times. Then she got up and moved to leave.

"Counselor," he said. "We should schedule your procedure before you go."

Troi ignored him. She got up and made her exit; his office door and windows reverted to their normal, transparent state as the portal slid open. She crossed sickbay at a hurried pace and was out the door without a look back at the concerned surgeon.

Her refusal of his medical advice put him in a precarious position. Ree had no doubt that Troi would have the support of the captain, and that Riker would obstruct any effort he might make to exert his medical authority for Troi's own good. Worse, he was appalled at the idea of performing a surgical procedure on a patient against her will. In his opinion it would be little different from assault, his good intentions notwithstanding.

On the other hand, his responsibilities as *Titan*'s chief medical officer were unambiguous and defined in stark terms by Starfleet regulations and the Starfleet Code of Military Justice. He could not, either by action or omission of action, allow personnel under his medical charge to bring themselves to harm or to death—and by law he was empowered to protect them, if need be, from themselves. The counselor's disregard for her own safety had made this his responsibility.

The fact that his patient was the captain's wife made the situation rather more incendiary than he was accustomed to, however. If he was going to make a stand, he would need to make certain he wouldn't be standing alone.

He sealed the door of his office and reset the windows to their frosted privacy mode. Then he used the companel on his desk to open a secure, person-to-person channel to the one individual he most needed to be certain he could trust.

"Ree to Commander Vale."

The first officer answered moments later. *"Yes, Doctor?"*

"We need to talk. In private."

Tuvok didn't need to look up from his work to know who had just entered the science lab behind him. Heavy, rapid footfalls and a faint hint of an obscure Risan cologne had told him who it was. "Good evening, Mister Keru."

"Pazlar says you two found something," said the Trill chief of security.

"Her report may have been premature," Tuvok said. "I am still conducting my analysis."

Keru sidled up to Tuvok and eyed the starmaps on several adjacent monitors. "Tuvok, you've definitely got something here. Fill me in—I want to know whatever you can tell me about this."

It was clear to Tuvok that Keru would not be willing to wait for his official report at the start of the next shift. He suppressed a surge of negative emotions and pointed out details as he spoke. "Lieutenant Commander Pazlar suggested that we narrow our investigation to those energy pulses that directly intersect known star systems. As she suspected, very few systems satisfy that criterion." He began augmenting the images on the screens with illustrative overlays. "The first, which led us to this method, is a remnant of the supernova that created the Azure Nebula. So far, we've identified three others." Pointing from each monitor to the next, he continued, "An uncharted system in the Delta Quadrant. A periphery system in globular cluster Messier 80. And an un-named system in the Gamma Quadrant."

"What about the other energy pulses?" Keru asked. "There had to be dozens of them."

"If we assume that each one is targeted at a specific star or planet, then the remaining pulses appear to be focused on subjects outside of our galaxy."

A dubious look creased Keru's brow. "What if *we* have assumed wrong? What if the pulses are passageways that open in deep space, away from prying eyes?"

"Then we would need to modify our research accordingly."

Keru narrowed his eyes and lowered his chin, signaling his apparent displeasure with Tuvok's answer. "All right, then," he said. "Let's examine the facts in hand. Have you uncovered any connections between these four locations?"

"I have found no direct connections," Tuvok replied.

Displaying the interrogatory style that had served him so well as a security officer, Keru asked, "What about *indirect* connections? Or suspicious coincidences?"

"I had hoped to conduct a more thorough investigation before sharing my initial discoveries," Tuvok said, "in part because I am not yet convinced that they are relevant, to either the phenomenon ahead of us, or to the crisis currently unfolding within the Federation."

His attention fully engaged, Keru pushed, "So you did find some kind of link?"

"Possibly," Tuvok said. He changed the images on one of the monitors. "The beam intersection in the Gamma Quadrant falls inside a star system where, eight years ago, the *Starship Defiant* discovered the wreckage of the Earth ship *Columbia*."

"I read about that," Keru said. "It went missing right before the Earth-Romulan war."

"Correct," Tuvok said, and he pointed at the monitor showing the first intersection point. "They vanished in 2156, while traveling from the Onias Sector with a convoy near this supernova remnant, which at that time was a main-sequence star."

Visibly intrigued, Keru asked, "When did it supernova?"

"In 2168," Tuvok said. "Which is most unusual, because main-sequence stars typically expand and cool for billions of years before such an event."

Now the security chief looked puzzled. "And what's the connection between that and the beams hitting those points now?"

"I do not know," Tuvok replied.

Keru was animated with enthusiasm for the mystery. "Is it possible these beams had something to do with how the *Columbia* got to the Gamma Quadrant? Could *Columbia* have made it out here, only to get tossed all the way across the galaxy?"

"Anything is possible, Mister Keru," Tuvok said. "Sensor readings made by *Defiant* indicated that the *Columbia*'s hull had been subjected to extreme subspatial stresses before it crashed.

Consequently, the Starfleet vessel *Aventine* was dispatched over a week ago to recover the wreck for analysis."

The burly, bearded Trill leaned over Tuvok's shoulder to skim the mission reports about the downed *Columbia*. "Those subatomic fractures in the hull are pretty intense," he said. "Any theories on what could've done that?"

"There are some hypotheses," Tuvok said. "Including a few that bear pronounced similarities to the phenomenon we are now moving to investigate."

Keru nodded. "I'll bet." He folded his arms and leaned back from the bank of computer screens. "So, what about that beam intersection in the Delta Quadrant? Is it inside Borg space?"

"Not as such," Tuvok said. "But it falls very close to the known limits of their conquered territory. It would take them only a matter of weeks to reach it without the benefit of their transwarp network."

"Then this is a whole lot of coincidences," Keru said. "A mysterious power source with an energy profile that resembles transwarp, shooting beams that point at Federation space, Borg space, and a planet in the Gamma Quadrant where an old Earth ship has been sitting for nearly two centuries."

Tuvok arched one eyebrow to convey his incredulity. "I understand your zeal to draw links between the phenomenon and the recent Borg incursions into Federation space. However, I fail to see the relevance, if any, of the disappearance and rediscovery of a twenty-second-century Earth starship."

A crooked grimace tugged at Keru's mouth, though it was hard to see his expression behind his beard. "Yeah," he said, "I'm drawing a blank on that, too. I feel like that ship has to fit into this somehow—that it's not just a random fluke that it's sitting on a planet with one of these beams pointed at it. But I'll be damned if I can see the connection."

Tuvok sighed softly. "Indeed."

Riker's eyelids fluttered and drooped with fatigue. Catching himself sinking into sleep, he jolted awake at his desk with a shudder. It was late, almost 0400, and his body craved sleep.

He took another sip from his third mug of half-sweet *raktajino* and savored the tingle of its caffeine infusing his bloodstream. Then he realized that he'd started drifting off again—he'd been dreaming of himself enjoying the Klingon coffee. He shuddered awake and sipped his now-tepid beverage for real.

His ready room's door signal chimed. Wiping the itch of exhaustion from his eyes, he said, "Come in."

The door opened and Christine Vale entered. He recalled the awkwardness of their last private meeting, several hours earlier, and he straightened his posture as she approached.

"Sorry to bother you so late," she said, "but since we're both up, I decided not to put this off."

That didn't sound good. "Put what off?"

Vale sat down in one of the chairs on the other side of his desk. "I just met with Dr. Ree. He's worried about Deanna."

Suspicion edged into Riker's voice, despite his efforts to remain calm. "I know about his concerns. Why is he discussing my wife's medical condition with *you*?"

"Because you and Deanna have made this into a crew-safety issue," Vale said. "Regulations require him to intervene—and they give him the authority to do so."

"I still don't see what—"

"And if he makes it an order, I'm required to enforce it," Vale cut in. "Whether you like it or not."

He was out of his chair and pacing like a caged animal. "Dammit, Chris, we talked about this a few hours ago. I'm not letting him force her to terminate her pregnancy."

She remained calm and seated. "It'd be best for everyone if it didn't come to that. If she doesn't have the procedure now, she'll need to have it when she becomes incapacitated. Except then there's a chance she'll die." Vale got up and stepped into Riker's path, disrupting his frantic back-and-forth. "Why let it come to that? Can't you talk to her?"

"No," Riker admitted. "I can't." He sighed. "I don't know what to say, and she wouldn't want to hear it if I did." Faced with the hopelessness of the situation, he turned away to gaze out the ready room's window. "She's not stupid, Chris—and she's not crazy. She knows her life's in danger, but that's not enough to change her mind." He stared at his dim reflection and realized it made him look the same as he felt—like he was only half there, half the man he used to be. "Our first miscarriage hit her so hard," he continued. "I think she just can't stand the idea of losing another baby."

Vale nodded. "I understand, Will. I really do. But if she's in that much distress, should she still be on active duty? And if her grief, or her depression, or whatever she's struggling with . . . if it's so overwhelming that she can't take action to save her own life, is she really fit to be making medical decisions?"

"Maybe not," Riker said. He turned from the window to face Vale. "But I am."

The first officer steeled her gaze. "Are you, sir? Do you really think you can be completely objective about this?"

"I don't need to be objective," Riker said. "I'm in command, and I'm not letting Ree force this on her."

"I see," Vale said, her temper starting to show. "This is *exactly* the kind of conflict of interest I was worried about when you told me your wife would be part of your command team. You promised me that your personal feelings wouldn't get in the way when it came to ship's business. But the first time there's a tug-of-war between what she wants and what the regs demand, the book goes out the window, doesn't it?"

Riker shot back, "This isn't about ship's business! We're talking about my wife's health, and maybe her life!"

"What if she collapses in the middle of a crisis situation? Have you thought about that?" He tried to turn away, but she kept after him, putting herself in front of him, hectoring him with increasing fury. "What if we're in combat, or handling an emergency, and she starts bleeding out? You think you'll be at your best when that happens? Think you'll stay focused on the mission when your baby's dying and taking her with it?"

He bellowed, "That's *enough*!" The force of his voice silenced Vale's harangue and made her take a step back. "I know what's at stake here, Chris—I don't need you to lecture me. Do I know my unborn child's going to die? *Yes*. Do I know that Deanna's risking her life by not ending the pregnancy? *Yes*. Am I going to let Dr. Ree force a solution on her? *No*." His face and ears felt feverishly warm. "If the doctor overrules me and makes the surgery compulsory, Deanna won't comply. If he declares me unfit for command, I'll refuse to step down. Then you can put me in the brig—and decide for yourself how *you* feel about terminating a woman's pregnancy against her will."

The captain and first officer regarded each other in a tense standoff for several seconds. Vale's eyes burned with resentment. She took a breath, calmed a bit, and seemed to be searching for the right words with which to reply.

Then a deep shudder of impact resonated through the deck and bulkheads, and a jolt of arrested motion hurled Riker to the deck as Vale slammed against the side of his desk. Darkness hiccupped in and out for a few seconds before settling on them. Outside the ready room's window, the slow pull of warp-distorted starlight had vanished, replaced by a static starfield. As the captain struggled back to his feet, dim emergency lights snapped on overhead and at regular intervals along the bottoms of the bulkheads. Vale clutched her ribs and had trouble straightening her posture. Riker asked, "You all right?"

"Just bruised," she said, and she glanced toward the door to the bridge. "I guess we ought to go see what happened."

"Might be a good idea," he said, patting her shoulder as he stepped past her.

She followed him and said, "You know we're not done talking about this, right?"

"I know," Riker said. "One thing at a time, though."

They stepped back onto the bridge, him first and her close behind, and found the gamma-shift team shaken and still out of sorts. Lieutenant Commander Fo Hachesa, the gamma-shift officer of the watch, was about to sit down in the center seat when he saw Riker and Vale. "Captain," said the trim, muscular Kobliad, "we've lost warp drive and main power."

"I've gathered that," Riker said. "What caused it?"

"The source of those energy bursts we've been tracking," Hachesa said, worry lines creasing on either side of his broad naso-cranial ridge. He nodded to the young Cardassian officer at the ops console. "Ensign Dakal picked up a high-power sensor beam directed at us from the energy source. On the chance it might be a Borg early warning system, I had Lieutenant Rriarr raise shields." The golden-furred Caitian at the security console nodded in confirmation to the captain and first officer. Hachesa gestured to the other side of the bridge, where a Benzite engineering officer stood at an auxiliary companel. "Ensign Meldok is analyzing what hit us after we raised shields."

Riker nodded once to Meldok. "Ensign? Any damage?"

"Yes, sir," the Benzite replied, with seemingly misplaced enthusiasm. "A broad-spectrum, high-nutation sensor pulse caused degenerative feedback loops in our warp field and shield grid, collapsing both in point-zero-zero-four seconds. I am still running diagnostics on all systems, but preliminary results suggest serious damage to our subspace communications array and weapons grid, and main power is offline. There may also be coil failures in the warp nacelles."

Vale asked Rriarr, "Casualty report?"

"Minor injuries in engineering," Rriarr said.

The captain nodded. "Understood. Commander Hachesa, carry on with repairs and keep Commander Vale informed of your progress. Let me know as soon as we have warp speed."

"Aye, sir," Hachesa said.

Riker looked at Vale and gestured with a subtle tilt of his head that she should follow him. He led her off the bridge, into the turbolift. The doors closed and he said, "Deck Five."

"Deck Six," Vale added. As the turbolift began its descent, she quipped, "Hachesa finally got the hang of verbs, I see."

Riker chortled under his breath as he recalled the well-meaning Kobliad's propensity for mangled conjugations. "Took him long enough." He folded his arms and looked at his shoes. "I'll try and talk to Deanna. Tonight, if she's awake, in the morning if she's not. I can't promise she'll change her mind, but maybe we can find a compromise."

Vale nodded. "I'll ask Dr. Ree for more options."

They rode together in silence until the turbolift stopped, and the doors parted to reveal the Deck Five main corridor. Riker stepped out. Before the doors closed, Vale stepped between them to hold the lift. "Am I the only one who finds it hard to believe we just got our ass kicked by a *sensor beam*?"

Riker cocked his head. "What are you saying?"

"That I don't think what that beam did to us was an accident. Think about it: Someone or something goes to a lot of trouble to black out a whole star system. We start flying toward it, pelting it with sensor sweeps, and what happens? It knocks us out of warp, frags our weapons, and fries our comms. If you ask me, I'd say whatever's out there doesn't want to meet us, and it doesn't want us talking about it to anyone else."

"Then it shouldn't have messed with my ship—because now I'm *really* curious."

"You and the cat, sir."

He chuckled softly. "Go get some sleep. I get the feeling tomorrow's gonna be a very busy day."

# 2168

## 13

Veronica Fletcher popped her head around the corner from the foyer and said to Erika Hernandez, "We're ready, Captain."

Hernandez lifted her feet from a reasonable facsimile of an ottoman and got up from the wraparound sofa that bordered three sides of the penthouse suite's sunken main room. She climbed the few stairs in quick steps and passed the open dining area. It was well stocked with fruits and a wide variety of faithfully recreated Earth foodstuffs. Before she left, she stole another look at the warm, natural light slanting through the suite's panoramic windows, which rose to great arches near the vaulted ceilings. As gilded prisons went, this one, intended for her and the rest of the landing party, was truly first-rate.

She joined Fletcher in the foyer and followed her out to the floor's central corridor, where a transparent pod waited for them in an alcove. They stepped inside. It began a swift descent, devoid of any sensation of movement, into a glowing shaft of pale, pulsing rings. In seconds they emerged into what seemed like thin air, dropping in a controlled manner toward a pool of water shimmering with rippled sunlight.

The towers of the city surrounded them, and through slivers between the platinum spires, Hernandez caught flashes of the jagged mountaintops in the west. Peach-colored clouds were pulled taut across the sky.

"It really is a beautiful city," Fletcher said.

Hernandez allowed herself a moment to admire the scenery. "Nice place to visit. Wouldn't want to live here."

Their pod touched down on the surface of the water without so much as a ripple. The dancing sparkle of sunlight on wind-teased water transformed into a dull glow of reflected illumination on a solid, matte surface, and the pod itself sublimated and dissipated into the hot summer air.

Fletcher led the way across a sprawling plaza paved with white marble. Hulking granite sculptures and massive, flowering topiaries depicted alien creatures unlike any the captain had ever seen before.

At its far end, flanked by densely grown trees, was a rectangular reflecting pool. Its surface was serene and black, and it cast razor-sharp reflections of everything in sight. At its farthest end, a tall, thick-trunked, droop-boughed tree stood on a low, wide island of earth, whose mossy shores reached to within a meter of the low wall that bordered the pool.

The rest of the landing party was gathered in a cluster on the miniature island in the shade of the tree, crouched like ancient primates wary of abandoning their arboreal redoubts.

Fletcher and Hernandez hopped across the narrow channel of water to the tree's island and slipped into the middle of the huddle. Hernandez folded her arms across her bent knees. "What did we learn?"

Before anyone else could speak, Major Foyle asked, "Captain, are we sure it's safe to talk here?"

"Why wouldn't it be, Major?"

He looked at the other MACOs and then replied, "What if we're being monitored?"

Fletcher fielded the question. "If the Caeliar want to listen in, I don't think it matters where we go in this city. Or on this planet, to be honest. With technology like theirs, I don't think we could stop them."

"Then maybe we shouldn't make plans verbally," Foyle said. "Maybe we should do it all in writing and destroy the notes."

Hernandez exhaled sharply. "They know about Earth, they've accessed the *Columbia*'s computers, and they speak English without translation devices. I think they can probably read our writing. So let's just get on with it, shall we?"

"As you wish, Captain," said Foyle. "But I object to this unnecessary risk to our operational security."

"Noted," Hernandez said, hopeful that she'd heard the last of Foyle's paranoia. "You spoke up first, so why don't you make your report first? How's our access to the Caeliar's city?"

"Almost unlimited," Foyle said, and he nodded to Yacavino, his second-in-command, to continue.

"Our men had no trouble coming or going from our residence tower," Yacavino said. "The Caeliar admitted us without search or challenge to a variety of spaces, both indoors and outdoors."

Hernandez nodded. "Good. At least we have mobility."

"Until they decide to take it away," injected Sergeant Pembleton. "All they have to do is turn off our see-through elevators and we'll be stuck in that four-star penitentiary."

"One problem at a time," the captain said. She looked to her first officer. "Veronica, what did you and Dr. Metzger find out about our hosts?"

Fletcher arched her eyebrows and frowned, as if she found her own report hard to believe. "They can change shapes."

Metzger added, "And they can turn into vapor or liquid."

"Change shapes?" Hernandez threw a quizzical look at Metzger and Fletcher. "Can you be more specific about that?"

The *Columbia*'s middle-aged surgeon pushed her short, gray bangs from her forehead and replied, "I saw them get larger and smaller, change from bipeds to quadrupeds—one of them even seemed to think it was funny to mimic the two of us down to the last detail."

The first officer nodded. "It was impressive," she said. "And a bit troubling, to be honest."

"That's an understatement," Hernandez said. "They can impersonate us?"

Fletcher waved her hand. "Not our behavior, just our appearance and voices. They don't seem to have any sense of personalities."

"Thank heaven for small mercies," Foyle quipped. He added, "Though what worries me is their ability to levitate."

Around the huddle, several heads nodded, and Hernandez's was among them. "Do we know how they do it?"

"Yes, sir," Fletcher said. "Catoms."

"I'm sorry, could you repeat that?"

Graylock cut in, "Claytronic atoms—also called programmable matter. They're like nanomachines, but more complex, and a lot more powerful. Bonded together, they operate on a human scale instead of a microscopic one. They can change their density, energy levels, a whole range of properties. Teams in Japan and the United States made a few prototypes about ninety years ago. Proof-of-concept models. It was all very primitive, never made it out of the lab. It was supposed to change telepresence, but it was scrapped after the last world war."

Hernandez asked, "And this is the same thing?"

"*Nein*," Graylock said, stifling a laugh. "What we had was a spark. *This* is a supernova. They can change their mass, their state, anything—all on a whim."

That made the captain think. "What's their power source?"

Graylock shook his head. "They wouldn't say. I'd guess it's an energy field generated at a remote facility."

"Let's make identifying that energy source a priority," Hernandez said. She looked to Foyle. "Did you or your men find any access to the underground regions of the city?"

"No," Foyle said. "On the surface we moved freely. But there's no sign of any way into the guts of this thing. Of course, we've had only a few days to search. It's a big place."

"True." The captain turned to her communications specialist. "Sidra, what's your take on Caeliar culture?"

Valerian pondered the question a moment. "Complicated," she said. "They don't seem to mind answering questions, which helps. A lot of the public spaces I've seen have been dedicated to the arts—mostly music and singing, but also some dance and visual performance art. They used to have narrative arts like theater and literature, but they fell out of favor a long time ago."

Fletcher asked, "How long?"

"Maybe a few thousand years," Valerian said. "They also don't seem to have anything resembling economics, and there's no agricultural production or animal husbandry that I could find."

"What about politics?" asked Hernandez.

The Scottish woman shrugged. "They have a ruling body here in Axion called a Quorum, with members from each of their cities, but they're all picked by lottery. I'm not sure how often they hold lotteries, but no one campaigns for it."

A balmy breeze carried the scent of green things and flowers in bloom, but made no ripples on the reflecting pool. Hernandez wondered if she was the only one who noticed. She turned her attention back to Valerian. "What else? What are their habits? We know they're pacifists; what else do they believe?"

"They hold art and science in the same esteem," Valerian said. "All the ones I talked to are both artists *and* scientists. One who makes mosaics in the plaza is also an astronomer; one who composed a symphony I heard is also a physicist."

Crichlow, a MACO from Liverpool, said, "They're also really polite. And they all seem to know who we are—I mean, these blokes knew me *by name*. Caught me by surprise, it did."

"Me, too," Pembleton said.

"One of them asked me to try sculpting," Graylock added. "Said I should nurture my creativity. But when I asked to learn more about their sciences, he lost interest in my artsy side."

"Our loss, I'm sure," Hernandez said. "Kiona, did you see anything we could use to send a subspace message back to Earth, or even just a signal up to the ship?"

Thayer shook her head. "Nothing. I tried using my hand scanner in case the scattering field didn't extend inside the city itself, but I think the Caeliar drained its power cell. It's been dead since yesterday."

"Everybody check your gear," Hernandez said. "Weapons, hand scanners, all of it. Quickly."

Hernandez inspected her own equipment while the rest of the landing party did likewise. A minute later, everyone looked up and around with the same flustered, dumbfounded expression. Her inquiry was almost rhetorical: "All drained?" Everyone nodded.

Fletcher tucked her hand scanner back into its belt pouch. "Captain," she said, "it's been almost three days since we contacted the ship. If we don't signal them by 1600 today—"

"I know," Hernandez said. "They have orders to break orbit." She gazed in dismay at the gleaming city. "Except they can't, because the Caeliar are holding them here." She sighed. "I guess all we can do is hope el-Rashad follows orders and doesn't try to send down a rescue team." With one hand she started smoothing out a patch of dirt in the middle of the huddle. "So much for fact-finding. Let's start working on—"

"One more thing, Captain," Major Foyle said. "It might interest you to know that the Caeliar never sleep."

That news silenced the group.

The captain blinked once, slowly. "Never?"

"Assuming they told me the truth," Foyle replied. "I figured they were being so helpful that I might as well ask how much sleep they needed and how often. That's when they told me."

"Well, that's *wonderful* news," Hernandez said with soft sarcasm. "For a moment there, I was afraid our escape would be too easy. Thanks for setting me at ease on *that* point."

Foyle dipped his chin, a half nod. "You're quite welcome."

"Now, let's start talking about—"

Private Steinhauer interrupted in a whisper, "Captain." Everyone looked at the MACO, who flicked his eyes to his right, toward the reflecting pool. "Company."

The group turned to face the pool. In its center, Inyx rose from the black water without a ripple of disturbance on its surface or a drop of moisture on his person. He ascended with an eerie floating quality and a perfect economy of motion. Then, once his body was fully in view, he strode across the pool without seeming to make actual contact with it. Hernandez found the spectacle quite surreal.

As he neared the tree's island, he spread his long, gangly arms and gesticulating tendril-fingers in a pantomime of greeting. "Hello again," he said to the landing party. "Are all of you well? Do you require anything?"

Hernandez stepped out of the tree's dappled shadows to meet the Caeliar at the edge of the tiny island. "Aside from our freedom and a way to contact our ship and our home? No."

His inquiry and her rejoinder had already become a ritual. Since the landing party's arrival, Inyx had visited them twice per day, always asking the same bland question and receiving the same pointed answer in return. It didn't seem to bother him.

"I have important news," Inyx said. "The Quorum has agreed to grant you an audience, Captain. It's a most unprecedented turn of events."

Fletcher grumbled behind Hernandez's ear, "Took them long enough. You've been asking to see them for three days."

The captain ignored her XO's grousing and asked Inyx, "When do they want to talk?"

Inyx reached out toward her with one undulating hand.

"Now, Captain."

At the heart of Axion, concealed by a ring of delicately complex interlocked towers and slashed with stray beams of late-afternoon sunlight, stood an intimidating, colossal pyramid of dark crystal and pristine metal: the Quorum hall.

Inyx stood at the leading edge of the transportation disk that was ferrying him and Hernandez toward the pyramid. She didn't know whether he was guiding the disk or merely riding on it as she was. He did seem more confident in its safety than she was;

he was perched on its rim, while she preferred to remain near its center. Like every other conveyance she had used since coming to the alien city, it imparted no sensation of movement—no lurch of acceleration or deceleration—and there was far less air resistance than she would have expected, given the speed at which it traveled.

The disk slowed and drifted at a shallow angle toward a broad opening in the middle of one side of the pyramid. From a distance it had looked to her like a narrow slash in the building's façade, but as she and Inyx were swallowed into the structure's interior, she appreciated how huge it and the pyramid really were.

Somewhere close to what Hernandez guessed was the core of the building, the disk eased into a curved port. As it made contact, Inyx stepped forward. Under his feet, the disk and platform fused into a solid structure with no visible seam.

Hernandez followed her Caeliar guide down a cavernous thoroughfare that cut all the way through the pyramid. In the distance, another narrow, rectangular opening framed a strip of cityscape aglow with daylight. Halfway between her and it, the massive passageway was intersected by another; the two paths formed a cross. Then she became aware of moving faster, as if in a dream, and she realized that she and Inyx were on an inertia-free moving walkway. Within seconds they slowed again and came to a stop at the very center of the intersection.

She looked at Inyx. "Let me guess: Now another disk takes us up to the top of the pyramid."

No sooner had she spoken than the disk started to ascend, through a vertical shaft that hadn't been there a moment before.

Inyx crossed his arms in front of his waist and bowed his head slightly. "I apologize if our civil engineering aesthetic has already grown monotonous for you. If you like, I can task an architect to prepare some surprises for your next visit."

"That won't be necessary," Hernandez said.

They reached the top of the shaft in a blur, slowed just as quickly, and rose the last few meters with languid grace. The sunlight was blinding in the pyramidal Quorum chamber, whose four walls were composed of towering sheets of smoky crystal suspended in delicate frames of white metal.

Four tiers of seating surrounded her, one sloping down from each wall, each suspended more than a dozen meters above the main level, which was open and empty except for her and Inyx. The floor was decorated with a fractal starburst pattern, each grand element echoed in millions of miniature designs. Hernandez strained to see how intricately the pattern had been reduced and surmised that it might well continue to the microscopic level.

A masculine voice resonated in the cathedral-like space. "Welcome, Captain Erika Hernandez." She turned until she saw the speaker, a Caeliar in scarlet raiment, standing in the middle of the lowest row of seats on the eastern tier. He continued, "I am Ordemo Nordal, the *tanwa-seynorral* of the Caeliar."

Hernandez tried to conceal her confusion. "*Tanwa* . . .?"

Inyx whispered to her, "An idiomatic expression. You might translate it as 'first among equals.' Call him Ordemo."

She nodded her understanding and then addressed Ordemo. "Thank you for meeting with me."

Ordemo's reply was cool and businesslike. "Are your accommodations and provisions acceptable?"

"They are," Hernandez said. "But our captivity is not."

"We regret that such measures are necessary," said Ordemo.

Keeping her anger in check was difficult for Hernandez. "Why are they necessary? We pose no threat to you."

"Your arrival on the surface of Erigol left us little alternative, Captain. As Inyx already told you, we greatly value our privacy. Once it became clear that you were aware of our world, we were forced to choose between banishing you to a distant galaxy and making you our guests. The latter option seemed the more merciful of the two."

Hernandez rolled her eyes and let slip a derisive huff. "Don't take it personally, but we don't see it that way."

"That's not surprising," Ordemo said.

Reining in her temper, Hernandez said, "If it's isolation you want, we can arrange that. I could have your system quarantined. None of our people would ever return."

"Not officially," Ordemo said. "However, in our experience with other species and civilizations, we have often found that telling people not to come here inevitably attracts visitation by those who disregard authority—hardly the sort of guests we'd want to encourage. I'm certain you can understand that."

"Yes, of course," Hernandez said. "But if it's anonymity you want, we could wipe our records of your world from our computers—"

Inyx interrupted, "Forgive me, Captain, but we have already done that. And we have rendered them blind to any new data about our world and star system." When she glowered at the lanky alien, he added, "It seemed a sensible precaution."

"Do not be angry with Inyx," Ordemo said. "The decision to tamper with your ship's computers was made by consensus. He only carried out the will of the Quorum."

Diplomacy had never been Hernandez's strong suit, and the Caeliar were making this overture more difficult for her than she had expected. Through gritted teeth she said, "All right." After a deep breath, she continued, "So, if my ship's databanks are clean, and I swear my crew to secrecy, there's no reason you can't let us go on our way."

The *tanwa-seynorral* seemed unconvinced. "Except that when you reached your people, they would expect an explanation for your absence. And you and your crew would still know the truth, Captain. Coaxed by threat or temptation, one of you would talk."

"Then erase our memories!" She knew she was getting desperate, but she had to press on. "We can't reveal what we don't know. With all this crazy technology of yours, I bet you've got something that could whitewash our minds, make us forget we ever saw you. You could erase everything since the ambush of our ship, send us back, make us think we blacked out—"

"And that twelve of your years passed in the interval?" Now the first-among-equals sounded as if he was mocking her. "How would you and your crew react to *that,* Captain? Would you accept a circumstance so bizarre without seeking an explanation? And if you did, who's to say that once taken back to that moment, you wouldn't make the same choice you did before, and set course once again to our world?"

Hernandez felt tired—of arguing, of plotting, of all the little battles that had marked every hour of her command since the ambush. Softening her approach, she said, "You make good points, Ordemo. I really can't refute them, so I won't try. But I just don't understand your motives. You cite this need for privacy as the reason my crew and I are being held prisoner. Why are you so afraid of contact with other races?"

"Our impetus is not fear, Captain," Ordemo said. "It is pragmatism." He looked at Inyx, and Hernandez did likewise.

Inyx turned to her and explained, "When less-advanced species become aware of us and what we can do, they tend to respond with either intense curiosity or savage aggression—and sometimes both. In the past, alien civilizations have inundated us with pleas for succor, expecting us to deliver them from the consequences of their own shortsightedness. Others have tried to steal the secrets of our technologies or force them from us. Because we will not take sentient life, even in self-defense, it became increasingly difficult to discourage these abuses. Some sixty-five thousand of your years ago, we concluded that isolation and secrecy would best serve our great work, so we relocated our cities and people here, to what was, at that time, a relatively untraveled sector of the galaxy. However, the recent development of starflight by several local cultures and your arrival on Erigol have reminded us that while changes are never permanent, change is."

"Yeah, life is hard," Hernandez said to Inyx. "Cry me a river." While the scientist struggled to parse her sarcastic idiom, she aimed her ire at Ordemo. "So let me get this straight: My ship, my crew, and myself are doomed to spend the rest of our days here because you don't like getting hassled?"

The angrier she became, the calmer Ordemo seemed. "It is not quite so simple a matter, Captain. These conflicts tend to escalate, despite our best efforts to contain them. Often, as we take bolder steps to defend ourselves and our sovereignty, several less-developed civilizations will band together out of fear or avarice. When that happens, we often must take . . . extreme measures, up to and including their displacement."

She held up a hand to interrupt him. "Displacement?"

"A shifting, en masse, of an entire civilization and its people, often to another galaxy. To use an analogy from your own world, it's like catching a spider in your home and expelling it to the outdoors rather than killing it." He paused and grew more somber. "It's a tactic we find distasteful and distressing. Having been forced to it in the past, we now choose to conceal ourselves rather than risk provoking another such travesty."

Begging and pleading both had proved ineffective. All that Hernandez could do now was try to lay groundwork for a future opportunity. "If my people and I have to stay here, we'd at least like to get to know more about your culture," she said. "In particular, I'd like to learn more about this thing you keep referring to as 'the great work.'"

Inyx looked up at Ordemo. "With the Quorum's permission?"

"Granted."

"The great work," Inyx said, "is a project that has spanned several millennia and is only now reaching its fruition. Reduced to its core objective, it is our effort to detect, and make contact with, a civilization more advanced than our own."

Hernandez arched her brow at the irony. "Finally . . . something we have in common."

Inyx left the humans' penthouse suite after escorting Captain Erika Hernandez back to her fellow guests. He guided his disk along the outer edge of Axion, to a narrow promontory that extended beyond the city's edge and faced the setting sun.

Sedín, his companion of many aeons, waited for him at the end of the walkway. They met frequently at this place to watch the sky's ephemeral changes. Often they eschewed conversation, having long since run out of anything new to say. Silent presence now passed for friendship between them.

The disk under Inyx's feet melded back into the memory metal of the city, and he stepped onto the walkway and willed it into motion beneath him. It whisked him with speed and precision to within an arm's reach of Sedín, and then it halted. With an ease born of many thousands of years of practice, he strode off the walkway and took his place at Sedín's side.

Beyond the mountains, the ruddy orb of the heavens made its descent, its colors bleeding into the darkness above it.

"You brought the human ship commander to the Quorum," Sedín said, her enunciation neutral but still intimating disapproval.

"She asked to see them," Inyx replied. "They consented."

The sky grew darker and swallowed the jagged silhouette of distant mountaintops. Stars peppered the sky before Sedín spoke again, her affectless manner betraying her disdain.

"They could have been displaced."

Inyx countered that statement of fact with another. "That was not the Quorum's decree."

"I audited the debate through the gestalt," Sedín said. "You shaped that decree. If not for you, they would have been displaced, like all the others. You advocated custody."

"Displacement was not warranted," Inyx argued. "They had no means of communication—"

"I've already heard your justifications," Sedín said. "And I know they swayed the Quorum. The matter is decided."

Darkness swallowed the last glimmers of twilight, and overhead the cold majesty of the galaxy stretched across the dome of the sky. Soon it would be time for Inyx to return to his research for the night, before paying another visit to the humans at daybreak. Tired of the hostility in his discourse with Sedín, he turned to leave.

He paused as she asked, "Why did you bring them here?"

"They came of their own accord," Inyx said, turning back.

"But you secured them permission to make orbit and come to the surface. *You* welcomed them to Erigol. Our *home*."

In time, Inyx knew, it might be possible to persuade Sedín to let go of her anxiety toward the unknown. That time, however, would not be this night. For now, he could only tell his comrade the truth and hope that it would suffice to postpone the rest of their discussion until the next sunset.

"I argued my conscience," Inyx said. "Nothing more."

Sedín was not appeased. If anything, she sounded more suspicious. "Your conscience? Or your curiosity?"

A new transportation disk appeared beside the end of the platform. Inyx stepped onto it and faced toward the city. He chose to ignore his friend's question—not out of guilt or anger, but because he did not, in fact, know the answer.

He willed the disk forward. "Good night, Sedín."

In the shade of the tree by the pool, violent ideas were taking root.

Most of the landing party was still asleep back at the penthouse suite. The MACOs, however, had risen at dawn, stolen away in silence, and gathered here. They circled around Major

Foyle, who used a green twig snapped from a low branch to draw designs in the rich, black earth of the tree's island.

"Our biggest challenge right now is the scattering field around the city," Foyle said, etching a circle in the dirt. "We can't transport through it, and we can't get signals out."

Lieutenant Yacavino tumbled three small stones in his hand while he stared at the circle Foyle had drawn. "Depending on our objective, we need to either get outside the field or collapse it. It's fifteen klicks to get clear, and we don't even know how to get back to the planet's surface from up here, so I'd suggest we focus on knocking out the field."

"That's a good plan," said Sergeant Pembleton. "Except for the fact that we don't have any power left in our gear."

Foyle waved away the complaint with his twig. "There are ways to fix that," he said. "Worst-case scenario, we can use solar power to recharge the rifles."

"That would take weeks," Crichlow protested.

Pembleton deadpanned, "Are you going somewhere, Private?"

"The city has to have some kind of power-generation," said Yacavino. "Maybe we can find a way to tap into it."

"Talk to Graylock," Foyle said. "But let's remember that we have options. The rifles and hand scanners might be out cold, but we still have chemical grenades, flares, and our hands."

Private Steinhauer said, "I don't want to sound negative, Major, but CQC with the Caeliar sounds like a bad idea."

"He's right," Pembleton said. "Going hand-to-hand with a shape-changer that can levitate is a good way to get killed."

"Except that the Caeliar are pacifists, Sergeant," said Private Mazzetti. "They won't kill."

"Not on purpose," Foyle said, feeling the urge to clarify the situation for the younger men. "But accidents happen. Just because they aren't trying to kill us doesn't mean they have to save us when we make mistakes." The three enlisted men nodded.

Yacavino massaged his stubbled chin with his thumb and forefinger. "We need an objective." The Italian-born MACO looked at Foyle. "I assume we're trying to get back to the ship?"

"Yes," Foyle said. "And from there, out of orbit."

"And home," Pembleton added.

"Then we have to take down the scattering field," Yacavino said. "That's job one. Then we need to neutralize the Caeliar's ability to hurt the *Columbia*. Once that's done, we contact the ship, beam up, and get the hell out of here."

Foyle nodded. "It sounds like there's a good chance we could achieve the first two goals by causing a major disruption of the city's power supply. Do it right, and we might gain a useful distraction while we're at it."

"A useful distraction?" parroted Yacavino. "An explosion?"

"Correct," said Foyle. "Is there a problem?"

The second-in-command looked troubled. "We don't know what kind of damage we might do with demolitions. We might be talking about a lot of collateral damage." His jaw clenched and he swallowed. "I don't think the captain will go for that, sir."

"No," Foyle said. "I don't imagine she will. Which is why we're treating that part of the plan as need-to-know information until further notice—and the captain doesn't need to know."

That seemed to mollify the privates, but Yacavino looked away to hide his agitation, and Pembleton had a cautious air about him as he asked, "What if she finds out anyway?"

"Funny thing about collateral damage," Foyle replied. "It can happen to anyone. Even captains."

# 2381

## 14

His cup of Earl Grey was long since cold, and Jean-Luc Picard stared at the padd in his hand and found no answers, only the gnawing emptiness of unanswered questions.

Why had the Borg changed their tactics against the Federation? What was the reason for their mad frenzy of murder, the wholesale slaughter of worlds?

Picard had thought he knew the Borg, understood them even as he'd loathed them. He'd been perplexed by their desperate pursuit of the mysterious and elusive Omega Molecule as an emblem of "perfection," but at least their obsession with it had been consistent with their cultural imperative toward the assimilation of technology and biological diversity. Genocide, on the other hand . . . It *didn't fit*.

The pragmatist in him didn't want to look beyond the surface. From a practical standpoint, all that mattered now was fighting the Borg, halting their advance, and ending the war.

But the part of him that was still an explorer needed to know *why*. Something had changed, and he needed to understand.

He paced in front of his desk, padd in hand, trying to reassemble the pieces of the puzzle into something that made sense. The timing, the targets—he saw no patterns in them.

His door chime sounded, and he was grateful for the interruption. "Come."

The portal hushed open, and Worf entered, followed by La Forge. "Captain," Worf said, "we have something." He nodded to the chief engineer, who continued the report.

"Sensor analysis of the Borg cube we just destroyed picked up something odd," La Forge said. "Traces of sirillium."

Picard lifted an eyebrow. "Sirillium? Out here?"

"That's what I said." La Forge stepped beside a wall companel and activated it. He accessed the ship's computer with touch commands as he continued. "I figured there were two likely explanations. One, the Borg might've started using it in their ships or weapons."

That struck a chord in Picard's memory. "The Tellarites used to arm torpedo warheads with sirillium, back in the twenty-second century."

"Right," La Forge said. "So did the Andorians. But that'd be a fairly primitive solution for the Borg, so I took a closer look at the samples we detected." He called up a series of images on the companel screen. "All the traces we found were on external hull fragments from the Borg ship, or floating free with other atomized matter. We recovered debris from their weapons system, and it had no traces of sirillium. Neither did interior bulkhead plates, or sections of their life-support system. And that led me to my second possible explanation: They picked it up in transit."

With a flick of his finger, La Forge changed the display to a starmap of the surrounding sectors. "There are only two sites near Federation space with high enough concentrations of sirillium gas to leave deposits that rich on a Borg cube. One is the Rolor Nebula, on the Cardassian border, past the Badlands."

A glance at the starmap revealed the Rolor Nebula to be, quite literally, on the far side of the Federation from the *Enterprise* and the recent spate of Borg attacks. Picard asked, "And the other?"

La Forge enlarged a grid of the map—the sector adjacent to the *Enterprise*'s position. "The Azure Nebula, precisely twenty-point-one-three light-years from here. I ran an icospectrogram on the Borg cube's most likely route from there to here, and I found sirillium traces at regular intervals."

Picard looked to Worf. "ETA to the nebula at maximum warp?"

"Twenty-two hours," Worf said. "Course plotted and laid in, ready on your command."

Picard gave his XO a curt nod. "Make it so." To both Worf and La Forge he added, "Excellent work, gentlemen."

"Thank you, Captain," La Forge said. "I'm heading back to engineering—see if I can push a few more points over the line and get us there in twenty-*one* hours." He nodded to Worf and the captain, and then he made his exit from the ready room. Worf, however, remained behind.

"Something else, Worf?"

The XO frowned. "If Commander La Forge is correct, we can

expect to face significant resistance when we reach the nebula." He looked Picard in the eye. "Permission to speak freely, sir?"

"Granted."

In a quiet but still forceful baritone, Worf said, "You need to rest, sir."

Picard turned to walk back to his desk. "Your concern is appreciated, Commander, but I—"

"Captain," Worf said, blocking Picard's path. "You have been on duty for more than twenty hours. I suspect you have been awake for at least twenty-two."

The captain stiffened in the face of his first officer's confrontational behavior. Even though Worf generally respected human customs and courtesies, moments like this served to remind Picard that having a Klingon for an XO would take some getting used to. Taking care not to blink or demur, he looked into Worf's eyes and replied gravely, "Do you mind, Mister Worf?"

Worf made a low growl of protest and stepped aside. As Picard walked by him, the brawny first officer grumbled, "You know I am right. Sir."

Picard stood behind his desk and rested his hands on the back of his chair. "What I *know,* Mister Worf, is that you've been awake even longer than I have."

Worf grunted. "True. It would be best if you and I were *both* well rested before taking the ship into battle."

The dead weight of his own feet and the dull aching in his muscles persuaded Picard to admit that his first officer was right. "I trust you've assigned new watch commanders for the next two shifts?"

"Yes, sir," Worf said. "Commander Lynley is on the bridge now, and Lieutenant Commander Havers will relieve him at 0800."

Picard sighed. He found Worf's new ability to anticipate his decisions both reassuring and irritating. "Very good. I'll be in my quarters—and I'll see you back on the bridge at 1600."

"Aye, Captain." He walked toward the door and paused before stepping in range of its motion sensor, so that he could turn back and add, with his unique brand of irony, "Sweet dreams."

Picard's valediction was a good-natured warning: "Good night, Number One." Worf answered with a wry smirk and left the ready room. Picard sighed and returned to his desk. He picked up his half-consumed cup of tea, carried it back to the replicator, and keyed the matter reclamator. The cup and its cold contents vanished in an amber swirl of dissociated particles.

Around him, the *Enterprise* resonated with the swiftly rising hum of the warp engines rapidly pushing the ship to its maximum rated velocity, and perhaps even a fraction beyond. The stretch of starlight outside the ready room window, normally a soothing backdrop, now raced by in frantic pulses. Even the stars knew that the *Enterprise* was headed into danger.

Picard had promised Worf he would rest, but he doubted he would sleep tonight, with the Collective looming on the horizon.

The voice from the overhead comm roused Miranda Kadohata from her troubled, fitful slumber a few minutes shy of 0500.

*"Bridge to Commander Kadohata,"* said Lieutenant Milner, the gamma-shift operations manager.

Kadohata's eyes snapped open. Her heart was palpitating furiously, and the muscles in her chest and arms twitched with nervous energy. Rescued from one of a night-long series of anxiety dreams, she was grateful to be woken. "Kadohata here."

*"You asked for notice when we had a comm window,"* Milner replied. *"I have one coming up in twenty seconds. It'll be short— a couple minutes, tops. You still want it?"*

She was already out of bed and scrambling into her robe. "Yes, Sean. Patch me through as soon as the channel's up."

*"Will do. Stand by."*

Leaning left, she caught her reflection in the mirror beside her bedroom desk and finger-combed her straight, sable hair into a smooth ponytail and twisted it into a knot on the back of her head. Her eyes were a bit red, and the circles under them were too dark to hide. *It doesn't matter,* she told herself. *There's no time. It'll be fine.*

She had left standing orders with the junior operations managers to let her know whenever there was an opportunity for her to get a real-time signal out to her family on Cestus III. When she'd first come aboard the *Enterprise*, she'd made a point of speaking to her husband and children via subspace every day. Their infant twins, Colin and Sylvana, couldn't understand her words, of course, but she wanted them to hear her voice as much as possible while she was away. She had recorded herself reading them bedtime stories while she had been pregnant, and Vicenzo, her husband, made a point of including those recordings in the twins' nightly routine.

Aoki, their first born, was another matter. It was chiefly for the five-year-old's benefit that Kadohata was so diligent about these comms home, however brief they might be. The girl was old enough to miss her mother, to feel the ache of absence, and for Kadohata it was worth any amount of lost sleep and expended favors to keep herself in Aoki's daily life.

Her comm screen snapped to life, the bright blue-and-white Federation emblem almost blinding in the night-cycle shadows of her quarters. Milner's voice filtered down from overhead as a string of numbers and symbols flashed past along the bottom edge of her screen. *"Hang on,"* he said. *"I'm routing the signal through about four different boosters in the Klingon Empire."*

"How'd you swing that?"

*"I know a bloke who knows a bloke who has friends on the High Council."* She understood his meaning: Worf had used some of his old diplomatic connections with the Klingon chancellor's office to secure this extraordinary favor.

She made a mental note to thank Worf the next time she saw him privately. Then the screen in front of her blinked to an image of her husband, Vicenzo Farrenga. She smiled at the sight of his round, jovial face and immaculate coif of dark hair. "What time is it there, love?"

*"We're just sitting down to dinner,"* he said. With a quick tap of a key, he switched the comm's feed to a wider angle that revealed him, Aoki, and the twins around the dining room table. *"How 'bout there?"*

"Middle of the night, as always." She hadn't worried about the differences in local times. As her calls home had become less frequent, Vicenzo had made it clear that he didn't mind being woken at any hour. Ringing in at dinner had been a lucky break, though; it meant she got to see the children.

Sylvana grabbed up fistfuls of strained-something and flung it in globs on the floor. Colin seemed content to smear his dinner on his bib. Aoki waved frantically from the far end of the table. *"Hi, Mummy,"* she said, her bright voice echoing.

"Hello, sweetheart." Kadohata wished she could teleport to her daughter's side and just hold her. "Have you been helping Daddy with the twins?"

Aoki nodded, and Vicenzo replied, *"I couldn't do it without her."* He winked at the girl, then continued, *"She's a natural."*

"I'm happy to hear that, love. What's for dinner tonight?"

Vicenzo pointed out each dish. *"Colin's turning mashed peas into a fashion statement, Sylvie's doing some redecorating with her strained carrots, and Aoki and I are enjoying some vegetable moussaka, fresh corn, and spinach salad."*

"Impressive," Kadohata said, nodding her approval. With a teasing lilt, she asked, "Real or replicated?"

He gave a small shrug. *"Mostly real. I think the dairy products are replicated, but all the vegetables were grown here in Lakeside, and the pasta's made fresh at a market in town."*

"Glad to see my lectures about eating healthy have stuck with you," she said.

Nodding, he replied, *"We're being good, I promise. Looks like you have, too. You look great."*

She shook her head. "I look horrid."

*"No,"* Vicenzo insisted. *"You really don't."*

It was true that she had lost weight in recent weeks, restoring the fine angles of her mixed European-Asian ancestry. What she didn't want to tell him was that most of her weight loss had been stress-induced, as the *Enterprise* had become the Federation's principal instrument of defense against the Borg.

"Thank you, love," she said, lowering her eyes. On the other end of the channel, Vicenzo sensed her fatigue and her fear, and like her he masked it with a sad smile of quiet desperation, for the sake of the children.

Oblivious of the unspoken tension, Aoki asked in a loud and shrill voice, *"When are you coming home, Mummy?"*

*"Inside voice, honey,"* Vicenzo murmured, hushing the girl.

Kadohata shook her head. "Don't know, love. Soon, I hope."

Aoki pressed on, *"Where are you?"*

*"She can't tell us that, sweetie,"* Vicenzo said, circling the table to pluck Aoki from her chair and into his arms. *"It's not safe for her to say things like that over the comm. Bad people might be listening."* Watching him comfort her made Kadohata miss the embrace of her little ones that much more.

The little girl locked her arms around her father's neck and rested her head on his large, rounded shoulder. *"I'm sorry, Mummy,"* she mumbled.

"No need to be sorry, love," Kadohata told her. Forcing a smile, she said to Vicenzo, "Happier thoughts, right? Big day coming up next month."

"*I remember,*" he said. "*Eight years.*"

"What's the gift for that anniversary?"

He chuckled. "*Bronze. Had a devil of a time thinking up a gift for that one.*"

"You've already bought my gift?" He nodded, and she grinned. Vicenzo had never been one to leave things until the last minute. "I should've known." Feigning seriousness, she added, "I suppose you'll expect me to get you something, now."

"*I wouldn't want you to go to any trouble.*"

She almost laughed. "Liar."

A double-beep over the channel heralded an interruption. From the overhead speaker in her quarters, Lieutenant Milner warned, "*Twenty seconds, sir.*"

Kadohata looked away from the image of her family on the screen and said, "Thank you, Sean." Then she looked back. "Time's up, loves. I have to go."

Vicenzo looked as if he'd had his heart cut out. "*Stay safe, Miranda. We miss you.*" Aoki lifted her head from his shoulder and crowed, "*We miss you, Mummy!*"

"I miss you all, too," Kadohata said. "Very much. I'll comm again as soon as I can, but I don't know when that'll be."

"*We'll be waiting. . . . Love you.*"

"Love you, too."

She and Vicenzo reached out and each pressed a fingertip to their comm screen, an illusion of contact transmitted across light-years, for the last few seconds before the signal was lost and the channel cut to black and silence.

A sinking feeling became an emptiness inside of her as she plodded back to her bed and slipped under the covers. It had been barely two hours since she'd watched the Borg lay waste to Korvat. If they weren't stopped, sooner or later they would reach Cestus III. It would only be a matter of time.

Visions of her beautiful children being turned to fire haunted her when she closed her eyes. There was nothing she wouldn't do to prevent that, she was certain of it. She would kill, die, or sacrifice the ship and whoever or whatever was necessary, if doing so saved her children.

But tonight, alone in her quarters, her face buried in the soft clutch of a pillow, all she could do was sob with rage for the lives she had already failed to defend.

From dead asleep to wide awake—Beverly Crusher blinked her eyes open wider and inhaled. There had been no sound, no sudden change in her surroundings. She had been on the edge of slumber's gray frontier, inching her way over the border, when a jolt and a shiver had pulled her back.

Rolling over, she looked for her husband. Jean-Luc's side of the bed was empty, his pillows untouched. He hadn't come to bed yet. It was just after 0500. She had gone to bed at 0315, after the ship had secured from general quarters. *I guess I did doze off,* she realized. *For a little while, at least.*

A small, soft bump of a sound carried into the bedroom, through the doorway that led to the suite's main room. Crusher pushed off the lightweight but pleasantly warmed sheets and blanket and eased herself out of bed, into the relatively chill air. She suspected that Jean-Luc had been at the climate controls again; he preferred a crisp coolness in their living quarters, a temperature a few degrees below where she was comfortable. And so they wrangled. It had been the same way with her first husband, Jack, decades earlier.

The skin on her arms and legs turned to gooseflesh until she shivered into her bathrobe and tied it shut. She was grateful that at least the deck in their living area was carpeted. The plush, synthetic fabric was warm under her feet as she padded to the doorway and peeked into the main room.

Jean-Luc sat on the floor with his back to her. He was still wearing his uniform. On the floor beside him, a tarnished, engraved copper box with a foam-pad interior lay open and empty. In his hands he held his Ressikan flute, a keepsake recovered from an alien probe that years earlier had gifted the captain, in the span of a few minutes, with the memories of another lifetime, the last message of a dying world and people.

In that other life, he'd lived as a man named Kamin, raised a family, and learned to play the flute. Its music, he'd told Crusher, often soothed his nerves and dispelled his sorrows. She knew how much he treasured that instrument. He turned the narrow, bronze-hued flute in his hands and gently straightened a twist in the silken cord of its white tassel.

Taking sudden note of her presence, he looked over his shoulder. "Beverly," he said in a hushed voice. "I'm sorry. I didn't mean to wake you."

"You didn't," she said. "I just woke up. Don't know why."

Jean-Luc nodded once and looked back at the flute. He pulled the tassel cord taut with one hand and placed the instrument back into its custom-cut indentation on the foam pad, taking care to lay the silken thread parallel to the metal body of the flute. Then he closed the lid gently, picked up the box, stood, and carried it to a nearby shelf. He bore it as if it were a holy relic. Setting the box beside some leather-bound volumes of classic works, Jean-Luc was somber, like a man moving with great care because he might be doing everything for the last time. Crusher found the deliberateness of his manner worrying.

"You look exhausted," she said. "Are you coming to bed?"

He sighed. "To what end? I can't let myself sleep. Not with the Collective waiting for my guard to fall."

"I could prescribe a sleep aid that would—"

"No," Jean-Luc said. "No drugs. I have to be ready."

She stepped beside him and put her hands on his shoulder. "How ready will you be if you don't sleep?"

"Worf said the same thing." His eyes became distant, disengaged from the moment. "Neither of you can hear them, not the way I do." He frowned. "I can't sleep. Not now."

Crusher let him shrug off her hands. She didn't take it personally. Instead, she walked toward the replicator. "All right," she said. "If you're not sleeping, neither am I. Computer, lights one-half."

"Beverly," he said in protest as the room brightened.

"Shush." She stopped in front of the replicator. "Two peppermint herbal teas, hot." A singsong whine filled the room; two delicate porcelain cups took shape in a spiral of glowing matter inside the replicator nook. When the sequence ended, Crusher lifted the cups and carried them back to Jean-Luc. She offered him one.

"I'm not thirsty," he said.

"It'll soothe your nerves," she countered, but still he made no move to accept the tea. She set the cup down on an end table beside the sofa. "When was the last time you ate?"

He took a few steps into the middle of the room and gazed out the window at the passing streaks of starlight. "I don't recall," he said. Then he added, "Breakfast, I think."

"Jean-Luc, you have to make time to take care of—"

"Beverly," he said. There was a deadness in his voice. Crusher had heard it before, in combat veterans suffering from shock. "In the past twenty-four hours, I've seen two worlds destroyed. Billions of lives, each one unique and irreplaceable, all extinguished." He turned to face her. "And it's only just started. Something terrible is coming, I can feel it. Watching Korvat burn was like seeing an omen."

She inched closer to him. "An omen? Of what? A disaster?"

His jaw trembled. "An apocalypse."

Closer now, she took his hands, tried to anchor him, keep him from being swept away by the undertow of his fears. "You don't know that," she said. "The worst of it might be over."

"No, Beverly. It's not." His voice fell to a whisper, as if he feared eavesdroppers. "The worst is still out there, waiting to fall, like a hammer in the dark." She watched his eyes glisten with tears as he freed his right hand and placed it softly against her cheek. "We're out of our depth now."

"I can't believe that," she said. "I won't. Starfleet's destroyed six Borg cubes in the last few weeks, and five more today. We can stop them."

"And what have we lost in the bargain?" He lowered his hand from her face, and his tone became harder. "More than a dozen ships of the line. Three major starbases. Four worlds. *Worlds,* Beverly! *Billions* of lives." Pacing away from her, he continued, "I've read Kathryn Janeway's reports from her years in the Delta Quadrant. Her encounters with the Borg. They have *thousands* of ships." He stopped near the replicator and turned back to face Crusher. "They control vast regions of space, have almost unlimited resources at their command. Beverly, the Collective *dwarfs* the Federation. They're gearing up to fight a war of attrition. That's a war we can't win. We just don't have the numbers. Not enough ships, not enough people. Not enough *worlds.*" His voice deadened again. "We can't win."

Crusher crossed the room and stood in front of him. He looked up at her with a vacant, fearful expression.

She slapped his face.

The smack was sharp and loud against the quiet hum of the engines and made contact with enough force to knock Jean-Luc back half a step and leave her palm stinging. She fixed her husband with a feral glare. "Snap out of it, Jean-Luc! The man I married is a *starship captain*. He doesn't declare defeat when he's still fighting the war."

To her surprise, he smiled. Almost laughed. "You don't think I'm the man you married?"

"The Jean-Luc Picard I know would never talk this way."

His smile soured. "'Do I contradict myself? Very well, then, I contradict myself. I am large, I contain multitudes.'"

"Don't quote Whitman at me. You don't even *like* Whitman." She sighed. "Do you want to know what I've always liked about you, right from the very first time we met?"

"Tell me," he said sincerely.

"Your faith that there was more good than bad to be found in the universe. I heard you once tell Jack on the *Stargazer,* 'That's why we do this—it's what makes going to the stars worthwhile.'"

Jean-Luc massaged his reddened cheek. "Perhaps I was wrong," he said. "Those are the beliefs of a young man. A man who hasn't felt the harsh embrace of cruel machines." He collapsed on the sofa. Crusher sat down beside him. "Words will never capture the horror of losing myself that way, Beverly. I can't describe what it's like to be erased. Absorbed. To have everything I am become lost inside a force untouched by love or joy or sorrow. To know that it's *stronger* than I am."

"That's where you're wrong, Jean-Luc," she said. "It's not stronger than you. It's not stronger than us." She grasped his hand and lifted it, moved it onto her belly, above her womb. "We'll survive as long as we have hope," she said, trying to project her shaken optimism onto him, hoping he would reinforce it with some small gesture, however minor. "As long as we don't let them take that from us, we can still fight. And they can't take it if we don't let them." She touched his face as tears rolled from her eyes. "Don't let them."

His free hand closed tenderly around hers. "I won't," he said, but some part of her knew that he was lying. He was clinging to hope for her sake, but she felt it slipping from him, as the Borg drove it from him by degrees.

"Don't let them," she said.

# 15

Federation President Nanietta Bacco led a procession out of her chief of staff's office on the fourteenth floor of the Palais de la Concorde. "Don't tell me there aren't any ships available, Iliop," Bacco snapped at her secretary of transportation. "Your job is *making* ships available."

As soon as she stepped through the door, a phalanx of four civilian security guards fell into step around her. Iliop—a tall Berellian man whose spectacles, mussed hair, and ill-fitting toga made Bacco think of him as a cross between an absentminded professor and a Roman senator—lingered half a step farther behind her as he followed her out of the office. "Madam President, my mandate was to restore the avenues of commerce and normal—"

"We're way past 'normal,' Ili," said Esperanza Piñiero, the president's chief of staff, who was the next person to exit the office. "Here's your new mandate: Get those twenty-nine thousand survivors off Korvat in the next three days." The Berellian opened his mouth to argue, and Piñiero cut him off. "Get it *done,* Ili." He nodded and slipped away down a side corridor as Safranski, the Rigellian secretary of the exterior, and Raisa Shostakova, the secretary of defense, followed Bacco and Piñiero from the office and down a central hallway to the turbolifts.

"Korvat's the least of our worries, Madam President," said Shostakova. "FNS is whipping up a panic with images of the attack on Barolia."

"The Borg are making the panic, Raisa," Bacco said. "The media just report it. Besides, corralling the media is Jorel's problem." To Safranski she said, "Any word on the summit?"

The Rigellian replied, "No."

As ever, his brevity bordered on the passive-aggressive and added frown lines to Bacco's brow. "Why not?"

"No one's taking our calls."

"Not good enough," Bacco said. "Keep trying."

Shostakova shouldered her way past Safranski—not an easy

feat for the squat, solidly built human woman from the high-gravity colony planet known as Pangea. "We've got an antimatter problem," she announced as Bacco turned a sharp corner.

Piñiero replied for Bacco, "What kind of problem?"

"A shortage," Shostakova said. "We need fuel for the Third Fleet and the reserves are tapped out."

The chief of staff pulled a personal comm from her jacket pocket, flipped it open, and pressed it to her ear. "Ashanté," she said, addressing one of her four deputy chiefs of staff. "We need an executive order authorizing Starfleet to commandeer civilian fuel resources, on the double. Work up a draft with Dogayn and have it in the Monet Room in thirty minutes." She slapped the device closed and tucked it back into her pocket in a fast, well-practiced motion.

The group passed through a set of frosted double doors into a comfortably furnished reception area. Its honey-hued wood paneling and warm lighting cast a pleasant glow over the off-white carpet, which was adorned by a pale blue outline of the Federation emblem. Long sofas and a few armchairs surrounded a C-shaped formation of coffee tables.

Standing between them and the bank of turbolifts was a presence as austere as the surroundings were relaxed. Shoulder-length gray hair framed his proud countenance, and the pristine blacks and grays of his Starfleet uniform flattered his tall, heavily muscled frame. He nodded to Bacco, who strode ahead of her security detail, hand outstretched to greet him.

"Admiral," she said, shaking the hand of Leonard James Akaar, the official liaison between Starfleet and the Office of the Federation President. "Any good news to report?"

He pressed his lips together, making his chiseled features appear even more stern. "I am afraid not, Madam President."

She frowned. "Why should you be any different?"

The doors of a large turbolift gasped open a few meters away. A burly Zibalian man from Bacco's security detail stepped inside, made a quick scan with a handheld device, and motioned everyone inside. Bacco entered and moved to the back of the turbolift. Akaar, Piñiero, Shostakova, Safranski, and the other three security men followed close behind. The doors hissed shut. The senior agent on the detail, an ex–Starfleet officer named Steven Wexler, issued the turbolift command with a whisper via his subaural implant. The lift began a swift descent.

Bacco said to Akaar, "Give me the bad news, Admiral."

"We've lost three critical starbases near the tri-border," Akaar said in his rich rumble of a voice, referring to the region of space where the territories of the Federation, the Romulan Star Empire, and the Klingon Empire collided. "In the past hour, Epsilon Outposts 10 and 11 have gone dark. We're proceeding on the assumption that they've been destroyed."

"What about Khitomer?" asked Shostakova. "What went right at Khitomer?"

Akaar directed his reply to the diminutive defense secretary. "The *Starship Ranger* used phase-inversion technology to penetrate the Borg's shields and sacrificed itself as a single, massive warhead to vaporize the cube."

Shostakova recoiled, shut her eyes, and inhaled sharply, almost as if by reflex. Safranski, unfazed by the report, replied curtly, "Can we do it again?"

"Too late," Akaar said. "Captain Calhoun tried to sacrifice the *Excalibur* using the same strategy, but the Borg had already adapted. His chief engineer rigged a salvo of torpedoes with phase-inverters, each set to a different variance. Enough made it through to destroy the cube, but it's safe to assume the Borg will be ready for that tactic next time."

The doors sighed open, revealing a windowless corridor with soft, indirect lighting. Agent Wexler was the first person out of the turbolift, followed by another agent, an Andorian *thaan*. They sidestepped clear of the others who were exiting the lift, and remained just ahead of Bacco on her left and right as she led the rest of the group toward the Monet Room.

Bacco said to the admiral, "What's Starfleet doing before there is a next time?"

"The *Enterprise* is following a lead that may reveal how the Borg are reaching our space," Akaar said. "We've deployed every available ship to reinforce the *Enterprise*, but it will take a couple of days before they arrive. Until then, she'll be on her own, out by the Azure Nebula."

From behind Bacco and Akaar, Safranski inquired, "That's near the tri-border, isn't it?"

"It *is* the tri-border," Akaar replied.

Anticipating the president's next order, Safranski said, "I'll have K'mtok and Kalavak summoned to the Palais." Bacco nodded her approval; she expected that she would soon have an urgent need to talk to the Klingon and Romulan ambassadors.

She turned left at an intersection and neared the door to the Monet Room. "Admiral," Shostakova said, "we need an update from Starfleet on its evacuation plan for the core systems in the event of a full-scale Borg invasion."

"We don't have one," Akaar said, and his matter-of-fact tone made Bacco bristle. "If the Borg get past us at Regulus, there will be nothing between them and the core systems. In essence, Madam President, if the Federation had what was once called, in Earth history, a 'doomsday clock,' its hands would now be set at one minute to midnight."

A grim pall settled over the group, which became very quiet as they strode the final few paces to the Monet Room. Agent Wexler stopped just shy of reaching its door, letting President Bacco move past him.

Bacco resolved not to surrender to the paralysis of despair. "All right, Admiral," she said. "If we can't evacuate the core systems, we damned well better find a way to defend them. Which is why I've brought you all down here to meet my new deputy security adviser." She stepped to the door, which slid aside with a soft swish, and she led the group into the Palais's unofficial war room.

On one wall hung an impressionist painting from Earth's preunification period, *Bridge over a Pool of Water Lilies,* by Claude Monet. Panoramic viewscreens dominated the other walls. Most of the middle of the dimly lit room was taken up by the long, dark wood conference table, which comfortably seated up to twenty people. The group filed in and spread out to Bacco's left and right on one side of the table.

Standing on the other side were two people. The middle-aged Trill man was her senior security adviser, Jas Abrik. An irascible former Starfleet admiral, he actually had managed the presidential campaign of Bacco's opponent, Fel Pagro, during the special election the previous year. In exchange for his silence on a potentially explosive matter of national security that had emerged during the election, she had appointed him to this key position in her cabinet. He had treated it like a coup.

He didn't seem quite so enthused about his new deputy.

Bacco introduced the statuesque, fair-haired human woman, who had jarring patches of silver machinery grafted to her left hand and temple. "Everyone," said the president, "this is Seven of Nine. She's here to help us stop the Borg."

Struggling bodies and flaring tempers added to the musky heat of the Klingon High Council Chamber. Shouts of "Federation lackey!" were met with angry retorts of "Traitorous *petaQ!*"

Instead of calving into partisan ranks on either side of the dim, sultry meeting space, as the councillors normally did, they were a shoving, bustling mass in the brightly lit center of the room, atop the enormous red-and-white trefoil emblem that adorned the polished, black granite floor.

Elevated above the mob, on a dais at the end of the chamber, Chancellor Martok struck the metal-jacketed end of his ceremonial staff on the stone steps before him. Explosive cracks of noise resounded off the angled walls and high ceiling, to no avail. With his one eye he glared at the disgraceful thrashing and longed for days of honor that had long passed into history.

Martok stepped forward and hammered the end of his staff down on one of the marble tiles, harder than before. This time the percussive banging was loud enough to halt the melee and shatter one of the square tiles into dusty, broken chunks. The councillors all set their feral gazes on him.

"This is war!" he boomed. Then his voice turned to gravel. "The hour for debate is over. You stand for the Great Houses of the Empire. It's time you showed our enemies what *greatness* is!"

The chancellor descended the stairs and prowled forward through the muddled ranks, which parted, disturbing the humid air and creating a current that was rich with the odors of sweat and *warnog*-tainted breath, and the traditional scents of *targ*-tallow candles and braziers of sulfur and coal. "Some of you"— he aimed a lacerating stare at Kopek, his longtime bitter political rival—"say this is not our war. That it's an internal matter for the Federation. *Use our strength for conquest,* you say, *and let the Federation defend itself.*" He spat on the floor and scowled at Qolka and Tovoj, who in recent months had become vocal backers of Kopek's verbal sabotages. "I never want to hear that excuse again." He continued stalking through the knot of councillors, making eye contact with each one as he passed—with Mortran and Grevaq, Krozek and Merik. "Don't pretend you haven't heard the news from Khitomer," Martok growled. "The Borg came gunning for *us*. It was no *accident*. No *coincidence*."

On his way back to the dais steps, he passed Kryan, the youngest member of the Council. Behind him, and closest to the dais, were Martok's three staunchest allies in the chamber: K'mpar, Hegron, and Korvog. He nodded to them, ascended the steps, and turned to face the assembled councillors en masse.

"When the Borg came to destroy one of our worlds, our allies *bled* for us. They died *defending* us. Three Federation starships sacrificed themselves for Khitomer, a colony world of less than half a million Klingons. Do you remember the last time that happened? I do." He let the implication sink in before he pointed at his nemesis, Kopek. "And so do you." Over his opponents' shamed silence, Martok said simply, "Narendra III."

Grunts of acknowledgment came back to Martok in reply.

He pressed on, "Blood shed for a friend is sacred, a debt of honor. And if you won't stand and fight beside a friend in blood, then you are not a Klingon. You are not a warrior. Run home to your beds and hide, I have no use for you! I won't die in the company of such *petaQ'pu*. The sons of our sons will sing of these battles. Time will erase our sins and fade our scars, but our names will live on in songs of honor.

"The Borg are coming, my brothers. Stand and fight beside me now, and let us make warriors born in ages to come curse *Fek'lhr* that they were not here to *share our glory!*"

His partisans in the chamber roared the loudest, but even Kopek's allies joined the chanting war cries, their bloodlust inflamed with rhetoric. Martok would never admit it aloud, but he suspected that a full-scale conflict with the Borg might be enough to push the Empire past its breaking point. It did not matter; better to die in the struggle than to surrender. As long as he and his people perished with honor and not as *jeghpu'wI'*, he would not consider it a defeat.

Unity in the Council would be critical to the war effort, Martok knew. He saw Kopek step forward, away from the others. Martok took one step down to meet him, maintaining his one-up power position for its symbolic and psychological advantages. Making eye contact with his adversary, he said, "Choose, Kopek."

He saw that the choice was galling for Kopek, and that pleased him. Despite years of political maneuvering, Martok had never been able to halt Kopek's dirty tricks. It had taken a Borg invasion to outflank the ruthless *yIntagh*. Where scheming and coercion had failed, circumstance had prevailed.

With a clenched jaw and bitter grimace, Kopek extended his open right hand to Martok, who took it. "*Qapla'*, Chancellor." A feral gleam shone in his eyes as he released Martok's hand, turned, and declared with a raised fist, "To war!"

The councillors roared their approval, and Martok flashed a broad, jagged grin. "It is a good day to die . . . for the Borg."

Lieutenant Commander Tom Paris sat alone in his quarters aboard the *U.S.S. Voyager* and picked lethargically at his dinner. He had ordered a platter of deep-fried clams with a side salad of spinach and sliced tomatoes. The clams were rubbery and tough, but he knew that was because he had let them sit too long and get cold. *Can't blame the replicator for that.*

More troubling to his palate was that the clams seemed to have no flavor. They were just a texture without a taste. He felt the same way about the salad. The leaves were the perfect color and crispness, but they were an empty crunch. The grape tomatoes felt right as his teeth cut through them, but they delivered none of the sweetness that he'd expected.

*Can't blame that on the replicator, either.*

He didn't figure there was anything wrong with the food itself. The problem was him. Nothing had been right since B'Elanna had left and taken Miral with her.

Food no longer tasted good. Synthehol had no effect. Sleep brought no rest, only dreams of loss and regret.

It had been several months since he'd last seen his wife and daughter. He had wondered if B'Elanna would return for Kathryn Janeway's memorial service. Captain Chakotay had been there, of course, along with Seven, and just about everyone else who had served with Janeway on *Voyager*—with the exception, of course, of Tuvok, who by that point was already hurtling away into sectors unknown as the new second officer of the *U.S.S. Titan* under Captain Riker.

During the outdoor services, Paris had stood with his friend and shipmate Harry Kim. Tom's father, Owen Paris, though he'd come to the memorial, had remained distant and avoided him.

Despite the cool, breezy weather that had graced the event, the skies over San Francisco had been unusually clear that day, and the sunlight had beaten down on their dress-white uniforms with great ferocity.

The crowd had been packed with familiar faces, including people Paris hadn't seen since graduating from the Academy. He'd even stolen a glimpse of captains Picard and Calhoun, standing together in front of the gleaming pillar that had been erected in Janeway's honor.

But there had been no sign of B'Elanna.

He'd understood her reasons for leaving. The fact that their child had been hailed as the messiah—aka the *Kuvah'magh*—by an obscure Klingon religious cult was a better reason for separating than most couples could claim. But it didn't make her absence or her silence any easier to bear.

If the separation had plunged Paris into new depths of melancholy, it had rocketed his father to new heights of recrimination and wrath. The admiral had excoriated his son without mercy when Paris had first broken the news, and only the strict decorum of Janeway's military funeral had likely prevented Owen from an encore performance at their last meeting.

They hadn't spoken since. Paris had received a few messages from his mother, each carefully crafted to make no mention of his father, except one noting his transfer to take command of Starbase 234. A few times, he had considered writing to the old man, but he'd never been able to find anything to say. The situation with B'Elanna was what it was, and nothing he could tell his father was going to change it.

So he sat alone in a compartment of gray bulkheads, darker-gray carpeting, and institutionally drab taupe furniture replete with rounded corners for his safety. His food tasted like cardboard, and going to sleep meant waking up to find each day a little bit darker than the one before.

*And I'm supposed to be in charge of morale on this ship,* he thought with grim amusement. *How's that for irony?*

He stood, picked up his plate, and carried it back to the replicator to dispose of it. As he placed it back in the nook from which it had come, a soft double tone from the overhead comm preceded the voice of Ensign Lasren, the ops officer.

*"Bridge to Paris."*

"Go ahead," Paris said, activating the matter-reclamation sequence. The plate dissolved and vanished in a whorl.

*"You've received a priority signal from your—"* Lasren changed course in midsentence. *"—from Admiral Paris, sir."*

Paris wondered what would be important enough to make his father break his silence after all these months. He assumed the worst. "Patch it through." He crossed the room quickly to his desk and activated the comm screen.

A prerecorded image snapped to life in crisp colors and sharp shadows. His father sat at a desk in an office; Paris presumed it was his father's office at Starbase 234. An unsteady percussion of explosions was like a subliminal track underneath Owen's halting words.

*"Tom,"* he began. He paused and looked around in confusion before he continued. *"I had meant to do this the right way, son. Not like this. But we don't always get to choose, do we?"*

Objects trembled on the shelves in the background of the shot as Owen continued. *"I said terrible things when you told me about B'Elanna, Tom. Stupid things. It wasn't my place."* Lights stuttered for a few seconds, distracting the admiral. *"I was so upset about my granddaughter being taken from me that I forgot it was your* daughter *being taken from you. It's just that—dammit—we were all so happy not so long ago. How'd it go so wrong?"*

The question, though probably rhetorical, stung Paris. It was something he'd asked himself daily since B'Elanna and Miral had left him behind on Earth, a family man with no family.

*"Can you forgive a dumb old man for words spoken in anger? Can you believe me when I tell you that it kills me to know how much you must miss your wife and little girl?"* In the space of a breath, Owen was on the verge of tears. *"I don't know how I'd live if I lost your mother. I don't think I'd want to."*

Owen rubbed his eyes and forced himself back into a state of composure. *"I was wrong to blame you for what happened. It's your marriage, not mine, and I shouldn't have said anything, except that I'm sorry . . . and that I still love you, no matter what. But most of all, just that I'm sorry."* He flashed a bittersweet smile at the screen. *"For everything."*

His composure began to slip again as louder, closer explosions rocked the image. *"No matter what happens, Tommy, you'll always be my boy. Take care of yourself."* A dark expression descended on him. He reached forward, said, *"Good-bye, son,"* and terminated the recording.

The screen cut to black, and Tom Paris had the icy feeling of gazing into the depths of a grave. Unable to contain his alarm, he called out, "Paris to bridge!"

Harry Kim replied immediately, *"Bridge. Go ahead."*

"Harry, get me a channel to Starbase 234, *now*!"

The delay before Kim's response was long enough for Paris to anticipate what his old friend would say, and dread swelled in his heart even as he prayed that he was wrong. But he wasn't, and he was already sinking into shock, tears streaming down his face as Kim broke the news, his voice freighted with remorse.

*"Tom . . . Starbase 234 is gone."*

# 16

The desert swelled around Lieutenant Lonnoc Kedair and seemed poised to reclaim the husk of the *Columbia* in its shifting embrace. She stood near the top of the downed ship's saucer section, watching the evacuation grind forward by degrees.

She tapped her combadge. "Kedair to Hockney. How much longer till you're ready to beam up?"

Through the beige veil of the growing sandstorm, she looked aft and saw the harried engineer turn and look her way as he answered over the comm, *"A few more minutes."* The wind howled and whistled, and he had to shout to be heard over the wail. *"We're rounding up the last of the small stuff."*

"Quickly, Ensign," Kedair said. "We're scheduled to break orbit in an hour. It'd be a shame to have to leave you here."

Hockney replied, *"Just a few minutes, I promise."*

"Notify me the moment you're ready. Kedair out."

Below, the engineer turned away and resumed work, helping researchers and their enlisted assistants carry equipment out of the *Columbia* through an aft hatch on one of the lower decks. The crates were gathered in a neat, stacked cluster several meters from the ship, between its broken and off-kilter warp nacelles. Through it all, the wind whipped sand at Kedair's face.

Raging winds, shifting sands . . . the desert was ever-changing, but the desert never changed, as if it were a cousin of the sea.

Kedair had remained on the surface during the overnight shift and through the dawn. The deep watches of the night had settled, starry and frigid, on the broken bones of the *Columbia* until it coaxed out the away team's breaths in huffs of thin mist. The gray majesty of predawn twilight had been short-lived, blasted away by the swift ascent of one sun and then another.

Another blistering afternoon had seemed to be in store until minutes earlier, when the leading edge of a kilometers-wide sandstorm hove into view, turning the sky the color of burnt umber. It was hurling the desert at Kedair and the away team, and the force of it felt like millions of flying insects slamming against her uniform from every direction. She felt the sand working its way into everything—her boots, her uniform, her hair, her ears, her mouth, her nostrils—and it was still better than spending even another minute inside the *Columbia.*

She preferred the blinding stings of the storm to the rank odor of decaying flesh and blood, the grotesque perfume of scorched tissue, and the sharp stink of burned hair. After spending the night belowdecks with the forensic investigators, Kedair was relieved to be free of the bowels of the *Columbia,* and she had no intention of going back inside, not even if this damned storm buried her alive.

The section of D Deck where Chief Komer and Crewman Yott were killed had been sealed less than an hour earlier. The investigators had collected so many samples and scrapings that they'd nearly scoured the deck plates clean. All that evidence was now secured aboard the *Aventine,* where it was being subjected to an endless, ad nauseam battery of tests—none of which had so far yielded a single clue to the identity or even the nature of the killer.

Kedair blamed herself. As far as she was concerned, her shipmates were all under her protection, and it was her job to prevent tragedies like this. And she'd failed.

*If only they weren't all so fragile,* she lamented. Of all the moments of culture shock she had endured when she made the decision, upon reaching adulthood sixteen years earlier, to emigrate to the Federation and apply to Starfleet Academy, none compared with her discovery that most of her classmates—indeed, most of the species she would meet from then on—were absurdly delicate organisms when compared to Takarans. Specialized internal organs, limited disease and toxin resistance, no cellular stasis abilities—their myriad shortcomings astounded her. She had assumed that all species were like hers, with distributed internal anatomy, resilient hides, and tissue-regeneration genes. Instead, she had found herself living in a galaxy of hopelessly vulnerable people. Even relatively sturdy species, such as the Klingons, the Vulcans, and the Andorians, could be slain easily enough if only one knew where to strike.

Defending them, she'd realized during her first year at the Academy, was her charge to keep, her purpose for being. The deaths of Komer and Yott had been a painful reminder of that duty. In the hours since the attack, she had tripled the security presence in and around the *Columbia*. Armed guards had shepherded every research team, open channels had been maintained, and everyone had been made to stick together.

The last warm bodies on the planet's surface now were herself, the two rifle-toting guards down below, and the four engineers and two scientists they were protecting.

*"Hockney to Kedair."* The engineer's voice, filtered through her combadge, was all but lost in the roar of the wind and the white noise of sand scouring the hull of the *Columbia*.

She shielded her eyes and squinted aft through a crack in her fingers. If Hockney was still down there, she couldn't see him. "Go ahead," she said.

*"Stand by to beam up in sixty seconds,"* Hockney shouted over the storm. *"Cupelli and ch'Narrath are upgrading the cargo transporters to quantum resolution to preserve our biosamples. As soon as they're done, we're outta here."*

Lifting her own voice, she replied, "Thank you, Ensign. Kedair out."

She hated to leave while the deaths of her shipmates remained unsolved. Abandoning the ship, letting it be swallowed up by the sands, felt to Kedair like a dereliction of duty. If the answer was still in there, it might be lost by the time the wind next deigned to liberate the *Columbia* from its shallow desert grave. But orders were orders. It was time to go.

Another voice squawked, weak and hollow, from her combadge. *"Aventine to away team: Stand by for transport."*

Her muscles tensed and she closed her eyes while she waited for the hazy white embrace of the transporter beam. Buffeted by the dry, hot gale and stinging granules, she held her breath and focused on continuing the investigation, by whatever means were available, when she returned to the ship.

*Did we find anything here that was worth two people's lives?* Kedair wondered. *Or was this all for nothing?*

She suspected that, at that very moment, on the *Aventine,* Captain Dax was learning the answer to that question.

"That doesn't answer my question, Lieutenant," said Dax, who was starting to think the briefing was going in circles.

Helkara stood in front of a diagram of the subspace tunnel phenomenon on the conference room's wall monitor, his mouth slightly agape. "I'm sorry, Captain," said the Zakdorn science officer. "Which question didn't it answer?"

"Any of them," Dax said. "We've suspected since day one that a subspace phenomenon carried the *Columbia* here from the Beta Quadrant. I want to know how it entered the phenomenon, as well as where and when."

Another stymied pause. Helkara cast bemused looks at the other officers seated around the table behind Dax: Mikaela Leishman, Sam Bowers, and Nevin Riordan, a young computer specialist with a slight build and a disheveled bramble of short, spiky white hair. Then the Zakdorn said, "I don't have the data to answer that question right now, Captain."

*And we're back at square one,* Dax grumped to herself. "Why not?" She directed her next statement to Riordan. "I thought we recovered all of *Columbia*'s logs and databases."

"We did, Captain," Riordan said. "But as I was saying before you—" He stopped as he noticed Bowers's warning glare, but he'd already crossed the conversational Rubicon and had to continue. "—before you cut me off—we detected a gap in their log chronology. Eight months separate their last data on the ambush from the start of their sensor logs about the phenomenon."

As much as Dax wanted to be upset with the ensign for his impolitic reproach of her, she knew, in hindsight, that he was right. She had run roughshod over him in her impatience to reach some answers. To make some progress before the clock ran out and it came time to break orbit.

She asked Riordan, "Is it possible that it was a malfunction, or the result of damage?"

Riordan shook his head. "No, sir. No sign of damage or erasure. It's as if the ship's sensors just got turned off for eight months, then snapped back on inside the phenomenon."

Turning back to Helkara, Dax said, "What are the last regular entries in the *Columbia*'s log?"

"A Romulan ambush," Helkara said. "Based on the dates, it looks like the Romulans were testing some new tactics right before the start of their war with Earth. The ship's chief engineer tricked the Romulans into thinking the *Columbia* was destroyed, but it was left without communications or warp drive, a few light-years from Klingon space."

Dax drummed her fingertips on the tabletop. "Any indication what their next plan of action was?"

"None," Helkara said. "The last entry in Captain Hernandez's log is that their engines and subspace antenna were irreparable."

Leishman leaned forward and added, "The damage in their warp reactor and the internal components of their comm system still hadn't been fixed by the time they crashed here."

Helkara continued, "For what it's worth, Captain, the data from their passage through the phenomenon was completely intact, and as detailed as sensors of that era could be."

"All right," Dax said, surrendering to the realization that her other questions would have to wait for another time. "What, exactly, do we know about their journey through subspace?"

Bowers took over the briefing from Helkara, who returned to his seat as the first officer got up and stepped over to the wide companel monitor. "The *Columbia* was inside the phenomenon for just over forty-five seconds," he said. "There were thirty-one human life signs on board at the start of its journey, and one Denobulan. That leaves ten of its crew unaccounted for."

Dax interrupted to ask, "Could they have been killed during the Romulan ambush?"

Bowers looked to Helkara, who said, "The logs identified fifty-three ambush casualties and forty-two survivors."

Satisfied, Dax nodded to Bowers, who continued. "Once the ship passed inside the phenomenon, it got kicked around pretty good. The subspatial stresses were more volatile than those inside a wormhole or a controlled warp bubble."

"I can see the difference between this and a warp bubble," Dax said. "But what makes this different from a wormhole?"

Again, Bowers nodded to Helkara. The Zakdorn used a touch-screen interface in front of him on the tabletop to display animations on the large wall monitor. "Topologically, not much. Both, in essence, serve as passages for rapid travel between distant points in the same universe, or possibly different universes. Both are tubes with a topology of genus one, with a mouth, or terminus, at either end, and the throat, or tunnel, between them. The chief difference is where and how they exist."

He enlarged one of the schematics. "This is the Bajoran wormhole, a relatively stable shortcut through normal space-time. Its structure is made possible by a twelve-dimensional, helical verteron membrane and a series of verteron nodes, which tune its as-yet-unknown energy source to maintain its tunneling effect through space-time."

Switching to the second schematic, Helkara continued, "This is the subspace tunneling effect the *Columbia* encountered. Its shape is basically identical, but there are two major differences between this and the Bajoran wormhole. First, it doesn't exist in normal space-time, it only exists in subspace. Second—and I just want to say that this next point is pure conjecture, because no one has ever seen this work before—all of the *Columbia*'s data suggest this phenomenon is powered by dark energy drawn from normal space-time." He highlighted part of the display. "We think that's what led to the deaths of the crew."

Dax asked, "They were killed by the dark energy?"

"Not directly," Helkara said. "It was the by-product that did them in: hyperphasic radiation."

Bowers made a clicking noise with his tongue against the roof of his mouth. "That would do it. How fast did it hit?"

"I'd estimate every organic particle on the ship was disintegrated within twenty seconds of entering the subspace tunnel," Helkara said.

"But the ship spent forty-five seconds inside the phenomenon," Dax said. "Yesterday, Mirren said the ship's autopilot had been engaged. When did that happen?"

Bowers answered, "About fifteen seconds after the ship exited the subspace tunnel and returned to normal space-time."

"In other words," Dax said, doing the math in her head as she spoke, "about forty seconds after every living thing on that ship was dead."

Her first officer cocked one eyebrow and responded with a slow nod. "Give or take."

"And there's no record of who or what triggered the autopilot," Dax said, and Helkara and Riordan nodded in confirmation. "Maybe it's some kind of creature that lives out of phase most of the time. Could it be the same thing that attacked Komer and Yott last night?"

With a shrug, Bowers said, "We don't know yet."

"Captain," Helkara said, "there's one more important note I'd like to share about the subspace tunnel."

She nodded. "Go ahead."

He got up and walked to the companel and pointed out some details as he spoke. "The energy field inside the tunnel was remarkably stable, much more than a conventional wormhole would be. If my analysis of its graviton emissions is correct, I think there's a very good chance the subspace tunnel is *still there*."

Dax looked at Bowers, who seemed as surprised by this news as she was. Intrigued, she asked Helkara, "Are you sure?"

"I'm almost positive," he said. "If we can locate the terminus and make a successful passage of the tunnel, we might be able to figure out how it was created. It could open up new areas of the galaxy for exploration—maybe the whole universe."

As if Dax needed more convincing, Bowers added, "If it leads back to a point in the Beta Quadrant, it might also be a major strategic discovery for Starfleet."

"Okay," Dax said. "How do we find the terminus?"

"I have a few ideas," Helkara said. "It's too soon to say which approach will work. But if I'm right and it's still there, with Lieutenant Leishman's help, I'm fairly certain I could track it down in a few hours."

She frowned. "We're supposed to be heading back now. I can hold us here for an hour, maybe two at the most. You have that long to find the subspace tunnel and figure out how to open it."

"You know," Bowers said, striking a hopeful note, "if we find it and it still works, we could be back on the line in Federation space today instead of next week."

"Let's not get ahead of ourselves," Dax said. "The tunnel's still flooded with hyperphasic radiation."

Leishman waved away the problem. "I can work around that. A properly harmonized multiphasic frequency channeled into the shields should be able to cancel out their effects." She flashed an expectant look at Dax. "So what's the word, Captain?"

"The word is go. Mikaela, get to work on those shields. Gruhn, start looking for the subspace tunnel. Sam, think up some excuse I can give the admiralty for why we're not out of orbit yet." She got up from her chair. "If there's—"

An alert whooped once over the shipwide comm.

*"Kedair to Captain Dax."*

"Go ahead," Dax said.

*"Captain, I need to see you and Commander Bowers in Shuttlebay One, right away."*

Bowers followed Captain Dax out of the turbolift on Deck 12 and followed her at a quick step toward the shuttlebay. At the first curve in the corridor, they were met by four security officers armed with phaser rifles. The quartet of guards fell into step around the two command officers and walked with them until they approached the open door to Shuttlebay One, which was blocked by another duo of armed security officers. The pair stepped aside and let Dax and Bowers pass.

The first clue that something was amiss was the odor. Bowers wrinkled his nose at the sickly stench, which only became stronger as he and Dax neared the cluster of armed security personnel that surrounded the runabout *U.S.S. Seine*.

Security chief Kedair noticed their arrival. She stepped away from the group to meet them. Her complexion was an even richer shade of blue-green than Bowers was accustomed to, and he took it as a sign of agitation. "Captain," she said, "I think we have an intruder."

Before Dax could ask Kedair to elaborate, the guards between them and the *Seine* parted, revealing a troubling sight through the runabout's open side hatch.

It was the slagged remains of a humanoid body, mixed with the burned tatters of a Starfleet uniform. Much of the victim's skin was gone, exposing jumbled viscera, half-dissolved muscles, and bones wet with liquefied fats and spilled blood. The half of its face that Bowers could see looked normal from the scalp to the nose, but everything from the upper lip to the chin looked as if it had been blasted away, down to the morbid grin of the skull. Its tongue was draped across its throat.

Forcing himself to remain detached and businesslike, he asked Kedair, "Have you identified the victim?"

"Crewman Ylacam," Kedair said. "Flight technician, first class. He was logged in for routine maintenance on the *Seine*."

Dax stepped forward, studying the scene with the eyes of a scientist. "How much do we know about what happened?"

"Not much more than we know about what happened to Komer and Yott on the *Columbia*," Kedair said. "Mirren's pulling the internal sensor logs and starting a forensic review."

Bowers averted his eyes from the stomach-churning carnage inside the runabout. "Are we sure it's the same cause of death that we saw on the *Columbia*?"

"All but certain," Kedair said. "I'm just waiting on final confirmation." Looking over Bowers's shoulder, she added, "And here it comes now."

Dr. Tarses entered the shuttlebay, followed by a female medical technician with a stretcher. The CMO paused as he saw the state of the body inside the runabout. He looked back at the medtech and said, "We don't need the stretcher. Go back and get some sample jars and a stasis pouch." The technician nodded and reversed course, quick-timing her way out of the shuttlebay and looking relieved for the opportunity.

Tarses approached the runabout with a wary frown. "Not again," he mumbled as he passed Kedair. He opened his satchel, removed a medical tricorder, activated it, and started a scan of the half-burned, half-melted corpse. "Molecular disruption," he said, reading from the tricorder's screen. "Acute thermal effects. Major breakdown in all organic material."

On a hunch, Bowers asked, "Is the damage consistent with hyperphasic radiation exposure?"

"No, it's not," Tarses said, putting away his tricorder. "Hyperphasic radiation desiccates organic matter and disperses it into subspace. Basically, it turns people into gas and dust. Whatever did this turns people into soup."

Dax asked the doctor, "Was this done by the same thing that killed our people on the *Columbia*?"

As he considered his answer, Tarses crossed his left arm over his torso and tugged gently with his right hand at the lobe of one of his pointed ears. "The effects are all but identical," he concluded. "So I'd have to say yes, it was."

"Lonnoc," Dax said to the security chief, "sound a shipwide intruder alert. All nonessential personnel are restricted to quarters. Have your people sweep the ship, bow to stern. Use sensors, hard-target searches, whatever it takes. Something followed us up from the planet, and I want it found, now."

Turning to Bowers, the captain added, "Sam, tell Starfleet Command we're not going anywhere—not until I find out what we're dealing with."

# 2168

## 17

An electric charge in the air raised the fine hairs on Commander Veronica Fletcher's forearm. She gazed into the chasm beyond the catwalk and felt humbled.

"This is as close to the apparatus as I can permit you," said Inyx, who led Fletcher, Karl Graylock, and Kiona Thayer on a guided tour of the enormous machine at the center of the Caeliar's "great work." They had come here by way of a disk ride and a swift descent through a nondescript tube set into a promenade beside a vast, darkly translucent dome. It wasn't until they'd reached the catwalk that Fletcher realized their destination lay beneath the hemispherical shield, which from this side appeared to be transparent.

A massive, clear cylinder with dozens of meter-wide vertical gaps placed asymmetrically along its entire length was connected at its top to the dome's center, two hundred meters overhead. Suspended from it was a huge, circular platform whose surface was divided into a silver ring around the cylinder and a black outer ring of equal thickness. Both surfaces were polished to mirror brilliance and reflected the steady, pulsing display of prismatic energy inside the central column.

"It's magnificent," Thayer said, awestruck.

Fletcher continued to study the platform's other large details. From her vantage point, she could see five of what she presumed was a total of eight narrow arms with chisel-shaped ends reaching down and away from a second layer of the platform; the arms were mounted on broad, ring-shaped joint mechanisms and spaced forty-five degrees apart. Between them were bevel-edged, blocky structures that resembled docking ports. From the center of each squarish mass bulged a black hemisphere set inside a bright metallic ring.

Underneath the thick lower ring of the platform was a shimmering globe of incandescent coils. The top of the sphere was

connected by a weblike conglomeration of machinery and cabling, all of it silhouetted by the blinding ball. Its glow illuminated the distant sides of the silo-shaped abyss, but it was not
powerful enough to reach the bottom, from which came an echo
of the low, throbbing pulse of the machine.

"The apparatus serves two major functions," Inyx said. He
walked forward, and the *Columbia* officers followed him along
the curved, railing-free catwalk that ran the perimeter of the silo.
"It is a means of observation, and a tool for communication. With
it, we can listen for signals from the farthest extremities of the
universe, and we can establish real-time contact with anyone or
anything we discover."

As Fletcher's eyes adjusted, she discerned the shapes of
Caeliar moving about in pairs on the surface of the sprawling
platform. Watching them move in and out of portals in the blockhouse structures, she asked Inyx, "So, this is how you plan to
talk with something more advanced than yourselves?"

"Yes," Inyx said. "We realized several thousand years ago that
many of the galaxies we were investigating were either long dead
or had never been capable of supporting life. In order to find
a civilization that meets our criteria, we limited our search to
those billions of galaxies that were not inherently hostile to life,
and that had remained stable for the estimated billions of years
that might be necessary for it to develop."

"I'm sorry," interrupted Thayer. "Did you say you searched
*billions* of galaxies?"

Inyx faced the dark-haired young woman. "Yes. We were extremely selective. I confess that limiting our candidates in this
manner might have led us to overlook viable systems, but I felt
the risk of oversight was statistically insignificant."

Fletcher watched a trio of Caeliar levitate and float from the
platform, across the hundred-meter-wide void, to a catwalk
below the one on which she walked. "So now you're looking
for contacts at the end of the universe," she said to Inyx, to keep
him from making note of her silent observations. "At what range?
Fourteen billion light-years?"

"Slightly less," Inyx said. "Approximately thirteen-point-
eight-seven billion light-years, using your metrics."

Graylock took his turn drawing their host's attention. "Hmmph.
Must take a lot of power to send a signal that far."

"More power than your species has harnessed so far in its entire history," Inyx said.

Graylock pointed at the distant platform and asked in amazement, "All through *that* machine?"

Inyx bowed his head in a stiff imitation of a nod, a habit he'd picked up from interacting with the *Columbia*'s landing party. "Yes," he said.

Goading the Caeliar, Graylock inquired, "What if that generator on the bottom overloads?"

"As that is not the generator, there is little possibility of that," Inyx said.

Thayer cut in, "See, Karl? I told you. They generate the power remotely, just like for everything else around here."

"Quite correct, Kiona," Inyx said in a patronizing tone.

She replied, "You must use up a lot of that power punching through the scattering field, though."

"*Nein*," Graylock said before Inyx could answer. "They use a subharmonic to collimate the signal after it leaves the field."

"Hardly, Karl." The visage of the Caeliar always seemed to convey hauteur, but Inyx's tone was rife with it. Graylock visibly tensed whenever one of the Caeliar addressed him by his given name. Inyx continued, "At the power levels involved here, a phase-shifted soliton pulse is the only choice."

"Really?" Graylock's feigned ignorance was painfully obvious to Fletcher, but the Caeliar seemed so oblivious of human behavior that they took the landing party's statements at face value. In this case, Graylock had made good use of the Caeliar scientist's almost reflexive habit of correcting erroneous hypotheses. Had the question been left for Inyx to answer, his reply would have been vague. To correct Graylock's blatant "errors," however, Inyx seemed frequently compelled to elaborate and underscore his superior expertise.

Part of Fletcher's task was to keep changing the subject, in the hope of distracting Inyx from the purpose of their many inquiries and ruses. "Assuming you locate a culture more advanced than yours," she said, "what do you hope to learn?"

"We don't know, exactly," Inyx said. "One might say we are in search of our next step as a culture."

Thayer said, "Are you certain there's nobody worth talking to anywhere closer than the edge of the universe?"

"It has been hundreds of your millennia since we eliminated all the habitable galaxies within one billion light-years as viable candidates," Inyx said. "Every failed search has spurred us to press on and look deeper into space and time. We believe that we are only days from opening contact with the civilization we have sought. If my analysis is correct, I have located a harnessed galaxy, an achievement unlike any I have ever seen."

Fletcher regarded the giant machine, brilliant and held aloft over a pit of midnight blue shadows. She looked at Inyx. "That thing really must be one of a kind."

"Not at all," Inyx said. "There is an identical apparatus in each of our cities." Conspiratorial glances passed between Fletcher and the other two officers, unnoticed by Inyx. He continued, "If your curiosity is now sated, may I suggest we—"

"Can we go to the platform for a closer look?" asked Fletcher. It had taken her months of pleading and assurances to secure permission from the Caeliar for this tour, and she wasn't going to let it end without trying to make the most of it.

Inyx stiffened at the request, and his normally cordial demeanor chilled. "I'm afraid that would be quite out of the question," he said. "It's time to go back. Please follow me."

The lanky alien led the three humans off the catwalk and down a narrow passage, one of several that radiated away from the vast empty chamber of the apparatus. Their visit to the Caeliar's signature achievement had been brief but educational. Fletcher hoped that she and her officers had learned enough to find a way off this planet—and a way home.


Sheltered under the gnarled boughs of the tree at the end of the black reflecting pool, the stranded members of the *Columbia*'s flight crew sat in a circle around their captain.

"The clock is definitely ticking, folks," Fletcher said. "Inyx says they're only days away from powering up this super gadget of theirs, so if there's any way it can help us get back to the ship, we need to figure it out fast."

Graylock and Thayer reached into the pockets on the legs of their jumpsuits and removed three hand scanners each. It had taken Graylock months to jury-rig a solar cell and then recharge the drained devices. From then until that day's tour of the "apparatus," the landing party had kept the scanners powered down and hidden to avoid detection by the Caeliar. As Thayer had hoped, the scattering field was configured as a shell around the city; the hand scanners functioned normally inside the protected zone but were blind to anything beyond it.

"We had these set for passive scans," Graylock said as he handed two of them to Hernandez and Fletcher. "Each scanner was set to look for something different."

Metzger and Valerian each accepted a scanner from Thayer, who noted, "Security on the 'apparatus' is tighter than other spots we've been to. It's completely sealed in and underground."

A warm breeze tossed locks of Hernandez's black hair into her eyes, and she swept it away with a pass of her hand. "Karl, what is this thing?"

"The final word in subspace radio," said the Austrian. "Inyx says it can make real-time contact between here and the end of the universe."

Lifting her eyebrows in mild surprise, the captain asked, "Any idea how it works?"

Graylock tapped at the screen of his hand scanner. "The platform creates an intense subspace phase-distortion field. And the pulses inside the column—" He looked around, made a hasty swap of scanners with Thayer, and continued. "—are soliton waves, just like Inyx said. I think this thing sends the waves through subspace, uses them like a drill to make a hole. Then the phase distorter . . ." He leaned forward and traded scanners with Valerian. "The phase distorter acts like a nut and bolt, pulling the two ends of the hole together, until they meet."

"Now my brain hurts," mumbled Dr. Metzger.

Hernandez turned off her hand scanner and looked at Thayer. "Thoughts, Kiona?"

"With all the power that thing uses, it might make a hell of a feedback pulse if it got disrupted during their big event, maybe enough to knock out their power source and drop the scattering field so *Columbia* can beam us up and break orbit."

Graylock let out a derisive snort of laughter. "Or it might blow up the city—or maybe the planet."

"That's not the only flaw," Fletcher said. "It would have to take the Caeliar out of commission for at least six minutes: one minute for *Columbia* to find us after the scattering field falls, four minutes to beam us up three at a time, one minute to break orbit at full impulse. And that's assuming the crew on the ship is standing by and ready to act on a moment's notice."

"Actually," Hernandez said, "we don't even know if the rest of the crew is still up there. They might have abandoned ship and beamed down to the planet by now."

Thayer added darkly, "Or the Caeliar might have displaced them." Grim stares around the circle confirmed that she wasn't the only one who had considered that scenario.

Valerian said, "Even if we do get back to the ship, what then? We're still at least twenty light-years from the nearest friendly system, and there's no tellin' what's moved into the space between while we've been tootlin' around for the last twelve years. Are we just gonna limp home, show up thirty-four years late, and ask if we have any messages?"

Speaking like a man who knew a secret, Graylock asked, "Who says we have to get home late?"

Hernandez was not in a mood for a mystery. "Explain."

"The tunnels the Caeliar are making through subspace are a lot like Lorentzian wormholes," Graylock said. "Even though they're in subspace, most of the rules still apply. If it makes a shortcut through space, it can make a shortcut through time— forward *or* backward."

"Whoa," said Hernandez, dragging out the word like she was reining a wild horse to a halt. "Time travel, Karl? Are you out of your mind? We've barely got the hang of warp speed, and you think you're ready to break the time barrier?"

The chief engineer got red in the face. "Why not? If this thing's as powerful as Inyx says, we can get back to Earth—not today, but twelve years ago, when it might make a difference!"

"He's right," Thayer said. "If we go back, we could warn Earth about the Romulans, tell them about the ambush. It might save who knows how many lives."

Captain Hernandez frowned. "And it might destroy the time line. The Vulcans *warned* us about this kind of thing."

"Oh, screw the Vulcans," Thayer said. "Us getting back might be the thing that decides who wins the war. We have a duty to try and get home."

Graylock nodded. "*Ja,* and for all we know, Captain, it's what's *supposed* to happen. Maybe we've already done it. And if we prevent our earlier selves from coming here, the Caeliar would never *know* that we did it."

On some level, Hernandez found the idea tempting. It would be a chance to erase the biggest mistake of her career, maybe even save the convoy, hundreds of lives, and change the course of the war. . . . Then she reminded herself that tampering with history and with temporal mechanics might be a task with zero margin for error; the slightest mistake could destroy everything and everyone that she cared about. And then there was the reaction of the Caeliar to consider, whether they succeeded or not.

"No," she said. "Messing with time is too damn dangerous. We might end up making things worse. For all we know, we were meant to be lost in action twelve years ago, and we're meant to be here now. I want to go home just as much as the rest of you, but I'm not willing to risk undoing twelve years of history— twelve years of *other* people's successes and sacrifices—just so I can feel like I didn't miss anything." She scanned the reactions of the group as she added, "Even more important, if we actually escape and get home, think about what the Caeliar will do—not just to us, but to Earth. We might end up condemning our entire world to oblivion. And I can't allow that." She let go of a heavy, dispirited sigh. "I'm sorry, but our first duty is to protect Earth, and in this case that means making a sacrifice and accepting our fate. Is that clear?" Thayer and Graylock gave reluctant nods, in contrast to the easy assent from Valerian, Fletcher, and Metzger. "All right," Hernandez said.

"So, what now?" asked Fletcher. "If we're really giving up on escape, what's left for us?"

Hernandez shrugged. "I'm not sure. Maybe I'll ask for permission to bring down the rest of the crew. Let the Caeliar decide what to do with the *Columbia.*" She looked around at the city. "It's not exactly where I'd planned on spending my retirement, but I can think of worse places."

"If we're staying here," Fletcher said, "there'll have to be some changes."

Hernandez arched one eyebrow. "Such as?"

"For starters, I want my own apartment."

Major Foyle stood on the penthouse suite's terrace and stared beyond the sharp edges of the Caeliar city, to the distant peaks of mountains hidden under blankets of autumn fog. "So . . . she's lost the will to fight?" He turned and regarded his visitors.

The *Columbia*'s chief engineer and senior weapons officer both looked and sounded nervous—appropriate enough reactions for officers going behind their captain's back.

"They've broken her," Thayer said. "Not only is she telling us not to try and escape, she wants to bring down the rest of the crew. She's talking about *abandoning the ship*."

Foyle's brow creased with intense concentration as he pondered the situation. He asked Graylock, "Do you concur with Lieutenant Thayer's assessment?"

"*Ja, Herr* Major," said the broad-shouldered Austrian.

Behind the two flight officers, the rest of the MACOs perched like gargoyles along the lip of the penthouse's roof, which was a jumble of odd shapes and angles. It was lunchtime, and the men were all snacking on small pieces of fruit, as well as on sticks of dried, synthetic meat that they had conserved and rationed from their provisions for the past few months. The switch to a predominantly vegetarian diet had given all the members of the landing party a distinctly lean and hungry look.

"I wish there was some satisfaction in being able to say I told you so, Lieutenant, but there isn't." Foyle sighed and turned back toward the faraway range. "If Captain Hernandez isn't willing to use force to secure our freedom, then I have to question her fitness to command." At the edges of his vision, he saw Graylock and Thayer stake out positions on either side of him, leaning on the terrace's railing. "If I place this mission under military authority, will I have your support?"

"Absolutely," Thayer said.

"*Jawohl*," said Graylock. "It's why we came to you."

The major nodded. "And the others?"

"*Nein*. They won't go against the captain."

"I'd suspected as much," Foyle said. Turning his head toward Thayer, he said, "Tell me about your diversion."

There was excitement in her eyes as she detailed the plan. "It entails coordinated strikes on the 'apparatus' in two of the other cities, preferably ones as far as possible from Axion."

"I don't have that much manpower," Foyle argued.

She pulled a hand scanner from her jumpsuit's leg pocket and handed it to him. "We only need to seize one node of the apparatus in person. In the second city, we'll use a timer-detonated munition to blow up a different node while it's all juiced up for their big experiment. The tachyon pulse alone should be enough to collapse the scattering fields worldwide."

"For how long?"

Thayer glanced at Graylock, who said, "No idea. We hope it'll last for at least six minutes so we can beam back to the ship and break orbit."

Foyle considered the power that their captors had already displayed on the planet's surface. "Once we're on the ship, what then? Do we really think we can outrun the Caeliar at impulse?"

"We may not have to," Graylock said. "The technology they're using for their 'great work' could be modified to send us back home in a snap."

The major gritted his teeth and twisted his mouth into a rueful grimace. "Let's remember what the good captain said about our hosts' bad habit of 'displacing' entire civilizations. Do we want to risk bringing that kind of attention to Earth?"

"If we do this properly, the Caeliar might never know we were here."

"That's the other proposal the captain rejected," Thayer said. "The Caeliar's machines can move us through time *and* space. We'd have to run afoul of the predestination paradox, and deal with meeting ourselves, and about a dozen other temporal no-nos . . . but we could go back, warn Earth about the Romulans, and save ourselves from getting stuck here in the first place."

From behind the trio came the scuffle of men climbing down from the rooftop. Foyle and the *Columbia* officers turned to see Pembleton and Yacavino stride toward them, while Crichlow, Mazzetti, and Steinhauer scrambled over the edge and sought purchase with their hands and feet.

"Did I just hear that?" asked Pembleton. "We can go back? I can see my wife again and watch my boys grow up?"

"In theory," said Graylock.

The MACOs gathered around, a wall of intense focus and dark forest camouflage, as Foyle asked the engineer, "What will it take to make your theory a reality?"

"Phase two of the plan," answered Thayer. All eyes turned to her, the only woman on the terrace, as she continued. "Karl has a good idea what the Caeliar's machines are capable of, but he doesn't know how to make them do what he wants. I think the Caeliar do know how, and if they're properly motivated, they might be . . . *persuaded* to assist us."

Pembleton threw a sidelong stare at Foyle. "That does sound like our specialty, Major."

Foyle was torn. Mucking about with time was dangerous business, no matter how cavalierly his men embraced it. He hadn't been trained for decisions such as this. Small-unit tactics, SERE protocols, psy-ops, boarding procedures—those were his areas of expertise. Altering the flow of history had not been covered at the war college in Credenhill. But the human cost of his decision was staring him in the eye. This was a chance to reunite his sergeant with his family, bring his men and the crew of the *Columbia* home to their friends and loved ones, and spare all those people back on Earth the grief of believing the ship and its crew lost in action.

A chance to go home to Valerie. To his life. Their life.

*For all I know, the Romulans conquered Earth because we couldn't get a warning out. What if everyone we care about is gone because of that mistake? What if our going back in time is Earth's only hope?*

He climbed up from the deep well of his thoughts to find everyone staring at him and waiting for his answer. "Graylock, if my people get you into one of those machines and compel the Caeliar to cooperate, are you sure you can pull this off?"

"I'm certain it's our only chance, *Herr* Major."

Foyle studied Thayer's eyes, looking for the resolve of a soldier. He asked her, "When this turns ugly—and I promise you, it will—can I count on you to go the distance?"

"Whatever it takes, sir," Thayer said. "I refuse to die as a prisoner, here or anywhere else."

That was an answer Foyle could accept and respect. "All right, then," he said. "Forget what Captain Hernandez wants. If we're going to make a go of this, we have to hit the Caeliar where it'll hurt them most." He worked his way around the circle with speed and certainty. "Yacavino, you and Crichlow get munitions in place before they start their big experiment. Have Lieutenant Thayer tell you which site to mine. Pembleton, go over the scans of the Caeliar with Lieutenant Graylock and see if we can bring them down to our level and hurt them once we get them there. Mazzetti, Steinhauer—you're both with me."

Yacavino looked worried. "What will you be doing, sir?"

"I expect Captain Hernandez will object to our plan," Foyle said. "She and the other flight officers will have to be kept in sight and out of the loop. When it's time to attack, they'll have to be contained until we're ready to beam up." He saw Yacavino's expression of concern mirrored on the faces of Thayer and Graylock. "Trust me," he added. "She'll thank us after we all get home." That seemed to mollify the three lieutenants. Foyle snapped everyone into action with a clap of his hands. "We have a lot to do. Let's get to work."

The group moved off and segregated into duos according to the assignments that Foyle had made. The lone straggler was Sergeant Pembleton, who waited until the others were out of earshot before he confided to the major, "You know containment won't be enough, don't you? She won't stand for it."

"I know," Foyle said. "And we can't take a chance on her alerting the Caeliar before we break orbit." He patted the taller man's shoulder. "I'll handle it."

"One more thing bothers me, sir," Pembleton said. Foyle nodded for him to continue. "What if the Caeliar have taken the rest of the ship's crew prisoner? What if there's no one up there to beam us aboard?"

Foyle looked to the horizon. "Then we're already dead."

# 2381

## 18

Commander Geordi La Forge walked through the mechanical jungle of assembly lines that occupied three converted cargo bays on Deck 23 of the *Enterprise*. A tang of overheated metal filled the ozone-rich air, and the long, open space buzzed with the hum of motors, plasma welders, and industrial replicators.

*The death factory.* That was La Forge's secret nickname for this hastily erected manufacturing complex. Here was where the crew struggled to produce a steady supply of the one weapon that so far had proved consistently effective against the Borg: transphasic torpedoes.

Flashes of light from the welding teams pierced the blue haze that lingered between checkpoints on the line. Lighting in the munitions plant was kept glare-free and diffuse, to avoid hard shadows and reduce eyestrain. Most of the line was powered by antigravs, which kept the noise to a low rumble.

For those who toiled here, the only relief from the monotony was to be rotated between different stations each day. Watching the dull routine, the grind of repetition, La Forge found it hard to believe that it made much difference. One set of rote tasks was as mind-numbing as another.

He stopped to check the phase variance circuit on a finished warhead that was awaiting delivery to the forward torpedo room. He used the warhead's built-in touch-screen interface to perform a quality-control inspection of its internal systems. The data was still crawling up the screen as he noted someone approaching from his left.

"Geordi," said Beverly Crusher, who had a medical satchel slung at her hip. She stopped beside him and noted the inspection in progress. "Am I catching you at a bad time?"

It was a terrible time, but the chief engineer shook his head and replied, "Not at all. What can I do for you?"

"Actually, I'm here to do something for you," she said,

opening her satchel. She removed a small gadget that La Forge recognized as a recalibration tool for his ocular implants. "I'm sorry I didn't have time to tend to your injuries personally when you came to sickbay." Lifting the device to his temple, she continued, "Dr. Tropp said you left sickbay before he could fix the damage to your implants."

La Forge tried to dismiss her concern with a halfhearted smile. "It's no big deal, Doc. Just some false-spectrum artifacts in the ultraviolet range. I just tune it out."

"Mm-hmm," she mumbled, adjusting the calibrator's settings. "I'll have it fixed in a few seconds, so just hold still." With a mischievous gleam she added, "And don't say I never make house calls."

As promised, the distortion cleared instantly. Crusher switched off the device, and he nodded to her. "Much better. Thanks." He turned to resume his diagnostic of the warhead he'd been inspecting when she came in. A moment later he noticed that Crusher didn't seem to be making any move to depart. Over his shoulder, he asked, "Want to tell me why you're really here?"

"Because I don't know who else to talk to," she confessed.

He turned and folded his arms. "This sounds interesting."

Now that she had his full attention, Crusher looked very self-conscious. "It's about the captain," she said, copying La Forge's guarded stance, arms crossed in front of her chest. "I'm worried about him. About what this mission is doing to him."

"Are you sure I'm the right one to talk to?" he asked. "If it's a command issue—"

"It's not," she interrupted. "And it's not something for the counselors, or for Starfleet Command. I don't even want to take any action, I just want to talk to someone about it. Someone who won't have to file a report."

Crusher didn't mention Worf by name; she didn't have to. All at once, Geordi understood her dilemma. Worf, by nature, would always err on the side of supporting his captain, and if Crusher raised an official concern, Worf would be required to note it in his log. The same would likely be true of the ship's staff of counselors. With the recent departures of so many of Crusher's longtime friends on the senior staff—including Will Riker and Deanna Troi—La Forge was probably the last of the "old guard" whom she felt she could trust to lend a discreet and sympathetic ear to her concerns.

He conveyed his understanding with a single, slow nod. "If anyone asks, this conversation never happened."

"Thank you," she said.

He gave a final glance at the warhead's data readout and was satisfied that all its ratings were nominal. He shut it down and moved on, walking between two long lines of automated machines cranking out a steady parade of warhead casings. Crusher followed along. As she fell into step beside him, he asked, "So what is it we aren't talking about?"

"Obsession," she said. "Specifically, Jean-Luc's fixation on eradicating the Borg. I guess I'm worried because I'm hearing him advocate strategies that I never thought he'd endorse."

La Forge rolled his eyes at the understatement. "I know what you mean. Every line I think he won't cross, he goes over in a broad jump. Truth is, it's starting to scare me."

She reached out and touched his arm in silent affirmation. "Me, too," she said. Gentle pressure from her hand brought him to a halt with her as she continued. "One minute he seems ready to surrender, just throw himself on his sword, and the next he's channeling Henry the Fifth, 'once more unto the breach,' and all that. And neither seems like him."

"Except when he deals with the Borg," La Forge corrected her. "Then everything he's ever done and said goes right out the window. Logic, discipline, principles . . . he burns 'em all when he's up against the Collective."

"I know," she said. "When he fights them, he becomes like them—an extremist. A conformist one moment, a radical the next. And I feel like he's pushing us and Starfleet into a full-scale confrontation, no matter what the cost. He keeps talking about a 'clash of civilizations' as if it's inevitable, but then he says we can't win that kind of war with the Borg. So what is he trying to do? Is he just looking to end it, even if it means dying and taking the Federation down with him?"

La Forge resumed walking, and Crusher stayed by his side. "I wouldn't say the captain has a death wish," he said. "Not yet, anyway. But I look at this place"—he gestured around them at the munitions plant—"and I feel like he's already decided there's only one way the war can end, and it's in fire."

"It's not like the Borg are giving us much choice, Geordi, especially now that they're bent on extermination instead of assimilation. Shutting down the Collective might be our only chance of survival."

A gust of heated air washed over them as they kept walking. Shielding his face, he replied, "It's not as simple as shutting them down, and you know it. The Borg aren't just machines. Most of the drones in the Collective used to be individuals, just like us." La Forge raised his voice as they passed a noisy bank of plasma cutters. "We've seen drones come back from that—Hugh, Seven of Nine, Rebekah Grabowski, even the captain himself. No matter what the Borg look like on the outside, there are still people in there, Beverly—people who've been enslaved. I know the Collective's the enemy, but I can't help but feel like killing the drones is just punishing the victims without getting to the source of the problem."

They turned left at the end of the aisle and circled around to walk past a row of specialists who were performing precision calibrations on magnetic containment cores for variable-phase antideuterium. One mistake here could spark a blast that would destroy the *Enterprise* in a microsecond. Ion fusers in constant operation cast dull, ruddy glows beneath thick, rodinium glare shields while technicians monitored their work via nanocams.

Crusher walked with one hand pressed protectively over her abdomen. The sight of Beverly, as the bearer of a new life, surrounded by instruments of death and destruction made La Forge want to hurry her out of the munitions plant and as far away from these infernal machines as possible.

She sounded worn out as she asked, "What are we going to do if Jean-Luc loses control, Geordi? Where do we draw the line?"

"I don't know. I'm not even sure I'm qualified to say if or when he's crossed it. He's always been hard to gauge when it comes to the Borg. One minute he's ready to kill them all, the next he says wiping them out is wrong . . . and then, when you least expect it, he turns himself back into Locutus." He stopped next to one of the photon chargers and stared into the rhythmic workings of the assembly line until his sense of depth flattened and its details fused together. "I'm just afraid we won't know which Captain Picard we've got this time until it's too late."

\* \* \*

"Whatever we're flying toward, it's big," said Miranda Kadohata, "and eight minutes ago it started jamming all known subspace frequencies within thirty light-years of the Azure Nebula."

The announcement by the ship's second officer added to the already grave mood of the emergency staff briefing. Dismayed glances were volleyed across the conference table, from Choudhury to Worf, and then from Kadohata to the captain. Absent from the meeting was Commander La Forge, whom Worf had excused so the chief engineer could give his full attention to making the ship itself ready for combat.

Worf decided to try and preserve a sense of momentum in the meeting. He asked Kadohata, "What is our ETA to the nebula?"

"Nine hours. We're following the sirillium traces from the Borg ship we destroyed at Korvat, but the jamming field is blocking our sensors. We could be heading into a trap."

Captain Picard sat at the head of the table and regarded the senior officers with his careworn frown. "I think it's safe to say that we'll be facing stiff resistance when we reach the nebula," he said. "We need to be prepared."

Lieutenant Choudhury replied, "The security division is good to go, sir. With your permission, I'd like to post extra guards on all decks, in case we get boarded."

"Granted," Picard said, "but you might find their effectiveness limited against the Borg."

"I'm aware of that, sir, but in combat, sometimes a few extra seconds make the difference. My people are ready to give you those seconds if you need them."

Worf noted the captain's dour nod of approval but no change in his mirthless visage. "Well done," was all Picard said to the security chief. Then he turned to Lieutenant Dina Elfiki. "Can you break through the interference at short range?"

"I think so," Elfiki said. The soft-spoken science officer—whose brown hair framed her tanned, elegant cheekbones and dark, beguiling eyes—looked younger than her years. "The subspace interference shouldn't stop us from finding transwarp signatures or anything similar. Once we close to within a few billion kilometers of the nebula, I can start my sweep."

"Good," Picard said as he got up from his chair. He seemed pensive as he paced behind it and laid his hands on top of its headrest. After a few moments, he said, "Before we lost communications, I received a message from Starfleet Command. It was a reply to my request for reinforcements to rendezvous with us at the nebula." He stepped to the wall panel and activated it with a touch of his hand. A starmap of the surrounding sectors appeared. "Starfleet's losses have been heavier than expected," he continued. "Less than an hour ago, a previously undetected Borg cube destroyed Starbase 24, along with the starships *Merrimack, Ulysses,* and *Sparta.* The only ship besides us in this sector is the *Excalibur,* and she's all but crippled after stopping the attack on Starbase 343. Which means we'll be facing this threat alone."

Tense anticipation filled the room. Worf could almost smell the anxiety—he was too polite to call it *fear*—of his human shipmates. "The *Enterprise* is ready, Captain. As are we."

"Of that I have no doubt, Commander. But I need to make clear that combat is not our principal mission. Our assignment is to find out how the Borg are reaching our space undetected, and then deny them that ability. Furthermore, we, and this ship, are to be considered expendable in the pursuit of that goal." The captain looked at the faces around the table. "Clear?"

Everyone nodded in confirmation.

Picard's already serious manner turned grim. "I've made no secret in the past of my . . . *unusual* connection with the Borg Collective, or that it's as much a liability as an asset." He strolled behind the officers seated on Worf's side of the table as he continued, talking as if to himself. "I can sense them now. The voice of the Collective is getting stronger as we get closer. There are at least three Borg cubes waiting for us. Maybe more." The captain avoided eye contact with everyone else as he paced around the far end of the conference table. "And they know we're coming. We won't enjoy the element of surprise." Returning along the other side of the table, Picard stared into some deep distance only he could perceive. "If we had the luxury of time, I'd wait for the fleet. But I can feel the fury that's driving the Borg. It's like a whip of fire on their backs."

The captain returned to the head of the table, eased his chair aside, and stood tall before the group. "We don't have long— hours, perhaps days—to stop this invasion before it goes any further. The Federation has suffered more casualties from hostile action in the past five weeks than in all the previous wars of its history combined. And it's only going to get worse, unless we put an end to it. This ship is the Federation's last line of defense, and nine hours from now we will have to hold that line, outnumbered by an enemy that doesn't negotiate, won't surrender, and never shows mercy. It's an impossible mission."

Picard's mien brightened as he added, "Fortunately, we have some experience with those here on the *Enterprise*."

# 19

"Of course you don't like it," Vale said to Riker, Troi, and Ree. "I don't like it, either. That's how I know it's a good compromise: We're all equally unhappy."

Troi shifted uncomfortably on the end of the biobed where she was sitting. Riker stood beside her. They were both sullen, and their eyes searched *Titan*'s sickbay for everything except each other. Vale watched them, worried they might reject the agreement she had negotiated with Dr. Ree on their behalf.

Ree carried himself with an even greater aura of menace than usual. The dinosaur-like physician's tail waved behind him in slow, steady swishes, a Pahkwa-thanh affectation that Vale intuited was indicative of suppressed irritation.

Standing between the vexed doctor and the unhappy couple, Vale was determined not to say anything more until one side or the other broke the standoff. As she'd hoped, the captain took the initiative. "How long will the stasis last?" Riker asked.

"Strictly speaking, it's not stasis," Ree explained. "The treatment will slow your child's growth almost to the point of halting it, but she will still draw nourishment from—"

Troi interrupted, "Did you say 'she'?"

The doctor's tail halted in mid-swing, and he seemed frozen, as if he were trapped by invisible amber.

Vale knew from some of her earlier conversations with Ree that he had been avoiding using gender pronouns when referring to Troi's terminally mutated fetus, because he felt that calling the child "it" would somehow depersonalize her and make her loss easier for Riker and Troi to cope with. Although Vale had no medical or psychiatric training to speak of, she was convinced that Ree was crazy if he believed that his choice of pronoun would ease Troi's and Riker's pain one damn bit.

A low rasp rattled deep inside Ree's long, toothy mouth, and his head dipped in a gesture that Vale thought might suggest shame, disappointment, or perhaps both at once. "Yes," he continued, with an air of resignation. "She will continue drawing sustenance from your body, even as her growth is impeded by the targeted synthetase inhibitor."

Riker nodded. "Is this a onetime treatment?"

"Unfortunately, no," Ree replied. His tongue darted from between his front fangs, two quick flicks. "To avoid harming the fetus—and your wife—I have to keep the dosages very small. She will need daily injections to maintain a safe equilibrium. I also wish to make clear that this is not a solution, merely a delaying tactic. It will postpone the imminent risk of the fetus growing and puncturing the uterine wall, but it doesn't change the fact that the pregnancy itself is unviable."

Troi asked, "How long can we use this treatment?"

"I don't know. It's experimental, and there are many variables. We might be able to stall your pregnancy for months, or your body could reject the TSI, and we'd be back where we started. I can't guarantee it will work for long, or at all."

"Until it does," Vale said to Ree, "I need to insist you remove Commander Troi from active duty."

The captain cut off Ree's reply. "Absolutely not. If this works, there won't be any imminent threat to her health, so what would be the point?"

Vale modulated her voice into a diplomat's tones. "The point is that until Dr. Ree can observe her reaction to the treatment, we won't know how safe she really is."

"Commander Vale is correct," Ree said to Riker. Then, to Troi, he added, "A period of observation would be in your best interests, my dear counselor."

"Fine," Troi said. "Monitor my bio-signs with a transponder and let me go about my business. I don't need to be confined to a bed—here or in my quarters."

Riker added, "Would that be acceptable to you, Doctor?"

"It won't be ideal," Ree said. "But it will be sufficient." He reached over to a nearby surgical cart and picked up a hypospray and a biometric transponder implantation device. "Are we agreed, then, on this futile and utterly—"

"*Doctor,*" Vale snapped, terminating another potentially inflammatory elocution of the doctor's sarcastic rant about patients ignoring his advice.

Ree's tongue flitted twice in the cool, antiseptic-scented air of sickbay. Ostensibly accepting defeat, he sagged at the shoulders and said to Troi, "May I proceed?"

The counselor nodded her assent, and Ree went to work. A gentle press of the hypospray against Troi's left bicep injected her with her first dose of TSI. He switched to the transponder implantation device, manipulating it and the hypospray with one clawed hand, whose digits, Vale saw, were capable of surprising dexterity. Ree placed the tip of the squat, cylindrical device against Troi's left forearm, a few centimeters above her wrist. "This might sting a bit," he warned.

A soft popping sound from the device was overlapped by Troi's stifled yelp of discomfort. Then it was done. Ree put away his tools while Troi massaged her forearm. The doctor turned back with a medical tricorder in hand. He activated it, made a few adjustments, and mused aloud, "Yes, it's working. Signal is strong and clear. Very good."

Riker sounded edgy as he asked, "Are we through here?"

"You may leave any time you wish, Captain," said Ree. "I need your wife to remain a few moments longer while I gather baseline data from the transponder."

"Just go," Troi said to her husband, in a tired, resentful monotone. "I'll be fine." Riker seemed both angered and relieved by her dismissal, and he marched out of sickbay without so much as a glance backward.

The door sighed closed after his departure, and Ree turned off his tricorder. "I'm finished," he said to Troi. "Please come back for a more detailed checkup tomorrow at 0900."

"Thank you," Troi said, without sounding the least bit grateful. She got up from the biobed, glared at Vale, and walked out of sickbay in a hurry.

Vale waited until she was gone and the door once again closed before she berated the doctor. "A biometric transponder? Thanks a lot, Doc. I wanted her relieved of duty, not tagged for research."

"And I wanted her pregnancy terminated, not stuck in slow motion." Ree plodded away from her in heavy steps. "As it is, we are only postponing the inevitable."

The first officer sighed. "Story of my life, Doc."

* * *

As the phaser blasts started flying, Ranul Keru almost forgot that it was only a holodeck simulation.

The passageways of the Borg transwarp hub complex were so close that he could touch both sides at once by extending his elbows. Through the open-grid framework that surrounded him, Lieutenant Gian Sortollo, and Chief Petty Officer Dennisar, he saw the fast-moving silhouettes of Borg drones. The enemy was converging on them from every direction, swarming on levels above and below them, harrying them with a steady barrage of energy pulses that screeched through the thin air and stung the back of his neck with hot sparks as they flashed off the dark bulkheads around him.

Keru filled the corridor ahead of him with covering fire as he yelled to Dennisar, "Block the side passage!"

The Orion security guard pulled a finger-sized metallic cylinder from his equipment belt, thumbed open its top cap, and pressed its arming button. Then he pitched the capsule underhand down an intersecting corridor that led to a ramp from the upper level. He leaped past the corner and yelled, "Fire in the hole!"

Sortollo and Keru ducked against a solid block of infrastructure and turned away.

A thunderclap and a brilliant flash. The plasma blast rocked the structure, and a rolling cloud of fire spilled out into the main passage, between Dennisar and Keru. Through gaps in the walls, Keru watched several levels of the Borg facility collapse inward, glowing hot and dripping with slag.

Then a deep groaning resonated around the three men, and a powerful tremor robbed them of solid footing. A grinding of metal was underscored by a deep, steady rumble. The walls around them began moving, reshaping themselves, sealing off the damaged area and making new paths inside the complex.

"Sortollo," Keru shouted over the din, "send in the scouts."

The human security officer detached a hexagonal block from his equipment belt and pressed a button in its center. Then he hurled it with a sideways toss and sent it skidding along the deck ahead of them. In the span of seconds it seemed to break apart into thousands of pieces—and then all the pieces skittered away in different directions, vanishing into the tiny spaces between the machines, the slots in the deck grilles, and the open ports of various machines.

Moments later, the lights began to flicker, plunging entire levels of the complex into darkness. Some of the deep hum of machinery faded, making the clanging footsteps of approaching drones all the more ominous.

Sortollo pulled his phaser rifle from its sheath on his back and checked the tactical tricorder mounted on the top of the weapon. "Nanites are working," he said. "I've got a signal. Ahead and right to the central plexus."

Keru motioned the two men forward. As he followed them, he plucked a cylinder from his own equipment belt, twisted its two halves each a half turn in opposite directions, and lobbed it behind them. He heard its soft pop of detonation and knew that Ensign Torvig's cocktail of virulent neurolytic pathogens was spreading in a thick, syrupy puddle across the deck, a lethal greeting for any Borg drone that came into contact with it. Then he drew his own rifle and quickened his step.

Ahead of him, Dennisar stopped short of passing a T-shaped intersection, poked his rifle around the corner, and fired off a fusillade of shots to cover Sortollo, who jumped forward and tumble-rolled to safety on the other side.

It was Sortollo's turn to lay down cover fire as Dennisar waved Keru to continue past him. "Go ahead, sir," the Orion said. "We'll cover your—" His eyes went wide and his body started to twitch. Then snaking tubules erupted from the wall behind him and mummified him in a blur of black movement. The wall split open, transformed into a biomechanoid maw, and the hideous tendrils pulled Dennisar inside.

Sortollo lurched away from his corner as more assimilation tubules sprang from it, writhing like ravenous bloodworms. He fired frantically at the wall, vaporizing chunks of it.

Keru sprinted forward, trying to find a position from which he could cover Sortollo, but then the floor was no longer beneath his feet. He fell forward into a pit of churning cables, tubing, and wiring that coiled like serpents around his legs and pulled him downward. Struggling to steady his aim and avoid shooting off his own foot, Keru pumped a dozen full-power shots into the tangled mass that held him. The blasts had no effect.

"Go forward!" he shouted to Sortollo. "Get to the plexus!"

Sortollo hesitated, clearly torn between a desire to try and save Keru and his training to obey orders. As the synthetic tentacles of the Borg complex yanked Keru's rifle from his hands and pulled him down until only his head was left exposed, Sortollo turned to continue down the pitch-dark corridor—and was felled by a single, massive pulse of green energy.

Only after the shot had struck home did the telltale red targeting beam of a Borg's ocular implant slice the darkness.

Then everything halted, frozen in time and space.

From behind Keru came the deep thunks of magnetic locks being released, followed by the hiss and whine of the holodeck doors opening. A broad shaft of warm light from *Titan*'s corridor spilled into the chilling, hostile darkness of the simulated Borg facility. Then a long shadow bobbed into view, and Ensign Torvig said, "Computer, end program."

The industrial architecture and biomechanical trappings of the Borg complex vanished, along with the security trio's simulated weapons and equipment. It took a moment for Keru's perception to adjust, because the simulation had fooled his senses into believing he had been pulled to a lower elevation than Sortollo and Dennisar, but now all three of them sat on the deck and massaged their aches and pains.

"Maybe it's just me, Vig," Keru said, "but I think you went a little overboard with this program."

Torvig responded with a bemused tilt of his head. "Odd that you would say so, sir. If the mission reports from *Enterprise* and *Voyager* are accurate, then this simulation might not be aggressive enough."

The other two security officers cast alarmed looks at each other. Sortollo said to Torvig, "You've gotta be kidding me."

"I'm not, Lieutenant," Torvig said. "Borg drones are now capable of very fast individual action in combat, and there is reason to believe that Borg ships and structures have become active combatants during battles to repel invaders."

Dennisar looked stricken. "Even the walls are going to attack us? How are we supposed to fight that?"

"That's what we're here to figure out," Keru said, forcing himself to stand. "Torvig's right. The Borg are getting faster and smarter all the time. If we underestimate them, we won't have a chance. So we train until we're ready for anything." He turned and said to Torvig, "Good work on those new gadgets, by the way. Can you protect us from getting eaten by the walls?"

The young Choblik engineer waggled his bionic fingers. "Avoiding or preventing physical attack may not be possible," he said. "However, my research indicates that neural-suppressant injections once rendered persons temporarily immune to the psychological effects of assimilation. Implanted neutralizer chips performed a similar function, as did nanites developed by Lieutenant Commander Data and Dr. Kaz. Though all these methods are known individually to the Borg, I have synthesized a hybrid that they will not yet have adapted to. Even if the Borg inject you with nanoprobes, you will not submit to the Collective."

"Won't stop them from just killing us," Keru said, "but I'll have Dr. Ree inoculate the away team, just in case."

That seemed to trouble Torvig, who replied, "Sir, a neural suppressant will prevent my body from interacting with my cybernetic implants. I would, in effect, be incapacitated by the injection. If you still wish me to be a part of your away team, I will have to forgo that protective measure."

Keru frowned. "Is that a risk you're willing to take?"

"If necessary, yes."

"In that case," Keru said, "stay close to me and Dennisar, and load us up with as many of your gadgets as we can carry."

Torvig's tail flipped anxiously behind him. "Sir . . . I should warn you that my devices are made to exploit weaknesses of the Borg that might already be known to the Collective—and which they might already have remedied. There is no guarantee that any of the devices I've created for your team will be effective."

Sortollo muttered to Dennisar, "Now he tells us."

Ignoring his comrades' pessimism, Keru said, "Don't worry about that. Now that you've given us some tools for offense, we need to focus on defense. Any ideas on that front?"

"Yes, sir," Torvig said. "I've sent you a new deployment plan for your people here on the ship. It should enable your team to defend the same areas with fewer personnel, freeing up additional strength for such key locations as the bridge, sickbay, and main engineering."

Keru nodded. "Sounds good. Anything else?"

"Defending *Titan* from external attack by the Borg will be very difficult," Torvig said. "The difference in power between a Borg cube and our vessel is too great to overcome. Assuming we evade destruction by overwhelming force, the Borg will likely resort to infiltration and sabotage." The Choblik shifted his weight from side to side, like an anxious child. "I have a response strategy," he continued, "but I don't think Commander Ra-Havreii will like it."

"Don't worry about him," Keru said. "What's your idea?"

"We need to isolate system functions throughout the ship," Torvig said. "Not with firewalls, but by shutting down the data network. Each console must be dedicated to one task, so that Borg drones can't seize low-priority stations and use them to access the ship's main computer and command systems."

Imagining the potential consequences of Torvig's strategy, Keru winced. "That could be a real handicap in combat, Vig. If a dedicated station goes down and we can't reroute its functions to a working console, we could end up in big trouble."

"As I said, Commander Ra-Havreii will not like it."

Dennisar grumbled to Sortollo, "He'll like being killed by the Borg even less."

"We all will," Keru said, shooting a silencing glare at the human and the Orion. Turning back to Torvig, he said, "Write up a contingency plan for combat situations. We'll bring it to the XO and let her decide."

"Yes, sir."

The Choblik looked at the deck, then away from Keru, which gave the Trill security chief the impression that there was something else on the engineer's mind. "What's wrong, Vig?"

"I am concerned that I might be a liability to the away team," Torvig said. "While I'm honored to help you and your team prepare, I'm not sure how much help I'll be inside a Borg facility. My talents are better suited to working in a lab than fighting in a battle."

Keru patted Torvig's back. "Relax, Vig. You'll be fine. Most of my people can only hold two phasers at a time. You can hold three. You'll be a natural."

Torvig seemed unconvinced. "I will do my best, sir." He glanced at the doorway. "With your permission, I will draft my contingency plan for Commander Vale."

With a nod, Keru said, "Dismissed."

The young engineer bounded out of the holodeck. Keru looked

at Dennisar and Sortollo, who were still sprawled behind him. "Go get some chow, and be back here at 1800," he said. "We're running this sim again until we can get past the first level."

The two security officers pushed themselves to their feet and limped out of the holodeck. Watching them go, Keru had to wonder if maybe Torvig was right. He was starting to feel as if he was asking too much of him. After all, Torvig had been an ensign for less than six months.

Doubts plagued Keru's thoughts. *How can I expect someone so young to face something like this? What if he's not ready? Do I really want to risk getting him killed just so he won't think I've lost faith in him?* He shook off that notion. *I haven't lost faith in him. He can do this, I'm sure of it. He'll be fine.*

Then he imagined his friend falling into the hands of the Borg, just as his beloved Sean had fallen years ago.

*No,* Keru promised himself. *Not this time. Not to Vig. I talked him into joining this mission, and I'm making sure he comes back from it . . . even if that means I won't.*

He had an hour before Dennisar and Sortollo returned.

"Computer," he said. "Restart program. From the top."


Riker stepped out of the turbolift onto the bridge and was met with anxious stares. Vale, who was manning the center seat, rose to surrender the chair to him. He nodded and said, "Report."

"Warp drive and main power are back online, but long-range communications are down for the count, along with most of the sensor array." Vale handed him a padd with a summary of the ship's status. He skimmed it as she continued. "Ra-Havreii networked the subspace transmitters on the shuttles, only to find out that the subspace booster relays we've been leaving behind us are all offline."

He almost had to laugh. "Of course they are." Settling into his chair, he ruminated aloud, "Whatever we're moving toward just muzzled us, but it left our tactical systems alone. Why?"

Lieutenant T'Kel looked up from the security console and offered, "Perhaps because it doesn't see us as a threat."

"Then why did it disable us?" asked Riker.

The Vulcan woman shrugged. "A warning shot?"

From the other side of the bridge, Tuvok added, "It might also have been an accident. An entity with such power could easily have destroyed us while we were incapacitated. The fact that it did not suggests that its intention was not to kill."

"Or that it thought it *had* killed us," Vale offered.

Sariel Rager swiveled her chair away from the operations console and joined the conversation. "Sir, I think it's worth noting that the pulse that hit us did so only after we'd run some fairly high-energy scans of our own. It's possible we provoked the target's curiosity, and it may not have realized we'd be so vulnerable to its sensors."

"All good points," Riker said. "Cease active scanning of the target. Passive sensors only from this point forward."

Rager nodded. "Aye, sir."

"Ensign Lavena," Riker said to the Pacifican flight controller, "resume our last course, maximum warp."

The thrumming of the engines grew louder and pitched quickly upward as the stars on the viewscreen shot past.

"Course laid in and engaged, sir," replied Lavena, her voice filtered through her aquatic breathing mask. "ETA to target is approximately seven hours, nine minutes."

To Vale, Riker added, "Get ready for a hostile reception."

Vale turned to T'Kel. "All security personnel to stations." Then she pivoted toward Tuvok. "Shields to ready standby, weapons hot." As the two officers carried out her orders with cool, quiet efficiency, Vale turned back to Riker and lowered her voice. "Without comms, we won't be able to report our findings to Starfleet. If we get into trouble, we won't even be able to send a Mayday. We'll be completely alone out here."

"We're already alone out here," Riker replied in the same hushed tone. "But I'm not breaking off or going back. Whatever's hiding out there in the dark, it's got my full attention."

# 2168

## 20

Erika Hernandez awoke struggling and flailing as a gloved hand clamped over her mouth and nose.

A German-accented voice snapped, "Quick, tie her!"

She lashed out and cuffed Private Steinhauer on the ear before someone else snared her wrist and yanked it backward.

Steinhauer and Mazzetti pulled Hernandez from her bunk. The German's hand slipped from her mouth, and she inhaled, a prelude to a shout—then Mazzetti wedged a rolled-up sock between her teeth, muffling her panicked cry for help.

There were sounds of struggle in the rooms adjoining hers, more sharp-but-hushed orders, heavy thuds of bodies striking the floor, the meaty smack of fists against flesh.

Her attackers flipped her facedown on the floor. One of them, she couldn't see which, kneeled on her back and held her wrists behind her while the other bound them. The odor of their exertion was heavy in the air. She kept trying to pull free, and they tightened their hold. Beads of sweat rolled from beneath her hair, soaking her forehead and neck.

Mazzetti and Steinhauer each grabbed one of her arms, under the shoulder, and dragged her backward out of her quarters, into one of the corridors of their penthouse suite. At the same time, Commander Fletcher was dragged, bound and gagged, from her room by Sergeant Pembleton and Private Crichlow. Lieutenants Yacavino and Thayer pulled the similarly restrained Lieutenant Valerian into the hallway, while Major Foyle and Lieutenant Graylock towed Dr. Metzger from her chambers.

"Bring them to the main room," ordered Foyle. The group did as the MACO leader said and pushed, pulled, and prodded their four prisoners into the suite's sunken living area, near the terrace entrance. Foyle released his hold on Metzger and said, "Seat them back-to-back and tie them together."

Hernandez eyed Foyle as he stepped away and watched Pembleton and the three privates lash the four *Columbia* officers together, each of them facing out, like points on a compass.

The major conferred in whispers with his second-in-command for a moment before he acknowledged Captain Hernandez's baleful glare. "I won't insult you by apologizing," he said. "And I can't say as I mind our conversation being a bit one-sided in my favor, for a change." He stepped down and kneeled beside her. "You understand why I had to do this, don't you?"

She wanted to spit at him, but the sock was in the way.

"Yacavino," said the major. "I'll brief our guests on what happens next. Deploy the others and wait for my signal." As the group began to leave, he added, "Pembleton, hang back."

The MACO sergeant turned and halted while the rest of the mutineers departed. Hernandez caught a backward, regretful glance from Lieutenant Thayer, but only a stern mask of resolve on Graylock. She was profoundly disappointed in both of them, but especially in her chief engineer.

*I never should've let Tucker transfer back to* Enterprise, she jokingly berated herself. *It's so hard to find good help these days.*

After the Caeliar elevator pod had departed, carrying the others back to street level, Foyle waved Pembleton over. "Take their communicators," he said. "And anything else you find."

Hernandez had suspected that Foyle would remember she had ordered everyone to carry communicators at all times, in case the scattering field ever lifted. All the same, as Pembleton plucked hers from her pocket, she felt a twinge of irritation at the MACOs' efficiency and thoroughness. The sergeant concluded his pat-down search of the four female officers and held up four communicators. "This is all they had."

"Stack them over there, against the wall." Pembleton did as Foyle instructed. Then the major added, "Frag them."

Pembleton tugged the strap of his phase rifle and swung it off his back and into his hands. He squeezed off a burst of charged plasma and reduced the four communicators to smoking, sparking sludge.

Then he aimed his rifle at Hernandez.

"Give the order, sir," said Pembleton, his index finger poised over the trigger, steady and certain.

Foyle absorbed Hernandez's murderous, defiant stare. His face was an icy cipher. After several seconds, he said to Pembleton, "Lower your weapon." He strode toward the elevator pod. "We'll leave them here."

Pembleton let his weapon's muzzle dip toward the floor as he watched Foyle walk away. "Sir, that wasn't the plan."

The major stopped, turned, and snapped, "I know that, Sergeant. Sling your rifle and get in the lift." He watched Pembleton engage the safety on his weapon and quick-step toward the returned elevator pod. Then he looked at Hernandez. "I've chosen not to kill you, Captain," he said. "Please don't make me regret my decision."

He followed Pembleton to the pod and stepped inside. Its transparent shell sealed itself around them, and then it vanished through the floor on its way to the plaza below.

Hernandez assessed her situation with dour cynicism. *I'm bound hand and foot, unarmed, with no communicator. And I've got a sock in my mouth.* She felt her nostrils flare as she sighed through her nose. *I wish he had shot me.*

Time was dragging for Kiona Thayer even as the wind whipped her long, dark hair above her head like Medusa's serpents.

She still had a sick feeling in her gut from helping Major Foyle and his men assault and restrain her four fellow officers. Everything had unfolded so quickly once the MACOs had set themselves in motion. Within minutes she and Graylock had been roused and pressed into service to restrain the captain and the others.

In the hour that had elapsed since they'd left the penthouse and persuaded the Caeliar to provide them with an automated transportation disk to the nearby city of Mantilis for "cultural research," Thayer had felt her pulse throbbing in her temples. At any moment her four betrayed shipmates would be discovered trussed like animals in the penthouse, she was certain of it. And then all of this would be for nothing.

Towers and spires blurred past in the darkness. Then the lines of the metropolis sharpened as the disk settled to a soft landing in the midst of a great plaza across from the opaque dome that shielded this city's majestic Caeliar apparatus.

The disk melted into the marbled stone of the plaza, and the eight-person team moved quickly toward the dome. A violet radiance shot up from the top of the dome and soared skyward.

"Nice thing about a species that never sleeps," Crichlow said softly. "They don't ask why you'd want to take a trip in the middle of the night."

Pembleton smacked the back of Crichlow's crew-cut head, and said in a whisper laced with menace, "Shut up."

At the base of the dark hemisphere that loomed large before them, the group halted. The MACOs unzipped side pouches on one another's packs and removed rolls of wide medical tape from their first-aid kits. They worked strips of tape between their fingers and wrapped a few loops, adhesive side out, around their palms and the toes of their boots.

Pembleton handed a roll of tape to Thayer. "Just enough to give yourself some traction," he whispered. "Once we're past the first half, we should be okay without it."

Thayer tried to wrap her hands and boots with the tape; it was clumsy work, holding one end in place while manipulating the rest of the roll. After it slipped from her grasp for the third time, Pembleton and Steinhauer did the work for her. When they finished, Pembleton asked her, "Ready?" She nodded. "All right," he said. "Let's climb."

The sergeant and Major Foyle led the way, scrambling and fighting for purchase on the smooth surface. The rest of the group hurried behind them. In moments they were scratching and kicking their way up the dome like drunken bugs. Just as Pembleton had predicted, after they reached the halfway point they were able to move more quickly, jogging in a knuckle-dragging slouch, occasionally padding their palms against the dome for traction or balance. Recalling that the domes appeared transparent from inside, Thayer hoped that none of the Caeliar working on Mantilis's apparatus were looking up at that moment.

At the top of the dome, the eight-person team perched at the edge of the fifty-meter-wide aperture to the crystalline shaft that linked the dome to the enormous circular platform two hundred meters below. "Moment of truth," Foyle said as he stared down into the glittering empty space and the constantly moving mass of dark machines at its nadir.

All six MACOs doffed their packs, opened them, and began extracting coils of high-tensile microfiber rope and carabiners that they snapped into reinforced loops on their standard-issue tactical vests. Their hands worked faster than Thayer could follow, threading ropes through the steel loops, tying knots, and securing pockets and packs.

Graylock carried a tube of cyanoacrylate from his emergency repair kit and moved down the line, stopping behind each person to affix a carabiner on the surface of the dome with a thick wad of the polymer superadhesive. Thayer eyed the fat dollop of glue with suspicion. "Will that hold?"

"*Ja,* but not long. Six, maybe seven decades." As Graylock moved on, Thayer reflected on the truism that there had never been any great German comedians.

Yacavino tapped her on the shoulder. "Lift your arms, *signorina,*" he said. "I need to tie you a harness." She did as he asked and watched as he worked careful loops in a cross over her torso and then secured them with a strong simple knot through the carabiner at her feet. Then he threaded her descent rope through a carabiner on her makeshift harness. "You know how to use this, *sì?*"

"I think I remember, yes," she lied.

A few meters away, Steinhauer finished strapping Graylock into his own jury-rigged harness. The MACOs secured their rifles and gear, slung their packs back into place, and looked to Foyle for orders. "Let's go," he said. "We're running out of time."

Yacavino whispered to Thayer, "Do as we do."

He turned his back to the aperture and took hold of the rope between himself and his glued-on anchor. Thayer mimicked his actions but lacked the Italian man's ease or confidence as they began backing up in small steps toward the edge behind them. Watching and copying his every movement, she set her heels precisely over the edge, pulled her rope taut, and leaned back until she was almost horizontal, with only her grip keeping her from free fall. On either side of her, the others hovered over the shining abyss. Then Foyle said, "Now."

Reflex kept her in motion with the MACOs. She bent her knees just enough to coil up some energy, then she pushed away from the wall and let the slack rope fly through the carabiner. Then her old combat training came back to her, and she was right beside Yacavino and the others, plummeting and bouncing and feeling the exhilaration of acceleration, the rush of falling without losing control, all her focus on the present moment, the angle of her body, the placement of her hands, the tension in the rope, the rebound in her feet.

In less than a minute, they were standing on the narrow perimeter rim at the bottom of the shaft and unhooking their carabiners from their rappelling lines. Speed was paramount now. They had to act before the Caeliar had time to respond.

They slipped through a close grouping of meter-wide slits in the columns and sprinted across the giant, deserted circular platform, toward one of the entrances to the facility hidden within. Beyond the luminous halo of the platform, Thayer saw nothing but shadows and heard only the vital pulsing of great machines and the endless echoes of the yawning silo.

A portal irised open on the blockhouse as Foyle and Pembleton approached it, weapons held steady and level. Thayer was stunned by the lack of security. *Guess the Caeliar figured we'd never get this far, so why lock the door?*

Beyond the portal was a long, spiral-shaped ramp that led down and doubled back beneath Thayer's position. Foyle motioned Pembleton to take point, and the sergeant stalked forward in a low crouch until he was almost out of the team's sight. With a low wave, he ushered the rest of the team forward.

Mazzetti and Crichlow were the next to proceed. Then Foyle gestured for Thayer and Graylock to advance, placing them in the protected middle of the formation. Next, the major and Private Steinhauer followed the two flight officers, while Yacavino lingered a few meters back as the squad's rear guard.

Near the bottom of the ramp, the team halted while Foyle and Pembleton surveyed the situation. Thayer peeked over the low half wall that bordered the ramp and stared agape at the Caeliar laboratory. Beside her, Graylock was stealing a peek of his own.

Machines of crystal, light, and fluid ringed the nearly hundred-meter-wide open space, and a dancing sphere of light several meters in diameter hovered in the chamber's center. The ceiling was dozens of meters overhead, lending a cavernous aspect to the facility's total enclosure. But its real wonder were the Caeliar themselves.

There were only thirteen of them overseeing the entire works. Some stood and interfaced with the apparatus by contact, while others hovered in midair and manipulated two-dimensional screens that seemed to be made of silver liquid that rippled at their touch. A slow, oscillating song emanated from the machines, eerie and almost hypnotic in quality.

Pembleton looked back at Foyle, who nodded. It was time.

The team charged into the open, the MACOs brandishing their rifles, as Pembleton shouted, "Stop what you're doing!" His voice echoed back to him twice as the rest of the MACOs spread out around him. The Caeliar, if they were surprised or alarmed, gave no appearance of it. They regarded the invaders with the same curious annoyance that a human might have at discovering a troublesome pet in a forbidden room of the house.

Foyle stepped out in front of the group and addressed the Caeliar in a calm, even manner. "We are here because we desire your cooperation. And before you start vanishing in puffs of smoke or floating away, I should warn you that if you don't cooperate, there will be grave consequences."

The nearest Caeliar scientist said, with almost pitying boredom, "Your weapons pose little threat to us, Stephen Foyle."

"Yes, I'm aware of that." Foyle looked at Pembleton. "Sergeant, if you would."

Pembleton turned, fired, and shot Thayer's left foot.

She collapsed to the floor, screaming and bleeding.

Her ragged cries of horror and agony resounded in the vast enclosure, bringing her pain and shock back to her threefold. The initial needlelike blast of pain in her now-crisped foot became an unbearable burning that spread from her ankle into her entire leg. *"Putain de merde!"* she raged at Pembleton. To Foyle she added, *"Con de crisse!"* Blood flowed from the stump of her leg, forming an irregularly shaped puddle on the floor.

No one had told her this would be part of the plan.

Graylock tried to come to her, but Yacavino held him back.

The Caeliar crowded forward as if attracted to her pain. Foyle waited until they had circled around the squad and said, "Any closer and my sergeant will kill her."

"And if we drain the power from your weapons?" inquired another Caeliar.

Steinhauer pressed a combat knife against Thayer's throat.

"Then he cuts her from ear to ear," said Foyle.

Thayer fought to blink through her kaleidoscope of tears.

She saw Graylock struggle against the MACO lieutenant's hold. "You're all *verrückt*!" shouted the furious Austrian.

"Be quiet, Mister Graylock," Foyle said. "We've come here to do a job, and I will see it done, by any means necessary." Returning his focus to the Caeliar, Foyle continued, "My chief engineer is going to ask you to make some adjustments to your apparatus. First, however, I want you to weaken the scattering field in a narrow radius around this facility, with a clear line of transmission to our ship in orbit. Do you understand?"

The Caeliar watched Thayer as she squirmed in agony on the floor and flailed desperately in a pool of her own blood. A few seconds passed before the first Caeliar who had spoken to Foyle replied, "We understand."

That was when Thayer understood Foyle's logic. Unable to overpower the Caeliar, he had exploited their only weaknesses: their compassion and pacifism. Several times over the past six months they had reminded the *Columbia* team of their aversion to violence and their cultural prohibition against taking sentient life, through "action or omission of action."

It was a noble philosophy, in Thayer's opinion, and it was therefore completely unsuitable for dealing with such a ruthless political actor as Foyle, who had just put it to the test and found it wanting. He snapped at Graylock, "Stop staring at her and get to work on the time tunnel home." While Graylock stepped away and conferred with three of the Caeliar scientists about the modifications he wanted to make in their apparatus, Foyle looked to his MACOs. "Yacavino, hail the *Columbia*. Pembleton, if he can't break through the scattering field and raise the ship in the next fifteen seconds, shoot Thayer's other foot."

His order brought back all her pain, and the fear of an encore made it worse. She wanted to crawl away and hide, but the cold edge of Steinhauer's knife was firm against her throat. Her leg felt as if it was on fire, and her mouth was parched. A sick feeling swelled in her stomach, and adrenaline overload was shaking her with the force of a seizure while she watched her lifeblood seep away.

Yacavino held up his communicator and called to Foyle, "I have the *Columbia,* sir."

"Tell them to fire up the transporter," Foyle said. "Fast."

One of the Caeliar made cautious gestures to Foyle and then

drew near. "Your engineer's time-travel formulae are crude," the scientist said. "We've made such adjustments as are necessary for your safe passage. However, I should warn you that the linked nature of the apparatus will make it obvious to the other loci in the network when we shift our focus to Earth. Also, the various stations all operate from a central command system, so your time-travel formulae will infect the system as a whole. These details will not go unnoticed. The Quorum will block your escape from orbit once your actions are noted by the gestalt."

"They'll try," Foyle replied. He pulled back one sleeve of his camouflage uniform and checked his watch. He tapped its face and smiled. "Which is why, when we set our timers, I chose this as the perfect moment for a distraction."

On the sunlit side of Erigol, in the city of Kintana, Auceo, poet-laureate and chief archivist of the Caeliar, worked with his colleagues in the core of the city's apparatus, awaiting the response to the hail they had projected across the universe, toward a civilization from the dawn of time.

"The aperture is steady," said Eilo, his research partner. She dragged the tip of one tendril across the liquid display that shimmered before her.

Attuning his will to the gestalt, Auceo rearranged the monads that infused the air around him. The same nigh-invisible cloud of raw matter surrounded all the Caeliar's cities and was free for the taking by all who could perceive its existence.

Subatomic particles coalesced at his behest and formed a curving liquid-silver sheet that he molded until its vista of images, all as sharp as reality, filled his peripheral vision. Streams of data flooded his senses, some of it numeric, some of it visual. "Subspatial harmonics are stable," he said. "Data stream integrity is—"

Errors and failures cascaded from every system, and Auceo and the others in the Kintana locus abandoned their previous tasks to attend the emergent crisis.

"The Mantilis node is misaligned," reported Noreth, the interlink engineer.

Auceo observed the feed from Mantilis. It fell farther out of synchronization with the other loci the longer he watched.

Then a hue of alarm resonated in the gestalt, and Auceo caught only the most fleeting sense of its warning—the humans had interfered in the Great Work somehow. Before he could learn more, a discordant wail of pain and terror engulfed the gestalt and drowned out all the other voices. At the same time, a surge of chaotic signals and unchecked power spikes blasted through the apparatus network, disrupting its global frequency.

For the first time that Auceo had ever known, the gestalt was silenced by its shared pain and horror.

Far beyond the horizon from Kintana, halfway between it and Axion, the city of Feiran had just vanished in a flash of fire.

"Massive detonation on the planet's surface," reported Ensign Claudia Siguenza, the *Columbia*'s gamma-shift weapons officer. "One of the alien cities just exploded."

"Hexter, report," said Lieutenant Commander el-Rashad.

Lieutenant Russell Hexter, the alpha-shift officer of the watch who had been serving for the past few months as el-Rashad's XO, punched up a new screen of data on the science station's monitor. "The scattering fields on the surface just collapsed."

"Do we have a transporter lock yet?"

"Almost," replied the lanky, rudder-nosed, red-haired American. "The explosion kicked up a lot of interference."

From the communications station, Ensign Remy Oliveira called out, "I have a lock on Major Foyle's communicator. Relaying coordinates to the transporter room now."

El-Rashad thumbed a switch on the arm of the command chair and opened an intraship comm to the engineering deck. "Pierce! Power up the transporter, and stand by for full impulse!"

"Aye, sir," said the acting chief engineer. "We're patching in the coordinates now. Energizing in sixty seconds."

"Acknowledged, bridge out." El-Rashad closed the comm channel and said to the entire bridge crew, "Look sharp, everyone. I get the feeling this one's going to be close."

At first, Erika Hernandez thought she and the other captive officers were being visited by a swarm of fireflies. Then the gently buzzing cloud of glowing motes fused together and formed an incandescent sphere, which swiftly reshaped itself into Inyx.

The looming Caeliar scientist took a moment to assess Hernandez's predicament. Then he extended his hand, conjured a small cluster of radiant particles that descended on her and the others, and sent the glowing specks into a dizzying spin. Seconds later the tiny lights faded away to nothing, and the ropes that had held her were gone. She plucked the sock from her mouth and looked for any trace of the ropes behind her, but there wasn't so much as a loose thread or a stray fiber.

Hernandez turned to Inyx and massaged her rope-burned wrists. "Foyle and his men are planning an attack."

"Their scheme is already set in motion," Inyx said. "They have destroyed one of our cities by sabotaging a node of the apparatus, and they have seized another."

Fletcher, Valerian, and Metzger gathered at Hernandez's sides. "Can't you stop them?" Fletcher asked Inyx.

"They are threatening one of their own to keep us at bay," Inyx said. "For her sake, we are exercising caution."

Hernandez fumed to think of Foyle and his men using Thayer as a pawn. Although Thayer had betrayed her by siding with the MACOs, she was still one of Hernandez's officers. "Is she okay?"

"No," Inyx said. "She's badly wounded. She may die."

Dr. Metzger said, "Take me to her, please, I can—"

"Unacceptable," Inyx said. "Allowing you to regroup with the others is forbidden by order of the Quorum. I am here only because the gestalt saw that you four were not with the others, and we feared for your well-being."

The doctor looked ready to argue with him, but Hernandez silenced her CMO with a raised hand. "Inyx, take us to the Quorum, as fast as you can. We'll help you stop Foyle and his men before this gets any worse." She saw him bristle at the notion. "Please, Inyx. I'm begging you. Let us try to help. Bring us to the Quorum."

Inyx pondered her request for a few seconds. He turned away and bowed his head ever so slightly, then he extended his arm toward the terrace outside the penthouse and summoned a pool of quicksilver from the dark marble tiles.

Valerian stared at the shifting metallic liquid and muttered, "Talk about taking blood from a stone."

Thousands of drops of shining fluid floated upward and conglomerated a few centimeters above the terrace into a mirror-perfect, razor-thin transportation disk. Inyx walked forward, stepped onto the disk, and looked back at Hernandez.

"Events are accelerating," he said. "We should go."

Major Foyle's vision pierced the white haze of the transporter effect as he rematerialized on D Deck inside the *Columbia*.

To his left was Lieutenant Yacavino, and in front of them, with their rifles in his back, was a Caeliar scientist. As soon as the rematerialization sequence finished, Foyle prodded the lanky, bulbous-headed alien forward. "Move."

The two MACO officers and the Caeliar stepped off the small transporter pad and were met by Corporal Hossad Mottaki and Private Ndufe Otumbo. Mottaki nodded at the Caeliar and asked Foyle, "Who's your friend, sir?"

"He's not a friend, he's a prisoner," Foyle said. "Put him in the brig and keep an eye on him at *all times*. Understood?"

"Yes, sir," Mottaki said, and he aimed his rifle at the Caeliar. "Follow Private Otumbo." The corporal nodded to the private, who led them out of the transporter bay.

Standing behind the transporter control console was Ensign Katrin Gunnarsdóttir, from the ship's engineering division. The wide-eyed Icelander asked, "Are you all right, sirs? I've never had to run a transport sequence that fast before."

"We're fine," Foyle said. "Thank you, Ensign. I'm just glad you were ready when we needed you. Start scanning for the next round of transports, we don't have much time." He signaled Yacavino with a nod toward the door. "Let's get to the bridge."

As the two men headed for the exit, Gunnarsdóttir called after them, "Sirs? I'm only reading six communicator signals at the transport site. I can't get a lock on the captain, the XO, the doctor, or Ensign Valerian. Where are they?"

Foyle ignored his lieutenant's accusing stare and replied calmly, "They didn't make it. Let's get the rest of our people home as soon as we can, Ensign."

She averted her eyes and focused on her console. "Aye, sir," she said, with a vibrato of grief in her voice.

As he and Yacavino left the transporter bay, Foyle noted his lieutenant's tensed jaw and brooding glower. They didn't speak of his lie to the ensign as they moved down the corridor and entered the turbolift, and with every step they took, Foyle became more certain that they never would—because Yacavino was a good soldier, and he knew that war made its own demands.

Karl Graylock had only the vaguest idea what the machines in the Caeliar apparatus were, and he had no idea how the aliens made the system work. The Caeliar seemed to direct it by thought alone; so far as he could tell, it had no physical interface. The symbols that streamed past on the enormous liquid sheets that the Caeliar had produced in midair were gibberish to him.

He cast a wary look at the alien closest to him. "How do I know you're programming the variables I asked for?"

The scientist had to twist his upper body to look at Graylock. With their ever-frowning, impenetrable visages, the Caeliar always looked disdainful, and their hauteur always conveyed a degree of condescension. As this one answered him, however, he couldn't mistake his obvious contempt. "Shall I have the formulae translated into your primitive alphanumeric code?"

"If you wouldn't mind," Graylock said, answering sarcasm with more of the same.

On the silver sheet above and in front of him, a ripple transformed the alien script and symbols into Arabic numerals and Earth-standard mathematical expressions. It was the most beautiful thing Graylock had ever seen. It was elegant and economical, it was mathematics and physics and temporal mechanics fused into one and reimagined as poetry.

He looked around, hoping to share his wonder with one of the other members of the *Columbia* landing party—and then he saw Thayer, lying on the floor, her jumpsuit soaked with her own blood, which still seeped from the ragged and meaty mess that used to be her left foot.

A Caeliar scientist said, "It is ready."

Graylock turned back to the formula and its creators. "Then let's proceed. Open the passage."

The apparatus resonated with a deep droning, and Graylock felt it vibrating the fillings in his molars. Several liquid displays indicated sharp increases in power output, and another set its puzzle of Caeliar symbols racing. As they began to melt into a blur, he imagined he could almost see in it numbers and notations he understood. Then the image dissolved into a view of a dazzling rift in space-time, in orbit of Erigol. Looking like a speck poised on its event horizon was the *Columbia*.

"*Mein Gott*," Graylock said under his breath. "We did it." For a moment he could only stare in fascination at the temporally shifted subspace tunnel. He was unable to fathom how much raw energy was being expended to keep it open and stable. Recovering his wits, he called over his shoulder to Pembleton, "Hail the ship! The road is open."

The last time Hernandez had visited the Quorum, the Caeliar had seemed aloof and reserved. Now, as she and her loyal officers ascended with Inyx into the center of the hall's main level, the clamor in the soaring space was deafening. Scores of sliver-thin, levitating liquid screens raged with riots of color and sound. The hall was lit by thirty-six sunlike orbs, arranged in a circle high overhead, near the pyramidal chamber's peak.

None of the Caeliar spoke. Instead, they filled the air with an atonal humming punctuated by deep, vibrato drones, like the low groan of a didgeridoo she had once heard on Earth, in the silence of the deep Outback.

Fletcher stood on her right, Metzger on her left, and Valerian was close at her back. Inyx stepped a few paces ahead of Hernandez and spread his arms in a submissive gesture before the eastern tier, where the scarlet-robed *tanwa-seynorral* looked down at them. Ordemo Nordal appeared to be the only member of the Quorum who wasn't lost in the throes of a droning swoon.

"Captain Hernandez," said the first-among-equals, "you told us a short time ago that you and your kind posed no threat to us." A wave of his hand united the many liquid screens around the hall into one enormous floating wall of quicksilver. An image rippled into focus—it was a Caeliar city being consumed in a fiery flash. When the blinding glare faded, it revealed an image of the MACO-led hostage crisis taking place in another city's apparatus control center. Her cheeks burned with shame as she watched her mutinous crew coerce the Caeliar by threatening the already wounded Lieutenant Thayer. "It seems you underestimated your people's capacity for brutality."

The Caeliar leader continued, "Inyx, these savage beings were welcomed into our home at your urging. Now they have extinguished countless lives, minds that were integral to the gestalt, and they have interfered at a critical moment during the great work. Our link to the far galaxy has been corrupted."

Inyx bowed low from the waist. "Forgive me, *tanwa-seynorral*. I sought only knowledge and understanding."

"I trust that you will remember this the next time you are tempted to indulge your curiosity at the expense of our safety."

"I will," said Inyx, the top half of his body still parallel with the floor.

Hernandez stepped forward. "Can we play the blame game later, please?" Inyx straightened and looked back at her in surprise, and Ordemo seemed taken aback by her tone. "We need to act quickly if you want to stop this from getting worse."

Ordemo's contempt was bilious. "What do you propose?"

"Let me talk to them," Hernandez said. "Now."

"That seems ill-advised."

She gritted her teeth and sighed to dispel the swell of anger in her voice. "They're manipulating you," she said. "You're not used to dealing with strangers, so your people told us anything we wanted to know. My men are using that knowledge to make you help them. You don't understand us well enough to put an end to this. But I do. Stop cooperating with them and open a channel, and I'll try to end this."

Ordemo replied, "I find it difficult to believe you are so concerned with our well-being."

"You're right," Hernandez admitted. "I'm not. But I know how seriously you take your privacy, and I have a good idea what you'll have to do to my homeworld if I don't put a stop to this. I like Earth where it is. I'd rather not see it displaced."

Inyx interjected, "She sounds sincere, Ordemo."

Hernandez got the impression that Inyx's support did little to bolster her position with the *tanwa-seynorral*. Regardless, a few seconds later Ordemo turned toward the image of the ongoing hostage situation and declared, "Your people in Mantilis can hear you now, Captain."

She surveyed the scene, noted that Foyle and Yacavino were both absent, and surmised that the two MACO officers had likely already beamed up to the *Columbia*. Technically, Graylock was the ranking officer on the scene, but the one in charge was obviously Sergeant Pembleton. He was in command of the MACOs, and the one with whom she would have to negotiate. "Sergeant," she snapped, "this is Captain Hernandez. Stand down."

Pembleton looked up and around until he obviously found a screen near him that was displaying the captain's face. *"I'm sorry, Captain. I can't do that."*

"Yes you can, Pembleton. Ask your men if you're still in contact with the *Columbia*." She waited while he looked to Private Mazzetti, who fiddled for several seconds with a communicator, then shook his head and frowned at his sergeant. Hernandez continued, "The scattering field's back up, isn't it? Take my word for it, Sergeant: The *Columbia*'s not breaking orbit today. You've failed. Tell Private Steinhauer to let Thayer go."

He seemed ready to falter, just for a moment, and then he lifted his weapon to his shoulder and pointed it at Thayer. *"No, Captain. Major Foyle's orders were clear."*

"What did the major order you to do?" she asked.

*"Whatever I had to,"* Pembleton said. *"As long as I secured the Caeliar's cooperation."*

Hernandez found it telling that Pembleton was reluctant to elaborate on Foyle's orders. She suspected that part of him regretted what he was doing. His hesitation and general unease told her he was rationalizing his way through this mess. "So," she said, "you were prepared to wound Thayer. But are you ready to kill her? Because she's bleeding out, you know. A wound like that's fatal if it's not treated."

*"We'll treat her as soon as we reach the ship,"* he said.

"You're not going to reach the ship, Sergeant. And neither is she. So you might as well kill her now, and let her death be quick instead of drawing it out like this."

Ordemo interrupted, indignant, "Captain, we cannot permit your sergeant to—" A vicious glare from Hernandez quelled his protest, and the *tanwa-seynorral* cast a long, silent look at Inyx, who responded with his own icy stare of reproof.

Pembleton intensified his focus on Thayer as he said to Hernandez, *"Don't bother trying to bluff me, Captain. I'll do what I have to. I'm going home. I'm gonna see my boys again."*

"No, you're not, Gage. I've asked the Caeliar not to cooperate with your demands. But I can't stand here and watch Kiona's life drain away like this. Let me make it easier for you. This is an order, Sergeant: Kill Lieutenant Thayer."

He looked perplexed. *"Sir?"*

"You heard me, Sergeant. Kill her. When she's dead, you've got nothing left. You can't kill Graylock, you need him to help the ship make the trip through the subspace tunnel. I don't think you and your men are ready to start killing one another. That makes Kiona your only pawn. So let's just end the game here, shall we? Kill her." Hernandez waited a few seconds. When, by the end of that interval, Pembleton had done nothing, she feigned disgust. "Fine, pass the buck, Sergeant. Private Steinhauer: Cut the lieutenant's throat. That's an order."

Only now did Hernandez notice that the din of the Caeliar had faded to silence and that a tense silence hung over the Quorum as everyone waited for the reaction to her stratagem.

Steinhauer removed the blade from Thayer's throat, dropped it on the ground, and sank to a sitting position on the floor. Without him to hold her torso upright, Thayer collapsed onto her back. Pembleton, sensing the surrender of his men, lowered his weapon and pulled his hand over his face, wiping away sweat, grime, and fatigue. In the background, Graylock leaned against one of the machines and covered his eyes with one hand.

"Private Mazzetti," Hernandez said, "get a first-aid kit and start treating Lieutenant Thayer's wound. We'll get the doctor to you as soon as we can."

*"Aye, Captain,"* said Mazzetti, who took off his backpack, opened it, and removed the first-aid kit. He jogged over to Thayer and started taking steps to stanch her bleeding.

One of the Caeliar scientists in the Mantilis facility neared the comm interlink and addressed the Quorum. *"It will take time to dissolve the temporally shifted subspace aperture,"* she said. *"The Earth ship should be restrained until the phenomenon has been disincorporated."*

"Understood," said Ordemo. "Proceed with haste, Sedín." The massive silver screen vanished, leaving a faint mist that lingered in the air like a rain shadow. Ordemo looked down at the visitors and said, "Inyx, see the humans' physician to their wounded comrade in Mantilis."

Hernandez cut in, "One thing first: Let me talk to my ship. I need to have a few words with Major Foyle."

Foyle didn't seem to care that he was making a scene on the bridge. "I'm not interested in excuses, I want answers!"

Lieutenant Commander el-Rashad, the nominal commanding officer of the ship, shoved past Foyle on his way to the science console, which had once been his regular station. Punching buttons to skim several screens of data, he said, "If I had answers for you, Major, I'd give them to you. But all we know right now is that the scattering field is back, and we can't get a transporter lock."

"What about the subspace tunnel?" Foyle asked, pointing at the image of the dazzling passage on the main viewer.

"Stable," said el-Rashad, who lurched away from the science console to join Ensign Oliveira at the communications panel. "For now." To the ensign he added, "Patch in the boosters. Maybe there's a lingering frequency gap we can exploit."

The major stayed close behind el-Rashad, who was quickly tiring of his irate shadow. "We should go now," Foyle said, "while we still can."

"That wasn't the plan," el-Rashad said. "We've already lost the captain and the XO, I'm not leaving any more of our—" He was interrupted by the beeping alert of an incoming comm signal. "Oliveira, report," he said, moving back to the command chair.

Oliveira made some quick adjustments on her panel. "Signal from the planet's surface, sir."

"On-screen."

The image of the subspace tunnel was replaced by the faces of Captain Hernandez and Commander Fletcher, who stood with Ensign Valerian and Dr. Metzger inside a huge, ornate chamber. *"Mister el-Rashad,"* said Hernandez. *"Nice to see you again."*

"Likewise, Captain," el-Rashad said, confused at seeing his commanding officer and XO alive after receiving Foyle's report of their demise. "What are your orders?"

*"Don't take the ship into the subspace tunnel, Kalil. If you do, the Caeliar will have to retaliate against Earth, and I can't allow that. Understood?"*

El-Rashad nodded. "Aye, Captain." He felt the two MACO

officers on the bridge staring at him, their malice a tangible presence. "Captain," he began, uncertain how to phrase the next part of his report, "Major Foyle . . ."

*"Ah, yes,"* said Hernandez. *"Major Foyle. He and Lieutenant Yacavino are charged with mutiny, conspiracy, assault on a superior officer, assault on flight officers, and the attempted murder of Lieutenant Kiona Thayer. And tack on disobeying the orders of a superior officer."*

"Aye, sir," said el-Rashad, his resolve galvanized by the captain's surety. He turned to his acting XO. "Mister Hexter, place Major Foyle and Lieutenant Yacavino under arrest. Ensign Siguenza, help the XO take our prisoners to the brig." Siguenza drew her sidearm and faced Foyle and Yacavino. It was a testament to the two MACOs' respect for military tradition that they showed no sign of resistance. Both men surrendered their sidearms with care to the XO, who directed them with a nod into a waiting turbolift.

After they had departed, el-Rashad felt a moment's regret that the plan to go home and erase the *Columbia*'s lost years would have to be abandoned. Then he cast aside those selfish desires and reminded himself that this was the captain's call to make, not his. The *Columbia* was her ship; he was just watching over it until she came back. "Sir?" he said, easing into his question. "We're running low on provisions up here. Is there any chance the Caeliar might let us settle on the planet's surface if we stay out of their cities?"

Hernandez sighed. *"I don't know, Kalil. That's a ver—"*

The signal went dead.

Then something hammered the *Columbia,* and el-Rashad realized that the ship's near-empty galley had just become the least of his problems.

Hernandez had sensed the reduction in tension among the Caeliar in the Quorum hall as soon as Pembleton had lowered his weapon. She hoped that her role in ending the crisis might persuade the Caeliar not to take punitive measures against her ship or against Earth for the crimes that Foyle and the others had committed.

Her thoughts drifted while she watched el-Rashad direct the

officers on the *Columbia* to arrest Foyle and Yacavino. *How am I supposed to make amends for this? How do I apologize for the deaths of millions?*

She was pulled back into the present moment by el-Rashad asking, *"Sir?"* She blinked once and looked up at his larger-than-life image on the liquid wall high above her. *"We're running low on provisions up here,"* he said. *"Is there any chance the Caeliar might let us settle on the planet's surface if we stay out of their cities?"*

*After what we just did?* She sighed. "I don't know Kalil. That's a very good—"

A thunderclap rent the air, the glowing orbs at the top of the chamber were extinguished, and a flash reddened the night sky beyond the crystal-walled pyramid. Tremors shook the floor under Hernandez's feet and knocked her down. The other *Columbia* officers fell beside her. The liquid screens evaporated and rained down like stardust. Inyx and the other Caeliar levitated upward, and then Hernandez saw why—the tiers on which they had been seated were collapsing, shearing away from the crystal walls of the pyramid with sharp splintering sounds.

An earsplitting crack made Hernandez wince, and when she opened her eyes again, a ragged fissure had bifurcated the magnificent, fractal starburst pattern that adorned the floor.

Over the steady rumble of an earthquake, she called out, "Inyx! What's happening?"

Despite the tumult erupting around them, Inyx's voice resonated clearly, as if it were amplified. "It's a feedback pulse from the galaxy we contacted," he said. "A million times more powerful than we expected."

The reddish glow that suffused the chamber brightened. Outside the pyramid, the night sky had become almost bloodred.

Valerian shouted to Inyx, "A feedback pulse did this?"

"It disrupted all our technology, including our deep-solar energy taps," Inyx said. "The gestalt is trying to contain the damage, but the signal appears to have been crafted with malicious intent. Please excuse me while I commune with the gestalt." Inyx turned away and stared into space with the other Caeliar. Outside, lightning blazed across the sky. Then Inyx looked back at Hernandez and her officers. "We are unable to contain the reaction. We have very little time left."

Fletcher traded a terrified look with the captain and asked their Caeliar liaison, "Until what?"

"Until this star system is destroyed."

Karl Graylock stared in anger and disbelief at the Caeliar scientist and asked, "Are you serious?"

"The feedback pulse from the extragalactic signal has caused a chain reaction in our solar and geothermal taps," the alien replied. "The core of our star has been pushed past its supercritical point. Its detonation is imminent, and the solar mass ejection will be propelled at faster-than-light velocity by a subspatial shock wave. At the same time, explosive conditions are being generated inside Erigol's core. The annihilation of this planet will be all but instantaneous."

Waving his hands at the darkened and sparking equipment in the sprawling laboratory, Graylock protested, "Can't you stop it?" A violent shuddering motion was followed by a low, metallic groan from the structures around them.

"It is too late to save Erigol," the alien said. "But if you will permit us to work without interruptions, maybe we can save this city—and you, as well."

Graylock stepped away from the machines and said, "Do whatever you have to do." As the Caeliar started moving atoms around by the power of thought, and another temblor rattled the apparatus control room, Graylock flipped open his communicator, in the hope that the impending calamity had once again disabled the scattering field. "Graylock to *Columbia*. Come in, *Columbia*."

Static and squalls of noise half buried el-Rashad's reply. *"Go ahead, Karl,"* said the second officer.

The chief engineer spoke loudly and slowly to improve the likelihood of his message being understood through the interference. "Kalil, the star and the planet are going to explode. Break orbit now! Get the hell out of here!"

*"What about the landing party?"*

"Forget us," Graylock said. "Save the ship!"

The channel was quiet for a few seconds before el-Rashad said, *"Good luck, Karl. To all of you."*

*"Danke,"* Graylock said. Then he lowered his voice, pressed

the communicator close to his mouth, and covered it with his free hand. "Kalil, the solar shock wave will be FTL. You can't escape on impulse. You know what you have to do. Graylock out."

He flipped the communicator closed and prayed that his warning to the *Columbia* had been delivered in time.

Hernandez was just starting to regain her footing when the violent shaking of Axion became a steady vibration, and then her sense of balance abandoned her and she tumbled backward. She expected to strike the floor and stop there, but she kept on rolling, tumbling sideways, realizing only after several disorienting seconds that the floor inside the Quorum hall was sitting at a steep angle and that she and her officers were being dragged across it by gravity.

All of this went unnoticed by the levitating Caeliar, who maintained their positions relative to the pyramid's walls.

Fletcher was the first of the group to slam into the pile of wreckage from one of the collapsed seating tiers. Hernandez plowed into the broken stone and metal behind her first officer, with Valerian and Dr. Metzger making impact seconds later. It was Fletcher who asked, "What the hell? Did the city fall over?"

"I don't think so," Hernandez said as she watched forks of lightning dance across the dark crystal walls of the pyramid, which was engulfed in glowing red mist. "I'd say we took off."

The four women clung to the apparently stationary wreckage as the ruddy clouds outside the pyramid cleared and revealed the broad sweep of the planet, from low orbit. Along the horizon, other Caeliar cities were rising from the surface, which was aglow with volcanic eruptions and wreathed in ashen smoke.

Above the cerulean halo of the thinning atmosphere, Erigol's once-golden star had turned bloodred and expanded to frightening proportions. In higher orbit of the dying world, numerous tunnels of light were forming, and when Hernandez looked to the apex of the Quorum hall's pyramid, she saw another such passage directly ahead of Axion. They closed the distance to it in moments—then they stopped, hovering at its aperture.

Valerian was trembling and wide-eyed as she muttered, "What are they waiting for?"

Inyx was far away, but his voice was close. "We are trying to purge the equations that your engineer forced us to put into the system. The damage caused by the feedback pulse is slowing our efforts, but it is not safe to enter the passage until we have stabilized the phenomena."

Fletcher pointed at the distant cities hanging in space. "Why aren't they leaving?"

"All our cities are linked nodes in the apparatus," Inyx said. "An error in one is an error for all. Harmony must be restored before we can proceed."

The star was enlarging at a rate swift enough to be seen by the naked eye. "I don't think we have that much time," she said.

Shaking her head in denial, Valerian sounded hysterical. "It's not real, it can't be real. How can it be real?"

Dr. Metzger snapped, "What're you talking about?"

"The sun," Valerian said. "The sun. We shouldn't be able to see the effects yet. The inflation just started, it's nine light-minutes away, we can't really see it, it's not real. . . ."

"Subspatial lensing," Inyx's voice explained. "The same phenomenon that will carry the supernova's eruption to us is telegraphing its effects."

His answer didn't seem to placate Valerian, who buried her face in her hands. Hernandez watched the red star dimming and swelling, and she felt her own anxiety swelling in equal measure. "Inyx, how much longer?" When he didn't answer right away, she hollered at his distant form, "How long?"

"Not long," he said, "but too long, all the same."

"Fifteen seconds to the subspace tunnel," said helmsman Brynn Mealia.

El-Rashad watched the coruscating phenomenon grow larger on the main viewer as the *Columbia* broke free of the Caeliar's tractor beam and accelerated toward freedom. The captain had told him not to do this, but she had been motivated by a fear of retaliation by the Caeliar against Earth. Based on the cataclysm that was unfolding in front of him, however, he doubted the aliens would be in a position to take their revenge, or that they would even notice the *Columbia*'s departure.

"Commander," said Ensign Diane Atlagic, who had taken over for Siguenza at tactical, "none of the Caeliar city-ships are entering the subspace tunnels. They're all holding station at the apertures." He looked back at the dark-haired Croatian woman, who added, "Maybe they know something we don't, sir."

He had only seconds to decide—proceed or hold? *If the Caeliar don't trust the passages enough to use them, do I really want to take us in there?* "Helm, all stop!"

"Answering all stop," Mealia said.

"Oliveira," el-Rashad said, "hail the Caeliar capital-ship, find out why they—" The main viewer whited out for a fraction of a second, and when it reset, Erigol was breaking apart like a marble struck by a hammer. A subspatial shock wave blasted scores of city-ships into vapors, and the subspace passages dissolved in its wake. "Helm! Go!"

Mealia punched in full impulse power, and the *Columbia* hurtled forward into the breach.

The ship pitched and rolled the moment it was inside the subspace tunnel. Darkness blinked in and out on the bridge as consoles erupted into flames and sparks showered down from overloaded relays in the overhead. A brutal jolt hurled el-Rashad from the command chair and pinned Mealia to the helm.

El-Rashad clawed his way across the deck, back to the chair, and jabbed the comlink to engineering. "Bridge to . . ."

The next word refused to leave his throat. A dry rasp rattled in his chest. His mouth felt as if it were carved from sand, and a burning sensation filled his eyes, his sinuses, and then every cell in his body.

Everyone on the bridge was in agony, just as he was. He saw their faces contort in horror, watched them fall to the deck beside him. They were all going through the motions of fighting for air, even though their bodies no longer had the ability to inhale. He felt his thoughts breaking down as his brain boiled and burned.

Mealia was the first to vanish in a cloud of ash, and Atlagic disintegrated into gray powder. Oliveira reached out to el-Rashad for one last moment of human contact before oblivion. He bridged the distance with his outstretched hand, but as she took it in hers, he couldn't feel it.

Then both their hands crumbled to dust, and a few seconds later he felt absolutely nothing at all.

Planetary debris slammed into the spires of the Caeliar city-ship Mantilis and pulverized swaths of its platinum-white majesty.

Behind it, Erigol was an expanding jumble of rocks and fire and gases, and a subspatial shock wave shattered dozens of city-ships in seconds.

Karl Graylock watched the mayhem on one of the Caeliar's liquid screens as the alien scientists tinkered with numbers and symbols and generally acted as if nothing was wrong. The chief engineer grabbed one of them, spun the looming freak around to face him, and shouted, "Go! Go now! Or we're all dead!"

"Temporal balance has not—"

Graylock shook him silent. "If you don't go, you're *killing* us! Go, *scheisskopf*! *Schnell*!"

The scientist became as insubstantial as a ghost and slipped from Graylock's grasp. A moment later he resolidified in front of a large console of glowing liquid surfaces, waved his tendril-like fingers over it, and declared, "It is done."

On the liquid screen, the images of the cataclysm were replaced by the swirling, blue-white chaos of the subspace tunnel. A slight tremble in the floor made Graylock wonder if they would face turbulence inside the passage.

Then a savage quaking gripped the lab, and the liquid screen showed him mighty towers being shorn from the city-ship and cast away into the uncharted realms of subspace, flotsam in the ether beyond space and time.

"*Mein Gott*," Graylock said as the buildings were swallowed in the subspace vortex. "Don't you have shields?"

The Caeliar scientist didn't look at him as he replied. "They failed when we entered the passage, as I feared."

The chief engineer was aghast. "Are you saying we're exposed?"

"No," the Caeliar answered. "This lab is a protected environment. It will protect you from the passage's effects."

"But what about the rest of the city?"

All the Caeliar in the vast facility turned and faced him with their permanent frowns and cold, metallic-hued eyes. In an ominous tone, the one closest to him said, "The rest of the city is dead, Karl Graylock."

The city-ship Axion hurtled through the subspace passage, buffeted by forces more powerful than Erika Hernandez could imagine. She hung on to a bent piece of wreckage from the tier. Veronica Fletcher hung on to Hernandez's legs, and Valerian and Metzger were both clinging to Fletcher.

Hernandez and her officers all had watched in terrified silence as Erigol's sun had exploded and the shock wave, propelled toward the planet at faster-than-light speed, had atomized scores of Caeliar cities hovering in orbit of the broken world. She had seen only two of the other cities escape destruction, by entering their swirling subspace passages scant moments before the shock wave dispersed their apertures. Then Axion had raced into its own subspatial rift and left its shattered legacy behind.

Outside the dark-tinted pyramid of the Quorum hall, lashes of blue-white energy tore away chunks of the city's periphery. Hernandez winced as massive slabs of metal and landscaping were ripped from its edges and impacts flared against its protective energy shield, which appeared to be contracting. As the field's outer edge shrank below the tips of Axion's loftiest spires, the towers were rapidly shorn away and scattered into the blinding swirl of chaos that surrounded them.

Then the whirling brightness fell away and darkness returned. Hernandez felt the strain of gravitational forces release its hold on her, and Fletcher let go of her leg. Looking back, the captain saw her people all safe on the floor, looking scuffed and mussed but generally unhurt. The crystal walls of the pyramidal chamber lightened and became transparent. Once her eyes adjusted, Hernandez saw the vista of stars. Axion had returned to normal space-time.

Fletcher was the first to get up, and she offered a hand to Hernandez. The XO asked, "Where are we?"

"No idea."

Valerian and Metzger were slow getting to their feet. The doctor rolled out a crick in her neck while the young Scotswoman brushed the dust off her blue jumpsuit uniform.

"I'm just glad we're still alive," Metzger said.

Valerian added, "Aye, I'll second that."

Above them, the hundreds of Caeliar, who had hovered undisturbed by the rougher moments of their subspace transit, floated down to the main level. They looked exhausted. As they descended closer, she realized that they actually appeared to be smaller than they had been before. Their bodies were emaciated and shorter, and the colors of their skin were blanched and dull. Once they touched down on the main level of the hall, the group quietly dispersed, wandering dazed like refugees from a war zone, singly and in small clusters. A few of them clung to one another for mutual support.

A lone figure emerged from the erratic, spreading crowd. Inyx limped in heavy steps toward the four humans, looking humbled and enervated. "Are any of you hurt?"

"No, Inyx," said Hernandez. "Thank you." Observing the slow, weary sway of his torso with every breath he drew and released, she asked, "How about you? Are you all right?"

"We are weakened. Much power was lost with our fallen cities. And the loss of minds has been a blow to the gestalt."

Fletcher said, "Looks like the city took a lot of damage."

"Nothing that can't be repaired," Inyx said, but the sorrow in his voice betrayed his optimistic words as a lie.

Valerian cast a nervous glance at the stars. "Inyx, how far did we travel?"

"In space, not far," Inyx said. "A few thousand light-years, by your species' reckoning."

His choice of words alarmed Hernandez. "*In space*?"

"Because your engineer's equations had polluted the neural network of the apparatus, the subspace tunnels we created were unstable. The induced detonation of our star introduced a cascade of high-energy tachyons that—"

Hernandez held up her hand. "No details, Inyx, just the summary. Where are we?"

"We are approximately half the distance from the galaxy's core to its rim . . . and, using your chronological units, we have been displaced six hundred fifty years, seven months, eight days, eleven hours, and forty-three minutes into what was the past . . . and is now our present."

Shocked reactions were volleyed between the four *Columbia* officers. It took Hernandez a moment to process the news. "Well, we can't stay here," she said to Inyx. "We have to go back."

"That will not be possible," Inyx said. "Not yet."

Commander Fletcher snapped, "Why the hell not? The subspace tunnel brought us here, it can take us back the way we came."

"It cannot," Inyx said. "Because it traversed time as well as space, it was extremely unstable. Only a focused effort by the gestalt was able to prevent its collapse before we reached its far terminus. As soon as we returned to normal space, it collapsed behind us. It no longer exists."

Ensign Valerian's temper flared, as well. "So? Moving forward in time can't be that hard! We skipped twelve years in two months on the *Columbia*. You lot must have somethin' better, what with all your fancy tricks and gadgets."

"It is not a matter of ability," Inyx said. "It is a matter of law. For as long as we have known the methods of time travel, it has been strictly controlled by the Quorum. Careless jaunts either forward or backward in time carry the potential for great harm. It was permitted in this instance only to save *your* lives. Had you not been among us, we would have let ourselves perish rather than risk the integrity of the time line."

Dr. Metzger inquired, "So, what happens now?"

"First, we heal," Inyx said. "Then we mask our presence, to avoid anachronistic encounters. When that is done, we will analyze the causes of our world's destruction, and we will attempt to determine if our presence in this earlier phase of the time line is an error that needs to be corrected."

"And what about us?" asked Hernandez. "We're just supposed to sit quietly while you do all this?"

"Yes," Inyx said. "We will not skip forward in time unless we are certain that doing so is necessary, nor can we permit you to leave or return to your time with knowledge of us. All we can do now is seek the truth and go forward."

As usual, Hernandez realized, there was little point in arguing with the Caeliar. Then another worrisome thought occurred to her. She asked Inyx, "Is the Quorum going to blame us for what happened at Erigol?"

The delay in his answer was both telling and troubling.

"That remains to be seen."

Sergeant Gage Pembleton's only clue that the city-ship of Mantilis had exited the subspace tunnel was that the blinding flurry pictured on the lab's liquid screens had changed from blue and white to red and black. The turbulence was the same.

Pembleton and the other humans were huddled under the ramp they had descended during their ultimately futile assault on the laboratory. Mazzetti and Steinhauer were devoting their full attention to treating Thayer's wounded foot and keeping her sedated. Crichlow hid in the shadows, wrapped in a fetal curl around his rifle while he prayed. Graylock stayed near the edge of the ramp and observed the silent Caeliar scientists at work.

Tapping the engineer's shoulder, Pembleton asked, "What's going on?"

"My professional opinion? We're crashing."

The energy sphere in the center of the control facility had dimmed greatly during the brief journey through the subspace passage, and the current crisis wasn't making it any better. Pembleton tried to edge past Graylock. "I'm asking them."

The engineer grabbed his arm. "Let them work."

He dislodged Graylock's hand with a brusque shake of his arm and walked away, toward the nearest Caeliar. "Hey," he called out. "What's your name?"

"Lerxst," the alien replied.

"Hi, Lerxst. We'd like to know what's happening."

The scientist didn't look at Pembleton as he replied, "Your friend Karl Graylock is correct. We're crashing."

"Where, exactly?"

A rectangle of metallic liquid assembled itself in front of Pembleton and rippled to life. It showed a world that, despite being half-obscured by the curtain of fire around the Caeliar's city, appeared Earth-like—but which, based on the shapes of its continents, definitely was not Earth. "There," said Lerxst.

Pembleton began to understand why Graylock had tired so quickly of talking with the aliens. "Does 'there' have a name?"

"None that is known to us. If it's inhabited by sentient forms, they might have one they prefer."

Now he was annoyed. "I don't suppose you could give me a sense of where we are relative to, for instance, *Earth*?"

"We are fifty-eight thousand, nine hundred sixty-one light-years from your world."

Pembleton heaved a disgruntled sigh. *So much for a shortcut home.*

On the screen, plumes of superheated gas from Mantilis's atmospheric entry blasted vast areas of the city-ship's surface bare. Gone were the spires, the plazas of art and trees, the reflecting pools and footbridges and elegant architectural flourishes. The city resembled little more than a metallic disk with molten edges and a million ragged scars.

"Graylock says you told him the rest of the city was dead."

"You six and we twelve are all that remain," Lerxst said, apparently without either regret or bitterness.

Pembleton was surprised by the scientist's sangfroid in the face of tragedy. "Aren't you upset about this?"

"Do not mistake stoicism for an absence of emotion," Lerxst said. "Our anger and sorrow are greater than you can imagine, but the sacrifice of our people outside the apparatus was a choice, not an accident."

"What does that mean?" Pembleton asked.

Lerxst said, "It means that we will not destroy sentient life, or allow sentient life to be destroyed, by action or omission. Not for revenge, not in self-defense. We do not kill."

"Are you telling me that millions of Caeliar agreed to let themselves die to save the six of us?"

"Correct," Lerxst said. "Though making the passage would cost them their lives and violate our people's laws against time travel, the gestalt concurred that—"

"Time travel?" Pembleton interrupted. "Forward or back?"

"Backward," Lerxst said.

"How far?"

Lerxst told him the numbers, in years, months, and days.

Pembleton staggered back to the others in a daze. Liquid screens throughout the vast circular facility showed the flattened disk of the city-ship. It was aglow within a nimbus of fire and slicing through the atmosphere, toward a rocky, icy expanse of arctic tundra whose details were coming into focus all too quickly for comfort. The sergeant slumped to the floor next to the chief engineer, who asked, "What'd they say?"

"They said we're gonna crash."

The rippling images of the horizon flattened and fell away, and then the liquid screens went dark and scattered. Pembleton felt the ground rising to meet them. It would be a disastrous crash landing, and their chances of survival were slim. But even if they did live through planet fall, it no longer mattered.

He closed his eyes but didn't bother to pray—because it was much too late for that now.

# 2381

## 21

Ezri Dax emerged, bleary-eyed and aching-limbed, from her ready room shortly after 0200 and was surprised to see many of her senior personnel still at work on the bridge.

Sam Bowers was settled in the command chair as if he had been melted into it. The steaming beverage he held in one hand while perusing a report on a padd seemed to have done little to reinvigorate him. He looked up at Dax as she entered and was half a second slower than usual snapping to attention.

"Captain on the deck!" he announced as he bolted to his feet—and spilled his hot drink across the back of his wrist. Swearing under his breath, he dropped the padd on the chair and swapped the mug into his unburned hand. He waved his scorched appendage in the air to cool it as Dax approached and smiled.

"As you were," she said to the bridge crew. Joining Sam at her chair, she added sotto voce, "Guess how much I want to make a joke at your expense right now."

"I can only imagine, Captain." He wiped the liquid from the back of his hand onto the pant leg of his uniform. "I'm required by regulations to remind you that we're now ten hours overdue for departure, as per our last orders from Starfleet Command."

Dax fought the urge to roll her eyes and said simply, "I'll note your reminder in my log, Sam, thank you." She stepped past him toward the security chief's station, where Lieutenant Kedair was busy reviewing a steady stream of incoming data and reports. Catching the Takaran woman's eye, Dax said, "Give me an update on the manhunt, Lieutenant."

Kedair's hands continued to manipulate data on her console as she replied, "We've finished two full sweeps of the ship, Captain. So far, no intruder." She called up Dr. Tarses's forensic reports on one side of her station. "No new leads on the cause of death, and no progress devising a defense against it—whatever it turns out to be."

"That's not very encouraging, Lonnoc."

"No, Captain, it's not. But I'd still like your permission to keep the ship in lockdown until we complete a third sweep of all compartments. We've switched to some fairly exotic detection methods this time around. It's a long shot, but I want to be as thorough as possible."

She admired Kedair's refusal to admit defeat. "All right. Let's hope the third time's the charm." Kedair nodded her understanding and resumed her work as Dax moved on to the aft station, where Gruhn Helkara and Mikaela Leishman were immersed in conversation about their wall of schematics and sensor data. "How's *your* search going?" she asked the duo.

"We haven't found the subspace tunnel yet," Helkara said. "But not for lack of trying. We've been through the full range of likely triggers, and now we're trying the unlikely ones."

"Sounds like a familiar refrain around here tonight," Dax said. She nodded at a screen showing a diagram of the *Aventine*'s shield emitter network. "What about the hyperphasic radiation inside the anomaly?"

"*That* we solved," Leishman said. "If we ever find this thing, we'll be ready to try it out."

Dax smiled at the pair. "Finally, some good news. Keep at it, and let me know when we get a fix on the phenomenon."

"Will do, Captain," Leishman said. She and the Zakdorn science officer returned to their hushed conference about exotic particles and technological arcana.

The captain continued her circuit of the bridge, past the relief conn and ops officers, who were occupying their time at the starboard duty stations compiling data for Kedair's manhunt and tagging sensor reports for Helkara and Leishman. Ensign Erin Constantino, a human woman from Deneva, manned the conn, while Lieutenant Mirren was on her second shift of the day at ops.

Stopping beside the ops console, Dax peeked at the display panel. Mirren looked up. She sounded anxious. "Yes, Captain?"

"Just curious," Dax said. "Have we learned anything new from the *Columbia*'s databanks?"

"Maybe," Mirren said. "Most of it is log fragments and snippets of internal comm chatter, but there was one interesting bit." She called up a recovered data file on her console. "The *Columbia*'s transporter had a redundant activity log from the main computer. It shows four outgoing transports, for twelve people. The first six beamed down at 1100, and the rest followed at 1300. The time stamp on those transports is roughly sixty-three days after the Romulan ambush." Mirren called up the last line in the log. "There's only one beam-up sequence, for three subjects, about six months later—less than twelve minutes before the ship's flight logs put it inside the subspace tunnel."

Intrigued, Dax asked, "What's the connection?"

"No idea," Mirren said. "But I have to believe it's more than a coincidence—and it accounts for nine of the ten missing personnel. Or maybe for all ten, if we assume that one of the three who beamed up wasn't a *Columbia* crew member."

Dax nodded. "Okay. What if something beamed up with two of *Columbia*'s people? Could that something have killed Komer and Yott inside the wreck and the crewman in the shuttlebay?"

"Two hundred years later?" Mirren said, incredulous. "It would have to be something *really* long-lived if it—"

An explosion thundered belowdecks and resonated through the bulkheads. The *Aventine* pitched wildly and knocked Dax off balance. Then the ship's inertial dampers reset themselves, and the heaving and rolling of the deck ceased. "Report!" Dax said.

Kedair replied from tactical, "Explosion in Shuttlebay One! Hull breach and explosive decompression in the bay."

"That bay was sealed after Ylacam's body was found," Bowers said. He joined Dax at ops. "Mirren, what the hell happened?"

Mirren reconfigured her console to assess the damage and review internal sensor logs of the explosion. "It was the runabout," she said, surprised. "The *Seine* destroyed the bay doors with a pair of microtorpedoes." She looked back at the captain and XO. "It's leaving the bay, Captain."

Looking back at Kedair, Dax said, "I want to know who's in that ship—*now.*"

"No life signs inside the runabout," Kedair said. "But I'm picking up some wild energy readings."

Mirren added, "It's accelerating to full impulse and breaking orbit, bearing three eight mark seven."

"Pursuit course," Bowers said. "Full impulse."

"Aye, sir," Constantino replied. The *Aventine* veered away from the planet and fell in behind the fleeing runabout.

Helkara bounded away from the aft station. His face was bright with excitement. "Captain! There's a massive energy buildup in the runabout's sensor array. I think it's been reconfigured to emit a soliton pulse!"

"Locking phasers," Kedair said, as if by reflex.

"Hold fire," Dax said, and then she turned to watch the runabout on the main viewer. A moment later a shimmering beam lanced out in front of the tiny ship and seemed to cut through space-time like a scalpel. The slash through reality parted and revealed a tornado-like passage of coruscating blue light.

The runabout accelerated toward the subspace tunnel.

"Captain," Bowers said, "we can catch it with a tractor beam before it crosses the aperture."

Dax shook her head. "No, Sam. Whatever's on the runabout, I think it could've killed us all if it meant to. But that's not what it wanted. I think it came here from the other side of that passage. Now it's on a journey, and I want to see where it leads. Lieutenant Kedair, raise shields. Helm, take us into the subspace tunnel, full impulse."

Seconds later, the *Aventine* plunged into the blinding maelstrom, close behind the fugitive runabout. Erratic fluctuations in the inertial damping system had Dax hanging on to the edge of the ops console for balance, while Bowers clung to the flight controller's chair to keep himself upright. Twenty seconds into the passage, Dax directed a questioning look back at Kedair, who reported in a calm voice, "Shields holding."

Less than a minute later, a pulsing circle of midnight blue appeared ahead of the *Aventine,* the darkness at the end of the tunnel of light. The runabout shot out of the subspace passage, and the *Vesta*-class explorer followed it back into normal space-time moments later. The two ships were completely engulfed in a deep-indigo stain, a rich cloud of violet supernova debris that was, depending on where one looked, steeped in shadow or lit from within.

Dax stared at the cerulean majesty on the main viewer as she said, "Position report."

"Beta Quadrant," Constantino replied. She checked her readings while stealing glances at the vista on the screen. "Near supernova remnant FGC-SR37–758, in the center of the Azure Nebula."

Kedair looked up from the tactical console. "Captain, the

runabout is reducing speed." She punched in a command on her console and added, "Its power levels are dropping fast."

"Helm, hold station at ten thousand kilometers," Dax said. "Mirren, put a tractor beam on it."

On the main viewer, a golden beam from the *Aventine* snared the runabout, which made no effort to evade it or break free. "Tractor beam locked, Captain," Mirren said. "Radiation levels inside the runabout are dissipating rapidly."

"It didn't even put up a fight," Bowers said. He lifted one eyebrow to express his suspicion as he said to Dax, "After all that, it's just giving up?"

"I don't know, Sam," Dax said. "That's what I'm beaming over there to find out."

The XO raised both eyebrows, bringing out the worry lines on his forehead. "With all respect, Captain, you should let a boarding team secure the runabout before you beam over."

She headed for the turbolift. "What? And miss all the fun? Not a chance." To Kedair she added, "Lieutenant, have two security officers meet me in transporter room one." The security chief nodded to Dax as she passed by. The turbolift door sighed open ahead of Dax, who stepped in and turned back to face the bridge. She leaned forward, just enough to poke her head out at Bowers. "Well? Are you coming or not?"

"Do I have a choice?"

"Not really, no."

Bowers walked to the turbolift, issuing orders along the way. "Mirren, watch the runabout and make sure the transporter room keeps a lock on the away team. Kedair, lower the shields *only* for transport. Mister Helkara, you have the bridge."

Helkara crossed to the command chair as Bowers stepped into the turbolift with Dax, who directed the computer, "Deck Four."

As soon as the doors closed and the lift began its descent, he said, "I'm required by regulations to remind you, Captain, that this is a really stupid thing to do."

"Sam, what's the point of being a captain if I don't get to do something stupid once in a while?"

His mien shifted from annoyed to bemused to stymied in just a few seconds. Then he frowned, sighed, and replied, "Touché."

\* \* \*

Shapes emerged beyond the white haze of the transporter beam, and Dax recognized the familiar close quarters of a runabout's empty aft compartment.

The transporter effect faded. She looked around to confirm that the rest of the away team was with her. Bowers was at her right side, and behind them were Ensign Altoss and Lieutenant Loskywitz from the ship's security detail.

Loskywitz and Altoss charged their phaser rifles. Bowers checked his tricorder and pointed the pair forward, toward the cockpit. The human lieutenant took point, with his rifle braced against his shoulder, moving in smooth, easy strides that kept his aim steady. His female Efrosian partner stepped to the control panel for the aft portal and, on Bowers's signal, opened the door to the middle compartment of the small ship. Then she aimed her rifle around the corner and covered Loskywitz as he stole forward, his body pressed close to the port bulkhead in the short connecting passageway.

Dax started to follow them, but she stopped when she felt Bowers's hand on her arm. He held out his tricorder so she could see the information on its screen. Although it wasn't reading any life signs in the forward compartment, its motion and air-density sensors had revealed a vaguely humanoid shape slumped against the cockpit's aft tactical console.

"Let them secure the ship first," Bowers said to Dax, with a nod toward the security officers. Loskywitz was keeping his weapon aimed at the hatch to the cockpit as Altoss advanced through the narrow passageway to the middle compartment.

As soon as both security officers reached the portal, they looked back to Bowers for the order to proceed. He motioned Dax to take cover near the corner, and she moved to a safe position from which she could still observe what was happening. Then the XO signaled Altoss and Loskywitz to advance.

Altoss reached up and tapped a button on a control panel. The hatch hissed open, revealing the darkened cockpit, whose only illumination came from the glow of the nebula outside.

Just as the tricorder's scans had indicated, a large, long-limbed alien figure was collapsed on the deck, its narrow torso resting against the support for the aft tactical console. The upper and rear portion of its head was enormous and round, but it had a fleshy quality, like that of a cephalopod. On either side of its head were tubules, whose ends dilated and contracted in a slow cadence. Pulsing in the same rhythm were ribbed, organic tubes that emerged from its neck and curved over its shoulders before tapering and vanishing into its chest.

At the ends of its gangly arms were limp tendrils, and its feet had two forward toes joined by a U-shaped curve and a prominently clawed third toe near the rear of its instep.

Its head swiveled slowly in Dax's direction. Lidless, almond-shaped black eyes stared at her from a narrow face with a mouth that seemed capable of no expression but a grimace.

Loskywitz and Altoss kept their rifles aimed at the weak and apparently defenseless being, even as they looked back to Bowers for new orders. Bowers, in turn, looked to Dax.

She emerged from behind the corner and walked forward before Bowers could tell her not to. "Lower your weapons," she told the security officers.

At the cockpit's threshold she stopped and examined the creature more closely. Its leathery hide was mostly gray and mottled with faint hues of violet and viridian.

"I'm Captain Ezri Dax, commanding the *Starship Aventine*."

The alien's mouth barely moved as it replied in a fragile whisper, "I am Arithon of the Caeliar."

Dax stepped inside the cockpit and squatted next to Arithon. "You were on the Earth ship *Columbia*?"

"Yes. Taken as a prisoner. Before entering the passage."

Following her flashes of intuition, she asked, "Was it you who set the ship's autopilot after the crew died?"

"Yes. . . . Hoped to control the vessel, use it to return home. Too much damage. Couldn't stop the crash." The arm that Arithon was using to hold himself in place slipped, and he slumped lower to the deck. Dax reached out to steady him. His skin was cold.

"And that's why you stole the runabout," Dax realized, thinking aloud. "You were trying to get home. But what happened to my people? Did you do that?"

"Forgive me," Arithon said. "Did not mean to kill. Weak without the gestalt. Centuries alone. Drained energy from the ship's batteries until none was left. Hibernated in the machines, waiting for power." The Caeliar finished his slow collapse to the deck. His voice became hollow and distant as he stared at the overhead. "So hungry, so cold. Saw heat and fuel. Had to feed. Was nothing but the hunger. Did not remember myself until this vessel's power restored me. Made me tangible again."

"I don't understand," Dax said. "Made you *tangible*?"

Arithon's head lolled in her direction and came to a heavy stop. "Needed power to rebuild myself for the return. But all for naught. Voices silenced. Gestalt is lost."

Dax leaned closer. "What does that mean?" The alien didn't respond. She reached out and cradled his head in one arm and laid a hand on his bony, thin chest. "What is the gestalt?"

No answer came. Before she could ask her question again, she realized that Arithon's head was becoming less heavy in her arm—and then it weighed nothing at all. It disintegrated on her sleeve, along with the rest of his body. It all became a cloud of sparkling particles of dust that shimmered for a moment and then transformed into a dull, superfine powder.

Dax lingered in the shadows and dust and looked at the gray residue on her hands. She was torn between remorse at Arithon's demise and relief at being rid of the entity that had killed three members of her crew.

Bowers stepped into the cockpit and stood beside her. "You live to make my job difficult, don't you?"

"Yes, Sam, it's all about inconveniencing you." She stood and clapped the dust from her hands. "I just don't get it. What did Arithon hope to find here?"

The XO shrugged. "Whatever it was, it probably got fried in the supernova."

"We don't know that. Maybe it left without him."

"Maybe," Bowers said. "What I want to know is, if this is where the *Columbia* entered the subspace tunnel, why don't its logs have a record of its journey here?"

"No idea." Dax nudged the powder on the deck with the tip of her boot. "But I bet *he* knew." She looked out the cockpit windshield at the chaotic beauty of the supernova remnant. "I feel like we're on the verge of a major breakthrough, Sam. I wish we could see where all this leads."

Bowers replied, "I get the feeling Starfleet Command has other plans for us. Speaking of which, we should probably check in, since we're back in Federation space ahead of schedule."

"We'll check in with Starfleet as soon as we get back to the

*Aventine,*" Dax said. "But I think we're on to something here, Sam—something *big.* One more ship defending Trill won't make any difference against the Borg. But this might."

"I have a new theory about you," Bowers said, his serious tone telegraphing his deadpan humor.

She mirrored his grave demeanor. "Let's hear it."

"You don't really like being a starship captain, and you're trying to get fired."

"You'd have made a good counselor. If you want, I can arrange a transf—"

A comm warble was followed by Lieutenant Commander Helkara's excited hail: *"Aventine to Captain Dax!"*

"Go ahead, *Aventine.*"

*"Captain, we've just received a priority-one distress call. We're reeling in the runabout and beaming up you and your team in ten seconds. Stand by for transport."*

"Hang on," Dax said. "A distress call from whom?"

*"From the* Enterprise, *Captain. They've engaged the Borg."*

# 22

In the heart of night, *Titan* had found an iron sun.

Riker marveled at the dark orb taking shape on the main viewer. "It reminds me of a Dyson shell the *Enterprise* found twelve years ago," he said to Vale, who was standing next to his chair and watching the black globe grow steadily larger. "Except smaller, of course."

"Naturally," Vale said. "Heck, this one's only two million kilometers across. You can barely fit a star in there."

He looked up and caught the hint of jest in her eyes. "Exactly," he said.

Melora Pazlar—or, as Riker had to keep reminding himself, her holographic avatar—turned from the aft science station and said, "Captain, we've picked up another sphere." She relayed her data to the main viewer, where it appeared as a small inset in the top right corner. "Equatorial diameter is eighteen thousand six hundred kilometers. Based on the gravitational field and subspatial displacement, it appears to be constructed of the same unknown alloy as the star-sphere."

Vale asked, "Distance from the star-sphere?"

"One hundred sixty-nine million kilometers," Pazlar said. "Orbital period estimated at four hundred nineteen days."

Riker asked Tuvok, "Any sign we've been detected?"

"None. I have detected no artificial signal activity in this system, Captain. No sensors, no communications."

"So far, so good," Vale said. "What about defenses?"

"Unknown," Tuvok said. "We remain limited to passive sensing protocols, and the spheres absorb a wide spectra of energy. Consequently, I have been unable to make detailed scans."

The captain felt his brow crease as he concentrated on finding the simplest and most direct solution to the issue. "What if we moved in closer? To within standard orbital range?"

Tuvok arched an eyebrow as he considered that. "That would enable me to make a more detailed visual analysis."

Riker nodded to Vale, who turned toward the conn and said, "Lavena, take us into orbit of the planet-sphere. Half-impulse approach, and have evasive patterns on standby."

"Aye, sir," replied the Pacifican through her liquid-filled respirator mask. "Sixteen minutes to orbit." The steady thrumming of the impulse engines lent an invigorating vibration to the deck, a tangible sense of impending action.

Riker swiveled his chair toward the other side of the bridge, where Lieutenant Commander Keru manned the security console, Ensign Torvig monitored the bridge engineering station, and Deanna Troi hovered at Keru's side. "Mister Keru, does any of this look like Borg technology to you?"

The brawny Trill security chief traded a glance with the deceptively meek-looking Choblik engineer before he answered, "No, sir. It doesn't look like anything I've ever seen."

"Ensign? Anything to add?"

"Yes, Captain," Torvig said. His tail undulated gracefully behind him. "I've confirmed that the planet-sphere is the source of the energy pulses we detected. Another such pulse has just been emitted, toward Federation space in the Alpha Quadrant."

Vale folded her arms across her chest. "That seals it. We have to go down there. Ranul, is your security team ready?"

"As much as they'll ever be," Keru said.

Tuvok interjected, "Whether there is a planet inside the

smaller sphere or its interior surface serves as a habitat, I suspect its shell will prove impervious to transporter beams."

"Then we'll find a gap in the shell and jaunt down by shuttle," Keru said. "Failing that, we'll *make* a gap."

Troi stepped from behind Keru, toward the middle of the bridge. "Have we considered hailing them? Opening diplomatic negotiations *before* we send armed personnel to their planet?"

"For all we know, it's the Borg inside there," Keru said. "If the shell makes it as hard for them to see out as it makes it for us to see in, then we might have the element of surprise on our side. We'll lose that if we hail them."

"They sent a pulse that knocked us out of warp and destroyed our communications systems," Troi said to Keru. "I'd say we lost the 'element of surprise' quite some time ago." She turned toward Riker. "Captain, I respectfully suggest we not abandon diplomacy before we've had a chance to try it. If it's not the Borg inside that shell, we should be prepared to greet its people in peace and make a proper first contact."

Riker was tempted to agree with everything Deanna said, but he didn't want to be too quick to side with his wife during a debate on the bridge. He also was unsure whether he might want to concur with her simply to avoid clashing with her again, to preserve some piece of common ground between them. Instead, he shifted his gaze to Vale and said, "Your opinion?"

"She's right," the first officer said. "There's no sign the Borg have been here, and our primary mission remains peaceful exploration and first contact. We may have come ready for a fight, but we don't have to force one."

Rising from his chair, Riker said, "I agree. Lieutenant Rager, open hailing frequencies to the planet-shell."

The operations officer keyed in the command on her console and replied, "Channel open, Captain."

He took a breath, then lifted his voice. "Attention, residents of the shelled planet. This is Captain William T. Riker of the *Starship Titan*, representing the United Federation of Planets. My crew and I have come in peace and wish to meet with your leaders or representatives. We intend to send a small, unarmed shuttlecraft to your world. If this is acceptable to you, please respond."

Several seconds passed in silence. Rager tapped at her console and cycled through all the known frequencies, searching for a

reply. Then she looked over her shoulder at Riker and shook her head. "Nothing, sir."

"I might have something, though," Pazlar said. She replaced the inset system chart on the main viewer with a close-up detail from the surface of the planet's shell. Blocks of its exterior seemed to slide or melt away, revealing hollow spaces underneath. "It looks like a passage through the shell is being created, sir. More than wide enough for a shuttlecraft."

Vale asked, "What about a transporter beam?"

"Sorry," Pazlar said. "No line of sight to the planet. I'd guess they're willing to let us fly down but not beam down."

"Or up," Keru muttered, his suspicion evident.

"It still looks like an invitation to me," Riker said. "Chris, have a shuttlecraft ready to fly as soon as we make orbit. We're going down there."

His first officer glared good-naturedly at him. "What do you mean 'we'? You're not going anywhere, sir."

"Captain's privilege," Riker shot back.

"Starfleet regulations," Vale countered. "And yes, I'm invoking them for real. We don't know who's down there, and I agree with Keru—I worry about why they've made sure we can't use the transporters. Until we know more, you should stay on the ship and leave the away mission to me."

He was about to argue when Troi stepped closer and lowered her voice to tell him, "Listen to her, Will. Your place is here, in command of the ship. We'll handle the first-contact mission."

"With all respect, Counselor," Vale cut in, "you're not going down there, either."

"Yes, I am, Commander. I'm the diplomatic officer on this ship, and first-contact assignments fall under my authority."

"Counselor, this isn't the time or the place—"

"Enough," Riker said. He suspected their disagreement was about to ignite into something much worse unless he intervened. "My ready room, both of you."

He ushered them off the bridge into his private office. Vale entered the ready room first, followed by Troi and then Riker. After the door closed behind him, he asked, "Chris, did Dr. Ree clear Deanna for duty?"

"Yes, as long as she stays close enough for him to monitor her condition. In other words, on the ship."

Riker felt Deanna's ire intensify even as her voice became very calm. "The requirement was proximity to Dr. Ree, not confinement to the ship. The doctor can join the away team and monitor my condition at all times. If anything happens, he can stabilize me long enough to get me back to the ship."

"Seems reasonable," Riker said.

Vale frowned. "I doubt the doctor will agree."

"I'll leave it to you to persuade him, then," Riker said. "Assemble your away team and be ready to fly in ten minutes."

As Tuvok piloted the shuttlecraft *Mance* into the newly opened path through the planet's dull, black shell, he maintained a wary vigil on the environment outside the craft. A passage so easily provided could be just as easily revoked.

Commander Vale sat on his left, in the mission commander's seat of the shuttlecraft's cockpit. She, too, seemed to be keeping her attention focused outward, looking for any sign of a trap being sprung. Then her stare connected with his, and she rolled her eyes. He imagined it was her way of expressing frustration at their vulnerability.

Behind them, their six passengers faced one another, grouped in rows along the port and starboard bulkheads. Commander Troi, Ensign Torvig, and Dr. Ree were behind Vale. On the other side of the cabin were Lieutenant Commander Keru, Lieutenant Sortollo, and Chief Dennisar. The bench seating was awkward for Ree and Torvig, who both perched uncomfortably on its edge.

Outside the cockpit window was nothing but a dark tunnel that curved and dipped and doubled back on itself several times, creating a winding course through the shell. None of the *Mance*'s sensors were functioning inside the passage. Not even proximity detectors registered any contact with the shell's mysterious, black alloy. That left Tuvok no choice but to navigate by eye and instinct, trusting in his perceptions of parallax motion to guide his hand as he steered through hairpin turns with only navigational thrusters to control the ship.

Vale peeked upward through the windshield. "How thick do you think the shell is?"

"Without sensors, I could offer only a vague estimate," Tuvok said. "I would speculate that, so far, we have made seven-point-three kilometers of vertical descent while navigating inside the shell."

The XO replied with gentle mockery, "That's a 'vague estimate,' Tuvok?"

"Indeed. I suspect it might be inaccurate by up to three-tenths of a kilometer. Its value as a computational variable for assessing the shell's mass and other properties is negligible."

"Noted," Vale said. She resumed her anxious visual survey of the environment outside the ship as Tuvok guided the *Mance* through another banking turn, into a much brighter area.

The cockpit windshield dimmed automatically to reduce the glare, enabling Tuvok to see that the passage came to an abrupt end roughly sixty meters ahead of the shuttlecraft, at the source of the light flooding into the tunnel. He slowed the shuttle's forward motion to less than two meters per second as it drew within twenty meters of the light. The windshield dimmed again, revealing a gap along the bottom of the passage, an opening just more than wide enough to let the *Mance* through.

He guided the shuttlecraft to a stop with its nose less than a decimeter from the terminal wall of the passage. Then he nudged its vertical thrusters into a descent profile and eased the *Mance* straight down, past what he guessed was more than twenty meters of the same black metal . . . and into open space.

Tuvok had too much control over his emotions to be amazed by the spectacle that stretched out ahead of him, but as a disciple of reason and as an explorer, he was impressed.

Before them lay a lush, bluish-green world swaddled in clouds and bathed in ersatz sunlight projected from the interior surface of the shell. From their vantage point on the edge of the planet's uppermost atmosphere, the shell looked like nothing more than a starless night, as if this was the only world orbiting the only star in the universe.

Checking his systems panel, Tuvok reported, "Sensor functions restored, Commander. Scanning the planet's surface."

"Any sign of habitation?" asked Vale.

"Life signs are extensive," Tuvok said as he reviewed the data. "The planet appears to be rich with plant and animal life in all regions and climates." He adjusted the sensors. "Scanning for artificial power sources and signal emissions." It took only seconds for the *Mance*'s sensors to lock on to something large. "Intense power readings, Commander. From inside a large mass of refined metals and synthetic compounds. Range, nine hundred eighty-one kilometers, bearing two two one."

"Take us in, Tuvok."

"Should I raise shields?"

Vale shook her head. "Negative. Not unless they give us a reason. Let's try to make this a friendly visit."

"As you wish." He adjusted the shuttlecraft's heading and keyed its thrusters, hurtling the small ship forward through the atmosphere. They punched through massive cloud banks and made a slight detour around a black-bruised stormhead that was bursting with rain and flashing with electric-blue lightning. Far below, the surface blurred past, a verdant landscape marked by dramatic rock formations and pristine, azure lakes.

Then the *Mance* passed over a range of jagged peaks capped with snow and cruised over a twilit arctic sea, toward a shimmer on the horizon. Tuvok reduced the shuttle's speed and altitude as a glittering metropolis took shape above a sea of pack ice. The city covered the entirety of a vast, bowl-like platform, which hovered hundreds of meters above the water. Most of its highest towers were clustered in its center, and the airspace above and between them teemed with thousands of small objects in motion.

"Wow," Vale said under her breath. "I'm guessing that's our energy source?"

"Affirmative," Tuvok said. He responded to a soft beeping on his console and saw that a signal was being transmitted to the shuttlecraft. "Commander, we appear to be receiving a repeating signal from the city. I believe it might be a beacon intended to guide us to a landing site."

Vale nodded once. "Follow it." She adjusted the sensor protocols. "The energy levels are making it hard to detect any life signs inside the city . . . except one. It's carbon-based, but it doesn't match anything in the computer."

"I've locked on to our landing coordinates," Tuvok said, guiding the *Mance* through a wide turn past twisting, organically shaped towers of dark crystal and delicate metalwork. He pointed at a circular platform situated at the end of a narrow causeway, a hundred meters past the edge of the city's outermost rampart.

The XO seemed amused. "All this high technology, but the

visitor parking lot's still out in the boondocks. I guess some things really are universal." She looked at Tuvok as if she expected him to return her volley of inane banter with one of his own. Noting his pointed lack of a response, she faced forward and muttered, "Tough room."

Tuvok centered the shuttlecraft above the landing pad and eased it downward. It made only the slightest bump of contact as it touched down and settled on the platform. As he switched off the thrusters and activated routine command lockouts to secure the craft during the away team's absence, Vale moved through the aft cabin and marshaled the passengers into motion.

"Everybody ready?" she asked. The others nodded. She opened the port hatch, letting in a blast of frigid air. "Let's go."

Troi and Torvig were the first to follow Vale out of the shuttlecraft, and then Keru, Dennisar, and Sortollo exited with their rifles slung diagonally across their backs. Tuvok paused at the threshold when he noticed Dr. Ree lingering in the middle of the passenger cabin. "Doctor? Are you all right?"

"Let's just say that extreme cold is not a friend of the Pahkwa-thanh," Ree replied.

"Your exposure will be brief," Tuvok said. "Scans of the city I made during our approach indicate that the average temperature inside its environmental maintenance field is thirty degrees Celsius. I suspect that our landing area has been placed outside the protected zone as an incentive for us to leave the ship and proceed inward."

Ree's tongue flicked twice from between his front fangs, and he rasped, "Doesn't mean I have to like it." Then he lumbered through the hatch and out of the ship. Tuvok followed him into the dry, arctic chill.

"What the hell took you two?" snapped Vale in between huffing warm breath onto her cupped hands. "We're freezing our asses off out here." She tucked her hands under her armpits. "Come on. Double-time, people."

She led the away team at a brisk jog across the causeway, toward the humbling majesty of the city, whose structures gleamed with reflections of the peach-and-indigo arctic sky and the silhouetted landscape of peaks flanking a virgin sea. Their breath billowed around their heads in short-lived gray plumes as they ran, dispersed by gusts of wind that roared in their ears.

It was not a long run, but the extreme cold made it seem like one. Ahead of Tuvok, a wave of exhaustion and relief seemed to wash over the away team members. Then he caught up to them and felt the balmy warmth of the city's protected climate. It was more humid than he would have preferred, but still mild by human standards.

Dr. Ree arched his head back until his long snout was pointed straight up, and he made several deep snorting sounds, followed by rich, trumpeting blares that sounded as if they had originated deep inside his torso. He relaxed then and noticed the surprised looks from the other away team members. "Warming breaths," he said. "Just something Pahkwa-thanh have to do after we're exposed to the cold."

Vale gave a tight-lipped smile and said, "Okay, then. If show-and-tell's over, let's get . . ." Her voice tapered off as she stared past the away team, back toward the shuttlecraft. Tuvok and the others turned to follow her gaze.

The causeway had vanished. A hundred meters away, past a gulf of open air hundreds of meters above an ice-packed arctic sea, the circular landing platform hovered without support. The *Mance* did not appear to have been damaged; apparently, whoever had removed the causeway had been satisfied merely to render the vessel inaccessible.

"Well . . . that's just great," Keru said. He looked at Sortollo and Dennisar. "I don't suppose either of you can do a hundred-meter long jump?"

Holding up her palms, Vale said, "All right, we came here to work some diplomacy. Getting our ship back will just have to be one of our negotiating terms—right, Counselor?"

"I think you'll have to ask them," Troi said, pointing.

Tuvok pivoted back toward the city and looked up, along the line of Troi's outstretched arm. Hundreds of meters above them, from a breezeway connecting two massive but delicate-looking towers, three figures floated downward with swift grace.

The away team watched in silence as the descending trio neared. Vale, Tuvok, and Troi stepped forward to meet them.

When the beings came within ten meters of the ground, they slowed and positioned themselves in a line. The two mottled gray-and-blue aliens at either end had their tendril-like fingers folded together in front of them. Their heads were bowed slightly forward, revealing the enormous globes of their skulls. Their generally humanoid shape made the ribbed tubing that ran from their chests to what Tuvok assumed were respiratory tubules near the backs of their heads all the more curious.

Most curious of all was the figure standing between them.

According to his tricorder, it was a carbon-based life-form of a kind not previously encountered by the Federation. What he saw was an athletic, healthy, and attractive young human woman with a long and unruly mane of black hair. Judging from her appearance, he estimated her age to be somewhere between her late teens and her early twenties.

The woman stepped forward and looked at Vale and Troi. Her voice sounded guarded and cautious—and perhaps secretly excited. "Humans," she said, apparently not discerning that Troi was half-Betazoid. Then she looked at Tuvok. "Vulcan." She glanced past them at the rest of the away team. "Orion," she said when she saw Dennisar. Looking at Keru, she said, "Trill."

After eyeing Torvig, she said nothing at all.

Tuvok studied the woman's face. Something about her seemed familiar to him. He searched his memory and found the reason.

Troi asked her, "You recognize our species?"

Before the woman could answer, Tuvok said, "I'm sure she does, Counselor. She is *from* Earth." Everyone looked at Tuvok for the explanation. He addressed the woman directly. "You are Captain Erika Hernandez of the Earth starship *Columbia,* missing in action for more than two hundred years."

"Yes," Hernandez replied. "I was the captain of the *Columbia.* And I've been missing much longer than you think." She raised her voice to address the rest of the away team. "Welcome to New Erigol."

# BOOK II

# MERE MORTALS

# HISTORIAN'S NOTE

The main narrative of *Mere Mortals* takes place in February of 2381 (Old Calendar), approximately sixteen months after the events of the movie *Star Trek Nemesis*. The flashback portions begin in 1519 and continue through 2381.

Our torments also may in length of time
Become our elements, these piercing fires
As soft as now severe, our temper changed
Into their temper.

—John Milton, *Paradise Lost,* book 2

# 2381

## 1

Blue fire preceded a crimson flash, as one of the Borg cubes on the main viewer erupted into a cloud of blazing wreckage. The two that had followed it from the indigo fog of the Azure Nebula barreled through its spreading debris, accelerated, and opened fire on their lone adversary.

Pitched alarums of struggle surrounded Captain Jean-Luc Picard, who sat in the bridge's command chair, stone-faced and silent, watching and hearing the battle unfold around him.

Over the thunder of energy blasts hammering the shields of the *Enterprise,* Commander Worf bellowed, "Helm! Attack pattern Echo-One! Tactical, target the closer cube and fire at will!"

Picard tried to focus on the voices of his crew—Worf barking orders, second officer Miranda Kadohata relaying damage reports, security chief Jasminder Choudhury confirming her targets, and the low buzz of several junior officers manning backup stations and sensor consoles everywhere he looked—but they all were drowned out by the one voice that was many: the dehumanized roar of the Borg Collective.

*Resistance is futile. You will be exterminated.*

It had been more than fourteen years since the Borg's voice had first invaded the sanctum of his mind, when the Collective assimilated him. Transformed into Locutus of Borg, Picard had watched through a dark haze, a spectator to his own life, as the Borg used his knowledge and experience against Starfleet and against Earth. Even after he had been physically liberated from the Collective, he'd remained yoked to its voice, attuned to its soulless group mind.

His bond to the Collective had faded with the passage of years. He had expected to welcome its permanent absence from his thoughts, but then the Borg returned with an unprecedented ferocity marked by aggressive tactics and a disturbing new motivation. It had been several months since, in a desperate bid to understand the true nature of the new threat posed by the Borg, he had attempted to infiltrate the Collective by posing as Locutus. He'd thought he could outwit them, that experience and innovation would protect him as he dared to plumb their secrets. *What a fool I was,* he castigated himself.

A powerful concussion threw the bridge crew to starboard and strobed the lights. A port-side console exploded into smithereens. Glowing-hot bits of smoking debris landed in Picard's lap, and the momentary jolts of hot pain on his legs broke the spell that the Collective had held over his thoughts.

He swatted the blackened embers off his thighs as he stood and moved to stand beside Worf. The Klingon executive officer remained focused on directing the battle. "Helm," Worf shouted as Lieutenant Joanna Faur scrambled back into her chair, "hard to port!" To Choudhury he added, "Ready aft torpedoes!" As Worf turned forward again, Kadohata switched the main screen to display the ship's retreating aft view. A Borg cube loomed dramatically into sight, dominating the screen. "Fire!"

Four radiant blue bolts flew from the *Enterprise*'s aft torpedo launcher and separated as they followed weaving, spiraling paths to the Borg ship. At the final moment they shot toward different faces of the cube. Two penetrated the Borg's shields and ripped through its hull. Within seconds, cerulean flames consumed the Borg vessel from within and broke it apart. A blinding flash reduced it to fading supercharged particles.

*Two down, one to go,* Picard mused as the main viewer image reverted to its normal, forward-facing perspective.

"Attack pattern Bravo-Eight," Worf ordered, and the bridge crew translated his words into action with speed and skill.

Picard heard the intentions of the Collective and saw the trap that Worf had just stumbled into. He snapped, "Belay that! Evasive maneuvers, starb—" The bone-jarring thunderclap of an explosion cut him off, and the deck felt as if it had dropped out from under him. He fell forward and landed on his forearms. A bank of large companels along the aft bulkhead blew apart and showered the bridge with a flurry of sparks and shrapnel.

Gray, acrid smoke lingered above the shaken bridge crew. "Continue evasive maneuvers," Worf said to Faur. He plucked a jagged bit of smoking debris from the rings of his metallic

Klingon baldric as he stepped behind Kadohata, who was struggling to halt the erratic malfunctions that flickered across the ops console. "Damage report," Worf said.

"Hull breaches, Decks Twenty-two and Twenty-three," replied the lithe human woman of mixed Asian and European ancestry. Her Port Shangri-La accent was just similar enough to a Londoner's inflections that Picard had to remind himself again that she wasn't from Earth. "Direct hit on our targeting sensors," she continued. Then she swiveled her chair to face Worf and added with alarm, "Sir, we can't lock weapons."

Another shot from the Borg cube rocked the *Enterprise.* "Break off, Number One," Picard said.

"Full evasive," Worf said, "maximum warp. Engage!"

As Worf stepped quickly from station to station, gathering status reports, Picard moved forward and stood beside Kadohata's console. In a confidential tone, he said, "Casualty report."

Reciprocating his quiet discretion, she replied, "Four dead in engineering, several dozen wounded. Still waiting on official numbers from sickbay, sir."

"Understood," he said.

Worf finished his circuit of the bridge and returned to Picard's side. "Captain, the transphasic shields are starting to overload. Lieutenant Choudhury estimates—" Cacophonous booms resonated through the bulkheads. When the echoes had faded, Worf continued, "She estimates shield failure in nine minutes."

"Commander," Picard said to Kadohata, "we need those targeting sensors. Devote all free resources to their repair. Mister Worf, help Lieutenant Choudhury find a way to target our torpedoes manually."

The XO nodded and said, "Aye, sir."

As Worf walked back to the tactical console, Kadohata confided to Picard, "Sir? The damage to the targeting system was major. I doubt it can be repaired in the next nine minutes. And manually targeting transphasic torpedoes is almost impossible. Without the targeting computer, we'll never adjust the phase harmonics quickly enough."

"What do you suggest, Commander?"

"With all respect, sir . . . a distress signal."

Picard frowned. "To whom? Our nearest allies are several hours away, at best."

Kadohata mustered a bittersweet smile and shrugged. "You have your desperate measures, I have mine."

He had to admire her grace in the face of danger. "Make it so," he said. Then, dropping his voice again, he added with grim resignation, "And prepare the log buoy."

Captain Ezri Dax was seated and steady, with her hands relaxed on the ends of her command chair's armrests, but in her mind she was pacing like a caged beast, feverishly circling her anxiety.

"Time to intercept?" she asked.

Lieutenant Tharp answered over his shoulder, "Two minutes, Captain." The Bolian conn officer returned to his controls and faced the main viewer, whose image was dominated by the retreating mass of the Borg cube that was pursuing the *Enterprise*.

Her first officer, Commander Sam Bowers, returned from his hushed conference with Lieutenant Lonnoc Kedair, the Takaran chief of security for the *Aventine,* and stood beside Dax. "I feel like a dog chasing a shuttle," he said, watching the Borg ship. "Even if we catch it, what do we do then?"

"Sink our teeth in, Sam," Dax said. "As deep as we can."

Kedair looked up from the tactical console. "We've just been scanned by a Borg sensor beam," she said, her deep-green face darkened half a shade by concern.

"So much for a surprise attack," Bowers said.

"Lieutenant Mirren," Dax said to her senior operations officer, "signal *Enterprise*. We need to coordinate our attack."

Mirren nodded. "Aye, sir. Hailing them now."

"Sixty seconds to firing range," Tharp said from the conn.

The cube was large enough now on the main viewer that Dax could discern the layers of snaking machinery and the haphazard network of grids, plates, and crudely grafted pieces of alien machinery that this ship must have assimilated in its past. She couldn't tell by looking how long ago each component had been acquired, or even guess at how new or old the cube might be. Every Borg cube, from the raw to the battle-scarred, had the same weathered, dull look, the same drab utilitarian aesthetic.

"Incoming signal from the *Enterprise*," Mirren said.

"On-screen," Dax replied. A blizzard of visual noise and

twisted images danced on the main viewer while banshee wails and the crackle-scratch of static muffled the words of Captain Picard, who Dax could recognize even through the storm of interference. "Mirren," she said, "can we clean that up?"

Mirren jabbed at her console and grimaced in frustration. "Trying, Captain. The Borg are jamming us."

Lieutenant Commander Gruhn Helkara, the ship's second officer and the head of its sciences division, called to Dax from one of the aft bridge stations. "Captain, I might have a way to bypass the jamming!" The wiry Zakdorn moved toward one of the starboard auxiliary consoles. "The Klingons use a super-low-frequency subspace channel to stay in contact with cloaked ships." He keyed commands into the auxiliary panel at furious speed. "I'll interlace an SLF signal on a subharmonic fre—"

"Less talk, Gruhn," Dax said. "Just make it work."

"Aye, sir," he said, and then he tapped in a few final details. "Channel ready. Try it now."

Dax waited while Mirren reestablished contact with the *Enterprise*. After several more seconds of garbled images and sounds, the visage of Captain Picard snapped into shaky but mostly clear focus. *"Captain Dax?"*

"At your service," Dax said.

*"I thought your ship was in the Gamma Quadrant."*

She was about to explain, then shook off the impulse. "Long story. We're coming up fast on the Borg. How can we help?"

*"We need you to be our eyes,"* Picard said. He nodded to someone off-screen, then continued, *"We're sending you a set of targeting protocols. After we fire the transphasic torpedoes, you'll have to arm them and guide them to the target."*

"Data received," Mirren said. "Decrypting now."

At the auxiliary console, Helkara studied the incoming data, frowned, and then looked up at Dax. "I'll have to recalibrate the sensors."

"How long?" asked Dax.

"Four minutes," Kedair said.

Dax expected bad news as she looked back at Picard, and he didn't disappoint her. *"Our shields will fail in three."*

"Gruhn," Dax said to her second officer.

"I know, three minutes," Helkara said without looking up.

"Hang on, Captain," Dax said. "We're on our way. *Aventine*

out." Walking back to her command chair, Dax said to Bowers, "Sam, let's give the Borg something new to think about for the next three minutes."

"Aye, sir," Bowers said. "Tactical, arm phaser cannons one and two, stand ready on quantum torpedoes. Helm, set attack pattern Alpha-Tango . . . and engage."

Dax settled into her chair and stared at the ominous mass of black metal that filled the bridge's main viewscreen like a spreading cancer. She wondered how close the Borg would let the *Aventine* come before the cube opened fire.

Then a searing flash of green light shot from the cube to the *Aventine,* and the *Vesta*-class explorer lurched forward like a ship at sea running momentarily aground over a sandbar. When the percussive din of impact finished resonating through the hull, Dax pushed herself fully back into her chair and said to her XO, "I think they're in range now, Sam."

"We'll only get one shot, Captain," Bowers replied. "I plan on making it count." He nodded to Kedair. "Fire at will."

Deep droning hums swelled rapidly in pitch and volume and ended in rushing thunderclaps of release as the *Aventine*'s experimental Mark XII phaser cannons fired their peculiar mix of supercharged high-energy particles at the Borg cube. The enemy vessel's shield bubble flared violet for a half second before it buckled. A series of blasts punched through the cube's hull and left fire and molten metal in their wake.

A volley of quantum torpedoes arced in alongside the phaser blasts, punching more holes in the Borg ship's dark exterior. Then the last two torpedoes impacted harmlessly against the Borg's resurgent defensive energy screen. Two more bursts from the phaser cannon were absorbed by the protective field.

"Hard to port," Bowers ordered, "full evasive!" The whine of the impulse engines grew louder as the *Aventine* veered away from the Borg ship. Bowers wore the slack expression of a man who knew all too well what would happen next. "Here's where the real fun begins," he said.

Then the Borg started shooting back.


Commander Geordi La Forge dodged through flames and smoke in the main engineering compartment of the *Enterprise,* trusting the enhanced-spectrum view provided by his cybernetic eyes to keep him a step ahead of the next catastrophe.

He grabbed the sleeve of a passing engineer and spun the dark-haired human woman back to face him. "Granados," he said, "shut down the starboard EPS tap, it's overheating!"

"The gauges read normal," the ensign protested.

"Maureen, they're wrong," La Forge shouted. He let go of her arm and pointed at the auxiliary control panel a few sections away, down the corridor. "Shut it down, now!"

She nodded. "Aye, sir." As she sprinted toward the control panel, La Forge continued on his original path and weaved around a running damage-control team in pressure suits.

The din of system-failure alarms, panicked voices, cries of pain and fear, and running footfalls all were drowned out by the overpowering percussive rumble of an energy strike against the ship's hull. A hurricane-force gust hurled La Forge several meters through the air for a few seconds, then it fell away and dropped him to the deck as emergency force fields and bulkheads engaged to isolate the breached compartment a few sections away.

A flash accompanied another ear-rending blast, this time from the already overtaxed electroplasma system energy tap, which routed power from the main reactor to the ship's internal power grid. Its magnetically sealed protective housing cracked and blew apart. The superheated plasma inside it jetted like lava from a volcano, engulfing a team of engineers who had been trying to prevent exactly that disaster. Even from a distance, the heat overpowered La Forge.

The lucky ones nearest the rupture were vaporized instantly, transformed into gases and trace atoms. The handful of technicians and mechanics who had been behind them were fighting to pull their maimed, burned bodies away from the fiery mess. Most of them had lost their legs in the first half-second of the explosion, as the falling tide of plasma cut their feet out from under them. One of them, a Benzite, had lost an arm.

Another hazard-suited damage-control team sprinted in from an adjacent compartment. La Forge pointed to the rupture. "Seal that breach, and raise the force fields!" His skin tingled with pain. *Great. Now we'll all need anti-radiation shots.*

When he turned around, he saw a lot of young enlisted engineers and fresh-faced junior officers staring at the wounded and the dead, and only a few of his more experienced people minding their posts. He stepped between the young gawkers and the horrifying spectacle and started snapping orders.

"Gallivan, rebalance the power load on the starboard PTC. L'Sen, make sure the SIF is compensating for the hull breach. Newaur, stop chewing your claws and start patching that hole in our shields. The rest of you, back to your stations!"

The engineers had just resumed work when another hit by the Borg roared and echoed inside the *Enterprise*. La Forge moved at a quick step down the line of consoles, glancing past his people at their work and assembling the glimpses of data into a mental picture of the ship's condition.

As he neared the impulse system's power relays, he was intercepted by his assistant chief engineer, Lieutenant Taurik. The Vulcan's uniform was torn and smudged, and his face was obscured by dark gray carbon dust. "Commander," he said, "the targeting sensors have been almost completely destroyed. Rebuilding them will take up to a day."

La Forge cringed as a resounding boom shook the ship. He heard the crack of exploding consoles behind him a moment before he felt a blast of heat and the sting of shrapnel on his back. The impact knocked him facedown at Taurik's feet.

Within seconds, Taurik was lifting La Forge back to his feet. "Are you all right, sir?"

"No," La Forge said, gritting his teeth against the burning pain shooting through shallow wounds on either side of his spine. He turned and looked back at the damage. A quick scan in several different wavelengths revealed no other imminent overloads, but the body-heat readings of several downed engineers were alarmingly unstable. Pain and anger overpowered his sense of decorum. "Where are the medics, goddammit?"

"Sir," Taurik said, trying to lead La Forge away from the scene, "you need to get to sickbay."

La Forge threw off Taurik's helping hand. "What I need, Taurik, is two more minutes of shield power. Focus on that."

The Vulcan betrayed no hint of umbrage at La Forge's sharpness of tone. "Aye, sir," he replied, and he walked quickly toward the engineering control center for tactical systems.

La Forge limped in the other direction, one painful step at a time, back through the haze of toxic smoke and bitter dust, toward his fallen engineers. At long last, he saw a team of medics rounding the corner from the far corridor.

Another pounding blow resounded through the hull.

"Just keep it going a little longer, people," he said, his mood grim and his voice strained by his fresh injuries. "One way or another, this'll be over in the next two minutes."

Helkara spun away from his console to report, "Sensors ready!"

"Signal *Enterprise*," Bowers said to Mirren.

The slender ops officer tapped a ready key on her console. It flashed red twice before it turned green. Mirren replied, "*Enterprise* confirms. Torpedoes away in ten."

"Helm, all ahead," Dax ordered. "We need to get in close and arm the warheads before the Borg realize what we're doing."

Bowers threw a look at the captain that she recognized as one of apprehension. Putting the ship into easy firing range of the Borg was something her XO had wanted to avoid, but in this case it couldn't be helped. To his credit, she thought, he kept his objections to himself and resumed directing the attack as if nothing was amiss. "Tharp, show the Borg our port side. Kedair, reinforce the port shields for the flyby." He looked to the relief tactical officer, a Deltan woman named Talia Kandel. "Lieutenant, arm the *Enterprise*'s torpedoes as soon as they're away, and lock them onto the Borg cube as fast as you can."

"Incoming!" called Kedair. Then an erratic series of hard impacts scrambled monitors and companels around the bridge, which dipped deeper into shadow after each blow. The high-pitched whine of the engines began to fall. "Shields buckling," the security chief said.

"Six torpedoes away!" Mirren shouted over the clamor.

"Acquiring control," Kandel said as she worked.

On the main viewer, Dax saw energy pulses from the Borg cube slice past the *Aventine* into seemingly empty space. She was about to be grateful for the missed shot when she saw the flare of a distant detonation.

"We just lost two torpedoes," Mirren said. "The Borg are locking on again—"

Kandel cut in, "Torpedoes armed!" Her fingertips danced lightly across her controls as she added, "Target acquired!"

"Resume evasive maneuvers," Bowers ordered.

The remaining four missiles became incandescent, shining bright and blue against the blackness of space. They traced corkscrew paths through the Borg's defensive fusillade of energy blasts. A blinding pulse of light washed out the image on the main viewscreen, and a gut-wrenching sensation of collision lifted the bridge officers several centimeters into the air. Then the artificial gravity kicked back in and dropped everyone roughly on the deck.

"Stations," Dax said, the edge in her voice cutting through the daze and shock of the direct hit. "Mirren, get the viewer back on. Tharp, new evasive pattern. Kandel, report!"

It took a few seconds for the Deltan woman to coax her console back to full operation. "The Borg neutralized three of the torpedoes while we were down. Adjusting the last torpedo to compensate." The main viewer flickered back to life as she added, "It's through their shields—direct hit!"

Sapphire flames blazed from an erupting rent in the cube's patchwork hull, and fissures traveled with surprising speed and ferocity across all its surfaces as it began to tumble through space like a cast die. Explosions peppered its surface, ejecting chunks of its exterior in its wake.

Bowers turned and said with dark satisfaction to Kedair, "Feel free to have a little target practice, Lieutenant."

"With pleasure, sir." Seconds later Kedair opened fire with the *Aventine*'s phaser cannons and quantum torpedoes. Piece by piece, she vaporized the debris of the disintegrating Borg vessel, which now looked like a hollow shell; it had been all but consumed from within by the transphasic warhead's electric-blue fires. Staring at the gutted hexahedron, Kedair said, "Permission to finish the job, Captain?"

"Permission granted," Dax said, noting a subtle nod of agreement from Bowers. They both watched as a volley of ten quantum torpedoes plunged into the smoldering wreckage of the Borg ship and obliterated it. Watching the fire cloud disperse into the unforgiving vacuum of space, Dax noted the heavy odor of scorched metal and burnt optronics that permeated her bridge.

Mirren silenced a beeping alert on her console. "*Enterprise* is hailing us, Captain."

"On-screen," Dax said.

Captain Picard's visage filled the screen. *"Captain Dax,"* he said. *"My thanks and compliments for a fine rescue."*

"The pleasure was all ours, Captain," Dax said. "We're still licking our wounds over here, but I have medics and damage-control teams standing by if you need them."

Picard sighed softly and nodded once. *"We're not too proud to say we're in need of assistance. Any help you can offer will be gratefully accepted."*

"Understood," Dax said. "Send us a list of any parts or equipment you might need. I'll have my chief engineer take care of the details."

Nodding, Picard replied, *"Very good. My second officer, Commander Kadohata, will apprise your crew of our needs. In the meantime, Captain, I'd like to invite you and your first officer to meet with me privately aboard the* Enterprise. *We came to the Azure Nebula on an urgent mission, and now that you're here, we need to ask for your help in completing it."*

"Of course, Captain," Dax said. "Commander Bowers and I will beam over as soon as you're ready to receive us."

*"At 0230, then,"* Picard said. *"Enterprise out."*

The main viewer blinked back to the serene vista of deep space. Dax turned to Bowers. "*Enterprise* took some heavy damage in that fight, Sam. Make sure Mikaela knows to make their repairs a priority."

"Will do," Bowers said. Quietly, he added, "I guess it would be awkward to ask if they could loan us a few of those transphasic torpedoes, wouldn't it?"

"Not as awkward as it'll be for me seeing Worf again," Dax replied. "With all that's been going on for the last five weeks, I haven't had a chance to talk to him since my promotion. Last time I saw him, I was congratulating him for accepting the XO billet on the *Enterprise*. That was before I transferred here, when I was still a lieutenant commander. Now I outrank him."

Bowers shrugged. "Don't worry about it, Captain. Maybe he'll just be happy for you, as a friend."

"Maybe," Dax said. "But you know what they say: Rank is like sex—it changes everything."

\* \* \*

Dr. Beverly Crusher moved quickly from one biobed to the next, supervising her staff of surgeons, nurses, and medical technicians as they tended to the scores of grievously wounded personnel being portered into sickbay by security officers, paramedics, and damage-control officers.

At one bed, Dr. Tropp, her Denobulan assistant chief medical officer, was already deep into a surgical procedure, trying to stabilize the vital functions of a Bajoran woman whose legs were gone, sheared away halfway between the waist and the knees, cauterized black and smooth by some hellish trauma.

Walking down the row of biobeds, Crusher saw only more of the same: the burnt and the broken, the amputated and the paralyzed. Her normally antiseptic-smelling sickbay was rich with the charnel perfume of scorched flesh and spilled blood. Pitiful moaning, wails of agony, the hoarse exhortations of the suffering and the dying dispelled the quiet ambience she had always taken for granted.

A woman's voice called out, "Doctor Crusher!" She turned and saw Dr. Rymond, a chestnut-haired female surgical intern, beckoning her into the triage center adjacent to sickbay. Crusher dodged past a pair of medical technicians carrying a wounded officer on a stretcher to the O.R., brushed a few sweat-soaked strands of her red hair from her face, and joined Rymond.

The patient, a youthful-looking man, lay on his side, facing away from Crusher. A jagged length of what looked like a fragment of a metal support beam skewered his torso. "Fill me in," Crusher said.

"Fell onto a broken railing segment," Rymond said. "The DC team cut him free and left us a few centimeters to grab on to, but it's stuck tight. He's in shock and fading fast. Pulse is one-forty and thready, BP fifty over thirty."

Crusher grabbed one end of the man's stretcher and nodded to Rymond to take the other. "Okay, front of the line, let's go." They carried him into sickbay, toward a biobed that had just been vacated. "Does our lucky friend have a name?"

"Lieutenant Konya," Rymond said as they set him down.

Hearing his name enabled Crusher to see past the blood and grime on the wounded man's face and recognize him. He was the ship's deputy chief of security. "Get a breathing mask on him. Try and bring up his pulse ox while we get a clearer picture of the damage. And watch his EEG, he's Betazoid." She called over her shoulder, "We need a surgical arch over here!"

She lifted her medical tricorder, which she kept holstered on her belt during crises like these, and began an exploratory imaging sequence of Konya's torso. "Damn," she muttered. "It's straight through the inferior vena cava." To the unconscious Betazoid she added, "You had to make it difficult, didn't you?"

A pair of technicians, one an Andorian *thaan* and the other a female Saurian, hurried over with a surgical arch for the biobed. They slipped past Rymond and Crusher, fitted the arch into place, then rushed away as Dr. Tropp called from across sickbay for a new pack of hyposprays.

Crusher powered up the arch, calibrated its settings for Betazoid male physiology, and downloaded Konya's medical history from the ship's computer, to serve as baseline data. "Activate the delta-wave generator and monitor his vitals for me," Crusher said. "I'm about to open the pericardium and put a circular constrictor field around the auricle of his right atrium."

Her touches on the arch's interface pad were delicate and precise. Its noninvasive surgical protocols were state-of-the-art medicine, but only if one knew how to use them. This seemed to Crusher like a good opportunity to pass on some of that skill to her fresh-faced intern. "Watch closely," she said to the younger woman. "We're going to constrict the auricle and create a virtual venous-return catheter from there to the IVC."

The procedure went exactly as Crusher hoped, with the surgical arch manipulating force fields and tissue regenerators in an intricately programmed sequence. "As soon as I detect resistance from the fragment, I want you to use the controls on your side to dematerialize it." She watched Rymond initialize the interface on the other side of the arch. "Ready?"

Rymond nodded and kept her eyes on her controls.

"Okay," Crusher said, watching the resistance gauges creep upward for the constrictor field, "now."

Rymond tapped in the micro-transporter sequence and removed all traces of the intruding metal fragment.

As soon as the transporter sequence ended, Crusher finished closing the constrictor field. "All right," she said. "The auricle's sealed, the catheter's functional, and we can start doing some repair work." She looked over at Rymond. "Feel up to finishing this one on your own?"

"Yes, Doctor." The young surgeon glanced at the display screens on the arch. "I'll need to transfuse him first." She turned her head and caught the eye of Nurse Mimouni, who was passing by. "Nurse, prep eight units of J-neg and two units of Betazoid plasma, stat." Mimouni nodded her acknowledgment without breaking stride.

"Let me know if you need a hand," Crusher said. Rymond nodded and continued repairing Konya's wounds as Crusher moved on, back through the chaotic hustle of bodies and equipment.

She paused in the open doorway to the triage center, which was packed almost to capacity. Patients lay on beds arranged in long parallel rows. Most of them were unconscious; a few stared blankly at the overhead. Multiple copies of the ship's female-personality EMH—Emergency Medical Hologram—moved from bed to bed, assessing the criticality of new patients as they arrived.

Closer to Crusher, the ship's senior counselor, a Bajoran man named Dr. Hegol Den, kneeled beside a wounded young medic and conversed in soothing whispers with the shaken Trill woman. Crusher admired Hegol's gentle bedside manner; for a moment she lamented that he lacked the surgical training to do more for the wounded, but then she noted the generally subdued mood in the triage facility, and she realized that much of it was likely the product of Hegol's calm attention.

From the main sickbay compartment, she heard Dr. Tropp's voice get louder and pitch upward with frustration. She turned back and watched a moment she had witnessed far too many times before: a surgeon fighting a losing battle against injuries so severe that nothing short of a miracle could fix them.

"Push one-twenty-five triox," Tropp snapped at his trio of assistants. "Cortical stims to two-eighty-five! Dammit, th'Shelas, that artery's bleeding again!"

"V-fib," said medical technician Zseizaz, through a vocoder that rendered the buzzes and clicks of his insectile Kaferian language into recognizable phonetics.

"Charge to three hundred," Tropp said.

"Belay that," Crusher cut in. "Your patient has total organ failure, and her EEG flatlined four minutes ago." She hated to pull rank, but Tropp could be obsessive in times like this, and she couldn't afford to let him fixate on one lost cause when there were a dozen other lives in need of his help.

Tropp stared back at her, wild-eyed, and his nurse, his technician, and his intern all watched him. Then his shoulders slumped and his head followed. When he lifted his head again, Crusher saw in his eyes that he knew what he had to do.

He shut off the surgical arch. "Time of death, 0227." Zseizaz and th'Shelas removed the surgical arch, and Tropp waved over a pair of medical assistants to remove the body. Then he nodded to Nurse Amavia and said, "Let's go see who's next."

Crusher watched the assistants transfer the body of the dead Bajoran engineer to an antigrav gurney. With decorum and gentility they stretched a clean blue sheet over the body from head to toe and guided it away from the living patients, into the recesses of sickbay, to the morgue, where it would be placed in stasis pending its final journey home to its next of kin.

Over in the triage center, Tropp and Amavia zeroed in on a patient and directed Zseizaz and th'Shelas to move the wounded Tellarite officer to a biobed in sickbay.

*The fight goes on,* Crusher told herself. Then she impelled herself into motion, and summoned medical technician Ellwood Neil to join her as she crossed the compartment to find a case of her own. "Look for criticals," she said to the sharp-eyed young man. "I'm in the mood to work miracles tonight."

"A subspace tunnel to the Gamma Quadrant," said Captain Picard, sounding intrigued by Captain Dax's account of how the *Aventine* had found itself in a position to charge to the *Enterprise*'s rescue. He reclined his chair from his ready room desk and continued, "That's a remarkable discovery, Captain."

"I'll tell my science officer you said so."

Commander Bowers, who had accompanied Dax on this visit to the *Enterprise,* added, "It was Mister Helkara's suggestion to look for the subspace tunnel in the first place."

Picard nodded at Bowers and replied, "It sounds like you're blessed with an excellent crew."

"The best in the fleet," Bowers boasted. Worf, who was standing on Picard's right behind the desk, shot a fierce, challenging stare at Bowers, who quickly and nervously added, "Present company excluded, of course."

Worf signaled his acceptance of Bowers's capitulation with a muted growl from the back of his throat.

Captain Picard turned his chair away from Worf, stood, and walked around his desk to face Captain Dax. "I cannot dismiss as coincidence your discovery of a subspace tunnel and the recent entry of Borg ships into Federation space, both within the Azure Nebula," he said. "My instincts—not to mention common sense—tell me that these events are related."

"We're in complete agreement, Captain," Dax said, speaking with authority and serenity. Listening to her, Worf thought for a moment that he could hear and see echoes of Jadzia Dax in Ezri—the same confident timbre in her voice, the same poise and grace. Then the shadow of his slain wife faded and he was left with only the present.

"It's important we act quickly," Picard said. "Starfleet's defenses are faltering, and I can sense that the Borg are on the move. Another assault is imminent, unless we prevent it."

Bowers said, "We can have the *Aventine* ready for action by 0630." He cast a questioning look at Worf.

"Most of our systems will be functional by 0630," Worf said. "But Commander La Forge reports that repairs to the targeting sensors will take roughly twenty hours."

Picard nodded. "I see. Until we finish repairs, then, the *Aventine* will have to lead the investigation."

"Our pleasure, Captain," Dax said. "If I might make a suggestion . . . ?" Picard nodded for her to continue. "I think we should start our search at the coordinates where my ship emerged from the subspace tunnel. If there is another passage with a terminus inside the nebula, I think the best place to look for it is in proximity to one we already know about."

"Agreed," Picard said. "But before we begin the search, I want to reiterate our objective. If there is another subspace tunnel being used by the Borg, our mission is first to obstruct and then to destroy that phenomenon. It's imperative we deny the Borg access to Federation space, at all costs. Is that clear?"

"Absolutely, Captain," said Dax.

A look of resolution passed over Picard's face. "Very well. Let's get to work. We'll return to the nebula together at 0630."

Bowers and Dax nodded their assent and got up from their chairs. As the two visitors walked toward the door, Picard shook Dax's hand and then Bowers's. The portal sighed open ahead of them, briefly admitting the gentle humming and chirps of work being performed at numerous duty stations on the bridge. Then the door closed after the departed officers, leaving Worf and Picard alone in the captain's ready room.

Captain Picard walked to the replicator nook behind his desk and said to the computer, "Tea, Earl Grey, hot." His drink took shape inside a tiny, short-lived blizzard of atoms. He picked up the cup and saucer and eased himself into his chair.

Worf watched the captain take a sip and wince slightly at the sting of it on his lips. He wondered for a moment whether Picard was aware that he hadn't dismissed Worf. Then he wondered if his commanding officer was even cognizant of the fact that he was still there at all. Finally, Picard looked at Worf and said with droll amusement, "I understand your pride in the *Enterprise*'s crew, Number One, but do you think it was polite to intimidate Commander Bowers in front of his captain?"

Worf scowled. "He should choose his words with more care."

"Perhaps," Picard said. "Though I have to wonder . . . was your display really about what he said? Or did it have something to do with seeing your former colleague precede you as a captain?"

Worf looked away from the captain. "I do not resent Captain Dax's promotion," he said, and it was mostly true. However, he had to admit there was a certain dark irony to the situation.

During the Dominion War, Worf had decided, during a vital military operation, to save the life of his wife, Jadzia Dax, rather than complete his assignment. The ensuing fallout of that botched mission had resulted in a black mark on his service record, one which Captain Sisko had believed would prevent Worf from ever receiving his own command.

Years of distinguished service in Starfleet and the Federation Diplomatic Corps had mostly overcome the stigma of that old reprimand, but there were times when Worf still felt pangs of guilt for all the other lives that had been lost in the war because of his selfish choice. Despite all he had achieved since then, Worf still harbored serious doubts that Starfleet would ever place him in command of a ship of the line.

And now Ezri Dax—for whose previous host Worf had committed his professional *Hegh'bat*—was in command of a starship. He didn't begrudge Ezri her success, but he had to wonder how long the universe intended to mock him for his actions on Soukara.

"Do you wish me to apologize to Commander Bowers, sir?"

Picard's expression brightened. "Definitely not. Everyone knows the *Enterprise* has the best crew in Starfleet." He sipped his tea and cracked a wry smile. "Dismissed, Mister Worf."

# 1519

## 2

The future was the past, and the past was the present.

On Earth, Cortés was leading a Spanish expedition in Mexico and triggering the New World's first pandemic by introducing it to the influenza virus; Babur was conquering northern India, as a prelude to establishing the Mughal Empire; Magellan had begun his circumnavigation of the globe; and in Europe, Martin Luther was challenging the infallibility of papal decrees.

Adrift in the cold light and deep silence of interstellar space, however, time began to feel like an abstraction to Captain Erika Hernandez. During the months that she and her landing party from the *Columbia* NX-02 had spent on the planet Erigol as "compulsory guests" of the reclusive aliens known as the Caeliar, she had accustomed herself to the rhythm of natural days and nights. As much as she had shared her crew's desire to escape the aliens' custody and return home to Earth, she had on some level enjoyed being back in a natural environment.

Now that lush world was gone, annihilated by a supernova along with much of the Caeliar's civilization—and, as far as Hernandez knew, the *Columbia* itself.

Without the rising and setting of the sun, Hernandez had no sense of the passage of days or weeks or months. She slept when she was tired, ate when she was hungry, and filled the indeterminate spans of her waking hours with nostalgic remembrances of a life left behind. Her only indicator of time's passing was the length of her hair, which had barely reached her shoulders when she'd first come to Erigol; it now fell in dark, thick tangles a few inches below her shoulder blades.

Three other survivors from the *Columbia* had escaped the cataclysm of Erigol with her, as passengers inside the fleeing capital city of Axion: Commander Veronica Fletcher, the first officer; Dr. Johanna Metzger, the ship's chief medical officer; and Ensign Sidra Valerian, the communications officer. None of them had adapted to the formless, unstructured existence of the Caeliar with any more ease than she had.

Hernandez stood alone in the middle of an empty, granite-tiled plaza, surrounded by the majestic towers and spires of the Caeliar metropolis. Its delicate metal-and-crystal architecture captured the feeble illumination of starlight, which cast the city in fathomless shadows, dull swaths of titanium white, and endless shades of gray.

The silence of the city pressed against her soul. It was so absolute, so unnatural. Despite the presence of millions of Caeliar denizens, the megalopolis appeared deserted. Its concert shells sat empty; shattered sculptures lay abandoned in the plazas and streets. Even the air was deathly still.

Footsteps, faint and distant, behind her. Drawing near by slow degrees. She felt no need to turn and look; she already knew that it was one of her officers. Only they ever walked in Axion. The Caeliar, with their bodies of catoms—sophisticated nanomachines—hovered and floated at will, and when the mood struck them, they could coalesce from glowing motes in the air.

A few minutes later the footfalls were crisp and close. Then they stopped, and in the perfect stillness of the city, Hernandez could hear the gentle tides of breathing behind her.

"Any idea what they're up to?" asked Fletcher, her New Zealand accent softened slightly by her years of service in the multinational Earth Starfleet.

The captain turned and regarded her blond, athletically toned XO with a dour look. "Considering I haven't even seen a Caeliar in . . ." She paused, momentarily at a loss for a unit of time she could be certain of. She gave up and continued, ". . . in God knows how long, I have no clue what they're doing."

"I don't suppose we could just ask Inyx," Fletcher said.

Hernandez shook her head. "I get the feeling he's not taking my calls right now. Can't say as I blame him."

"No, I guess not." Fletcher joined Hernandez in staring up at the stars. "It's not like we can send a fruit basket with a little card that says, 'So sorry our MACOs went haywire, blew up a city, and killed a million of your people.'"

"And then some," Hernandez said. "For all we know, by interrupting the Caeliar's work, Foyle and his men might have started a chain reaction that wiped out their planet."

An interval that felt to Hernandez like a long time and also like no time at all passed between the two of them while they watched the unchanging stars.

It was Fletcher who broke the silence. "So now what?"

"We wait," Hernandez said with placid resignation.

It didn't seem to be the answer Fletcher had hoped for. "That's it? We wait? For what?"

"Whatever comes," Hernandez replied. "We can't escape, Veronica. We don't have a ship, and even if we hitched a ride and somehow escaped the Caeliar, where would we go? Earth? We don't even know where we are, never mind which way to travel. And if, by some miracle, we actually got there, then what? It's the *sixteenth century*."

"Maybe we could catch a few Shakespeare plays."

"Sure, if you want to wait about seventy years."

Fletcher made exaggerated swivel-turns to her left and right, looked up at the deserted walkways and promenades, and then turned back and said to Hernandez, "I've got time."

The captain sighed. "We both do."

Another silence stretched out between them. At one point Fletcher started to shuffle her feet, creating a dry scraping sound that became too much for Hernandez to ignore. She glared at her XO, who put on a sheepish expression and stilled her fidgeting, restoring the city to eerie soundlessness.

After a time—how long, exactly, Hernandez couldn't say—a figure appeared on a distant walkway between two lofty towers. It moved at a languid pace, slowly crossing the yawning distance between its origin and the two women on the plaza.

When it was still more than a hundred meters away, it became clear to Hernandez that the figure was a Caeliar. She couldn't help but note the enormous, bulbous skull behind its long, distorted face. Its gangly arms swung awkwardly as the alien plodded on bony legs and broad, three-toed feet. There was a pronounced heaving of exertion in the ribbed air sacs that linked respiratory tubules on either side of its head to the anatomy inside its fragile-looking chest.

From the unique mottling of purple and green on his leathery gray hide, she recognized Inyx, the chief scientist of the Caeliar and her team's principal contact. Just a few months earlier, she had not been able to distinguish the majority of his people from

DAVID MACK

one another, but now she was able to recognize the individual
subtleties in the shapes of their ocular ridges and mandibular
joints.

Inyx halted a few meters in front of Hernandez and Fletcher.
"The Quorum wishes to speak to you, Erika."

"About what?"

"Many things," he said.

Fletcher scrutinized the alien, starting at his feet and ending
at his drawn, always-frowning face. "Nice to see you walking on
solid ground with us little people for a change."

"We're still weak from the wound to the gestalt," he said. "Our
power is being conserved to repair the city while we seek out a
new world on which to continue our Great Work."

Hernandez lifted one eyebrow in suspicion. "With all the
power you folks had to spare on Erigol, I find it hard to believe
you're this desperate now."

"We could marshal more," Inyx said. "However, it is imperative that we maintain a minimal energy profile, so as not to draw
attention to ourselves. We must be extremely careful not to disrupt the course of this timeline now that we are here."

Hernandez was bursting with questions. "But why—"

He cut her off with a raised hand. "There will be time for your
inquiries later. Now I must escort you to the Quorum."

She nodded toward her first officer. "Commander Fletcher is
coming with me."

"As you wish," Inyx said. "Please follow me." He turned his
back on the women and began his trudging return journey.

Hernandez fell into step behind him and motioned with a tilt
of her head for Fletcher to follow her. "Come on."

Fletcher caught up to Hernandez in a few steps. "Why'd you
have to drag me into this?"

"I'm sorry," Hernandez said with deadpan sarcasm, "did you
have something else to do today?"

Narrowing her eyes in mock frustration, Fletcher replied,
"Fine. But if they've changed their minds about executing us, I
get to say 'I told you so.'"

Hernandez shrugged. "That's fair."

The walk through the city was long and slow.

Before its expulsion into the void, Axion had been filled with conveyances subtle and fleet. Moving sidewalks had hurtled pedestrians along the boulevards; floating disks of razor-thin, mirror-perfect silver had ferried groups large and small from one end of the city to another in minutes, and even between cities, back when there had been other cities to visit. Vertical shafts had once spiraled open on command and shuttled passengers, safe inside invisible shells, from the city's highest vantages to its deepest recesses.

Now there were ramps and stairs, and bridges too narrow for Hernandez's liking. And everything seemed so far away.

She and Fletcher followed Inyx as he loped forward, his long arms swinging in rhythmic opposition, like metronome bars forever parted by one beat.

Hernandez's gait grew heavier and clumsier with each step. Her knees hurt, and her feet had started to ache.

And that was *before* they reached the pyramid.

It rose ahead of the three travelers, a geometrically perfect peak of dark metal and smoky crystal, each face of it subdivided into triangular quarters, each of those quartered again, and so on, through hundreds of shrinking iterations.

At its base, a triangular portal several meters high slid open far in advance of their arrival, while they were still traversing the forlorn emptiness of the square promenade that surrounded the pyramid. Through the opening, Hernandez saw stairs. "Inyx, tell me we're not walking up."

"It is an unfortunate but necessary consequence of our power conservation," he said. "Do you need to rest before we begin the climb to the Quorum hall?"

She glanced at Fletcher, who nodded energetically. "Yes," Hernandez said. "Just for a few minutes."

"Take such time as you require," Inyx said.

When at last the trio reached the mountainous structure, Hernandez and Fletcher sat down and leaned against the base of the pyramid to rest. "I didn't remember it being this far," Fletcher said between heaving breaths.

"Neither did I," Hernandez said, huffing for air.

Inyx stood in the open portal while he waited for the recuperating women, as still as if he were a statue rooted into the gleaming black granite. His ever-present frown betrayed nothing. Hernandez wondered if she would ever be able to read the moods of the Caeliar. If there was some external cue to be parsed, it certainly wasn't to be found in the leathery slack of their inexpressive faces.

Fletcher sighed and slapped her palms against her thighs. "Ready to go see the happy brigade?"

"I can hardly wait," Hernandez said. Pushing off the pyramid, she forced her aching body back to a standing position and stretched to dispel the leaden stiffness of fatigue and the tension that had coiled into a crick between her shoulder blades. It released with a gentle *pop,* and she turned to face the steep grade of stairs that receded to a point far above them. She looked at Fletcher. "Ready?" The first officer nodded, and Hernandez said to their guide, "Okay, let's go."

The awkwardly built Caeliar ascended the stairs with ease. He walked with an unflagging stride, and after the first hundred steps had easily outpaced Hernandez and Fletcher, who labored to follow him. After the fourth time that he found himself forced to pause and wait for them to catch up, he relented and slowed his climb to accommodate them.

Hernandez felt as if she had scaled Everest by the time the top of the staircase became visible. She could barely breathe, and the muscles in her legs and lower back had started tying themselves into a Celtic knot of pain.

At the apex of the climb, another triangular portal—this one only a few meters tall at its highest point—opened into the vast expanse of the Quorum hall, which occupied the uppermost level of the pyramid. Hernandez and Fletcher slumped against the edges of the doorway while they caught their breath.

The hall was a hollow pyramid, with towering walls of dark crystal over the lattices of metallic triangles. It had been quite some time—weeks, or maybe even months—since Hernandez and Fletcher had last been here, during the destruction of Erigol. From this room they'd witnessed Axion's desperate escape, through a subspace tunnel, to this remote corner of space and time.

Before the cataclysm, tiers of seating had been elevated above the main level of the hall; those had collapsed during the disaster. The wreckage was gone now, and the fissures that had marred the beauty of the fractal sunburst pattern adorning the polished marble floor had been repaired. The tiers, however, had not been repaired. Instead, the hundreds of Caeliar gathered in the hall milled about in clusters great and small on the main level, communicating by means of their atonal humming.

Then everything was silent, and the Caeliar turned to face the two women. Inyx turned toward them and said, "The Quorum is ready to receive you."

"Lucky us," Hernandez said.

"Follow me," Inyx said.

They walked with him toward the throng of Caeliar, who spread out into a half circle around the trio. At the center of the curved line was the crimson-garbed de facto leader of the Quorum, Ordemo Nordal. His own people called him the *tanwaseynorral,* which Inyx had explained to Hernandez meant something akin to "first among equals." All she knew for certain was that, in this chamber, Ordemo did most of the talking.

"Some members of this Quorum have suggested we should hold you and your three remaining companions accountable for the tragedy of Erigol," Ordemo said. "There also has been debate over a preemptive displacement of your homeworld and your species, to prevent future disruptions of our Great Work. However, I have agreed to postpone a final referendum on these matters until after Inyx presents his findings."

Inyx made a small bow from the waist toward Ordemo and then addressed the Quorum, in a voice that sounded artificially amplified despite the apparent absence of any means to do so. "I offer you the sum of my research," he said, spreading his arms wide. "The gestalt will attest to its veracity." A mellifluous drone coursed through the assemblage. "The humans' interference with the apparatus had no effect on the Great Work." A discordant buzzing undercut the group's melodious tones as Inyx continued. "Even as they interfered with the apparatus's locus in Mantilis, the other loci compensated for its loss. There was no disruption in, or corruption of, our transmission to the shrouded galaxy."

Ordemo lifted one arm, and the dissonant noise of the Quorum faded away. "How, then, do you account for the hostility of the response we received?"

"It was intentional," Inyx said. "The damage it inflicted upon the apparatus, and throughout our energy matrix, was quite precise and crafted with expert knowledge of our technology. It was intended to annihilate us, and to do so with such alacrity that we couldn't hope to respond in time. The most interesting fact, however, is that it also was made expressly to prevent us from purging the humans' time-travel formulae from the apparatus. This, as well as several unique characteristics of the signal pulse itself, leave no doubt as to the identity of the civilization that committed this barbarous act."

Hernandez heard the ire in Ordemo's voice as he demanded, "Who, Inyx? Who did this to us?"

Inyx faced the *tanwa-seynorral*. "We did."

Ordemo sounded stunned. "Why?"

"Two more of our cities escaped through time-shifted subspace tunnels, just as Axion has. One of them I have been unable to locate, but the other had a chroniton signature so profound that I couldn't help but see it. If my calculations are correct, it traveled back nearly to the dawn of time. Our own people, or perhaps their heirs, built a new civilization in the nascent universe, and then they waited nearly fourteen billion years to smite us—in order to create themselves."

"A predestination paradox," Ordemo said in a shocked hush.

"Technically, this would be considered a self-consistent causal loop," Inyx said. "Regardless, it absolves our human guests of ultimate culpability for the Cataclysm. And as we have already established that Captain Hernandez and her fellow survivors were as much victims of their renegade compatriots as we were, it would be unjust to treat them as accomplices."

The susurrus of debate charged the air in the Quorum hall for several seconds. Then the cavernous chamber fell silent again, and Ordemo stepped forward from the line. "Very well. The Quorum has consensus. Captain Hernandez and her companions will remain as our guests." To the captain herself he added, "I am certain you will understand, however, if we choose to exercise a heightened degree of caution in our future dealings with you."

"Of course," Hernandez said.

Ordemo brought his arms together and intertwined his tendril-like fingers. "This convocation is concluded. If you'll excuse us, Captain, we have much work to do."

Without awaiting her response, the *tanwa-seynorral* walked past her and merged into a line of Caeliar walking toward one of the four exits from the chamber.

Inyx lingered for a moment beside Hernandez and Fletcher. "Are you and your companions well? Do you need anything?"

"Physically, we're fine," Hernandez said. "But we could use something to keep our minds occupied."

With a flourish of raised arms, Inyx replied, "You could always take up art."

Hernandez couldn't help but be amused.

"I might just do that," she said.

# 2381

## 3

"Welcome to New Erigol," said the woman who Commander Tuvok had identified as Erika Hernandez.

Commander Christine Vale's first, unspoken reaction was to wonder what the hell had happened to Old Erigol.

Her next thought was that Hernandez looked amazing for someone who had been missing for more than two centuries. The woman's enormous mane of dark, unruly hair spilled over her shoulders and framed her youthful face, and her physique—loosely garbed in drapes of gauzy fabric that were barely equal to the demands of modesty—was equally trim and toned. If Vale hadn't known better, she'd have assumed Hernandez was barely out of her teens.

Even though Vale was the away team commander, Counselor Troi took the lead in speaking for the group. "I'm Commander Deanna Troi, senior diplomatic officer of the *Starship Titan*," she said. Gesturing back at the other *Titan* personnel behind her, she continued, "These are my shipmates and friends. Commander Christine Vale, first officer; Commander Tuvok, second officer; Dr. Shenti Yisec Eres Ree, chief medical officer; Lieutenant Ranul Keru, chief of security; Ensign Torvig Bu-kar-nguv, engineer; and Lieutenant Gian Sortollo and Chief Petty Officer Dennisar of our security division."

Hernandez nodded to the away team. "Hello," she said. Looking to the being on her right, she said, "This is Edrin, our chief architect." Turning to her other companion, she continued, "And this is Inyx, our chief scientist."

Inyx made a subtle bow toward Troi. "Welcome to the city of Axion, Commander Troi," he said, his voice a rich baritone.

Vale stepped forward and stood shoulder-to-shoulder with Troi. To their hosts she said, "Hi, nice to meet you. It seems you know quite a bit about us, no doubt thanks to Captain Hernandez. But I'm afraid you have us at a disadvantage."

Behind her, Tuvok quipped, "In more ways than one."

"Of course," Hernandez said, her voice strangely subdued in its inflections. "Inyx and Edrin are members of a species known as Caeliar."

"For simplicity's sake," Inyx interrupted, "you may use Caeliar as a singular or plural noun, or as an adjective." Vale thought she caught a fleeting look of mischief between the alien scientist and Hernandez.

"Good to know," said Troi. "Captain Hernandez? Forgive me for prying, but finding you alive raises many questions."

"Yes," Hernandez said, her face betraying no emotion. She looked at Inyx, who returned her gaze in silence, and then she looked back at Troi. "What do you wish to know?"

Troi lifted a hand and gestured at the magnificent city of platinum and crystal that towered behind them. "For starters, how you came to be here, so far from Earth."

"And why you're still alive two hundred years after your ship disappeared," Vale added.

Their questions provoked a sly look of amusement from Hernandez. "As the saying goes, it's a long story."

The two Caeliar turned and looked at each other. Then they looked at Hernandez, who shifted her downcast gaze back and forth between the aliens before she looked up at Vale and Troi.

"Forgive me," Hernandez said. "I was sent here to deliver a message, and I should do as I was instructed before I digress."

A chill of foreboding washed through Vale. "What kind of message?"

Hernandez's manner became cold and aloof. "At this time, your shipmates on *Titan* are being informed of what I have to tell you now. Although no violent measures will be used against you or your vessel, the Caeliar will not permit you to leave this place, nor will you be allowed to have any further external communications. Those of you who have come to the planet's surface must remain here. *Titan* will be expected to remain in orbit, though any of your compatriots who wish to join you here in Axion will be free to petition the Caeliar for entry."

With sour sarcasm, Vale replied, "How generous of them."

"The power has been drained from your weapons," Hernandez continued. "If the Caeliar detect any effort on your part to recharge them, they will disintegrate them. You may retain your scanning devices, provided you don't use them against the Caeliar or to jeopardize the safety of the city." She paused while gauging the away team's reaction. "It is important that you understand the Caeliar do not see you as prisoners."

Tuvok inquired in reply, "How, then, are we to perceive our incarcerated status?"

"Like me," Hernandez said, "you are all considered to be guests . . . with restrictions." Another glimmer of silent interaction passed between Hernandez and Inyx.

With acidic sarcasm, Vale said, "You've been away a couple hundred years, so maybe you don't know this, but English has a word for that now: It's called a *prisoner.*"

"I understand this will be a difficult transition for many of you," Hernandez said. "Some of you may find it impossible. But it's my hope, and that of the Caeliar, that you'll learn to accept this new paradigm." She nodded to the second Caeliar. "Edrin will escort you to your accommodations. If you need anything, just say it aloud. The Caeliar will do the rest."

Edrin extended his arm and waggled his tendril-like digits. Tiny droplets of quicksilver formed like dew on blades of grass, rose into the air, and fused into a sliver-thin disk of mirror-perfect metal four meters in diameter. The disk hovered a few centimeters above the ground. The Caeliar stepped onto it and gestured to the away team. "Please join me," he said in a melodic tenor. "It's quite safe."

Vale nodded to the rest of the away team. Keru was the first to climb atop the disk, which remained as stable as bedrock. The bearish, bearded Trill man nodded to his security officers, who shepherded Dr. Ree and Ensign Torvig onto the levitated platform. The reptilian physician alighted onto the disk, the talons of his nimble feet clicking against the metal. Torvig—who Vale thought resembled a wingless ostrich with a sheep's head, cybernetic arms, and a bionic hand grafted onto his prehensile tail—bounded lightly onto the disk beside Ree. Keru waved Dennisar aboard, and the Orion security guard complied. Lieutenant Sortollo followed him.

As Vale turned to walk to the disk, Troi asked Inyx, "Will we be allowed to contact *Titan?*"

"No," he said. "I'm sorry, but our past experience has made it clear that any contact you have with your ship would likely be used to collude in your escape. We don't wish to separate you from your friends and colleagues, but we can't risk allowing you to plan coordinated action that might be to our detriment."

The half-Betazoid counselor nodded, but her expression was forlorn. "I understand," she said. Then she followed Vale and Tuvok to the disk. As soon as the three of them joined the rest of the away team on the circular platform, it ascended several meters with no sensation of motion that Vale could detect.

Hernandez looked up at them with a longing gaze. "I'll come to see you once you're settled. And I'll tell you my story."

"I can hardly wait," Vale said, already stewing in her own anger. She made a flippant gesture at the two Caeliar. "Bring your friends. They're a hoot."

Troi, however, was gentler in tone and word. "I'll look forward to seeing you," she said.

Then the disk was hurtling forward in silence, through the gleaming canyons of the city, soaring over the plazas and under the causeways of the sprawling metropolis. Vale fought to take it all in as it blurred past, trying to remember the shapes of the city and the grid of its streets.

Because it was never too early to start planning an escape.


Captain William Riker was irate. "That's all they said?"

"Yes, sir," said Lieutenant Sariel Rager, *Titan*'s senior operations officer. She held one hand a few centimeters above the touchscreen interface of her console. "Do you want to hear it again?"

"That won't be necessary," Riker said. He stalked back to his chair and fumed at the arrogance implicit in the audio-only message *Titan* had just received from the Caeliar. In effect, the aliens had just declared the away team and *Titan* itself to be their prisoners. There had been no warning, no opportunity to discuss terms—just a standing invitation for those on the ship to change the setting of their incarceration.

Adding to his anger was the fact that this new crisis had deprived him of most of his senior officers, including his wife, Deanna Troi. His concern for her, especially in light of her fragile medical condition, was only slightly offset by the knowledge that Dr. Ree was with her.

He stood behind his chair and rested his hands on top of it.

On the main viewer, the world the Caeliar called New Erigol was concealed inside a spherical shell of dark metal. A similar hollow globe encased its star, rendering this system all but invisible to most detection protocols.

Lieutenant Commander Fo Hachesa, a Kobliad man who served as *Titan*'s gamma-shift officer of the watch, occupied the first officer's seat. He tracked the crew's ongoing efforts to repair the damage to the ship's sensors that had been inflicted a day earlier by one of the Caeliar's long-range scans.

Commander Xin Ra-Havreii, *Titan*'s chief engineer, handed off control of his engineering station console to a junior officer and joined Riker behind the command chair. The slender Efrosian man pensively stroked his long, flowing white mustache and stared at the forward viewscreen. "It's quite a feat of engineering," he said. "Whatever it's made of, I can't get a clear sensor reading from it."

From the tactical console, Lieutenant Rriarr called out, "Captain? The passageway through the shell that the shuttlecraft *Mance* used to reach the surface has closed."

Riker nodded to the Caitian, who was filling in for Keru. "Keep an eye open for any other changes."

"Aye, sir."

Ra-Havreii asked Riker discreetly, "Do you want me to look for a way to punch a hole in it? Maybe take a shot at beaming the away team back?"

Shaking his head, Riker said, "No. I doubt we'd even scratch it. And with the level of technology the Caeliar must possess, I'd rather not provoke them into a fight."

"Sensible," said Ra-Havreii, who then nodded past Riker, to Lieutenant Commander Melora Pazlar, the head of the ship's sciences division, who had just joined them.

The thirtyish blond Elaysian woman looked strangely incomplete to Riker's eyes, because he had become accustomed to seeing her limbs and torso surrounded by a powered exoskeletal armature. The mechanical suit—which Pazlar often jokingly referred to as "the armor"—had been necessary because she was a native of a world with a microgravity environment; in the Earth-normal gravity of most Federation starships, starbases, and worlds, her bones would snap under her own weight.

Now she stood beside him, at ease and unencumbered by

her armature, thanks to the latest innovation of Commander Ra-Havreii: holographic telepresence. The figure next to Riker was not the flesh-and-blood Pazlar but her holographic avatar, which could go anywhere aboard the ship by means of a network of holographic sensors and emitters. Meanwhile, the real Pazlar was safely ensconced in the microgravity environment of the ship's stellar cartography lab, interacting with perfect holographic simulacra of her shipmates in a real-time re-creation of the bridge.

"I presume we're not simply giving up," she said to Riker.

He felt his jaw tighten even as he replied, "Never."

Hachesa looked up from his work and joined the conversation. "If we cannot fight the Caeliar," he said, "and we do not wish to surrender to them, how shall we proceed?"

"As I see it," Riker said, "we have two paths left to us: diplomacy and deceit. Our best diplomat is already on the surface, so I'd recommend we leave any negotiations to her."

Pazlar folded her arms. "What kind of deception do you have in mind, Captain?"

"I don't know yet," he said. "What I want is for you and Ra-Havreii to go over everything we know so far about this system, this planet, and this species. Look for anything we can exploit, either tactically or politically. I don't want to use violence while our away team is down there, so focus on making contact with our people and gathering intel any way we can."

Ra-Havreii's snowy eyebrows twitched upward. "I should advise you, Captain, that this is a task whose progress will likely be measured not over the course of hours but of days, even under the best of circumstances."

"Then the sooner you get to work, the better," Riker said, in a tone that brooked no debate. "Don't you agree, Commander?"

Pazlar's avatar tugged at Ra-Havreii's shirtsleeve. "Come on, Xin. I have an idea where to start. We can work on it in your office."

"An excellent suggestion," Ra-Havreii said. "Fewer distractions down there." He followed the holographic Pazlar into the turbolift. Before the doors closed, Riker was certain that he caught sight of a smug leer on the lean, angular face of the Efrosian, whose reputation as a ladies' man was well earned.

Riker sighed. "Commander Hachesa, I'll be in my ready room. You have the bridge."

"Aye, sir," Hachesa said, and he returned to administrating the minutiae of the ship's business as Riker walked aft and withdrew to the privacy of his ready room.

After the door had hissed shut behind him, Riker collapsed heavily onto the sofa, tilted his head back, and stared blankly at the overhead. It had been a long couple of days for him and *Titan*'s crew. Weighing most ponderously in his thoughts was the emotional turmoil that had been wrought in his and Deanna's marriage by her miscarriage of their first successful pregnancy several months earlier, and the recent news, delivered by Dr. Ree only a few days earlier, that their second attempt had become not only nonviable but also a risk to Deanna's health and life. Talking about it with his first officer had proved explosive, and Deanna's refusal to heed Ree's medical advice had only made an already tumultuous situation even more volatile.

The tension and grief that filled every silence between himself and Deanna had made it almost impossible for them to communicate these past few days. All the same, he wished she were here now, even if only as his diplomatic officer and not as his wife, so that he wouldn't feel so adrift. At times such as this, he relied on sage advice from Deanna, Christine Vale, and Tuvok. Drawing on their experience and insight, he had come to think of command as a process of synthesis rather than one of genesis.

He closed his eyes and tried to focus on the tides of his breathing, because for the first time since he'd taken the reins of *Titan,* he felt the true loneliness of being in command.


Night had been falling on New Erigol's northern latitudes for weeks without quite arriving. Arctic twilight suffused the sky with a dusky haze along the horizon, and outside Axion's protective shield, fierce winds howled and whipped spindrifts across a dark and ice-choked sea.

Erika Hernandez stood next to Inyx on a circular platform at the end of a narrow walkway, which extended several dozen meters beyond the city's periphery. She sensed his influence on the invisible cloud of catoms that surrounded them, as he used them to extend and shape Axion's protective field around their just-created and temporary widow's walk.

She stared into the half-light and let the vista imprint on her consciousness. Its qualities of color and shadow changed by slow degrees. "Please ask the Quorum to take the city south," she said as mournful winds caterwauled between nearby glaciers.

"I thought you admired the austerity of the arctic," Inyx said, passively resisting her request.

"It's very pretty," Hernandez said. "But it's going to get darker soon, and I'm concerned about the effect that a prolonged night might have on the humans from *Titan*."

Inyx sounded almost contrite. "Yes, I should've considered that. I'll pass your request to the Quorum now." She felt a low crackle of energy surround him as he communed with the gestalt. For a moment she was tempted to eavesdrop, but she decided that it would be too risky. Instead, she waited for his response, which she knew was imminent when the tingle of psychic communion faded from the air between them. "The city will be under way very soon," he said. "We'll complete the transition while our guests are asleep, and we will try to match our longitudinal position with the proper phase in their endogenous diurnal cycle."

"Thank you," Hernandez said. "It should ease their adjustment to life in the city. And if I'm to be completely honest, I was starting to miss our sunrises."

"As was I," Inyx said. "Though if some in the Quorum have their way, we may not have many more to share." She felt a slight chill as he expelled all the free nanoscopic catoms from their immediate vicinity and configured those closest to them into a spherical scattering field to grant them privacy. "It has been proposed that if *Titan*'s crew accepts our invitation of sanctuary, our new guests should be exiled to remote settlements on the surface, and segregated by gender to reduce the risk of infesting the planet with a new civilization."

Hernandez remained calm as she replied, "I object to the use of the term 'infesting.'"

"As you should," Inyx replied. "However, I think the more important issue is to oppose this crude and repressive measure."

She was surprised to hear him speak out on behalf of *Titan*'s personnel. "I presume you have a different solution?"

"Absolutely," he said. "Though it would take greater effort, I think that more harmonious and sociologically balanced communities could be created if we segregate the visitors not by gender but rather by genetic incompatibility."

"Genetic incompatibility?" she repeated. She understood its meaning; she simply couldn't believe that Inyx had suggested it.

As usual, he rambled on, oblivious of her objection. "It's my hypothesis that a mix of male and female personalities, regardless of species, will help curb aggression in these new communities. By combining only those individuals who are not genetically compatible, however, we can achieve the desired state of negative population growth."

"In other words, they can pass their days pursuing futile labors until they die," Hernandez said with disdain. "Just like everyone else in the universe." She sighed and looked at the purple silhouettes of mountain peaks in the distance. "Why do your people always resort to such draconian measures? Why can't you try anything new?"

Inyx's tone became stern. "You've lived among us long enough to understand our ways and our reasons."

"Long enough to understand they're misguided," she said.

Undeterred, he continued, "I empathize with your desire to permit *Titan* into orbit, and even to let its emissaries come to the surface. But after what happened with your people on Erigol, we cannot risk such vulnerability again."

"Then why did you let them come here?"

"Because their civilization is too large to be displaced without drawing unwanted attention to ourselves. If we shifted the worlds and peoples of the Federation into another galaxy or quantum universe, we would be obliged to do the same for all the many powers that neighbor it. Likewise, all the astropolitical entities across the galaxy that know of the Federation would have to be displaced, as well. Ultimately, it seems to be a more prudent use of our resources to restrain and impound one starship and its crew than it would be to disrupt a significant fraction of all known galactic civilizations."

Hernandez considered Inyx's argument and realized that, in the centuries since the *Columbia*'s disappearance, Earth and its allies—its Federation—had become a formidable power in local space. When she and her crew had first come to Erigol, the Caeliar had not hesitated to level a threat against Earth if the *Columbia*'s personnel breached the Caeliar's precious secrecy. Now, however, they seemed reluctant to make such threats. It was the first sign of weakness they'd shown in all the time that she had known them—but she didn't believe it would be enough to make a difference.

After more than 860 years in Axion, Hernandez had learned to accept defeat as a given. The sooner *Titan*'s officers embraced that essential truth, the sooner they would be able to let go of the past and find a new modus vivendi here among the Caeliar.

With a thought, she directed the ever-attentive catoms in the air to disassemble the widow's walk. Inyx found himself standing on air, high above the churning sea. Hernandez strode away from him, followed by the vanishing edge of the walkway. "Call me when there's a sunrise."

# 4

Five hours had been barely enough time to make jury-rigged repairs on the *Enterprise* and render the ship strong enough to brave the volatile embrace of the Azure Nebula. The supernova remnant looked to Commander Miranda Kadohata like a bruise without a body as it grew larger on the main viewscreen. Then it swallowed the stars as the *Aventine* and the *Enterprise* moved inside it, less than a minute's flight from the coordinates at which the *Aventine* had exited a subspace corridor from the Gamma Quadrant.

Kadohata was finding the task of coordinating the effort complicated by her body's urgent desire for sleep. It took almost all of her concentration to stay awake as she tried to enter one more bit of data and assign one more damage-control task.

*"La Forge to ops,"* said the chief engineer over the comm.

Her eyes snapped open. "Go ahead, Geordi."

*"Miranda, we need some more bandwidth freed up on the subspace interlink."*

She scrambled to reorganize her interface to call up an inventory of available and committed computer resources. "How much more do you need?"

*"At least four megaquads,"* La Forge said. *"Five if you can spare it. The* Aventine*'s data-burst capacity is incredible."*

Even though La Forge couldn't see her, she shook her head

in dismay. "Even if I dump the nontactical systems from the primary network, the most I can give you is three-point-six mega-quads. Is there any way you can trim their signal?"

*"Not without reprogramming their main computer,"* La Forge said. There was a pause as he conferred with someone else, whose voice Kadohata couldn't hear clearly. Then La Forge continued, *"Lieutenant Leishman suggests we take all but our navigational sensors offline while we make repairs, since we'll be relying on the* Aventine*'s sensors inside the nebula, anyway."*

"I see," Kadohata said. "Does the *Aventine*'s chief engineer have any suggestions for how I should monitor our damage-control efforts without an internal sensor network?"

La Forge stammered, *"I, uh, I'm not sure I—"*

"Because if she's that interested in doing my job for me, I can knock off early, and maybe tell Ensign Rosado she can sleep in, too, since *Lieutenant* Leishman has the *Enterprise*'s operations-management needs well in hand."

She could almost hear him rolling his eyes. *"Getting a little defensive, aren't you? There's plenty of starship to go around, you know."*

Calling up some additional options on her console, she replied to La Forge, "This isn't about territoriality, Geordi. It's about balancing conflicting needs." She authorized some changes to the *Enterprise*'s status and added, "Speaking of which, I just isolated the internal sensors and comms on the emergency backup system, changed our protocol for incoming subspace radio traffic, and launched a subspace relay buoy to act as a signal buffer. That just bought you another point-six megaquads of bandwidth."

*"Thanks, Miranda,"* Geordi said, sounding grateful. *"You're the best. We're starting the relay from the* Aventine *now."* Adding a teasing quality to his voice, he added, *"I'll let* you *decide what to do with the data."*

"Don't test me, La Forge," she said with half-joking menace. "Routing it to aft stations one through four."

The row of consoles along the bridge's aft bulkhead came alive with mad flurries of data and imagery piped in from the *Aventine*'s sensors. Lieutenant Dina Elfiki, the *Enterprise*'s strikingly attractive, Egyptian-born senior science officer, took half a step back from the display, her dark brown eyes wide. "Wow," she said. "That's amazing." She turned toward Kadohata and flashed a smile. "Commander, you have to see this. The level of detail is incredible."

Kadohata got up from her chair and nodded to one of the relief officers to take over for her at the ops console. The young Saurian looked excited to finally be getting his webbed fingers on some real work as he slipped into her chair.

At the aft duty stations, Elfiki and two more lieutenants from the ship's sciences division—theoretical physicist Corinne Clipet and subspace-particle physicist James Talenda—watched in awe as a flood of raw information poured in from the *Vesta*-class starship that was leading the *Enterprise* into the nebula.

"Dina," said Kadohata, ever so gently, "is all that data going to analyze itself?"

The question snapped Elfiki back into motion. "Talenda, start looking for high-energy triquantum wave by-products. If there's another subspace conduit out here, that's how we'll find it." She turned toward the slender Frenchwoman. "Clipet, help Talenda filter out false positives by screening triquantum wave artifacts from any Borg ships still operating in this sector."

Kadohata watched the three scientists' hands fly across the consoles in a desperate and probably futile effort to keep up with the rapid crush of sensor input from the *Aventine*.

Clipet's hands kept moving as she reported, "The *Aventine* crew is already running a triquantum filter on the stream."

"Confirmed," Talenda said. "I'm finishing a sweep around the *Aventine*'s subspace tunnel terminus. If there's anything else like it within a hundred thousand kilometers of those coordinates, we should know in . . . a . . ." His voice tapered off as he finished, ". . . few minutes." He let his hands fall by his sides, and he stared slack-jawed at the complex schematic the computer had just rendered on the large display in front of him.

Kadohata waited for Elfiki to follow up, and then the second officer noticed that all three science officers had the same stunned expressions on their faces. "Ahem," she said with a loud and unnecessary clearing of her throat. Elfiki turned at the sound, prompting Kadohata to add, "What's going on?"

Elfiki nervously fiddled with a lock from her stylish coif of mahogany-brown hair. "I know we're looking for a different subspace tunnel than the one the *Aventine* used," she said.

"Yes," Kadohata said, "that's correct."

"Um . . ." Elfiki crossed her arms and leaned back a bit from the wall of consoles and screens. "Would you happen to know *which one,* exactly?"

*I don't like the sound of that,* Kadohata mused. "Dare I ask how many there are?"

The senior science officer stalled. "About . . . roughly . . ."

"Twenty-seven," Clipet declared.

Kadohata closed her eyes and wished that she were already asleep, so that this could be just a banal anxiety dream. Already braced for more bad news, she asked, "I don't suppose there's any way to tell which one the Borg have been using?"

"No, sir," Talenda said. "For all we know, they might be using more than one."

"Splendid," she said, rubbing her eyes gingerly.

The chrono on the console showed ship's time to be 0750. Her shift was scheduled to end in ten minutes, but sleep was going to have to wait, and there was no telling for how long, because the entire nature of their mission had just changed.

She tapped her combadge. "Captain Picard and Commander Worf, please report to the bridge."

Dax appreciated Captain Picard's courtesy in coming aboard the *Aventine* to meet with her in her own ready room, but his gesture wasn't making her any more receptive to his plan. The fact that she'd only been able to steal two hours of sleep since their last meeting wasn't improving her mood, either.

"I think you're making a mistake, Captain," she said. "It's like using a phaser to swat a fly."

Her metaphor seemed to fray the edges of Picard's already careworn patience. "I would hardly call the threat of a massive, genocidal Borg invasion 'a fly,' Captain Dax." He paced like a tiger not yet resigned to life inside its cage. "Whether we're talking about one hole in the Federation's defenses or several, our mission remains the same—close the gap."

"We will," Dax said, pulling back hard on the reins of her own temper. "But that's a short-term goal. We also have to consider long-term objectives." It was important to keep this discussion civil. Though they were both captains, Starfleet protocols clearly recognized his many years of command seniority and afforded him considerable privileges under circumstances such as these.

He narrowed his eyes. "I'd consider the survival of the Federation both a short- and a long-term mission priority."

"So is exploration," Dax replied. "Think of where some of those subspace tunnels might lead. What if some of them are passages to other galaxies? Or shortcuts across our own? Their value to science is immeasurable."

"As is the threat they represent to our survival," Picard shot back. "If there was some way to tell if the Borg had access to only one, and if we knew which it was, I might consider a surgical strike. But both our science departments concur: there's no way to be certain. For all we know, the Borg are exploiting several of these tunnels through subspace. And as far as I'm concerned, even one is too many. They *must* be destroyed."

Shaking her head, Dax ruminated aloud, "We could open them up, go through, and scout ahead. If we could save even a few safe passages—"

"We don't have that luxury, Captain," Picard said. "Your science officer wrote in his report that it could take hours to calculate the frequency for opening the aperture of one tunnel, and that they all resonate to different harmonics. It could take days to scout all these passages—and I have reason to suspect the Borg won't be giving us that much time. Collapsing the passageways is the swiftest means of ending this Borg invasion, and it lets us do so without further conflict or loss of life."

Dax turned away for a moment and looked out the window behind her desk, at the swirling violet and blue fog of the Azure Nebula. Like most officers in Starfleet, she had heard the rumors of Picard's bizarre mental link with the Borg Collective, and the advantages that it had given him in combat against them. He seemed convinced of the imminence of the Borg threat, and that was enough to persuade her. She swiveled her chair back to face him and folded her hands atop her desk.

"All right," she said. "I see your point. All the research opportunities in the galaxy don't mean much if we're not here to enjoy them. Do you have a plan for how to proceed?"

Picard stopped pacing and leaned on one of the chairs in front of Dax's desk. "I'd like our science, engineering, and operations teams to keep working together," he said. "This is a new phenomenon, and we need to comprehend it before we can find a way to dismantle it."

"Tall order," Dax said. "Learning how to take it apart might take as much time as scouting each passage. Or more."

"Perhaps," Picard said. "Certainly, it will take time to complete our analysis. Reinforcements are en route, but we should take aggressive precautions."

"Aggressive precautions," she repeated. "Is that one of those phrases I'm supposed to learn as a captain, or did you just make that up?"

"I have been known to coin a phrase once in a while," he said, with his own disarming charm. "As for securing these passageways, we can take advantage of the fact that all the apertures surround a central position. If we mine that zone heavily enough, we can prevent further incursions while we complete our research."

Something about his suggestion didn't sound right to Dax. "A minefield? Inside a nebula full of sirillium gas?"

"Exactly," Picard said. "We'll make the environment work for us, use it to amplify the potential impact of the mines."

Dax tried to remain calm as she considered the consequences of Picard's strategy, but anxiety set her index finger to tapping on her desktop. "At this range, the blast effects of a full-scale detonation would probably cripple both our ships."

Nodding and adopting a grave countenance, Picard said, "I've already made it clear to my officers and crew that the *Enterprise* is to be considered expendable if that's what it takes to seal this breach in the Federation's defenses. I need to know that you and your crew share this commitment."

*I must have missed the memo about this being a suicide mission.* She wondered for a moment what pointed words her symbiont's former host Curzon might have hurled at Picard in a moment such as this. Going along with Picard's plan to wipe out an invaluable scientific discovery in the name of security had already rankled her; now he was asking her to pledge her ship's destruction and her crew's collective demise to accomplish it.

*If he's wrong, this'll be a disaster,* she told herself. *But if he's right . . .*

"During the Dominion War," she said, "Deep Space 9 used self-replicating cloaked mines to prevent Dominion reinforcements in the Gamma Quadrant from traveling through the Bajoran wormhole. I'm not sure the cloaking technology will work here inside the nebula, but if we make the minefield self-replicating, it'll be able to sustain and rebuild itself even if our ships are destroyed or forced to retreat."

"An excellent suggestion, Captain," Picard said. "How soon can it be done?"

"We're still fabricating parts for your repairs," she said, thinking out loud, "but after that's finished, we can build the first dozen mines in a few hours. Then we can release them and let them do the rest of the work, replicating themselves to build a defensive cluster between the subspace tunnels. The entire zone could be filled in about four hours."

Picard stood tall and gave her a curt nod. "Make it so."


"It's a right awful shame, if you ask me," said Miranda Kadohata, keeping her eyes and her hands on her console at ops. "One of the most amazing things we've ever discovered, and the captain wants us to destroy it."

Worf had no wish to debate Kadohata regarding the wisdom of their assignment, and not just because she was right. The simple fact was that the Federation had once again found itself in a state of war with the Borg Collective. Discipline and morale were more important at times like this than at any other.

"I concur," he said. "It is an interesting phenomenon, and it is regrettable that we will not be able to study it. But the captain's orders stand."

From a few meters behind him, Worf heard contact specialist Lieutenant T'Ryssa Chen mutter to another junior officer, "If we really wanted to know what makes these things tick, we'd have found a way to avoid blowing them up."

Muscles in the Klingon's jaw rippled with tension as he bit down on the rebuke he felt Chen so richly deserved. He stalked toward her, his unblinking gaze locked with Chen's as her young confidant prudently slipped away to work at a different station on the other side of the bridge.

He loomed over the youthful woman of mixed Vulcan-human ancestry, and his voice became quiet even as it sharpened to a fine edge. "Do you have something to share, Lieutenant Chen?"

She swallowed once while staring up from beneath eyebrows lifted to steep peaks of anxiety. "No, sir," she said. "I'm just, you know, compiling sensor logs and collating data. Sir."

"I see," Worf said. He put a malicious gleam in his stare. "Carry on, and keep Commander Kadohata informed of your progress," he said. As he stepped away, he added, "The captains want regular updates."

"They always do," Chen mumbled under her breath, and Worf felt frustration force his hand to clench into a fist. With effort he had opened his hand by the time he reached the security console, where Lieutenant Jasminder Choudhury, the chief of security, was plotting the minefield's distribution pattern. She had been laboring at the task for some time—longer, in fact, than Worf had expected it to require. He watched the serene-faced woman work at it, her agile hands rearranging patterns and data on her console. A subtle knitting of her brow was the only evidence of her mounting frustration.

He asked, "Is there a problem, Lieutenant?"

Choudhury stopped working. "There are some challenges." Her face was emotionless, her voice low and controlled—all hallmarks of a bad mood for her. "The fluid dynamics of the nebula are making it very difficult to keep the minefield's position stable relative to the subspace tunnels. And I'm still waiting for an updated analysis from stellar cartography about the behavior of the apertures themselves, so I can correct for any distortions."

"We can request help from the *Aventine*'s crew," Worf said. He noted the dubious stare of his security chief—with whom he had also recently become more closely acquainted—and concluded that she wasn't embracing his suggestion. "Or I could let you take more time with it."

Her lips pursed into a frown, and she shook her head in small, slow motions. "I'm sorry, sir, I can do this—really. I just don't know that I agree with it."

"Why not?" It wasn't like Choudhury to question orders, and Worf began to suspect that Kadohata might not be the only member of the *Enterprise*'s senior staff who was balking at Captain Picard's tactical directive. Noticing Choudhury's reluctance to answer, he added, "Speak freely, Lieutenant."

"Commander Kadohata's right," she said. "Aside from their scientific value, the subspace tunnels would be a major tactical resource for the Federation if we could secure them."

"And if we cannot, they are a vulnerability," Worf said. "One of these passages is being exploited by the Borg. We have no way of knowing what threats lie beyond the others."

Choudhury's face flushed slightly. "For all we know, most of the passages might not need any defending at all. Why don't we explore them, figure out which ones the Borg have compromised, and conduct surgical strikes to collapse just those passageways? Then we'd still have the others for exploration."

"I agree . . . in principle," Worf said. "But that approach would take a great deal of time—which we do not have."

"But if we did," Choudhury said, "and we could target only the Borg's subspace tunnels—"

"It would make no difference," Worf cut in. "If the Borg found one passage, they can find others. And now that they know what to look for, they will not stop until they find it." He hardened his countenance to drive home his point. "The safest choice is to collapse *all* the tunnels."

The security chief sighed. "You're right." She closed her eyes, took a deep breath, then set herself back to work. "I'll let you know when I've stabilized the deployment pattern," she said, and then she let herself become consumed in her task.

As Worf returned to his chair, an ensign handed him a padd. The XO sat down, skimmed the padd's contents, and was pleased to see that the *Aventine*'s damage-control teams working on the *Enterprise* were beginning to get ahead of schedule. If all continued to go well, the *Aventine*'s engineering division would be able to repurpose its industrial replicators for mine production shortly before midday.

On a less encouraging note, he reviewed the casualty statistics from sickbay and imagined it must have seemed like an abbatoir in the immediate aftermath of the battle. Before he could dwell too long on that morbid thought, Kadohata called back from ops, "Commander? Can I show you something?"

Worf put down the padd on his chair as he got up, and he walked at a quick step back to Kadohata's side. "Report."

"The *Aventine* just sent over its telemetry from its trip through the subspace tunnel," Kadohata said. "Watch what the aperture does when it opens." She played a computer-simulated animation that graphed the phenomenon's behavior, and pointed out details of the tunnel's interaction with normal space-time. "Something tells me Choudhury won't like that."

"No, she will not," Worf agreed. Eyeing the display with a more critical eye, he asked, "Will this interfere with our plan to destroy the tunnels?"

"If by interfere you mean scuttle, then yes." Kadohata pointed at a string of data. "Maybe I'm off the mark, but I think these readings mean that collapsing those passages is far more dangerous than we thought." She swiveled her chair toward Worf. "Sir, I'd like to get a second opinion on this data from Commander La Forge and my counterpart on the *Aventine*."

Her request prompted a subtle double take from Worf. "I have never heard you ask Geordi for a second opinion before."

With quiet humility, Kadohata replied, "That's because I've never been on the verge of making a galactically catastrophic mistake before."

Jean-Luc Picard was always grateful for those rare days when everything went according to plan. Alas, this would not be one of those days.

He entered the Deck 1 observation lounge of the *Enterprise* to find Worf standing beside his chair near one end of the table. Next to Worf were La Forge and Elfiki.

On the other side of the table stood Captain Dax, Commander Bowers, and the *Aventine*'s science officer, Lieutenant Helkara. The normally warm-colored, indirect lighting of the conference room was overwhelmed by the violet illumination from the nebula outside its broad, sloped windows.

Picard walked in brisk steps to his chair at the head of the table, and as he sat down he said, "Please, be seated." Everyone settled in at the table and leaned forward. He looked at Dax and asked, "Why has production halted on the minefield?"

"Because it won't work," Dax said. She nodded to her science officer. "Mister Helkara, the details, please?"

The svelte Zakdorn used the touchscreen on the table surface in front of his seat to activate a brief presentation on the wall monitor opposite the windows. "Our sensor telemetry of the subspace tunnels reveals a curious feature of its apertures," he said, narrating as the computer-generated animation on the screen continued. "When they open, they cause a localized disruption of the space-time curvature, to a range of approximately a hundred thousand kilometers. The effect is subtle enough that a starship's navigational system can compensate with little difficulty. Position-stabilized mines, on the other hand . . ."

He triggered a new animation sequence of an aperture opening into a region occupied by the minefield cluster. In a brief blur, the area was swept clean. "The space-time distortion is powerful enough within one thousand kilometers to disperse any minefield we install. Most of the mines will collide with one another and detonate. Any that are left will be brushed aside and ejected from the nebula, into deep space."

"It's possible that a few might remain intact after the aperture closes," Bowers added, "but not enough to stop a Borg ship, or to regenerate the minefield."

"Plus," Helkara said, "the mines that get tossed from the nebula will become hazards to interstellar shipping and travel."

Captain Picard presented a calm and professional demeanor as he looked to his science officer. "Lieutenant Elfiki? Have you had a chance to review this data?"

"Yes, sir," she said. "Our own sims confirmed it. The subspace tunnels' apertures will violently disperse the minefield. Mister Helkara and I think it might be a deliberate safety feature of the passageways."

Worf asked La Forge, "Could the mines be altered to compensate for the distortion?"

The chief engineer shook his head. "No, they just don't have that kind of maneuverability."

"Could we build it in?" Picard asked.

"I doubt it," La Forge said. "We can remove the replication systems, but there still won't be enough room for the hardware and computing power these things'll need to make those kinds of adjustments on the fly. Even if there were, without the self-replication feature, each mine would have to be produced and deployed by us or by the *Aventine*. And once triggered, the field would be unable to regenerate."

Picard scowled, exposing his ire at seeing a perfect plan thwarted by incontrovertible facts. "Very well," he said. "We'll simply have to proceed without a safety net. Reinforcements will arrive within fifty-one hours. Until then, we'll have to hold the line while we work on collapsing the subspace passages."

Elfiki, who rarely spoke up in meetings, seemed cowed as she said to Picard, "Um, Captain?"

"Yes, Lieutenant?"

Her eyes darted nervously from Picard to Helkara and then back again. "There's just one problem with that plan. We should stop trying to collapse the tunnels."

The captain lowered his voice to mask his irritation, but in the hushed conference room, he still sounded upset. "Why?"

She took a deep breath and seemed calmer as she replied. "All the passages resonate at different subharmonics of one interphasic frequency, so any pulse that collapses one of them safely will cause a domino effect that'll collapse the others. But the uncontrolled implosions will have amplified effects that could resonate throughout galactic space-time."

Worf swiveled his chair toward her. "Such as . . . ?"

"Stars could explode," she said. "Whole systems could vanish. Spiral arms could be dispersed into the void."

Helkara added, "Pluck the wrong string on this instrument, sir, and you could wipe out a quadrant in one note."

Certain that he felt a headache forming inside his skull, Picard muttered, "*Merde.*" For a moment he let his mind go quiet, to see if he could hear the voice of the Borg Collective. He sensed no contact, but he felt as if the silence held its own menace. The Borg were out there, lying in ambush, waiting for him, awaiting some final call to action. He was certain of it.

It was Worf's voice that drew him back into the moment.

"What are your orders, Captain?"

Picard sighed. "Captain Dax, suspend production of the minefield—but I want both our crews to continue looking for ways to safely collapse the subspace tunnels."

"Aye, sir," Dax said.

Nodding to the group, Picard added, "I'll take all your recommendations under advisement and review them in my ready room. Captain Dax, I'll contact you as soon as I've reached a decision." He stood, and the others followed suit. "Dismissed."

Captain Dax stood as the door to her ready room opened and Captain Picard strode in. She smiled. "Two visits in one day," she said. "I feel special."

He seemed less enthused about this visit. "I had considered delivering my decision over the comm," he said as he stopped in front of her desk. "However, given the tenor of our last meeting, a follow-up visit seemed warranted."

"I appreciate that," Dax said. She motioned to a chair. "Have a seat, I'll get you something from the replicator."

Picard waved away the offer. "No, thank you." He sat and gestured for her to join him. "I've apprised Admiral Nechayev of our tactical options, and the unacceptable risks of trying to implode the subspace tunnels at this time."

Dax made a small nod. "And what did she say?"

"Teams at Starfleet Research and Development, the Daystrom Institute, and the Vulcan Science Academy are all working to find a safe means of destroying the subspace passages," Picard said. "But until one is found, Admiral Nechayev agrees we should shift the front line of this war away from Federation space."

"A counterattack," Dax said.

"Precisely. Admiral Akaar is petitioning President Bacco to rally our allies and assemble an expeditionary force to take this fight to the Borg."

Her brow creased with concern. "We can't possibly conquer all of Borg space," Dax said. "So what's the strategy here?"

"A holding action," Picard said. "We advance the front line to the other side of whichever aperture the Borg have been using to reach our space, and there we establish a stronghold. Our task then becomes to hold the line there until we have the means to collapse the passageways. Then we fall back and implode the subspace tunnels behind us."

She frowned as she imagined spending the next several months engaged in a brutal, nerve-wracking battle of attrition. "I'm going to make an educated guess here," she said. "Since we'll need to know which aperture the Borg are using before we can launch a counteroffensive, Admiral Nechayev wants us to start scouting ahead through the passageways until we find it."

"Correct," said Picard.

"Calculating the frequency for opening each aperture takes time," she said. "And it takes processing power. We'll need to suspend our own research into imploding the tunnels if we want to start making scouting runs before our reinforcements arrive."

"My second officer said as much before I beamed over," Picard said, nodding. "So be it. We need to start scouting ahead for the expeditionary force as soon as possible. The *Enterprise* is still fourteen hours away from completing its repairs. How soon can the *Aventine* be ready to proceed?"

Dax activated her desktop monitor and checked the latest readiness report from Commander Bowers. "We'll be done assisting your engineering teams in about five hours, but it might take longer than that to pick the lock on one of the passageways."

"Then we'd best get started," Picard said as he got up. "We have a long road ahead—but heaven help us all if the Borg strike the next blow before we do."

# 5

"Why does Captain Picard hate me? What did I ever do to him?"

"I have no idea, ma'am."

President Nanietta Bacco reclined her chair while her chief of staff, Esperanza Piñiero, stood facing her, barely inside the pool of amber light from the antique lamp on Bacco's desk. Bacco shook her head as she continued to work through her denial. "An expeditionary force? Is he out of his mind?"

"Shostakova doesn't think so," Piñiero said, invoking the name of the secretary of defense. "It's the first time Picard's called for reinforcements since the Klingon civil war."

The office comm made a soft double tone, which was followed by the voice of Bacco's executive assistant, Sivak. *"Madam President,"* the elderly Vulcan man said. *"Secretary Safranski is here."*

"Send him in," Bacco said.

To her right, across the curved room, one of the office's two doors to the reception area was unlocked by her senior protection agent, Steven Wexler, a trim and wiry ex-Starfleet officer who was shorter than average for a human male. What he lacked in height, however, he made up for with speed, security experience, and martial-arts expertise. As the door slid open, a broad slash of bright light poured in. Wexler stepped inside and moved to his left to admit the secretary of the exterior.

Safranski crossed the room in long strides as Wexler stepped out and shut the door behind him, once again steeping the

sprawling executive space in deep shadows. Seconds later, as the Rigellian secretary breached the penumbra that surrounded Bacco's desk, he nodded in salutation. "Madam President. We're almost ready."

Piñiero pounced, sparing Bacco the trouble. "How much longer till we get started?"

"Two minutes," he said. "Five at most. I have my undersecretaries wrangling diplomats."

Bacco arched one graying eyebrow in accusation. "And why didn't you wrangle with them?"

"Oh, but I did, Madam President," Safranski said. "I personally rousted Ambassador Zogozin from the Gorn Embassy in Berlin and escorted him back here, to the Roth Dining Room."

The president showed him a forgiving smile. "Criticism withdrawn. Who are we waiting for?"

"Tezrene," Safranski said with weary resignation.

"As always," added Piñiero, who rolled her dark brown eyes. "So much for the stereotype of Tholian punctuality."

Rising from her desk, Bacco replied, "There's a difference between being late out of negligence and being late on purpose. I get the feeling this is a case of the latter."

"Almost certainly," Safranski said.

"What about Ambassador Emra?" asked Piñiero.

The secretary shook his head. "He won't be joining us. The Tzenkethi recalled their entire embassy staff four days ago."

"And when were they going to tell *us*?" Bacco replied.

"When we asked," Safranski said. "Which was roughly fifteen minutes ago." A low buzzing emanated from his torso. He grimaced with embarrassment, reached inside his jacket, and retrieved a personal communicator. "Excuse me, Madam President," he said, accepting the incoming call with a press of his thumb. Into the device, he said, "Safranski. Go." He listened, nodded, and replied, "Good. We're on our way." He thumbed the device into standby, tucked it back under his jacket, and said, "Tezrene just reached the table."

Piñiero looked anxious. "Time to go to work."

"Let's get to it, then," Bacco said, motioning with a sideways nod for Piñiero to follow her. As they walked past Safranski, she said to him, "Thanks for the wrangling."

"My pleasure, Madam President."

The door to the reception area opened a few seconds before Bacco reached it, and as she passed through into the lobby, she squinted against the sudden change in brightness. Agent Wexler fell into stride a few steps ahead of her, on her right. Piñiero remained on her left, matching her relaxed stride and purposeful expression, but the frown dimples in Piñiero's cheeks betrayed her concern about the imminent summit.

They followed Wexler into a turbolift, which he set in motion with a whispered command through his implanted, subaural communicator.

The lift began its brief descent to the thirteenth floor of the Palais de la Concorde. "Esperanza," Bacco said. "The sound of gears turning inside your head is getting deafening. Out with it, before we reach the dining room."

Piñiero said, "Out of nine ambassadors, I can only think of two we can really count on."

"That many?" Noting her chief of staff's aggrieved frown, she continued, "K'mtok and who else?"

"I figured Kalavak kind of owes us, after last year."

"Don't be so sure," Bacco said. "Romulans aren't known for their deep sense of gratitude. And if Martok hadn't already ordered his fleets to our border, I'd tell you not to put your chips on K'mtok, either."

The turbolift slowed.

"Shostakova says we can't repel another full-scale attack without at least four of these states as allies."

Bacco harrumphed. "She's being optimistic. We need at least six of them on our side, or this war's already over."

Piñiero asked, "What are the odds of making that happen?"

"No idea. And if you find out, please don't tell me."

The turbolift doors opened, and Piñiero remained behind as Bacco and Wexler proceeded toward a towering scarlet curtain that concealed the lift from the rest of the dining room. Once she was through the artfully concealed gap in the curtains, it was only a few meters' walk to the raised dais on which stood the president's round table. It boasted fourteen seats around its polished, lacquered surface, which was composed of recycled wood recovered from sunken sailing vessels of ancient Earth. As Bacco had expected, the beauty of the table stood in stark contrast to the ire on the faces of those who surrounded it—nine ambassadors, all but one openly seething at having been summoned by Bacco on absurdly short notice.

Ambassador K'mtok was tall, broad, and brutish, even by Klingon standards. It had been Bacco's experience that he loved using his height and prominently sharp incisors to intimidate other humanoids. Kalavak, his counterpart from the Romulan Star Empire, on the other hand, relied on his cold and unyielding stare to unnerve his political opponents. The two diplomats regarded each other with profound suspicion.

The one person at the summit whom Kalavak was pointedly ignoring was Ambassador Jovis, of the Imperial Romulan State. The former warbird commander had been appointed by Empress Donatra several weeks earlier, after the recognition of her government by the Klingon Empire had left the Federation little choice but to demonstrate solidarity with its ally by doing the same. Though Bacco had been careful to keep her government neutral in the internecine Romulan conflict, her decision to establish diplomatic relations with the nascent state had led to unavoidable resentment from Praetor Tal'Aura and, by extension, her diplomatic representative.

On the far side of the table from Bacco were the two ambassadors whose moods and reactions she had the most trouble understanding. Zogozin of the Gorn Hegemony frequently eschewed the use of the universal translator he had been offered, preferring instead to express himself with a series of hisses and growls. The archosaur's facial expression seemed frozen, locked in a perpetual mask of predatory intensity. Because of her years of experience as the governor of Cestus III, Bacco knew that the emotional states of the Gorn were often expressed in thermal changes in the olive-scaled reptilians' faces. Without the ability to see in the infrared spectrum, however, that knowledge did her little good at that moment.

Equally inscrutable to Bacco was the ever-tardy Tholian diplomat, Ambassador Tezrene. Hidden inside a shimmering suit of loose, golden Tholian silk whose interior was filled with searing-hot, high-pressure gases, Tezrene's metallic shriek of a voice was translated by a vocoder that invariably rendered her speech into an ominous monotone.

Derro, the Ferengi Alliance's ambassador to the Federation, was quiet for a change—but only because he found himself caught between the imposing presences of Breen Ambassador Gren and Talarian Ambassador Endar, both renowned as ruthless soldiers.

Then there was the one diplomat at the table who favored Bacco with a polite smile, and he was the one who she found most unnerving of them all—the eloquent and alarmingly intelligent ambassador from the Cardassian Union: Elim Garak.

He lifted his voice and silenced the room. "Everyone! Order, please! Our esteemed host has arrived." He nodded to Bacco. "Madam President. I yield the floor."

"Thank you, Ambassador Garak," Bacco said, uneasy with the realization that he had already positioned himself as having done her a favor, thereby elevating his status in the room. *He's a crafty one,* she reminded herself. *Don't give him an inch.* "And my thanks to all of you for joining me here this evening."

Endar, ever the epitome of boldness, declared, "This is about the Borg invasion of your space."

Bacco made eye contact with the Talarian. "Yes, it is. The situation has escalated, and it now threatens all of us."

Derisive sounds filled the air—a rasping hiss from Zogozin, a crackling squawk from Gren's vocoder, and a shrill scrape of noise from Tezrene. "Do not drag us into your war," said the Tholian ambassador. "Your conflict with the Borg is an internal matter, and of no concern to us."

Tezrene's comments seemed to fuel K'mtok's anger, and it left both the Romulan representatives silent and guarded, watching with caution to see what happened next.

"Nothing could be further from the truth," Bacco replied. "In the past day, the Borg have launched an attack against the Klingon world of Khitomer, and they have a history of striking worlds inside Romulan space. Given the scope of their latest actions, it would be foolish to think their campaign would be limited to Federation planets."

Derro cowered and nodded, as usual aligning himself with the most recent strong opinion spoken aloud. Then he flinched as Gren spoke; the Breen's voice was harsh and mechanical through his helmet's snout-shaped speaker. "The Federation and its Klingon allies have a history of provoking the Borg," the Breen said. "And the Romulans' expansion in the Beta Quadrant may have done the same. But no Breen vessel or citizen has ever been a foe of the Borg."

"Of course not," said K'mtok, his gravelly voice like a cutting saw. "You've been too busy hiding."

Zogozin growled, and then he said through a razor-sharp smile of gleaming-white fangs, "Why does Qo'noS still send an ambassador here? Didn't the Federation annex your empire?"

K'mtok reached for his *d'k tahg* and found only its empty sheath on his belt. "Count yourself lucky," he said to the Gorn. "If our hosts hadn't disarmed us—"

"Enough!" snapped Garak. "This posturing is useless."

Kalavak narrowed his eyes at Garak. "Curious," he said, the cultured inflection of his voice rife with implied mockery. "I should not have expected the infamous Elim Garak to be such an ardent friend of the Federation."

Garak's stare bordered on maniacal, and he spoke with such soft courtesy that his words cut like knives. "My dear ambassador, I am an ardent friend only of self-preservation, common sense, and the general welfare of the Cardassian Union. We all share the same charge—to advocate and negotiate on behalf of our peoples. Petty bickering does not become us."

"Indeed, it does not," agreed Jovis, who met Kalavak's glare with his own cool gaze. "The Imperial Romulan State is willing to put aside past enmities and seek new alliances."

Unable to contain his contempt for Jovis, Kalavak asked, "And is Empress Donatra prepared to offer reparations to the Romulan Empire? Will she release the worlds she took hostage?"

Before Jovis could answer, K'mtok shouldered his way between them and jabbed at Kalavak with his index finger. "If any reparations are to be made, they will be made by your Praetor Tal'Aura for the attack on Klorgat IV!"

"Ah, yes," Kalavak said. "Because the Klingon Empire made itself the guardian of all Remans. What was Martok thinking when he did that? Was he running short of *jeghpu'wI'*?"

Bacco cast a summoning glance at Agent Wexler as K'mtok stalked toward Kalavak.

"At least when Remans go to war, they fight their own battles," the Klingon said, clenching his fists.

As the two ambassadors squared off, Jovis and the others moved back. K'mtok cocked his fist and threw a punch at

Kalavak, who deflected the attack, grabbed the Klingon's wrist, and twisted it as he reached for K'mtok's throat.

Then came a blur of movement and the rapid patter of falling blows, and both ambassadors were on the floor, meters apart, still conscious but dazed. Agent Wexler stood between them, his hands empty and his dark suit as pristine as ever.

Bacco's eyes hadn't been fast enough to note the details of Wexler's thrashing of the two men, but she was determined to take advantage of the precious seconds of shocked silence that followed it. "I didn't summon you people here to argue among yourselves," she said. "I called you here to make you understand your role in what's about to become our mutual fight for survival."

She began circling around the table, staring down each ambassador, one by one, as she continued. "The Borg invasion isn't an internal Federation problem, and it's not a localized threat. If the Federation falls, there will be nothing standing between the Borg Collective and all of you. The Borg have no allies. They don't make nonaggression pacts. They honor no truces, no cease-fires. They don't consider the enemy of their enemy to be anything except another target. The Borg conquer, assimilate, and destroy."

As she passed by Kalavak, she saw Wexler help the ambassador back to his feet. K'mtok, in a rare display of humility, permitted Jovis to lend him a hand. Stopping between the two bruised diplomats, she finished, "I'm not asking you to sign any permanent treaties. All I want you to do is be smart enough to know when we ought to unite for our common survival. This isn't politics, goddammit—this is life and death. Take up arms and fight, or lie down and die." She looked around the table and still found it impossible to gauge the nonhumans' reactions by visual cues, but she had no choice but to continue. "It's time to put this to a vote. Show of hands: Who's ready to stand with us? Who's ready to join the fight for survival?"

Bacco lifted her own hand high over her head. It came as no great shock to see K'mtok lift his hand, as well. Then, as she looked around the table, she saw Jovis's hand raised, as well as Endar's. To her surprise, despite his earlier displays of courtesy and support, Garak's hands remained at his sides.

She lowered her hand, and K'mtok, Jovis, and Endar did the same. "All right," she said. "Who votes no?" As she'd expected, Tezrene, Gren, Zogozin, and Kalavak each lifted a hand or its equivalent to vote nay. To her disappointment, Garak also lifted his hand. That brought Bacco's roving stare to the Ferengi ambassador, Derro, who cowered behind the Breen diplomat.

"Ambassador Derro," Bacco said. "How does the Ferengi Alliance vote?"

"We'd like to abstain, Madam President."

"And I'd like to be able to take a peaceful, month-long vacation on Risa, but we don't always get what we want, do we? This is a binary question, Your Excellency. You're either in, or you're out. Will the Ferengi Alliance stand with the Federation and its allies, or would it prefer to stand alone when the Borg come?"

Eyes darting from the Breen to the Gorn to the Tholian, Derro was like a bag of nervous flinches disguised as a pudgy, big-eared Ferengi. Finally, he stammered, "I, I mean we, I mean—the Ferengi Alliance votes yes."

"Yes to *what*, Ambassador Derro?" prodded Bacco.

"We're in," he said, suddenly firming his resolve against the hostile glares directed at him by Zogozin and the others. "The Ferengi Alliance stands with the Federation."

"Welcome aboard, Ambassador." She nodded to the motion's *yea* votes. "Ambassadors K'mtok, Jovis, and Endar. Thank you for your support. I'd like to ask each of you now to take your leave from these proceedings so that you can make arrangements with your governments to deploy ships and personnel to join our expeditionary force against the Borg."

Endar made a small bow in Bacco's direction. "Right away, Madam President. And might I add, it's a pleasure to hear a Federation leader who speaks a language Talarians understand."

"Her knowledge of *thlIngan Hol* is equally impressive," added K'mtok. He nodded to Bacco and followed Endar away from the table. Derro hurried out, close behind them.

Jovis paused long enough to offer his hand to Bacco, who accepted it. "Humans and Romulans have a long and troubled history, Madam President. But it's the hope of Empress Donatra that today we can begin a new era of amity between our peoples."

"You may tell Empress Donatra that the desire is mutual," Bacco said. Jovis bowed his head, released her hand, and slipped away, off the dais and out a side door.

Then, with her allies gone, Bacco turned back toward the table and faced the emissaries of her rivals and foes. "I suggest you all take a seat and get comfortable," she said. "The easy part is over. Now we get down to business."

"We've already made our decisions," Kalavak said, with naked malice. "This summit is over." He moved to step off the dais and found his path blocked by Agent Wexler.

The goateed human agent said, "Sit down, Your Excellency."

Angry chatter buzzed between Gren and Tezrene, and a steady growl resonated from Zogozin. As before, only Garak maintained an untroubled veneer of civility as Kalavak demanded in a heated tone of voice, "Madam President, what is the meaning of this?"

"The meaning, Mister Ambassador, is that we're going to continue discussing this matter until I'm satisfied that all diplomatic possibilities have been exhausted."

A wail of staticky noise spewed from Gren's vocoder, but it was Zogozin who growled with rage and bellowed, "How dare you hold us hostage!"

In her smoothest and most annoyingly diplomatic timbre, Bacco replied, "Don't be so melodramatic, Mister Ambassador. You're not hostages. For the time being, let's just call you 'compulsory guests,' shall we?"

The Gorn roared with indignation, adding his fury to the cacophonous protests of Gren and Tezrene. Kalavak, for his part, fumed in menacing silence.

None of their reactions troubled Bacco. The only one who worried her was Garak.

Because he was utterly serene . . . and smirking.


Admiral Edward Jellico couldn't remember the last time he'd slept. A mixture of adrenaline and desperation fueled his continuing struggle to keep his eyes open.

Sequestered inside his office on the top floor of Starfleet Command Headquarters in San Francisco, he was surrounded by a panorama of holographic displays, all of them crowded with information that had long since begun to bleed together in his vision.

Fleet deployments. Casualty figures. Probable targets. Projected losses. And an ever-growing queue of communiqués to which he had lost the will to respond.

He turned away from his desk and plodded to the replicator on the rear wall. "Coffee, hot, double-strong, cream and sugar," he said, planting one hand against the wall and leaning forward with fatigue. He closed his eyes and for a moment almost drifted into a reverie while listening to the musical drone of his latest caffeine fix swirling into existence. Then, with great effort, he opened his leaden eyelids, picked up his coffee, and shambled back to his desk.

Sagging back into his chair, he knew that he had no one to blame for his circumstances but himself. *You always wanted to be top dog,* he chided himself. *Should've been more careful what you wished for.* He sipped his coffee. The sweet liquid warmth felt good in his scratchy throat—he wondered if he was coming down with a cold—but it did nothing to sharpen his dulled senses.

His door chime sounded.

He winced, groaned, and said, "Come in."

The door slid open, and Admiral Alynna Nechayev stepped inside. She recoiled as soon as she got a good look at him. "Sir, have you been here since last night?"

"I liked you better when you called me Ed."

Nechayev moved farther into his office, and the door closed behind her. "You sound terrible, sir. Let me call a medic."

"No," he said, his voice roughened by the pain in his throat. He planted his stubbled face in his hands and sighed. "They'll just tell me I need to sleep."

"Might be sound advice, sir."

"Dammit," he said, looking up. "Stop calling me that."

She put on a mocking air of affront. "Well, excuse me, but you *are* the appointed C-in-C, aren't you?"

"Yes, and I'm giving you a direct order: When we're alone, *call me Ed.*" He tried to scowl and ended up coughing instead.

"Aye-aye, Ed," said Nechayev, smiling back at him. "Permission to speak freely, Ed?"

He was too tired to argue, even in jest. "Oh, go ahead."

"You're hanging on too tightly," she said. "Loosen up. Take a few hours' downtime—you need it."

His head lolled backward against the headrest of his chair. "Not yet," he said. "There's too much to do."

"And you're surrounded by thousands of highly trained officers who are ready to get the job done," she replied. "You need to delegate, Ed. You can't fight this war by yourself, no matter how much you might want to." She circled behind his desk and eyed the wraparound wall of holographic data. Pointing at one screen after another, she said, "Let Nakamura handle deployment orders. T'Lara can cut through the red tape with the Council. I'll take over on strategic planning."

"Hang on, now," Jellico said. "I haven't authorized—"

"Ed," she cut in, "how long has it been since you took off your boots?" She paused while Jellico looked down at his own feet, and then she continued, "By my best estimates, you've been awake and cooped up inside this office for almost sixty-one hours. Have you taken off your shoes even once?"

He tried to make sense of her question and failed. "What are you driving at?"

"Take off your boots and tell me what condition your feet are in," she said. "I'll wait." The blond woman folded her arms and stared at him, her expression stern and unyielding.

Ignoring the pain in his back, he bent forward, reached down, and struggled to pull off his left boot. "This is the dumbest thing I've ev—" The smell hit his nostrils and silenced him. Then he noticed the itching, burning sensation that spread like a brush fire from his toes across the top of his foot.

"One to go," Nechayev quipped.

"No thanks," Jellico said.

His longtime friend and colleague shook her head. "Ed, you're so tired, you couldn't remember to air out your boots once a day, and you gave yourself a case of what used to be called trench foot. Now get serious—if you couldn't see *that* coming, how ready do you think you are to plan a major, multinational counteroffensive against the Borg?"

Jellico's head drooped as he felt the inevitability of his surrender close in on him. He really had lost count of the hours as the Borg's invasion had escalated, and it was time for him to admit he'd gone not only to the limits of his effectiveness but far beyond. And he was simply so very, very tired.

"I wish I'd never been promoted," he said grimly.

Nechayev nodded sympathetically. "I understand," she said. "Everything seemed so much easier when all we had to worry about was the ship under our feet."

"Yeah, that too," Jellico said. "But mostly I meant that if I hadn't leapfrogged over you in the chain of command, you could be the one sitting here with trench foot instead of me."

All traces of mirth and charity left her face as she departed his office. "Go home and get some sleep."


Seven of Nine was alone in a room filled with strangers.

She knew their names and their titles, but that was all. In the ways of knowing that mattered, they were mysteries to her.

"We need to see what's worked so far and figure out what'll work next," said Raisa Shostakova, the secretary of defense. The highest-ranking person in the Palais de la Concorde conference room, she was human by ancestry but Pangean by birth, and her high-gravity upbringing showed in her short, squat physique. "The crew of the *Ranger* innovated a phase-shifted attack at Khitomer—"

"To which the Borg have already adapted," Seven cut in.

Jas Abrik, the senior security adviser to President Bacco, and Seven's direct superior in the governmental chain of command, replied in a tense whisper, "Let her finish first."

Shostakova continued, "And, as noted, a subsequent attempt by the *Excalibur* to repeat the tactic failed. Captain Calhoun and his crew compensated by creating a salvo of variably phased quantum torpedoes, but we have evidence the Collective has already learned to counter this, too."

"Undoubtedly," muttered Seven, who noted Abrik's glare and added in a confidential tone, "I am reasonably certain she was finished." Abrik rolled his eyes and looked away.

Seven held her tongue as the meeting dragged on, rehashing one failed weapon after another. Every time she opened her mouth to offer advice, Abrik silenced her with a look and a wave of his hand. It perplexed her to wonder why these seemingly intelligent individuals were so convinced that the formula for success must lie hidden in the legacy of their myriad failures.

She longed for her days aboard *Voyager* in the Delta Quadrant. Despite the awkwardness and loneliness that had come with her separation from the Collective, she had been able to rely on Kathryn Janeway to show her the way back to a human life. It had been as if Janeway had adopted her, instinctively replacing the mother who had been taken from Seven by the Borg.

Then, after all the travails Janeway had endured to lead her crew home, she herself had been ripped away from Seven by the Borg, and turned into the enemy she had so despised and against which she had struggled so ferociously.

That loss had left Seven with no comfort except her aunt, Irene Hansen, who now was being stolen from her, day by day, by an incurable, progressive neurological disease. Watching her aunt's persona disintegrate was like witnessing a slow-motion assimilation. *Soon, I will have no one left,* Seven realized.

An irritating voice disrupted her lonely reflections.

Participating in the meeting via one of the conference room's wall-mounted viewscreens, Admiral Elizabeth Shelby pursed her lips into a narrow frown. *"What about regenerative phasers?"*

The president's Starfleet Intelligence liaison, Captain Holly Hostetler Richman, shook her head. "Sorry, Admiral. Those failed in the Battle of Acamar."

Shelby huffed angrily. *"But the transphasic torpedoes still work, don't they? Why are we being so stingy with them?"*

"Admiral Nechayev's orders," Shostakova replied. "She thinks if we use them too much, the Borg might develop a resistance, like bacteria to antibiotics."

The fair-haired admiral folded her arms. *"Oh, give me a break,"* she said, her mouth hinting at a sneer. *"How do you develop immunity to something that kills in one shot?"*

Galled by Shelby's ignorance, Seven replied, "Even death is a learning experience for the Borg. Every time your new weapon destroys another cube, the Collective learns more about it. It is only a matter of time before they adapt a defense."

*"You almost sound like you admire them, Miss Hansen,"* said Shelby, whose narrowed stare conveyed utter contempt for Seven.

It wasn't Shelby's glare that stoked Seven's ire. "I prefer to be addressed as Seven," the former Borg drone said, the coldness of her warning leaving no room for debate. The use of her former name was a privilege Seven reserved for her aunt.

Shostakova picked up a padd from the conference table and used it to call up a tactical display on a secondary viewscreen. "Let's move on, please, everyone," she said. "I suggest we leave tactics and weapons development to the experts. For now, I'd like to stay focused on big-picture strategy. Any ideas?"

Seven folded her hands on the table as she spoke up. "Yes, in fact. Redeploy all your forces to the Azure Nebula."

Abrik, seated next to her, coughed as he aspirated a small mouthful of his coffee. Wiping the splatter from his chin and the front of his shirt, he replied, "*All* of them?"

"If you are committed to exploiting the transphasic torpedo to its fullest extent, you will have to land a decisive blow as quickly as possible," Seven said.

Shelby looked horrified by the suggestion. *"Your plan would leave our core systems completely undefended."*

"They are all but undefended now," Seven said. "If you wish to prevail against the Borg, you should do exactly as Captain Picard has suggested—go on the attack. Once the Borg enter your space, the momentum of the battle will turn against you."

Hostetler Richman threw a dubious look Seven's way. "If we do send a force through one of those anomalies and find a Borg invasion fleet, how many ships are we likely to face?"

"That depends," Seven said.

"On . . . ?" prodded Shostakova.

Turning to the secretary, Seven replied, "On whether the Borg intend merely to destroy Earth, or to destroy every world in the Federation and those of all its allies."

"Could they really do that?" asked Hostetler Richman.

Seven met the woman's fearful stare. "Yes. They can."

"Then we ought to seek every advantage," interjected Captain Miltakka, the president's liaison to Starfleet Research and Development. The Rigellian amphiboid got up from his chair, picked up a padd, and changed the tactical display on the secondary screen. He pointed out details as he spoke. "Though our ships' phasers are not compatible with transphasic modulation, their shield emitters can be. I have compiled some upgrade plans that should be compatible with the defensive systems of most of the vessels currently active in Starfleet." As he sat down, Seven mused that the mottled skin on the back of his head reminded her of a Borg's complexion.

"That is a good first step," Seven began. "However, it will not be enough. To halt the Borg invasion on your own terms, you will have to resort to more drastic measures."

Suspicious stares fell upon Seven from every direction. It was Abrik who dared to ask, "Such as . . . ?"

"You will need to replicate the thalaron weapon that the Remans made for Shinzon," Seven said.

Abrik shot back, "Are you out of your mind?"

She was barraged by overlapping rebukes from all sides. "It'd violate our treaty with the Romulans," said Shostakova. Shelby protested, *"Do you have any idea what will happen if the Borg capture it?"* Hostetler Richman said, "Never mind the risk of it being copied by the Tholians," and Miltakka added, "It'd defeat the whole point of destroying it in the first place!"

"It is your only chance," Seven said, her voice sharp enough to cut through the opposition.

"It's illegal," Shostakova replied. "It's *immoral.*"

"That is irrelevant," Seven said. "Without it, you do not possess the firepower to stop a full Borg attack fleet."

Her insistence was met by denial in the form of shaking heads and closed eyes. *They do not trust me. None of them wants to be the first to agree with me.*

"When you find the Borg's staging area, you will have only one chance to destroy it," Seven said. "The only weapon you possess that is powerful enough to do so in a single shot, and to which the Borg have not yet adapted, is the thalaron array."

Shostakova slammed her palms flat on the tabletop. "I don't care, Seven," she said. "Thalaron weapons are an abomination, which is why we signed a treaty outlawing them. The Federation won't endorse the use of genocidal tactics."

"Then I cannot help you," Seven said, "because the Borg have no such reservations—and they will exterminate you."

# 1519

## 6

There were no hours or days in Axion, only what felt to Erika Hernandez like interminable years of night as the metropolis made its slow transit of the void.

Hernandez and her fellow survivors from the *Columbia* basked in the honeyed glow of artificial sunlight. An array of solar lamps had been installed above the courtyard that lay between their respective living quarters. In the long drag of time since they had become stranded in the past, Inyx had arranged new, more spacious accommodations for them at "ground level" in the city, to remove the need for the Caeliar's energy-intensive version of a turbolift.

The last piece of advice that Inyx had given to Hernandez and Fletcher was that they should pass the time by taking up art. Hernandez had yet to find a creative outlet that suited her, but Fletcher had submerged herself in her new hobby: writing. Using an ultrathin polymer tablet and a feather-light stylus, she had lately spent most of her waking hours scribbling and revising a novel that she refused to let anyone else read until it was finished. Remembering the often muddled state of Fletcher's mission reports, Hernandez had decided to keep her expectations low for Fletcher's prose.

"What's another word for 'oozing'?" Fletcher asked, and Hernandez's hope of reading one more great novel in her lifetime diminished by another degree. Before anyone could answer, Fletcher looked to Valerian, who sat in an arched window portal, staring out at a cityscape surrounded by a star-speckled dome of deep space. "Sidra, you must know a good synonym for 'oozing.'"

Valerian said nothing. Her face was blank, and she didn't give any sign of acknowledging Fletcher. The young Scotswoman sat with her knees against her chest, arms wrapped tightly around her legs, face half hidden from view. It had been a long time since she had said anything to anyone. She often had to be coaxed and half-pulled from her residence by Dr. Metzger for regular sessions of solar therapy, which all four women needed in order to stave off the onset of seasonal affective disorder and make at least a passing attempt at preserving some of their bodies' natural diurnal rhythms.

Metzger, who was meditating in a lotus position an arm's reach from the younger woman, opened one eye and glared with mild annoyance. She extended her arm and poked Valerian. "Sidra," she said. "Veronica asked you a question."

The mentally fragile redhead recoiled from Metzger's touch. Trembling, she cast fearful looks at her shipmates, and then she bolted from the window and jogged across the courtyard and out an open door, disappearing around a corner into the city beyond.

Fletcher looked mortified. "Should I go after her?"

"I'll do it," Metzger said, standing slowly.

"Be careful," Hernandez said. "If she seems like she might be out of control, ask the Caeliar for help."

Metzger's mood darkened. "I don't need their help," she said, and then she was out the door, in slow pursuit of the runaway communications officer who didn't talk anymore.

Silence descended once more on the courtyard.

Hernandez sat on a bench and watched Fletcher tapping at a virtual keyboard on her tablet, committing words to the device's memory, losing herself in a world of her own making. It was hard for Hernandez not to envy her friend. Whatever aesthetic value her writing might possess or lack, it had one undeniable virtue: it offered Fletcher a means of escape, however temporary or illusory, from the monotony of their imprisonment.

*Lucky her,* mused Hernandez.

At one end of the courtyard sat a mutilated block of granite and a set of diamond-edged chisels that Hernandez had found too unwieldy for comfort. She had chipped and chopped and hammered at the dark slab, at first without even an image in her mind of what she meant it to become. Choosing a shape—in this case, a spiral—hadn't helped, even after Fletcher had offered her teasing, inexpert advice, "Just chip away everything that doesn't look like a spiral."

Music hadn't come naturally to Hernandez, either. Inyx had crafted her a Caeliar instrument that seemed reminiscent of an old Earth device known as a theremin, but the only sounds she had been able to elicit from it had sounded like the crystal-shattering whines of feedback or chaotic, bloodcurdling wails.

She had told herself she would keep trying to master the instrument despite her difficulties—and then she'd produced two unnerving pulses of sound in quick succession. The first had been a high-frequency screech that sent torturous vibrations through her teeth; the second was an almost inaudible low-frequency drone that had shaken her from the inside out and left her trembling and terrified, shaken to the very roots of her soul, as if she had discovered the sound of true evil.

Other artistic talents whose total absence Hernandez had confirmed included painting, drawing, and singing.

The fact that Caeliar society had abandoned the theatrical arts more than a thousand years earlier had tempted her to focus on acting. Even if she turned out to be the worst actress in Axion, as the *only* actress in the city she would also, by default, be its best. As her comrades had pointed out, however, they would likely be her only audience, and they had no desire to suffer through whatever one-woman dramatic atrocity she might be tempted to inflict upon them.

So she passed her days as stagnant as the windless city.

She thought of Fletcher writing, Metzger meditating, and Valerian going mad by leaps and bounds. The future, which she constantly reminded herself was a replay of the past, promised more of the same. Routine without purpose. Night without end.

"I'm taking a walk," she said.

Fletcher didn't look up from her tablet as she waved. "Have a nice time. See you at dinner."

Leaving the blonde to her unfolding fiction, Hernandez left the courtyard through the same door by which Valerian had fled. She walked away into the ashen sprawl of the silent metropolis.

A new understanding came to her as she walked. She'd failed at art not for lack of talent or effort, but because she had a greater need for something else. Not a hobby—a job. She didn't want to just pass the time anymore; she wanted to contribute. To do something that mattered.

Ordemo Nordal would likely object. So would the Quorum. That left her only one option.

She had to persuade Inyx.

\* \* \*

"I fail to see what meaningful contribution you might make to our efforts," Inyx said, his ungainly stride swaying his body side to side like a sailing vessel at sea. "You lack the knowledge and technical expertise to assist us."

"Only because I haven't been taught," said Hernandez, who followed him through a glowing, hexagonal tunnel.

The Caeliar scientist made a derisive-sounding bleat of air from the tubules on either side of his bulbous cranium. "Perhaps, if your species was longer-lived, we could impart the fundamentals of our Great Work, but it would be for naught."

"Why?"

"Our tools," he said. "They are not operated with buttons and levers and dials, as on your vessel. We direct them with infinitely more subtle measures, by means of the gestalt."

Unfazed, she insisted, "So? Teach me to do that."

Near the end of the corridor he paused and looked back at her. "I doubt that your mind would survive the experience."

He led her out of the passage and into a vast chamber deep inside the city's foundation. Like the corridor they had traversed, the room was hexagonal in shape, resembling a single cell from a honeycomb laid flat. The walls, ceiling, and floor shimmered with stars. For a moment, Hernandez wondered if the room even had a floor; for all she knew, this was a vantage point on the reaches of space beneath Axion. As she stepped forward, however, her perception of stars passing underfoot was too swift for normal parallax with very distant objects, and she concluded that it was a starmap.

Several clusters of Caeliar huddled in ostensibly arbitrary locations throughout the chamber. Inyx walked toward one trio, who stood in a tight group several dozen meters away.

"Is this where the Great Work gets done?" she asked.

"Its current phase, yes," Inyx said. "Though a separate inquiry of equal importance is also in progress."

His choice of terms intrigued her. "Equal importance? What ranked high enough to horn in on the Great Work?"

"I prioritized an investigation into the temporal effects of Erigol's destruction. One of our other cities traveled to the distant past, and its descendants triggered our cataclysm. Another city might have made a similar though less drastic journey, as we did. If our analysis indicates that the past has been altered, then we might need to risk taking steps to prevent the catastrophe, regardless of the paradoxes it might create."

Stepping over an asymmetrical red nebula, Hernandez said, "How would you be able to tell? If the past changed, wouldn't we have changed with it?"

"Not necessarily," Inyx said. "All our cities have long been temporally shielded to guard against potential changes in the timeline. Our data archive contains detailed records of this era's chroniton signature. By comparing the universe's current chroniton dispersal pattern to the one we have on record for this period, we can identify any variances that would suggest the timeline has been changed by the passage of our cities into the past. If significant changes are detected, the Quorum might consider initiating corrective measures."

"Sounds important," Hernandez said.

"Very much so."

Looking around at the murmuring groups of Caeliar standing far apart in the massive chamber, she remarked, "Too bad the others don't seem to share your sense of urgency."

"By our standards, this is a frantic burst of activity."

They were a few meters from the trio, which turned to face them in unison, like birds changing direction in flight. The three Caeliar bowed to Inyx, who reciprocated. Then all four of the aliens began making noises that were part groan, part hum. The tonal pitch of the chorus oscillated, and the intensity of the vibrato rose and fell. As quickly as it had started, it stopped, and Inyx said to the others, "Are you certain?"

"Yes," said the shortest and bulkiest of them.

The tallest, who was nearly three meters in height, added, "I verified the results several times. We await your permission to apprise the gestalt."

"Proceed," said Inyx, who turned away from the trio and resumed walking.

Hernandez hurried after him. "What'd they say?"

"They have already concluded the temporal analysis," he said. "There is no variance in the chroniton signature."

She didn't know whether his reluctance to elaborate was evidence of boredom with her questions or a misguided display of faith in her ability to know what the hell he was talking about. "Okay, no variance," she said. "What does that mean?"

"It means that all is as it was, and is as it should be." This time he seemed to sense her unspoken desire for clarification. "Because the passage of our cities and the others into the past has resulted in no detectable change of the timeline, we have deduced that these events must have occurred in the timeline that we consider standard. Consequently, the destruction of Erigol and our own exile in the past appear to be part of the natural flow of events. Therefore, no steps will be taken to alter the outcome we have witnessed. Instead, we will move forward with the Great Work from this new vantage point."

He was still a few steps ahead of her, so she knew he couldn't see her jaw hanging open in disbelief. "How can you do nothing? You know that a few hundred years from now your world and millions of your people will be destroyed, and you're just gonna let it happen *again*? Why?"

"Because that is the shape into which time has unfolded," Inyx said, as if he was explaining the matter to a child. "Once time has chosen its form, it is not our place to change it."

"So, you're saying you won't save your people because it's their destiny to get blown up?"

He stopped and turned back to face her. "That is a crude reduction of a complex issue, but in essence . . . yes."

She shook her head. "Sorry, but I'll take free will over fatalism any day."

"As would we," Inyx said. "Free will exists in the present moment. But the present is always in flux, slipping on one side into the past while pulling from another on the leading edge of the future. We only accept as predestined the events that we know will transpire between this moment and the last moment before we entered the past. When we return to that moment in our subjective future, we will once again treat time's shape as a revelation in progress. Until then, our work continues."

Inyx walked away, and Hernandez stayed close behind him. He stopped in the middle of a broad swath of what seemed to be empty space in the middle of the starmap. When he squatted to study an image on the floor more closely, his long, bony legs folded up on either side of his narrow torso; he reminded Hernandez of a grasshopper perched on a lawn. She watched with great curiosity as he tapped at several points of light on the floor. Ghostly symbols twisted upward from each mote, as if written in curling smoke. They snaked between his tendril-like fingers and were absorbed into his mottled gray-blue skin.

"What are you looking for?" she asked.

He rested his long arms across his knees and gazed at the map of the sky inscribed under his feet. "A new world to call home," he said. "A system where we can finish the Great Work."

"Well, there must be plenty to choose from," she said. "Hell, if the Drake Equation is right, there are millions of Minshara-class planets you can colonize."

The Caeliar scientist straightened and shuffled his huge, three-toed feet. "It is not so simple," he said. "We have many criteria for a world on which to settle. Its star must be the right age, neither too young nor too old. Its planets cannot be too recently formed to sustain life, nor must they be past the ability to do so; they cannot be geothermally inert, nor overly volatile. A viable star system will need to be rich in many rare elements and compounds. Most important of all, no part of the star system can be populated by sentient life, indigenous or otherwise, in any form—including cosmozoans."

"I'm sorry, hang on," Hernandez said. "Cosmo-what?"

After making a few clicking sounds, Inyx said, "My apologies, I'd forgotten your species hasn't encountered their kind yet. The galaxy is home to a great variety of spaceborne life-forms, many of which are sentient. They tend to thrive near stellar clusters, so we are focusing our search on star systems that are relatively remote in nature, in order to avoid them."

Hernandez quipped, "Glad to see you're not being picky."

"If we are selective, it is not without reason," Inyx said. "At this point, our discretion is as much for our privacy as for the safety of the galaxy at large. We must remain unknown."

"Good thing you're not doing anything conspicuous, then," she said. "You know, like moving an entire city through space."

Inyx regarded her with his pupil-free eyes. "Do you think that because I am physically incapable of what you call laughter, I don't understand humor? Or sarcasm?"

"I hadn't given it that much thought," Hernandez said. "Mostly, I just like ribbing you."

"I see," he said. "If I agree to teach you the methods of our search for a new homeworld, and include you in the process, I would appreciate fewer gibes at my expense."

She nodded. "Sounds fair. When do we start?"

Gesturing at the vast, star-flecked chamber that surrounded them, he said, "We already have."

Dinner was finished, and Fletcher, Hernandez, and Metzger sat together at a round table in their courtyard. As usual, Valerian had refused invitations to come out and eat, preferring instead to sequester herself and mumble the story of her-life-that-was at the walls inside her bedroom.

"Your turn," the captain said to Fletcher, who picked at the remains of yet another bland and texturally unsettling Caeliar interpretation of vegetable lasagna.

Setting down her fork, Fletcher thought for a moment and said, "Meat, to be honest. Tonight, it's meat."

The game was called *What do you miss most tonight?*

Fletcher forced another bite of the slightly soupy casserole into her mouth, swallowed, and looked at Metzger. "You're up, Jo," she said.

The doctor, who had already cleared her plate, was sitting with her arms folded behind her head. She leaned back in her chair and stared at the stars that were always overhead. "Constellations I recognize," she said. "Back to you, Erika."

Fletcher had lost track of when they had all started calling one another by their first names. It had begun not long after they had surrendered to the proposition that the four of them would spend the rest of their lives here, in this alien city roaming deep space, lost in the gray mists of history.

"Wine," Hernandez said, closing her eyes. "Red or white. Merlot, Chianti, Rioja, Cabernet, Zinfandel, Riesling, Malbec, Pinotage, Chardonnay, Sauvignon Blanc. All of them. I'd do anything for one glass of good Burgundy right now." She tilted her head back, closed her eyes, and sighed. "Go, Ronnie."

Certain subjects had always felt too awkward to broach, given their circumstances, but the truth was straining to be free of Fletcher's conscience. "I'm sorry, I have to say it. I bloody miss men. The way they look, the way they sound, the way they *feel*. I'd trade you ten cases of wine for one strappin' lad willin' to give his ferret a run, know what I mean?" She felt a bit guilty when Metzger and Hernandez glared at her, but the damage was done. "I know, I know. We're not supposed to bring it up. I said I was sorry."

"And then you brought it up anyway," Metzger said.

Hernandez held up a hand and cut in, "It's fine. We had to talk about it eventually. We can't ignore it forever."

"I can," Metzger said, rising from the table. "If you two want to negotiate some kind of deviant relationship, that's your business, but count me out." The gray-haired physician walked away to go check on Valerian, at whose side Metzger had spent most of her waking hours since the younger woman's breakdown.

Fletcher rolled her eyes. "Back to the river in Egypt."

"What's wrong with you?" Hernandez said. "Couldn't you just lie and say you missed Vegemite? Or margaritas? Or jazz?"

"I do miss margaritas and jazz, but you can keep the Vegemite," Fletcher replied. "Look, this is daft. We're all going crazy in this place without any lads"—she cast a look in the direction of the departed doctor—"those of us who don't hate them, anyway, and I think it's mad we can't say it." She kicked away her chair as she stood and hollered to the silent heavens, "I want a hard shag, and I don't care who knows it!"

With droll calm, Hernandez said, "Keep your voice down. You'll scare the natives." She motioned for Fletcher to sit. As the XO pulled her chair back to the table, the captain continued, "If you're really this hard up, I'm sure we can work something out."

"No offense, Erika," Fletcher said, "you're flash and all, but I just don't see us that—"

"Not with me," Hernandez chided her. "Remember what you told me about the Caeliar—a long time back, before the disaster? How they shape-change and mimic us? Maybe one of them can stand in for one of the MACOs." She put on a teasing smile. "I know I saw you checking out Yacavino a few times."

Horrified, Fletcher stared aghast at Hernandez. "Are you mad? You think I'd let myself get rogered by one of *them*?"

"Funny, I thought some of the MACOs were rather dashing."

"Not the MACOs!" She lifted her chin and looked away to indicate she was talking about the Caeliar. "*Them*. The enemy."

Hernandez rolled her eyes. "Don't you think you're being a little bit melodramatic?"

"Oh, I see. They give you a job, and suddenly you forget they're holding us prisoner, hundreds of years and thousands of light-years from home." She regretted it as soon as she'd said it. *Apparently, it's my night for putting my foot in my mouth.*

"I haven't forgotten anything, Ronnie," Hernandez said. "Earth, my ship, my crew . . . Jonathan. Do you really think I could forget him? The way he used to touch me? Or the sound of him whispering in my ear when I was half asleep?" A bitter mood replaced her previous joviality. "We're all stir-crazy here, Ronnie, but torturing ourselves over it doesn't make it any better. Ranting about how badly you want to get laid doesn't make the days go by any faster, either. If you want to let off steam, go running. Do a thousand pull-ups. Find a place with a nice echo and take up primal screaming. Or shut your door and just be your own best friend, like the rest of us do."

Contrite, Fletcher sank back into her seat. She draped her limbs over the seat as if she were a rag doll. "Sorry. Guess I was a bit 'round the bend there."

"Forget it. We're all bound to snap sooner or later. You just got it out of the way early."

Fletcher chuckled softly through an abashed smile. When it faded, she felt a crushing sense of loneliness pressing in on her from all sides. "Erika? Tell me the truth. . . . We're really never going home, are we?"

Hernandez's smile was sympathetic and bittersweet.

"Never say never."

# 2381

## 7

Worf was surprised by the sharpness of Captain Picard's voice as the captain dropped the padd on his ready room desk and said, "These numbers are completely unacceptable, Mister La Forge."

The chief engineer shrugged and lifted his palms in a gesture of surrender. "They're the best we have, Captain. All engineering teams are working around the clock, even the walking wounded. We're at the limit."

"Then go past the limit, Geordi," Picard said. "Suspend any other operations that use computer power and focus everything on the task at hand." He picked up the padd again and waved it as an object of contempt. "If we have to spend six hours trying to open each of these passages—"

La Forge interrupted, "It may take longer than that, sir. On this side, we have the *Aventine* to help us. Once we split up, whichever ship goes through the tunnel will have to calculate the return frequency on its own. If we're lucky—"

Picard held up his hand. "Split up?"

The chief engineer looked to Worf, who explained, "Until reinforcements arrive, either we or the *Aventine* will have to remain here, as a sentinel against the Borg."

The captain nodded. "I see."

"In any case," La Forge said, "processing power is only half the problem. After we analyzed the logs from the runabout that opened the passageway the *Aventine* used, we found out that the creature who'd hijacked the runabout altered its deflector output somehow. He stabilized the subspace aperture by emitting a triquantum wave—something we're not set up to do."

Folding his hands together, Picard asked, "How do we plan to remedy this?"

"I'm working with the *Aventine*'s chief engineer to design and install some upgrades to our sensor grids. We should be ready to start opening tunnels in less than three hours."

"Very well," Picard said. He turned to Worf. "How soon will the *Enterprise* be battle ready, Number One?"

With grim regret, Worf replied, "It will require at least another eight hours."

"Why so long?" Picard asked.

Worf traded a knowing look with La Forge before he answered, "Personnel and resources are currently . . . limited, sir."

La Forge added, "What he's too polite to say is that I've commandeered all the engineers and damage-control teams to make the modifications to the sensor grid. When those are done, we'll move the tactical system repairs to the front of the line."

"See that you do, Mister La Forge. If we're to stay behind as sentries, I'd prefer not to do so unarmed."

The chief engineer nodded. "I understand, sir."

"Dismissed, Mister La Forge. Mister Worf, stay a moment."

Worf clasped his hands behind his back as La Forge left the captain's ready room. When the door closed, Picard said to Worf, "I want your honest opinion, Worf. Is this crew really ready to face the Borg?"

"They have already done so several times," Worf said, perplexed by the captain's question.

Shaking his head, Picard said, "I'm not talking about starship combat, Number One. I'm referring to close-quarters combat. There's no telling what we'll find when we uncover the tunnel that leads to the Borg's invasion staging area. Starships might not be enough to win the day—we may find ourselves tasked with infiltrating and destroying anything from a unimatrix complex to a transwarp hub. So, if it comes to that, I need to know: In your professional opinion, are Lieutenant Choudhury's security personnel equal to the task?"

"Some are," Worf said. "Some are not. But until they are tested in battle, there is no way to know who will falter."

Picard seemed dubious. "Simulations—"

"—are unreliable," Worf said. "Some trainees will not commit themselves, masking their true abilities. Others will indulge in bravado, inflating their egos while learning nothing. The only true measure of a warrior is combat."

"Very well," Picard said. "Putting aside the readiness of the individuals, how would you rate the department as a whole?"

"Exceptional, sir."

The captain leaned forward. "Splendid. Tell Lieutenant

Choudhury to start scheduling drills for her most experienced combat personnel. I want multiple small units capable of independent action. See to it that they're briefed on all our latest intelligence about the absorptive properties of Borg cubes—just in case. And, at the risk of fueling their bravado, have them conduct intensive training simulations as soon as we get the holodecks functional."

"For what objective should they be trained, sir?"

Picard's aquiline visage tensed, and his frown lines deepened as he said, "To seek and destroy the Borg Queen."

The door sighed open ahead of Bowers, and he walked into the *Aventine*'s gymnasium to find Captain Dax laboring to swing a *bat'leth* through a simple series of parries and strikes. She wore an off-white gi, and her feet were bare. As the pixyish Trill woman pivoted through a turning slash, she saw Bowers and lowered the crescent-shaped Klingon blade.

"Sam," she said, sounding exhausted and annoyed.

"Captain." He nodded at the *bat'leth*. "Looks a bit on the heavy side for you, don't you think?"

"It was a gift," she said. "One of these years, I'll get the hang of it, the way Jadzia did."

He decided not to mention that, from all accounts he had heard, Jadzia had been several inches taller than Ezri and had begun her martial-arts training at a much younger age. "I just wanted to let you know we're less than two hours away from our first scouting run. Helkara says we'll have the ingress frequency for the nearest tunnel by 2100 at the latest, and Leishman's team is almost done modifying the sensor grid."

Dax plodded to a bench along the side of the compartment, rested the *bat'leth* against it at an angle, and picked up a towel to dab the perspiration from her forehead and the nape of her neck. "How long until the *Enterprise* is ready?"

"Not till 0200, but they have to hang back to watch for the Borg, anyway," Bowers said, partly distracted by the exquisite workmanship of the engraving on the side of the *bat'leth* and the fine temper of its edge. "We're on our own for the first run."

She noticed his attention to the blade. "Want to spar?" she asked, toweling sweat from her short, dark hair. "We can replicate one for you, go a few rounds. . . ."

"No, I don't think so," he said with a self-deprecating wave of his hand. "Not really my weapon of choice."

The captain shrugged. "What's your preference? I'm flexible."

Bowers wondered if he was just imagining a note of manic desperation in Dax's manner. Then he saw the anxiety in her wide-eyed gaze, and he knew that something wasn't right. "Are you feeling okay, Captain?"

"We have the gym to ourselves, Sam, you can drop the rank."

Her attempts at familiarity felt like more deflection, but if it helped her open up, he'd take advantage of her offer. "It just seems a bit weird, this sudden need to spar. Have you tried using the holodeck?"

"What's the point of sparring in the holodeck? There's no satisfaction in it." She tossed her towel on the bench, picked up the *bat'leth,* and lugged it back to the middle of the gym.

He watched her arms quake with the effort of heaving the blade level with her shoulders and holding it steady. "Why can't you get satisfaction sparring on the holodeck?" he asked. When she made no attempt to answer, he speculated, "Is it because a holodeck character can't hang out in the lounge and tell the crew he got his ass kicked by the captain?"

She closed her eyes as her concentration broke, and the sword dragged her buckled arms halfway to the deck. "Goddammit, Sam," she exclaimed. "I'm just trying . . . I just want to get my focus back so I can feel like I'm in control." Dax turned away, and then she dropped the *bat'leth*. She planted one hand on her hip and used the other to cover her eyes. "Maybe you won't understand this, but I feel like I'm faking my way through every minute of the day, and that everyone around me knows it." Her hand dropped from her face, which was pale except for the circles under her eyes. "Five weeks ago, I was the second officer on this ship. Third in the chain of command. Then one direct hit by the Borg, and it was like I was watching Tiris Jast die on the *Defiant* all over again."

Bowers recalled the death of *Defiant*'s female Bolian commander, during an attack by rogue Jem'Hadar ships several years earlier. That incident had been a key moment for Ezri, then still a counselor. She'd tapped into the Dax symbiont's past lifetimes of experience, taken charge of the *Defiant,* and proved adept at rising to the challenges of command.

"If your moment on this ship was anything like the one you had on *Defiant,* you deserve to be in the center seat," he told her, because it seemed to be what she needed to hear.

Dax shook her head. "It wasn't just that incident. It feels like my whole career's been like that. Just one lucky coincidence after another. What if they'd found another host for the Dax symbiont on the *Destiny*? Then I'd just be Ezri Tigan now, counselor un-extraordinaire. If Jast hadn't been killed in that attack on Deep Space 9, I might still be wearing medical-division blue. Or what if Captain Dexar or Commander Tovak had survived the Battle of Acamar?"

Bowers rolled his eyes and sighed. "Bullshit." Her head snapped toward him, and the fiery anger in her eyes confirmed that he had her attention. He continued, "Who cares how or why you ended up in those situations? What matters is what you *chose* to do each time you faced a challenge." He stepped toward her. "You could've refused to host the Dax symbiont, but you didn't. You could've let someone else call the shots on *Defiant* when Jast fell, but you took command and saved the ship. During that crisis with the alternate universe, and the fallout that came after it, *you* were the one who stepped up when it mattered the most. And from what I've read in this ship's logs, you did *exactly* what you were supposed to do at Acamar."

He stopped in front of her, kneeled, and picked up the *bat'leth* from the deck. It was a perfectly balanced weapon, and it rested in his hand with a reassuring heft.

Then he straightened, rotated the blade with both hands, and offered it grip-first to Dax. "You're in command because you're a natural leader. When others shrink, you rise. And you've got the advantage of *eight lifetimes* of experience—that's seven and a half more than most captains."

She looked up at him with grateful eyes and hesitantly accepted the *bat'leth*. As she took hold of it, he added, "You're a hell of a good CO, Ezri. And I bet the man who gave you that sword would tell you the same thing—if you let him."

Geordi La Forge braced himself inside the steep, nearly vertical crawl space that led to the *Aventine*'s sensor control nexus and reached down toward the ship's chief engineer, Lieutenant Mikaela Leishman. "Gravitic calipers," he said.

The slender, thirtyish woman passed the tool up to him. "How's it going up there?"

"Almost done," he said. "I have to say, I almost envy you. This is quite a ship you've got here."

"Yeah, she's a beauty. I still feel like I'm getting to know her, though. I only came aboard a few weeks ago, with the other replacements." She chuckled. "There are systems on this ship I still haven't read the manuals for."

"That's confidence-inspiring," quipped Lieutenant Oliana Mirren, the *Aventine*'s senior operations officer, who stepped up behind Leishman and peered up the crawl space at La Forge.

Leishman cast a sour frown at her colleague, then asked, "Shouldn't you be on the bridge?"

"Finished my double shift a few hours ago," she said. "Now I'm checking up on the damage-control teams." Looking up, she called to La Forge, "Hope our prototype systems aren't giving you too much trouble, sir."

"Not at all," La Forge replied, even as he wondered what had led to so much tension between the two women.

Folding her arms, Leishman said to Mirren, "Geordi has everything under control, so you can go find someone else to hassle." La Forge wondered when he and Leishman had come to be on a first-name basis, but since he wanted to stay clear of her cross fire with Mirren, he let that go for the moment.

"I'm sure Mister La Forge is an excellent engineer," Mirren said, "but we're equipped with a lot of test-bed systems. It would be a good idea to monitor his work a bit more closely."

Leishman replied defensively, "He doesn't need me to show him around a sensor grid, Oliana."

"Actually," La Forge cut in, pointing at a series of linked components, "I have no idea what those are. A heads-up before I disconnect something that ought to stay online might not be such a bad idea."

Mirren's smug glance at Leishman said, *I told you so.*

The *Aventine*'s chief engineer flashed an insincere smile in return, and then she clambered swiftly up the crawl space toward La Forge. He tried to wave her back. "Whoa, hang on! Space is a little tight up here right—" The last word of his sentence caught in his throat as Leishman pulled herself up beside him in the narrow tube and let her body press firmly against his.

She reached past him, which pushed their torsos together even more than before. A subtle, floral scent of shampoo in her hair teased his nostrils. "That," she said, pointing at one bundle of optronic cables, "is a multidimensional wave-function analysis module." Using her outstretched hand to grab a support, she extended her other arm over his opposite shoulder. "That bulky thing over there is an experimental sympathetic fermion transceiver, whose counterpart is currently being installed in a secure facility somewhere ultra top secret." She pulled herself a bit higher than La Forge, placing her bosom in front of his face as she pointed at a complicated apparatus. "And this marvel of modern science is a chroniton integrator, which in theory will let us take sensor readings from several seconds in the future when our slipstream drive is engaged."

"Very impressive," La Forge said, only half certain that he was talking about the ship.

Leishman smiled. "Believe it or not, there are actually a few more things up here that are so secret that if I told you what they were—" She lost her grip suddenly on her handhold and whooped in surprise as she fell. Without thinking, La Forge caught her, and she held on to him, her arms around his neck, her legs wrapped around his waist. "Nice catch," she said.

"All part of the service," La Forge said, a grin brightening his own features.

From below the two chief engineers came an exasperated huff. La Forge and Leishman looked down and were met by the censorious glare of Lieutenant Mirren. "Heaven defend us from engineers in love," she groused. "Let me know when you're done."

The operations officer walked away, leaving the engineers to their strangely intimate clutch in the crawl space. After a few seconds, Leishman cast a wide-eyed look of amusement at La Forge and broke out laughing. "She's so easy to tweak!"

"I take it this is a running gag for you?"

The sylphlike brunette shrugged. "It's getting to be." As if she'd suddenly become self-conscious now that no one was looking, she averted her eyes from La Forge's and said, "We'd probably better get back to work."

"Yeah, I guess so," La Forge said as he helped Leishman disentangle herself from him. "Besides, it usually takes me three or four dates before I go this far." Flashing a grin, he added, "I might be a cheap date, but I'm not easy."

She climbed back down to the corridor and looked up at him. "Well, then, we might have a problem. Because I'm easy—but I'm not cheap." She reached into her roll-up bag of specialty engineering tools, pulled out a flux coupler, and passed it up to him. "Take this," she said. "You'll need it to balance the plasma flow to the triquantum coil."

Taking the tool, he didn't know what to make of Leishman. Was she just goofing around to annoy Mirren, or had she actually been flirting with him? The question nagged at him from the back of his thoughts while he finished his adjustments to the new systems in the *Aventine*'s sensor grid. "That ought to do it," he said as he deactivated the flux coupler. "Thanks for letting me go hands-on with this. It'll make refitting the *Enterprise*'s grid a lot easier while you guys are off on your scouting run."

"My pleasure," Leishman said as La Forge climbed down and out of the Jefferies tube. He handed the coupler back to her. She turned to tuck it back into its pocket in her equipment roll-up, but then she turned back toward La Forge with a deeply thoughtful expression. "I just want to say, in case there was, you know, any confusion or anything about that whole business with us in the tube . . ."

"It's okay," La Forge said. "I understand. You were just kidding around."

"No, I was totally hitting on you." She turned away, jammed the flux capacitor into her bag, rolled it shut in a blur of motion, and fastened its magnetic strap. When she turned back, La Forge was still at a loss for words. "But I get it, sir. You're just not that into me. It's no big deal." She picked up her bag and walked past La Forge, away down the corridor.

He called after her, "Can I buy you a drink sometime?"

She stopped and turned back. With a raised eyebrow, she asked, "Just a drink?"

He spread his arms in dismay. "Dinner?"

Her eyes narrowed in mock suspicion. "Appetizers?"

"Of course."

Planting a hand on her hip, she asked with exaggerated doubt, "*And* dessert?"

"Naturally," La Forge said, liking her style.

"And I'll expect flowers or something pretty," she said.

"Pushing your luck, aren't you?"

"Easy but not cheap," Leishman said. "Take it or leave it."

He laughed and said, "Sold."

"All right," she replied. "As soon as this war's over, you've got yourself a date." Patting a bulkhead, she added, "You've got my number." Then she turned and walked away around a bend in the corridor, leaving Geordi La Forge to wonder why this sort of thing didn't happen to him more often.

His elation was short-lived as he considered the obstacle that lay in front of him. *All I have to do to get a date with Mikaela is end the Borg invasion. If that's her idea of being easy, I don't even want to know what "not cheap" really means.*

Dax followed the instructions of the *Enterprise*'s computer as she moved through the ship looking for Worf. Her visit to the 1701-E was unannounced, and she wanted it to stay that way, but it was making it hard to find her old Deep Space 9 comrade.

When she'd first beamed aboard, the computer had dutifully informed her that he was in the forward sensor control center. By the time she'd walked there, however, he'd long since gone. Another query of the computer had led her to the auxiliary phaser control compartment, where she was told by a helpful young Bolian chief petty officer that she'd just missed the XO.

Now she was riding in a turbolift down to the main engineering compartment, in the hope of catching up with him at last. The doors hushed open, and she stepped out into the frenetic activity of a massive repair effort. The sharp smell of scorched metal was heavy in the air, and the clangor of voices, plasma welders, and echoing announcements over the shipwide comm fused into a gray din of noise.

A team of engineers moved past her, escorting a convoy of antigravs loaded with newly fabricated replacement parts and stacks of optronic cable. Everywhere she looked, there were panels open on the bulkheads, revealing the ship's inner machinery. She dodged clear of a hazard-suited duo of damage-control mechanics laden with tools.

"Excuse me," she said to a passing ensign. "Have you seen Commander Worf down here?"

The frazzled-looking young Tellarite pointed back the way he'd come. "By the main reactor with Lieutenant Taurik." Noticing the four rank pips on Captain Dax's collar, he added belatedly, "Sir."

"Thank you, Ensign," Dax said, and continued on her way.

She found Worf exactly where the Tellarite had said, and the Klingon was still conversing with the *Enterprise*'s Vulcan assistant chief engineer. Not wanting to intrude or interrupt, she lingered several paces shy of being able to eavesdrop on them—not that she could have heard much in the clamorous bustle of the all-hands repair effort.

Taurik nodded and stepped away, and Worf turned to head toward the turbolift. His eyes widened as he saw Dax watching him, but he didn't break stride as he passed her. "Are you returning my chief engineer?"

"He'll be back any minute," she said, falling into step beside him. "But I'm actually here to talk to you."

His dark brows furrowed as he glanced sideways at her. "Is there something you need, Captain?"

She followed him into a waiting turbolift. "Can we drop the ranks and just go back to being friends for a minute?"

The doors closed, and Worf's shoulders relaxed by only the slightest measure. He lifted his chin and softened his voice to a less authoritarian baritone. "Computer, hold turbolift." A feedback tone from the overhead comm confirmed his order, and he looked at Dax. "I apologize," he said. "Tracking the repairs is time-consuming. . . . Are you all right?"

"I'm fine," she said, touched as ever by his terse but genuine concern for her well-being. "It's just that you and I haven't talked since before I transferred to the *Aventine,* and suddenly I'm a captain. Must be weird for you."

"How so?"

Dax didn't know how to answer. In two words, he'd worked a dexterous bit of conversational judo and left her speechless. Reflecting on her feelings, she saw that she'd been wrong in her assumptions, and she decided to be honest with herself and with Worf. "Let me start over," she said. "The truth is, I have no idea how you feel about my promotion. I was projecting my feelings about it onto you, and I shouldn't have. I'm sorry."

"You do not need to apologize," he said.

She held up her palms, as if to deflect his gracious words.

"No, I do, Worf. I should've given you more credit, but I was afraid you'd resent me for making captain ahead of you."

He nodded. "Because of the reprimand I received after saving Jadzia on Soukara," he said.

"Yes," Dax said, relieved to have the matter in the open.

His sharp inhalation and heavy exhalation gave Dax ample notice that he was on the verge of saying something important. "I regret nothing that I did for Jadzia," he said. "I accepted the consequences then, and now." His stern features brightened. "You earned command by leading in battle. Jadzia would be proud of you—as I am. Your success honors her, and vindicates my decision to save her."

The decorum of command was the only thing keeping Dax from becoming completely overwrought at Worf's rare expression of his feelings for her, and for Jadzia. "Thank you, Worf. It means a lot to me to hear you say that. And for what it's worth, I've never seen you look more relaxed and contented than you do right now." A moment of self-doubt prompted her to ask, "I'm not just imagining that, am I? Are you happy with your life?"

He looked away for a moment, his demeanor pensive. Then he looked back and said, "The *Enterprise* is where I belong, and I consider it a great honor to be Captain Picard's first officer."

She reached out and rubbed his shoulder. "I'm glad." Flashing a broad smile, she added, "Don't get too settled in, though. I bet you'll prove Captain Sisko wrong and have a ship of your own before long."

"I am in no hurry."

"Of course not," Dax said. "You always did take your time."

A low grunt rumbled in his chest before he said, "Computer, Deck Five," and the turbolift hummed into motion.

Dax folded her hands behind her back as the lift made its rapid ascent. "It's funny, isn't it? Just at the point you and I are finally living up to our potential, the Borg are trying to exterminate us. What would you call that? Irony? Or tragedy?"

Worf grimaced. "Bad timing."

# 8

"Strike team ready," reported Lieutenant Pava Ek'Noor sh'Aqabaa, the tall, sinewy, and breathtaking Andorian *shen* who was filling in for the absent Ranul Keru at *Titan*'s security console.

Captain Riker wanted to be on his feet, moving from station to station, but he knew his role called for him to stay in the command chair and project certainty to his crew. His acting XO, Commander Fo Hachesa, double-checked the readouts on sh'Aqabaa's console and nodded his confirmation to Riker.

At the aft science stations, chief engineer Ra-Havreii and the holographic avatar of science officer Pazlar were racing through their final adjustments. Ra-Havreii pivoted away from the console and declared, "Ready, Captain!"

"Engage!" Riker ordered.

Lieutenant Rager keyed in commands on the ops console. "Charging the inverters now," she said.

"Power levels steady," Pazlar said, watching the gauges on her station's monitor. "Initializing subspatial trajector."

"Calibrating targeting beam," Ra-Havreii said, his own hands moving with speed and grace across his console's controls.

Riker crossed his fingers. This was a plan that had a lot of ways to go wrong. Distilled to its essential elements, *Titan* would use a folded-space transporter—a technology with proven deleterious effects on organic tissue—to bypass the protective shell of black metal around the Caeliar's hidden planet and sneak a strike team inside.

Because they had no way to scan the planet's surface, Pazlar had estimated the likely size of the planet and the approximate thickness of the hollow sphere that surrounded it. The strike team, outfitted with orbital skydiving gear, would be shifted past the sphere into the planet's atmosphere and free-fall to the surface. Once on the ground, they would don isolation suits to cloak themselves from the Caeliar, seek out the away team, and then, once they found them, trigger a transdimensional recall beacon.

Listening to the rapid volleys of technical information from one bridge officer to the next, Riker fixed his mien into a mask of calm resolve.

"Trajector at full power," Pazlar said.

"Sensor module buffers holding," Rager added.

Ra-Havreii chimed in, "No lock for the targeting beam." He poked at the console controls. "There's a multiphasic scrambling field inside the sphere," he said.

Riker asked, "Can you break through it?"

"I'll need more power," Ra-Havreii said. "Increasing to five-eighty . . . five-ninety . . . six hundred."

A droning whine began vibrating the deck. It made the bulk-heads ring like a struck tuning fork.

"Feedback pulse," Pazlar said, raising her voice over the rising hum. "We need to reduce power!"

"Negative," Ra-Havreii said. "Increase to six-twenty-five, we're almost through!"

Rager interjected, "Buffer overload!"

"It's a transition rebound effect," Ra-Havreii shouted back. "Negate it with a canceling frequency, quickly!"

A port-side engineering station erupted in a storm of shattered black polymer shrapnel and jetting sparks. The blast knocked Ra-Havreii off his feet and peppered his drooping white mustache and flowing white hair with smoldering motes, which he frantically finger-combed away before brushing clean his shoulders and chest.

Overhead, the lights flickered, and several consoles stuttered under the hands of people trying to keep them working. Pazlar reported with rising frustration, "Cascade failures in the sensor module! We're losing the trajector's targeting system!"

Hachesa stood close to Riker and bent low to offer in confidence, "I recommend we abort the mission, sir."

Riker frowned at the Kobliad, even though he knew the acting XO was right. Then he nodded and said in a voice that cut through the din, "Abort mission. Rager, shut down the inverters. Lieutenant sh'Aqabaa, tell the strike team to stand down. Secure from Yellow Alert." He saw Hachesa help Ra-Havreii stand up, and he said to the chief engineer, "Commander, deploy damage-control teams to the sensor module."

"Aye, sir," Ra-Havreii said, shaking off Hachesa's hand and walking stiffly toward a functioning duty station.

All around *Titan*'s bridge, Riker saw dejected expressions, faces reflecting failure and disappointment. Looking over his shoulder, he saw Pazlar switch off a mission-command screen as she grumbled, "I guess that's it, then."

The bad morale had a toxic quality, one that Riker was determined not to grant a foothold on his ship. He stood and stepped forward to the center of the bridge. "Rager," he said, "put me on a shipwide channel."

The ops officer keyed in the command, turned her head back in his direction, and replied, "Channel open, sir."

"Attention, all decks," Riker said. "This is the captain. By now you're very likely all aware that our latest rescue mission has not gone as planned.

"Though we've only been at this a short time, I'm sure some of you are beginning to harbor doubts about our chances for saving the away team—and ourselves. Given the obstacles that the Caeliar have left in our path, I can certainly understand why you might feel that way.

"But we aren't going to give in to doubt or frustration or fear. I know that each time another plan fails, it seems like we're running out of options. But I assure you, we're not.

"Every step of the way we're learning. Every failure teaches us something new. And if there's one thing I know about Starfleet—and especially about this ship, and this crew—it's that we've got a million tricks up our sleeves. If none of them work, we'll pull out a million more. And a million after that.

"As long as our away team continues to be held prisoner on the surface, we will keep looking for a way to free them, and ourselves. We will use every means at our disposal, every technology we possess, to free ourselves.

"We will never relent, and we will never yield, no matter how long it takes—and we'll *all* go home, together."

He signaled Rager with a small slashing gesture beside his thoat to cut the channel, and then he returned to his chair. Pazlar and Ra-Havreii stood next to it. The science officer's holographic avatar flickered and wavered a moment. "So," Riker said to the pair, "what's your next plan?"

"The way you were talking, I figured you already had one," Ra-Havreii said, pinching another charred granule of companel composite from his singed mustache.

"Not yet," Riker said. "But give me time, Commander. Give me time."

Ranul Keru tried to keep an open mind as he wandered with Ensign Torvig through the deserted avenues of Axion, but there was something about the city that put him perpetually on edge. The morning was bright and beautiful, its air temperate, sweet, and mild in humidity. Sunlight glinted off surfaces in every direction. It was as pristine an urban environment as Keru had ever seen, yet everything about it sent a chill through him.

Torvig, on the other hand, gamboled from one discovery to the next, his curiosity insatiable. His sleek, ovine head bobbed and swiveled as he trotted along several meters ahead of Keru, with a tricorder clutched in one cybernetic hand. He pivoted back toward Keru just long enough to report, "I'm reading a new energy wave ahead." Then he was off again, loping along through the gleaming canyon of bright metal and smoky crystal.

"Slow down, Vig," Keru called ahead to his friend. "It's a recon, not a race."

The Choblik engineer didn't seem to be listening to him. It was several minutes before Torvig halted long enough for Keru to catch up to him, and only then because he was engrossed in his study of a peculiar Caeliar construct by the side of the road. The three-meter-tall object was composed entirely of perfectly polished obsidian. Its base had a distinctly organic shape, but from a height level with Torvig's shoulder—and Keru's midriff—it became an asymmetrical fusion of hard angles and irregular polyhedrons. Some of its surfaces seemed to have been arbitrarily inscribed with symbols or characters of the Caeliar language.

Keru waited until he caught Vig sneaking a look back at him with one eye, and he asked the engineer, "Any clue what it is?"

"I have hypotheses," Torvig said. He circled the object and kept his head only centimeters from its surface as he continued. "The shapes might be directional indicators. The inscriptions may denote the names of locations in the city, or perhaps distances to known places from this point."

Narrowing his eyes at Torvig's knack for complicating the simplest of answers, he replied, "You mean it's a road sign."

"Maybe," Torvig said. "That's only one possibility." He stopped on the far side of the object from Keru, reached forward, and removed a loose piece, which was formed from the same ultrasmooth black stone. Shaped like a spike, it caught the sunlight and gave off indigo flashes as Torvig turned it in his left bionic hand while scanning it with the tricorder held in his right. His small mechanical appendages handled the object with tremendous dexterity and gentleness. "There is another piece like this one," he said. "Identical in every way. Thirty-one centimeters in length. Weight, one hundred forty-one-point-seven grams. Variable diameter, from two-point-one centimeters along the majority of its length, tapering to zero-point-four centimeters before widening again at the end, before a final tapering. Most interesting."

Circling around to stand beside the ensign, Keru said, "Vig, can I see those a minute?"

Torvig handed Keru the first slender object, and then he grabbed the other and passed it to the burly Trill security chief. Keru held the two stone sticks at their broader ends and felt the weight of them. He paid particular attention to the narrowing of each rod, and the slightly bulbous barrel tip that bulged at the end of that taper.

"I know what these are," Keru said. "Step back a little."

Keru took a moment to examine the tall object for flat surfaces. He imagined which angles of attack would feel most natural. Cautiously, he reached out and used one of the spikes to tap on an inscribed panel of the obelisk.

A rich, gonglike tone pealed from inside the black object and resonated in the towering buildings all around him. It sounded as if he'd struck a colossal xylophone with the hammer of the gods, yet all he'd done was tap the thing. He didn't listen to the instrument's phenomenally sustained note so much as he felt it vibrating through his flesh and bones.

When he looked back, Torvig cocked his head to one side. "Perhaps you should strike it again, sir. Someplace different."

Choosing another spot, Keru gave it a gingerly tap with one of the stone sticks, and a brighter note rebounded off the cityscape. Feeling bolder as the sound overwhelmed him, he began a slow exploration of the device, and he was astounded to find that, no matter how randomly or arbitrarily he percussed the black statue, he couldn't sound a discordant note. As he continued, his pace accelerated to a frenzy, and he was all but dancing around the object like a wild shaman, seeking out some new note to play, some new melody to coax into existence.

It was difficult for him to stop, but he knew that he had to. The instrument's sounds felt addictive to him. With great effort and more than a touch of remorse, he stopped playing, took a deep breath, and put the obsidian sticks back into their storage slots on the side of the instrument as the last note echoed and faded to silence. He stroked his beard pensively.

"Why did you stop?" asked Torvig.

"I felt like I was losing myself in it," Keru said. "I can't really explain it. I was taught at the Academy that the effect of sound on the humanoid brain is minimal. Certain infrasonic frequencies can produce anxiety and physical effects, like blurred vision or shortness of breath, but this wasn't like that. It was . . . something else."

Torvig sounded concerned. "Are you all right, Ranul?"

"I'm okay, Vig, thanks. I just want to get away from this thing as soon as we can."

"Of course," the engineer said. He pointed himself toward a boulevard that led to the city's outskirts. "There is an energy surge in this direction." Before Keru could protest, the Choblik was trotting away, eyes glued to his tricorder screen.

A few kilometers and minor detours later, Keru caught up to his diminutive friend once again. Torvig was perched on the edge of an overpass, supporting himself with his spindly bionic arms while he leaned over to stare at something of interest below.

Keru lowered himself to the ground and crawled over beside Torvig to peer into the space beneath the footbridge. Several dozen meters below, a Caeliar hovered above a dark, oval pool of liquid. Globes of the black fluid rose from the pool's surface without making a ripple of disturbance. In the air, a few meters away from the Caeliar, the dark spheres semisolidified, fused, and were reshaped into something new, which rotated slowly and on more than one axis as more matter accreted on its surface. Although the Caeliar made no motions or sound, and there was no visible connection between it and the object taking shape, Keru was certain that the alien was driving the process, directing its outcome.

His friend whispered to him, "Isn't it interesting how they manipulate forms? Their methods are economical and precise."

"Just like machines," Keru said, straining to keep his own voice a whisper.

"Not quite," Torvig said. "It's true that claytronic atoms enable them to mold their bodies and environment, but it would be a mistake to equate the Caeliar with cybernetic organisms such as myself." After a tense pause, he added, "Or the Borg."

Far below, the Caeliar transformed into a shimmering golden mist that fused with the black sculpture and vanished inside of it. The bizarre creation began changing shapes, shifting into ever more unusual configurations while the two Starfleet officers observed its mutations.

Torvig continued, "The Caeliar and their city are far beyond even our most advanced understandings of cybernetics. They represent a nearly perfect organic-synthetic harmony."

The Choblik paused as the golden mist flowed out of the abstract shape below. The Caeliar had turned the piece into something that reminded Keru of a ball of energy with countless ribbons of current dancing across its surface.

Finishing his thought, Torvig added, "The Caeliar have achieved everything to which my people aspire."

Keru grimaced. "Really? Do the Choblik daydream about taking innocent people hostage?"

That gave the engineer a moment of overtly self-conscious pause. "Perhaps the Caeliar are less than *ideal* role models. . . ."

"Vig, that's like saying the Gorn are less than ideal vegetarians. Or that Chalnoth make less than ideal nannies." He pushed himself back from the edge and stood. "Come on, let's keep moving. We need to finish this recon and get back."

Torvig sprang back from the edge of the bridge and fell into step beside Keru. "With proper dietary supplements, a Gorn *could* subsist on a vegetable-based diet, Ranul."

"So not the point, Vig. So not the point."

Melora Pazlar hadn't meant to fall asleep. She'd wrapped herself in a wispy sleep-cocoon, intending only to relax while listening to the musical emanations of the crystal sculptures that adorned the high walls of her vertically oriented quarters. She felt safe and comfortable in the microgravity environment, which simulated that of her native Gemworld, but days of overwork and sleep deprivation had finally caught up with her, and she'd found herself chasing multicolored giant insects over a lush dreamscape of ruggedly beautiful lapidary spires.

She awoke with a shudder and looked down to see someone gazing up and watching her. "Computer! Lights!"

The glow strips set into the walls gradually brightened, adding fire to her sculptures' facets while giving her eyes time to adjust to the increasing brightness. When the illumination had increased to roughly fifty percent of full, she recognized her unannounced visitor as Counselor Huilan Sen'kara.

On a ship packed with a staggering variety of life-forms, the S'ti'ach was one whom Pazlar found especially memorable. His four short arms, two squat legs, and stubby thick tail, coupled with his large-eyed, broad-eared visage, bright blue fur, and sub-meter height, reminded her of a child's plush animal toy. The illusion was belied, however, by the row of sharp spines on his back—and by his fangs.

"Sorry to wake you," he said, sounding insincere.

She unfastened the safety loop of her cocoon and rolled free of it. Falling slowly, she asked sharply, "What are you doing in my quarters?"

"I think we need to have a talk," Huilan said.

"Do you?" Spreading her arms as if to catch the air, she kept her angry gaze directed squarely at him as she neared the deck. "I don't recall making an appointment, Counselor. I also don't remember inviting you in."

Her toes touched the carpeted floor, and she let her calf muscles tense just enough to spring her back into the air, where she hovered over Huilan.

He flattened his spines against his back and pivoted awkwardly, apparently preferring to keep his feet planted on the deck. After surveying the narrow room, he looked back up at Pazlar. "I would invite you to sit down with me, but you don't seem to have any place to sit."

"My people don't have much use for chairs or anything like them," she said. "We find floating more comfortable." With a small push off a protrusion from one of the bulkheads, she sent herself a few meters higher. "Feel free to come up to my level if you want to keep talking."

The S'ti'ach made a sound that was part growl, part purr. "Not my first choice, Commander," he said. "My species evolved in a high-gravity setting. Neither floating nor flying comes naturally to us."

"Fascinating," Pazlar said. She reached the overhead and halted herself by pressing her fingertips against it and resisting ever so gently, bending at the elbows to absorb her momentum. The artificially generated pull of a few centigees of gravity slowly reeled her back toward the deck. She glared at Huilan. "You came to talk. So talk."

The spines on his back bristled back to full attention, betraying his reaction to her brusque tone. "Several of your shipmates have noticed that you spend an inordinate amount of time inside the stellar cartography lab," he said. "Since the introduction of your holographic avatar, none of your colleagues have seen you in the flesh."

"So? That was kind of the whole point."

As she touched down in front of him, he asked, "What was?"

"Being able to go anywhere, anytime, holographically," she said. "That's why Xin built it for me—so I could experience life on the ship just like everyone else does."

Huilan's sigh was tainted with mockery. "Well, that's a relief. And here I thought you were using it to shut yourself off from contact with other people. Silly me."

"That's ridiculous," Pazlar retorted. "Now that I'm free to move around the ship, I've had more face time with the rest of the crew than ever before."

"At a comfortable remove, no less," Huilan shot back. "It must be nice. Safe."

She backed up half a step from the counselor and launched herself up and away once more. "It is nice," she said, more defensively than she had meant to. "It's a great invention. Why do you have to go and make it into something dysfunctional?"

"That's not my intention, I assure you." Huilan watched her with keen attention as she continued to ascend. "And in principle, I don't disagree. I am happy to see you freed from your constraints. But too much of a good thing can be a cause for concern, Melora."

The metal of the overhead was cold against her fingertips as she pushed off it and began another descent. "What're you trying to say? That I need to spend less time using the holopresence system? Why? I spend most of my time working in stellar cartography, anyway. And clunking through the ship in my armor is hardly my idea of a good time, Doc."

"I sympathize," Huilan said. "But I think you need to stay in practice, so to speak, at living and working in the higher-gravity parts of the ship. If you don't use those skills, they'll atrophy—and you know it."

She landed a bit more firmly than she had intended, and she let the momentum carry her forward a few steps, toward Huilan. "I've heard the spiel before," she said. "Use it or lose it—blah, blah, blah. But it's not like I'm barricaded inside my quarters with the gravity off. I get around just fine."

"Is that a fact?" The small, blue S'ti'ach gazed at her with an almost feral intensity, as if accusing her with a look.

She taunted him with a shake of her head and thrust her empty palms upward in frustration. "What?"

"Where do you store your gravity-assist armature?"

She pointed toward the custom-built frame on the bulkhead. "Right over—" Her armature wasn't there. "What the . . . ?"

"Computer," Huilan said. "Deactivate holopresence module." As soon as he'd said it, Pazlar's quarters vanished, and she found herself standing on the observation platform inside stellar cartography. The walls of the spherical chamber were dark, dull, and blank. Her armature and cane rested against one railing of the catwalk that linked the platform to the entrance portal. "I'm glad you don't think you've blurred the line between illusion and reality," Huilan continued. "But you've been in here for thirty-nine consecutive hours."

He turned and shuffled a few paces toward the exit before he stopped, turned back, and added, "If you'd like to talk about this a little more, you know where my office is. But if you come by, do us both a favor—come in person."

"Here they come," Tuvok said, activating his tricorder. As he ducked behind a low wall for cover, Vale crouched beside him.

She peeked over the wall's edge. Several dozen meters away, a trio of Caeliar were crossing an open courtyard surrounded by flowering trees. Their long, bony limbs moved with more grace than Vale had expected. They walked directly toward a solid wall of dark crystal in a frame of immaculate, polished metal.

"Watch for a device or a trigger," Vale whispered.

Her brown-skinned Vulcan colleague arched one eyebrow into a dubious peak, but he said nothing. Instead, he did as she'd asked and kept his attention on the Caeliar.

As the three aliens made contact with the wall, it seemed to offer no resistance to their passage. "They walked through it like it was a hologram," she said.

Tuvok lifted his tricorder and checked its readings. "Negative, Commander. No sign of holographic projection. But I did pick up a momentary, localized surge in baryonic particles."

"And that means . . . ?"

His expression was exquisitely neutral, but Vale was certain she saw a hint of irritation in Tuvok's eye. "That something powered by dark energy affected either the particles in the wall, those in the Caeliar, or both."

"So that wasn't just an illusion," she said. "They really did just walk through a wall."

He turned off his tricorder. "In essence, yes."

From far behind them came the swift patter of footsteps. Vale looked back and saw the away team's two security officers, Lieutenant Sortollo and Chief Dennisar, jogging toward her and Tuvok. Their footfalls echoed off the dizzying vertical faces of the Caeliar's majestic towers. Vale looked askance at Tuvok and remarked, "The acoustics out here would make it damn hard to sneak up on someone."

"Indeed," Tuvok said. "I heard them several minutes ago."

She considered chiding him for boasting, but she knew he would say that he was only making a statement of fact. Then he would insinuate that her accusation was rooted in insecurity. *You know you've meshed with your people when you can have the entire argument without saying a word,* Vale mused.

The two security officers slowed as they drew near to Vale and Tuvok. "Commanders," said Sortollo. "We finished our recon. What do you want first, the good news or the bad news?"

"Life is short," Vale said. "Give me the good news."

Sortollo nodded. "The shuttle's still on the platform, about a hundred meters from the city's edge," he said. "So, at least the Caeliar didn't ditch it at sea."

That was something, at least. "And the bad news?"

An anxious glance passed between Sortollo and Dennisar. The lieutenant replied, "We haven't found a single door anywhere in the city. Not at ground level, at least. The Caeliar seem to levitate from place to place, or just appear out of nowhere."

"And they're watching us," said Dennisar. "And listening to everything we say. All the time."

Doubt creased Vale's brow. She asked the Orion, "Are you sure you're not just being a little paranoid?"

"I'm sure," Dennisar said. Looking up and away, he raised his voice and said, "Who's observing us right now?"

To Vale's surprise, a gentle breeze moved past her, warm and pleasant on her skin, and then a slow, gentle swirl of luminescent pinpoints formed behind the two security officers. The glowing motes spread and cohered into the shape of a Caeliar. Within seconds the figure solidified, and then it spoke with a pleasing, feminine voice. "I am Avelos," she said.

Tuvok inquired, "Have you been observing us?"

"Yes," said Avelos. "For a time."

"She isn't the one we met," Sortollo said. "His name was Bednar." He added, to Avelos, "Are there others watching us?"

"There are many of us," Avelos said. "We share the responsibility. Bednar followed two of you here, but once the four of you were together, there was no need for two monitors. So I volunteered to stay and released Bednar."

Thinking aloud, Vale said, "There are monitors with all our people, right?"

"Correct," said Avelos. "Our intent is not malicious, merely vigilant. The Quorum feels that precautions are prudent, given the outcome of our last dealings with your kind."

"Do you refer to the crew of the *Columbia*?" Tuvok asked.

The Caeliar turned toward him. "Yes. Members of its crew, whom we'd welcomed as guests here in Axion, resorted to violence in their bid for escape. Their methods caused the deaths of millions of Caeliar, and the loss of one of our cities."

Vale cut in, "There are other cities?"

Avelos's reply was heavy with resentment. "Not anymore." She calmed herself before she continued. "The gestalt has made its adjustment to the new paradigm, and your predecessors' actions, though tragic, ultimately proved necessary in the larger scope of the timeline. However, we have only this city now to defend, and we cannot allow you or your shipmates on *Titan* to put us at risk. We wish you no harm, but we have learned from experience not to assume the reverse is true."

"Most logical," Tuvok said.

His reply seemed to satisfy Avelos. She said, "Do you have any other questions you would like to ask me?"

"How do you walk through walls?" Vale asked.

"Programmable matter," Avelos said. "We and the city are composed of the same kind of malleable subatomic machines, and powered by a shared energy field. . . . I'm afraid I'm not permitted to share any information more detailed than that."

Sortollo visibly tensed. "Hang on a second—you and your people . . . are all *machines*?"

"We prefer to think of ourselves as synthetic life-forms. Our catoms mimic much of our original biology, in both form and function. Though your scanners probably don't see us as organic beings, from our perspective, life looks and feels as it ever did. We are as we were . . . and as we shall remain."

The four Starfleet personnel stood in silence and absorbed Avelos's information. Finally, Vale looked at her and said, "Thanks. You can go back to being a breeze or whatever it is you do. We'd like the illusion of a little bit of privacy."

"As you wish," Avelos replied. She became semitransparent, and then she grew blurry and faded away in a balmy rush of air.

Vale looked at Tuvok. "Time for Plan B."

"I was not aware that we *had* a Plan B."

"We don't," she said. "But we'd better get one. Fast."

Deanna Troi leaned against the balcony wall, her weight on both her hands. From her lofty vantage point she gazed beyond the spires of Axion into the distance, out across fog-draped tropical forests and low clouds dragging dark rain shadows.

She heard the air displaced behind her as much as she felt it against her back, and she wasn't surprised to hear Erika Hernandez's voice. "The Quorum will meet with you soon," she said. "I should warn you now not to expect much. The Caeliar tend to resist change—and suggestions."

Troi didn't turn around. Instead, she swiveled her head just enough to catch sight of Hernandez over her shoulder. "We just want to talk to them," Troi said.

Behind her unannounced visitor, Dr. Ree sauntered out of the corridor that led to the away team's respective private quarters. The therapodian physician flicked his forked tongue at Hernandez, no doubt tasting the woman's scent on the air. "I heard voices," he said. "I didn't mean to interrupt."

Hernandez tilted her head in a birdlike manner as she stared at Ree. "May I ask what your species is called?"

"Pahkwa-thanh," Ree said.

The youthful brunette nodded. "Humanity hadn't met any life-forms like yours when I was a starship captain. If it's not too forward of me, I think yours is a very handsome species."

"Well, we've always thought so," Ree replied, sauntering

closer to the two women. "But it's nice of you to say." He stopped at a large, rough-textured boulder, which sat beneath a square light fixture that bathed it in a warm, white radiance. In a graceful hop, he was atop the beige-hued rock, and he stretched out to sun himself. "Don't mind me," he said.

"The Caeliar certainly saw to our comfort," Troi said, in a derogatory tone.

Hernandez didn't take the bait. She joined Troi on the balcony and stood forward against the low wall, her fingertips resting lightly on its ledge. "They try to be good hosts."

A fleeting stab of pain swirled inside Troi's abdomen. She masked her profound discomfort with an intensity of anger she didn't really feel. "Don't you mean 'jailers'?"

"My landing party and I felt much the same way when we first came here. Some of us got over it. Some didn't."

The pain faded slightly, and Troi regained more of her emotional control. She didn't want to give Hernandez or the Caeliar any more information than she had to about her condition, but she was even more intent on concealing her symptoms from Dr. Ree and Commander Vale until the mission was done. The last thing she wanted was to be relieved of duty and treated like a casualty. "You've been living with the Caeliar for quite some time," she said. "Do they trust you?"

"To a point," Hernandez replied. "I have more liberties than you do, but I'm still subject to many restrictions."

Troi's half-Betazoid empathic skills sensed the veracity of Hernandez's words. It was a relief to Troi that whatever change had imbued Hernandez with nigh-eternal youth and rendered her biology unrecognizable to the tricorders had not hampered Troi's ability to detect her emotions. She asked Hernandez, "Have you ever tried to defy them?"

The question colored Hernandez's mood with regret and contempt. "Many times," she said. "More than I could count."

"And how did the Caeliar respond?"

Hernandez cast a sly look at Troi. "Gauging your own risk before you challenge them?"

"I just want a sense of what kind of civilization they've created. Their values, their beliefs . . . their point of view."

Now it was Hernandez's turn to stare out across the mist-dappled tropical mountain slopes as Axion roamed the skies.

Troi watched the sunset paint the sky amber and scarlet along the horizon for a few minutes while Hernandez pondered her query. The sweet, refreshing scent of rain and earthy perfumes from the jungle below reached Troi in a soft, humid upswell.

"The Caeliar," Hernandez said at last, "are very often just what they seem to be: reclusive xenophobes with a frightening amount of raw power. They can be distrustful and stubborn."

Everything she'd said had the ring of truth, as far as Troi's empathy could tell. "How do they punish disobedience?"

"They don't," Hernandez said. "All they ever do is stop the action that bothers them and then lecture you about why it's in your best interest to do as they say."

"And they don't resort to threats or punitive measures?"

Hernandez shook her head. "Not on a personal level. They're pacifists—they won't kill, and they hate violence. Besides, even if they weren't, they'd hardly need to use force to get their way. You've barely seen a fraction of what they can *really* do." In a more ominous timbre, she added, "Trust me, it's a waste of time butting heads with them. You won't win. Ever."

There wasn't a single trace of deception or exaggeration that Troi could sense behind Hernandez's words—just a deep and profound despair, tinged with bitterness. Troi decided to try and coax something more substantial from her hostess. "You say they're nonviolent. But are they fair?"

"They can be." A sullen mood took hold of Hernandez, and Troi felt the other woman's resentment being stoked by her reminiscences. "Though I have to admit . . . in recent centuries, their decisions haven't always been as reasonable as they'd like to think. Some of their decrees have seemed . . . arbitrary."

Pushing a bit more, Troi asked, "Did they seem malicious?"

"No, just selfish."

"I see." Another pang of sickly discomfort made Troi wince. Hernandez didn't seem to notice, and a glance back at the boulder confirmed that Ree's eyes were still closed while he basked in his artificial sunlight. To Hernandez, Troi continued, "I'll just have to hope I catch the Quorum in a good mood."

"Don't count on it," Hernandez said. "Visitors always make them edgy." She turned as if to leave, then she stopped. "I'll be back to escort you to the Quorum hall when they're ready for you. In the meantime, can I ask you a favor?"

Fighting to suppress the sick feeling in her stomach and keep her poker face steady, Troi replied, "It depends."

"Would it bother you if I stopped pretending not to have abilities that you've already seen me use?" She looked back across the residence's open great room. "I could use the pod lift to come and go if it makes you feel better, but . . ."

Troi gave her permission with a sweep of her arm. "Be my guest."

"Thanks," Hernandez said. She walked to the railing, rolled her hips over the low barrier with a gymnast's grace, and pushed away from the edge into open air. Troi peeked over the wall and watched Hernandez make her slow descent, arms wide, her diaphanous raiment and sable hair billowing in an updraft.

Watching her float to the ground, Troi envied Hernandez's freedom . . . until she remembered that, for all her powers and privileges, Hernandez was as much a prisoner as she was.

# 1525–1573

## 9

The years had flowed like water, one into the next, until Erika Hernandez no longer knew where one ended and another began.

Axion was a mountain moving through an ocean of night. Its slow passage of the void between stars was motivated in part by the Caeliar's obsessive need to conceal their presence from the galaxy at large, which necessitated a reduced energy signature. Hernandez's work with Inyx had also given her reason to suspect another cause for their languor: they had no idea where to go.

She stood half a meter behind Inyx in the center of the vast hexagon that she had nicknamed the Star Chamber. The alien scientist's bony limbs were doubled over on themselves as he squatted above a holographic representation of a star system on the black, nonreflective floor. He teased it with his tendril-fingers. Smoky symbols curled up and away from the tiny, orange sun-sphere. "Stable," Inyx declared. "Energy output . . . adequate."

"What about the planets?" asked Hernandez, who waited to enter notations on a sleek, paper-thin polymer tablet.

Inyx enlarged the system as he pushed it high above their heads. Six worlds formed. "Four iron-cored inner planets, two gas giants," Inyx said. "One planet in the habitable zone. Mark this one for further investigation. System D-599."

"I'm naming it Xibalba," Hernandez said.

"You may name it anything you wish, provided you log it in the catalog under the heading System D-599." The simulated star system overhead dissolved and vanished. Inyx strolled toward some other speck of light, several meters away.

Hernandez followed him as she jotted the system's bland catalog designation on the tablet and added her more colorful appellation as a footnote. "That's the second possibility you've found this month," she said. "You're on a roll." Her estimate of time's passage was approximate at best. There were no days in Axion, no changing of seasons, no moon to wax and wane like a celestial timepiece. Just the enduring darkness.

"This latest discovery was most unexpected," Inyx said. "Unfortunately, it's also quite distant. It will be some time before we can reach that sector."

Carefully excising all eagerness from her voice, Hernandez said, "You could build a scout vessel and send a small team to survey the system."

Without deigning to look back, Inyx replied, "I presume you would volunteer for that survey? And that your three companions would be ideal assistants?"

"It is the sort of mission we were trained for."

As she caught up to Inyx and walked beside him on his left, he asked, "What do you think are the odds that the Quorum will give you its permission for such an endeavor?"

"Zero," she said as they passed over the image of a bright stellar cluster on the floor. "Because you won't even present it to them as an option."

"Correct," he said. "I'm glad you've learned that much."

"I told you: I'm a quick study."

"Yes, you have absorbed a great deal of information more quickly than I'd expected," Inyx said. "Though I still have much to teach you, I must admit I've enjoyed your enthusiasm . . . and your stories. You've led a colorful life for one so young."

"Kind of you to say," she said, appreciating his flattery.

He slowed, stopped, reached up, and pulled down a yellow marble of fire from high overhead. "I hope you can sustain your zeal," he said. "It would make the next several decades far more pleasant for all of us."

It took her a few seconds to let herself hear what he said, and even then she was still somewhat in denial. "Decades?"

"Yes," Inyx said. "Many of these candidate systems are quite distant from one another. Given the limitations on our power output, and the need to avoid detection in regions where contact with starfaring races would be a risk, it will take some time for us to complete all our surveys."

Hernandez felt stunned. She had been mentally prepared to spend a few years, or even several years, aiding the Caeliar in their search for a new homeworld. Decades were another matter.

Inyx extracted more smoke-symbols from the burning dot that hovered between his undulating tendrils. After the vaporlike sigils vanished into his mottled skin, he released the tiny orb, which drifted upward, back toward the ceiling. "Not enough essential elements," he said. "It also had only one terrestrial planet, which was too close to the star to be habitable." He moved on, oblivious of Hernandez's state of shock.

"I have a question," she said.

He halted and turned toward her. "Ask."

"If we found a habitable world, but in a star system that didn't suit your more exotic needs, would the Quorum consider letting me and my companions settle there, in exile?"

The tubelike air sacs that ran from Inyx's neck to his chest swelled and then sagged, a Caeliar equivalent to a heavy sigh. "I suspect they would refuse such a request," he said. "There would always be the risk, once you left our custody, that another starfaring species might rescue you, or find you when it came to colonize. Even the discovery of your remains, long after your demise, might raise unfortunate questions. And then our security would be in peril."

"Well, what about displacing us?" she said. "Your Quorum threatened to do it before—fling us to an Earthlike planet in some distant galaxy. Why not do that now?"

He seemed caught off guard. "We'd have to expend a great deal of energy to move you so far. Because we are presently unshielded, doing so would attract significant attention to us. Someone would almost certainly investigate."

"All right," she said, unwilling to surrender. "Then leave us here and move yourselves to another galaxy, one with no one else in it. Then you can have all the privacy you want."

"Why do you have this sudden need to get out of Axion?"

The rusty wire that held the cork on her bottled-up anger finally broke. "There's nothing sudden about it, Inyx! I've wanted out of this place since the moment I got here! I brought my crew here to get help, not become inmates." She paced away from him, then pivoted back. "Human beings aren't meant to live their whole lives in space," she said. "We need a break once in a while. Some fresh air, a walk on the grass, a swim in the ocean. And now you tell me I can look forward to several more decades of night in this wandering ghost town? I'm not sure I can take that, Inyx. I'm not sure my friends can take it."

He sounded genuinely contrite. "I'm sorry. I didn't realize how hostile this environment must seem to you." He looked around at the Star Chamber as he continued, "Holographic simulation is a fairly simple art. Perhaps our chief architect, Edrin, could construct some therapeutic artificial environments for you."

"Holograms?" she replied, unconvinced. "I know they say a picture's worth a thousand words, but I doubt a trick of the light can stand in for a night on the beach in Cancún or a day spent rock-climbing in Clark Canyon."

"You may be surprised," was Inyx's last word on the subject. And despite his permanent frown and unreadable body language, Hernandez was certain that something in Inyx's tone rang unmistakably of mischief in the making.


Johanna Metzger sat slumped in her chair, with her head tilted over the back so she could stare straight upward. "Is it my imagination," she asked, "or are there a lot less stars than there used to be?"

Veronica Fletcher stopped poking at what felt like her millionth plate of bland Caeliar vegetable gruel and looked up at the sky above their courtyard. "That's been happening for a while now," she said. "According to Erika, it's 'cause the Caeliar moved the city a few thousand light-years above the galactic plane. Most of what we're seeing from here are close globular clusters and other galaxies."

"They never do anything the easy way, do they?"

Pushing her plate aside, Fletcher replied, "Why would they, when they have all the time in the universe?" She reached up and released her golden hair from the French knot that kept it from getting in her way. It fell the entire length of her back, to her waist. Metzger had refused to indulge in such extravagances and had kept her hair shorn to a utilitarian crew cut.

The doctor stiffened as Erika Hernandez walked through the open archway into the courtyard and quipped, "I'm home."

Metzger got up and avoided contact with Hernandez, as usual. "I have to go check on Sidra," she said. "Find out if she felt like eating any of her dinner tonight."

Hernandez eyed Metzger's exit with a weary stare, but she said nothing. In the long, dark blur of indistinguishable days and nights, the reasons behind grudges and resentments had long since been lost. The four women, in Fletcher's opinion, were all stuck in a loop, going over the same ground from moment to moment and year to year. Sidra had taken refuge in her psychological meltdown; Metzger had made a fortress of her anger and resentment; Hernandez had submerged into work, as always; and Fletcher sat on the sidelines, trying and failing to think of a way to quit this pointless game.

She watched Hernandez sit down across from her and stir the vegetable paste in the ceramic pot that sat on the table between them. "Another failed attempt at soup?" the captain asked. "Why don't they ever listen to us and put in more water?"

"Because we're just humans," Fletcher griped. "What the hell could we possibly know about cooking our own meals?" She tilted her head back and gazed at the sparse starfield. "Find any good planets today?"

Hernandez shook her head. "We thought we did, but when we looked closer we picked up radio signals."

"Off-limits, then," Fletcher replied.

"Exactly. Another day, another system off the list." She picked up a clean bowl and spooned some greenish vegetable goop into it. "How was your day? Do anything interesting?"

"I finished my novel."

"As in, you finished a first draft? Or as in, it's done?"

"Well," Fletcher replied with a shrug, "great works of art are never finished, only abandoned."

"I see," Hernandez said, lifting a spoonful of accidentally condensed soup. "Glad you're so modest about it." As soon as she had the spoon in her mouth, she winced. Then, with effort, she swallowed. "So," she continued, twisting her tongue in disgust, "what is this great work of art?"

Trembling with excitement, Fletcher picked up her writing tablet, which also doubled as the storage and retrieval device for her manuscript. She was about to proffer it to Hernandez, but she hesitated and hugged it to her chest instead. "Do you want to read it?"

"Do I really have a choice? I mean, come on—it's what, the early sixteenth century? You've just written the first modern novel by a human being. I'd say that makes it required reading, from a historical perspective if not a literary one."

"Thanks for the vote of confidence," Fletcher said, thrusting the writing tablet across the table to Hernandez, who took it and stared at its title page with raised eyebrows.

"*Revenge of Chaotica: A Captain Proton Adventure?*" Disbelief or disapproval creased Hernandez's brow. "The first work of long-form modern human prose is an unauthorized space-fantasy *sequel?* Please tell me you're kidding."

"Well, since you've already decided that you hate it . . ." She reached across the table to take back the tablet.

Hernandez leaned back and pulled the tablet beyond Fletcher's grasp. "Hang on," she said, holding up her free hand. "You're right, I should read it before I judge it. And I'm honored that you're letting me be the first to see it."

"Well, you're the second, actually," Fletcher said, feeling sheepish. "I had Johanna proofread it. You know, just for style and spelling and all that." A slackjawed look from Hernandez made it clear to Fletcher that she'd hit another nerve.

The captain protested, "English isn't even her first language! Unless you penned your magnum opus in German, I can't imagine why you'd let her see it before I did."

"Because I wanted it to be bloody great when you saw it," Fletcher said sharply. Then, more modestly, she added, "I wanted it to be perfect."

Then it was Hernandez's turn to hang her head in shame. "That's sweet of you," she said. "I'm sorry if I got all high and mighty on you there."

"No worries," Fletcher said, shrugging it off.

"I'll start reading it tonight," Hernandez said. She looked at her bowl of vegetable food product and grimaced. "I get the feeling I won't be sleeping too well, anyway." She set down the tablet and resumed poking at her dinner. "What are you doing tomorrow night after dinner?"

"Let me check my calendar," Fletcher deadpanned. "Why?"

"I have something to show you," Hernandez said. "And Johanna and Sidra, too. I think you're all gonna love it."

"What is it?"

Hernandez could barely hide her excitement. "A surprise."

Fletcher felt a surge of curiosity and dread. "I don't like surprises."

"You'll like this one."

She looked up at the empty spaces of the void. "We'll see."

* * *

"Keep your eyes shut," Hernandez said as she led her friends through the sublevel passage toward the threshold. "No peeking."

Fletcher and Metzger walked on either side of Valerian, each of them cupping one hand over the younger woman's eyes. Metzger whispered to the nervous young redhead, "Relax, Sidra. It's going to be all right. Breathe."

Inyx and Edrin stood on either side of the broad portal, awaiting the foursome's arrival. As they had agreed beforehand with Hernandez, they said nothing as she led the other three women to the edge of the world that lived beneath the city.

"Stop here," Hernandez said, and the women halted. "Take a deep breath. Hold it. . . . And on the count of three, let it go and step forward. One. Two. Three." She backpedaled ahead of them as they passed through the wide, oval doorway. Radiant warmth, a roar of white noise, the cawing of circling birds, and the scent of salt air swept over them as she said, "Open your eyes."

Metzger and Fletcher did as she'd asked, and they removed their hands from Valerian's eyes. In contrast to Hernandez's excited smile of expectation, Fletcher and Metzger reacted with wide-eyed stares of shock. Valerian, on the other hand, shrieked with joy and sprinted forward, across the white-sand beach, toward the frothing breakers that surged in on a high tide.

"Sidra, wait!" cried Metzger, who stumbled forward in belated pursuit, arms futilely outstretched.

Hernandez caught Metzger's sleeve. "It's all right, Johanna, she's safe." She turned and watched Valerian, who doffed her clothes and waded through the crashing waves before diving headfirst through a churning white breaker.

Fletcher pivoted in a slow circle, taking in the scene. High, white cliffs rose behind them, and wind-sculpted towers of limestone ascended majestically from the teal sea, bleached fingers poking up from the deep, some as close as a few dozen meters from shore. Farther out, almost halfway to the horizon, stood jagged islands of gray rock dotted with gnarled, anorexic trees.

"Where are we?" Fletcher asked, sounding wary.

"In a special chamber beneath the city," Hernandez said. "Inyx and Edrin built it for us."

Valerian had shed the last of her clothing, some of which floated behind her as she propelled herself away from shore with a choppy crawl stroke that had once been well practiced.

Shaking her head, Metzger said, "I don't understand."

"When they told me we might be in deep space for several more decades, I told them I couldn't take that—and I didn't think any of you could, either," Hernandez said. "They thought we only needed artificial sunlight, because it's all we ever asked for. Once I explained that we need a planetary—"

"No," Metzger interrupted, "I don't understand how they built us an ocean."

Before Hernandez could explain, Fletcher cut in, "It's some kind of high-tech simulation, isn't it?"

"Yes," Hernandez said. "Holographic, I think. I don't really get all the technical details, but it has something to do with force fields and optical illusions."

Twenty meters from shore, Valerian switched to a backstroke as she crested a rising swell of blue-green water, and she paddled easily into the trough behind it.

On the beach, Fletcher looked back at the white stone cliffs and asked, "Where's the bloody exit?"

Stunned, Hernandez replied, "What? You're *leaving*?"

"Tell the Caeliar they can keep this, whatever it is," Fletcher said. She started running her hands over the chalky cliff face. "What do I have to do, say 'open sesame'?"

A moment later, Metzger joined Fletcher's search.

"Johanna!" Hernandez protested. "You, too?"

Metzger looked back at her and scowled. "This is a trick, Erika. And you're falling for it."

She began to suspect her friends were crazy. "What're you talking about? Exactly how is this a trick?"

Fletcher gave up probing the cliff and turned back toward Hernandez. "Don't be so thick, Erika. I know a gilded cage when I see one." Metzger abandoned her own search and stood by Fletcher in solidarity as the XO continued, "It might look like home, but it's not."

"No one ever said it was," Hernandez said, frustrated with Fletcher's accusatory manner. "So it's a gilded cage. So what? Endless night was turning us all into basket cases, Ronnie, and you know it. We *need* this."

"I don't," Fletcher said, folding her arms.

Holding out her arms, Hernandez replied, "Don't you? Smell that air, Ronnie. Feel the sand under your feet. Listen to the wind and the water. Who cares if it isn't real? What difference does it make that we're still prisoners? Would you really rather be an inmate in that dark, gray box we've been living in? Or would you rather serve your time in the tropics?"

Fletcher laughed, but it was a mean-spirited chortle. "You just don't get it," she said. "It's not about whether it's real. It's about them wanting us to be happy as prisoners."

"You're right," Hernandez said. "I don't get it. What the hell are you talking about?"

"I'm talking about surrender, Erika. That's what accepting gifts from them would be. A bunk to sleep on, basic nutrition, clean water, sanitation—those are basics any prisoner ought to expect. I can take those and feel like I'm not letting them do me any favors. The solar therapy was pushing it, but Johanna made it a doctor's order, so that's that." She kneeled and picked up a handful of sand that spilled between her fingers. "But this? This is a gift, from *them*, with a big shiny bow on top. Living in here would be a lot easier; I know that. But it would also be the same as telling them, 'I give up.' And if I give them that last ounce of my pride, I'll have nothing left." She opened her hand and turned it to let the last grains of sand fall back onto the illusory beach. "I won't give them that, Erika. Not now. Not ever." She squinted into the bright blue dome of the sky. "Not even for this."

A ball of fire, red as an ember, lay in Hernandez's wrinkled palm. Gray ghosts condensed above it. In their serpentine motions and changes, Hernandez read the star system's life story.

"One-point-three billion years old," she said while Inyx stood behind her and listened. "Rich in actinides, very rare for a system this old." A long and especially complex symbol split and snaked in a double helix around her index finger. "All the building blocks for unbihexium-310." A short parade of simple glyphs traveled up the side of her left hand. "No terrestrial planets, only gas giants. Forty-eight natural satellites, including one rich in lead-208. All but one exhibit profound geological instability. The only stable one is a cold hunk of silicon and carbon at the edge of the system."

Inyx asked with the quiet satisfaction of a proud teacher, "What about life-forms?"

"None," she said, studying the slow unspooling of smoky sigils. "Not even cosmozoans. I'm guessing the heavier elements made this system a bit rich for their tastes."

"Recommendation?"

A turn of her index finger set the crimson sphere spinning in her cupped hand as she gave it a push back into the virtual heavens of the Star Chamber. "Unsuitable for colonization, but it's rich in the elements you've been looking for. You should exploit this system for resources while colonizing another." She pointed up at a brilliant yellow-orange dot near the red orb she'd just released. "Have we looked at that one?"

"It's on the short list, as you would say." Inyx reached up and summoned the bright spot down to Hernandez's waiting hands. "I thought I might let you do the honors."

She placed her hands on either side of the warm-hued star's miniaturized doppelganger and puffed a small breath across it. A misty stream of data curled upward from it like smoke from a snuffed taper. Her eyes widened at the tale it told. "K2V main sequence star, mean temperature 4,890 degrees Kelvin. Seven planets, four terrestrial, two in the habitable zone, one at optimal distance. No sign of cosmozoan activity."

"Hardly surprising," Inyx said. "It's rather far from the nearest OB cluster. In fact, I'd daresay it's remote from most everything in this sector." He passed his undulating tendrils over the glowing orb in her hands and changed the image to a blue-green world streaked with white. It turned slowly before her. "Tell me about its third planet," he said.

"Minshara-class," she replied, reading more grayish-white Caeliar runes as they formed above the tiny globe. "Nitrogen-oxygen atmosphere. Gravity is ninety-eight percent of Erigol-normal. No artificial satellites, no radio emissions. No sign of industrial pollutants in the oceans or atmosphere. No evidence of synthetic electrical power generation on the surface. Geothermal activity is minimal, but it still has a molten iron core." She was almost giddy as she looked up at Inyx. "It's perfect."

"Perhaps," Inyx said. "We'll still need to survey the surface to make certain there are no sentient life-forms there. If there are, we mustn't interfere with their habitat."

"Of course," Hernandez said. "You know, I have to admit: On the one hand, it makes me happy to find out so many Minshara-class worlds are populated by sentient species. But I have to wonder why so many of the races we've found have been humanoid. Even some of the more exotic ones we've seen have been bipedal and demonstrated bilateral symmetry."

"The result of an ancient bit of genetic interference," Inyx said. "I'll tell you about it someday, after Axion is settled and secure." Before she could pester him for details, he looked away. When he turned back, he said, "I've petitioned the Quorum for a survey of that world. Efforts are under way."

She released the planet, which floated languidly back into the darkness above. "I want to join the survey," she said.

"It's not a literal visit to the world's surface," Inyx said. "We'll use a number of subspace apertures to make undetected inspections of the planet, from its core to its oceans to its highest elevations. Noninvasive scans will be made of any life-forms we encounter."

"And how long will that take?"

"Not long," Inyx said. "No more than two of your years."

Once upon a time, she might have laughed at the Caeliar's conception of human time scales. Now she just swallowed her sarcastic remarks and moved on. "I presume we'll keep looking for new candidate systems while the survey is conducted?"

"Yes," Inyx said, "though we can stop for today, if you're feeling fatigued."

Her eyes itched as though they'd been rubbed with sand, but she lied, "I'm fine. What's next?"

He reached up, and a bluish-white fireball the size of a grape answered his call and floated down to Hernandez. It came to a gradual stop in front of her, and she interpreted its fleeting dance of wispy pictograms. When she'd finished and released it, Inyx remarked, "I have been meaning to commend you for the way you've mastered our written language."

"All it took was time," she said. "And I had plenty of it."

He gestured for her to follow him as he moved toward the nearest exit from the Star Chamber, and she walked beside him. "I don't think you appreciate how special your achievement is," he said. "You are the first non-Caeliar to learn our language in more than eighty thousand years."

She responded with a veiled accusation. "Did you ever give anyone else the chance?"

"Well . . . no, not as such," Inyx said.

"Then I can't feel that impressed with myself."

He turned his bulbous head just enough to glance down at her. "You seem to be learning some of our other abilities, as well," he said.

Unable to discern what he was talking about, she furrowed her brow in confusion. "What other abilities?"

"Transmogrification," he said. "Your changes in form."

"Okay, you've lost me."

He waved his arm in a slow arc, and a metallic pinpoint formed in the air ahead of them. They stopped and watched as it grew, flattened, and expanded into an immaculate silver mirror that hovered before them. Gesturing at their reflections, Inyx said, "Your change has been quite gradual, but it's no less impressive for its subtlety."

It was the same face she saw in her own mirror every morning now. Her face was wrinkled and marked by dark brown age spots, and her once mostly black hair had long since turned a leaden gray. Her cheeks sagged beside her chin, under which drooped a small waddle of loose flesh. A stroke of genetic good fortune had preserved her eyesight all these decades, and though her eyes now were sunken within age-darkened sockets, they were the only part of her that still resembled the woman she had been when she had come to Axion a lifetime ago.

"Inyx, are you talking about the changes I've gone through since I came to Axion? The deterioration of my skin, the fading of my hair, the compression of my spine?"

"Of course," Inyx said.

She sighed because she was too tired to actually get angry anymore. "It's not a conscious shape-change," she explained. "It's just cellular breakdown. Or, as my people like to say, it's called getting old."

"I know," Inyx said. "I was just trying to make a joke."

Hernandez detoured around the mirror and continued toward the exit. Inyx loped along and caught up to her. She scowled at him. "If you need a hobby, stick to sculpture," she said. "'Cause you're *definitely* not cut out for comedy."

Johanna Metzger held Sidra Valerian's hand and walked with her onto the beach that wasn't really a beach but was real enough for the younger woman's daily escape from reality. A long time ago, it had been Valerian who'd needed the reassurance of contact, the steady guidance from the bleak confines of their quarters to this blinding, sunlit lie.

Age had taken its toll on them both since then. Valerian's fiery red hair had faded to a dull rusty hue flecked with gray, and Metzger's own gray crew cut had turned bone-white and now spilled far beneath her shoulder blades. It was Valerian, the silent athlete, the mute woman-child, who supported Metzger now. Frail and doddering, the elderly Swiss doctor could barely see. To her, the world had become little more than soft-edged shapes and blurs of color, washes of light and darkness, elusive shades and specters. She relied on Valerian to escort her through the labyrinth of Axion's streets each day, to and from this refuge.

They crossed the threshold, and the false sun warmed her skin and reduced her world to a red glare through her closed eyelids. With wordless tenderness, Valerian touched Metzger's face, then released her hand. Beyond the wall of white noise, Metzger heard her surrogate daughter's soft steps in the sand, then the splash as Valerian plunged headlong into the crashing surf for another day of aquatic reverie.

Swimming was all Valerian did anymore; it was all she had done for as long as Metzger could remember. Once, the Scotswoman had been young and beautiful. Now she was age-worn, like Fletcher and Hernandez, and the extra time that Valerian spent in the glow of the Caeliar's artificial tropical sun had blemished her once-milky skin with a million brown freckles and several dark spots that Metzger was certain would eventually become malignant melanomas. And she never spoke. She had been silent for so long that Metzger no longer remembered her voice.

Metzger added that to the ever-growing list of things she no longer recalled.

Routine and repetition were all that Metzger had left, and all that Valerian had left. In the mornings, they walked to the beach.

Sometimes, Metzger had stayed the entire day, until the sun set and Valerian took her arm and guided her home again, to the courtyard.

Before Metzger's vision had deteriorated, however, she had often left Valerian to enjoy the ersatz paradise alone, excusing herself to take refuge on the top level of a nearby tower, one of the highest vantage points in Axion. Elevated above the spires of the metropolis, Metzger had lost herself against the vast canvas of space and stars.

"The outer darkness," she had called it, in the days before darkness had become her norm.

She breathed in the salty air and tried to make herself believe that it was real, but she couldn't. There was no cure for knowing it was a lie—a hoax, just like the sand and the surf and the sun. There was nothing here worth believing in.

*Except for Sidra.*

Turning around was a labor of small steps, uncertain pauses, calculated risks. It felt as if it took forever before she was facing the cliff wall that concealed the exit. Metzger could have sworn that the angle of her shadow was moving faster than she was. Then she nudged herself forward through an act of sheer will, and said to the Caeliar's machine, "Let me out."

The exit appeared. The oval aperture was wide, and its bottom was perfectly flush with both the beach and the corridor floor on the other side. Metzger was grateful to be spared the need to step over anything; she left the simulation with weak, shuffled steps. She doubted that Valerian would even note her absence until dusk. Maybe not even then.

*I've held on for so much longer than I thought I would,* Metzger thought, shambling along. *I must be a crone by now.*

Minutes passed, or maybe hours, while Metzger forged ahead in quaking steps, her weight supported by a simple cane. As much as she had disdained the Caeliar's moving walkways and pod lifts in the past, she depended on them now. Once she'd reached the city's pedestrian network, it whisked her along in ease and comfort, straight into the main level of her favorite tower.

Calling down a pod lift was effortless; she stood in the empty, illuminated ring, and a pod formed around her. "To the top," she croaked, her voice brittle and breathy. Without delay, the transparent cocoon surrounded her. She was hurtled upward, past the blur of one level after another, until she found herself on the tower's top floor. The pod dissolved, and she stepped forward, through an arched portal onto a balcony surrounded by black sky and stars.

*A blank slate,* she thought, peering into the endless night. *I stared into it so long that I became it. I gazed into the abyss and erased myself.*

Her past was gone, fled from her, and had been for a long time. *I can't remember the faces of my children,* she lamented. *My sweet, lovely Franka . . . why can't I see you when I dream? Jörn, my little man . . . you looked so much like your father, but I've lost you both.* Tears ran from her half-blind eyes, down her slack and fissured cheeks. She couldn't even remember her own past— the images of herself as a child and as a young woman were faded and out of reach. Her life was a gray memory, dim and lost.

Metzger had tried to be strong and defiant like Fletcher, but Fletcher had never had a family. At first, Metzger had thought that the hope of returning to her kin might be a source of strength. Then months had turned into years, and years had become a lifetime . . . and hope had become despair.

*There's nothing left to hope for,* Metzger told herself. She'd held on longer than she'd wanted to, and she knew that it was because of Valerian. She had found some measure of meaning in her life by caring for the emotionally fractured younger woman, but it no longer felt like enough. *I can't live for someone else,* Metzger admitted to herself.

She had told herself the same thing every day for what felt like months now, during her daily retreats to this perch above the city. Her intentions had been clear from the beginning, but one thing or another had held her back. A lifetime of losses, grudges, and mistakes had burdened her and rooted her in place.

One by one, she had made her peace with them all. Day after day she had come to the top of this tower, stared into the void, and shed her emotional ballast.

Fear was the first burden she'd cast off into the night. Guilt was the second. Then all that remained had been a legion of regrets: words left unspoken, wounds left unmended, debts left unpaid. The last was one that could not be helped—there was no way she could explain herself to Valerian.

*She won't understand. But that's not my fault.*

Looking up, she let the fathomless darkness consume her final lamentations, the end of her hope, and the vestiges of her memory, until nothing remained. There was no more cause for joy or weeping, no more grieving for the life she had lost or the one she had lived in exile.

There was only blessed emptiness.

Metzger leaned forward, over the balcony railing. Her stiff, arthritic back protested as she forced herself to double over. *The pain is an illusion,* she reminded herself. *It's just the last hurdle. Up and over.* Tucking her chin toward her chest, she felt her toes come away from the balcony deck. Then gravity took hold, tugged the rest of her body over the railing, and pulled her in its steady, loving embrace toward the ground—toward release. For a moment, she felt weightless.

Then she was free.

Hernandez looked down into Valerian's glassy blue eyes and saw no spark of life left in them. The mute woman's chest expanded and contracted with slow, shallow breaths, and her heartbeat was barely palpable when Hernandez pressed her palm on Valerian's sternum. "It's been almost three days," she said. "She can't last like this, not for much longer. She'll dehydrate."

"I just can't believe it," Fletcher said, standing on the other side of the bed. "I wasn't even sure she heard what we were saying when we told her about Johanna."

Stroking a wild tangle of Valerian's unkempt hair from her forehead, Hernandez was struck by the prospect of losing two of her only three friends in less than a week. After Inyx had broken the news of Metzger's suicide, it had fallen to Hernandez to go to the simulated beach and collect Valerian.

The change in the daily routine had immediately made Valerian edgy. Neither Hernandez nor Fletcher had meant to confront the fragile younger woman with the tragedy right away, but the empty seat at their shared dinner table, and their own grave moods, had made the subject unavoidable. The consequences had proved worse than they'd feared; the revelation that Metzger had taken her own life and was gone forever had pushed Valerian into a denial so profound that she sank into catatonia.

Inyx stood at the foot of the bed and waited on Hernandez. "What do you wish to do?" he asked.

"I haven't decided yet," Hernandez said, torn between what she felt she could live with and what she thought was merciful.

Fletcher took Valerian's left hand in hers and squeezed it. She looked at Inyx. "What could you do for her?"

"I'm not entirely certain," Inyx said. "Our examinations of her through the years have always suggested that her malady is purely psychological in nature. As such, we would advise against any pharmaceutical interventions."

Bitterly, Fletcher replied, "In other words, with all this power and all these gadgets, there's nothing you can do."

"On the contrary," Inyx said, "there is a great deal that we can do. I only doubt that the great majority of it would be of any therapeutic benefit to her affliction. In the end, I suspect that anything short of our most invasive efforts would serve only to prolong her current, isolated existence." He directed his next words to Hernandez. "But if that is your wish, Erika, we will do as you ask."

She reached down and clasped Valerian's other hand. "I don't know what to do, Ronnie. I want to save her. . . ."

"Why?" Fletcher's grief was as raw as Hernandez's own, but her defiant spirit was as strong as it ever had been. "What would be the point, Erika? She'd be alive, but that's not the same as living, and you know it."

"I don't know anything of the sort," Hernandez said. "Inyx, she has brain wave activity, doesn't she?"

He made a slight, concessionary bow, arms apart. "Of a very limited kind," he said.

"So, who knows what kind of life she's living inside her head? Maybe it's paradise in there."

"And maybe it's limbo," Fletcher said. "Or purgatory. Or hell, or just plain, simple oblivion." Sorrow moistened her eyes as she looked down at their stricken friend. "Face the truth, Erika. She's gone, and you know it. We have to let her go."

Hernandez shook her head. Valerian's hand was still warm to the touch, and even if the light had gone from her eyes, there was still blood coursing in her veins and breath moving in her lungs. Her heart was beating, and her synapses were firing—even if it was only a lonely few of them holding the fort until true consciousness returned. It didn't matter to Hernandez that Sidra Valerian was old—she was alive and worth fighting for.

"Inyx," she asked, "can you do more than just keep Sidra's body alive? Is there anything you can do to help her heal her psychological injuries?"

The question made the lanky alien think for several moments before he answered. "It's difficult to predict," he said. "Our methods would involve making significant alterations to her biology and linking her mind to our communal gestalt."

Fletcher was horrified. "You'd turn her into one of you?"

"Not truly one of us," Inyx said. "But she would become integrated into our community. If we can achieve a balanced communion with her consciousness, we might be able to quell her emotional turmoil and restore her to a greater semblance of her former self." His enthusiasm waned as he added, "The process would, however, entail a significant risk. We've never tried to fuse our catoms with non-Caeliar life-forms before."

That earned a contemptuous snort from Fletcher. "I take it back. You wouldn't be turning her into one of you. You'd be turning her into a bloody guinea pig." She glared at Hernandez. "Don't let them do it, Erika. She's not a piece of meat to be experimented on. Let her die with some dignity."

It was tempting to think of Valerian being restored to the woman she'd been fifty years ago—at least, in terms of her personality. And it was the very sense of temptation that told Hernandez she had to resist. There was something wrong about it, something unnatural. And maybe Fletcher was right—perhaps it was also, in some distinctly human-specific way, undignified.

Still pondering her options, she asked Inyx, "What about sedating her into a gradual cardiac arrest?"

"The word you're avoiding," Inyx said with sharp sarcasm, "is 'euthanasia,' and its practice is forbidden here. We will not engage in it, nor will we tolerate its use in Axion."

"But suicide seems to get the stamp of approval," Fletcher sniped. Hernandez threw a silencing glare at her old friend.

Inyx continued, "We can apply pain-blocking medications and protocols as a precaution, in case the patient's mind is still conscious on some level and cognizant of the body's suffering or discomfort. However, this prevention of pain is accomplished without the risk of aggravating the patient's condition."

"Sounds reasonable," Hernandez said, short-circuiting any further dissent from Fletcher. Pointedly, she asked the other woman, "Any problem with that?"

Fletcher sighed and averted her eyes back toward Valerian. "No," she said. "No problem."

Inyx folded his tendril hands in front of him. "Of course, to impose a medical procedure on someone without proper consent would be an act of violence. Because Sidra is not competent to make an informed decision, and you're her commanding officer, we consider you to be her guardian, Erika—and we will engage no medical efforts without your permission."

Hernandez looked at Valerian, and then she looked up at Fletcher, who said simply, "It's your call, Erika."

She looked to Inyx. "You promise she won't suffer?"

"We will do all that we can to prevent it."

She palmed tears from her puffy, wrinkled cheeks and nodded in the face of the inevitable. "Let's get on with it, then."

The waiting was the worst part. Encamped at Valerian's bedside with Fletcher, all that Hernandez could do was sit and be numb as she watched Valerian deteriorate. Only a week earlier, despite being in her seventies, Valerian had been vital, able at least to savor her moments in the Caeliar's ersatz sea.

Now her cheeks were gaunt, her eyes sunken. Her skin had become sallow and flaky. "Maybe we should give her water," Hernandez said, second-guessing all her decisions.

"It'll only prolong her decline," Fletcher said. "Ketosis is a good way to go if you let it take its course. If she is conscious of anything, there's a good chance she's semi-euphoric from all the fat her body's burning."

It had been six days since Hernandez had made her decision to let Valerian fade away. Since then, either she or Fletcher had been at Valerian's side, and usually it was both of them. They'd taken turns eating, napping, and using the lavatory so that, in case Valerian regained consciousness, there would be someone there to halt the process. That moment hadn't come.

Valerian had gone all these days without food or water. Hernandez knew that renal failure must be imminent for Valerian, if it hadn't already occurred. Once Valerian's kidneys failed, the end would come within a day or two as toxins in her blood disrupted her heart.

Time had crawled during Hernandez's decades in Axion, and it also had flown. Trudging through the monotony of routines and rituals had felt like slow time, a life sealed in amber sap, barely moving, trapped in stasis. But then, one day, she'd looked up to find forty years had passed. Now nearly fifty.

*Most of my life went by before I knew what happened,* she realized. *Measured against that, a few days should be nothing. But this feels like forever.*

There were no clocks to watch, no calendar pages to turn. In the cosmic scale of the Caeliar's search for a new world to claim as their own, nothing marked the lost hours and seconds. Valerian's irregular gasps for breath made it clear that these insignificant increments of time were all that were left to her; she'd see no more days, no more years.

An upwelling of panic impelled Hernandez to her feet. Trembling in her steps, she shuffled away from the bed at a pace only the elderly would consider hurried. Her hands shook as she reached out for something to steady herself.

From behind her, Fletcher asked, "Where are you going?"

"To call for Inyx," she said.

Fletcher's tone was sharp. "Why?"

"I've changed my mind." She reached the doorway and was gathering her strength to cross its threshold when Fletcher stopped her with the piercing anger in her voice.

"Stop, Erika," Fletcher commanded. "Don't do this, not like this. It's almost over, and she's not in any pain."

Hernandez shut her eyes and leaned against the doorway. "I can't just let her die, Ronnie. We can't know what Sidra really wants. What if she wants to live? What if she's in there, wishing she could wake up?"

"No, Erika, stop." She heard Fletcher get up from her chair and walk toward her in slow steps. "If Sidra wanted to be here, she would be. But she's been running away for a long time, ever since Erigol was destroyed. This is just the last step for her. Let her take it in peace."

She opened her eyes to find Fletcher beside her. "What if the Caeliar can help her, Ronnie?"

"They can't do anything without changing her," Fletcher said.

"What they're proposing would make her something not quite human anymore. It'd be invasive and would violate the very core of what Sidra is. Is saving her life worth taking away her humanity, Erika? Is death that frightening?"

Turning away, Hernandez looked to the stars and said, "Inyx, are you listening? I need you. Please."

Fletcher grabbed Hernandez's shoulders. "Think about what you're doing! Sidra's ready to go—don't force this on her!"

Specks of airborne dust seemed to catch the starlight for a moment, and then they coalesced into glowing motes. In seconds the flurry of tiny lights swirled together and fused into a white radiance that faded to reveal Inyx on their doorstep. He gave a small, courteous bow and said, "How can I help, Erika?"

Guilt made her look to Fletcher for forgiveness, but she found only seething resentment and disappointment in the other woman's gaze. To Inyx she said, "I've reconsidered your offer. I want you to help Sidra, any way you can."

Inyx looked past her, toward Valerian. "Her condition has worsened. The process would be challenging for her, under the best of circumstances. She's very fragile. Are you sure you want to change course now?"

"Is there any chance that you could save her? That she could talk to us again?"

The tall, gangly Caeliar scientist crossed the room to Valerian's bedside, reached out, and let the tendrils of his right arm caress the dying woman's face and throat. Then he looked back at Fletcher and Hernandez. "There is a chance."

"Then do it," Hernandez said. "Hurry."

He pushed his arms under Valerian's emaciated body and lifted her from the bed. Fletcher was sullen as Inyx carried Valerian into the courtyard, where he summoned one of the Caeliar's signature silver travel disks. He stepped onto the disk and said, "Erika, you'll need to come with me. Veronica, you may attend the procedure if you wish."

"No, thanks," Fletcher said, and she walked away.

Hernandez joined Inyx on the silver disk. She gently took Valerian's hand as the platform ascended from the courtyard, hovered above their residence, and accelerated into the heart of the city. Traveling above dark boulevards in a city of perpetual night, and seeing Valerian cradled in Inyx's skeletal arms, gave

Hernandez the troubling sensation of being a passenger on the ferry of Charon, crossing a black river into the underworld.

"Hang on," she whispered to Valerian. "It'll be all right." She knew what Fletcher would call this, and she didn't care.

Forced to choose between letting Valerian die or letting her be transformed by the healing gifts of the Caeliar, death no longer seemed like a victory, and she no longer thought of surrender as a defeat.

It was simply the price of survival.

Despite having spent most of her life in Axion, Hernandez had never before seen the chamber into which she followed Inyx.

It was long, narrow, and high-ceilinged. Bizarre, semi-organic-looking alien machines were crowded into the tight space. Silvery cables drooped on long diagonals high overhead, and at the top of the laboratory was a broad, clamshell-shaped skylight through which she saw the black sky dotted with stars.

Inyx carried Valerian to a long, flat metallic table that Hernandez grimly thought of as a slab. Its surface was dark gray, several centimeters thick, and unadorned. As he set the dying woman on the table, a sepulchral droning began to fill the echoing silence. Looking around, Hernandez saw several of the machines in the room begin to pulse with a violet light.

"Please watch from behind that barrier," Inyx said, pointing to a transparent wall that curved around a large, odd-looking console. "You will be safer there."

She did as he asked and walked behind the protective shield. Motion from overhead caught her eye. It was an ungainly contraption, long and asymmetrical and covered with alarming protuberances. It glowed with the same purple radiance as the other machines in the lab, and it glided through the air without any obvious means of support or locomotion. She tensed as it settled into position directly above Valerian.

Watching the device move into place, she noticed more subtle movements, much higher up along the far wall. There she saw a row of wide observation windows, in front of which more than a score of Caeliar had gathered. That was when she understood that this wasn't simply a lab—it was an operating theater, and Valerian was to be that night's main attraction.

On the other side of the barrier, Inyx levitated himself a few meters off the floor and made some minuscule manual adjustments to the large machine. Apparently satisfied with his modifications, he floated back to the floor and joined Hernandez behind the see-through wall. "We're almost ready," he said. "I just need to make some detailed scans of her brainwave pattern to be certain the catoms are set to the correct frequency."

"What's going to happen to her?"

Manipulating the console's controls with his tendrils, Inyx replied, "I'm going to infuse her body with the same sort of catoms that now constitute Caeliar bodies. In Sidra's case, the concentration will be infinitesimal, but it should be enough to let us repair any damage to her vital organs. Once that's done, we'll bring her back to consciousness and let her mind make contact with the gestalt."

"What if she doesn't understand what's happening?"

"The gestalt has gentle ways of making itself understood," Inyx assured her. "Whether she will be able to understand the message will depend greatly on her frame of mind." He turned and eyed a wall of liquid-textured panels that were strobing with information faster than Hernandez could decipher. "Excuse me a moment," he said, moving toward the rippling screens. "I have a few more details to check before we begin."

While he worked, she busied herself with studying the master control panel. Unable to discern most of its operational components, she looked up again at their Caeliar audience and saw a familiar figure lurking behind one of them. It was Fletcher, who Hernandez deduced must have changed her mind about boycotting the procedure. *One of the other Caeliar must have brought her here,* she figured.

"It's ready," Inyx said. "This is your last chance to change your mind, Erika. Once the procedure begins—"

"Do it," Hernandez said.

His tendrils moved over the console and never seemed to make contact, yet toggles changed positions and functions were triggered. Ominous churning noises filled the operating room, though Hernandez had no idea what was causing the sounds, which were followed by deep, rhythmic percussions that shook the floor. The incandescent core of the machine above Valerian turned a blinding shade of magenta.

Valerian was bathed in rose-colored light.

Her physical transformation was subtle—her skin regained its healthy color, and her eyes suddenly seemed less sunken.

"Now we rouse her," Inyx said. "This will take a few seconds." He made more fine adjustments to a delicate crystal console in front of him and Hernandez. Then he looked up and waited to see what would happen, his own sense of nervous anticipation as tangible to Hernandez as her own.

Valerian's blue eyes fluttered open.

And she screamed.

Her piercing wail, pure terror as sound, filled the lab.

Then she began thrashing, pounding her fists on the metal slab, kicking wildly—all as she kept on screeching.

"Turn it off!" Hernandez cried. "Make it stop!"

"It's too late," Inyx said. "We—"

Panicked, Hernandez bolted from the console, tried to run to Valerian, hoping to pull her off the table. Before she could round the safety wall, Inyx snared her in his grip, which was stronger than she had ever imagined it would be. "Don't, Erika. It's not safe."

"Let me go!" she pleaded. "I can't just let her—"

Then the screaming stopped, and Valerian curled in upon herself, hands pressed over her face like a mask, her eyes wide with horror and shock. Hernandez froze in place, and Inyx let go of her and returned in a flurry of motion to the console.

"Synaptic failure," he said, his dismay and surprise evident. "Something in her mind rejected contact with the gestalt." His hands began to work faster.

"What's going on?"

Growing more concerned, he replied, "Her disharmony with the gestalt is causing the other catoms in her body to fall out of sync with the city's quantum field."

Frustrated by the opacity of his reply, she angrily prompted, "Meaning . . . ?"

"Her body's rejecting the infusion," Inyx said. "The catoms are becoming chaotic." He turned, stepped between Hernandez and her view of Valerian, and tried to lead her away from the console. "You should step out, Erika, quickly."

She shook off his guidance. "Don't tell me what to—"

Words caught in her throat as Valerian started screaming

again. Shrieks of agony, primal and inchoate, erupted from her . . . and then her body began to dissolve. Her skin sagged and her torso caved in. She clawed at her face with skeletal hands as her eyes sank into her skull. Then her cries of pain and fear rattled into silence, and what was left of her collapsed into a boiling froth that turned to black dust.

Hernandez stood paralyzed, in anguished silence, and stared at the carbonized stain that was the only evidence of Valerian's gruesome demise. Beside her, Inyx shut down the machines, which returned to their dormant state with a long, dwindling groan.

He looked up at the Caeliar spectators. Then he turned away from them in what Hernandez could only imagine was shame. "The Quorum demands my presence," he said in a subdued voice. "I'll send someone to escort you back to your residence."

Like a pile of leaves blowing away in an autumn wind, Inyx disincorporated in a rush of warm air. Reduced to a flowing stream of golden motes, he rose like smoke and vanished into the dense machinery that lined the high walls.

The other Caeliar who had gathered along the observation deck's windows departed, leaving only Fletcher, who stared down with cold anger at Hernandez.

Tears of guilt and rage streamed down Hernandez's face. *My God, what have I done? Sidra was at peace. All I had to do was let her go. Why couldn't I just let her go?*

She looked up at Fletcher and said, "I'm sorry."

Fletcher turned her back and walked away.

Alone in the darkened lab, Hernandez stood in silence. Failed and friendless, overwhelmed by sorrow and shame, she felt that she finally understood what it meant to be in exile.

The tree was long dead, its branches bare and brittle after decades in the dark. It sat on a mound of dusty earth that once had been a miniature island at the end of a long, rectangular pool of dark water. The pool was gone now. In its place was a dry stone cavity some two meters deep.

Hernandez stood beneath the expired tree and remembered it as it used to be, before Axion's panicked flight into the past. She and her landing party had met in the shade of its leafy boughs to weigh their chances of escape. Its shelter, however illusory, had been a comfort to her and to the others. Now its exposed, gnarled roots and fissured bark served to remind her only of life's fragility—and its brevity.

Something unseen stirred the air. She inhaled, caught a faint hint of ozone, and felt a warming tingle on the back of her neck. They were familiar sensations to her now. An illumination from behind her brightened the tree trunk, but she didn't need to turn around to know that Inyx had joined her.

"I thought I might find you here," he said.

She drew a line with her bare left foot in the coarse sand. "It's not like I have anywhere else to go."

He stepped forward to stand beside her. "I came to say that I'm sorry. For my failure, and for your loss."

"Thank you," she said. "But it wasn't your fault. It was just an accident."

"I still feel responsible," he said.

She sighed. "Don't. The decision was mine. You only did as I asked. If anyone's to blame, it's me." They stood together for a short time, saying nothing. Her mood took a melancholy turn. "I wonder sometimes if every decision I've made since the day the Romulans ambushed my ship has been wrong."

Inyx sounded perplexed. "Why would you think so?"

"Why wouldn't I?" she replied. "I risked traveling at relativistic speeds to seek a safe haven instead of waiting for a rescue. I took my ship to an unknown world instead of setting course for home. I led my people into captivity here." She paused as the wrenching impact of her recent tragedies hit her in full force. Her voice caught in her throat as she continued, "I missed or ignored all the warning signs that Johanna was planning on committing suicide. And instead of letting Sidra die with peace and dignity, I made her final moments agonizing and humiliating . . . because I was too scared to just let her go."

Inyx asked, "Did your decisions seem rational at the time?"

She shrugged. "I suppose."

"In that case, unless you've secretly possessed the power of precognition all this time, I would posit that you made the right decision in at least some of those moments. Even if you feel the outcomes were negative, it could be argued that some of the alternatives might have been far worse."

"In my mind, I know you're right. But part of me can't shake the fear that all I've been doing since the ambush is failing the people who depended on me, who trusted me. Maybe it's not rational to think so, but it's how I feel."

He made a strange grunt of acknowledgment. "I understand, Erika. After your shipmates' interference helped spark the destruction of Erigol, I grieved for millions of my brothers and sisters—including Sedín, my friend of several millennia. She'd castigated me for persuading the Quorum to grant you and your crew sanctuary on Erigol. In her eyes, I had defiled our home. At the time, I was certain I had made the right and merciful decision, but after Erigol was lost, I . . . I wasn't sure anymore. I felt that I'd failed my people and jeopardized the Great Work."

The profound pathos of his confession moved Hernandez. She turned toward him and let herself look at him, in an effort to see past his stern, alien visage. His grim countenance remained inscrutable, but she could hear the changes in his voice and his breathing, and she saw the vulnerability and openness of his body language. It was the first time that she felt as if she could understand the nonverbal cues of his species.

He continued, "Even when the Quorum exonerated me, I didn't believe I deserved to continue as Axion's chief scientist. Not after my lapses in judgment."

"But you went on," she said. "You found a reason."

He looked at her. "Yes, I did. It was you."

She was caught off guard. "Me? I don't understand."

"Because you sought me out, in the Star Chamber," he said, calling Axion's observatory by the name she had given it in jest. "You came and asked to help us, and to be taught. I knew that you were burdened by losses, as I was. But you coped with your suffering by seeking to aid others. You reminded me that sometimes the way to heal oneself is to tend to others first."

"Wow," she said. "And I thought I was just trying to make the days go by a little faster. I had no idea I was such an inspiration." Flexing the stiffness from her fingers, she winced at the brittle dryness of her skin, a reminder of time's ravages and her advancing years. She masked her anxiety with glib humor. "What'll you do when I'm gone?"

"Do you intend to leave the city?" he asked with genuine

surprise. She wasn't sure if he was joking, sincere, or just especially obtuse as a consequence of denial.

"In a manner of speaking, yes," she said. "I probably don't have much time left, Inyx."

A somberness settled upon him. "You mean you're dying."

"I don't know that I'd put it quite like that," she said. "I'm not saying I'm at death's door, for heaven's sake. My body's just starting to wear out, is all. It's part of life, Inyx. Everything that lives has to die eventually."

"Yes," he said. "Eventually. But some die sooner than others, and many before they should or need to."

Hernandez nodded. "On Earth, we call that Fate." She reached out and rested her hand on his bony, grayish arm. "I'm sorry. I didn't mean to upset you by bringing up dying."

His voice sounded smaller, softer than usual. "I'd prefer that you didn't."

"Talk about it?"

"No," he said. "Die."

His earnestness almost made her laugh. "No offense to you and your supertoys, but I don't think it's your call to make."

"You're absolutely right," he said. "It's yours."

It had been several weeks, or possibly even months, since the twilight had descended on Fletcher's friendship with Erika. Though they continued to live in residences off the same courtyard, Fletcher had taken pains to avoid contact with her captain since Sidra's grotesque desecration by the Caeliar's untested technology and Erika's clouded judgment.

Whenever Fletcher saw Erika dining alone in the courtyard, she made a point of sequestering herself in her residence until after Erika had left, no doubt for another turn of collaboration with the Caeliar scientist in his observatory. Once, a few weeks earlier, Fletcher had emerged after Erika's departure to find that one of the white pawns on the chess board she'd carved had been moved from its starting position at c2 to c4.

*So,* Fletcher had mused. *She wants to play.*

Unwilling to indulge Erika's feeble attempt at contact, Fletcher had picked up the board and pieces and taken them back into her suite of rooms and tucked them inside a drawer.

The thought of the chess set inside the dresser had nagged at her ever since, to the point that she had begun having recurring dreams about chess. In one she played against a hooded opponent. The outcome of that game, she knew, had been preordained. Playing it to its end was merely a formality. She'd tried to take the inevitable loss in stride.

In another nightmare, she was a piece on the board, trying to exert her queenly power by dashing diagonally across the ranks to strike down a haughty bishop, only to stumble and fall over her own feet. When a cavalier reached down from his steed to help her back up, he'd laughed. "What were you thinking?" he said. "You know pawns can't move diagonally except to attack, and there's no one here within your reach."

There were as many variants on her nightly reveries as there were strategies for chess. She'd look down to find all her pieces missing except her king, who stood completely exposed. Or her king would betray his own army and cut them down, one by one. Or she would pick up a piece to move it, only to discover that all her pieces were carved of sand, which would crumble between her fingers and be carried away in a whisper of wind.

Her pieces burned and turned to ashes. They'd rebel and cut her fingertips. The entire board would turn black and become a portal into the void, and all the pieces, white and black alike, would fall through it and vanish into the emptiness of nothing.

That day Fletcher had awakened, opened her eyes, and gritted her teeth against the cramps and pains that had become as familiar to her as old friends whose company was obnoxious but was tolerated for lack of an alternative. Seeing no sign of Erika in the courtyard and no lights on in the other woman's residence, Fletcher retrieved the chess set from her drawer, carried it out to the table in the middle of the court, and set it up, with the white pieces facing herself.

Then she waited.

Lost in her thoughts, she had no regard now for time's passage. It slipped past as it always had: seeming to move impossibly slow in the present, the future always so far at bay, until the day when one looked back on uncounted expired moments and realized how few must then remain.

Fletcher had played both sides of an entire game of chess in her thoughts by the time Erika stepped through the entryway into the courtyard. The captain hesitated, as if fearful of intruding on Fletcher's privacy. For a moment, Fletcher considered picking up the chess pieces and retreating again into her private spaces. Instead, she made eye contact with Erika and allowed the moment to linger. Then she reached forward and moved the king's knight to f3—a clear invitation to play.

Erika's manner was cautious as she approached the table and, with some effort and apparent mild discomfort, eased herself into a seat across from Fletcher. She gave a shallow sigh, studied the board, and advanced her queen's pawn to d5.

Moving a pawn to g3 beside her knight, Fletcher said nothing and waited for Erika's reaction.

The captain lifted one eyebrow. "The Réti Opening?" she said. "With the King's Indian attack? Really?"

Exhaustion made it easy for Fletcher to betray no reaction to Erika's brazen inquiry. She spent those moments picturing the likely next sequence of moves, the captures of pawns, the development of pieces for the middlegame. If Erika remained as predictable as always, in five moves Fletcher would be ready to fianchetto the king's bishop to g2, assert command of the center, and set the stage for a kingside castling.

A sharp pang in Fletcher's side made her wince as she reached forward to advance another pawn.

Although Erika's eyes never seemed to leave the board, she asked, "Are you all right?"

"Just a cramp," Fletcher said.

The game continued in silence for several minutes, until Erika perplexed Fletcher by making a number of irregular moves. Suddenly, Fletcher's plan to control the board's center from its wings with her bishops and knights began to seem unworkable. With equal measures of amusement and irritation, she said, "Don't tell me—Tayvok's Gambit?"

It was Erika's turn to give away nothing. She folded her hands and continued eyeing the ranks and files of the board.

"I finished another novel," Fletcher said. "The sequel to *Lightning Shy*."

Erika steepled her fingers in front of her chin. "Finally. I've been waiting for you to resolve that story for ages." She looked up. "What's the new book called?"

"*Flashpoint Sinister*."

The answer stoked Erika's simmering curiosity. She moved her queen's bishop to a6. "What does the title mean?"

"Read it and find out."

Before she could take any satisfaction in prolonging Erika's suspense, Fletcher looked again at the board and saw that she'd been lulled into a careless blunder two moves earlier—a mistake that had become apparent only as more of the pieces were developed by both sides. Within three moves she would either have to risk losing significant pieces or watch her pawn structure collapse under a skewer attack that Erika had developed with remarkable subtlety.

While Fletcher pondered some strategic adjustments that might let her recover her tempo, Erika remarked casually, "I learned today that a star system I singled out for investigation has been selected as the site of New Erigol. Inyx tells me we'll reach its Minshara-class planet in less than a year."

"That's great," Fletcher said, swallowing her anger. It rankled her every day to know that Erika was helping the Caeliar in their search for a new homeworld. As far as Fletcher was concerned, as long as the Caeliar remained her captors, they were the enemy, not to be aided or abetted in any way. But the fact remained that Erika was the captain, and it was up to her to follow the dictates of her own conscience.

Fletcher let her queen's knight brave the center as a lure for Erika's queen. If the bait was taken, Fletcher could capture black's queen with her bishop; if Erika responded in a more conservative fashion, it would become possible to weaken her kingside pawn structure as a prelude to a check scenario.

"Once we reach the planet, Inyx says the Caeliar will let us leave the city and live on the surface if we want." Erika's tone seemed to be imploring forgiveness from Fletcher. "We could have grass under our feet again, Ronnie. Breathe fresh air." Getting no reaction from Fletcher, she continued more earnestly. "We could wade in the ocean—a real ocean, not a Caeliar simulation. It wouldn't be a gift. It'd be more like a well-earned parole." She had the cautious expression of someone expecting a harangue. "Would that be okay?"

Fletcher shrugged. "I suppose."

Erika shifted her queen to a position from which she could better defend her center, but Fletcher knew that she'd developed her own knights and rooks in ideal positions to pick off Erika's queen if it tried to interfere with her knight's burning-and-salting march through Erika's rear ranks.

Looking up from her move, Erika said, "The Caeliar would also be willing to build us a house on the surface. Is that an act of charity you could live with, or would you rather build a lean-to and sleep on the ground out of principle?"

Before answering, Fletcher captured Erika's king's bishop with her knight, exposing an important weakness on that flank of Erika's formation. At the same time, Erika's previous move, combined with this latest attack, now presented Erika with another imminent threat, this time to her king's rook. If she moved it to spare it from this discovered attack by Fletcher's queen, she would lose her queen's knight and see her king placed in check on the next turn. Or she could let the rook be captured, move the king to delay the inevitable, and—in the most favorable scenario for black—fight on to a stalemate.

"Sure, build a house," Fletcher said, as Erika assessed her tactical vulnerabilities. "I'm sure you'll be very happy in it."

Angrily, Erika asked, "What does that mean? You'll sit here in your 'cell' and rot rather than share a real house with me?"

Fletcher frowned and looked at Erika with tired eyes. "No," she said, choking down the sickening sensations that swelled upward from her gut. "It means I think I'm dying."

# 2381

## 10

Ezri Dax's eyes had just adapted to the rings of bluish-white light flashing by on the *Aventine*'s main viewer when the pulses vanished and released the ship back into normal space with a nerve-wracking shudder.

"Confirm position," Dax said.

Lieutenant Ofelia Mavroidis tapped at the conn and replied, "Delta Quadrant, between the Perseus and Carina arms."

Bowers leaned forward in his chair and asked, "Distance from the Azure Nebula?"

The Ullian woman checked the conn display and replied, "Sixty-four thousand, five hundred ninety-two light-years."

Unable to stay seated, Dax got up and moved toward the science station, where Helkara worked with quiet, singular focus. "Gruhn," Dax said. "What's the word on the subspace tunnel? Do both ends open to the same frequency?"

"No, Captain," Helkara said. "It seems to need a unique frequency pulse for each aperture, just like the passage that brought us from the Gamma Quadrant to the nebula. It's likely this'll be true of all the tunnels."

Turning his chair toward the tactical console, Bowers asked, "Any sign of the Borg out here?"

Ensign Padraic Rhys, the gamma-shift tactical officer, replied, "Negative. But we're picking up a massive debris field bearing three-three-one mark one-five." The fair-haired, broad-shouldered young Welshman made rapid adjustments on his panel as he continued, "Lots of refined metals—duranium, rodinium, terminium, and semirigid polyduranide."

Dax asked Rhys, "Enough mass to suggest a starship?"

"More like a hundred thousand ships, sir," Rhys said. "It's pockets of pulverized metal orbiting the nearest star system."

Curiosity nagged at Dax. "Range?"

"Just under a light-year," Rhys said.

Mavroidis swiveled her chair around from the conn. "At top speed, we could reach the debris ring in about an hour."

"I don't think we can afford the distraction," Bowers said, rising from his chair. He walked over to join Dax. "We should hold station while Gruhn works out the aperture frequency for our return trip."

The lithe Zakdorn science officer looked up and flashed a crooked smile that lifted his facial ridges. "Don't hang around on my account. This'll take a few hours, at least."

"Ofelia," Dax said, "set a course for the debris field. I want to check it out."

Leaning in close, Bowers said in a quiet voice, "Captain, if something did destroy hundreds of thousands of ships, we could be heading into a trap."

"Or maybe we just found an archaeological treasure," Dax said. She noted the grim frown that was deepening the creases on Bowers's face, and she relented a bit in her enthusiasm. "A little caution never hurts, though. Mister Rhys, scan the region for subspace radio activity and any other artificial signals."

"Aye, Captain," said Rhys.

While the tactical officer executed his sensor sweep, Mavroidis reported, "Course plotted and laid in, Captain."

Rhys finished his scans and said, "No short-range signal activity, Captain. Minimal subspace radio traffic at long range. No sign of transwarp signatures or other vessels."

"Glad to hear it," Dax said. "Helm, maximum warp. Engage."

The *Aventine* resonated with the rising hum of its warp engines accelerating to their limits, and the stars on the main viewer became snap-flashes of light coursing past the ship. "Warp nine-point-nine-seven," Mavroidis said, reading from her gauges. "Warp nine-point-nine-eight. Warp nine-point-nine-nine and holding steady, Captain."

Dax walked back to her chair, and Bowers followed her. As she sat down, she said to him, "Don't look so glum, Sam. We might actually learn something while we're stuck out here."

"It's not the learning that worries me," Bowers said as he settled into his own seat beside hers. "I just have to wonder if any of that debris is from ships whose captains also got a little bit curious."

She teased him, "Y'know, Sam, for someone who likes to think of himself as 'a man of action,' you sure don't—"

"Long-range contacts," interrupted Rhys. "Multiple bogeys leaving the debris-ringed system."

Bowers called back, "Speed and heading?"

"Warp two," Rhys said. "Intercept course. At that speed, they'll reach the debris field around the same time we will."

The first officer narrowed his eyes as he looked back at Dax. "I suppose this'll go in your log as a coincidence."

"Maybe," Dax said, conceding nothing to her XO's anxiety.

Ensign Svetlana Gredenko—a woman whose mixed human and Rigellian ancestry was betrayed only by her eyes' disturbing, crimson-hued irises—swiveled around from the ops console and asked Dax, "Captain, should we consider breaking off our investigation of the debris field?"

"No," Dax said. "Whatever's on its way out to meet us knows we're here. If it's friendly, I want to make contact."

The XO kinked one eyebrow. "And if it's not . . . ?"

"Then we'll have to hope we can outsmart it, outrun it, or outgun it, in that order. Steady as she goes." As the rest of the bridge crew returned to work at their posts, Dax leaned toward Bowers and added in a low whisper, "However, it might not be a bad idea to take the ship to Yellow Alert."

He triggered the intraship klaxon, which whooped once and left golden warning-status lights activated on bulkheads around the bridge. "I thought you'd never ask," he said.


Beverly Crusher heard someone limp into the *Enterprise*'s sickbay and grunt with pain. She looked up from the padd in her hand to steal a glance out her office door.

It was Commander Worf. He was garbed in a loose, off-white exercise garment, similar to the gi he usually donned during martial-arts training. This one was scuffed and torn in places. His nose and upper lip were bleeding, and his right arm dangled limply beneath his drooped shoulder.

"Worf!" she said, bolting from her chair and jogging to him. "What happened?"

"I was exercising." He tried to turn his head to the right, stopped, and winced. "I fell."

She picked up a medical tricorder from an equipment cart and made a fast scan of his injuries. "Looks like you fell several times," she said with a teasing gleam. "In addition to your broken clavicle, you've got four cracked ribs and multiple deep bruises all over your body."

"It was a very good workout," he said.

"I'm sure it was," Crusher said. She nodded to the closest biobed. "Have a seat. I'll get the osteofuser." Worf eased himself onto the bed as Beverly rooted through the lower drawers of the equipment cart.

"Once we fix the break, I'll take the swelling down on those bruises," she said. With the surgical implement in hand, she stepped in front of the seated Klingon and asked, "Do you want any anesthetic before I reset the bone?"

He shook his head once. "No."

"Suit yourself." She placed the surgical device on the bed. Then she put her left hand behind his right shoulder and tensed her right hand in front of his broken clavicle. "This'll hurt. A lot. You need to promise not to hit me."

His glare betrayed his fraying sense of humor. "I will try not to. Please proceed."

She slammed her palm into his jutting clavicle and hammered it back into place with one strike.

His bellow of agony and fury was deafening. Crusher recoiled from his roar and covered her ears. Averting her eyes from his, she saw that his hands were clenched white-knuckle tight on the edges of the biobed.

Then he was silent and gasping for breath to relax himself. "Thank you," he said.

"You're welcome," she replied.

He sat with his eyes closed while she used the osteofuser to mend his clavicle. "I haven't seen you do this to yourself in a while," she remarked. "Are the holoprograms getting tougher, or are you getting a bit careless?"

Her observation opened his eyes, and he pondered her words for a moment before he replied, "I felt it was time for a greater challenge." She finished fixing the bone and adjusted the fuser. He rotated his arm forward once and twice in reverse, and he seemed satisfied. "Much better."

"Good. Open your jacket and let me fix your ribs."

As he untied his black belt and opened his jacket, Worf said, "I did not expect to find you here so late."

"I wasn't *planning* on being here," she said, starting work on his left side, which was purpled with bruises. "But we didn't stabilize the critical cases from last night's battle until after 0800, and it was almost 1300 by the time I scrubbed out of surgery." Switching her efforts to the cracked ribs on his right side, she continued, "I didn't get to sleep until almost 1400, and I woke up a few hours ago. Now my sleep cycle's completely turned around. I'll probably be up all night."

Satisfied that his ribs were healed, she switched off the fuser and traded it for a tissue regenerator. "You know, Worf, as your doctor, I really have to suggest you ease up on your calisthenics programs. You're not getting any younger, and—"

She was interrupted by the opening of the sickbay door. The ship's security chief, Lieutenant Jasminder Choudhury, stumbled in looking haggard and disheveled. Her long, wavy black hair was a wild mess, and the left side of her face was an indigo bruise. Rips, bloodstains, and streaks of dirt marred her flowing, orange athletic garment.

Crusher rushed to Choudhury's side and helped her to the biobed next to Worf's. "And what's your story?" she asked.

"I fell," Choudhury said. "In the holodeck."

The lieutenant's choice of words made Crusher throw a curious look at Worf. Then she said to Choudhury, "Let me guess: a 'calisthenics' program?"

"Rock-climbing simulation," Choudhury replied.

Reaching for her tricorder, Crusher mumbled, "I'll bet." She scanned the security chief and was not surprised by what she found. "Seven cracked ribs, a hairline fracture of your skull, and a mild concussion. Plus, more bruises than I can count." Closing the tricorder, she added, "Ever heard of safety protocols, Lieutenant?" Choudhury seemed content not to respond to that query. "Mister Worf, I'm afraid you'll have to live with your bruises for a few minutes while I see to the lieutenant."

"I can wait," Worf said.

Crusher retrieved the osteofuser and set herself to work on closing up the microfissures in Choudhury's ribs and skull.

Worf and Choudhury's situation seemed so transparent that Crusher couldn't help but be amused. Odd as it seemed at first, she understood it. In the face of so much death and horror, it was natural to want to affirm life in the most potent ways possible.

Seeing the two of them together, she appreciated for the first time that, for all of their superficial differences, the XO and the security chief had a great deal in common. It made sense to her that they would be drawn to each other.

A few minutes later, as Crusher treated Choudhury's concussion, she chided her, "When it comes to using holodecks without safeties, I expect that kind of thing from Worf. But I thought security personnel were smart enough to know better."

"I admit, I was careless," Choudhury said. "Maybe I just got a bit overconfident."

"That's possible." She switched off the subdural probe and looked at Worf. "What's your excuse?"

"An error," he said. "I misjudged the skill level of my . . . new holoprogram."

"I have a simpler explanation," Crusher said. "I think you two beat each other up."

Worf shot an intense look at Choudhury, who remained as serene as ever. The security chief's cool discipline over her passions went a long way toward explaining why she won so many more hands than Worf did at the senior staff's poker games.

"Relax," Crusher said to Worf. "I won't tell anyone. But if you two keep *this* up, I won't have to."

Cooling his glare to a frown, Worf said, "Thank you. For your discretion."

"Please," Crusher said, with raised eyebrows, a reassuring smile, and a weary chortle. "I'm married to the *captain*. Discretion's my middle name."

The closer the *Aventine* got to one of the vast pockets of dark, metallic debris, the more anxious Sam Bowers became.

"Two minutes until the alien craft enters optimal sensor range," reported Ensign Gredenko.

Bowers looked to his right and caught the attention of Ensign Rhys at tactical. "I want a detailed threat assessment as soon as possible."

"Aye, sir," Rhys replied.

Captain Dax stood in the middle of the bridge and watched blackened wreckage tumble on the main viewer. Her gaze was focused, and Bowers could see by the expression on Dax's face that she was troubled by the image on the screen. "Sam," she said as he stepped beside her, "do you notice anything unusual about all the wreckage in that cluster?"

He looked at it with as much intensity of focus as he could muster, but if there was some insight to be found, it eluded him. "No," he admitted. "It all looks the same to me."

"That's exactly what I mean," she said. "The color, the composition, the forms—it's obviously a starship graveyard, but I've never seen one this uniform, have you?"

Inspecting the spaceborne flotsam and jetsam, he realized that Dax was right. There was no variation in the debris field's contents. He asked Gredenko, "Are there more pockets like this?"

"They're *all* like this, sir," the operations manager replied. Her red eyes widened as she added, "Exactly like this."

He turned to Dax. "Could it all be from the same ship?"

"My guess is that it came from thousands of *identical* ships," she said. The anxious peaking of her eyebrows conveyed her meaning to him with perfect clarity.

"Gredenko," Bowers said. "Run an icospectrogram on the debris and tell us if it came from the Borg."

"Aye, sir," Gredenko answered as she started the scan.

From tactical, Rhys interjected, "Sixty seconds until the alien vessel enters optimal sensor distance."

Dax folded her arms and confided to Bowers, "I'm beginning to think this might've been a bad idea."

"Do I get to say 'I told you so'?"

"Only if you want to get court-martialed."

Gredenko swiveled halfway around from the ops console and said to Bowers and Dax, "All of the debris shows subatomic decay consistent with exposure to tetryons and high-energy chroniton exposure—just like the hulls of Borg ships."

"Good work," Bowers said to the ensign. To his captain he added, "Looks like we're definitely in Borg territory."

"Maybe," Dax said. "Maybe not. The Borg may have made it here, but judging by the number of ships they must've lost, I don't think they've set foot in that star system."

Bowers was cobbling together a response when he saw Mavroidis stand up slowly from her post at the conn. The Ullian woman made an awkward turn to face the rest of the bridge crew. She regarded them with a blank, wide stare. Her voice sounded deeper and oddly resonant as she declared, "You are not Borg."

Everything about the young conn officer's body language and enunciation gave Bowers the impression that the woman was being used as a puppet. *Probably by something that tapped into her native telepathic abilities,* he reasoned.

"To whom am I speaking?" inquired Dax.

"The children of the storm," something said via Mavroidis.

Rhys beckoned subtly to Bowers, who slipped away to the tactical station as Dax continued to converse with the entity that was using their flight controller as a medium.

"I'm Captain Ezri Dax of the—"

"You are trespassers," the voice said. "But you are not Borg, so you may live—if you depart now."

On the tactical console, Bowers saw the deep-resolution scan of the entity that had intercepted them. As far as he could tell, it wasn't any kind of vessel, nor was it a creature native to the vacuum of space. What the sensors revealed was an energy shell without any apparent power source or means of being projected. Inside that spherical force field was an atmosphere of incredibly dense, superhot, semifluid liquid-metal hydrogen laced with trace metals. Suspended within that volatile, hostile soup of radioactive atmosphere were hundreds of individual energy signatures that had the cohesion of life signs.

He whispered to Rhys, "Patch in an exobiologist, *now.*"

While Rhys covertly signaled the ship's sciences division for an expert consultation, Dax said to the entity that was speaking through Mavroidis, "We only wish to establish peaceful contact and communication, on behalf—"

"Contact is not desired," the entity insisted. "It has taken many centuries to purge these systems of Borg. We will not permit them to be defiled again. Reverse your course, and make no attempt to violate our possessions."

Rhys handed Bowers an in-ear subaural transceiver, and then placed one in his own ear. Bowers did likewise, and Rhys opened a muted channel to one of the science labs as Dax continued her futile back-and-forth with the entity.

"Could we return at a specified future time and—"

"We do not wish you to return. Ever."

Lieutenant Lucy D'Odorico, one of the *Aventine*'s exobiology researchers, appeared on a small inset screen on the tactical console. Bowers and Rhys heard her through their transceivers. *"Based on the composition and pressure inside their enclosure,*

*I'd posit this species evolved in the middle atmospheric region of a gas giant,"* she said. *"Also, their brainwave patterns are consistent with species that demonstrate high-level telekinesis and other psionic talents—and it looks like you've detected the same frequencies in their energy field. I think this species might have mastered space travel and warp flight through the power of thought alone."*

Dax sighed in resignation, apparently having lost hope of making any meaningful contact with this potent but xenophobic entity. "Very well," she said. "We'll reverse course and leave—as soon as you release your hold on our conn officer."

"It is done," said the child of the storm. Mavroidis's eyes closed and fluttered for a moment. She swayed, as if afflicted with vertigo. Dax lunged forward and caught the young Ullian, who had begun to lose her balance. Mavroidis shook off the side effects of having been manipulated like a marionette and nodded to Dax. "I'm all right, Captain."

"Resume your post, Lieutenant," Dax said. "Then reverse course, back to the subspace aperture, maximum warp."

Mavroidis sat down and entered the commands into the conn. On the main viewer, the starfield swept past in a blur as she pivoted the ship 180 degrees from its previous heading. "Course laid in, sir," she confirmed.

"Engage," Dax said, and the ship jumped to warp speed.

At the tactical station, Rhys examined the sensor logs of the aliens' force-sphere, and he looked perplexed. "I don't see anything that looks like a weapon," he said. "And according to my readings, one good shot from a phaser should have been enough to burst their bubble. So how did they ever fight off that many Borg ships?"

"Rhys," said Bowers, "I think this is one of those times we should just be glad we didn't find out the hard way."

# 11

"According to the Breen domo," said Esperanza Piñiero, "our compulsory summit is an insult to his people's sovereignty, and the Tholian Ruling Conclave is calling it a war crime."

President Bacco faced away from her chief of staff, reclined her chair, and regarded the dreary, gray morning outside her office window. Thick fog and a misting rain had settled upon Paris. "What did the Gorn Imperator say?"

"Only part of it translated," Piñiero said. "The gist was that Zogozin might try to eat you, or a member of the cabinet."

"Let's hope I get to choose," Bacco replied, turning her chair away from the urban vista of spray and sprawl.

The door to her office opened. An aide entered to collect from a side table the tray on which Bacco's breakfast of French toast, strawberries, and coffee had been served. As he gathered the linens and cutlery and glasses, under the watchful eye of protection agent Alan Kistler, Bacco continued her conversation with Piñiero. "Zogozin makes a fuss in front of the others, but I think I made some progress with him last night. If we can get him to talk in private, we might sway him."

"Sounds like a long shot," Piñiero said.

"So is a counteroffensive against the Borg."

Tray in hand, the aide exited Bacco's office through the north door. Agent Kistler secured the portal behind the man.

Piñiero checked her data padd. "If you've got such a warm-fuzzy for Zogozin, why is your first one-to-one with Garak?"

"Because he's the one I least want to talk to," Bacco confessed. "Plus, if I can win over the Cardassians, we'll have a better chance with the Gorn—and it'll cow the Tholians and the Breen, so we won't have to watch our backs so much."

A doubtful expression sent Piñiero's eyebrows climbing toward her hairline. "On the other hand, if Garak leaves us high and dry, there's a good chance the Breen and the Tholians will be annexing our border systems by dinnertime."

"Thanks for the pep talk," Bacco said with a dour grimace. "I knew I could count on you to bolster my confidence." She pressed the intercom switch to her executive assistant. "Sivak, we're ready for Ambassador Garak."

The droll old Vulcan replied, *"So soon, Madam President? His Excellency has been waiting less than an hour."*

Bacco's fists curled shut. "Now, Sivak."

*"The ambassador is on his way in, Madam President."*

In the anticipation-filled moment before one of the doors opened again, Bacco straightened her posture and pulled her chair up closer to her desk. She folded her hands in front of her as loosely as she could, in an effort to appear calm and states-manlike. Images and impressions were critical in politics, and she expected to call upon all her years of experience in order not to be outmaneuvered by the wiles of Elim Garak.

The south door opened, and Garak was ushered in by another of Bacco's protection agents, a tall Andorian *chan* whose face looked as if it had been chiseled by wind from a slab of blue ice. As the lean, smiling Cardassian diplomat crossed the room, he was closely shadowed by Agent Kistler.

"Good morning, Madam President," Garak said.

Bacco got up and stepped out from behind her desk to meet him. "Good morning, Your Excellency. Thank you for coming."

"The pleasure is entirely mine."

She gestured to the chairs in front of her desk. "Please, Mister Ambassador. Have a seat."

He eased himself with grace and impeccable balance into the closest chair, while Bacco returned to her high-backed, padded pseudo-throne behind her desk.

Once they were both settled, she forced herself to establish and maintain eye contact with Garak. The intensity of his stare made Bacco want to avert her eyes. She cheated by staring at the intersection of cranial ridges above his nose. "Would you mind if we dispensed with the usual obfuscations and denials and skip ahead to the real reason I asked you here?"

Garak leaned forward and smirked mischievously. "I'd be delighted," he said.

"After all the strides we've made since the end of the Dominion War, why did you vote against joining our counterstrike against the Borg? And spare me the flimflam about politics, because we both know you aren't earning any favors from the Tholians or the Breen just for turning your back on us. So what's the real reason, Garak?"

He seemed to be highly amused by her question. "My," he said. "You're every bit as direct as I'd been told. It's an unexpected quality in a political leader, I must say—and a refreshing one, at that."

"You won't distract me with compliments, Ambassador," said Bacco. "So drop the flattery and answer my question."

The glimmer in his eye lost its humor and became one of cold, ruthless calculation. "You say you want the truth?" At her nod,

he continued, "It's simply this, Madam President. We aren't joining your war because we can't afford to."

"If your castellan is worried about reprisals by the Breen or
the Tholians, we—"

"I wasn't speaking figuratively, Madam President," Garak cut
in. "My meaning was quite literal. Even now, Cardassia has yet to
recover from the Dominion War. As dire as your conflict with the
Borg certainly is, my people face more imminent crises. Housing, for one; starvation, for another. Without foreign aid, we can't
even secure our borders or enforce the law inside them. The
Romulans withdrew their forces months ago when their empire
fractured, and now your forces and those of the Klingon Empire
have deserted us in order to prosecute your war with the Borg."

Bacco leaned forward. "I think you might be exaggerating a
bit, Mister Ambassador," she said. "Cardassia is more than capable of maintaining order in its core systems, and allied security
patrols were always limited to your border sectors. I also happen
to know you have a full battle group deployed on a training exercise to the Betreka Nebula. They could reach the Azure Nebula
and join the expeditionary force in sixty hours."

Garak conceded the point with a slow, single nod. "I can suggest that to the castellan," he said. "You might find the crews
of those ships woefully inexperienced, however. They are on a
*training* exercise for a reason, after all."

"True," Bacco said. "But we all have to learn sometime."

He weaved his fingers together in front of him and relaxed
back into his chair. "It seems prudent to caution you, Madam
President, that the castellan will likely refuse your request. Unlike her predecessor, she has little interest in foreign affairs unless they translate into immediate gains for the well-being and
survival of the Cardassian people."

Nodding, Bacco replied, "And you say that, right now, the
Cardassian people are most in need of . . . ?"

"Land and food," Garak said. "The Dominion's retaliation for
our rebellion at the war's end left several of our worlds radioactive and wiped out key agricultural resources. It will take decades to find, colonize, and cultivate new worlds."

"Unless we give them to you," Bacco said.

Her apparently offhand comment seemed to catch Garak off
guard. "Excuse me, Madam President?"

She nodded to Piñiero, who had been standing a respectful few meters behind Garak. As the chief of staff approached the desk, Bacco said to Garak, "I'm quite serious, Ambassador Garak. We're well aware of the Cardassian Union's troubles, and of your new castellan's political inclinations." She paused as Piñiero reached over Garak's shoulder to hand him a padd, which he scrutinized as Bacco continued. "Your people face grave times and have serious needs. The same is true of my people. Events are in motion, Your Excellency, so permit me to be blunt. If your castellan will order Gul Erem's battle group to join our forces at the Azure Nebula, the Federation will transfer three star systems to Cardassian authority."

Piñiero chimed in, "Specifically, Argaya, Lyshan, and Solarion—all on the Cardassian-Federation border, with stable Class-M planets and numerous exploitable natural resources."

Bacco added, "That would go a long way toward easing some of Cardassia's difficulties, wouldn't it, Mister Ambassador?"

"Indubitably," Garak said. "Though considering the role that Cardassia played in destroying your previous colony on Solarion IV, your generosity seems rather difficult to believe."

"The offer is genuine," Bacco said. "The question now becomes, do you think it's good enough to recommend to your castellan? And is risking one battle group of starships an acceptable price to pay for three new worlds?"

Garak's eyes widened, along with his smile. "Perhaps. Though a commitment to also provide us with new ships for our internal defense would be an even more magnanimous gesture."

"Yes, it would," Bacco said. "But I doubt the Federation Security Council would approve." With a tilt of her head she added, "If security's your concern, we could petition the Bajoran Militia to step in and patrol your trouble spots."

That drew a scathing glare from Garak. "Oh, I'm sure the castellan will *love* that idea."

"Indubitably," Bacco said, mimicking his inflection. "Maybe we'd best stick to the offer of planets for support, then."

"I have to ask why the Federation is willing to pay so high a price for what seems like a comparatively small boon."

"We're not paying you for the service of your ships and their crews," Bacco said. "You aren't mercenaries. It's your public show of support that makes this worthwhile. Emphasis on the word 'public.' Do I make myself clear?"

He bowed his head without breaking eye contact with her. "Unmistakably clear, Madam President." He stood up and handed the padd back to Piñiero. "With your permission, I'll return to my embassy and relay your offer to the castellan."

"By all means, Your Excellency." Bacco stood, stepped around her desk, and offered her hand to Garak, who shook it. "Can you speculate as to when we might have her answer?"

His grip was firm and feverishly warm. "Soon," he said, releasing her hand. "Good day, Madam President." Nodding to the chief of staff, he added, "And to you, Ms. Piñiero." Both women nodded their farewell to him, and he turned and walked to the north door, escorted by Agent Kistler.

As the door closed behind Garak, Piñiero's shoulders slumped, and her whole body sagged as if she had just been partially deflated. "I don't trust him," she said.

"He's not the problem," Bacco said. "Ambassador Garak is a lot of things, but foolish isn't one of them. He knows a good offer when he hears it. The problem is going to be his castellan. If she turns us down, his hands will be tied."

Piñiero shook her head. "It's not his hands I'm worried about; it's our necks."

The combat operations center on the uppermost level of Starfleet Command was frantic with activity. Uniformed officers hurried past Seven of Nine and the other high-ranking Federation government visitors, who were gathered around a central strategy table with a handful of senior admirals.

"We're too damned spread out," insisted Admiral Nakamura. He gesticulated angrily at the two-dimensional starmap that currently dominated the table's surface. "If Picard's right, then we need to start redeploying everything we've got toward the Azure Nebula."

A chorus of shouting voices tried to respond and fell silent only when one succeeded in drowning them out. "We've given Picard everything we can," Admiral Jellico said. "But we still have to be ready for a dozen other scenarios. And if we learned anything from the Dominion War, it's not to leave the core systems undefended."

The conversation devolved into another round of side-by-side debates between admirals and undersecretaries from the

Department of the Exterior. Bored with the round-robin argument, Seven considered walking away and returning to her regeneration alcove, just to see if anyone noticed.

All the admirals looked crisp and polished, while their subordinates had the frazzled, harried look of people who had been worn down by dodging a nonstop fusillade of enemy fire. Fearful looks haunted their faces.

The spacious, high-tech facility was rank with the odors of stale sweat and unwashed uniforms. Plastic cups, half full of cold coffee, littered every level surface. Against the backdrop of gleaming machines and towering display screens, the biological occupants of the facility looked soft, fragile, and slow to Seven's unforgiving eye.

Her patience expired, and she timed her declaration to fill an anticipated conversational lull. "Captain Picard's plan is fatally flawed," she said in a raised voice, silencing the admirals and the politicians alike.

"Finally, we agree on something," Jellico grumbled.

Admiral Nechayev cocked an eyebrow and adopted a defensive tone and posture toward Seven. "Would you care to explain that assertion, Miss Hansen?"

She ignored Nechayev's dismissive use of her former appellation. "Captain Picard—and by extension, this admiralty—proceeds from a false assumption. Your expeditionary force will not be sufficient to repel a full-scale Borg invasion."

Admiral Hastur—an olive-skinned, red-eyed, white-haired Rigellian flag officer with a reputation for strategic prowess— protested, "President Bacco is recruiting more allies for the task force right now. When we're ready, we'll have enough firepower to hold the line."

"No, Admiral, you won't."

Flustered, Hastur replied, "It's not as if we're trying to invade Unimatrix 01! All we have to do is hold one choke point until we can seal the breach in our defenses."

"Irrelevant," Seven said. "If your task force fails to find the Borg staging area before they begin their final invasion, your preparations will be for naught. And if they do locate the staging area, they will be forced to engage hundreds of Borg cubes. Your recent losses should make it clear that you are ill-equipped to fight even *one* Borg cube at a time."

"Aren't you forgetting something?" asked Nakamura, who looked far too smug for his own good. "We have the transphasic torpedo. One shot, one kill."

She directed her stern gaze at Nakamura, and for a moment she almost felt pity for him. "The Borg will adapt to your new weapon, Admiral. The only question is how long it will take. To survive a full-scale counteroffensive, your fleet will be forced to expend hundreds of transphasic warheads in a matter of minutes. The Borg will sacrifice as many cubes as necessary to devise a defense."

Seven paced slowly behind the admirals and civilian security advisers, all of whom tensed as she walked by. "There is no way that you can destroy the entire Borg Collective quickly enough to prevent them from adapting." She dropped her voice and spoke into Nakamura's ear as she passed him. "They will learn to defend themselves from your weapon." To Hastur, she said, "Then they will assimilate it." She continued past Nechayev, the only one of the admirals who had been sensible enough to demand moderation in the use of the transphasic warheads, and told Jellico, "And then they will turn it against you, and destroy you."

He bristled at her prediction. "So what do you suggest we do? Retreat?"

Without humor, she replied, "Yes."

Jellico lifted his arms and looked around in feigned confusion. "To where?"

"Anywhere you can," Seven said. "Some of the subspace tunnels the *Enterprise* discovered might lead to other galaxies. If you can isolate such a passage and collapse the others before the Borg have a chance to invade, you could organize a mass evacuation of the Federation."

Seven's governmental superior, security adviser Jas Abrik, looked horrified. "Are you insane?" the Trill man bellowed. "You want us to abandon the Milky Way galaxy to the Borg?"

Jellico, who was standing next to Abrik, rolled his eyes away from Seven, shook his head in disgust, and said, "This is why we don't let civilians write the battle plans." Snorts and chortles of dismissive laughter spread like a virus through the room, all of it at Seven's expense. Then Jellico turned his back on her and said to the others, "Let's keep working."

Seven had no conscious plan or moment of premeditation.

In a snap of action, she locked her right arm around Admiral Jellico's throat. She pulled him backward, off balance. Borg assimilation tubules extended from the steely implant still grafted to her left hand as she pressed her fingertips against his jugular. The tubules hovered above his skin but did not penetrate it—yet.

Around her and the admiral, the combat operations center became deathly quiet.

"If you do not escape beyond the Borg's reach, you will never be safe," she said, all but hissing the words into the trembling man's ear. "They know where you are, and they are now committed to your annihilation. Even if you collapse the subspace tunnels, they can still reach you by normal warp travel. It may take them decades. Perhaps even a century. But they *will* come. And when they do, your civilization will be eradicated. All that you have built, all that you have labored to preserve, will be erased from history. You cannot stop them, ever. As long as they exist, you will never be free."

The terror in Jellico's eyes was the same one she saw in her own when she awoke from nightmarish hallucinations during her regeneration cycles.

It was her only real fear: *I will never be free.*

Behind her back, the rising whine of charging phaser rifles cut through the silence. A security officer said in a carefully mannered voice, "Professor Hansen, let the admiral go. Now." She looked over her shoulder at the man, who met her gaze with his own unblinking stare. "Please release the admiral, Miss Hansen."

*They will not listen to reason,* Seven decided. *So be it.* She retracted her assimilation tubules and removed her arm from Jellico's throat. "I trust I made my point clearly, Admiral?"

"Get out of here before I have you shot," Jellico said, massaging his bruised windpipe.

The security guards advanced to within a few meters of Seven and kept their weapons aimed at her. One of them said, "Please proceed to turbolift four, Miss Hansen."

She met Jellico's furious stare. "You are only postponing the inevitable. When the Borg have the Federation by the throat, they will not release it—they will destroy it."

Jellico scowled. "Over our dead bodies."

"Precisely," Seven said.

* * *

Ambassador Derro was an old-fashioned Ferengi. He liked his profits large, his females naked, and his lobes stroked every night before bed.

All those pleasures had been in short supply during the reign of Grand Nagus Rom, however. Rom had granted Ferengi females the privilege to walk about in all manner of garb, and they had been invested with the right to work and earn profit. With those opportunities they had gained a new independence, and Derro's harem of solicitous females had evaporated all but overnight. Worst of all, he had spent the past few years cut off from the vast profits of the arms trade, as a consequence of being relegated to the pacifistic, economically backward world known as Earth.

He searched his memory for any clue as to what he might have done to anger Grand Nagus Rom. A grudge was the only explanation he could think of for his exile on this rock without profit. Rom, of course, had saddled Derro with the diplomatic posting as if it were a gift. As the Grand Nagus had smiled and waxed ecstatic about how much he expected Derro to learn about humanity and the Federation, Derro had suspected that Rom was either the most diabolically clever charlatan ever to occupy the nagal residence, or he was the most dangerous simpleton ever to stumble lobes-backward into power.

Derro's shuttlepod pilot, a Bolian woman named Doss, snapped him back from his bitter reverie by asking, "Is everything all right, Mister Ambassador?"

"Yes, Doss, I'm fine." He watched the rain slash against the shuttlepod's cockpit windshield. "This weather just makes me think of home, is all."

A male comm voice squawked from the overhead speaker, *"Ferenginar Transport, you're cleared to land on pad three."*

Doss activated the reply channel. "Acknowledged, Palais Control. Down in T minus ten. Ferenginar Transport out."

Outside the cockpit window, Derro saw nothing except a gray curtain of fog and rain. Then the façade of the Palais de la Concorde emerged like a phantom that quickly became solid, and Doss guided their two-seat transport pod inside the Palais's lower-level docking area. Ground crews with lit batons waved the transport to an air-soft landing.

The side hatch unlocked and opened with a loud pneumatic hiss and a hydraulic whine. Derro unfastened his safety restraint and got up. "Keep the engine running," he said. "I won't be long." He slipped between their seats and made his way out of the pod and down the ramp, to a waiting detail of four Federation plainclothes security personnel.

One of them, the leader, was a tall human female who had pale skin and a tightly wrapped bun of chalk-white hair. She hid her eyes with a black, wraparound sunshade, and her lean physique was concealed by the kind of dark suit that served as a uniform for President Bacco's protection agents. "Your Excellency," she said. "The president's expecting you. Please follow me to the transporter station." Without waiting for his reply, she turned and began walking in long strides toward the core of the Palais.

Derro followed her, and he heard the other three agents—all men: a Vulcan, an Andorian, and a Trill—fall into step around him. He was uncertain whether their presence was intended to make him feel protected or intimidated. In a peculiar way, it managed to do both at the same time.

They reached an internal transporter node, the kind that was used for secure site-to-site beaming inside a protected environment such as the Palais, which was surrounded by a scattering field to prevent unauthorized transports in or out. The albino female ushered Derro onto the platform. As soon as he'd found his place on the energizer pad, he turned back and saw the Vulcan initiate the dematerialization sequence. *Good,* he thought. *I hate long good-byes.*

A white haze erased the transport level from his sight and replaced it in a slow fade with the luxurious confines of the lobby on the uppermost level of the Palais. As the shimmer of the transporter beam faded and its confinement field released him, he found himself being greeted by a beefy, dark-haired human male who wore a familiar style of dark suit. "Welcome, Ambassador," the man said, motioning Derro toward the nearby door to President Bacco's office. "We apologize for the short notice." At the door, they stopped. "Just a moment, sir."

On the far side of the lobby, the other door to Bacco's office opened, and Zogozin, the Gorn ambassador, was escorted out by a man whom Derro recognized as Bacco's senior bodyguard, Agent Wexler. Zogozin halted, turned, and looked directly at

Derro, who reacted with a nervous smile. The archosaur answered the gesture with bared fangs.

Then a transporter effect began dissolving Zogozin, and the door in front of Derro opened.

Derro stepped inside, followed by the agent. President Bacco crossed the room to meet Derro. She pressed her wrists together, palms up, fingers curled inward. "My house is my house," she said, offering a traditional Ferengi salutation.

"As are its contents," Derro replied, imitating her gesture of greeting. He was secretly impressed that Bacco had made the effort to learn this peculiar domestic ritual of his people. In keeping with tradition, he reached inside his jacket pocket, removed a strip of latinum, and handed it to Bacco as the price of admission for a private audience in her official sanctum.

"Thank you for coming, Your Excellency," she said, pocketing the strip. She walked back to her desk. "Come, sit."

He followed her and settled into one of her guest chairs. "The Grand Nagus has ordered all armed Ferengi ships to your aid," he said. "Though he regrets their numbers are so few."

"I'm grateful to the Grand Nagus for all his efforts," Bacco said. Despite the fact that she was swathed in clothes, and that her tiny lobes were mostly concealed by her close-cut, paper-white hair, she radiated authority. "However, I've asked you here to discuss a more urgent and . . . *sensitive* matter."

She waved over a young Trill female and an Orion man who had been lingering on the far side of the room. The pair approached carrying trays that were loaded with foodstuffs. Only when they had reached the president's desk and set down the trays did Derro realize he had been presented with a smorgasbord of Ferengi delicacies: jellied gree-worms, live tube-grubs, soft-shelled Kytherian crabs, and an ice-cold Slug-O-Cola.

"Now I know you want something big," he said, flashing a snaggle-toothed maw and plucking a crab from the plate.

"Correct," she said, as the aides withdrew and left the room. "I've persuaded Ambassador Zogozin to remind Imperator Sozzerozs that the Gorn Hegemony stood with the Federation against the Dominion, and benefited from that decision. Zogozin believes that Sozzerozs will choose to side with us again."

Derro's teeth had pierced the crab's tender shell just before Bacco began her revelation about the Gorn. Now the feisty crustacean writhed in his jaw as he sat paralyzed by the news that she had completely reversed Zogozin's position. He withdrew his bite from the pincered delicacy in his hand. "How, may I ask, did you *persuade* Ambassador Zogozin of this?"

"The specifics aren't important right now," she said. "What matters is that we have our coalition for the expeditionary force. However, there's another matter for which the Federation needs the help of the Ferengi Alliance, and we'll be *extremely* grateful if you and the Grand Nagus can assist us."

He took a solid chomp out of the crab. Masticating the crunchy treat into paste, he asked, "What do you need? A loan?"

"Not at the moment. What we need you to do is cut the Tholians off at the knees, and quickly."

His throat tensed as he tried to swallow, and he struggled to force the mouthful of food down so he could speak again. "Excuse me, Madam President? I'm afraid I don't understand."

Bacco got up and walked around to his side of the desk. "We've made our deal with the Cardassians, and I expect to have Gorn ships in the Azure Nebula the day after tomorrow." She sat back against the edge of the desk. "But I know the Tholians, Your Excellency. They've been waiting for a chance to stab us in the back, and now is probably the best chance they've had in decades. The only way to stop them is to isolate them—contain them on all fronts, without angering the other local powers."

He washed the dry, sour taste of fear from his mouth with a sugary, slimy swig of Slug-O-Cola. "What does that have to do with Ferenginar, Madam President?"

"I'm glad you asked," she said. "The best chance the Tholians have of undermining us is to ally with the Breen and harass our border. But that won't happen if the Breen have already committed the bulk of their forces to another battle."

Every time she spoke, the situation seemed to get worse. "I'm still not following, Madam President. Are you suggesting the Ferengi Alliance start a war with the Breen Confederacy?"

"Of course not," Bacco said. "I'm saying you have so few ships at your disposal that you need the Breen's help to press the fight against the Borg." She reached over and pinched a fingerful of tube grubs from the bowl on the tray. "The Federation Council would never let me hire Breen mercenaries for the expeditionary force. But the Grand Nagus can take whatever steps he deems necessary to protect his people."

Derro was flabbergasted. "Striking bargains with the Breen is risky business, Madam President."

"The riskier the road, the greater the profit, Your Excellency." Before he could compliment her invocation of the Sixty-second Rule of Acquisition, she continued, "If the Grand Nagus's foresight—and yours—leads to the continued safety and survival of the Federation . . . the Ferengi Alliance would prove itself to be a steady and trusted ally. Naturally, allies rank ahead of neutral powers when the Federation Council determines which states receive most-favored trade status." She popped the grubs into her mouth.

He took another healthy bite out of his crab, savored it, and swallowed. "So . . . what you're saying is, you'd like us to subcontract your war and leave the Tholians with no friends."

"Exactly."

"Sounds profitable." He sleeved the greasy bits of shell from his mouth. "What about that loan? I can guarantee very good terms, and I have a few ideas about modernizing the Federation's economy that I'd love to share with you."

"Maybe next time," Bacco said.

"Suit yourself," he said with a shrug. He got up. "If you'll excuse me, Madam President, I have to go make a business proposition to Ambassador Gren."

She pressed her wrists together to bid him farewell. "Don't let him try to charge you extra for torpedoes."

"Give my lobes more credit than that," Derro said, returning the valedictory gesture. "When I get done with Gren, the Breen will be buying their torpedoes from *me*."

Less than two hours after Ambassador Derro had left her office, Nanietta Bacco's attention to a report from Starfleet was broken by the sharp buzzing of the intercom.

It was followed by the voice of her assistant, Sivak. *"Madam President, Tholian Ambassador Tezrene is here to see you. She appears to be in a rare state of heightened dudgeon."*

On the other side of Bacco's desk, Piñiero looked up with a droll countenance. "That didn't take long," she said.

"Send her in, Sivak," Bacco said.

The intercom switched off, the southern door opened, and Ambassador Tezrene swept into the room, her scorpionlike body wrapped in a golden shroud of silk that was taut from the high-pressure, searing-hot gases it contained.

Agents Wexler and Kistler followed close behind her, and two more protection agents, Lovak and de Maurnier, entered through the office's other door. All of them kept their eyes on the agitated Tholian diplomat, who was following a direct path toward Bacco. The president stood and held her ground.

"You'll regret this," Tezrene said through her vocoder, which barely muffled the metallic shrieks it was translating.

Bacco replied with transparently insincere concern, "Is something wrong, Your Excellency?"

First came a string of angry scrapes and clicks the vocoder couldn't parse, then Tezrene said, "Your backroom deals with the Gorn and the Cardassians were expected. But sending the Ferengi to do your dirty work—you disgust us."

"Forgive me, Madam Ambassador," Bacco said. "I don't know what you're talking about. There was nothing secretive about my meetings with Ambassadors Zogozin and Garak. As for the Ferengi, they're a sovereign power who can do as they wish."

A flurry of furious clicks and scrapes telegraphed Tezrene's ire. "Using them to marginalize us, contain us . . . you have overstepped your bounds."

Piñiero leaned forward to join in the conversation. "Excuse me, Madam President. I think the ambassador might be referring to the Ferengi's recruitment of Breen and Orion mercenaries to serve as their proxies on the expeditionary force."

"Oh, I see," said Bacco, feigning sudden understanding. Then she changed tack. "No, I don't see, actually. Why would the Tholian Assembly take offense at that, Madam Ambassador? You weren't planning to use those same mercenary forces to launch proxy attacks on *our* territory, were you?"

"Our concern was merely for the defense of our borders from the Borg," Tezrene said. "You've deprived us of our allies when we need them most."

It took real effort for Bacco not to laugh with contempt. "Do you really think the Breen would hold the line for you against the Borg?" she asked. "If the Collective comes for you, who do you plan on asking for help? The Orions? The Tzenkethi? Do either of them have a history of benign foreign intervention that I've just never heard of?"

A threatening twitch jerked Tezrene's stinger-tipped tail to and fro, lending her seething a mesmerizing quality. "The Tholian Assembly does not need the Federation's help."

"Maybe not," Bacco said. "But you should know that Starfleet won't sit by and let the Borg attack Tholian worlds. If your people send distress signals, we will answer."

"Your gestures change nothing," Tezrene said. "Hollow promises do not erase the sins of the past. We remember the crimes of the Taurus Reach."

Bacco turned her palms upward and spread her arms, hoping that the gesture would not be misunderstood or ignored by the Tholian diplomat. "Madam Ambassador, history is offering us a unique opportunity. We're faced with a common enemy, a shared need. This is a chance to put aside old hatreds."

"Not for us," Tezrene said.

Without another word, the Tholian ambassador turned and stalked away, flanked by all four of the presidential security agents. Bacco and Piñiero watched Tezrene exit. The last agent out of the room was Wexler, who nodded to Bacco as he shut the door behind him.

"Well," Piñiero said. "That went better than I expected it to. Now all we have to do is keep the ships of two warring Romulan factions from shooting at each other, find a way to reimburse the Ferengi Alliance for all the privateers they hired, and figure out how to make the Klingons give back eight systems they took from the Gorn over a century ago."

Bacco relaxed into her chair. "Let Safranski squeeze concessions from the Klingons," she said. "As for paying the Ferengi, get Offenhouse up here. It's about time he started earning his keep as secretary of commerce." She picked up her black, sweet coffee and enjoyed a long sip.

Piñiero asked, "What about the rival Romulan fleets meeting at the Azure Nebula?"

"That's Picard's problem, now," Bacco said. "He asked for everyone, and he's got 'em. The next move is his."

# 1574

## 12

A lifetime of night surrendered to the day. The icy sterility of the starry reaches of space faded from view as the city of Axion descended into the pale corona of a planet's upper atmosphere.

Veronica Fletcher stood at the edge of the city and peeked over its rocky rim, at the lush green orb flattening beneath her. Fiery wisps danced past the city-ship's invisible sphere of protection, and a great roar, like that of an engine, chased away all the stray thoughts that had been lingering in the forgotten tenements of her mind.

Next to her, Erika Hernandez perched on the corner of the precipice and watched the Caeliar's new world rising to meet them. Fletcher recalled how different she and Hernandez had looked in their youth—Fletcher had been pale and golden-haired, in contrast to Hernandez's black hair and olive complexion. Now they looked all but identical: pale, snow-maned, withered, and ravaged by time and gravity. Their stooped, fragile bodies were both clothed in silvery-gray wraps that reminded her of both togas and saris. Even their shoes had been replaced by flexible, synthetic-fiber slippers made by their captors.

She had never forgotten. Not even now, watching mountains of clouds race past into a blue sky, did she forget where she was, how she'd come to be there, and who was responsible. All the beauties of creation wouldn't have been enough to make her forget that she was a prisoner, a dying bird in a gilded cage.

The city broke through the bottom layer of cloud cover, and the details of a majestic landscape were revealed below them. Rugged, reddish-brown cliffs flanked abyssal canyons, and in the distance lay a range of charcoal-hued mountains topped with sun-splashed snowcaps. In the middle distance, a verdant landscape of rolling hills and broad plains was cut by wide rivers.

Hernandez sounded awed. "Amazing, isn't it?"

"It's everything I'd hoped it would be," Fletcher replied in her ancient rasp of a voice.

A knifing jab of pain pushed between her ribs, and she fought for breath as a fierce pressure clamped around her heart. *Not here,* she commanded her failing body. *Not yet. I won't die in this damned city.* Slowly, the pain faded.

The horizon became all but level as the city-ship of Axion settled into a stable, hovering position above the planet's surface. Then there was a subtle change in the air around them. A soft hush of moving atmosphere. The natural perfumes of flowers and green plants and living things. Thousands of tiny olfactory details came to Fletcher, like whispers half heard.

She became aware of warmth on her skin, and she looked up at the yellowish-orange sun high overhead. It was the first time she had felt natural solar radiation in more than fifty years. "The Caeliar must have turned off the shields," she said.

On the surface, a herd of graceful-looking animals gamboled across the open plains and stopped every few paces to graze on grass and flowers.

Hernandez stretched her arms over her head and smiled. "It's like paradise," she said.

An electric tingle on the back of Fletcher's neck served as a herald of Inyx's arrival. She turned, regarded him sourly, and said, "Yes, it's paradise. Complete with an apple salesman."

Inyx, who looked exactly as he had when Fletcher and the *Columbia*'s landing party had first come to this city decades earlier, ignored her comment and bowed to Hernandez. "We have completed the transit," he said as he straightened. "Thanks in no small part to your efforts, Erika."

"You're quite welcome," Hernandez said. "But it was only possible because of everything you've taught me."

Watching her captain curry favor with the enemy made Fletcher feel ill. Or homicidal. Sometimes both simultaneously. "I hate to break up your mutual admiration society," she said, "but can Erika and I make a visit to the surface? Now?"

The looming Caeliar scientist extended his arm, waved the three cilia at its end, and conjured a large-diameter, razor-thin, levitating disk of quicksilver. He stepped up onto it and gestured for Fletcher and Hernandez to join him. "It would be my pleasure to bring you there."

"Thanks," Fletcher said, forcing her arthritic knees to bend and propel her aching body up the short step onto the disk. Beside her, Hernandez was having almost as much difficulty mounting the transportation platform. It took several seconds, but they soon were safely in its center.

Hernandez nodded. "Let's go."

The forward motion was slower and gentler than it once had been. Fletcher presumed that Inyx must have realized how frail his passengers were and adjusted his control of the disk to a more appropriate velocity. They drifted away from the city in a slow turn, taking in the panorama of pristine wilderness that surrounded them. In a pleasant change from past rides on the circular platforms, gentle winds teased Fletcher's face, tossed her hair above and behind her head, and fluttered her clothes. It felt good, like a memory of freedom.

She pointed toward a low rise in the smooth plain, a knoll graced by a stand of three thick-trunked trees topped by proud green crowns of leaves. "There," she said. "Set us down on top of that hill, will you?"

"As you wish," Inyx said, altering the disk's path.

Less than a minute later, the disk touched down without any vibration of contact on the grassy hilltop and dissolved like a mirage. Fletcher felt the pliant sensation of grass bending under her feet, the cool touch of a gentle breeze scented with flowers and warm earth. She reached over and took Hernandez's hand. "Come with me," she said, leading Hernandez forward. Looking back at Inyx, she added, "You stay here."

He responded with an obedient nod.

Fletcher and Hernandez moved away from him in small, careful steps. Their slow progress gave Fletcher time to savor all the small details of this serene spot. The lilting of birdsong in the boughs above. A bright rhythm of sawing insect noise. The rustling of leaves, whose gentle dance in the wind dappled the sunlight falling between the three mighty trees.

When they reached the center of the trees' irregular, triangular formation, Fletcher stopped. She breathed in the air, nodded in confirmation to herself, and permitted herself a bittersweet smile. "This'll do," she said.

"For what?" asked Hernandez.

"My grave," Fletcher said. "When I die, this is where I want to be buried."

\* \* \*

Back in the embrace of a planet, it became easier for Hernandez to measure time. Sunrises and sunsets were novelties again. Each new dawn was another mark on Hernandez's calendar, and she noted the passage of weeks, and then months.

The Caeliar had wasted no time admiring the scenery. Instead, they'd set to work acclimating to their new home. Soil and plant seeds had been harvested from the planet's surface, to restore the landscaped sections of Axion that had been destroyed in its hasty flight from Erigol. Trees, shrubbery, and flowers were transplanted; water was taken from the rivers to replenish the city's many fountains and artificial waterfalls.

Edrin, the quiet and modest chief architect of the Caeliar, had supervised the design and construction of a residence for Hernandez and Fletcher. It was a spacious home of cedar-like wood and rough-hewn gray stone, with an open floor plan. Broad windows on its walls and strategically placed slanted skylights set in its sloped roof filled its common areas with large amounts of natural illumination throughout the day.

In the evenings, voice-activated lights concealed in the walls lent a warm glow to the two women's shared living space. Though neither of them had seen any sign of plumbing while the house was being constructed, it nonetheless featured clean hot-and-cold running water from a variety of locations, including both of their bathrooms and the kitchen.

Because neither of them had much interest in or energy for cooking, Edrin had provided them with a food synthesizer. As Hernandez had come to expect living in Axion, its entire menu consisted of vegetables and nondairy vegetarian dishes. Only after many experimental mishaps had Hernandez been able to help the Caeliar devise a leavening agent for bread that didn't contain eggs or anything patterned on them. The result was less than successful, but it was at least recognizable as bread, and it had opened the door to making noodles and other pasta, providing a much-needed respite from the Caeliar's endless variations of ratatouille.

In the back of the house there was a brick patio and a wading pool. Though their home had been built on a hill with a commanding view of the surrounding landscape, the vista from the back of the house, facing west, was the only one not obstructed by the looming mass of Axion close overhead. That one fact made the western view Fletcher's favorite. Hernandez found it harder to enjoy, however, because it looked out on the adjacent hilltop, where three trees stood their silent vigil over Fletcher's self-selected grave site. It was a daily reminder for Hernandez of an inevitable truth she didn't want to face.

*Put it from your mind,* she told herself. *Focus on each day as it comes.* Hernandez regretted not having been able to find a hobby during her long decades on Axion, because now that the Caeliar had settled upon this world as New Erigol, she no longer had a job to perform in the observatory. As dark and as imposing as the Star Chamber had seemed to her, now that it was in her past, there was a hole in her life.

It was about an hour past dawn. Hernandez set two plates of toast with jam and fresh fruit on the patio dining table, across from each other. Moving in slow, measured steps, she made her way back to the kitchen and retrieved a tray on which sat a pot of tea, a dish of sugar, and two delicate cups. As she carried it past Fletcher's bedroom door on her way out to the patio, she called out in a brittle voice she still couldn't believe was really hers, "Breakfast is ready."

A few minutes later, after she'd spread the jam on her toast and stirred a spoonful of sugar into her tea, she looked up and wondered what was keeping Fletcher.

Nagging concern impelled her from her seat and back into the house. *Let me be worrying over nothing,* she prayed to no one. *Let her just be sleeping in, or deaf under a hot shower.*

She pushed open the door to Fletcher's bedroom suite. In a timid voice, she called out, "Ronnie?"

Fletcher lay supine in her bed, one arm dangling half off the side. She lolled her head and stared blankly in Hernandez's direction. Though her mouth moved, no sound issued from her throat, only hollow gasps.

Hernandez wanted to run to her friend, but panic rooted her feet to the floor. It took all her strength to draw a breath and make a desperate cry for help: "Inyx!"

Fletcher's end was close, closer than Hernandez had thought only a few minutes earlier. Sprawled on a quicksilver disk, cradling

her friend in her lap, it was all Hernandez could do to stay focused on the details of the moment. The cool kiss of the wind.
The fragile, parchmentlike quality of Fletcher's skin, and the
golden radiance of the morning shining on this hideous moment.

"We're almost there," Inyx said, looking back and down at
them. "Just a few seconds more."

Looking around in confusion, Hernandez saw that Axion was
far behind them, and slipping farther into the distance with each
moment the disk spent in flight. Nodding toward the city-ship,
Hernandez shouted, "Inyx, we're going the wrong way!"

"No," he said. "We're not."

Then she looked past him, ahead of the disk, and saw the
three trees on the hill directly ahead. "Inyx," she demanded as
they passed under the trees' branches, "what are you doing?"

"Exactly what Veronica asked me to do," he said. The disk
touched down with preternatural grace and seemed to soak into
the dark, rich earth. Beside the two women was a freshly excavated grave with near-perfect corners and a neatly piled mound
of dirt waiting to be returned whence it came.

Hernandez shook her head, denying what was right in front of
her. "No, Inyx. You can't just let her die! There has to be something you can do!"

"There are many things we can do," Inyx said. "But it's Veronica's wish that we do nothing."

With a weak grip, Fletcher clasped Hernandez's hand. "It's
okay, Erika," she said. "It's what I want."

"How can you say that?" She clutched Fletcher's hand with
both of hers. "The Caeliar could give you medicines we've never
dreamed of, synthetic organs, gene therapy—"

Fletcher cut her off with a derisive laugh that became a hacking cough. A moment later she steadied herself and replied,
"Gene therapy? Like in the Eugenics Wars? No, thank you."

"All right, forget I said that," Hernandez said. "But try the
medicine, at least, or a synthet—"

"No, Erika," Fletcher said, more gravely. "This is my choice.
It's my time. Accept it, and say good-bye."

"Veronica, as your captain, I'm *ordering* you to let the Caeliar
try to help you."

Sardonic humor lit up Fletcher's wrinkled visage. "Pulling
rank, eh? Go ahead—court-martial me, Skipper."

Hernandez let go of Fletcher's hand and twisted so she could glower up at Inyx. "She's being irrational," she insisted. "She needs help, but she won't admit it."

Inyx shrugged by raising and lowering his gangly forearms. "She seems perfectly lucid to me," he said. "And the refusal of medical treatment is an entirely valid decision."

"You can't be serious," Hernandez said. "After all your speeches about the sanctity of life and not letting it come to harm, you'll just stand by and watch her die?"

The Caeliar lowered himself into a deep squatting stance, putting his bulbous head and stretched face on the same level with the seated Hernandez. "Everything dies, Erika," he said. "Sometimes, death can be thwarted and kept at bay. At other times it's natural and logical, and should not be resisted with too much vigor. Veronica has chosen to accept the natural life span of her biology."

"But you can fix that, can't you? Extend it?"

"Just because we can do a thing, it does not follow that we should do a thing. Veronica made her wishes clear long ago. For us to defy her stated desires and impose our cures upon her would be a violation of her personal sovereignty, and an act of unforgivable violence."

Tears of rage fell from Hernandez's eyes and were warm against her cheekbones. "You 'violated' Valerian, didn't you?"

"Only with your permission," he said. "As her guardian, you assumed the right and responsibility for making that decision. But Veronica is capable of making her own choice, and she has."

Fletcher's faint whisper, like a breath across dried leaves, commanded Hernandez's attention. "Don't fight it, Erika. Let me go. . . . I beg you."

Hernandez's thoughts were trapped in a storm of chaotic emotions—remorse and denial, rage and guilt. She picked up Fletcher's hand again and held it more tightly than before. Her sorrow was a tourniquet around her throat, and her voice quavered as she choked out the words, "I don't want you to go."

"Promise . . ." Fletcher's voice faded as she ran out of breath. She wheezed as she inhaled and continued, "Don't be seduced, Erika. Refuse their gifts. Don't take their medicine. *Please.*"

It wasn't the last request she had expected. "Why not?"

"Because the price . . . is too high."

A spasm jerked Fletcher's body into grotesque poses and blocked her airway. Her eyes squeezed shut as her face tensed, and her hands clenched like spiders shriveled in a flame.

All that Hernandez could do was weep and wail as Fletcher twitched in her death throes. Then the seizure stopped, and the tension left Fletcher's body. A soft gasp escaped her mouth, and she looked up at Hernandez with a beatific smile.

"It's okay," she said. "I'm free."

From that moment to the next nothing seemed to change, but Hernandez felt the difference, and she knew that everything had. Fletcher's eyes were still open, but they no longer saw. The warmth was still in her hand, but it would soon fade. Life had become death cradled in Hernandez's arms.

Inyx reached out and caressed Fletcher's brow with the delicate cilia that the Caeliar used as fingers. "I'm sorry, Erika," he said. His visage was as stern as ever, but the tilt of his head and the timbre of his voice emoted sympathy. "Would you like to say something before I inter her remains?"

She let go of Fletcher's hand, closed her friend's eyelids with a gentle pass of her fingertips, and lowered the body to the ground. As she stood on trembling legs, Inyx straightened to his full height beside her. Hernandez looked again at the dark pit in the ground that was waiting to receive her friend.

"I have nothing left to say," she declared, and then she turned and walked away from the three trees, and down the hill.

He called out, "Can I take you back to your house?"

She didn't answer him. There were no words.


No place felt like home for Hernandez.

The house on New Erigol was too big for her to live in alone. Though she and Fletcher had resided there for less than half a year, it had been built for the both of them. It was theirs, and with Fletcher gone, its open spaces had taken on a conspicuously empty quality. Hernandez's footsteps echoed when she crossed its hardwood floors; the pattering of rain resounded on the roof, reminding her that what had been meant to serve as a home was now just another hollow cage.

Worst of all, no matter where in the house Hernandez went, her eyes were drawn to the world outside her windows, and it seemed as if every view was of the three trees on the hill, where Fletcher lay buried. She tried to shut it out, ignore it, look away, pretend she didn't see it, and go on with her life. But it was always there, the defining element of the landscape.

After six days sequestered in her house, Hernandez stood in her kitchen and called out in a loud voice, "Inyx!"

It took him a minute to answer her summons. She'd expected another of his trademark light-show entrances. Instead, she heard a knock at the front door. Doddering steps carried her there. She opened the door to see Inyx standing with his head atilt. "Is everything all right?"

"No," Hernandez said. "I want to come back to Axion."

He pulled back and sounded confused. "Are you certain?"

"Yes." She turned and felt overcome with melancholy as she looked at the barren confines of her house. "I can't stay here."

Inyx stepped back from the door, onto the edge of a travel disk. "I will do as you ask," he said. "But I would like to know why you've chosen to abandon your home."

"It's not a home," she said. "It's just a house." She stepped outside, intending to leave without a look back, but she couldn't help herself. As she turned to take a final gander at the house, she said, "I always knew that, barring some event that killed us both, either I or Veronica would die before the other. I used to tell her I didn't want to die first, because I refused to let her have the last word. But the truth is, I didn't want her to die first, either—because I just don't want to go on without her."

She offered a silent valediction to her short-lived house in the country and stepped onto the silvery disk with Inyx.

He asked, "Is there anything I can do to help?"

"Yes," she said, looking at the house. "Raze it."

Night in Axion was never silent. The Caeliar didn't sleep, and their labors respected not the hours.

Large crystalline pods had departed the city-ship weeks earlier and fanned out across the star system, to begin the Herculean labor of preparing the next phase of the Caeliar's all-consuming Great Work. Inyx had kept the details of their task from Hernandez at first, but when she saw the thin dark line being traced across the dome of the sky, she began to suspect the nature of their new project. "Are you building a planetary ring?" she'd asked, full of renewed hope and wonder, eager to witness the creation of such a marvel.

Then Inyx had dashed her optimistic fantasies by telling her the truth. "No," he said. "We're building a shell."

"Around the entire planet?" she'd protested.

"And its star," Inyx said. "Privacy is essential now."

In the weeks that had passed since that conversation, on those rare occasions when she was able to sleep, she'd been plagued by nightmares of being sealed in a brick wall, buried alive, or trapped in a covered well. The smothering terror of being confined alone in the darkness had roused her again this evening. Driven by lingering fear and adrenaline, she rose from bed and drifted like a shadow through her compact quarters.

Her body felt lighter than air, insubstantial. She'd lost the will to eat days earlier, and the gnawing feeling in her stomach had abated quickly. Since then, her senses had taken on a dreamlike surreality; her vision felt softened at the edges, and sounds were muffled, as if underwater. Air smelled sweeter, and she was convinced it was because part of her essence had begun to transcend the mundane limits of sensation.

Walking the boulevards of Axion, surrounded by the milling packs of Caeliar, Hernandez felt as if her own passage had become as effortless and graceful as theirs. She let herself stare freely at all of them; wide-eyed and slack-jawed, she displayed all the bewilderment they'd provoked in her since her first day in their city.

Not one of them looked at her.

She realized that to most of them, she was a nonentity. Except for Inyx, and occasionally Edrin, none of the Caeliar regarded her as anything more than a nuisance and a burden—a pet they had been duped into adopting, and whom they either resented or ignored, depending on whether she misbehaved.

A crowd of them gathered in an open amphitheater, hovering in tiered rank and file, listening to a mournful musical performance that resonated from beneath a perfectly engineered acoustic half shell. There was only one performer on the stage far below, but she sounded like a quartet.

It had been so long since Hernandez had seen the city at its best that she'd forgotten the wonders it contained. The Caeliar, with their staggering gifts of art and science . . . their casually dynamic habit of coming and going in flurries of light, or just floating away, like soap bubbles on a warm summer breeze . . . their unaging bodies and unfathomable machines . . . they were power personified.

Standing alone among them, Hernandez saw herself as she really was: tiny, weak, old, and fragile.

She looked up at the stars, which once again flickered on the other side of an atmosphere, and her eyes were drawn to the empty patch of black sky where the view of the starfield had been obstructed by the Caeliar's shell-in-progress. *A bigger and better prison. They'll even take the sky from me.*

Eyeing the towers that loomed overhead, she thought of Johanna Metzger's fatal leap. Then she pictured Sidra Valerian, reduced to a screaming puddle of burning flesh. Desperate to exorcise that horrible memory, she forced herself to remember Veronica Fletcher's dignified, quiet exit, but it brought her no solace. Envisioning her friends in happier times yielded no comfort, either.

Hernandez had only the most tenuous grasp of her present moment as she wandered and explored the empty avenues and plazas of the darkened city. Her mind cast itself back to her life-that-was: the *Columbia* NX-02, her crew, the people she'd left behind on Earth . . . Jonathan. They were all hundreds of years in the future, and from her perspective they were all long gone.

She stood at the top of a steep staircase of white granite, high above a circular plaza. In the plaza's center was an inverted fountain, a circular cavity into which water poured from a surrounding ring. A geyser of spray shot up from the hole's center, dozens of meters into the balmy night air. The falling mist caught the pale starlight while it still could.

Holding out her arms as level with her shoulders as she could, Hernandez felt for a fleeting instant as if she could fly. Vertigo twisted her thoughts even as it seemed to lift her bare feet from the cold ground. She gave a push with her toes, shifted her weight incrementally forward, and hoped she was strong enough to do what she should have done so long ago.

Gravity made her its slave and tugged her into a tumbling plunge down the staircase. Delirious and feather-light with hunger and dehydration, she barely felt the easy snaps of her brittle old body breaking with every rolling impact, with every hammering collision against the corner of a step. The pummeling was unrelenting and overwhelming, and it pushed her to the brink of euphoria. Then she slammed to a halt on the plaza and lay very still, her body throbbing with the tactile memory of violence. She focused on the icy caress of the stone under her twisted body and imagined it bleeding away her last ounce of heat and life, snuffing her out with a cold and gentle embrace.

As she lay on the ground waiting for death, an amber shimmering of light formed on the periphery of her vision. At first she hoped it was her final hallucination before expiring.

Then the light began to assume a familiar shape.

*Please let him be too late,* she prayed, as she let go of awareness and sank into what she could only hope was oblivion.


"Are you in any pain?"

Inyx's question awakened Hernandez. She opened her eyes and was partly blinded by the flood of white light that was focused on her. It took her a moment to realize that she could see only with her left eye. She thought about his query, took stock of herself, and said, "No, I don't feel anything at all."

He leaned forward, blocking some of the light. She was relieved to have a respite from the glare. Staring up at his enormous, silhouetted head, she asked, "Where am I?"

"A sterile facility," he said. "I was concerned about a risk of infection by organisms from the planet's atmosphere."

A wave of his hand conjured a rectangular sheet of reflective liquid metal above and parallel with Hernandez's supine body. At first it showed only her reflection—broken, bruised, and bloody—but as Inyx spoke, the image on the sheet rippled and shifted to reveal scans of her internal organs, deep tissues, and endoskeleton.

"Your fall caused great damage, Erika," he said. "You've suffered compound fractures in both femurs, as well as simple fractures in your left tibia, right fibula, right humerus, the left ulna and radius, and the pelvis. In addition, you've cracked the parietal and occipital bones of your skull, concussed your brain, detached your right retina, and ruptured your liver and spleen. You'd also collapsed your lungs, but I took the liberty of repairing them and blocking your pain receptors so that I could discuss your options with you."

Lolling her head away from him, she muttered, "What's there to discuss? I'm dying, Inyx."

With another gentle sweep of his arm, he dispelled the reflective liquid screen as if it were nothing more than smoke. Gradually, the bright lights dimmed. When he spoke again, his voice was quiet and close to her ear. "You will die today if I don't treat your injuries," he said. "Is that what you want?"

Part of her wanted so badly to cry, but she felt emptied out, desiccated. "I don't know what I want," she said. "But I feel like I can't go on. Not alone."

Inyx stepped behind her head and walked around to the other side of the metal surface on which she lay. He passed out of her field of vision for just a moment. When he reappeared, she saw him completing the final details of his physical transformation into the likeness of Veronica Fletcher, as she had been in her youth. The sight of him wearing her friend's appearance like a cloak filled her with fury. "Don't do that," she snapped at him.

"I'm sorry," he said in Fletcher's voice. In a blink he altered himself into the semblance of Fletcher as she had been only weeks before her death. "Is this—"

"Stop it! I don't want your imitations, or your illusions."

Fletcher's face and form expanded and changed color and texture until Inyx stood beside her again. "Forgive me," he said. "I only meant to offer some comfort."

"Well, it didn't help," she said.

He pivoted away from her for a few seconds, apparently feeling chastened. Then he turned back and said, "You have not answered my question. Do you want medical treatment?"

"What good would it do? It's not like I have long to live."

"That might not be true," Inyx said.

She harrumphed. "Of course it's true. Look at me, Inyx, I'm an old woman. How long do you think I've got?"

"As long as you want," he said. "If you let me help you."

"The way you helped Sidra? No, thanks."

He squatted beside her and dropped his voice to a whisper. "After the incident with Sidra, Ordemo and the Quorum ordered me to cease my research into your species' physiology and genetic structure. I acknowledged their order. And I disobeyed it."

The intensity of his words alarmed her. "Why?" she asked.

"Because I had to know the truth about what happened to

Sidra," he said. "I needed to know if she died because of my error, my negligence. But I found no evidence to support that." His tone brightened. "As a result of my investigation, however, I learned a great deal about your species and how to treat its myriad diseases—including what you call 'natural' death."

Hernandez rolled her good eye. "Death isn't something you cure, Inyx. Death is a constant, not just another illness."

"In your species, natural death is the end result of unchecked cellular senescence," Inyx replied, with profound earnestness. "Most of the problem is related to the shortening of your cells' telomeres, which are sacrificed, bit by bit, to prevent the loss of your working DNA during cell division and replication. But these losses lead to your aging process, and, eventually, you run out of telomeres. That triggers your cells' preprogrammed senescence—cell death. Then your organs fail."

"That's a long way of saying humans get old and die."

"What I'm saying is that I believe I can correct that flaw in your genetic program. Aging and death are a disease, Erika. Don't you want the cure?"

She considered the implications of what he was saying. Beyond mending her shattered bones and ruptured organs, he was offering her something that humanity had searched for and dreamt of for eons: eternal youth and near immortality. A bite of the fruit of the Tree of Life itself.

"No," she said. "It's too much. I can't."

He lowered his head and sounded despondent as he said, "I wish you would reconsider."

Fletcher's defiant warnings echoed in Hernandez's thoughts, and she gave them voice. "Inyx, if I accept that kind of gift from you, it would be the same as sanctioning my captivity and that of my crew. I'd be dishonoring all their sacrifices."

A note of desperation crept into his voice as he replied, "Erika, your crew and your friends are gone. Only you remain. And no matter what they might have wanted or believed, you should make the choice that's best for you, here and now."

"I think I am," she said, feeling her strength ebb.

He reached out and transformed his waggling cilia into more human-looking fingers and a thumb, and took Hernandez's hand. "I've seen how much death frightened you in the past," he said. "But I don't want to appeal to your fear, and I won't ask you to set aside your resentment of me and my people for having imprisoned you. I'd like you to consider an entirely different rationale for accepting my help."

Hernandez's curiosity overcame her guilt. "Which is . . . ?"

"By your reckoning, I've lived for tens of thousands of years," Inyx said. "In all that time, I have encountered very few sentient life-forms from outside of my society. But of all the beings I have met, you are one of the most . . . vital."

She tried to swallow the saliva pooling in her mouth, but her tongue and throat felt like poorly lubricated gears grinding to no avail in a dusty machine. "Ironic of you to say so," she said in a hoarse croak of a voice.

"Even in your present state, you're more vibrant than any of the millions of Caeliar in Axion. And though our association has so far been—from my perspective—incredibly brief, I have come to think of you as my friend. And so . . . for purely selfish reasons . . . I want you to survive, and enjoy living, and help me continue the Great Work." His words were heavy with sorrow as he added, "I don't want you to die, Erika. So I'm begging you to let me help you. Please don't make me stand aside and watch you die. If I cannot give you your freedom . . . at least let me give you back your life."

His heartfelt plea would have brought her to tears had her eyes not been as red and dry as the Martian desert. "All right," she said, flashing a sad smile. "But only because you're doing it for selfish reasons." Noting his confused silence, she explained, "It makes you seem a little more human."

"I'll try to take that as a compliment," he said.


Hernandez was only partially conscious as Inyx levitated the metal slab on which she lay and guided it telekinetically through the vaulted, cathedral-like spaces of Axion.

As they passed a long line of massive, narrow open archways that looked out on the landscape of New Erigol, she caught the sweet, heavy scent of a gathering storm. She turned her head and saw the hills and trees strangely luminous with bright sunlight, beneath ominous clouds that were black and pregnant with rain.

Then she and Inyx turned down a dark, narrow passage that led to a dead end in a circular chamber. The ceiling spiraled open above her, and the walls rushed past as she and Inyx were lifted in silence to the top of one of the city's towers.

She asked, "Where are we going?"

"To my operating theater," he said, evoking heartbreaking memories of Valerian's ugly demise. Perhaps sensing Hernandez's unspoken reaction, he added apologetically, "It's the only facility equipped for the procedure."

Their ascent slowed.

"What will the Quorum say?"

"They'll forbid it," Inyx said. "Which is why I won't tell them until after it's done."

Hernandez chuckled softly at Inyx's insolence toward his superiors. "I knew there was a reason I liked you."

They arrived in a circular room much like the one at the start of their vertical journey, and Inyx guided her steel stretcher down another passage that was far shorter. At its end, a door slid open, admitting them to his laboratory.

Nothing had changed about the lab since her last visit, except that the carbon-black stain on the metal operating table had been expunged. The tall and narrow space was still packed tightly with machines throbbing with low-frequency sounds and pulsing with scarlet light. Overhead, a web of slack, silvery cables surrounded the room's periphery. The only gap in the tangled mess was directly above the operating table, where the long, irregular machine hovered without support beneath the closed, clamshell-shaped skylight.

Inyx guided the stretcher onto the operating table, and out of the corner of her eye, Hernandez saw the two metallic surfaces fuse into one.

Above her, the protruding implements of the surgical machine began to glow with crimson energies, and a surge of terror coursed through her.

"It's important you understand the procedure and the risks," Inyx said. "I want you to make an informed decision."

"So, inform me," Hernandez said, hiding behind bravado.

He gestured to the hovering contraption. "With this machine, I will introduce a limited quantity of catoms into your body. These nanomachines will effect repairs to your damaged bones and organs, and they'll modify your genetic code."

Hernandez swallowed her anxiety. "Sounds okay so far."

"Because of certain immutable limitations of organic cellular replication, the catoms will need to remain part of your body to monitor the Change's effects. Once incorporated into your body, the catoms will be sustained partly by your biology, but primarily by Axion's zero-point quantum field."

"You talk like you're selling me a used car," she said. "Skip ahead to the risks."

Her rebuke silenced Inyx for a moment. Then he continued, "My chief concern is that you will not be able to commune with the gestalt. Sidra died because her mind rejected contact with the Caeliar. The catoms in your body will not stabilize unless they can form a bond between your mind and the gestalt."

"Bond? Commune with the gestalt? What does that mean?"

A long huff of breath puffed the sacs that curled over Inyx's shoulders and dilated the ends of the tubules on his head. "It's difficult to explain, Erika. It's about becoming part of something greater than yourself and accepting your place in it. Reduced to its most basic level, you must surrender or perish."

Fletcher's warning came back to Hernandez: *They want our surrender.* "And if my subconscious mind resists . . . ?"

"Then what happened to Sidra will happen to you, as well."

New waves of anxiety christened her forehead with sweat. She glanced nervously at Inyx. "How hard is it to surrender?"

"That depends on you." He looked up at the machine, then back at her. "We don't have to do this. I can mend your immediate injuries and forgo the rest of the procedure."

She shook her head, feigning defiance and resolve. "No," she said. "If I back away from this now, I might never have the courage to come back. I'm ready now."

"Are you sure?" he asked, sounding doubtful.

"Yes," she said.

Inyx levitated up from the floor. "Very well," he said, and he began making his final adjustments to the machine.

A guilty voice inside Hernandez's head justified the rashness of her choice: *If it goes wrong, and I die like Sidra did, it'll be justice. I'll get what I deserved.* As the device looming directly above her face thrummed with power and glowed with light, she lost herself in its ruby glare. *No turning back now,* she told herself. *Whatever happens . . . happens.*

Inyx rested his cilia on her shoulder and spoke in a soothing baritone. "I'm going to use a low-power energy wave to guide your brain into an unconscious state. Most of the changes to your body will take place while you're sedated. When the catoms have completed their fusion with your genetic matrix, I'll bring you back to consciousness. Those first moments will be critical, Erika. As you awaken, you must open yourself to the gestalt and accept its embrace. Do you understand?"

She nodded. "Yes. And, Inyx . . . ? Thank you."

He gently nudged a few snowy-white hairs from her eyes. "Breathe deeply," he said to her. "We're about to begin." Then he withdrew, floating like a ghost to the master control panel behind the transparent wall to her right. She did as he asked, and slowly inhaled, filling her lungs. Then, as she let the air escape, her senses faded, and she knew that she was being sedated. When she opened her eyes again, it would be to face either a new life or an instant death.

Darkness fell for a moment that might have lasted forever. Then the distant glimmer of light and life beckoned her upward, out of an abyss of shadow.

She felt like flowing water, free and moving in the current of something greater than herself, a fluid with no boundaries, no beginning and no end, just momentum and union. For a moment, part of her mind cried out in alarm that she was drowning. Through an act of will, she silenced her fear and gave herself a new frame for the experience: *I'm in the womb.*

There were voices, millions of them, each distinct, none exalted over the others. Ideas and forms and concepts filled Hernandez's thoughts, every one of them hers for the taking if she wanted it, but if she averted her thoughts they fell away, forgotten. Images and sounds buoyed her. She was afloat in a sea of memories and daydreams, all equal in substance and value.

All of it was hers to enjoy, but none of it was hers. It wasn't anyone's, and it was everyone's. Information and power were all around her, as abundant as the air she breathed. She was immersed in it, was part of it, and gave it a focal point. Other loci were moving throughout the city, and one was beside her. They and she were like stars orbiting Axion.

Sound returned. "Open your eyes," Inyx said softly.

Her eyelids parted with reluctance. Above and around the operating table, Inyx's lab looked exactly as it had before the procedure, but Hernandez saw it with a new vision. She felt a reciprocal tug from the machines that surrounded her—a give and take that enabled her to sense their energy levels and, she presumed, direct their function by thought alone.

Rain slashed against the clamshell skylight directly above her, and the storm-blackened sky flashed with lightning. Half a second later, thunder rocked the city.

Inyx stood at her side, his cilia-fingers waggling together in front of him. "Your catoms are stable. How do you feel?"

"I don't know," she whispered. Then she looked down at her hands. Their skin was rosy and taut and their muscles toned, and all the scars she had acquired in her youth as a rock climber had been erased. At first, she sat up slowly, in the cautious manner to which age had made her accustomed. None of her old aches and pains were with her, so she pivoted and swung her legs off the side of the bed, appreciating all of a sudden how lean and firm they were beneath her delicate silver-white raiment.

As she leaned forward to stand up, her hair spilled in front of her face—in long, lustrous black coils. She touched her face and throat. Gone was her brittle and age-loosened skin. Her fingertips found only the soft, graceful lines of her jaw. In a moment of vanity, she wished for a mirror . . . and one took shape in front of her, coalesced from billions of motes of nanoscopic, programmable matter that lingered in the air.

"Did I do that?" she asked, staring in wonder at the free-floating oval mirror, which reflected back the sight of her as she might have been at the age of eighteen, had she worn her hair in an epic, wild mane that fell to her lower back.

"Yes," Inyx said. "You did. And you can do much more, if you want to. I can show you how."

Giddy with excitement, she tore her eyes from the lissome echo of her youth in the mirror and looked at Inyx. "Show me everything," she said.

"Look up," he said. She did as he asked. Above them was the skylight, rattling beneath the fury of the wind and rain. "Open it," he told her. "See it open in your mind."

The moment played in her imagination and became clear.

Then it became reality. The skylight opened.

Rain, warm and pure, surged through the open space and doused Hernandez and Inyx. She closed her eyes and reveled in the sensation of the droplets pelting her face and bosom.

He placed his arm against her back. "Rise with me."

Her feet lifted from the floor of the lab.

She and Inyx levitated together, ascending into the downpour. They passed through the frame of the open skylight, into open air. Until that moment, she'd thought Inyx alone had lifted her up. Then he removed his arm . . . and she soared.

Violent gales buffeted her with rain, and twists of blue lightning split the shadows and cracked the heavens with thunderclaps. She cried out in a panic, "Inyx!"

He was nowhere to be seen, but she heard his calming counsel close by. "Don't be afraid . . . it can't hurt you now."

And she knew that it was true.

She opened herself to the power that radiated up from the city and unlocked the potential that now suffused her body. Gaining speed, she shot upward, slicing through the stormhead, fearless, baptized by the storm as she flew like a bullet.

She wept with joy; it felt like freedom incarnate.

Like an arrow piercing a target, she burst free of the tempest and exploded into blue sky and golden light. Spreading her arms wide to embrace it all, she turned in a slow spiral, feeling the wind and the sun warming her rain-drenched body, and her head lolled back to glory in her transformation.

Then came the gentlest tug of restraint.

It was subtle but undeniable, as if an invisible, silken cord had been tied around her ankles, anchoring her to Axion and rescuing her from her inner Icarus.

"Everything has a limit," explained Inyx's disembodied voice. "Our gifts are made possible by Axion's quantum field. Beyond a certain distance, our powers diminish greatly. Within and near the city, however, you'll have nothing to fear."

His words haunted her thoughts as she looked again at the sky and saw the dark scar of the planet's growing shell taking shape in high orbit. *This is what Veronica was warning me about,* she realized. *How could I have been so stupid?*

The Caeliar had granted her eternal youth and functional immortality—but only as long as she remained in Axion. It was nothing less than a life without end in captivity. She would never be freed, not even by death.

Her joyful tears turned bitter as she confessed the truth to herself: *I just made myself a prisoner forever.*

# 2381

## 13

"Aperture two-alpha, opening now," reported Lieutenant Sean Milner, the *Enterprise*'s gamma-shift operations manager. "Ship emerging. It's the *Aventine*. They're signaling all clear."

Picard nodded. "Noted, Lieutenant."

A demonic whispering stole the captain's attention for a moment: it was the voice of the Borg. He tried to see through the cerulean churning of the Azure Nebula on the main viewer. The susurration had no words, no message he could discern. After a few seconds he realized that the Collective wasn't speaking to him; it didn't even seem to be aware of his presence . . . yet. But he knew that it was nearby, somewhere on the other side of one of these shortcuts through space.

An electronic tone warbled from the operations console. Milner, a tall and square-jawed Londoner, checked his console and pivoted around to report, "It's Starfleet Command, sir."

"On-screen," said Picard, rising from his chair.

Admiral Nechayev's image appeared on the main viewer. *"Good news, Captain,"* she said. *"Reinforcements are on the way."*

"Glad to hear it, Admiral. Who's with us?"

She arched one eyebrow in apparent amusement. *"Everyone except the Tholians, apparently. The Ferengi even paid off the Breen to send a fleet. I don't know how President Bacco did it, but if we get through this, I might ask her to turn some water into wine."*

Picard feigned high spirits. "How long until our force assembles?"

Nechayev checked something off-screen before she replied, *"The Klingons and the Romulans will have several dozen ships at your position in less than thirty-six hours. Our forces start arriving in forty-eight. A Cardassian battle group will reach you in fifty-six hours, and the Talarians, Ferengi, Breen, and Gorn will be the last to arrive, in about four days."*

"Understood," Picard said. "We'll continue scouting the sub-space tunnels and holding the line until they arrive."

*"Good luck and godspeed, Captain,"* Nechayev said. *"Starfleet Command out."* The main viewer blinked back to the cloudy sprawl of the nebula.

Picard looked at Worf. "Commander. Status report."

Worf checked the display on the end of one of his chair's arm-rests. "Repairs complete," he said. Looking up, he added, "Lieu-tenant Elfiki is ready to open tunnel three-alpha."

"Very good," Picard said. To Milner, he added, "Put me on in-ternal speakers, Lieutenant."

Milner keyed in the command. "Channel open, sir."

"Attention, all decks, this is the captain," Picard said. "The *Aventine* has just returned from its first jaunt. In a few minutes, we'll be making our own first trip through one of the subspace tunnels. Please report to your primary duty stations. Senior com-mand officers, report to the bridge. Picard out."

As Picard settled back into his command chair, Worf said to tactical officer Abby Balidemaj, "Sound Yellow Alert. Raise shields, transphasic torpedoes to standby."

"Aye, sir," Balidemaj replied, executing the order.

Picard threw a questioning look at his first officer. "Feeling anxious about our first scouting run, Mister Worf?"

"No, sir," Worf said, with a ferocious gleam. *"Eager."*

Drawing strength from Worf's confidence, Picard sat up a bit straighter in his chair and fixed his eyes on the main viewscreen. Far away, beyond a veil of shadows, the voice of the Collective still whispered . . . and he vowed that he would silence it—soon, and forever. No matter what the cost proved to be.

Miranda Kadohata looked up from the desktop monitor in her quarters as Captain Picard's voice echoed over the intraship comm. *"Attention, all decks, this is the captain,"* he said. *"The* Aventine *has just returned from its first jaunt. In a few minutes, we'll be making our own first trip through one of the subspace tunnels. Please report to your primary duty stations. Senior com-mand officers, report to the bridge. Picard out."*

The comm clicked off, and Kadohata resumed staring at the blue-and-white Federation emblem on the screen in front of her.

*Connect, dammit,* she fumed. *Can't wait much longer.* An icon in the lower right corner of the screen changed, indicating that the real-time signal had been routed to its destination. *Pick up, Vicenzo! Hurry!*

An image blinked onto the screen: her husband, Vicenzo Farrenga, looking frazzled and standing in a sunlit corridor of Bacco University, on Cestus III. *"Miranda? They pulled me out of a lecture. Hope I didn't keep you waiting."*

"I have to make this quick, love," she said. "I can't explain, but this might be the last time . . . for a while . . . that I get to talk to you, and I need you to pay attention."

He reacted attentively to her urgent tone. *"I'm listening."*

Kadohata wanted to shout, *Run! Take the children and go, and don't look back!* But she knew that all communications were monitored at times like this, and Starfleet regulations forbade her from sharing what she knew of the rapidly worsening tactical threat against the Federation. Fomenting fear and panic about the imminent Borg invasion would only serve to destabilize the situation. To save her family, she'd have to be more discreet.

"Do you remember Judi and Adams?"

Vicenzo thought for a moment. *"You mean that nice couple who lived out on Dundee Ridge? Didn't they move?"*

"Yes," Kadohata said. "They started a farm on Kennovere."

*"Right, Kennovere,"* he said, nodding in confirmation. *"That crazy, low-tech organic colony out past Typerias."*

"Organic, yes. Crazy, maybe not. That's a way of life I'd really like the kids to see."

He rolled his eyes and combed his fingers through his unruly dark hair. *"Okay,"* he said. *"I'm not sure I can fit that in during spring break. Maybe when the semester's over—"*

"They ought to see it as soon as possible," Kadohata said, more sharply than she'd meant to. "Before the growing season ends on Kennovere next month."

She recognized the look of slowly dawning understanding that was changing Vicenzo's face. *"It'll be tricky getting out there in time,"* he said, doing a poor job of pretending to be nonchalant. *"We'd probably have to hop a transport out first thing tomorrow to have a chance at seeing the harvest."*

"Trust me, love," she said, her eyes misting with tears as she fought to bury her fears. "It'll be worth it."

The overhead comm beeped twice and was followed by Commander Worf's irate baritone. *"Commander Kadohata, report to the bridge immediately."*

"On my way, sir," she answered. "Kadohata out." Then she looked back to her husband and touched her fingertips to his lips on the screen. "Duty calls, love. Safe travels."

He touched his screen and replied, *"You, too, sweetheart."*

The signal ended abruptly, and her monitor went black.

Kadohata stood, tied her hair back in a utilitarian knot, and smoothed her uniform while looking in the mirror.

*It'll be all right,* she assured herself. *He'll get the kids out of Federation space. Out of the war zone.*

As she left her quarters and hurried to the bridge, she kept telling herself that everything would be okay, but she knew that unless the Borg invasion was halted soon, having her family flee their home wouldn't be enough to save them. Because when the real invasion came, there would be nowhere left to run to.

Worf detested sitting still. All around him, the *Enterprise* felt as if it was shaking itself to pieces while making its transit of the subspace tunnel Elfiki had opened. At flight control, Joanna Faur fought to steady the *Sovereign*-class vessel's passage, and from ops Commander Kadohata called out over the rumbling of the engines and turbulence, "Shields weakening."

Defying his instincts, Worf looked at the captain and said, "Sir, I suggest we route phaser power to shields."

Picard assented without hesitation. "Make it so."

Worf delegated the order with a glance at Choudhury, who nodded and entered the command on the tactical console.

"Picking up speed," Faur reported, reacting quickly to the changing data at the conn. "Full impulse plus ten percent."

Lieutenant Elfiki looked up from the starboard science station to add, "We're reading an extreme-gravity environment ahead, past the tunnel's terminus. We should be able to compensate for it with a low-power subspace field."

"Bridge to engineering," Worf said.

La Forge answered. *"Go ahead, bridge."*

"Stand by to generate a low-power subspace field, on Commander Kadohata's signal."

*"We're on it,"* La Forge said. *"Engineering out."*

Instead of the proverbial light at the end of the tunnel, Worf saw a circle of darkness growing larger and emptier with each passing moment. Then the *Enterprise* shot out of the subspatial anomaly, and it seemed to be bashed in three directions at once. The force of the impacts hurtled Worf out of his chair onto the deck. As he struggled up onto one knee, a mournful groaning of stressed duranium resonated through the hull. Over the deep, metallic howls, Worf bellowed to Kadohata, "Initiate subspace field!"

Kadohata was half on the deck, clinging with one arm to her station and manipulating its controls with her free hand. Seconds later, the banshee moans of the hull ceased. Everyone clambered back into their chairs. Once they were settled, the captain said with stern equanimity, "Report, Mister Worf."

"No damage, Captain," Worf said, checking the status screen beside his chair. "A few minor injuries in the cargo bay." He looked toward the conn officer. "Lieutenant Faur—position."

"Still calculating, sir," Faur replied. "I'm not reading any of the nav beacons." As she continued, Captain Picard got up from his chair and walked slowly toward the main viewscreen. "There's a lot of signal interference, too. Background radiation's off the scale."

Picard stood behind Kadohata and Faur and stared in silence at the image on the massive screen at the forward end of the bridge. Worf looked past the captain and realized why: There were practically no stars anywhere to be seen, just a few lonely dots of light separated by unimaginable reaches of icy void.

"Where are we?" Picard wondered aloud.

Worf stood and stepped forward to stand with his captain. "Perhaps we are in a region between galaxies," he said.

"Negative," said Elfiki. "The gravimetric disturbances we're reading are from massive numbers of black holes, including a few that are bigger than any ever seen before." She tapped commands into her station's controls. A false-spectrum image was superimposed over the emptiness on the screen, so that violet-hued rings of various sizes could represent the black holes. "In addition to the singularities, we've detected enough mass to suggest that there are billions of very old stars in this galaxy."

Kadohata gestured at the black screen. "So where are they?"

Elfiki layered another computer-generated image over the first, this time stippling the view with brilliant points of light. "All around us," said the science officer. "The reason we can't see them is that they've all been shrouded."

Picard turned aft to face her. "Elaborate."

"If the nearest star is any indication," she said, "the shells are some kind of neutronium composite. I'm sorry I can't be more specific. The one shell within sensor range is proving resistant to most of our detection methods."

The captain glanced at Worf, as if to confirm that he wasn't the only one hearing Elfiki's report. Then he asked the young lieutenant, "What about planets?"

She shook her head. "So far, we aren't reading any. No nebulae or interstellar dust, either. It's like someone vacuumed up all the loose matter in this galaxy—and probably from a few neighboring galaxies—to make those shells."

Dread and awe both showed in Picard's eyes. "What is the purpose of these shells, Lieutenant? Energy? Concealment?"

"Maybe both," Elfiki said. "But I can't imagine what anyone would need that much power for."

"Some acquire power for its own sake," Worf said.

Faur swiveled away from the conn. "I hope they didn't do it to impress the neighbors, because it's a long way to the next galaxy," she said. "It's hard to be certain, but this could have been one of the first proto-galactic clusters. It might date all the way back to first light."

"Remarkable," Picard said, his voice reverentially hushed. "One of the universe's first galaxies, completely harnessed." He looked back at Elfiki. "Can you determine which galaxy this is, Lieutenant?"

She shook her head. "I'd doubt it, sir. Our records of the early proto-galaxies are based on redshifted images that date back nearly thirteen billion years. Comparing those images to this shrouded galaxy would be like using a baby picture to try and identify an old man wearing a bag over his head."

"Lieutenant Choudhury," Picard said. "Transmit a standard greeting hail, on all frequencies, and in all directions."

"Aye, sir," replied Choudhury.

Worf tensed as the security chief carried out Picard's order. It was difficult for Worf to suppress the urge to tell Choudhury to belay the captain's command, but he knew it would be wiser to reserve such a blunt tactic for a moment when it was more critically needed. Instead, he stepped closer to Picard and lowered his voice. "Sir . . . discretion might be a more prudent choice, in this situation."

Emulating the XO's muted tone, Picard replied, "What's your objection, Mister Worf?"

Before he could answer, Choudhury cut in to report, "No reply to our hails, Captain. Shall I try again?"

Taking note of Worf's clenched jaw and intense stare, Picard responded with a small shake of his head. "No, Lieutenant." He met Worf's glare and said, "This might be one of the oldest civilizations in the universe, Mister Worf. And it is the mission of the *Enterprise*—in times of both war and peace—to seek out new life-forms and attempt peaceful first contact."

"Perhaps," Worf said. "But imagine what kind of a people would wield technology like this in such a brute manner. Then ask yourself: Is this the kind of civilization whose attention we want to attract?" While the captain pondered that, Worf added, "In any case, our mission is to seek out the staging area for the Borg invasion. This is not it. For the safety of the ship, and the sake of the mission, I suggest we reopen the subspace tunnel and return home as soon as possible."

The captain looked unhappy. "Very well," he said. "Have the astrometrics teams continue their research until it's time to head back. There's no telling when a Starfleet vessel will get another opportunity like this one."

"Aye, sir," Worf said.

Picard wore a grim expression as he walked toward his ready room. "You have the bridge, Number One."

After the ready room door closed behind the captain, Worf settled into the command chair. He had just started reviewing the results of the ship's last combat-readiness drill when Lieutenant Elfiki stepped beside his chair. "I wonder why there was no answer to our hail," she said.

"There are many possibilities," Worf said.

Elfiki tilted her head and crossed her arms. "Well, yes. Maybe they don't listen to the frequencies we transmit. Or maybe they're unable or unwilling to respond."

"Or perhaps they are extinct," Worf said.

The science officer looked taken aback. "Would that make you *less* anxious about being here, sir?"

He looked at the great swath of blackness and imagined a hundred billion stars held captive inside dark metal spheres.

"No," he said. "It would not."

# 14

Deanna Troi had thought that having Erika Hernandez stand beside her while she addressed the Caeliar Quorum might be encouraging. Instead, as Troi had feared, Hernandez said nothing while Troi stood before the eerily hovering throng of the Quorum and faced off in a futile dialogue with the Caeliar's *tanwa-seynorral,* the officious Ordemo Nordal.

"All of your suggested resolutions have been proposed here before," Ordemo said, his stately voice resounding in the vast, crystal-walled, and pyramidal space of the Quorum chamber. "Interdicting our sector by means of your laws will only inflame others' curiosity and draw the attention of precisely the sorts of visitors we most wish to avoid.

"Altering your logs and even your memories would seem to be a viable tactic," he continued, "until one considers that certain immutable laws of physics would inevitably give the lie to our ruse, and your subsequent investigation would, in all probability, lead you and your ship directly back to us."

The throng of Caeliar that surrounded Troi on three sides murmured in low concurrence with Ordemo's statement.

Troi looked to Hernandez for some kind of cue as to how she ought to proceed, but Hernandez stood with her eyes averted, staring down at the fractal pattern that adorned the chamber's floor. Finding no help, Troi turned back toward Ordemo and waited for the Quorum's susurrus to abate. "Answer me this," she said to him. "If your people are so averse to contact with other species, why don't you just leave the Milky Way? There must be a few million galaxies quieter than this one."

"Indubitably," said Ordemo. "However, we have yet to find another that is blessed with the sheltering effects that this spiral formation takes for granted."

At a loss for understanding, Troi shrugged and raised her eyebrows. "Sheltering effects?"

Hernandez interjected, "He means the galactic barrier."

"Correct," Ordemo said. "We explored other galaxies as platforms from which we could continue the Great Work. However, all such efforts to establish ourselves met with resistance."

"By whom?" asked Troi. She couldn't name many species that would be capable of mounting significant resistance against a people as technologically advanced as the Caeliar.

Ordemo turned away to huddle with his colleagues. The teeming mass of Caeliar that was levitating several meters above the hall's floor filled the cavernous space with a muffled, low-frequency groaning and rapid clicking noises. Then the *tanwaseynorral* rotated back to face Troi and said, "We think it would be best to tell you only that, beyond the confines of this galaxy, there are many powers of varying degrees of malevolence. The only sanctuary we've found from their malicious interferences has been here, within the protective embrace of the galactic barrier."

Troi fought to hold the reins of her temper. "So what you're saying is, since you can't leave, neither can we?"

"Well," Ordemo said, slightly recoiling from her, "that's a crude reduction of an extremely complicated situ—"

"Yes," Hernandez interrupted. "What he's trying to say is yes. Whether you should think of it as 'You're stuck on this planet with them' or as 'They're stuck in this galaxy with all of us,' is entirely up to you."

A new, acute twinge of pain inside Troi's abdomen made her wince just a bit, and she did her best to conceal it by putting on an exaggerated frown. "Thanks for the translation," she said.

"My pleasure," Hernandez said, with a flicker of amusement.

Troi realized that Hernandez's mannerisms had become less stilted as she'd spent more time interacting with the members of *Titan*'s away team. *Maybe I'm looking for allies in the wrong places,* she speculated.

"Deanna," Ordemo said, "unless you have further proposals, we consider this discussion to be at an end."

"Fine," Troi said, concealing her irritation at being addressed with her given name by a being who had no right to affect such a degree of familiarity.

"Then, on behalf of this Quorum, I thank you for your input, and I hope that the rest of your residency in Axion, or on New Erigol, is pleasant and comfortable. You may go."

As Troi tensed in a prelude to a protest, Hernandez took Troi's shoulder in a gentle grip and steered her away from the Quorum and toward the circle in the chamber's center. "Trust me when I say they weren't giving you permission," she said. "They were giving you an order."

The two women stepped into the middle of the circle, which began its swift drop back to the entrance level of the pyramid. As the dark walls blurred past with just a hint of displaced air, Troi sighed. "You were right. They're very stubborn."

Troi's empathic senses felt Hernandez's aura of sympathy as she cracked a bittersweet smile. "I told you so."


Xin Ra-Havreii yawned. It had been twenty-four hours since Captain Riker had tasked him and Pazlar with finding a way to penetrate the Caeliar's cloak of secrecy; in that time, the chief engineer had stolen less than thirty minutes for a nap, sometime just after eating dinner.

He was certain that he was on the verge of a breakthrough. Somewhere in the flurry of subspace emissions and energy pulses, he knew there was a pattern. It was elusive, though. The harder he worked to pierce the clutter of noise to find the truth of the signal, the more chaotic everything seemed.

Worst of all, it was so close. *If only I could see it,* he fumed, rubbing the itch of exhaustion from his eyes. Then he scratched his bushy white eyebrows and massaged the dull ache from his temples.

A new bundle of data packets appeared on his lab's status display. It was a wealth of new sensor readings compiled and annotated with painstaking precision by Pazlar. *The answer's in this batch,* he told himself. *This time for sure.*

He had drained the last dregs of iced *raktajino* from his insulated mug and had started browsing through the new data when he was interrupted by the buzz of the door signal. "Come in," he said, too tired to mask his irritation.

The door opened, and Dr. Huilan waddled in. The diminutive S'ti'ach blinked his large, black eyes and presented himself as the very picture of innocence. "I hope I'm not interrupting."

"Actually, Counselor, I'm in the middle of working on a priority assignment for the captain," Ra-Havreii said.

Ambling closer, Huilan replied, "I'll be brief, then. I've come to talk to you about the holopresence system you built for Melora Pazlar."

Ra-Havreii turned away from Huilan, back toward his work, and asked in a dismissive tone, "What of it?"

"I'd like you to shut it off," Huilan said, sidling up behind the Efrosian. "Maybe even dismantle it."

A flash of temper spurred Ra-Havreii to pivot and loom angrily above his meter-tall visitor. "I'll do no such thing."

Huilan reacted defensively, raising the fearsome spikes that lined his blue-furred back. "There's no need to get upset, Commander," he said.

"Sorry," Ra-Havreii said, feeling self-conscious. He took a deep breath, smoothed his snowy, drooping mustache through the loop of his thumb and forefinger, and backed off half a step. "What's your objection to the holopresence module?"

The counselor's dorsal spines retracted gradually as he answered, "I'm concerned that it's serving as a new kind of crutch for her—and another crutch is the last thing she needs."

Shaking his head, Ra-Havreii said, "That's ridiculous. It's not a crutch at all. It's *freedom* from crutches."

"I see," Huilan said, easing forward, his large ears twitching with interest. "What was your reason for building it?"

The chief engineer recoiled from what he inferred was an impugning of his motives. "I designed it and created it to help Melora live more freely and more fully aboard *Titan*."

"I'm just curious, Commander. What part of interacting with holographic phantoms—or acting as one—is helping her live more fully? How is her life enriched by having her body weakened?"

Ra-Havreii held up his hands, palms facing Huilan. "Stop right there. What're you talking about?"

"Melora seems to think that your clever invention has absolved her of the need to brave the ship's one-gee spaces," Huilan said. "Instead, she's content to live and work in a centigee simulacrum of *Titan*. If she doesn't occasionally push herself to stay acclimatized, the physical abilities she worked so long to acquire will atrophy."

Getting angrier by the moment, Ra-Havreii shot back, "So what? When was the last time any of us one-gee natives tried to make ourselves function in a fifty-gee environment? Or even a ten-gee field? We can't adapt to that any more than she can adapt to our standard gravity, so why try?"

Huilan was quiet for a few seconds. "You may be right," he said. "But that still doesn't explain why you went to such absurd lengths to build a holopresence network inside *Titan*."

"I'm not seeing your point," Ra-Havreii said.

"There are easier ways to help Melora adapt to *Titan*'s environment," Huilan said. "All our shipboard gravity is artificial, so why not just program the graviton emitters to sense her combadge, or even her unique biosignature, and reduce the local gravity field wherever she goes?"

To keep from laughing, the chief engineer smiled. "That might seem like a good idea—until she and a regular-gravity crewmate step on the same deck plate at the same time, and the other person winds up embedded skull-first in the overhead. And may the spirits help her if the main computer gets overloaded or loses track of her—she'd be crushed under her own weight."

"All right," Huilan said. "I'm no engineer, but I'm sure you could equip Melora with a graviton-deflecting module for her uniform. You could make her immune to most of the ship's synthetic gravity without affecting anyone else. Right?"

As much as he wanted to dismiss Huilan's second idea, he had to think about it. Though it would be a tedious process to find exactly the right settings for such a device, it would be a fairly elegant solution to Pazlar's gravitational vulnerability. "That's not a bad idea," he admitted. "With the right adjustments, it might even let her move freely on a planet."

"Which brings me back to my earlier question," Huilan said. "Why did you build the holopresence system? I'll give you a hint: I don't think you really built it for her."

"Don't be absurd," Ra-Havreii replied. "Of course I did."

Huilan shrugged. "I don't doubt that you believe you did."

"If I didn't build it for Melora, then who is it for?"

"For yourself."

The chief engineer crossed his arms. "This I have to hear."

"I think the solution you concocted for her is just a proxy for your own issues," Huilan said. "I know that Efrosians are a very empathetic people—not in the telepathic sense, of course, but definitely in the emotional one. It makes you keenly aware of others' needs—but in this case, I think the need you're responding to is your own."

Ra-Havreii sighed. "Counselor, I have a lot of work to do, so if you're not going to get to the point—"

"Melora's vulnerability in the months after Tuvok assaulted her reminds you of your own emotional weak spots," Huilan said, his manner more aggressive than Ra-Havreii would have expected from such a small being. "So you tried to help her cope in much the same way that you do—by keeping personal interactions at a figurative distance, so they'll seem 'unreal.' You treat your emotional relationships like holograms—as purely superficial amusements—to shelter yourself from loss. To stay safe."

"You're half right about one detail," Ra-Havreii said. "I was trying to help Melora. Speaking of whom—when you came in, you said this was about her. So how did this conversation suddenly become about me?"

Huilan flashed an unnerving grin full of fangs. "Isn't everything all about you?"

"Well, yes—I can't fault your reasoning on that point," Ra-Havreii said, not too proud to accept the barbed compliment. "But tell me, do you counselors always try to make people feel bad about doing something good?"

"I'm just trying to help you understand your own motives," Huilan said. "You spent weeks building the holopresence system. Why did you go to so much effort for the benefit of one person? Why work so hard to reshape *Titan* just for her? What does it mean for you to make a gesture like that?"

Something about the question demanded a genuine answer and not just another flip remark. Ra-Havreii pondered it carefully, and then he said, "It makes this ship into something tangibly good that I've done for someone . . . instead of a reminder of a mistake I made that cost good people their lives."

"To be honest, Commander, I don't really fault you for what you've done here," Huilan said. "But I don't think you were trying to improve the ship—I think you were trying to improve yourself, and Melora's a big part of the reason why. All I want you to think about is whether, in the long run, the holopresence module is really the best thing for her—and whether you might both benefit from a life that's a little bit more . . . real."

Huilan walked away, leaving Ra-Havreii to mull over what the S'ti'ach had said.

*Have I made an illusion of my life? Did I just pretend to care about the women I've known?* The notion that his many and varied fleeting romances might all have been as emotionally sterile as a holodeck simulation troubled him—no, it *disgusted* him. And yet, he couldn't dispel it from his mind. In the passion of those moments, it all had seemed like harmless erotic fun, and he couldn't bring himself to regret any of it.

*But if Huilan's right,* he cautioned himself, *if I have been reducing romance to a superficial game to isolate myself, then Melora deserves better than that. She deserves something real.*

He began imagining all the ways he might express this revelation to Melora. Then his search for perfect words was interrupted as he stared blankly at a wall companel, across which raged the flood of data she had sent him.

In the moment he had stopped looking for it, he'd found a sudden flash of insight.

He saw the pattern.

"Ra-Havreii to Lieutenant Commander Pazlar," he said, putting aside his personal epiphany for a professional one. "Please report to my lab immediately. We have a breakthrough."

Most of *Titan*'s away team gathered around Christine Vale as they sat down in their common dining room to a late-morning breakfast, which had been provided to them by the Caeliar.

For the humanoid members of the team, the meal consisted of pancakes, fruits, nuts, and juice. Ensign Torvig's plate, however, was piled high with fresh greens, a variety of raw tubers, and a colorful assortment of wildflowers.

The one member of the team absent from breakfast was Dr. Ree. He had been granted special permission by the Caeliar for a visit to the planet's surface. There he was being allowed to hunt prey animals for his sustenance, because his biology couldn't be sustained by the vegetarian diet that the Caeliar insisted upon within the confines of their city.

Chief Dennisar and Lieutenant Sortollo wolfed down their tall stacks of hotcakes with gusto. Vale arranged her two pancakes and wedges of sliced fruit into something that pleased her eye. She nudged Tuvok. "Pass the syrup."

He handed her a small ceramic pitcher. She poured a small reservoir of the amber fluid into an open space she'd left at the edge of her plate. Then she cut off a small wedge of pancake with her fork, speared it, dipped it in the viscous liquid, and tasted it. It was more like a clover honey than a maple syrup, but it was pleasant enough.

Across from her, Deanna Troi picked at her breakfast without actually eating much of it. Vale asked, "How did your meeting with the Quorum go?"

"They're not interested in negotiating, if that's what you're asking," Troi said. A small, pained grimace played across her face as she broke eye contact with Vale, who made a mental note to have Ree give Troi a medical exam when he returned.

*Letting her die isn't worth it just for the right to say "I told you so,"* Vale mused.

"All right, we know they're listening to everything we say," Ranul Keru said. "And they're watching us every minute. So what's our game plan here?"

Vale swallowed another mouthful of syrup-drenched pancake. "Just like they taught us at the Academy," she said. "It's the Tanis scenario."

Keru shot her a look that made it clear he recognized the reference. The Tanis scenario was named for a plan that had used sabotage as a diversion to enable the theft or recovery of a vehicle for making a fast escape from hostile territory.

"Okay," he said. "Assume you're right. We're still stuck with a Pollux IV situation."

"True," Vale said, understanding that the security chief was talking about *Titan* being held by the Caeliar. "But Starfleet didn't gather laurel leaves then, and I don't think we ought to start now." *In other words, we're getting the hell out of here, no matter what it takes.*

Lieutenant Sortollo leaned forward, to look past Chief Dennisar at Vale. "Sir? Maybe we should hold off on making plans until we see if the captain has anything in the works."

"No," Vale said. "We have to assume we're on our own."

Ensign Torvig craned his long neck forward, mimicking Sortollo. "Erika Hernandez has lived with the Caeliar for a very long time," he said. "And we know she has some of their abilities. Maybe we should ask her for advice."

Tuvok replied, "That would be inadvisable. She seems to identify more readily with them than with us. For now, we should consider her an agent of the Caeliar."

"I disagree," Troi said firmly. "She's a prisoner like us, and I think we ought to reach out to her—for her sake, as well as our own."

Keru shook his head. "She may be a prisoner, Counselor, but she's *definitely* not like us. I have to concur with Tuvok—she's been compromised, and she can't be trusted."

"Agreed," Vale said. To Troi she added, "Leave Hernandez out of the loop. Until further notice, we need to stay focused on the Tanis scenario."

Another tiny wince at the corner of Troi's left eye made Vale suspect that a profound discomfort was continuing to plague the counselor. Vale wondered if anyone else at the table was noticing it. Then Troi set down her utensils on her plate, stood, and said to Vale, "Can I speak to you in private?"

"Of course," Vale said, pushing away her own plate and rising from her chair. As soon as Vale was on her feet, Troi was already walking away, out of the dining room and across their residence's great room, toward the terrace.

As she stepped outside and followed Troi to the far end of the broad balcony, Vale squinted against the bright morning sun and took a deep breath of the crisp, cool air.

*What a lovely day for an argument,* she mused, stepping with false confidence into Troi's harangue.

"You're being an idiot," Troi said. She had meant to take a more diplomatic tack with Vale, but the pain in her stomach had left her with a short fuse—which Vale had unwittingly ignited.

Vale continued smiling, but her narrowed eyes and furrowed brow belied her pleasant façade. "Care to rephrase that?"

Troi leaned with one hand on the terrace's low barrier wall and rested her other hand as casually as she could over her aching abdomen. "You're making a mistake, Chris."

"I'm doing my job, Deanna. If you don't approve, I'm willing to hear your objections, but once I've made my decision, the discussion's *over.*"

Irked by Vale's sudden display of authoritarian behavior, Troi couldn't help but frown. "You haven't spent any time with Hernandez, and neither have Tuvok or Keru. None of you know her, and none of you can sense her emotions the way I do. So why are you dismissing my opinion?"

"I can't speak for Keru or Tuvok," Vale said, "but I'm worried *your* judgment might be a bit impaired right now."

Pointing at her belly, Troi snapped, "Because of this?" Vale looked away, visibly discomfited. Troi pressed on. "If you think a few cramps are enough to wipe out twenty-six years of Starfleet experience and cloud my empathic senses, you're sorely mistaken, Commander."

"Cramps aren't the kind of pain that worry me, Deanna."

If there was a glib retort for that, Troi couldn't think of it. She paused, took a deep breath, and quelled her temper. "Let's not make this personal," she said. "We need to be careful what we do. The Caeliar's technology is extremely advanced. A mistake could have disastrous consequences for all of us. And it seems like a violation of Starfleet ethics to use force against a race of avowed pacifists."

Vale rolled her eyes. "They can call themselves pacifists if they like," she said. "But that doesn't change the fact that they're holding us, our ship, and Hernandez against our will. No matter how they try to excuse it, that's a hostile act, and one that merits a proportional response."

"The Caeliar make a compelling case for their right to protect their privacy and territory from outsiders," Troi said. "They believe they're acting in self-defense."

"So are we," Vale said, cutting off Troi's reply to add, "Not another word about this, Counselor. And don't talk to Hernandez or the Caeliar—that's an order."

A surge of resentment and anger left Troi feeling tense, as if her body wanted to defy her mind and lash out at Vale. She clenched her left hand into a fist behind her back. "Yes, sir."

The XO started to move back toward the residence, but then she turned around. "One more thing. If you're wondering whether I've noticed you're in pain, I have. As soon as Ree gets back from his morning hunt, you're getting a checkup."

Vale walked away as Troi protested, "I don't need one."

"It wasn't a request, Counselor."

Before Troi could reply, Vale went back inside.

Alone on the terrace, Troi watched sunlight shimmer across the titanium-white towers of Axion. The city was so beautiful but so cold—she couldn't imagine being confined to it for even one lifetime, never mind the hundreds of years that Hernandez had dwelled there. It would be enough to break anyone's spirit.

*I don't care what the others say,* Troi decided. *Erika's not the enemy. If we get a chance to escape, we have to at least try to bring her with us. She deserves a chance to go home, too.*


Will Riker entered the Deck 1 conference room. His eyes were bleary and his hair was slightly tousled. He was met by Commander Ra-Havreii and the holographic avatar of Lieutenant Commander Pazlar.

"It's three minutes past 0400," Riker said. "Why doesn't this crew ever make any progress during alpha shift?"

The chief engineer shrugged. "I wish I knew, Captain." Nodding to Pazlar, who turned and activated the wall companel, Ra-Havreii added, "But I think you'll forgive us this time."

"We'll see about that," Riker said, settling into his chair at the head of the table. "What have you got?"

Pazlar called up a screen of complicated and very colorful diagrams and equations. "The energy pulses we detected from the Caeliar's planet are soliton waves that have been tightly focused and amplified to a degree we never thought possible."

Ra-Havreii interrupted, "The soliton pulses, as we're calling them, tunnel through subspace."

"Drilling might be a better metaphor," Pazlar cut in.

The Efrosian nodded. "Quite right. They bore through the fabric of subspace much like a wormhole punches through normal space-time." The door slid open and a young, male Bolian yeoman entered. He moved toward the replicator as Ra-Havreii continued. "We believe that each tunnel is held open by a subharmonic resonance between the frequencies of its apertures."

Over the musical *whoosh* of the replicator, Pazlar said, "The same resonance also compresses the distance between the apertures by folding them toward one another across a subspatial curvature." She paused as the yeoman handed Riker a mug of piping hot *raktajino*. "We thought you might like to have a quick jolt before we got too deep into this," Pazlar said.

"I'd prefer a peppermint tea," Riker said. With speed, agility, and silence, the yeoman spirited away the mug and returned to the replicator.

"Despite the astronomical energy levels we've been reading, the tunnels being generated by the Caeliar are minuscule in diameter," Ra-Havreii said.

The replicator hummed again with activity as Pazlar said, "The passages would be barely large enough for a person to move through, so we know they aren't being used by the Borg fleet."

Accepting his mug of mint-flavored tea from the yeoman, Riker asked the engineer, "Then what are they for?"

Ra-Havreii raised his white eyebrows. "They're just large enough to transmit a compressed data stream."

Riker set down his tea without taking a sip. "A subspace crystal ball," he muttered.

"Exactly," the Efrosian replied. "A perfect espionage tool. Point it anywhere in the galaxy and see anything you want, in real time—and be all but undetectable while doing it."

"All right, I'm impressed," Riker said. He got up and stepped between Pazlar and Ra-Havreii to study their schematics on the companel. "Is there some way we can tap into this, see whatever it is the Caeliar are spying on?"

An anxious look from Pazlar drew a frown from Ra-Havreii, who said, "Maybe, but it won't be easy."

"It never is," Riker said.

Pazlar pointed out some details on the screen. "Tapping into the soliton pulse will mean matching its frequencies and resonance harmonics."

Ra-Havreii interjected, "The hard part is putting that much power into the sensors without blowing them to pieces. They're just not made for that. We'd have to rebuild the grid to handle the stress."

"And rewrite the software," Pazlar added. "If we don't, one feedback surge could cripple the ship—or worse."

Riker had heard enough caveats. "Yes or no," he said to Ra-Havreii. "Can we do it?"

The chief engineer shrugged. "In theory, yes."

"Then it's time to put the theory into practice," Riker said. "I want those soliton pulses tapped in twenty-four hours."

Pazlar threw a wide-eyed glance at Ra-Havreii, who looked at Riker and asked, "Do you care whether we blow up *Titan*?"

"I'd prefer we didn't."

"Then I'll need at least forty-eight hours. Sir."

He gave Ra-Havreii an encouraging slap on the shoulder. "Clock's ticking," he said. "Get started."

Vale stood behind Dr. Ree as he examined Troi with a medical tricorder. The counselor sat on the edge of the bed in her private room, and Ree was crouched in front of her. Beneath the tricorder's high-pitched whine, Vale heard the reptilian physician's rumbling growl of dissatisfaction.

"Forgive me, Counselor," he said. "The news is not good." The tricorder went silent as he switched it to standby mode. "Your body has rejected the targeted sythetase inhibitor," he said. "As a result, your fetus has resumed growing. This new scan suggests that it will rupture your uterine wall in less than forty-eight hours."

Troi leaned forward and planted her face in her palms. It was painful for Vale to watch her friend crumple under the weight of such a tragedy. She wanted very much to say something comforting, something not trite, but she couldn't think of anything. *It's not fair,* she lamented. *After all Deanna and Will went through, why did this have to happen to them?*

Ree reached forward, and with what looked like a surprisingly delicate touch, took Troi's hand. "Deanna," he said, his voice a deep whisper, like a breath through an oboe. "We need to operate, soon."

The counselor lifted her head, and Vale saw tears streaming from Troi's eyes. "No," she said to Ree. "Not here. Not yet. I'm not ready. . . . *Please.*"

The doctor turned his long head so that one side faced Vale. "Operating here would not be my choice, either," he said, revealing chunks of fresh red animal tissue caught between his fangs. "Not unless the Caeliar have a sterile facility."

"I'm sure they can make one if we ask," Vale said.

"No," Troi said. She continued with uncharacteristic ferocity, "I want to be with my *Imzadi* when it's time. We're doing this on *Titan.*"

Vale folded her arms and said, "Our hosts might have other plans, Deanna. And if you're counting on me to get you back to the ship, you're not leaving me much time to do it."

"Call this an incentive to work more quickly," Troi said.

A derisive noise—like a cross between a laugh and a cough—issued from Vale's throat. "No pressure," she said. "What about not ticking off the Caeliar?"

"To hell with them," Troi said, grimacing as she pulled her hand away from Ree and stood up. "I'm not ending this without Will, and I don't want him coming down here and winding up a prisoner." She walked with halting steps to her bedroom window and glowered at the sunny, pristine cityscape outside. "Get me home, Chris. Before it's too late."

Vale stepped past Ree on her way to the door. "Let me know if her condition changes."

"I will," Ree said with a dip of his scaly snout.

She contemplated the task ahead of her as she went in search of the rest of the away team. *I've got less than two days to outsmart an enemy that sees everything we do and hears every word we say. Two days to outmaneuver a foe that can be anywhere, lurking in thin air.* She shook her head. *Why do I get all the fun jobs?*

# 1574–2095

## 15

Sleep was the first casualty of Hernandez's former life.

After her rejuvenation, she had returned with Inyx to Axion. He'd left her at her residence while he went alone to face the censure of the Quorum. Daylight had faded, night had fallen, and she had waited for a tide of fatigue and exhaustion that never came. Then the sun rose again, and the previous day bled into the next. As did every day that followed.

Days lost their meaning for her. Light and darkness were no more than ephemeral conditions in what she quickly began to perceive as a steady continuity of experience. Time flowed as it ever had, but she no longer felt caught up in its currents. The past seemed deeper. The present was sharper. The future was closer at hand than it had ever been.

The second casualty of her humanity was her appetite.

"Your catoms manufacture your body's needs now," Inyx had explained one evening, while watching the sunset with her. "They fuel your cells and stabilize your neurochemistry. You will never hunger again."

She stared directly at the descending sun and was amazed to find that it wasn't painful. The fiery orb looked as bright as it ever had, but its fire was no longer blinding. "You haven't told me everything about my transformation, have you, Inyx?" Turning her head toward him, she asked, "What else can I do?"

"A great deal," he said. "But it would be best if you learned it in stages."

Gazing back at the orange blaze on the horizon, she smiled. "In other words," she said, "you're not going to tell me."

"No," Inyx said. "I'm not. Not yet."

Hernandez didn't mind waiting. She had time.

\* \* \*

As her routine became a rhythm, Hernandez expected she would eventually lose count of the number of sunrises and sunsets that she witnessed from the ramparts of Axion. Instead, she found that she could remember every one in exquisite detail. In fact, all her memories since the Change were clear and immediately at hand. She could compare them, contrast them, and replay them in her mind's theater without losing focus on the present moment.

On the occasion of her seven-hundred-eighty-first sunset since the Change, she emerged from a newly composed concert in the city's main amphitheater, looked to the horizon, and realized that the city was moving.

Reaching out with her thoughts, she located Inyx. He was on a widow's walk, on the edge of the city, facing in the direction of its movement. She summoned a quicksilver disk and sped over the boulevards and between the towers until she hovered above him. He glanced upward. "You're just in time," he said. "The sun's going down."

She lowered her disk to within a few meters of the widow's walk and stepped off. Envisioning herself as a feather, she drifted gently down to his side. The landscape blurred as it disappeared beneath the edge of the city, which raced westward in pursuit of the falling sun.

"We're on the move," she said. "Is there a reason?"

"I thought it was time," Inyx said.

The city gained altitude as it cruised toward a range of mountain peaks whose caps burned with the dying light of day.

Hernandez was silent while she admired the beauty of the passing moment. Then she asked, "Time for what?"

"For you to stop staring at the three-tree hill," he said.

Dusk smothered the shallow degrees of the sky. "A clean break, then," she said.

"A new horizon," Inyx said.

Darkness loomed over Axion and sparkled with stars—except for one widening strip of the sky, which was blank and black, as if someone had erased the heavens with malice aforethought. Hernandez sighed. "Fine," she said. "No more sunsets, then. From now on . . . all I want to see are sunrises."

"I think that sounds like an excellent idea," Inyx said.

\* \* \*

The city roamed New Erigol like a nomad. Hernandez and Inyx continued to time their meetings to coincide with the sunrise, which dimmed by slow degrees as the decades passed.

Over lush jungles and glaciated alpine slopes, above the deep deserts or the fathomless seas, every new dawn made Hernandez feel as she had at the moment of her rebirth, breaking free of the storm into the blue sky and sunlight. It reminded her to focus on beginnings instead of endings.

"Clear your mind and listen," Inyx said.

Hernandez closed her eyes. "I'll try."

"Focus," he said, guiding her through an exercise they had practiced many thousands of times since her Change. It had become part of their daily ritual, a catechism meant to improve her control over the gifts granted to her by the Caeliar. "You should hear the voices of the Quorum, guiding the gestalt."

She shook her head. "I'm sorry, I don't hear anything."

Inyx seemed to deflate, as usual, at her reported failure. "Perhaps it will take more time," he said. "I don't understand how you could master so many of the catom-based powers so quickly, yet not have a conscious link to the gestalt."

"Maybe it's because of a difference in our brain anatomy," Hernandez said. "Or it could be linked to the fact that you and your people are almost entirely synthetic, while I'm still mostly organic."

The Caeliar scientist sounded perplexed. "I thought I had compensated for those differences," he said. "It's possible, I suppose, that when the catoms altered your genetic structure, they shielded you from the gestalt in response to your own subconscious desire for privacy."

"Who knows?" She shrugged. "We can try again tomorrow."

"Yes," Inyx said. "These things don't always work right away. We should give it a little time."

The absurdity was almost too rich for her to bear. *A little time,* she mused. It had been 14,387 sunrises. Thirty-nine years, five months, and two days. *And he wants to give it more time.*

"Whatever you say," Hernandez replied. "You're back to the Great Work, now?"

Levitating from the widow's walk, Inyx replied, "Yes, it's time. Will you be continuing to work on your mural today?"

"As I do every day," Hernandez said.

"Until the next sunrise, then," Inyx said, conjuring a disk under his feet. It shot away, carrying him back toward the city.

Hernandez watched him go, and she kept her preternaturally keen eyes fixed on him until he vanished inside one of the platinum towers. Then she quieted her inner voice and opened her mind to the conversation that was all around her.

Brighter and clearer than the muddled rumble of the masses of Axion, the Quorum's debate was like a beacon. She picked out dozens of individual voices, including the *tanwa-seynorral* himself, Ordemo Nordal. It was a day of mundane details, as the tedium of the Great Work was engaged with unflagging attention and passion.

The numbers and details were difficult for her to follow; though she had learned the Caeliar's written language during her years working in the Star Chamber with Inyx, until the Change she had never had unfettered access to their native tongue. She suspected that she could translate it easily if she used her body's catoms to filter the discussion, but she worried that doing so would draw the attention of the gestalt.

She didn't know how long she could continue lying to Inyx, or how long she could keep this ability hidden from the gestalt at large or the Quorum in particular.

For the moment, however, it was her secret, and she intended to keep it that way.

No sooner had the sun crested the horizon than it was swallowed by the black edge of the planet's dome, which now encompassed more than fifty percent of New Erigol's sky.

"This is unacceptable," Hernandez said. "I won't live in the dark again, Inyx. I can't."

Her companion gazed to the horizon, arms folded in front of him. "You will not live in the dark, Erika. None of us will."

"How do you figure? Is that dome of yours going to turn invisible from the inside?"

"No," he said. "But we are taking steps to replicate the illumination and beneficial radiation effects of this planet's star, using a traveling artificial solar generator on the interior surface of the shell."

Hernandez deadpanned, "The sun will rotate around the

planet. How Ptolemaic of you." Looking back at the masked sky, she said, "How long until it's finished?"

"Soon," Inyx said, without elaborating.

By her own estimations—including information she had gleaned by eavesdropping periodically on the Quorum—the shells around New Erigol and its star would be complete in less than another thirty years. The Caeliar had dismantled scores of worlds, harvested entire Oort clouds and asteroid belts, and even stolen superdense strange matter from distant neutron stars to construct these monstrous cocoons. Whenever she looked at the one above New Erigol, she thought of it as the lid of a coffin, slamming shut forever above her head.

Even as she contemplated the possibilities of eternal youth, she found that the wonders of an endless galaxy still held less appeal for her than the dream of her long-lost home.

In the deep watches of the night, perched alone like a bird of prey atop the city's highest spire, Hernandez often dreamed of infiltrating the apparatus that the Caeliar employed for their Great Work, and using it to send a desperate SOS to Earth. Then she would remember that her dreams of escape and rescue were ultimately futile: there was no one on Earth who could hear her cry for help. On the world of her birth, the current year, according to the Gregorian calendar, was only 1645.

John Milton's "L'Allegro" was being published. The English Civil War was tearing Britain to pieces. The Black Death was spreading out of control in Europe. The great Japanese swordsman Miyamoto Musashi was soon to die in his sleep. Humanity was still two centuries away from harnessing electricity and nearly five hundred years shy of inventing subspace communications.

There was nothing she could do but wait and learn. And she vowed that when the time came to act, she would be ready.


By day the sky was the same. The sun wasn't real and hadn't been for centuries, but its light was just as bright and its heat as genuine. Hernandez understood only the slightest fraction of the holographic manipulations that the Caeliar had created to preserve the illusion of a distant star, so that none of the planet's delicate ecosystems would be disturbed.

In fact, the surface of New Erigol was safer than it had ever been. It was protected now from such hazards as asteroid impacts or bursts of cosmic radiation. Phenomena that would extinguish all life on an ordinary Minshara-class world posed no danger to New Erigol.

At night, however, the illusion was revealed. New Erigol had never had a moon, and now its nights were starless. When the last rays of the ersatz sun faded away, the planet's surface disappeared into an absolute, unnatural darkness. Its purity made Hernandez ache for the light's return, and when the horizon betrayed so much as the slightest hint of indigo, she made her way to whichever peripheral platform faced the dawn.

Violet bands crept from the edge of the sea, beginning their slow climb to the midheaven. In the ascending twilight, Hernandez sensed Inyx taking form beside her.

"I heard part of your opus in rehearsal last night," Inyx said. "It sounded quite stirring."

Hernandez frowned. "It needs more work," she said. "Your people have a lot of skill as musicians, but not much feeling. And my piece is all about evoking an emotional response."

"Are you trying to stir any emotions in particular?"

"Yes," she said. "Sorrow. And regret."

The sky brightened, and pastel colors bathed the misty streaks of cloud that raced past the city. Neither Inyx nor Hernandez had anything else to say that morning, and when the false orb of day breached the horizon, they parted ways.

She overheard enough conversations through the gestalt—after more than five centuries, she understood enough of the Caeliar's language to make sense of what she heard—to know that Inyx and his colleagues spent their time fine-tuning their new apparatus, which had been moved out of the city and ensconced in the protective shell high above the planet. Much of what she'd heard led her to believe that the machine was ready to resume the Great Work, yet the Caeliar seemed to be procrastinating. Hernandez wanted to ask Inyx why, but she knew there was no way she could pose the question without betraying her ability to eavesdrop on the Caeliar's communal dialogue.

Her own days since the Change had been spent in such artistic pursuits as painting murals, sculpting abstract stone forms, and composing instrumental music. Freed of the need for sleep or any sense of time's limitations, she learned through repetition or trial and error. She remained convinced that she possessed no natural talent for any of her hobbies, but she now had more than five hundred years of experience and skill, which masked her dearth of true inspiration.

Being able to shape molecules and tint pigments by thought alone also made it a bit easier to master the fundamentals of her visual endeavors.

Music, on the other hand—she couldn't force it or coax it into doing her bidding. Drawing the melodies from her mind was like hunting an elusive prey in the dark. It was the single most difficult thing she had ever tried to learn, and her obsession with it was a welcome distraction from her fixation on the slow machinations of the universe.

Centuries had passed while she was searching for the elegiac tune that she felt inside herself every time she closed her eyes. When she tried to hum it, her voice broke or veered off-key. Trying to produce it on a range of instruments created by the Caeliar had proved equally fruitless. The song was locked inside some vault she didn't know how to open.

Another in an endless string of daybreaks brought her back to a place she hadn't visited since before the Change. At the end of the long rectangular pool of jet-black water, the dead tree stood atop its dusty isle. Gnarled and blackened, it had a peculiar shine to it. Hernandez drew close to it and saw that its bark had the glossy sheen of stone. It had been petrified.

*A dead relic, preserved forever. Just like me.*

With her hand pressed against cold stone where life had once flourished, she felt a deepening grief. The tree would stand here, unchanging but unfeeling, impenetrable but isolated, unbowed but alone. *Once I might have cried,* she realized. *Now I don't know if I remember how.*

The glassy bark felt like ice, and she recalled the fates of traitors in Dante's *Inferno.* Those found guilty of betrayal weren't condemned to an eternity of fire and brimstone; they were cast down to Hell's lowest level, the Ninth Circle, and sealed into Cocytus, a frozen lake where all human feelings and memory died. The few who cried went blind as their tears froze and sealed their eyes shut forever.

Hernandez wanted to weep, but she didn't dare. She had lost

the way to her grief, and she was certain that the only way to find it again was to return home.

It would be another seventy-three years before she caught up to her own history. Then time's shape would no longer be in jeopardy, and she would feel free to plan whatever rebellion she could manage.

Seventy-three years. A few grains of sand through the neck of the glass. A blink in the stare of eternity.

She could wait.

She had time.

# 2381

## 16

Tuvok worked quickly, manipulating the tricorder's settings into a decidedly nonstandard configuration. There was little time to spare; Ensign Torvig was waiting for his signal, and it was imperative that they act before the Caeliar realized what was happening. He heard the shallow breathing of Lieutenant Sortollo and Chief Dennisar, who stood behind him keeping watch for any sign of the Caeliar or Erika Hernandez.

Keeping the plan a secret from the ever-attentive Caeliar had demanded a personal sacrifice on Tuvok's part. He had mind-melded with Commander Vale to devise the plan, and then with Lieutenant Commander Keru to refine its details.

Vale's mind had been a tumult of contradictory impulses. Despite her professional demeanor, Tuvok now understood that she was driven by powerful inner conflicts. Keru's psyche, on the other hand, was remarkably disciplined and focused. Tuvok was duly impressed at the Trill man's emotional equanimity, given the tragedies of his past.

*Remain focused,* Tuvok reminded himself. *Timing is critical.*

Their captors had confiscated the away team's weapons but allowed its members to retain their tricorders, on the condition that they not be used against the Caeliar. The *Titan* personnel were about to violate the letter and spirit of that agreement. Tuvok had made a detailed analysis of the structure and composition of a helically twisted tower of smoky glass and immaculate titanium, half a kilometer from his position, on the far side of an open and unoccupied plaza.

He evaluated the results of a rudimentary simulation he had just conducted, and he judged it adequate for his purpose. A tap of his thumb sent an encrypted signal to Keru's tricorder, several kilometers away. A moment later he received Keru's confirmation. The second team was in position and ready to proceed. From his tricorder, he transmitted a hypersonic oscillation that was calibrated specifically to induce a resonance wave inside the spiral-shaped tower, which would then amplify it by several orders of magnitude.

It would take a few seconds to build up to full power. While he waited, Tuvok appreciated a breath of warm, dry air and admired the powerful heat of the sun, high overhead. The city of Axion was cruising over a stretch of deep desert, and for a moment it made Tuvok nostalgic for the serenity of his home on Vulcan. Then a shiver traveled through the ground under his feet, and he heard a growing buzz of quaking metal and glass.

Watching the reflections of the cityscape quiver on the disturbed glass of the spiral tower, Tuvok tapped his combadge. "Tuvok to Ensign Torvig. Acknowledge, please."

*"Torvig here, sir. Go ahead."*

The buzzing became a bright, metallic ringing. Then it turned to thunder, and every pane of dark-gray crystal on the tower exploded outward, pelting its neighboring buildings and the plaza below with jagged shards of glassy shrapnel.

"Proceed," Tuvok said.

Torvig had known his part of the away team's escape plan for exactly sixty seconds. His friend, Lieutenant Commander Keru, had revealed it when he'd tapped Torvig's flank, offered him a tricorder, and said, "Hey, Vig. Take a look at this."

On the tricorder's screen was a miniaturized replica of the operations control panel of the shuttlecraft *Mance*. Somehow, Keru had reprogrammed the handheld device into a remote control for the shuttlecraft's command systems. The small vessel's one-person emergency transporter had been powered up and readied for a beam-up sequence, and it was targeted on Keru himself.

"Not until it's time," Keru said.

The young Choblik engineer clutched the tricorder in both bionic hands as he looked up at the burly Trill. "How will I know when it's time?"

"You'll know," said Keru.

They stood together atop a rampart at the city's edge, directly across the hundred meters of empty space separating them from the *Mance* and its platform, which were being towed on an invisible tether behind Axion. Dunes the color of nutmeg and cinnamon stretched across the landscape to the horizon in every direction. Torvig saw no vegetation or animals in the parched land; if not for the dull roar of hot, moving air, there would have been only the silence of a wasteland.

Then came a voice, tinny from being filtered through his combadge: *"Tuvok to Ensign Torvig. Acknowledge, please."*

"Torvig here, sir. Go ahead."

A distant *boom* echoed through the metallic canyons of Axion, and Torvig hoped that it was part of the plan and not a sign that something had just gone terribly wrong.

*"Proceed,"* Tuvok said, and Keru nodded in confirmation.

Torvig initiated the transporter's dematerialization sequence. A mellifluous drone filled the air. Keru was enveloped in a cocoon of shimmering particles. In seconds, the Trill officer was gone from sight. According to the tricorder, he had rematerialized safely aboard the *Mance*.

Then all that Torvig could do was turn off the tricorder and wait to see what the next step of the plan was.

Keru had called it a stupid plan from the beginning, but it was the only real option available to them, and risking their lives on a desperate scheme had seemed preferable to surrendering.

As soon as the transporter's confinement beam released him, he bounded off the lone pad and sprinted to the cockpit. The air inside the shuttlecraft was stuffy from having been sealed off for more than two days. He planted himself in the commander's seat, next to the pilot's station, and powered up the craft's sensors and communications suite.

His first task was to verify their position, relative to the gap in the planet's shell through which they had entered. Then he checked to see if the passageway was still open. It wasn't. He began a sensor sweep of the observable surface of the shell, looking for another egress point. There were none.

*So much for flying out,* he grumped in silence. *Can't get a signal out, either. Time to explore tactical options.* He reached forward to raise the shuttlecraft's shields—and every console in the ship went dark. His shoulders slumped. *That's not good.*

A tingling sensation raised the fine hairs on the nape of his neck. The darkened companels reflected a magenta glow that was emanating from behind him. Keru swiveled his chair to see Inyx hunched over, his tall form awkwardly confined in the tight quarters of the *Mance*. "Fancy meeting you here," Keru quipped.

"I must confess, I'm impressed by the versatility of your equipment," Inyx said. "It's a vast improvement over that of your recent predecessors." He paused, apparently expecting a reply, which Keru didn't give him. "I have to take you back, Ranul." He opened the shuttlecraft's side hatch with a wave of his arm and motioned for Keru to step out.

Keru walked to the open hatchway and looked out at the silver disk waiting at the end of its extended ramp. "I feel like I'm walking the plank," he said. He looked at the doubled-over Caeliar, and said, "After you."

"Gladly," Inyx said, squeezing his gangly limbs through the exit. As soon as he was over the threshold, he straightened to his full height and seemed to be a great deal more relaxed. He walked onto the silver disk and beckoned Keru forward. "Your chariot awaits," he said.

Stepping down the ramp, Keru said with guarded interest, "Did Erika teach you that phrase?"

Inyx seemed immediately self-conscious. "Yes, she did," he replied. "Did I use it correctly?"

"Yup," Keru said, wondering just how close Hernandez's bond with Inyx really was. He boarded the disk and moved behind Inyx. "I suppose we're all facing some kind of punishment now."

"No," Inyx said. "A degree of rebellion is expected. In time, you will grow out of such behavior—as Erika did."

Troi felt as if a balloon filled with acid had just burst inside her stomach. Hot bile was being pushed up her throat, the pressure in her head was dizzying, and a rush of fever alternated with waves of chilling cold. Determined to hide her symptoms, she steadied herself with one hand on the terrace railing and funneled all her pain into a steely glare at Hernandez. "This is unacceptable, Erika."

"It's done," Hernandez said. "Inyx warned you not to use your scanners for hostile action, but you did anyway."

Another bloom of toxic pain stirred inside Troi's belly, and she turned her grimace of pain into a scowl. "We need those tricorders," she said, "and you disintegrated them."

"I did no such thing," Hernandez said.

"Fine," Troi replied. "The Caeliar destroyed them."

Hernandez nodded. "Yes, in self-defense."

"But they destroyed the medical tricorder," Troi said.

"If you require medical attention, the Caeliar are fully equipped to provide—"

"We don't want their help," Troi snapped. For a moment, her anger was stronger than her pain, and it felt good.

Her remark seemed to provoke a melancholy reaction from Hernandez, who looked away from Troi, out past the cityscape to the desolate beauty of a violet sunset over desert canyons. In a soft voice, she said, "I used to feel as you do. My first officer was especially vocal on the subject. She used to tell me that accepting the Caeliar's help was like sanctioning what they did to us. And maybe she was right. There have been times when I feel like I betrayed her by letting the Caeliar change me. But it's not as if the Caeliar forced any of this on anyone. No one made us visit their homeworlds. It's just bad luck we invaded their privacy, that's all." With a sad smile, she looked at Troi. "They're not evil, Deanna. They just want to help."

Troi felt the sincerity of Hernandez's words. She didn't have to ask if Hernandez believed what she said; it was obvious that she did. "You identify with them, don't you?"

That caught Hernandez off guard. "What? No, of course not."

"It's perfectly understandable, Erika," Troi said, affecting her most sympathetic tone. "In a situation such as yours, it's a normal defense response to seek an emotional connection with the most powerful figure, for protection. It's what infants do naturally."

Looking offended, Hernandez replied, "I'm not an infant."

"No, you're a prisoner," Troi said. "And you wouldn't be the first person to succumb to Stockholm syndrome. Is that why you gave up trying to escape, or to contact Earth?"

Hernandez turned sullen. "I gave up because there's no way out. You can't outsmart them. They're always a step ahead."

"Really? Even with your abilities?" Noting the apprehensive glance her question provoked, Troi continued, "I know you were at a disadvantage facing them alone, first without powers, and then without your ship. But we have a ship in orbit, and our technology's come a long way since your time."

Shaking her head, Hernandez mumbled, "It won't be enough."

"How do you know until you try?" She grabbed Hernandez's sleeve and made her turn to face her. "You've been slapped down so many times by the Caeliar that you've gotten used to defeat."

The look on the other woman's face became one of pity. "It'll happen to you, too. It's just a matter of time."

"Time is what we don't have, Erika. Earth is in grave danger, and so are hundreds of other worlds."

At the mention of Earth, Troi sensed a profound surge of emotion from Hernandez, who replied, "In danger? From what?"

"Something worse than I can describe. We came here because we thought it might help us save Earth. Now we have to escape for exactly the same reason." Watching doubt and hope struggle against each other in Hernandez's eyes, Troi added, "If you won't take a risk to help us, take one to help Earth."

Conflicting emotions played across Hernandez's face, and for a moment Troi thought that she might have reignited some dormant spark of fighting spirit in the youthful-looking woman. Then Hernandez levitated up and over the terrace's railing. "I need to think," she said, drifting down and away.

"Earth needs you," Troi replied.

Hernandez was silent as she descended into the gathering darkness. As she vanished into the shadows, Christine Vale stepped out onto the terrace with Troi and peeked over the railing. "Nice try," she said to Troi. "But I don't think we can count on her."

"Maybe not," Troi said. "But I get the feeling we shouldn't count her out, either."

# 17

Dax watched the blurred rings of light on the main viewer as the *Aventine* neared the end of its tenth journey through a subspace tunnel in forty-eight hours.

After unlocking several subspatial apertures each, the crews of the *Aventine* and the *Enterprise* had detected patterns that helped accelerate the decoding process. At their current rate, Dax figured, they were less than half a day from finding the Borg's staging area and launching the allied counterattack.

From the conn, Ensign Erin Constantino called out, "Clearing aperture twenty-one alpha in three . . . two . . . one."

A slight lurch accompanied the ship's return to the Azure Nebula. As a flicker of electrical discharge lit up the roiling blue cloud, Dax saw the shadows of many starships, most of them holding position in tight formations. A few cruised in patrol patterns behind opaque swells of dense, semiliquid gases.

Bowers said, "Lieutenant Nak, report."

Gaff chim Nak, the beta-shift operations officer, reviewed a cascade of data on his console and replied, "All systems nominal, sir." A signal beeped on the Tellarite's panel, and he silenced it with a tap. "*Enterprise* is hailing us."

"On-screen," Dax said.

Nak patched in the signal, and the image of the nebula was replaced by the aquiline visage of Captain Picard, on the bridge of the *Enterprise*. "*Welcome back,*" he said. "*Any luck?*"

"Negative," Dax said. "Passage twenty-one leads to the intergalactic void, roughly nine hundred eighty-two thousand light-years from NGC 5078." She added, "I see we have a few more friends than when I left."

"*Yes,*" Picard said. "*Unfortunately, this group of vessels represents the last of Starfleet's battle forces in this sector. Everything else is being held back to defend the core systems.*"

Dax frowned. "It'll have to do. How long until the Cardassian fleet arrives?"

"*Twelve hours,*" Picard said.

"Time enough to run a few more sorties," Dax said.

Picard nodded. "*Perhaps more. If we go through together, our computers can share the work of unlocking the return aperture and reduce our round-trip time by a third.*"

She signaled her approval with a smile. "Sounds like a plan, Captain." Pointing upward, she added in jest, "Will our reinforcements be able to hold the line with both of us gone?"

"*There are only three hundred forty-two ships here, but I think they'll muddle through.*" His serious demeanor returned. "*In fact, I've ordered five pairs of ships to help us open and scout the remaining passageways. We're also taking additional precautions: We've sent all our data about the subspace tunnels, and*" *what we found on our scouting runs, to Starfleet Command and the Klingon High Command."*

Her eyes widened with surprise. "The Klingon High Command?"

*"President Bacco's orders,"* Picard said. *"We've also been directed to share all Borg-related tactical data with the Klingon Defense Force."*

"Understood," Dax said. She looked to Bowers, who nodded and moved off to delegate the necessary tasks. "We'll start transmitting our logs now. As soon as we're done, we'll be ready for the next jaunt."

Picard replied, *"We've already unlocked aperture twenty-two alpha. Enterprise is standing by to proceed, on your signal."*

"Acknowledged," Dax said. *"Aventine* out."

Nak cut the channel, restoring the nebula to the main viewer. Klingon and Romulan battle cruisers moved in and out of the turbulent sapphire mists, like predators of the deep circling before the kill.

Bowers returned to his chair and sat beside Dax. He muffled a quiet chortle and shook his head as he looked at his feet.

Dax had seen that reaction from him before, and she knew that it wasn't good. "Something wrong, Sam?"

"Twenty-one passages checked, six to go," he said. "It reminds me of a famous Earth game."

Eyebrows lifted with curiosity, she asked, "Hide-and-seek?"

"No. Russian roulette."

The trip through subspace passage twenty-two was shorter than Captain Picard had expected, but only because its end came with no warning. Instead of the circle of darkness that he and his crew had seen on their previous jaunts, this time there was only light—followed by the deafening thunder of impact.

"Shields collapsing!" declared Choudhury, whose hands moved quickly over the security companel. "Hull temperature forty-two hundred Kelvin and rising fast!"

Kadohata raced to orient herself at ops. "We're caught in a plasma stream, between a binary pair!"

Picard shouted over the wail of the alert klaxon, "Helm! Full impulse! Move us clear!"

Lieutenant Faur answered, "Full impulse! Aye, sir!" The engines whined and groaned as the *Enterprise* struggled to break free of the stellar inferno. Explosions rocked the ship.

"Hull breaches, Decks Five through Eight and Twenty-one through Twenty-four," Kadohata called out as the overhead lights stuttered and failed. She cringed and ducked as the starboard auxiliary stations erupted and shot sparks across the bridge. "We're losing main power."

"Clearing the stream in six seconds," Faur reported.

Worf threw a look at Choudhury. "Position of the *Aventine*?"

"Bearing one-nine-seven mark twelve," the security chief replied. "Following us out at full impulse."

The white-hot blaze on the main viewer faded to yellow, then dimmed through shades of orange and red before yielding to the star-flecked blackness of space. As the ship made a slow turn, Picard saw the crimson glow of a red-giant star, from which a blazing river of coronal mass was being torn by its black-hole companion. "We're clear," Faur said, "but the conn's sluggish because of interference from the singularity."

"Weapons are offline," Choudhury said. "Overloads in the tactical power grid."

La Forge's voice crackled from the overhead comm. *"Engineering to bridge."*

"Go ahead," said Picard.

*"Captain, we've got a lot of damage down here. I need to take warp power and the main impulse reactor offline, now."*

Worf cut in, "For how long?"

*"I don't know,"* La Forge said. *"But if we don't shut them down now, we'll have a containment failure in sixty seconds."*

"Do what you have to, Mister La Forge," Picard said. "Make a full report as soon as you can."

*"Aye, Captain. Engineering out."*

Faur swiveled her chair to face aft, toward Picard and Worf. "Position verified, Captain. We're on the outer rim of the Carina Arm, near the meridian of the Delta and Gamma Quadrants."

Kadohata turned her chair aft, as well. "No sign of Borg vessels within sensor range," she said.

"That could change," Picard said. He suspected she might be mistaken, because he heard the voice of the Collective, and it was getting louder and drawing closer with every moment. "We need to remain alert," he added, "given our present condition."

On the main viewer, he saw the scorched and scarred hull of the *Aventine,* and he wondered whether his own ship looked as distressed. "Commander Kadohata, hail the *Aventine.*"

"Aye, sir," Kadohata said. She and Faur turned their chairs forward and resumed work. "I have Captain Dax for you, sir."

"On-screen," Picard said.

Dax and Bowers appeared on the main viewer, wreathed in gray smoke and backed by a bulkhead of smoldering, sparking companels. *"I think we took a wrong turn somewhere,"* Dax said.

"What's your status, Captain?"

*"Shields are fried, main power's down, and we've got some major hull damage,"* she said. *"A dozen of my crew are seriously injured, but no fatalities."*

Worf handed Picard a padd showing the casualty report from sickbay. Picard blinked, and suddenly his vision was bathed in sickly green light and muddy black shadows.

The conversation between Worf and Ezri was continuing in front of him, but he could barely hear it. It was like trying to eavesdrop from underwater. His ears were filled with the roar of the Collective, and its sinister palette had tainted every facet of his perception, from the taste of tin on his lips to the sharp odor of chemical lubricants in his nose and the clammy sweat on the back of his neck.

Marshaling his senses into revolt was a single word.

*Locutus.*

He heard it being whispered beneath the raging tide of the Collective, and he knew the speaker's voice even by intimation. It was *her*—the Borg Queen. She was aware of his presence, he was certain of it. He concentrated on blocking her out. It took all his willpower to restore the sanctity of his thoughts.

Then Picard snapped back into the conversation with Captain Dax, and he became aware that Worf—and everyone else on the bridge of the *Enterprise*—was staring at him. Worf regarded Picard with an attentive gaze that made it clear Picard had been asked a question which deserved a response. Rather than ask for the query to be repeated, Picard volleyed the request to his XO in an interrogative tone. "Mister Worf?"

Worf said, "I concur with Captain Dax's recommendation, sir. Modifying the shields would be a prudent step."

"Very well," Picard said. "Make it so."

"Aye, sir," Worf replied, delegating the job with a look and a nod to Kadohata. To Dax, he added, "These repairs will take time. We should use it to start looking for the frequency to re-open the subspace tunnel."

*"Already on it,"* Dax said. *"Tell Clipet and Elfiki they're free to jump in anytime."*

"Understood," Worf said. *"Enterprise* out." The screen switched back to the placid vista of stars.

Picard stood and nodded to Worf. "You have the bridge."

As he retired to his ready room, Picard was relieved to be able to seek some privacy while Worf managed the business of directing the ship's repairs. Alone with his thoughts, however, Picard fell to brooding. The Borg Queen's voice haunted him.

*You should not have come looking for me, Locutus,* she taunted with cold menace. *I'll be with you soon enough.*

He put on his bravest face and whispered with false courage, "I killed you once. I look forward to doing it again."

*Bravado doesn't suit you, Locutus,* she replied. *And you know as well as I do that the next time we meet, it won't be my neck that gets snapped.* She pulled her thoughts away from him. *Soon, Locutus, soon. Until then . . . dream of my embrace.*

Terrible events were in motion; Picard felt it.

A shadow had gathered. Its hour was at hand.

*"Shields are fried, main power's down, and we've got some major hull damage,"* Captain Dax said. *"A dozen of my crew are seriously injured, but no fatalities."*

As Worf handed a padd to Captain Picard, he saw the captain blink and take on a blank, anxious stare. In a glance, Worf realized that Captain Picard had become mired in one of the dark fugues inflicted on him by the Borg.

Raising his voice to draw attention to himself, Worf said to Dax, "The *Enterprise* has sustained similar damage and casualties." He looked toward ops. "Commander, recommendations?"

Kadohata looked up and said, "We have to focus on repairing our shields—we can't get back without them."

Nodding, Dax said, *"My science officer suggests we modify our metaphasic shielding protocols, to compensate for the relativistic properties of the plasma jet."*

"Sounds reasonable," Kadohata said. She looked up at Picard. "With your permission, Captain?"

Worf froze as he waited to see if the captain would react. Kadohata's query had turned everyone's eyes to the captain, and if it became apparent that he had been distracted, it might undermine the crew's already damaged morale.

Picard blinked, and Worf noted a spark of alarmed recognition in the captain's eyes as he saw that he'd become the center of attention. As if reaching for a lifeline, the captain looked toward him and said, "Mister Worf?"

Instinctively covering the captain's momentary lapse, Worf replied, "I concur with Captain Dax's recommendation, sir. Modifying the shields would be a prudent step."

"Very well," Picard said. "Make it so."

Worf divided his focus between the continuing conversation with Captain Dax, directing the *Enterprise*'s bridge officers, and keeping a discreet watch on Captain Picard's reactions. As soon as Worf had concluded the conversation with Dax, Captain Picard stood, said, "You have the bridge," and excused himself to his ready room, leaving Worf in command.

Coordinating damage-control teams was a task Worf normally found tedious. Tonight he felt that a profound urgency was driving the *Enterprise* crew to speed its repairs for the return journey to the Azure Nebula. He knew the crew was talking about Picard. "If he's hearing the Borg, they must be close," he overheard contact specialist Lieutenant T'Ryssa Chen whisper to relief tactical officer Ensign Aneta Šmrhová.

The focus and intensity of the repair efforts felt almost like a battle to Worf, whose chief role was to set priorities for the various departments. The sciences division was devoting its time and resources to unlocking aperture twenty-two beta for the trip home. Engineering had been instructed to restore shields first, warp drive second, and weapons last. The medical group had been directed to send out roving teams of medics and nurses to perform first aid on personnel who were too busy—and too vital—to be sent to sickbay for minor injuries.

He was about to forward the latest status reports to Captain Picard in the ready room, when a silent communiqué appeared on the command panel next to his chair. It was a message from Lieutenant Choudhury at tactical, summoning him and

Commander Kadohata to the tactical station, where Choudhury huddled with Ensign Šmrhová.

Kadohata looked up from her work at ops and glanced back at Worf, who stood and motioned with a subtle, sideways nod of his head for her to follow him to tactical. She got up and walked aft to join him, Choudhury, and Šmrhová.

Choudhury pointed at the tactical display. "Šmrhová picked up multiple signals on long-range sensors," she said. "They're on an intercept course, at warp nine-point-nine-seven."

Worf anticipated the worst. "Borg?"

Šmrhová replied with a mild Slavic accent, "No, sir. Hirogen." The pale, dark-haired woman tapped the screen and called up a dense page of data. "Based on the energy signatures, it's an unusually large hunting pack—ten ships."

"Pretty far from their home territory," Kadohata said.

"They could be renegades," Choudhury said. "Or they might just be more adventurous than other Hirogen."

Cutting off further speculation, Worf said, "The reason for their presence is not important. What matters is the danger they pose to us and the *Aventine*." He asked Choudhury, "What is the hunting pack's ETA?"

"One hour and fifty-three minutes," she said.

Nodding, Worf continued, "Then we have just less than that to complete our repairs and make the return jaunt. The Hirogen must not learn about the subspace tunnels."

Kadohata asked, "Won't the plasma jet from the binary pair mask our exit?"

Choudhury replied, "Yes, as long as the Hirogen aren't within weapons range. But if they get that close, their sensors could pierce the interference and detect our frequency for opening the tunnels. Then they'd have a free pass to bring their hunt to Federation space whenever they want."

"Not today," Worf said. "Commander Kadohata, tell Mister La Forge that his priorities have changed: shields first, weapons second, warp drive last. Ensign Šmrhová, begin combat drills as soon as we have weapons back online. Lieutenant Choudhury, tell your people to prepare to repel boarders. I'll notify the captain and alert the *Aventine*."

The three female officers acknowledged his orders with curt nods and stepped away to start preparing for battle. He returned to his chair and opened a comm to the ready room. "Captain Picard, please report to the bridge."

*"On my way,"* the captain replied. *"Picard out."*

Worf had never fought the Hirogen, though he had read of their ferocity, prowess, and strength. As the first officer of the *Enterprise,* he hoped that his ship and the *Aventine* escaped before the battle was joined. But as a Klingon warrior, his heart swelled with anticipation.

The Borg were a plague, an infestation to be stamped out from a distance. A Hirogen hunter, on the other hand—that was a foe he had often tested himself against on the holodeck. Even there, they were formidable; in fact, he had yet to defeat one.

*There is a first time for everything,* he mused darkly.

# 2168–2381

## 18

An eerie silence pervaded Axion. It was sunset, and the city had halted its aimless wanderings of the sky. Hernandez felt the change in the air as the shield was raised, quelling the wind. From her favorite vantage point, clinging to a spire high above the towers of the Caeliar's last metropolis, she saw the city's denizens turn out en masse into the boulevards and amphitheaters.

Hernandez had never seen them do anything like this before. Opening her mind to the gestalt, she listened for its voice. It, too, was silent. Then she reached out with her senses and found Inyx among a throng gathered in a great plaza. She let go of the spire and floated down, hundreds of meters, guiding herself between the buildings, by what had come to feel like instinct.

Her feet touched the ground, bringing her to a stop at Inyx's side. He and the thousands of other Caeliar in the plaza gazed skyward, all looking in the same direction. There was something reverential about their united attention, and through the gestalt she felt an overwhelming collective sorrow.

All at once, the spell was broken, and the crowd began to disperse in seemingly random directions. Hernandez took Inyx's arm to prevent him from leaving. "What just happened?"

"We observed the moment of the Cataclysm," he said.

It took her a moment to grasp his meaning. "The destruction of Erigol?" she asked.

"Yes," Inyx said. "It just happened, moments ago."

After drifting like a ghost through centuries, fearful of causing the slightest disruption to the timeline, Hernandez was surprised to find herself feeling so rooted in the present moment. It was December 23, 2168. Erigol had just exploded. Her ship had just been destroyed. And her earlier self had just been flung six hundred fifty years into the past. Now she and Axion had come full circle, back to the present, and once again were forging ahead through time's uncharted waters. It was the end of history and the beginning of the future.

She let go of Inyx's arm. "What happens now?"

"The Great Work goes on," he said. "As it always has."

He began rising from the ground, en route to one of his arcane tasks, whose details he rarely shared with Hernandez. Not content to let him escape from her so easily, she willed herself into the air alongside him, the catoms in her body and the air drawing power from Axion's quantum field to free her from the hold of mere gravity. "If we're past the Cataclysm, then we no longer pose a danger to the timeline, do we?"

"No," Inyx said. "All is as it was."

"Then there's no harm in letting me see what happened to Earth during the years I was out of contact."

Inyx's reply sounded both cautious and dubious. "Are you certain you want to know?"

"Why wouldn't I?" she asked, as they drifted toward the great dome that shielded the Apparatus.

He replied, "What is the boon of wisdom when it brings no solace to the wise, Erika?" He looked at her, and perhaps noting her confused expression, added, "If your people have suffered, you'll feel guilty that you didn't share their misfortunes. If they've thrived, you'll feel cheated out of your portion of their happiness. Would it not be better to make a clean break from the past and embrace the future you've chosen?"

She halted herself in midair and let him continue alone. Watching him grow smaller against the massive bulk of the dark crystal dome, she kept her bitter rumination to herself.

*I didn't choose my future. It chose me.*


It was like sensing heat or a chill—Hernandez knew the airborne catoms in her vicinity were dormant. There were no Caeliar minds lurking unseen in the shadows. Though she lacked their ability to transmit herself from one cluster of molecules to another, or pass unseen like a breath on the wind, she moved through the night as if it was natural to her.

The portal to Inyx's laboratory wasn't secured. None of the few doors in Axion ever were, it seemed. She coaxed it open with an impetus of thought, and it spiraled apart as she stepped through into the darkened research space.

Ahead of her was the metallic slab on which Valerian had died and Hernandez herself had been Changed. Droops of metallic cabling reached from corner to corner around the tall, narrow room. Beneath the skylight, hovering, was the principal machine of the lab, the one into which all the others fed power and particles and data. All the occult instruments of Inyx's private labors were dark and cold.

Hernandez closed the entrance behind her, then concentrated on awakening the lab, one component at a time. She needed no instruction to know which machine was which; the catoms that infused her body gave her a link to all these devices. If she wanted to know what one was, she merely thought of the question, and the object provided its own answer.

*I know they've spied on Earth before,* she reasoned. *They knew about us—they even spoke English when we got here. And they've probably been watching thousands of other worlds, too. I just have to figure out how they do it.*

She thought about looking far away, across space, for tiny details, and her mind took the measure of the various implements available to her. It was as if the objective in her mind was an unfinished puzzle. All she needed was the missing pieces.

One by one, they revealed themselves.

A soliton projector. A triquantum stabilizer.

A chroniton generator. A subspace transceiver.

A subspace signal amplifier.

She told the machines what she wanted, and they obeyed.

Hernandez shaped them, granted them energy from Axion itself, and focused them with her mind. Then she was surrounded by fleeting, holographic images and a flood of data. Had she still been merely organic, it would have been far too much to witness, never mind comprehend. But she felt the catoms in her brain accelerating her synaptic responses, to help her mind keep pace with the whirlwind of information she'd tapped.

Within seconds she was perusing Earth's current historical archives and learning the entire chronology of the Earth-Romulus War. It had started shortly after her ship's ambush by the Romulans, and it had lasted nearly five years. In the end, it had led to a bloody and bitter stalemate, and the creation of a no-man's-land between the Earth Alliance and the Romulan Empire—the Neutral Zone.

*If only I could have warned them,* she lamented. *Earth's early losses could have been prevented. We might have saved thousands of lives. We might even have won the war.*

But if Earth had been unable to claim victory, neither had it conceded defeat. And the alliances it had forged to repel the Romulans had led to something new: a coalition of many worlds, and soon after that, the establishment of the United Federation of Planets. Finally, in all that perilous darkness, Earth was no longer alone. Humanity had grown up and become part of something bigger than itself. *Maybe some good did come of the war,* she admitted to herself. But then she felt a wave of deep sadness at being so far away from such a wondrous time in human events. *Life goes on without me,* she realized.

A morbid pang of fear nagged at her from the dark corners of her memory, and she plumbed Earth's archives for information about her lost love, Jonathan Archer. She hoped and prayed that he hadn't been a casualty of the war. . . .

Then his biography was at her fingertips, and she breathed a sigh of relief. His service during the war had earned him numerous commendations and a seat with the admiralty. He was still alive, and had just announced that he would retire his post as Starfleet chief of staff on the first day of the new year, to accept a diplomatic assignment as the Federation's newest ambassador to Andoria.

*Jonathan's done all right for himself,* Hernandez mused. Then she was gripped by a powerful temptation. *If he knew I was alive, he'd come for me. He'd never leave me here.*

She was tapped into Earth's planetary information network, which was utterly vulnerable to the Caeliar's superior technology. Finding Jonathan's personal contact information would be as easy as wishing for it. In a moment she could be speaking with him, seeing his face, his distinguished gray temples, those wistful smile lines. She could be hearing his voice, his laughter, the wonder and relief he'd feel at learning she was alive. . . . It was all a thought away.

Then all of it vanished, and Hernandez was alone in the dark surrounded by cold machines. The dream had been there in front of her, the lifeline had been in her hands. In the space of a breath, it all had been torn asunder. She had nothing.

A grave and booming voice came from nowhere and assaulted her senses as if it had come from everywhere. *"Erika,"* said

Ordemo Nordal, the Caeliar's perpetually arbitrary first among equals. *"We are very disappointed in you."*

"That's a shame," she said, her eyes narrowed and her brow creased with naked contempt.

Ordemo continued, *"The Quorum wishes to speak with you and Inyx. Come to us at once."*

She rolled her eyes, uncertain if the entity behind the disembodied voice could even see her. "Aren't you going to send someone to collect me?"

*"You know the way, Erika. Do not make us ask you again."*

"Or else what?" she taunted him. "You'll ask me again?"

*"Don't test our patience. Even our courtesy has limits."*

She knew that the Caeliar's pacifistic ethos wouldn't permit them to harm her or kill her, but she reflected somberly that it hadn't stopped them from taking her prisoner and holding her for what might effectively be forever. *They won't kill me,* she thought, *but there are plenty of ways to punish someone without touching them.* Then she thought of Valerian, who went slowly mad and lived out her days inside an illusion.

Deflating with a sigh, she replied to the *tanwa-seynorral,* "I'll be there in a few minutes, Ordemo."

Inyx stood before the Quorum and waited for Hernandez to arrive. The ruling body radiated condemnation, and he expected little from them in the way of understanding.

As the Quorum members conferred through the gestalt, Inyx sensed their impatience at Hernandez's absence. He wanted to speak in her defense, remind the Quorum that she wasn't able to move her mind from one catom cluster to another. But acting as her apologist would do nothing to appease the *tanwa-seynorral* or the Quorum at large. Instead, Inyx remained silent and watched the portals that had been prepared for Hernandez's arrival.

Then the Quorum looked up in surprise, and Inyx turned to face the cause of their alarm. It was Hernandez, hovering high above them, in an open frame of one of the pyramidal Quorum hall's walls. She had dissolved the triangular pane of crystal without making a sound. With her arms at her sides and her ankles crossed, she floated down toward the shocked mass of the Quorum and said with prideful insolence, "You called?"

Concealing his amusement from the gestalt, Inyx marveled at how intuitively Hernandez wielded the powers he had given her.

"Stand next to Inyx," said Ordemo Nordal.

Hernandez glared at Ordemo as she descended to the main floor of the hall. "As you wish," she said. She took her place with Inyx in the center of the fractal-pattern mosaic. "But only because I know how much you enjoy looking down on others."

A murmur of disapprobation coursed through the Quorum. Ordemo muted the protest with a calming wave of emotion through the gestalt. "Recent events have made it clear that we have been too permissive with both of you," he said aloud, his voice amplified and thunderous. "Inyx, you defied our wishes by Changing her, and you jeopardized our new homeworld by failing to impart the proper respect and self-control to your new disciple. From this time forward, we will hold you accountable for her actions. It is your responsibility to secure your lab from intrusion, and to see that Erika respects our laws."

Inyx wanted to protest, *Am I a mere watchman now? Shall I abandon my work and spend my every moment lording over her?* Instead, he made a small bow to the *tanwa-seynorral* and replied, "I understand, Ordemo." He felt Hernandez's hateful stare.

Directing his next verbal barrage at Hernandez, Ordemo continued, "As for you, Erika . . . it troubles us to see you abuse such powerful gifts. If it were possible to revoke them without harming you, we would do so. Unfortunately, your catoms are part of you now, and to forcibly remove them from you would be fatal. Because the Change cannot be undone, it is imperative that we ensure your compliance with our laws. Do you understand?"

"No," Hernandez said. "I don't." She threw an angry look at Inyx, then continued to Ordemo, "Why can't I learn about events on my homeworld? You spy on the galaxy. Why can't I?"

"Because you cannot be trusted not to try to contact your people," Ordemo said.

Hernandez pressed her palms against her forehead and pushed her fingers through her hair. "So what? The timeline's not at risk anymore. Would it be such a tragedy if I sent one message, one farewell to tell someone I'm okay?"

"You know our laws, Erika," Ordemo said. "Our privacy is of paramount importance to our work. Letting you send messages home risks exposing us to outside scrutiny. We can't allow that."

Nodding, Hernandez replied, "I see. It was never about the timeline. It's always the same thing with you people: fear."

"That's a simplistic—"

"Spare me, Ordemo," Hernandez interrupted. "Don't you understand that your obsessive need for privacy is completely incompatible with your Great Work?" Inyx turned to listen more closely as Hernandez made the argument he had long wished to espouse but had never had the courage to speak aloud.

"You say you're looking for civilizations equal to or more advanced than your own, but you act as if you live in fear of the less-developed cultures that are thriving all around you. Can't you see that your self-imposed isolation is making you narrow-minded and provincial? How can you devote yourselves to seeking out new worlds when you shrink and hide from the ones in your own backyard?"

She turned and scowled at Inyx. "And what about you? I know this is what you've been thinking all along, so why don't you speak up? Why don't you say something?"

Paralyzed by her accusation in front of the Quorum, Inyx hesitated, then said, "I wouldn't know where to begin, Erika."

"No," she said, looking away from him in disgust. "I suppose you wouldn't."

Ordemo hushed another susurrus of the scandalized Quorum. Then he fixed his gaze on Hernandez. "You are an outsider," he said, "and you've been with us only a short time. Perhaps in a few thousands of your years, you'll gain a deeper understanding of our motivations. For now, however, it is clear that we'll need to be more vigilant in policing your actions." He looked at Inyx. "See to it that this incident is not repeated, Inyx."

"Understood, Ordemo."

"Erika, you may go," said the *tanwa-seynorral*. Hernandez took immediate advantage of the dismissal and ascended in a swift arc, back through the open pane, which reappeared, solid and unblemished, as soon as she was outside the Quorum hall.

Alone before the Quorum once again, Inyx said, "Will that be all, Ordemo?"

"For now," Ordemo replied. "But if you cannot control her, Inyx, we will—in the only way open to us. Do you understand?"

Dread and resentment welled up within him; the Quorum was threatening to banish Hernandez to some distant galaxy, where she would be cut off from Axion's sustaining energies. She would weaken, grow old, and die alone on an uninhabited world. It was a sentence of lifetime solitary confinement and certain death.

He swallowed his fury. "I understand," he said.

Hernandez chafed at the notion of being leashed, and it wasn't long before she put Inyx's vigilance to the test.

She had thought she was being subtle. Her first challenge to the Quorum's edict was a message embedded in the matrix of one of their soliton pulses. It was a simple message, a basic SOS coupled with a Fibonacci sequence, to get the attention of whoever might receive it. Once decoupled from the soliton pulse, it would have propagated on several frequencies, both in subspace and on regular light-speed radio waves.

Inyx had appeared before Hernandez one morning to report the failure of her attempt. "It was elegantly simple," he'd said. "However, it was intercepted by the signal filters I've implemented for all outgoing energy pulses."

Years elapsed while she investigated the nature of Inyx's data filters, and eventually she concluded that she couldn't fool them. That left her only one reasonable course of action: She would have to bypass them by altering the configuration of the transmission hardware and software.

Unfortunately, almost all of the stations were permanently supervised by the Caeliar. By the time she had clandestinely followed the soliton generation network to an automated backup relay, decades had passed since her first attempt at subversion. During all those years, she had presented Inyx with a pleasant façade, to allay his suspicions. Pretending to trust him and treating him like a boon companion had secretly vexed her, but she reminded herself after every encounter, *Think long-term.*

With patience and effort, she had converted the backup relay into a primary transmitter, one with an unmoderated uplink to the soliton emitters. To evade detection of her transmission, she had been forced to wait until a scheduled emission surge in the service of the Great Work. By listening to the Caeliar's plans via the gestalt, pinpointing the time to act was easy.

On the night she'd chosen for her plan's fruition, however, she'd arrived at the backup relay to find it sealed off. Forcing her way through the seals, she'd received another rude surprise: a hollowed space. Not only had her modifications been undone, the auxiliary system itself had been removed.

She'd returned to her residence that evening to find Inyx waiting for her, with two of her rebuilt components, one in each hand. "Fine workmanship," he'd said, dropping them on the floor. "It was all that I've come to expect from you, and more."

"The backup relay was a lure," she'd replied.

"Yes. I wanted to see how far your skills had progressed."

"And are you satisfied?"

"Quite," he'd said, before vanishing in a flare of sparks.

Resentment had fueled her surreptitious efforts for several more decades. She had long used the Caeliar's technology without really understanding how it had been built. Even a grasp of its essential operating principles proved elusive, and she'd dedicated the better part of a century to probing them, molecule by molecule, to unlock the secrets of their construction. Then she'd undertaken her boldest stroke of defiance yet: crafting her own soliton emitter, one that would interface with the systems in New Erigol's shell without utilizing the Caeliar's data network. Each component had been painstakingly crafted from the subatomic level, shaped by Hernandez's obedient catoms.

One month before she'd heard of the approach of the *Starship Titan*, Hernandez had finished her machine and was ready to infuse it with power and bring it online. She had taken every imaginable precaution, and had dispelled the Caeliar's surveillance catoms from her vicinity whenever she'd traveled to her hidden, underground lab deep inside Axion's core. She'd built each part separately, never bringing any two of them together until all had been made and were ready to be assembled.

Then, as the last element had been fitted into place, Inyx had appeared from a smoky swirl in the darkness and with a wave of his arm disintegrated Hernandez's machine. A human lifetime's worth of labor was turned to dust in an instant.

"Why?" Hernandez had cried in anguished rage. "You said you were my friend! They've censured you, too—so why do you betray me? Why are you doing their dirty work?"

For the first time in the centuries that she'd known him, he had sounded afraid. "It's for your protection, Erika. If I don't enforce their laws, you'll be exiled, left to grow old and die in some remote corner of the universe." Sinking into his own despair, he had seemed to diminish before her. "I can't let them do that to you, Erika. I couldn't bear to lose you."

In that unguarded moment, she had realized how much Inyx cared about her, and she for him. Their threatened punishment had been sobering enough, but the realization of its potential impact on Inyx was what had swayed Hernandez. He had done so much for her, had taught her so many things, that she couldn't conscience inflicting such sorrow upon him. For the sake of her friend, she had surrendered. After more than eight centuries of low-intensity resistance to the authority of the Caeliar, Hernandez had buried the last ember of her fighting spirit.

But she'd learned something she hadn't known before: She could survive outside of New Erigol, despite the Change. *Grow old and die,* Inyx had warned. And she'd dreamt anew of escape.

Then *Titan* had come to New Erigol.

Inyx had arranged permission for their away team to visit the planet's surface. At his request, she had joined him and Edrin to greet them, and had appointed herself as their liaison.

Now, less than three days later, she stood under a starless night, beside the petrified tree and the deathly still black pool, and she asked herself what she had done.

For all the Caeliar's talk of her being a "guest with restrictions," despite the role she had played in helping them find this new world to call their home, regardless of the superhuman abilities bestowed upon her by the Change, looking at her reflection on the preternaturally still water, she saw herself as she was: a prisoner with a nigh-eternal sentence.

And, as the instrument selected to impose the Caeliar's rules on *Titan*'s crew, she had become a jailer, as well.

"All things considered, I think the op went fairly well," Vale said as she paced. "Right up to the point where it fell apart."

Tuvok stood in the main room of the away team's Axion residence, apart from the rest of the group, while Vale led the post-mission debriefing. Several hours had passed since Keru had been intercepted aboard the shuttlecraft *Mance*. Rather than meet immediately after their return to the residence, when the group was still agitated by its setback, Vale had suggested that everyone take some time alone to consider what had gone wrong, so that they could discuss the details later, in a calm and professional manner. Now it was later, and no one was calm.

"It was a total bungle," said Lieutenant Sortollo, who sat on a sofa with fellow security personnel Keru and Dennisar. "The Caeliar saw us coming a hundred klicks away."

Tuvok stepped forward and replied, "Not necessarily. If they had, it is unlikely they would have permitted us to beam Mister Keru onto the *Mance*. The fact that we did so would suggest that at least that much of our plan was a success."

Keru nodded. "I agree. That caught them looking. But once they knew where I was, it didn't take them long to shut us down. And now we've lost the element of surprise."

"More important," said Ree, who, with Torvig, flanked Troi's chair, "we've lost our tricorders. And the shuttlecraft."

Vale closed her eyes and pinched the bridge of her nose for a moment. Then she sighed and opened her eyes. "It could be worse," she said. "At least they didn't destroy it."

"So they say," Keru replied. "For all we know, they ditched it in the ocean. Or blew it to pieces."

Sortollo, Dennisar, Keru, and Vale overlapped one another with vitriolic remarks, but Tuvok ignored them. Something else drew his attention. A psionic pain shadow was lingering in the group's midst. It was a dull suffering, the kind of malaise produced by illness or deep discomfort. He quieted his thoughts and reached out with a gentle telepathic touch, seeking the source of the pain. Within moments, his mind focused on the source: Commander Troi.

As the discussion continued, he kept his psionic senses attuned to Troi's condition.

"All I'm saying," Dennisar snapped, "is that there's a lot of planet down there, and searching it for the shuttlecraft without tricorders or *Titan*'s sensors is going to take a *very* long time."

Sortollo rolled his eyes at his Orion colleague. "And what we're saying is, we'll need to use the Caeliar's technology to locate the *Mance*."

"And the only way to access that is to get Hernandez to help us," Keru added.

Torvig raised one mechanical hand. "Commander Vale? Did you not prohibit us from soliciting aid from Erika Hernandez?"

"Yes, I did," Vale replied, shooting a glower at Keru and Sortollo. "I considered her unreliable before the mission, and I haven't seen anything since then to change my mind."

"We're not saying it'll happen overnight," Keru argued. "If we want her help, we'll have to cultivate a relationship with her, win her over."

Dr. Ree signaled his disagreement with a rattling rasp. "You'll find that difficult with the Caeliar watching us every minute of the day," the reptilian physician said. "It stands to reason that if they consider us dangerous enough to merit constant surveillance, they must be doubly cautious of her."

Troi looked up. Her face was ashen and her voice hoarse. "Doctor Ree is correct. The Caeliar don't trust her much more than they trust us. Besides, I've tried reaching out to her, and she doesn't seem interested. Unless she comes to us, we shouldn't think of her as an ally."

The security personnel raised their voices in a clamor of protest, which Vale silenced by raising her hands and barking, "Enough!" She waited until the group fell silent. "Does anyone have any ideas about how we might apply what we've learned today? Or what we might do next?"

Keru mumbled, "We can start by building new tricorders."

"I'll take that as a 'no,'" Vale said. "Let's call it a night, then. But tomorrow at breakfast, I want to start hearing new ideas. We all know what the challenges are. Let's start coming up with solutions." With a nod, she added, "Dismissed."

Most of the away team members split up and plodded off toward their respective bedrooms. Tuvok watched as Dr. Ree hovered close behind Troi, shadowing her down the corridor to her quarters. Then the Vulcan tactical officer turned back and observed Commander Vale walking outside, onto the terrace. He made a discreet survey of the others' positions, and then he joined the first officer on the wide, open-air balcony.

She noted his approach but did not turn around. "Taking the air, Tuvok?"

He stood next to her and rested his palms on top of the broad railing. "Commander Troi is in serious physical distress," he said. "And she is masking her symptoms."

"I know," Vale said.

"Is her condition serious?"

"I'm not at liberty to say," Vale replied. "But Doctor Ree is aware of the situation. Please keep this information private."

He nodded once. "Of course. If there's anything I—"

"That'll be all." She threw a guarded look at him. "Thank you."

"I could be of assistance to the doctor," Tuvok said. "Counselor Troi and I have compatible telepathic gifts. Perhaps I could help her to control her pain until such time as—"

"I said that'll be all, Tuvok. *Thank you.*"

He stiffened and took half a step back from the railing. "Understood, Commander. Good night." He turned and went back inside, concerned for Deanna Troi's safety but bound by the chain of command. It had been a long day for the away team, but by the time Tuvok reached his quarters, he had already decided he would not be sleeping tonight. If necessary, he could forgo sleep for several days or longer. Until he was convinced that Troi was no longer in danger, he would remain awake and monitor her unconscious telepathic emissions for any sign of distress.

And if Troi's condition demanded that the chain of command be broken, that was a decision Tuvok could live with.


Hernandez held herself aloft through will alone. Feet together, arms wide apart, head bowed in concentration, she levitated many kilometers above the Quorum hall and immersed her thoughts in the hubbub of the gestalt.

There were hundreds of voices vying to be heard, expressing themselves in images and feelings as often as in words, and when they did speak in concrete terms, it was in the ancient tongue of the Caeliar. Fortunately for Hernandez, her centuries of scholarship, aided by her catoms, made it easy to understand.

Much of the argument receded as Ordemo asked, "Why have we not known of these passages until now?"

"Because," Inyx replied, "until mere weeks ago, they had been dormant. Lying fallow in the ubiquitous realms of subspace, they were all but invisible to our sensors." He offered the members of the Quorum a visual representation of the tunnels through subspace; it reminded Hernandez of a wheel with uneven spokes, and Erigol's former position was the hub. One of the spokes shone much more brightly than the others. "This was the first of the passages to be accessed, and it has been the most frequently traveled. In the past few days, all but a few of the remaining passages have been exposed, as they were transited by one or more vessels."

Low drones and rumbles of anxiety coursed through the hovering ranks of the Quorum. Above the din, Ordemo replied, "Inyx, the primitive civilizations of the galaxy cannot be trusted to use those passages wisely. If they should destabilize one or more of them, the effects would be catastrophic. Entire star systems could be annihilated."

"I am aware of that, Ordemo," Inyx said. "Now that the passages' recent usage has enabled us to pinpoint all their locations, I have begun calculations for a series of soliton pulses that will safely collapse them at their point of common intersection, without posing any risk to the galaxy at large."

Ordemo sounded assuaged. "Will it take long to effect?"

"No," Inyx said. "We'll begin the process momentarily. It should be complete within a matter of hours."

"Very good," Ordemo said. "Well done, Inyx, thank you."

Before Inyx could erase his catom-animation of the passages and their hub, Hernandez followed its data stream back to its source. She found herself gazing through a narrow pinhole in subspace, spying on events nearly half a galaxy away.

Hundreds of ships moved through her gestalt-vision, vessels of many different designs. Several she recognized as having the familiar configurations of Starfleet spacecraft, with their saucers and nacelles. Klingon ships were equally distinctive, and there were many of them, too. In addition, there were scores of ships whose provenances were unknown to her. All of them seemed to move in concert, unified in purpose, rallied around the clustered apertures of the subspace passages.

*This has something to do with the threat Deanna was telling me about,* Hernandez intuited. *The passageways,* Titan, *the threat to Earth. It's all connected somehow. But how?*

A moment later, one of the passageways spiraled open inside the blue night of the distant nebula. Fear like a fist of cold steel seized her heart. And she had her answer.

*Madre de Dios.*

\* \* \*

Deanna Troi awoke in a panic, a fugitive from a nightmare of knives and vipers. Gasping for breath and drenched in her own sweat, she lurched to a sitting position in her bed and was restrained by scaly talons locked around her arms.

"Easy, my dear counselor," said Ree through his maw of fangs. "Your symptoms are getting worse."

She struggled frantically in his grasp. "Let me go!"

"Counselor, please, you're in no—"

Troi spat in his left eye and tried to lift her foot to kick at him. "Take your hands off me!"

He let go, and she fell backward into bed. "As you wish."

Rubbing her abraded wrists, Troi sat up. Then a rush of nausea hit her, and she doubled over. Ree stepped back as Troi vomited a thin stream of watery stomach acid on the floor.

As a wave of dry heaves convulsed Troi's abdomen and left her dizzy, the Pahkwa-thanh physician inched toward her. "Counselor, without my tricorder, I can make only an educated guess as to your condition. But it is my belief that you are suffering from an internal hemorrhage."

She gulped a deep breath and pulled herself back onto her bed. The room felt as if it were spinning above her.

"Deanna," Ree continued, "we need to ask the Caeliar if they have medical facilities that we can use to treat you."

Pursing her lips, Troi lolled her head side to side. "No," she insisted. "Don't let them touch me."

"Counselor, we have no choice," Ree said, looming over her. "Your condition is deteriorating. It's time to let me operate."

His heartfelt-sounding plaints didn't fool her. She saw the predatory gleam in his cold, serpentine eyes. "Liar!" she screamed. "Butcher! You want to kill my baby!"

"Counselor, please, you're delu—" Her foot struck his snout and shut him up. As he recoiled from the blow, she rolled out of bed and landed hard on the floor. Escape was all that mattered now. Crawling away from him toward the door of her room, she focused on pulling herself with her hands and pushing herself with her feet. Then the doctor's bony, three-taloned feet landed in front of her. He had leaped past her with ease and blocked her exit. Turning, he confronted her. "Your skin was very warm to the touch, Deanna. I believe you're running a fever, possibly as a side effect to your body's rejection of the synthetase inhibitor. And the fever is making you delusional."

Scuttling backward on her palms, she rasped, "Get away from me! Monster!"

"Counselor, I don't have time to argue with your mental infirmities. Your life is in jeopardy, and you're not acting rationally. If I have to, I'll relieve you of duty."

The door swung open behind him and rebounded off the wall. He turned and was confronted by Sortollo, Dennisar, and Keru.

"We heard shouting," Keru said.

Troi pointed at Ree. "He attacked me!"

"I did no such thing," Ree said to Keru. "Counselor Troi is feverish, and I believe she's suffering an internal hemorrhage."

"He wants to give me to the Caeliar!"

Ree spun and hissed at her. "I need their help so I can operate on you."

Cowering in a corner beside her bed, Troi kept an accusing finger leveled at Ree. "Keep him away from me."

Dennisar and Sortollo stepped into the room between Ree and Troi. Keru reached forward and took hold of Ree's shoulder. "Okay, Doc, let's all just take a step back and—"

"There's no time for this!" Ree growled. "Her pulse is thready, her blood pressure is dropping—"

Dennisar and Sortollo began herding Ree backward, toward the exit. Behind the doctor, Keru said in a cajoling manner, "Just step out for a few minutes, Doc, let her calm down."

"She could be bleeding out! I need to operate!"

"No!" Troi called out. "No surgery!"

Dennisar shrugged at Ree. "You heard her. No surgery."

The therapodian physician stopped retreating, lowered his head, and fixed his jeweled-iris glare upon Troi. "Fine."

He burst forward, trampling over Sortollo and Dennisar. Keru lumbered after the lunging Pahkwa-thanh, but the Trill seemed to be moving in slow motion and lagging meters behind. Troi, paralyzed with terror, could only cringe and stare in mute horror as Ree descended upon her, his long jaw of razor-sharp teeth wide open.

Vale, Tuvok, and Torvig appeared in the corridor outside the doorway and looked on with shock and dismay as Ree pinned Troi to the floor—and sank his fangs into her chest.

# 19

Captain Picard stepped out of his ready room and onto the bridge of the *Enterprise*. The electric crackling of high-energy tools mixed with the low buzz of comm chatter and muted conversation. His bridge was crowded with engineers, junior officers, and his senior command officers, all of whom were working with great focus and alacrity to finish the ship's repairs.

Kadohata interrupted her report to Worf, who was seated in the command chair, and nodded to Picard. Worf stood and handed Picard a padd. "Captain, calculations for opening aperture twenty-two beta are almost complete. However, shields are at less than fifty percent, and engineering is having difficulty adjusting the emitters for the new metaphasic frequencies."

"Not ready to enter the plasma jet, then," Picard said. He noted a silent exchange of anxious glances between Worf and Kadohata. "How much longer, Number One?"

"At least thirty minutes," Worf replied.

The note of regret in Worf's voice compelled Picard to ask, "And what is the ETA of the Hirogen hunting pack?"

Worf looked at Kadohata, who folded her hands behind her back to affect a nonchalant pose. "Twenty minutes," she said.

"This is not the fight we came for," Picard said. He stepped past Kadohata and raised his voice to snare Choudhury's attention. "Hail the *Aventine*, Lieutenant."

The security chief tapped commands into her console and then looked up to respond, "Ready, sir."

"On-screen," Picard said.

The main viewer switched from an image of stars to the face of Captain Dax. *"You don't look like you're breaking good news, Captain,"* she said.

"I'm not," he replied. "The *Enterprise* won't be ready to reenter the plasma stream before the Hirogen arrive."

A worry line formed a single, wavy crease across Dax's brow. *"The metaphasic recalibration, right?"*

Picard nodded. "Has your crew finished the modifications? Can you extend your shields around the *Enterprise*?"

Dax shook her head. *"We'd have to be at full power to make it to the aperture and survive the jaunt back. Right now, we're at fifty-three percent."*

"We can't risk letting the Hirogen detect the frequency for controlling the apertures," Picard said. "If we can't make the return in the next fifteen minutes, we'll have no choice but to stand and fight."

*"Agreed,"* Dax said. *"I suggest we spend the time we have left restoring our tactical systems and preparing coordinated attack-and-defense protocols."*

Resigned to the coming battle, Picard consented with a grim nod. "Make it so. Good luck to you and your crew, Captain."

*"And to yours, sir. Aventine out."*

The channel closed, and the main viewer reverted to a backdrop of stars overlaid by a tactical display of information about the approaching Hirogen hunting pack. "Mister Worf," said Picard, "ready the ship for battle."

"Aye, sir." Worf turned toward Choudhury. "Hirogen use energy dampeners during boarding operations, to render phasers and internal security systems inoperable. Issue projectile rifles and bladed weapons to all security teams." To Kadohata he added, "Tell Mister La Forge to prioritize tactical repairs."

As the Red Alert klaxon wailed throughout the ship, Picard returned to his command chair, sat down, and steeled himself for the impending fray. A new degree of intensity drove the crew's efforts now, and it was almost enough to push all thought of the Borg from his thoughts.

Then Worf was at his side. "Permission to leave the bridge for five minutes, sir."

"Now? For what reason, Mister Worf?"

The Klingon averted his eyes from Picard's and frowned before he replied, "To retrieve my *bat'leth,* sir." Then he met Picard's gaze and added with stern surety, "As a precaution."

For once, Picard saw the logic of Worf's thinking.

"Permission granted."

Captain Chakotay had been itching for a fight for a long time. It had been several months since Kathryn Janeway had been taken by the Borg, and not a night had passed that he hadn't dreamt of vengeance. Payback. Blood for blood.

In the aftermath of the Borg's most recent, devastating sorties into Federation space, he'd persuaded Admiral Montgomery to petition Admiral Nechayev to reassign *Voyager* to combat duty on the homefront. When the call had gone out for a fleet to assemble in the Azure Nebula, to support the *Enterprise* in a daring counteroffensive against the Borg, he'd made certain that *Voyager* was the first ship assigned to the battle group.

*We've faced the Borg more than anyone.* Chakotay stared out his ready room window. *It should be us leading the scouting runs.* He clenched his fists and set his jaw. *Patience. Soon, we'll all get to fight. Until then, we hold the line.*

It was precisely because of Chakotay's personal experience against the Borg, and *Voyager*'s reputation in Starfleet, that Captain Picard had placed them in command of the allied expeditionary force while the *Enterprise* and the *Aventine* were off to who knew where on a recon run. Watching the silhouettes of hundreds of starships massing for a battle royal, Chakotay felt his pulse quicken. A red hour was close at hand.

A door signal interrupted his ruminations. "Come in." He turned as the portal sighed open to admit his first officer, Lieutenant Commander Tom Paris. "Tom," Chakotay said. "How're you holding up?"

"I'm fine, sir," Paris replied, with the demeanor of a razor's edge. It had been four days since he had received a posthumous message from his father, Admiral Owen Paris, who had been killed during the Borg's attack on Starbase 234.

Had such news come at any other time, Chakotay would have suggested his XO take bereavement leave, but a declaration by the Federation Council three days earlier meant that the UFP was now in a state of open war against the Borg. Starfleet no longer had the luxury of time for its sorrows.

Paris continued, "Captain T'Vala says the *Athens* is ready to open aperture twenty-three alpha, and the captain of the *Mendeleev* estimates his crew will open twenty-four alpha in less than an hour."

Chakotay nodded. "What about apertures twenty-five through twenty-seven? Any progress there?"

"Some," Paris said. "The warbird *Tiamatra* and the *I.K.S. veScharg'a* are working on twenty-five and twenty-seven. We've been trying to help the Gorn cruiser *Lotan* break the lock on aperture twenty-six, but it's not responding at all."

Suspicion and concern hardened Chakotay's already stern

expression. "Prioritize that," he said. "What about the *Enterprise* and the *Aventine*?"

"Three hours overdue," Paris said.

"That's long enough," Chakotay said. "We have the frequency for twenty-two alpha. Send the *T'Kumbra,* the *Templar,* and the *Saladin.* Make sure they treat it as a combat sortie, not—"

*"Captain Chakotay and Commander Paris, please report to the bridge,"* Lieutenant Harry Kim interrupted via the comm.

Paris threw a look at Chakotay, and they both moved at a quickstep out of the ready room, onto the bridge of *Voyager.* Paris centered himself behind the forward duty stations.

"Report," Chakotay said, dropping into his chair.

"Aperture twenty-six alpha's opening," Kim said. "But it's not us. Something's coming through."

Anticipation and dread entwined like snakes inside Chakotay's gut. "Red Alert," he said. "Battle stations. Alert the fleet, and get ready to target whatever comes out."

"Aye, sir," Kim said, arming weapons and raising shields as the alert klaxon whooped.

*Let it be a Borg cube,* Chakotay prayed. *Hell, let it be five. We've got enough firepower to pulverize* ten *of them.*

"Tare," Paris said to the conn officer, orchestrating the battle preparations, "bring us about, bearing one-three-one mark five. Lasren, tell the warbird *Loviatar* and the *I.K.S. Ya'Vang* to come about and guard our flanks."

Everyone reacted with quiet efficiency. Then all eyes turned toward the main viewer and the expanding circle of light that began to wash away the dreamlike cyan glow of the nebula.

A dark corner appeared in the blinding radiance, followed by another, and Chakotay prepared to sate his appetite for revenge. He was about to give the order to fire when the true scope of what he was seeing began to reveal itself. In that moment all his dreams of retribution left him.

"All ships, open fire!" Paris shouted, but it was too late.

Darkness fell upon *Voyager* like a hammer, and then all that was left were the flames, the terror, and the screaming.

Ezri Dax felt every blast that rocked her ship. The ten Hirogen attack craft swarmed the *Aventine* and the *Enterprise* and harried the Starfleet vessels with powerful subnucleonic beams.

Over the bedlam of explosions, Dax hollered to her first officer, "Sam! Return fire!"

"Aft torpedoes, full spread!" Bowers shouted through the din. "Helm, roll forty degrees port! Phasers, sweep starboard!"

Every command was carried out with dispatch, and the searing orange glow of phaser beams sliced across the image on the main viewer. Flashes from detonating quantum torpedoes were coupled with violent tremors in the *Aventine*'s hull.

"One enemy ship destroyed," Kedair reported from tactical. "Acquiring new targets."

Bowers replied, "Keep firing, Lieutenant."

Another fusillade of Hirogen fire raked the *Aventine*. An auxiliary tactical station on the starboard side of the bridge exploded, hurling Ensign Rhys backward in a jet of sparks and shrapnel. His scorched, bloody body fell in an unnatural pose in the middle of the bridge.

A Vulcan paramedic stationed on the bridge rushed forward, with a tricorder open in her hand, to Rhys's side. More blasts pounded the ship as she looked up at Dax and shook her head. There was nothing she could do—the man was dead.

Thunderous impacts buffeted Dax's ship and caused the overhead lights to dim. "Port shields failing," Kedair called from tactical. "Incoming!"

Bowers shot back, "Roll one-eighty to port! All power to starboard shields!"

It was too late. The Hirogen had spotted the weakness in the *Aventine*'s defenses and exploited it without hesitation. Dax held on to her chair's armrests as the bridge pitched sharply, knocking Bowers and the Vulcan medic off their feet. The ops console exploded, engulfing Oliana Mirren in superheated phosphors and shattered isolinear circuitry. When the flash faded, the reed-thin brunette went limp in her chair.

Casting off sentiment, Bowers shouted to the relief ops officer, Lieutenant Nak, "Reset science two for ops!"

"Aye, sir," replied the shaken young male Tellarite, who scrambled to reconfigure the bridge's backup science console.

The *Aventine*'s phasers shrieked as Kedair unleashed three barrages in rapid succession, and the torpedoes-away signal had never before sounded so sweet to Dax's ears. On the main viewer, another Hirogen ship was vaporized as it blundered into the *Aventine*'s tandem firing solution with the *Enterprise*.

"Eight Hirogen ships left," Kedair announced. "They're splitting up, four and four, on attack vectors."

"Tharp," Bowers said. "Hard about, let *Enterprise* cover our flank."

Phaser blasts slashed through two of the *Aventine*'s Hirogen attackers, but the last pair of enemy ships accelerated on an unswerving intercept course.

Kedair shouted, "Collision alarm!"

The two Hirogen ships made impact. A violent jolt shuddered through the deck and made Dax wince.

"Report," Bowers said.

From the new ops station, Lieutenant Nak replied, "Hull breach, Decks Seventeen and Eighteen, Sections Five through Nine. Force fields are up, damage-control teams responding."

"Intruder alert!" Kedair said. "Four Hirogen, moving in pairs on Deck Seventeen." She looked up at Bowers. "They're heading for crew quarters."

"Evacuate that deck," Bowers said. "And tell your people to shoot to kill. Hirogen don't take prisoners, so neither do we."

The bridge of the *Enterprise* was heavy with smoke and fumes. Sparks rained down from buckled overhead panels. Pressure-suited damage-control specialists jogged past behind Jean-Luc Picard, on their way to extinguish a fire in his ready room.

In front of him, off to starboard, a Kaferian medic was treating Lieutenant T'Ryssa Chen, whose right arm had been burned black when she'd pushed tactical officer Šmrhová clear of an overloading companel just before it exploded.

At the conn, a surge of electricity had stunned Lieutenant Faur, who had been taken to sickbay. Lieutenant Weinrib had taken over the ship's flight operations. In a pitched voice he declared, "Two Hirogen ships on ramming trajectories!"

Worf bellowed, "Evasive! Starboard!" He thumbed open the intraship comm. "All decks! Brace for impact!"

Two collisions in quick sequence pummeled the *Enterprise*. Choudhury held on to her console with one hand and worked its controls with the other. "Hull breach, Deck Ten! Ventral shields are down, and the last two ships are making another attack run."

Picard gripped his armrests so tightly that his knuckles turned white. "Helm, intercept course. On my mark, make a shallow, full-impulse dive across their path, then pull up."

"Aye, sir," Weinrib said.

"Divert phaser power to dorsal shields," Picard said to Choudhury. "Arm aft torpedoes, dispersal pattern Bravo."

"Weapons ready," Choudhury said.

Kadohata looked back from the ops console. "Dorsal shields are as strong as we can make them."

"Steady," Picard said, projecting unflinching confidence.

He watched the range and speed data on his chair's armrest tactical monitor. As he'd suspected, the Hirogen showed no sign of breaking off their attack or changing their course. They weren't going to surrender or relent.

*So be it,* Picard decided. "Now, Mister Weinrib."

The engines throbbed and whined as the *Enterprise* slipped below the Hirogen's glide plane at full impulse for just half a second. As the two enemy ships rolled to attack the *Enterprise* from above, it soared upward, ramming them from underneath. Bone-rattling concussions resounded through the hull as the massive starship slammed aside its smaller attackers. "Hard to port," Picard commanded over the hue and cry of explosions and damage reports. "Fire aft torpedoes!"

Bright feedback tones from Choudhury's console confirmed the release of the torpedo volley. Seconds later she reported, "Both Hirogen ships destroyed, Captain."

He threw a look at Worf. "Damage report."

"Hull breaches on Decks Two through Six, Sections Nineteen through Fifty-one," Worf replied. "Dorsal shields have failed."

It was no worse than Picard had expected. "Casualties?"

"Several," Worf said. "We also have nine crewmen missing from the breached compartments."

Picard watched the firefighting team shamble out of his smoky ready room. "Begin search-and-rescue operations, Mister Worf." He asked Choudhury, "What's the *Aventine*'s status?"

"They've been boarded," she said. Then her eyes opened wider as a signal shrilled on her console. "And they're not the only ones—we have four intruders on Deck Ten."

\* \* \*

Lieutenant Randolph Giudice led his security team into position on Deck 10 of the *Enterprise*. He ducked into a shallow recess along the corridor, hugged his TR-116 rifle to his chest, and held up a fist to halt the rest of the squad. Across from him, Lieutenant Peter Davila backed into another nook in a bulkhead, his own TR-116 clutched tightly.

A few meters behind them, past a curve in the passageway, four more security officers crouched, awaiting the signal to advance. Lieutenant th'Chun, Lieutenant Harley de Lange, and Ensign Manfred Vogel all were armed with the same kind of rifles as Giudice. In addition, th'Chun and Vogel carried collapsible stun batons for hand-to-hand combat, and de Lange wore a Nausicaan sword in a sheath across his back. The melee weapon was not a standard armament, but the TR-116s and bladed weapons had been issued from the armory on the XO's orders.

At the rear of the group was Lieutenant Bryan Regnis, the team's sharpshooter. He carried a specially modified TR-116. At the end of its muzzle was an inertia-neutral microtransporter, which was linked to an exographic targeting sensor that covered his left eye like a translucent crystal patch.

The sensor let him peek through decks and bulkheads, and the microtransporter enabled him to shoot through them as if they weren't there. His rifle fired ten-millimeter monotanium projectiles at nine hundred twenty meters per second—and materialized them ten centimeters from his target, with their kinetic energy unchanged. In essence, he was able to target his foes from several decks away and inflict damage as if he had shot them at point-blank range.

Giudice looked back at Regnis, made a "V" with his first two fingers, and pointed at his own eyes. Then he made a jabbing forward motion with his whole hand. The lean, boyish-looking sniper nodded, unslung his rifle, and peered through the exographic sensor, seeking out the Hirogen boarding party.

After several seconds of adjustments, Regnis frowned, met Giudice's questioning stare, and waved his hand up and down in front of his eyes: Something was blocking the exographic sensor.

*There's the dampening field,* Giudice figured. *So much for doing this the easy way.* He waved de Lange and Vogel forward.

The two men stayed low and skulked forward, rifles braced

and level. Davila and Giudice kept their own weapons aimed past the duo, ready to lay down covering fire. Regnis and th'Chun hung back, behind cover.

At the far end of the corridor, beyond the next curve, the overhead lights began going out. The leading edge of darkness moved swiftly closer, blacking out companels and even emergency lighting where the bulkheads met the deck.

A dull, heavy *thump* was followed by the sound of something rolling. Giudice saw a glint of light reflecting off a small, metallic orb the size of a baseball. It ricocheted off the bulkhead several meters away and rolled toward him and his team. A wall of darkness preceded it.

*An energy dampener.* "Back!" he snapped.

Vogel halted and stared forward into the darkness as it overtook him. A meaty *thunk* of metal striking bone followed a moment later. Lieutenant de Lange had turned back and was in the midst of his first sprinting stride when he was knocked forward. He fell facedown, revealing a sunburst-shaped throwing blade buried between his neck vertebrae, just beneath his skull.

Giudice and Davila scrambled backward as they opened fire, lighting up the darkened passage with tracer rounds from their TR-116s. Bullets sparked as they were deflected by the two Hirogen hunters' armor. The height and bulk of the invaders shocked Giudice; he and Davila were big men, broad-shouldered and thickly muscled, but they were dwarfed by the Hirogen.

Stumbling in reverse around the curve in the passage, Giudice almost ran into th'Chun, who was dashing forward. He tried to grab the Andorian. "Neshaal, stop!" He lunged forward to follow th'Chun around the curve, leading with his rifle.

The *thaan* rolled across the deck and came up shooting in full automatic mode. In a blaze of crimson tracers, he peppered one of the Hirogen with high-explosive rounds, blasting him to a dead stop. A handful of shots struck the hunter in the unarmored areas of his face, and he collapsed.

Then an ovoid hunk of metal arced out of the shadows and bounced across the deck toward th'Chun.

Giudice turned and dived for cover. "Incoming!"

Regnis and Davila retreated ahead of him. Behind him, th'Chun fought to go from a kneeling crouch to a standing run. He didn't make it. The explosion threw the Andorian forward and slammed him into Giudice and the others. Searing-hot shrapnel pelted them as they rolled in a jumble.

Giudice shook off the worst of the blast and pulled Davila back to his feet. One look at th'Chun confirmed that he was dead. "Redcaps," Giudice said to Regnis and Davila, using the slang term for high-explosive ammunition. "Suppressing fire. Fall back to Section Nineteen."

The trio quickstepped backward to an intersection that was still lit. Davila and Regnis switched their weapons' ammunition clips on the move. They ducked around the corner into Section Nineteen, and Giudice gave the signal to halt. He tapped his combadge. "Giudice to bridge. One hostile down. Need backup."

Lieutenant Choudhury replied, *"Acknowledged. Be advised, we've confirmed the Hirogen are using energy dampeners."*

The three men swapped angry, exasperated glares. "Thanks, bridge," Giudice said. "Noted." He looked across the passageway to note the bulkhead numbers. "I need force fields at Section Ten-nineteen Echo."

*"Negative,"* Choudhury said. *"The energy dampeners will just knock them out. Forget containment protocols. Shoot to kill."*

He pulled a clip of redcaps from his belt. "Acknowledged," he said. In a deft, practiced motion, he ejected his weapon's emptied magazine to the deck and slapped in the replacement. "Can you tell me if our blind spot's moving?"

*"Affirmative,"* said Choudhury. *"It's flanking you. Center of the scrambled zone is Section Ten-twenty-one Delta."*

The corridor to his right grew dark. "Copy that, bridge. Giudice out." He tapped Regnis's shoulder and motioned for the sniper to watch the dimming corridor. Then he gave a sideways nod to Davila to follow him to a panel that was marked as a storage space for emergency supplies.

Davila put his back to the wall and shifted his focus every few seconds, wary of an ambush from any direction. Giudice opened the bulkhead panel and retrieved a bundle of chemical emergency flares. He unrolled the bundle between himself and Davila. "Pop 'em, toss 'em, and make it quick," Giudice said.

The two men cracked the flares to life by the fistful and flung them wildly down the corridors. Even as the corridor's overhead lights faded to black with the Hirogen's approach, the pale lime and cyan glows of the chemical flares remained bright and un-dimmed. Lit only by the flares, the passageway took on a surreal cast of harsh shadows and unnatural hues.

Giudice watched the corridor opposite the one guarded by Regnis, and Davila monitored the intersection from which they'd come less than a minute earlier. "Stay frosty," Giudice whispered. "Check your targets, controlled bursts."

Waiting in the dark, lying in ambush, Giudice felt as if the seconds were being stretched by the adrenaline coursing through him. His pulse slammed with a steady tempo in his head, and the beating of his heart shook his entire body. Fat beads of sweat rolled from his thinning hair to his heavy eyebrows.

He thought he heard Regnis start to say something. Over his shoulder, he said in a hushed voice, "Bry? Report."

No answer came. Giudice looked back and strained to pierce the shadows. Then he saw Regnis dangling several centimeters above the floor, flailing desperately at his blood-drenched throat. The sniper looked as if he was levitating—until Giudice caught a glimmer of light on the monofilament wire that had been low-ered through a ventilation duct to garrote his comrade.

"Heads up!" Giudice unleashed a staccato series of short bursts at the overhead panels. The ceiling caved in.

Davila opened fire on the hulking forms of three Hirogen hunters, who let Regnis fall to the deck as they dropped into crouches, scythe-like blades in hand.

One hunter lunged at Davila, thrusting a dagger at the man's chest. Davila parried the blow with the stock of his rifle, only to get slashed across the chest by a curved blade in the Hirogen's other hand.

Giudice continued firing until his rifle clicked empty.

A hand locked on his throat, and cold steel bit into his gut and pierced his back. He'd been impaled on the sword of the Hirogen leader, the alpha. The alien, whose face was marked by broad stripes of bright war paint, yanked his blade free and tossed Giudice aside. The brawny security officer struck the bulkhead and fell bleeding to the deck.

A buzz-roar of weapons fire filled the corridor.

In the strobed light of tracer fire, the alpha convulsed as chunks of his armor were blasted from his body in a bloody spray. Giudice winced as he watched the stuttered-motion retreat of the other two Hirogen, one of whom hurled a fist-sized charge through an open escape pod hatch.

They ducked past the portal, and an earsplitting blast vomited fire and debris into the corridor. Then everything was drowned out by a terrifying howl of escaping atmosphere.

Water vapor condensed into white plumes racing toward space, and the sudden plunge in air temperature stung Giudice's eyes. He forced them open long enough to see the two Hirogen, whose armor suits were equipped with breathing masks and visors for survival in the vacuum of space, clamber out through the ragged new gap in the *Enterprise*'s hull.

The rush of air slowed, and Giudice's head swam. *We're running out of air,* he realized. Struggling to concentrate through his pain and hypoxia, he deduced that the Hirogen's energy dampener was preventing the ship's force fields from sealing the breach and repressurizing the isolated sections.

Several meters down the passageway, his rescuers had collapsed, robbed of breath. Regnis and Davila were down.

Lying next to Giudice was the dead Alpha-Hirogen. And on his belt was a spherical device like the one that had rolled out of the darkness minutes earlier. With weak, trembling fingers, Giudice detached the sleek, silvery globe from the alpha's belt. Barely able to see, unable to hear, he crawled forward on his knees toward the rent in the hull. To his relief, he felt the artificial gravity fail beneath him, lightening his burden.

He chucked the globe through the gap, out into the zero-g emptiness. It spun as it vanished into the eternal night.

The corridor lights snapped on, a force field shimmered into place across the rip in the ship's skin, and a flood of sweet air rushed over Giudice, who collapsed into the restored artificial gravity.

Boots clattered as a security team ran to Giudice and his men. Leading the reinforcement squad was Lieutenant Rennan Konya, the ship's Betazoid deputy chief of security. "Medics up here, stat!" he shouted back down the corridor.

"Good to see you back on your feet," Giudice said. From his vantage point lying on the deck, he noted the chrome stripe on the bottom of the ammunition clip in Konya's rifle: bullets with pointed monofilament tips—the ultimate armor-piercing rounds. "Silver bullets, eh?"

"When only the best will do." As a team of medics and nurses arrived to tend to Giudice and his wounded men, Konya eyed the damage in the escape-pod bay and tapped his combadge. "Konya to bridge: Hostiles have gone EVA."

Sam Bowers dodged through smoke and past a running engineer to join Lonnoc Kedair at the security console. "They're *where*?"

"Heading aft on the outside of the dorsal hull," Kedair replied. Her green, scaled hands moved with speed and grace over her dust-covered controls. "Four Hirogen wearing pressure-support gear. One of them has a pretty serious-looking piece of shoulder-fired artillery." An alert beeped and lit a pad high on her console. She silenced it with a quick tap. "Power failures are following them every step of the way."

Lieutenant Gaff chim Nak called across the bridge from the new ops station, "*Enterprise* also has two EVA hostiles."

"Our guests must be using magnetic boots," Captain Dax said, thinking aloud. "Can we electrify the hull? Maybe short out their armor?"

"It'd take about fifteen minutes to set up," interjected science officer Gruhn Helkara. "And with their energy-dampening field, there's no guarantee it would even reach them."

Kedair added, "We can't use phasers, either. Even if we target them manually, the beam would disperse before contact."

"What about the runabouts?" Dax asked the security chief.

She shook her head. "Same problem, sir. Phasers won't hit the targets, and even if their microtorpedoes explode on impact, shooting them at our own unshielded hull is a *bad* idea."

The captain heaved a frustrated sigh. "How soon can we send our own people out to engage?"

"Not soon enough," Bowers said, pointing at the enlarged image on the main viewscreen.

The Hirogen who carried the shoulder-fired weapon raised it, braced it, and aimed it at a central section of the *Aventine*'s secondary hull. His comrades moved behind him.

Dax tapped her combadge. "Bridge to engineering! Prep for hull breach!"

A fiery streak from the Hirogen's weapon left a trail of quickly dissipating expended chemical propellant. Then a flash on the main viewer coincided with a deep, angry rumbling in the hull. A port-side engineering status console became a chaotic scramble of symbols and static.

"Breach, Deck Twenty, Section Forty-one," Nak replied, before he covered his mouth and coughed painfully into his fist.

"They're heading for main engineering," Dax said. She snapped orders around the bridge. "Sam, get Leishman and her people out. Gaff, isolate all command systems on the bridge. Gruhn, lock down the engineering computer core. Lonnoc, we can't let the intruders control our warp core—get your people down there, and dead or alive, *get those bastards off my ship!*"

As the bridge officers scrambled to their stations to carry out their orders, Bowers saw Kedair summon relief tactical officer Talia Kandel to take over for her at security. Then the security chief walked briskly toward the turbolift.

Bowers intercepted her before she boarded the lift and snapped, "Lieutenant Kedair! Where are you going?"

"Main engineering, sir," Kedair said.

He folded his arms. "I don't recall you asking permission to leave your post, Lieutenant."

She bristled and then snapped to attention.

"Sir. Request permission to lead the counterattack and make our boarders sorry they ever set foot on Captain Dax's ship."

"Permission granted," Bowers said, stepping aside to let her enter the turbolift. "Give 'em hell, Lieutenant."

The doors hissed shut as Kedair replied with a determined glare, "That's the plan, sir."


Ormoch had earned his place as an Alpha-Hirogen through daring and resilience. Sacrificing his ship in order to breach the defenses of this exotic alien vessel had cost him many fine relics, but he was certain that, once subdued, this ship's crew would yield many superb trophies.

Kezal, his beta hunter, returned from one of the access corridors that led to the main engine compartment, which the two of them had commandeered without facing any resistance. "Scramblers and countermeasures are in place," the beta said. The muffled thunder of a distant detonation reverberated through the abandoned corridors.

"That should keep our prey busy until we've bypassed their computer lockouts," Ormoch said. "Then we can use their own antipersonnel systems to neutralize their energy weapons and test their skills in personal combat."

Something large and dense clanged heavily to the deck beside the matter/antimatter reactor and replied, "Why wait?"

Kezal and Ormoch turned to see a massive, reptilian biped with leathery brown scales, clawed extremities with opposable digits, and a face dominated by an ivory beak. Its round eyes were a solid, glossy black and utterly inscrutable. Fabric in the style of what Ormoch had come to recognize as this ship's uniform was fitted snugly across the creature's barrel chest. It hunched and prowled forward with an ornate and fearsome curved-blade axe clutched in one hand.

"This," Ormoch said to Kezal with a gleam of anticipation, "looks like worthy prey indeed." The alpha drew his own long blade and squared off against the greenish behemoth. "Stay clear, Kezal. This one is mine."

The alien shifted his grip on his axe. "Don't be greedy, friend," he said. "I'm willing to kill you both at the same time." He clicked his beak at Kezal. "Bring it on."

"Mind your place, Kezal," warned Ormoch.

Ormoch lunged at the alien. It moved quickly despite its bulk. The alpha's first thrust and slash missed completely, and he barely dodged a scalping blow from his foe's axe. He ducked under another lateral cut and chopped away a wedge of flesh from above the creature's knee. Dark blood ran down its leg.

Circling the reptilian, Ormoch studied its movements to see whether it favored its wounded limb or made a greater effort to defend it from further injury. To the alpha's surprise, it did neither. Either the creature had tremendous self-discipline or its species possessed an unusually high pain threshold.

*Best not to linger too long on this one,* Ormoch decided. A feint and a lunge slipped him inside the creature's circle of defense, and a well-placed stroke of his monotanium blade cut a deep wound across the creature's throat. He thrust his sword up, through the reptilian's gut and into its chest. As the creature twitched in its death throes, it tried to bring its axe down on Ormoch's neck. The alpha reached up and swatted the weapon from his foe's hand. It clanged and bounced across the deck.

Then the reptilian's other hand struck Ormoch's face like a spiked hammer, tearing ragged wounds across his cheek and brow. Blood drizzled over the alpha's eyes as the creature's last breath rattled from its throat. Ormoch lowered his blade and let his prey's corpse slide off, into a heap on the deck.

He wiped his blood from his face, looked at Kezal, and laughed. "Not the best I've ever fought, but not bad," he said. "Look at that beak and those claws. They'll make fine relics."

A woman's voice added, "Don't forget this."

Again, Ormoch turned to find an unexpected visitor. She was tall for a humanoid, slim but muscular, and not unattractive, in his opinion. Though her olive-hued hide was scaly, it was much finer in texture than that of the creature he'd just fought. And she twirled the first creature's weapon with ease and grace.

"You think you know how to handle that axe?" taunted Kezal.

The woman spared him only the briefest glance. "It's not an axe, it's a Rigellian voulge." Her smirk, Ormoch was certain, hid the subtle hint of a sneer. "And I wield it better than most."

She stalked around Ormoch in a wide circle. Her stride exhibited balance and confidence. Kezal fell into step directly opposite her, circling Ormoch.

"I'm sure you think yourself capable," Ormoch said to the woman. "But you're hardly what I'd call worthy prey."

"Are you sure?" She reached to the rear of her belt, detached two large pieces of metal, and tossed them at Ormoch's feet. He recognized them as Hirogen breathing masks. "Maybe you should ask Dossok and Saransk." Feigning forgetfulness, she added, "Oh, right, you can't. Because I killed them already, up at the engineering computer core—where *you* sent them, Ormoch."

*She knows our names.* The woman's detailed knowledge of him and his hunters lent credibility to her boasts. "Impressive," the alpha said. "And now you've come to fight me?"

That drew a snide chortle from her. "No." She pointed behind Ormoch, at Kezal. "I'm here to kill him."

Ormoch's temper flared. "I am the alpha!" he shouted, with such fury that it made his entire body tremble. "He is only the beta. Your life is *mine* to take, not his!"

The green woman stopped moving. "Not anymore. In a few seconds, he'll be the alpha. Because you'll be dead."

Quaking with rage, Ormoch felt like a spring that had been

coiled past its breaking point. "You think you can kill me?" He waved his sword erratically. "You're welcome to try!"

"I don't have to," the woman said. "My comrade, Lieutenant Simmerith, killed you ninety seconds ago." Her smile turned into a glare. "You have a few seconds left, so permit me to educate you. Simmerith was a Rigellian Chelon. In times of stress or combat, their skin secretes a deadly contact poison. And you got a faceful of it."

Ormoch was about to call her a liar when his knees buckled and dropped him in a quivering mass to the deck. Reduced to a helpless pile of flesh, he filled with shame.

Kezal wasted no time assuming his new status as the alpha. The young Hirogen hunter drew his sword and charged, leaping over Ormoch to attack the woman. The pair danced in and out of Ormoch's line of sight as he lay all but paralyzed on the deck. The engine compartment rang with the clashing of metal against metal, underscored by deep grunts of exertion.

Then the duelists loomed back into sight almost on top of him, and Ormoch saw the woman overextend herself into a fatal mistake. Kezal, to his credit, exploited it without mercy, driving his sword through the woman's chest.

Her voulge tumbled from her hands. She gurgled and gasped for air with a horrified expression as Kezal lifted her off the deck and admired his kill. When he raised his blade higher, her body went limp and slid down the blade until it came to a stop against the crossguard.

The new alpha breathed deep of the scent of his prey, committing it to memory. He brought her face level with his own and brushed her black hair from her shoulders, no doubt pondering where to begin her osteotomy for his newest trophy.

Then her eyes snapped open.

She plucked his short blades from the scabbards under his arms and lopped off his head with a scissoring cut.

His decapitated body fell limp at the green woman's feet. She discarded the two short blades and turned toward the fallen Ormoch, with the blade of Kezal's longsword still protruding from her back. Unsheathing it from her torso with a slow pull, she walked to Ormoch's side.

"Last lesson for today," she whispered in the former alpha's ear. "My species is called Takaran. We don't have vital organs, just a distributed physiology." She pulled open a rip in her uniform jacket and wiped the blood from her stab wound, which was no longer visible. "And, as you may have noticed, we're really good at healing."

He forced words past his dry, swollen tongue. "Your kind . . . are . . . worthy prey," he rasped.

The green woman wrapped her arms around Ormoch's head in an almost tender embrace. "Funny," she whispered. "That's how I feel about you." She torqued his jaw, and the last thing he heard was the crack of his spine snapping in two.


Worf's blood burned with anticipation, and he smelled the scents of the two Hirogen hunters who were climbing the port-side auxiliary turbolift shaft toward the bridge of the *Enterprise*.

"Power failures are moving up the shaft," Choudhury said, reading her tricorder. "Deck Six just went dark. Deck Five . . ."

"Here they come," said Captain Picard.

Kadohata herded the junior officers off the bridge and into the observation lounge. "Weinrib, Elfiki, Chen, let's go," she snapped, hustling them out of harm's way. Then she and tactical officer Šmrhová confronted the captain.

"You too, sir," Kadohata said.

"I belong here, Commander," Picard said with pride.

Choudhury called out in a steady voice, "Deck Four's dark."

"No time to argue," Kadohata said. She snapped her fingers at three of the ten security officers who had come to defend the bridge. "Mars, Braddock, Cruzen—front and center." The three security lieutenants stepped forward. "Give us your rifles, then fall back to the observation lounge and have the armory beam you three more." They traded confused looks, and Kadohata sharpened her tone. "That's an order, Lieutenants!"

Mars was the first to comply. The compact, gray-haired man handed his TR-116 and belt of spare clips to Captain Picard. Braddock, a trained sniper, reluctantly surrendered his weapon and rounds to Kadohata, and Cruzen seemed relieved as she passed her rifle and clips to Šmrhová.

"Right," Kadohata said. "Fall out." The three unarmed security officers exited the bridge. Kadohata looked at Picard and Šmrhová and nodded toward the mission-operations consoles to starboard. "Take cover there," she said. "Fire through the gaps in the console stands. Controlled bursts. I'll be close by."

Picard checked the settings on his weapon. "Very good," he said, and then he followed Šmrhová to cover.

Static filled the main viewer, which flickered and switched off, revealing the blank forward bulkhead. Consoles stuttered and went dark. The overhead lights failed, and the bridge's vast assortment of computers went silent.

Choudhury and Worf flanked the auxiliary turbolift doors. He kept his grip on his *bat'leth* firm but supple. She kept an equally lithe hold on her twin Gurkha kukri daggers. "Flares," Worf said to the security personnel who had taken cover around the bridge. Snap-cracks filled the deathly quiet, and then the bridge was aglow with pools of magenta- and lemon-hued light.

Fire and thunder tore through the doors of the auxiliary turbolift. Jagged hunks of the shattered portal caromed off the bulkheads and dormant companels, and a few slammed into random security personnel, who cried out in pain.

Amid the patter of falling debris, Worf heard two bright plinks of small metallic disks striking the deck. Searing flashes of light turned the smoky shadows of the bridge as bright as the sun, and for a moment he had to avert his eyes. He tried to stay alert as two Hirogen battle roars echoed on the bridge, but all he could see were purple retinal afterimages.

Tracer rounds filled the darkness, all of them targeted into the turbolift shaft. The strobing light and deafening buzz of gunfire were overwhelming to Worf's finely attuned senses, especially since he was all but standing atop the target.

His eyes and ears had almost adjusted when the barrage stopped, leaving the bridge steeped in dim shadows, acrid smoke, and tense silence. Nothing stirred in the turbolift shaft.

Then came the first choked-off scream, followed by the sickly gurgle of a humanoid with a slashed throat. Worf couldn't tell where the sound had come from, but his instincts told him that the Hirogen had slipped past him and Choudhury, probably in the moment of the first blinding flashes.

"Blades!" he shouted to the security team, and he heard the soft scrapes of combat knives being pulled from sheaths.

He stalked away from the blasted-open turbolift portal and hewed close to the aft bulkhead. On the other side of the bridge,

Choudhury followed his lead, moving at a quickstep in pursuit of foes who knew how to use the darkness.

Another wet crunch and muffled cry, from the port-side consoles. Choudhury leaped toward it as a yelp of alarm from the starboard side was cut short. Worf sprinted, hurdled over the command chairs, and found Ensign Carr from security with his throat slashed open—and no sign of his attacker.

One soft breath behind his back was Worf's only warning.

He spun, his *bat'leth* held vertically, and blocked what had been meant to be a silent killing stroke. Looking down at him was the scaled-and-painted face of a Hirogen.

The hunter snap-kicked Worf in the groin. Worf doubled over, sick with nausea, and the Hirogen kneed him in the jaw, knocking him through the air. The enraged Klingon landed hard and rolled quickly to his feet, ready to hit back.

Behind him, a battle cry preceded the agonized scream of Lieutenant ch'Kerrosoth, who tumbled wildly away from the second Hirogen hunter, into the middle of the bridge. The tall Andorian clutched at the stump of his left arm, which had just been severed a few centimeters above the elbow.

Pandemonium erupted on the bridge. Security officers broke cover and converged on the two exposed Hirogen, who cut them down with the smooth precision of butchers in a slaughterhouse.

Then the Alpha-Hirogen spotted Kadohata and Šmrhová trying to smuggle Captain Picard off the bridge to the observation lounge. He pointed at the captain. "Kill that one!"

Both Hirogen charged, knocking aside the security officers in their way. Worf sprinted to cut them off. Šmrhová and Kadohata closed ranks in front of the captain and fumbled as they tried to reload their TR-116s.

Choudhury buried one of her Gurkha knives in the charging Beta-Hirogen's unarmored knee joint. He spun and swung his own blade at her head. She ducked his slashing attack. He lunged forward, grasping at her throat. The limber security chief caught the beta's wrist, employed a move that was half judo and half *Mok'bara* to flip him onto his back, and used his own momentum to drive his dagger through his eye and into his brain.

Worf tackled the alpha, who jabbed an elbow backward, only to be blocked by Worf's *bat'leth*. The Hirogen rolled free of Worf's grip, and they came up facing each other. A feint by the hunter put Worf off balance. Next he felt the hot sting of a slash across his chin. He lunged and swung his *bat'leth* in a deadly downward stroke. It slammed impotently against the shoulder plate of the alpha's blue-black armor.

The alpha swatted the *bat'leth* from Worf's hands. Then he lunged and thrust his dagger forward and up, to stab Worf under his chin—exactly as Worf had hoped he would.

The rest happened in less than three seconds.

Worf pivoted away from the striking blade. He let himself flow like water, his limbs as free as the wind, and the dagger missed him. He ducked under the Hirogen's right arm, caught it by the wrist, and flipped the hunter over his shoulder.

The alpha struck the deck at Worf's feet, his wrist still caught in Worf's grip. Worf yanked the hunter's forearm taut and struck it with his knee. The elbow broke with a crack like a rifle shot. As the blade fell from the alpha's fingers, Worf landed a stomping kick on the alpha's neck. The fatal snap was muffled by the Hirogen's armor.

His dropped blade bounced across the deck and came to a stop as the Hirogen's body went limp.

"Turn off his energy dampener," Picard ordered, moving back toward his command chair.

Worf found the device on the alpha's belt and switched it off. Instantly, the overhead lights, companels, and main viewscreen became operational again. He noticed several of his crewmates recoil as the return of normal lighting revealed the copious amounts of blood that stained the deck around them.

Captain Picard, however, remained stoic and calm. "Hail the *Aventine*," he said. "Signal all-clear and confirm their status."

"Aye, sir," replied Kadohata, who stepped over the bodies of several dead security officers on the way to her post at ops.

Apprehensive looks and discomfited expressions marked the faces of the other bridge officers, who were led back in from the observation lounge. Elfiki lifted a hand to block the carnage from her sight as she hurried to the science station. Weinrib maintained a rigidly focused stare on the main viewer as he returned to his seat at the conn. T'Ryssa Chen looked as if she might become physically ill.

The main turbolift doors opened, and a team of medics emerged. As expected, they had come bearing a large number of blue body bags. The two who had actual medical equipment were led to the unconscious Lieutenant ch'Kerrosoth.

Kadohata glanced back at Worf and the captain. "*Aventine* confirms all-clear, sir."

"Splendid," Picard said, sounding enervated.

From the auxiliary science station, Lieutenant Chen stammered, "Um . . . sirs?"

Worf replied gruffly to the half-human, half-Vulcan contact specialist, "Report, Lieutenant."

"We have a new problem," she said, patching her sensor data onto the main viewer. "New readings from the subspace tunnel," she explained. "Long story short: It's becoming unstable. If we don't go back *right now,* we might never be able to."

Elfiki turned from her station, eyes wide with alarm. "Captain, without our shields at full power, we can't go back into the plasma stream."

"Bridge to engineering," Picard said.

"*La Forge here.*"

"Geordi, we need full shields, immediately."

"*After the beating we just took? Captain, we won't have full shields for at least six hours.*"

Everyone looked at Chen, who shook her head. "We don't even have *six minutes.*"

"Then we need a new solution," Kadohata said.

The normally shy Elfiki spoke up. "Mister Weinrib, how are your reflexes?"

The flight controller replied suspiciously, "Pretty good."

Elfiki threw a look at Kadohata. "And yours?"

"I've had no complaints," said the second officer.

"Well, you'd both better be fantastic if we want to get out of this." She shouldered aside Šmrhová from a tactical console and routed new information to the main viewer. "If we detonate two transphasic warheads—one *here* and the other *here*—we can create a six-second gap in the plasma stream. Which means we and the *Aventine* will have that long to emit the pulse that opens the aperture, navigate into it, and get both our ships inside the tunnel before the plasma stream catches up and slags us."

Chen added, "And we have about five minutes to do it."

Picard gave a fast nod. "Make it so."

The crew snapped into action. Worf settled into his chair

and sleeved a smear of blood from his chin. He looked left and caught the captain's eye. In a sub rosa voice, he said, "A pity she did not devise her plan *before* the Hirogen attack."

The captain lifted his eyebrows and sighed. "Starship command is like comedy, Number One. Timing is everything."

Dax stood in the center of the *Aventine*'s broken, smoldering bridge and felt precious seconds slip away. Her crew was racing to prepare the ship for its return journey while she stared at the main viewer and watched a raging flow of stellar plasma be siphoned from a red giant into its black-hole companion.

Bowers bounded from the science console to Dax's side. "We're ready," he said, wiping his soot-stained hand down the side of his grimy uniform jacket.

"Kandel, hail the *Enterprise*," Dax said. "Start the countdown. Nak, charge up the main deflector." Looking past Bowers to the ship's senior science officer, she added, "Get ready to pick that lock, Gruhn."

The svelte Zakdorn kept his eyes on his just-repaired companel as he palmed a sheen of sweat from his broad, high forehead. "Give the word and we're in, Captain."

Bowers confided to Dax, "Let's just hope the deflector's strong enough to shield the entire ship from the radiation inside the tunnel."

"If it's not, we'll know in about fifteen seconds," Dax said, watching the synchronized countdown on the main viewer.

A series of chirping tones sounded on the tactical console. Lieutenant Kandel reviewed the incoming data. "*Enterprise* is arming torpedoes and targeting the plasma stream," she said.

"Tharp," Bowers said to the Bolian conn officer, "full impulse, on my mark. Gruhn, open the subspace aperture on the same mark."

Kandel called out, "Torpedoes away in three . . . two . . . one . . ."

"Mark," Bowers said, as a pair of blue flashes sped from the bow of the *Enterprise* toward the plasma stream.

The vibration of full-impulse thrust resonated under Dax's feet as the *Aventine* accelerated instantly to one-quarter light speed, following the transphasic warheads toward a river of fire hanging in space. Six hundred meters to port, the *Enterprise* was pacing the *Aventine* in their race toward the subspace tunnel.

Electric blue flashes whited-out the main viewer. Then the image returned, and the first step of the plan had worked: The transphasic warheads had blasted a lacuna into the black hole's relativistic jet stream of superheated coronal mass.

Ahead of the two starships, the subspace aperture spiraled open as if rent from the fabric of reality itself. As it loomed larger on the *Aventine*'s main viewer, however, so did the tide of burning stellar plasma advancing from behind it.

"This is the fun part," Dax said, then inhaled sharply.

The blue-white rings of the subspace passage pulsed beyond its aperture's edges into the golden blaze of the plasma stream.

Then the *Aventine* was inside the passageway, shaking and pitching as strange energy currents hammered its hull. "Nak!" Dax hollered over the steady roar of turbulence. "Report!"

"Shields holding," the Tellarite shouted over the noise. "Hyperphasic radiation leaks on Decks Twenty-five and Twenty-six, Sections Thirty to Thirty-three."

Dax nodded. Nak had predicted leaks in those areas when he'd configured the deflector dish as a backup shield emitter, and they had been evacuated before the plan had been engaged.

A brutal tremor rocked the ship. Consoles stuttered light and dark, and white-hot phosphors rained down around Dax and Bowers as another EPS capacitor overloaded above them.

Bowers staggered across the heaving deck toward Helkara, and then a violent jolt of acceleration sprawled the first officer roughly against the science console. Through gritted teeth, he said, "Gruhn, what's going on out there?"

"The tunnel's imploding!" said Helkara, raising his voice so that Dax could hear his report, as well.

"What's causing it?" she demanded, falling awkwardly into her chair.

Helkara waved a drift of smoke away from his console. "Someone's bombarding it with high-energy soliton pulses," he said. "It's disrupting the tunnel's topology."

"Helm, all ahead full!" Dax yelled to Tharp.

"Almost there," the Bolian replied, even as he patched in every ounce of reserve power, including the ship's spacedock thrusters. "Clearing the passage in five . . . four . . ."

Ahead of them, the once-circular aperture of the tunnel had become deformed and irregular, like an amoeba. Its contours rippled, undulated, and began retracting and fusing together.

"I think it's trying to eat us," Nak blurted out in horror.

The melting edges of the aperture reached precariously close as the *Aventine* breached the subspace tunnel's threshold—and then the chaotic blue-and-white kaleidoscope was behind them, and the ship's main viewer was once more awash in the radiant, deep-blue serenity of the Azure Nebula.

"*Enterprise* is clear," Kandel reported over the relieved collective sigh of the other bridge officers. Then she gasped.

Dax glanced back at the Deltan woman to see what was wrong, only to see the shocked tactical officer raise her terrified stare toward the main viewer.

As she turned forward, Dax realized that all her officers were gazing at the viewscreen, looking transfixed and stunned.

Then she saw why.

The cerulean clouds and swirls of the nebula were aflame and littered with the wreckage of countless vessels.

Where she had expected to find the allied expeditionary force, all Dax saw was a smoldering starship graveyard.


Jean-Luc Picard didn't need sensor readings to know what had wrought the vast swath of carnage he saw on the *Enterprise*'s main viewer. The voice of the Collective was no longer distant; it was ubiquitous and deafening.

*We warned you, Locutus,* the Borg Queen declared. *We offered you perfection, and you refused us. Now you, Earth, and your Federation will suffer the consequences.*

"We're reading Borg weapon signatures everywhere," said Choudhury, whose console was only partly functional because of recent battle damage. "Massive subspace signal interference, too. I'll try to compensate for it."

Kadohata coaxed intermittent bursts of data from the ops panel. "I don't see any ships intact," she said. "Hang on—I'm picking up a Mayday on the emergency channel." Working quickly at her uncooperative controls, she added, "We have a visual."

Picard forced the Collective's voice from his mind and

struggled to remain stoic as he faced the maelstrom of destruction that surrounded his ship and the *Aventine*.

Then the image was magnified, and he saw the shadow of an *Intrepid*-class starship. One of its warp nacelles had been sheared away. Ragged chunks had been torn from its elliptical saucer, and sparking trails of half-ignited plasma streamed from its fractured secondary hull. It was trapped in a slow, random tumble, at the mercy of the nebula's currents.

With grim reverence, Kadohata said, "It's *Voyager,* sir."

He stood and tugged his uniform jacket taut. "Hail them."

The image on the main viewer sputtered in and out. Random signal noise hashed diagonally across the screen, and harsh static punctuated the high-frequency wail that tainted the audio. Even without the interference, however, Picard would barely have recognized the face of *Voyager*'s commanding officer.

Captain Chakotay's nose was broken, and the lower half of his face was caked with blood, some of it fresh and bright red, some dried and brown. All the hair had been scorched from the left side of his head, revealing burned, blackened skin. He was slumped at an awkward angle in his command chair, with his left arm pinned underneath him. A pink froth of bloodied saliva bubbled over his lip as he mumbled, *"Picard . . . ?"*

"Captain Chakotay," Picard replied. "Stand by to receive rescue teams from the *Enterprise* and the *Aventine*."

*"The Borg,"* Chakotay spluttered.

Nodding, Picard tried to calm him. "Yes, Captain. We—"

*"Rammed us,"* Chakotay continued, mumbling in a monotone born of severe shock. *"Smashed the whole fleet . . ."*

Picard nodded to Kadohata and Choudhury, who understood his unspoken intention and began discreetly directing the deployment of medics and engineers to *Voyager*.

*"Weapons did nothing,"* Chakotay went on, no longer looking at Picard but at some distant point in his imagination. *"Couldn't stop them. Too many."*

"How many?" Picard asked, not sure he wanted to know.

Chakotay didn't answer. He started shaking his head, and then kept on shaking it, as if denying the truth with enough vigor would make it go away.

Worf stepped forward beside Picard and said, "You need to see this, sir." The XO nodded to tactical officer Šmrhová, who split the main viewer image to present a sensor readout on the right-hand side. It was a long-range tactical scan. And the widening circular formation of red icons around the Azure Nebula stabbed an icy blade of fear through Picard's brave façade, down to his very core. "This is confirmed?"

"Aye, sir," Worf said. "At least seven thousand Borg ships have deployed into Federation, Klingon, and Romulan territory."

"Thousands," Picard mumbled, his voice barely a whisper. "Enough to send one to every inhabited world in known space."

Choudhury added, "With enough left over to target every starbase, outpost, and shipyard within a thousand light-years."

Under his breath, Picard said, "It's begun."

It was the day he had dreaded for sixteen years, since his first encounter with the Borg, in System J-25, during his command of the *Enterprise*-D. His inaugural experience with the Collective had spurred the Borg to step up their efforts to move against the Federation. But as horrific as the battles of Wolf 359 and Sector 001 had been, Picard had long suspected that they were little more than tests of the Federation's strengths and weaknesses—preludes for the true invasion that would bring Earth and its allies to ruin.

Now his greatest fear was made manifest, and there was nothing he could do to stop its deadly advance.

Kadohata tapped silent a comm signal on her panel. "The *Aventine* is hailing us," she said.

"On-screen," Picard said.

Dax appeared on the main viewer. She looked shell-shocked. *"Good news,"* she said. *"Helkara says all the subspace tunnels have collapsed, so there's no more back door to the Federation."*

Worf grunted. "Unfortunately, they have closed too late to make a difference."

*"Well, I guess making a difference is our job now,"* Dax replied. *"We're setting course for Earth."*

"To what end?" asked Picard, openly skeptical of Dax's proposed plan of action.

The headstrong young Trill woman shrugged. *"I'm playing it by ear. Maybe we can find the Borg Queen and take her out."*

Her naïveté inflamed Picard's temper. "It won't make any difference if you do," he told her. "They'll just raise another queen, and another."

*"Then we'll do something else,"* Dax said, her own ire coming to the fore. *"But I won't just sit back and do nothing."*

He stepped forward, hoping to make a stronger connection with Dax through virtual proximity. "Be rational, Captain," he urged her. "The Borg fleet numbers in the thousands, and it's moving away at speeds we can't match."

*"Maybe your ship can't,"* Dax said. *"Mine has a prototype slipstream drive, and this seems like a damned good time to fire it up."* She nodded to someone off-screen. *"There's a war on, Picard, and I plan on being part of it. Keep up if you can.* Aventine *out."*

The screen snapped back to the nebula full of broken starships and burning debris. The *Aventine* cruised past and then accelerated away, vanishing into the midnight-blue mists.

"*Aventine* is leaving the nebula at full impulse," Choudhury said, checking her console. "She's on course for Earth and powering up her warp drive."

Worf threw a sharp look at Picard. "Orders, sir?"

Picard knew that the logical response was to let the *Aventine* go on its quixotic tilt, keep the *Enterprise* hidden in the nebula, render aid to any survivors, and contact Starfleet Command for new orders.

He turned from the main viewer, walked back to his chair, and sat down. "Helm . . . go after them."

The news hit President Bacco like a gut punch.

"I need to sit down," she said, easing herself into the chair behind her desk. Outside the massive, curved window that served as a wall of her office in the Palais de la Concorde, Paris was resplendent beneath a blue sky and a golden sun, but Bacco felt as if someone had just turned out all the lights. "It's an entire fleet of Borg ships?"

Standing on the other side of Bacco's desk was Seven of Nine, who cocked her head and replied, "It would be more appropriate to call it an armada."

Flanking the ex-Borg security adviser were Bacco's defense secretary Raisa Shostakova, whose squat frame looked stouter than usual by comparison with Seven's trim, lanky physique; and Bacco's trusted chief of staff, Esperanza Piñiero, whose olive complexion and dark hair made Seven's fair skin and blond hair look almost albino pale.

Shostakova placed a padd on the desk in front of Bacco. "Long-range sensors have detected as many as seven thousand, four hundred sixty-one Borg vessels moving through our space, as well as in Klingon and Romulan territory."

Bacco read the intelligence estimate with growing dismay. "And the expeditionary force . . . ?"

"Wiped out," Piñiero said. "Their final transmissions were Maydays from *Voyager,* the *I.K.S. Chorbog,* and the *Antietam.*"

Pushing another padd across the desk to Bacco, Shostakova added, "The Borg have already started exterminating populations on Beta Thoridor, Adelphous IV, and Devnar IV. We project they'll launch attacks on Japori II and Gamma Hromi II in four hours, and H'Atoria within six hours."

A crushing despair settled on Bacco's shoulders. She looked to Seven. "How do we stop them?"

"You can't," Seven replied, her absolute certainty cold and unforgiving. "Without the subspace tunnels, there is nowhere you can go that the Borg will not find you."

The brutal truth and utter finality of Seven's words left Bacco with her head in her hands, pondering the possibility that she might have to preside over the end of the Federation.

"I need the room, everyone," she said, looking up.

Piñiero and Shostakova volleyed bemused glances before the chief of staff replied, "Ma'am . . . ?"

"Just for a few minutes, Esperanza. Please."

"Of course, ma'am," Piñiero said. Protection agents Wexler and Kistler appeared, as stealthy as shadows, behind the three women, and escorted them out of the president's office. Wexler was the last person out. He nodded to Bacco and shut the door.

Bacco was too keyed up to remain seated. She stood and paced along the panoramic window-wall, taking in what she belatedly realized might be Earth's final day.

As the elected leader of the Federation, there were so many events whose outcomes she could affect or direct that it made her dizzy sometimes to try and think of them all. Trillions of beings depended on her judgment. Countless technological marvels were at her command, tools she could use to shape the present and the future, to change the path of galactic destiny.

Not one of them was of any use against the Borg.

She stopped at her desk and pressed her palms flat upon its brilliantly lacquered surface. The true weight of her presidency settled upon her, an Atlas's burden, and she bowed her head as her late father's advice echoed in her memory: *Everything we do today defines us—because tomorrow might never come.*

Brushing a tear from her cheek, she whispered through a fearful grimace, "You didn't know how right you were, Dad."

# 20

William Riker hurried out of the turbolift onto the bridge of *Titan,* to find Pazlar and Ra-Havreii waiting for him at the engineering console. "What have we got?" asked Riker, walking quickly to join the exhausted, frazzled-looking duo.

"Just what you asked for," said Ra-Havreii, pointing at the upper display screen. "We tapped into the Caeliar's soliton pulses about an hour ago."

Pazlar lifted her arm to gesture at a different screen, and Riker noticed only then that the science officer was once again outfitted in her powered, musculature-assistance armature. "It's taken us since then to decode their signal patterns," Pazlar said. "We'll get the descrambled feed in a few seconds."

Ra-Havreii smoothed the top of his frost-white mustache with his thumb and forefinger. "Do you want to join their feed in real time or see it from where we first tapped in?"

"From the beginning," Riker said. The chief engineer nodded, and then he and Pazlar both keyed in commands as Riker added, "Excellent work, both of you."

They accepted the compliment with polite nods, and Pazlar said, "Here it comes." Garbled blurs and a stutter of sounds resolved quickly into a sharp and chilling spectacle.

A massive wave of Borg cubes was emerging from an anomaly that resembled a wormhole. The steady stream of black starships coursed like poison into an indigo nebula and rammed through a fleet of hundreds of ships; many of them were Starfleet and Klingon vessels, but there were also dozens of Romulan and Cardassian ships. The Borg crushed them all like children's toys beneath the boots of angry giants.

Even after the fleet had been pulverized and scattered into the blue storm, the anomaly continued to hemorrhage Borg ships.

Riker swallowed and pushed down the sick feeling that was rising from his gut. "Do we have a fix on those coordinates?"

"Aye, sir," Pazlar said. "It's the Azure Nebula."

He had seen enough of the slaughter. "Switch to real time," he said to Ra-Havreii.

A single tap by Ra-Havreii changed the image to one of quiet desolation. Broken hulls and fragments from a variety of ships drifted into random collisions, driven by the nebula's chaotic currents.

"Where's the anomaly?" asked Riker.

Radiant warmth filled the bridge behind him, and he noticed an overpowering smell of ozone. "It was a subspace tunnel," answered a female voice. "And it's gone."

He turned and saw an attractive young woman, ostensibly human and barely out of her teens. Her long, wild mane of black hair was out of proportion to her slender figure, which was garbed in silvery-white drapes of diaphanous fabric that were one trick of the light away from being scandalous. There was a steely quality to her eyes that belied her youthful mien.

Ensign Rriarr leveled his small sidearm phaser at the woman. "Don't move," he said.

She glanced at the Caitian security officer, and the weapon in his hand turned to dust as she strode forward to meet Riker. "There isn't much time, Captain, so please listen to me. My name is Erika Hernandez. I used to be the captain of the Earth starship *Columbia*. And I've been a prisoner of the Caeliar for more than eight hundred years." She waved away his unvoiced question. "I'll explain later. Right now, answer me this." Nodding at the science monitor that showed the Azure Nebula, she asked, "Do you want to take your ship there?"

Riker looked at Ra-Havreii and Pazlar, whose befuddled expressions offered him no guidance. He turned back to Hernandez. "Yes," he said.

"I can get you there," Hernandez said, "using the same device that helped me get here—but only if we leave *right now*."

Lieutenant Sariel Rager swiveled her chair toward the conversation and interjected, "Sir, the away team—"

Silencing his ops officer with a raised hand, Riker asked Hernandez, "What about my people on the surface?"

Hernandez shook her head. "They're all being watched," she said. "There's no way to free them without alerting the Caeliar." She glanced anxiously at the image of the nebula. "They've already shut down the subspace tunnels. Any second now they'll terminate this surveillance wormhole, and once they do there won't be any way out of here, for any of us—*ever*."

Torn by indecision, Riker clenched his fists. "You don't understand," he said. "My wife is down there."

"She's not going anywhere," Hernandez replied. "You can always come back to join her." She looked away, as if listening to something. When she turned back, there was fear in her eyes. "They know I'm missing. It's now or never, Captain. Call it."

Riker stared at the image of the nebula, wrenched between his desire to save his away team and his responsibility to save his ship; between his love for his wife and his oath to the Federation, which was about to face the darkest hour of its history. Acting for the good of the many was his sworn duty, but now it meant abandoning Deanna when she needed him most. No matter what he did, a sacred promise would have to be broken.

But a decision had to be made.

"Take us home," he said.

# BOOK III

# LOST SOULS

# HISTORIAN'S NOTE

The main narrative of *Lost Souls* takes place in February of 2381 (Old Calendar), approximately sixteen months after the events depicted in the movie *Star Trek Nemesis.* The flashback story occurs circa 4527 B.C.E.

Death closes all: but something ere the end,
Some work of noble note, may yet be done,
Not unbecoming men that strove with gods.

—Alfred, Lord Tennyson, *Ulysses*

# 2381

## 1

It was the hardest decision William Riker had ever made.

He cast a suspicious glare at *Titan*'s unexpected visitor, a human-looking young woman with a crazy mane of sable hair and delicate garments that showed more of her body than they covered. She had claimed to be Erika Hernandez, the commanding officer of the Earth *Starship Columbia,* which had vanished more than two centuries earlier, thousands of light-years from the planet where *Titan* was now being held prisoner. Her tale seemed implausible, but she had offered to help his ship escape, and so Riker was willing to accept her extraordinary claims on faith . . . at least, until *Titan* was safe someplace far from here and he could put her identity to the test.

Hers had been a proposition he couldn't refuse, but freeing his ship from the reclusive aliens known as the Caeliar would come at a price: His away team—made up of most of his senior officers, including his wife, his *Imzadi,* Deanna Troi—would have to be abandoned on the planet's surface.

But there was a war raging at home, and above all, he had a duty to protect his ship and defend the Federation. No matter what he did, he was certain his decision would haunt him for a long time to come.

"Take us home," Riker said.

Hernandez snapped into action and took command of the situation. Pointing at the display screen over the science station, she asked curtly, "Who set up this tap on the Caeliar's subspace aperture?"

"We did," answered Commander Xin Ra-Havreii, *Titan*'s chief engineer, gesturing to himself and the ship's senior science officer, Lieutenant Commander Melora Pazlar.

Hernandez stepped to the console and began entering data. The strange young woman's fingers moved with velocity and delicacy, as if she had mastered the Federation's newest technology ages earlier. "I need to change your shield specs to protect you from radiation inside the passage," she said.

"Our shields already do that," Ra-Havreii said.

"No," Hernandez replied, her flurry of tapping on the console unabated, "you only think they do. Give me a moment." Her hands came to an abrupt stop. "There." She turned and snapped at Riker's acting first officer, Commander Fo Hachesa, "Which station controls onboard systems?"

Hachesa pointed at ops.

"Thank you," she said to the stunned-silent Kobliad. Moving in rapid strides, Hernandez crossed to the forward console and nudged Lieutenant Sariel Rager out of her way. "I'm programming your deflector to create a phase-shifted soliton field. That'll make it harder for the Caeliar to shift the aperture on us while we're in transit." She looked across at Ensign Aili Lavena, the Pacifican flight-control officer. "Be ready to go at your best nonwarp speed, as soon as the passage opens. Understood?"

Lavena nodded quickly, shaking loose air bubbles inside her liquid-atmosphere breathing mask.

Watching the youthful Hernandez at work, Riker felt superfluous on his own bridge.

"All right," Hernandez announced, "I'm about to widen the subspace aperture into a full tunnel. When I do, the Caeliar will try to shut it down. Be warned: This is gonna be a rough ride." She looked around at the various alien faces on *Titan*'s bridge. "Everyone ready?" The crew nodded. She met Riker's gaze. "It's your ship, Captain. Give the word."

*Nice of her to remember*, Riker thought. He led Hachesa back to their command chairs. They sat down and settled into place. Lifting his chin, Riker said to Hernandez, "The word is given."

"And away we go," Hernandez said. She faced forward, fixed her gaze on the main viewscreen, and lifted her right arm to shoulder height. With her outstretched hand, she seemed to reach toward the darkness, straining to summon something from the void. Then it appeared, like an iris spiraling open in space: a circular tunnel filled with brilliant, pulsing blue and white rings of light, stretching away to infinity.

Lavena pressed the padd to fire the impulse engines at full power. One moment, Riker heard the hum and felt the vibrations of sublight acceleration through the deck plates; the next, he was clutching his chair's armrests as the ship slammed to a hard, thunderous halt and threw everyone forward.

"More power!" cried Hernandez over the alarm klaxons and groaning bulkheads. "I'll try to break their hold on us!" She closed her eyes, bowed her head, and raised both arms.

Riker had witnessed some of Deanna's psychic struggles in the past, and he knew that whatever Hernandez was enduring to free his ship, it had to be worse than he could imagine. "Give it all we've got!" he bellowed over the chatter of damage reports pouring in via the ops and tactical consoles.

*Titan* lurched forward, then it was inside the pulsating brightness of the subspace tunnel. Lieutenant Rriarr gripped the side of the tactical console with one paw as he reported, "High-level hyperphasic radiation inside the tunnel, Captain. Shields holding."

*That's why she had to modify our shields,* Riker realized. *Otherwise, we'd all be handfuls of dust by now.* Bone-rattling blows hammered the ship. "Report!" Riker ordered.

"Soliton pulses," Rriarr said. "From behind us."

"They're trying to bend the passage and bring us back to New Erigol," Hernandez said. "Keep that soliton field up!"

"Divert nonessential power to the deflector," Riker said.

"Belay that, sir," countered Ra-Havreii. "The gravitational shear inside the tunnel is rising. We have to reinforce the structural integrity field!"

Hernandez shot back, "Do that, and we'll lose control of the tunnel. We'll be taken back to New Erigol!"

"If we don't, the ship might be torn in half," replied the angry Efrosian engineer. Punctuating his point, a console behind him exploded and showered the bridge with stinging debris and quickly fading sparks.

Falling to her knees, Hernandez kept her arms extended and her hands up, as if she were holding back a titanic weight. "Just a few more seconds!" she cried in a plaintive voice.

The bluish-white rings of the tunnel began distorting as the black circle of its terminus became visible. "Lieutenant Rager, all available power to the deflector," Riker said. "That's an order." Another round of merciless impacts quaked the ship around him. "Hold her together, folks, we're almost out!"

An agonized groan welled up from within Hernandez as the egress point loomed large ahead of *Titan*. She arched her back and lifted her hands high above her head before unleashing a defiant, primal scream.

Outside the ship, in the tunnel, a massive ripple like a shimmer of heat radiation coursed ahead of *Titan,* smoothing the rings back to their perfect, circular dimensions and calming the turbulence. The shockwave rebounded off the exit ring as the *Luna*-class explorer hurtled through it.

Energy surges flurried the bridge's consoles, and displays spat out chaotic jumbles. A final, calamitous blast pummeled *Titan,* and the bridge became as dark as a moonless night. Only the feeble glow of a few tiny status gauges pierced the gloom in the long moments before the emergency lights filled the bridge with a dim, hazy radiance.

Smoke blanketed the bridge, and the deck sparkled with a fine layer of crystalline dust from demolished companels. The deck was eerily silent; there was no sound of comm chatter, no feedback tones from the computers.

"Damage report," Riker said. He surveyed the bridge for anyone able to answer him. He was met by befuddled looks and officers shaking their heads in dismay.

Ra-Havreii moved from station to station, barely pausing at each one before moving on to the next, growing more agitated every step of the way. When he reached the blank conn, he gave his drooping ivory-white mustache a pensive stroke, then turned to Riker and said, "We're blacked out, Captain. Main power's offline, along with communications, computers, and who knows what else. I'll have to go down to main engineering to get a better look at the problem."

"Go ahead," Riker said. "Power first, then communications."

"That was my plan," replied Ra-Havreii, heading for the turbolift. He all but walked into the still-closed doors before making an awkward stop, turning on his heel, and flashing an embarrassed grimace. "No main power, no turbolifts." He pointed aft. "I'll just take the emergency ladder."

As the chief engineer made his abashed exit, Riker got up and walked to Hernandez's side. In slow, careful motions, he helped her stand and steady herself. "Are you all right?"

"I think so," she said. "That last pulse was a doozy. Guess I didn't know my own strength."

Riker did a double-take. "You *caused* that final pulse?"

"I had to," she said. "It was the only way to close off the passage and destroy the machine at the other end once we were clear. That'll keep the Caeliar off our backs for a while."

"Define 'a while.'"

Hernandez shrugged. "Hard to say. Depends how much damage I did and how badly the Caeliar want to come after us. Could be a few days. Could be a few decades."

"We'd better get busy making repairs, then," Riker said.

She nodded once. "That would probably be a good idea."

Riker turned to Lieutenant Rriarr. "As soon as the turbolifts are working, have Captain Hernandez escorted to quarters and placed under guard." To Hernandez, he added, "No offense."

"None taken," she replied. "After eight hundred years with the Caeliar, I'm used to being treated like a prisoner."


Deanna Troi screamed in horror as Dr. Ree sank his fangs into her chest just below her left breast, and Ree felt absolutely terrible about it, because he was only trying to help.

The Pahkwa-thanh physician ignored Troi's frantic slaps at his head as he released a tiny amount of venom into her bloodstream. Then the half-Betazoid woman stiffened under his slender, taloned feet as the fast poison took effect.

Four sets of hands—one pair on each arm and two pairs on his tail—yanked him backward, off Troi, and dragged him into a clumsy group tumble away from her. He rolled to his feet to find himself confronted by the away team's security contingent, which consisted of Chief Petty Officer Dennisar, Lieutenant Gian Sortollo, and *Titan*'s security chief, Lieutenant Commander Ranul Keru. The team's fuming-mad first officer, Commander Christine Vale, snapped, "What the hell were you *doing*, Ree?"

"The only thing that I could, under the circumstances," Ree replied, squaring off against his four comrades.

Vale's struggle for calm was admirable, if unsuccessful. She flexed her hands and fought to unclench her jaw. "This had better be the best damned explanation of your life, Doctor."

A shadow stepped off a nearby wall and became Inyx, the chief scientist of the Caeliar. The looming, lanky alien tilted his bulbous head and permanently frowning visage in Ree's direction. "I am quite eager to hear your explanation as well," he said. The deep inflation and deflation of the air sacs that drooped over his bony shoulders suggested a recent exertion.

Ensign Torvig Bu-kar-nguv cowered outside the door of Troi's quarters and poked his ovine head cautiously around the jamb to see what was transpiring inside. Ree understood perfectly the reticence of the young Choblik, whose species—bipedal runners with no natural forelimbs—were descended from prey animals.

As Ree chose his words, Commander Tuvok, *Titan*'s second officer, entered and kneeled beside Troi. The brown-skinned Vulcan man gently rested one hand on Troi's forehead.

"I confess it was an act of desperation," Ree said. "After the Caeliar destroyed all of our tricorders—including mine—I had no way to assess the counselor's condition with enough specificity to administer any of the hyposprays in my satchel."

"So you bit her," Sortollo interrupted with deadpan sarcasm. "Yeah, that makes sense."

Undeterred by the Mars-born human's cynicism, Ree continued, "Commander Troi's condition became progressively worse after she went to bed. Based on my tactile measure of her blood pressure, pulse, and temperature, I concluded there was a high probability that she had suffered a serious internal hemorrhage." He directed his next comments to Inyx, who had moved to Troi's side and squatted low, opposite Tukov, to examine her. "She would not permit me to seek your help or request the use of your sterile medical facilities for the procedure."

"And *that's* why he bit her," Dennisar said, riffing on Sortollo's dry delivery. Commander Vale glared the Orion into a shamed silence.

Inyx rested his gently undulating cilia over Troi's bite wound. "You injected her with a toxin."

Menace was implied in Vale's every syllable as she said, "If you've got a point to make, Doctor, now's the time."

"My venom is a relic of Pahkwa-thanh evolution," he said to her. "It places prey in a state of living suspended animation. Its purpose in my species' biology was to enable sires of new hatchlings to roam a large territory and bring live prey back to the nest without a struggle, so that it would be fresh when fed to our young. In this case, I used it to place Counselor Troi in a suspended state to halt the progression of her hemorrhage."

Keru sighed heavily and shook his head. "All right, that does kind of make sense."

"What you did was barbaric and violent," Inyx said. A sheet of quicksilver spread beneath Troi like a metallic bloodstain. It solidified and levitated her from the floor. "Your paralyzing toxin, while effective in the short term, will not sustain her for long. If that is what passes for medicine among your kind, I am not certain you deserve to be called a doctor."

Inyx began escorting the levitated Troi toward the exit.

Tuvok lurked silently behind Inyx, his intense stare fixed on Troi's face, which was frozen in a look of shock even though she was no longer sensate.

Vale blocked Inyx's path. The security personnel regrouped behind her, fully obstructing the doorway. "Hold on," she said to Inyx. "Where are you taking her?"

"To a facility where we can provide her with proper medical care," the Caeliar scientist replied. He glanced at Ree and added in a pointed tone, "You might be surprised to learn that *our* methods do not include masticating our patients."

Ree was a gentle being by nature, but the Caeliar seemed committed to putting his goodwill to the test. "She needs the kind of medical care that I can provide to her only on *Titan*," he said to Inyx. "If you really were the beneficent hosts you claim to be, you'd let us return to the ship."

Inyx halted and turned back to face Ree. "I am afraid that is quite impossible," he said.

"Yes, yes," Ree groused. "Because of your sacred privacy."

"No," Inyx said, "because your ship has escaped and left you all behind." A gap opened in the ceiling above Inyx and Troi, who ascended through it into the open air of the starless night. Inyx looked down and added, "I will leave you to contemplate that while I try to save your friend's life." He and Troi faded into the darkness and were gone.

A shocked silence filled the room as the remaining away-team members regarded one another with searching expressions.

Dennisar asked no one in particular, "Do you really think *Titan* got away?"

Keru gave a noncommittal sideways nod. "The Caeliar haven't lied to us so far. Could be the truth."

Vale said, "If they did, good for them. And it's good news for us, too, because you know Captain Riker will send help."

Everyone nodded, and Ree could sense that they were all trying to put the most positive possible spin on the cold fact of having been abandoned by their shipmates and captain.

Torvig was the first to wander back to his quarters, and then Tuvok slipped away, his demeanor reserved and withdrawn. Vale left next, and Keru ushered his two men out of the room.

Ree followed the burly Trill security chief out of Troi's quarters into the corridor. Keru snickered under his breath. "I'm sorry, Doc," he said. "But for a second there, I really thought you were trying to eat Counselor Troi."

"I would never do such a thing," Ree said, affecting a tone of greater offense than he really felt. Then he showed Keru a toothy grin. "Though I have to admit . . . she was rather succulent." Noting the man's anxious sidelong glance, Ree added with a flustered flourish, "Kidding."

# 4527 B.C.E.

## 2

A fiery mountain fell from the sky.

Deep thunder rolled above the snowy landscape as the behemoth of scorched metal plunged through the low cover of bleak autumn clouds. Wreathed in flames and ashen smoke, its angle of descent shallowed moments before it caromed off the rocky mountainside. Eruptions of mud, splintered trees, and pulverized stone filled the air. The dark mass cut epic gouges into the alpine slope, and it broke apart on its descent to the rugged coastline of the ice-packed fjord below.

An avalanche rushed before it. Millions of tons of snow, dirt, and ice moved like water and then set like stone as they buried the shattered crags of blackened metal. The ground shook, and the roar of the collision and its consequences echoed and re-echoed off the surrounding peaks and glaciers, until it was swallowed by the deep silence of the arctic wilderness.

Twilight settled on the fjord.

And there wasn't a soul to bear witness.

"Stand back," MACO Sergeant Gage Pembleton said. "I'm almost through. One more shot ought to do it."

He stood, wedged in a jagged rent in the foundation of the Caeliar city-ship Mantilis. He aimed his phase rifle into the gap he had melted, through the densely packed ice and snow that had entombed the wrecked vessel after its calamitous planetfall on this unknown world, tens of thousands of light-years from Earth. A quick tap on the rifle's trigger released a flash of heat and light, and then he saw open sky. Frigid, pine-scented air surged through the new opening, and his whoop of celebration condensed into wisps of vapor in front of his face.

Waiting inside the remains of a laboratory complex, behind and beneath Pembleton, were the other five human survivors of Mantilis's hard landing. Three of them were privates from the *Columbia*'s MACO company: Eric Crichlow, a bug-eyed and large-nosed son of Liverpool; Thom Steinhauer, a German with chiseled features, close-shorn hair, and little sense of humor; and Niccolo Mazzetti, a handsome Sicilian with olive skin, black hair, and a reputation for never being lonely on shore leave.

Huddled between the MACOs was Kiona Thayer, the only woman in the group. She was a tall, raven-haired Québécoise with distant Sioux ancestry—and a bloody, hastily bandaged mess where her left foot once had been. Pembleton found her wound hard to look at—chiefly because he'd been the one who'd inflicted it, on orders from his MACO commander, Major Foyle.

At the front of the group was the *Columbia*'s chief engineer, a broad-backed Austrian man named Karl Graylock. He asked, "Is it safe to move outside?"

"I'm not sure yet," Pembleton said. He set the safety on his weapon and rubbed his brown hands together for warmth. "But I can tell you it's cold out there."

Graylock raised his eyebrows. "Coming from a Canadian, that means something." He glanced back at the others briefly before he added, "Maybe you and I should have a look first."

"Aye, sir," Pembleton replied. "I'll test the footing." Taking careful steps, he felt that the gravity was stronger than he was accustomed to. He made a careful climb through the icy passage he had carved one shot at a time. A few meters shy of the top, he called back to Graylock, "It's safe, Lieutenant."

The chief engineer followed Pembleton up the slope and out into the needle-sharp cold. The air was thin. As they stepped ankle-deep into the snow outside, Pembleton was awed by the sheer majesty of the vista that surrounded him: towering cliffs of black rock streaked with pristine snow; placid fjords reflecting a sky that glowed on the horizon with pastel hues of twilight; a few brilliant stars shining high overhead. It was so beautiful that he almost forgot that his fingers and toes had started going numb from the cold. "Quite a view," he said, his baritone voice reverentially hushed.

He looked sidelong at Graylock, who had turned to face in the other direction. The beefy engineer stared up the slope, his jaw slack. Pembleton did an about-face and beheld the swath that Mantilis had cut down the mountainside, through the upper half of the tree line. The devastation was impressive—in particular, the wounds that had been hewn into the mountain's rocky face—but it paled before the sight that filled the heavens above it. Ribbons of prismatic beauty wavered behind the distant peaks, against a black sky peppered with stars. The aurora was breathtaking in its intensity and range of colors.

"Wow," Pembleton muttered.

"*Ja,*" said Graylock, his voice barely a hush of breath.

Pembleton pushed his hands inside the pants pockets of his camouflage fatigues. "We should probably wait until it gets a little brighter before we bring the others out here," he said. Pointing at the fjord, he added, "Then we can head for low ground, by the shore. I'd suggest we make camp there and sort out the basics—shelter, fire, potable water, and as much food as we can stockpile. Then, if anything like spring ever comes, we can head for warmer weather near the equator."

"Why go so far, Sergeant?" Graylock asked. "Shouldn't we hold position until we figure out how to call for a rescue?"

Pressing his arms to his sides to quell his shivering, Pembleton said, "There's never going to be a rescue, sir."

Graylock folded his arms across his chest and tucked his hands under his armpits. "We can't think like that, Sergeant," he said. "We can't give up hope."

"With all respect, sir, I think we can." Pembleton tilted his head back to look up at the stars. He remembered what the Caeliar scientist Lerxst had told him just before Mantilis made planetfall. "We're almost sixty thousand light-years from home, and the year is roughly 4500 B.C." He turned his head toward Graylock and added, "This is where we're going to live the rest of our lives . . . and this is where we're going to die."

This nameless world had turned but once on its axis, and already Lerxst and his eleven fellow Caeliar felt the ebb of their vitality. "We should conserve our strength," he said to his colleague Sedín. "Reducing our mass will lessen the effects of this planet's gravity on our movement."

"Shedding some of our catoms is only a short-term solution," she replied. "Unless we find a new source of power, we'll weaken to the point where we can't recorporealize."

A pang of guilt impeded Lerxst's thoughts; he had decided to jettison the city's main power source and much of its mass into subspace, rather than risk inflicting its devastating potential on an unsuspecting world in the crash. But divorced from the gestalt, and with their city in ruins, he and the other Caeliar of Mantilis had no means of rebuilding their lost generators. Without them to power the city's quantum field, the Caeliar's catoms would swiftly exhaust their energy supply.

"At this extreme polar latitude, solar collection will not be a viable alternative until after our reserves have been depleted," Lerxst said. "Do we have enough strength to tap and develop this world's geothermal resources?"

Sedín's gestalt aura radiated doubt. "The bedrock here is deep, and we're far from any volcanic activity." She shared an image of the mountain atop which their city had been sundered. "There is a greater likelihood of mining fissionable elements."

"Not enough for our needs," Lerxst replied. "I am also concerned that their use might risk introducing toxins into this world's ecosphere." It had been aeons since he had felt so vexed. "If only we hadn't lost all of the zero-point aggregators, we might have had time to build a new prime particle generator."

Another Caeliar, an astrophysicist named Ghyllac, entered the darkened control center from behind Lerxst. He was followed by two of the human survivors, Gage Pembleton and Karl Graylock. Ghyllac said, "Visitors for you, Lerxst."

Lerxst turned to greet their guests. "Welcome, Gage and Karl," he said. "Have you reconsidered our invitation to use what's left of Mantilis as a shelter?"

"*Nein,*" Graylock said. "There is no food for us at this altitude on the slope. We need to move down to the fjord."

His statement seemed to perplex Sedín, who replied, "There is no greater variety of flora along the shoreline, Karl."

Pembleton said, "We'll try our luck at fishing."

Sedín was about to apprise the humans of the folly of such a labor, but Lerxst cut off her reply with a gentle emanation through their tragically reduced gestalt. He asked Graylock, "Then to what do we owe the privilege of this visit?"

"We need batteries," Graylock said. "Large ones for charging equipment and smaller portable ones."

Apprehension passed like an electrical charge among the

dozen Caeliar inside the demolished control facility. Parceling out any of their already scant stored energy to the human survivors would only hasten the Caeliar's fade into oblivion.

"We'll share what we can, limited though it is," Lerxst said, shutting out the swell of anxiety from his colleagues.

The humans nodded. Graylock said, "As long as we're here, we might as well ask if we can salvage parts and materials from the city's debris."

Lerxst bowed and spread his arms slightly. "Be our guest."

"Thank you," Pembleton said. He lowered his voice as he looked at Graylock and asked, "Anything else, sir?"

Graylock shook his head. "No." To Lerxst, he added, "You'll let us know when the batteries are ready?"

"Of course."

"*Danke schön,*" Graylock said with a nod. He turned and walked out, and Pembleton followed at his side.

After the humans were far from the control center, Sedín asked, "Was that a wise promise to make, Lerxst?"

"I obeyed the dictates of my conscience," Lerxst said. "Nothing more."

Ghyllac interjected, "We need that energy to live."

"So do the humans," Lerxst said.


The survivors' first full day on the planet barely deserved to be called a day at all, in Pembleton's opinion. The colorless sun barely edged above the horizon, turning the arctic sky marble gray above a wide, slate-colored sea.

One by one, the rest of the group followed Pembleton from the rifle-cut tunnel, out onto the wind-blasted mountainside. Everyone was garbed in warm, silver-gray hooded ponchos provided by the Caeliar. Their backpacks were jammed with blankets, a smattering of raw materials, and battery packs of various sizes.

Lieutenant Thayer lay on a narrow stretcher. The task of carrying her was shared by the MACO privates. At any given moment, two of them were handling the stretcher while the third rested between turns of duty.

To what Pembleton had decided was the west, an advancing storm spread like a purple-black bruise. "We'd better move if we want to reach low ground in time," he told Graylock.

"In time for what?" the engineer said.

"To build shelters and get fires lit," Pembleton replied. "Before the storm hits." Surveying the sparsely wooded slope, he added, "We sure don't want to get caught in that up here."

"Good point," Graylock said. "Lead us down, Sergeant."

The group trudged wearily toward the fjord, far below. In the slightly heavy-feeling gravity, each step gave Pembleton a minor jolt of shin-splint pain.

He glanced back to confirm that everyone else was faring all right. Crichlow and Mazzetti had the stretcher steadily in hand, and Steinhauer and Graylock were chatting amiably about something in rapid-fire German.

Along the way, the one resource whose supply exceeded demand was fresh water. According to Graylock's hand scanner, the snow that blanketed the landscape was remarkably pure and undoubtedly safe to drink. "At least we won't dehydrate," he said, trying to muster some optimism.

"That just means it'll take us longer to starve to death," Pembleton replied, in no mood to have his morale boosted.

Within less than two hours, they were far enough down the slope that other nearby peaks blocked out the feeble sunlight. Crossing into the steel-blue shadows, Pembleton felt the temperature plummet several degrees. His every exhalation filled the air ahead of him with ephemeral plumes of vapor.

It was late in the day and quickly growing dark by the time they reached the water's edge. "Steinhauer, help Graylock set up by those big rocks, up on that rise," Pembleton said. "It'll give us a break from the wind and keep us dry when the runoff comes down the mountain. Mazzetti, you and I will dig a latrine on the other side. Crichlow, take your rifle and a hand scanner. Hunt for any kind of small animal—bird, fish, mammal, I don't care. Anything edible."

"Right, Sarge," Crichlow said. He stripped off his backpack, tucked a hand scanner into a leg pocket of his fatigue pants, grabbed his rifle, and stole away into the sparse brush.

By the time Graylock and the MACOs had finished building the group's shelter—a tenuous structure of hastily welded scrap-metal supports overlaid by more of the Caeliar's wonder fabric—the sky was pitch dark. A vicious wind howled like a demon's choir between the cliffs that bordered the fjord, and the air was heavy with the scent of rain.

A snapping of twigs and crunching steps on snow turned Pembleton's head, and he aimed his rifle as a precaution. He lowered it when he recognized Crichlow, who emerged from the brush looking tattered, scratched, and dejected.

"Nothing out there?" Pembleton asked.

"Oh, they're out there," Crichlow said. The young private met Pembleton's disappointed gaze and shook his head. "But the little buggers are so spry, I can't get a bead on 'em."

Pembleton fell into step beside Crichlow as they walked toward the shelter. "Don't worry about it," he said. "Tomorrow, switch to snares. See how that goes."

"Right, Sarge," Crichlow said. "Will do."

They pushed through the front flaps that served as a door for the shelter. The ground had been covered with large squares of the Caeliar fabric, except for a circle in the middle, where large stones had been piled and heated to a bright red glow that filled the enclosure with smokeless warmth.

"Tighten your belts, folks," Pembleton said. "Looks like bark soup for dinner." Groans of dismay were his reward for honesty. "Look on the bright side," he continued. "After we enjoy our tasty broth, you'll all get to sleep, because I'll take the first watch, till 2100. Mazzetti, second watch, till 0100. Steinhauer, third watch, to 0500. Crichlow, last watch. We'll rotate the schedule nightly."

Mazzetti asked, "Can't we just set a hand scanner for proximity detection?"

"We're trying to save its power cell for things like finding food and figuring out what's toxic," said Graylock.

"Exactly," Pembleton said. "And Mazzetti? For asking that, you just volunteered for bark-collection detail."

The bark soup was hot but also bitter, like a raw acorn. Despite having drained his canteen twice in the hour after dinner and spitting furiously, Pembleton still hadn't expunged the taste from his mouth. *Fortunately, I have the rain to keep my mind off it,* he observed with dark humor.

Driven by brutally cold gales, a freezing spray slashed through the night and found every gap in Pembleton's salvaged-fabric poncho. His phase rifle was slung across his back, and his hands were tucked inside his camouflage fatigue jacket and under his armpits for warmth.

After Mazzetti had gone out for bark, Graylock had run a scan for any kind of edible plants near the shelter. Nothing had registered on the hand scanner. No berries, fruits, or nuts. Not even simple grasses. Just poisonous fungi and lichens.

*The weather's only going to get worse,* he predicted. *The nights'll get longer, and the cold'll get deeper.* He looked at the mediocre shelter that he and the others now depended on, and he frowned. *If that thing survives a winter in this place, it'll be a miracle.*

A short time before the end of his watch, the downpour was borne away on the shoulders of a biting wind. In minutes, the precipitation abated to a drizzle, and then it stopped. The air cleared, and as a parade of fast-moving clouds transited the sky, he saw the hypnotic radiance of the aurora behind the peaks. Then something beneath it, on the slope of the mountain, caught his attention. Pale glows of movement.

He fished his binoculars from his fatigues and trained them on the light sources high above his position. Magnified, the details of the scene became clearly visible. The Caeliar had come out from their buried, broken metropolis and were gathering atop a blackened crag that once had been part of its foundation.

Pembleton wondered what they were up to, so he increased the magnification of the binoculars to its maximum setting and looked again. Then he realized they were gazing back at him.

They looked different—sickly. There was a spectral quality to them, an otherworldly radiance and a lack of opacity.

He lowered the binoculars and thought of the millions of Caeliar who had willingly sacrificed themselves to send Mantilis through the subspace passageway, and through time, to this barren place; their city had become a necropolis.

Lifting the binoculars again, he saw the Caeliar for the ghosts that they'd become, and it filled him with despair.

*I guess we're not the only ones dying here.*

# 2381

## 3

"Hail them again, Commander," Captain Picard said to Miranda Kadohata, the *Enterprise*'s third-in-command and senior operations officer.

Her lean, attractive Eurasian countenance hardened with frustration as she worked at her console. "Still no response, sir," she said, her accent redolent of a Londoner's inflections.

Medical and security personnel worked with quiet efficiency around and behind Picard, clearing away the evidence of the ship's recent pitched battle with Hirogen boarders, two of whom lay dead in the middle of the *Enterprise*'s bridge. A thin haze of smoke still lingered along the overhead, and its sharp odor masked the stench of spilled blood on the deck.

On the main viewer, framed by streaks of warp-distorted starlight, was the *Vesta*-class explorer vessel *U.S.S. Aventine*. Under the command of Captain Ezri Dax, it was racing at its best possible warp speed toward Earth. They were in futile pursuit of a Borg armada that had, only hours earlier, slipped through a previously unknown—and since collapsed—subspace passage from the Delta Quadrant. Picard feared that at any moment Captain Dax's crew would activate their ship's prototype quantum slipstream drive and rush headlong into a suicidal confrontation.

Lieutenant Jasminder Choudhury, the *Enterprise*'s chief of security, directed four medical technicians entering from the main turbolift to the Hirogen's corpses. "Get those into stasis," she said. "We'll want them for analysis later."

"Aye, sir," said one of the technicians, and the quartet set to work bagging the enormous armored bodies.

While they worked, another turbolift arrived at the bridge, and four engineers stepped out. They carried tight, tubular bundles that unrolled to reveal long sheets covered with tools tucked into fabric loops and magnetically sealed pockets. In moments, the engineers all were at work, repairing ruptured duty consoles and bulkhead-mounted companels.

Commander Worf finished a hushed conference with junior tactical officer Ensign Aneta Šmrhová and returned to the command chairs to take his seat next to Picard's. Speaking at a discreet volume, he said, "Sensor reports confirmed, Captain. There are more than seven thousand Borg cubes deployed into Federation, Klingon, and Romulan territory. Several targets have already been engaged."

"Thank you, Number One," Picard said, though he was anything but grateful for the update. He raised his voice and asked the flight controller, "Mister Weinrib, time to intercept?"

"Actually, sir, the *Aventine*'s lead is increasing," Weinrib said. "They're now point-eight-five past our top rated speed."

Picard admired the sleek lines of the *Aventine* as it slipped farther away from the *Enterprise*. He was almost ready to abandon hope of reasoning with Dax when Kadohata swiveled her chair around from ops to report, "*Aventine* is responding, sir."

"On-screen," Picard said.

Captain Dax's face appeared on the main viewer. *"Changed your mind about joining us, Captain?"*

"Far from it," Picard said, rising from his chair and walking forward. "I urge you to reconsider this rash action."

The young, dark-haired Trill woman seethed. *"The Federation's under attack,"* she said. *"We have to defend it."*

"We will," Picard said. "But not like this. Sacrificing your ship and your crew in this manner serves no purpose. Going into battle against great odds can be brave or noble—but going into battle without a plan is worse than futile, it's wasteful."

She heaved an angry sigh, and he sensed her frustration, her desire to do anything other than stand and wait. *"So, what do you propose we do?"*

"We'll contact Starfleet Command and request new orders," he said. "They may not even be aware that our ships are still in service after the loss of the expeditionary force."

Dax seemed surprised by Picard's suggestion. *"Contact Starfleet Command? No offense, Captain, but that's not exactly the answer I expected, given your reputation."*

"I'll admit that when my orders have contradicted common sense, morality, or the law, I have followed my conscience," Picard said. "But at the moment, Captain, we haven't any orders at all—and I think we at least ought to see if Starfleet knows where it needs us before we commit ourselves to a potentially fatal course."

Dax relaxed her shoulders. *"I suppose it can't hurt to ask,"* she said.

"Then might I suggest we drop out of warp?" Picard said. "At least until such time as we know where we ought to go?"

She narrowed her gaze for a moment, and then she nodded to someone off-screen. *"We're returning to impulse,"* she said. *"Can you patch me in when you're ready to talk to Starfleet?"*

"Of course," Picard said. "*Enterprise* out." The screen switched back to the exterior view of the receding *Aventine*.

Picard nodded to Worf, who said to Weinrib, "Match their speed and heading." The conn officer nodded his confirmation.

On the viewscreen, the streaks of light shrank back to gleaming points as the *Aventine* and the *Enterprise* returned to normal maneuvering speeds.

*Another guarded victory for common sense,* Picard mused. "Commander Kadohata, raise Starfleet Command on any secure channel, priority one."

"Aye, sir," Kadohata replied.

He turned toward his ready room. "I'll take it in my—" He stopped in midstep and midsentence as he saw the burned and smoke-scarred interior of his office, which had been set ablaze during the assault by the Hirogen hunting pack. Picard frowned. The sight of his flame-scoured sanctum resurrected unpleasant memories he'd hoped were long buried.

*Time is the fire in which we burn.*

Looking back at Kadohata, he said, "I'll take it in the observation lounge, Commander." He walked to the aft starboard portal as he added, "Commander Worf, you have the bridge."

# 4

"Battle stations!" roared Captain Krogan. The bridge lights snapped to full brightness as the *I.K.S. veScharg'a* dropped to impulse one million *qell'qams* from the Klingon world Morska. Following close behind the *veScharg'a* was its battle partner, the *Qang*-class heavy cruiser *Sturka*.

A firestorm of disruptor blasts raged up from the planet's

surface and hammered the two Borg cubes in orbit. The impacts seemed to have no effect on the cubes except to silhouette them and give them blinding crimson halos. Then the Borg returned fire and wrought blazing emerald scars across the planet's surface.

Krogan's first officer, Falgar, bellowed, "Raise shields! Arm weapons! Helm, set attack pattern *ya'DIchqa*."

"Ten seconds to Borg firing range," answered the helmsman.

"All reserve power to shields," Falgar ordered.

*Time to find out if Starfleet's secret torpedoes work for us.* Krogan watched the Borg cubes grow larger on his viewscreen. His foes would have several seconds of advantage over his *Vor'cha*-class attack cruiser, whose effective firing range was a few hundred thousand *qell'qams* shorter than that of the Borg cubes. The *veScharg'a*'s goal was to survive the Borg's initial barrage and get close enough to target the cubes with the transphasic torpedo, which Admiral Jellico of Starfleet had just ordered to be distributed to ships of the Klingon Defense Force.

"The Borg are firing," Falgar said, sounding perfectly calm. Then explosions shook the battle cruiser with the ferocity of *Fek'lhr* himself. The bright battle lights flickered. Fire and sparks erupted from aft duty stations, and the stink of burnt hair assaulted Krogan's nostrils.

Qonqar, the tactical officer, shouted over the clamor, "Weapons locked!"

Krogan slammed a fist on the arm of his chair as he pointed at the Borg cubes on the screen. "Fire!"

A trio of blue bolts shot forth, spiraling erratically through the Borg's defensive batteries. As they closed on target, Falgar called out, "Helm! Break to starboard! Qonqar, all power to port shields!"

More blasts shook the *veScharg'a*. Krogan reveled as he watched the viewer and saw the aft-angle view of the torpedoes hitting home and blasting one Borg cube to pieces in a sapphire flash. As the blue fire cloud dissipated into the vacuum of space, another cerulean blast filled the starscape behind it, as the second Borg cube was annihilated.

The bridge officers cheered and roared at their victory. Krogan permitted himself a satisfied growl and a nod of his head. *It is a good day to die . . . for my enemies.*

The warriors' celebrations were ended by the shrilling of an incoming subspace message. Communications officer Valk covered his in-ear transceiver for a moment, then looked up at Krogan. "Signal from General Klag."

"On-screen," Krogan said, lifting his chin to project pride and confidence to his commanding officer.

The visage of General Klag, commander of the Fifth Fleet, filled the viewscreen. *"Report,"* said the general, who was now also hailed as a Hero of the Empire.

"Our foes are vanquished," Krogan said.

*"Excellent,"* Klag said. *"Your vessel is needed at a new battle. What is your status?"*

Krogan replied, "Minor damage but still battle-ready."

Klag nodded, and then he asked, *"What of the* Sturka?"

Qonqar routed an after-action report from the *Sturka* to Krogan's command monitor. "Captain K'Draq reports they've taken heavy damage," Krogan said, reviewing the details.

The general's brow creased beneath his scowl. *"We need every ship. Can they continue?"*

"Doubtful," Krogan said. "They've lost warp drive."

*"Leave them, then,"* Klag said. *"Rendezvous with the fleet in three hours, at the coordinates I'm sending you now."*

At a glance, Krogan knew that the meeting point lay on a direct line between the Azure Nebula, source of the Borg scourge, and the Klingon homeworld. "The Borg are coming for Qo'noS, then," he said.

*"If they do, they come to die,"* Klag said with bold eagerness. *"Get under way now. That is an order. Klag out."*

The screen returned to the wounded orb of Morska and the smoldering, battered hull of the *Sturka*, adrift in space. Krogan relayed the rendezvous coordinates to the helmsman's console. "Set a new course," he said. "Maximum warp. Go." Stars swept across the screen and then distorted into streaks as the *veScharg'a* jumped to warp.

Though Krogan would never say so—not to his crew, to his family, or to his superiors—he knew that it had been sheer luck that had preserved his ship even as the *Sturka* had fallen to the Borg. And if there was one truth that every warrior knew, it was that no one's luck lasted forever.

\* \* \*

Chancellor Martok stepped off the transporter padd and was glad to be back aboard his flagship, the *I.K.S. Sword of Kahless*. General Goluk, a high-ranking member of the Order of the *Bat'leth* and the commander of Martok's venerated Ninth Fleet, gave him a nod of greeting. "*Qapla'*, Chancellor."

In his cutting growl of a voice, Martok replied, "*Qapla'*, General. Report." He marched out of the transporter room, in a hurry to reach the bridge.

The gray-bearded general followed him and said, "Khitomer and Beta Thoridor have fallen. Beta Lankal and the Mempa system are under attack, as are several dozen smaller colonies."

"And Morska?"

"Defended by the *Sturka* and the *veScharg'a*," Goluk said. "The Borg are also laying siege to Rura Penthe."

"Who cares about Rura Penthe?" Martok said. "Is Klag gathering his fleet?"

"Yes, my lord," Goluk said, following Martok up a steep crew ladder to the command deck. "Our forces will assemble in three hours and engage the Borg in four."

Martok bounded up from the ladder and strode down the passageway toward the bridge. Despite the absence of his left eye and his limited depth perception, Martok knew the steps and corners of his ship so well that he could navigate its corridors blind. "Has there been any word from our forces at the nebula?"

"Not yet," Goluk said. He remained close behind Martok's shoulder as they walked.

The two grizzled warriors arrived on the bridge. The command center of the *Sword of Kahless* was packed with warriors, all of them intently busy preparing for rapid deployment. Deep, muted voices mixed with the comm chatter and the ambient hum of the ship's power-distribution systems. On the viewer, dozens of *Vor'cha*-class and *K'vort*-class cruisers moved in tight formations, turning in unison like flocks of birds.

Captain G'mtor, a seasoned officer who proudly bore a deep facial scar from his right temple to his chin, approached the chancellor and the general. "New reports from Federation and Romulan space, Chancellor," G'mtor said. "Battles have begun at Nequencia Alpha, Xarantine, and Jouret. The Borg armada is destroying all stray vessels it encounters."

"We'll find strength in numbers, then," Martok said. He took his place in the command chair. "How many ships are ready to follow us into battle, Captain?"

"One hundred seventeen are gathered here at Qo'noS," G'mtor said. "Another three hundred sixty-one will meet us at the rendezvous coordinates."

General Goluk asked, "And how many Borg vessels have we detected inbound?"

"Four hundred ninety-two," G'mtor said. "So already we enjoy an advantage."

Immediately, Martok could tell that Goluk was performing the arithmetic in his head. Then the general inquired of G'mtor, "How did you arrive at that conclusion, Captain?"

Martok loosed a short roar of laughter and answered for G'mtor, "Because we are *Klingons!*" Encouraging roars came from every warrior on the bridge. These men were sharp and ready for battle, and it filled Martok with pride to be among them. He stood and said to G'mtor, "Open a channel, all ships."

G'mtor nodded to another officer, who carried out the order with haste and nodded in reply. "Channel open," G'mtor said.

In a breath, Martok gathered himself and declared, "Warriors of the Empire! A great hour is upon us, a foe to test our mettle. The Borg have come not to plunder us but to destroy us—to leave our empire in flames, our bodies broken, our spirits disgraced at the gates of *Gre'thor*.

"This is a mistake they will not live to regret. We will meet their armada with our own and show them what it means to fight with honor. We shall whip the Borg from our space and crush them. Our empire has risen by the sword, and one day it might be felled by it. But if such a fate awaits us, let us fall to warriors—not to these *petaQpu'*.

"Today is a good day to die, for a warrior—but not for a way of life. The Klingon Empire *will not fall* today." He slammed his fist and forearm to his chest. "Fight well, and die with honor, sons and daughters of Qo'noS! *Qapla'!*"

A roaring "*Qapla'!*" came back to Martok from his bridge crew, who broke without preamble into a throaty and spirited rendition of "Soldiers of the Empire." Their proud voices echoed off the bulkheads and rang through the corridors, where new choruses of singers picked up the tune and carried it on.

General Goluk nodded to the communications officer, who

closed the channel as the singing continued. Martok settled into the command chair, which sat on a dais above the rest of the bridge. The general placed himself at Martok's right side. Over the hearty song, he said, "All ships ready to deploy, my lord."

"Break orbit," Martok said. "As soon as the fleet is in formation behind us, coordinate our jump to maximum warp."

Goluk let Captain G'mtor handle the details of marshaling the fleet into warp speed. Martok, meanwhile, savored all the sensations of shipboard life: the gruff singing voices, the warm aromas from the galley several decks below, the rumbling of the impulse engines pushing the ship out of orbit, the chimelike echo of boots stamping across duranium gratings.

This was not the war he would have chosen, but it felt good to be leading his people into battle, all of them united under one banner. The Kinshaya and the Elabrej had not been enough to give the far-flung worlds of the Empire common cause. But the Borg were a menace without equal in known space. The Collective's attack had galvanized the noble families and the common people, and it had quelled the resurgent internecine struggles of the High Council.

Barked commands across the bridge were followed by the flash of warp-distorted starlight across the main viewscreen.

*When this war is over,* Martok ruminated, *the Empire will be stronger than it's ever been . . . or it will lie in ashes.*

# 5

Starfleet's reports to the Palais de la Concorde grew worse with each passing hour, and President Nanietta Bacco had tired of reading them. She winced as her intercom buzzed, and her elderly Vulcan executive assistant, Sivak, announced, *"Admiral Akaar is here to deliver your midday briefing, Madam President."* Bacco was about to concoct an excuse to send the admiral away when Sivak added, *"Ms. Piñiero and Seven of Nine are with him."*

She sighed. "Send them in."

Bacco got up from her chair and turned around to look out the panoramic floor-to-ceiling window. Outside, the Tour Eiffel gleamed in the afternoon sunlight above the sprawl of Paris. Wispy clouds raced low along the horizon in the distance.

She pressed a padd on her desk to tint the window against the glare. As the electrochemical shade descended between her and the City of Light, the moment felt to Bacco as if it might be a tragically prophetic omen of the hours to come.

One of the doors behind her opened. It took all of her resolve to turn back and face her visitors, who she knew came bearing bad tidings. Leading them in was Bacco's chief of staff, Esperanza Piñiero, whose black hair and olive complexion contrasted with those of the two people who were following her.

Starfleet's liaison to the Federation president, Fleet Admiral Leonard James Akaar, was a tall, barrel-chested, and broad-shouldered man of Capellan birth. His pale gray hair fell in long natural waves on either side of his weathered face.

Beside him was Seven of Nine. She was fair-skinned and blond. Her striking good looks were marred by the presence of residual grafts of silvery gray metallic Borg technology on her left hand and eyebrow.

Seven, whose name had been Annika Hansen before her early childhood assimilation by the Borg, had been liberated from the Collective by the crew of the *Starship Voyager* during their long journey home from the Delta Quadrant. Now she was Bacco's top security adviser on all matters concerning the Borg.

"Good afternoon, Madam President," Akaar said, resembling a talking bronze statue in the honeyed light of her shaded window.

"Admiral," Bacco said with a polite nod. She offered one as well to her security adviser. "Seven."

Piñiero feigned offense. "No greeting for me?"

"I see you all day, every day," Bacco grumped.

Before Piñiero could continue their verbal volley, Admiral Akaar interrupted, "Madam President, we have important news."

"None of it good, I'm sure," Bacco said, easing herself back into her chair. She made a rolling motion with her hand. "Continue, Admiral."

A despairing frown darkened his expression. "The Borg are moving even faster than we could have imagined," he said.

Seven added, "They likely assimilated new propulsion technologies while replenishing their strength."

Bacco asked, "How fast are they moving, Admiral?"

"We have confirmed attacks on Yridia, Hyralan, and Celes," he said. "We project the Borg will siege Regulus in two hours,

Deneva in three, Qo'noS in five. At this rate, they are only nine hours from Vulcan and Andor and twelve hours from Earth. By tomorrow, they will be able to hit Trill, Betazed, Bajor, and dozens of other worlds. Most of our simulations suggest the collapse of the Federation in ten days, and the fall of most of our neighbors in local space within a month."

Bacco let her head fall forward into her hands. "Dear God."

Piñiero pushed her fingers through her hair, back over her scalp. "We have to evacuate those worlds," she said. "Now."

"Actually, Madam President," Akaar interjected, "that will not be feasible. It would entail trying to move tens of billions of people in a matter of hours."

Seven added, "It would be a futile effort. Any ships that fled those worlds would be hunted down by the Borg."

The ex-drone's calm certainty only inflamed Piñiero's anger. "So? Should we just tell our people to sit quietly and wait for the end to come? What kind of plan is that?"

Akaar's shoulders slumped. "I agree in principle, Ms. Piñiero. But we no longer have enough ships at our disposal for an evacuation effort. All civilian ships that are able to flee have already done so, and all armed vessels and their crews have been pressed into service for core-systems defense."

Bacco lifted her head and said to Akaar, "How many lives have we lost so far, Admiral?"

"Ma'am?"

"How many civilian lives, Admiral?" She hardened her anger to hold her despair at bay. "Do we even know?"

The admiral looked ashamed. "We have estimates."

"How many?"

He asked, "Since the first Borg attack?"

"Yes," Bacco said. "Since the beginning."

"Including non-Federation worlds . . . approximately thirty billion."

It was too vast a number for Bacco to grasp. Thirty billion was too large even to be a statistic; it was an abstraction of death writ on a cosmic scale. "Can Starfleet muster enough ships to intercept the Borg armada?"

"It is not that simple, Madam President," Akaar said. "There are no isolated thrusts of enemy forces to intercept. The Borg have dispersed on thousands of vectors across known space. We had organized Starfleet's defenses to shield the core systems. Unfortunately, the Borg have committed enough ships to attack all our worlds at once." He cast his eyes downward. "I regret to say we have no defensive plan for that scenario."

Fixing her weary glare on Seven, Bacco said, "Care to offer any strategic or tactical advice?"

"Our options are limited," Seven said. "I have been unable to help Starfleet pinpoint which cube is carrying the Borg Queen, which hinders our ability to launch a surgical counterstrike. Fortunately, none of the ships in the Borg armada has displayed any of the absorptive properties of the giant cube we faced last year. That suggests the *Enterprise*'s mission to stop the assimilated vessel *Einstein* was a success."

Piñiero threw a sour look at Seven. "Good thing," she said. "Otherwise, the Borg might have presented a threat." The snide remark drew a stare of cold fire from Seven.

Bacco frowned at Akaar. "Admiral, do you have any news to report *besides* the end of the Federation as we know it?"

"Yes, Madam President," he replied. "We have reestablished contact with the *Enterprise* and the *Aventine*. They were in the Delta Quadrant on a recon mission when the Borg armada attacked. They've returned and report that all subspace passages have been collapsed. Admiral Jellico is cutting them new orders now."

At that news, Bacco leaned forward. "Can you pass along a message for me to Captain Picard?"

"Of course, Madam President."

"Tell him that if he has *any* idea how to stop the Borg, no matter what he has to do, he has my unqualified authority to do it. If he has to toss Starfleet regulations and Federation law out an airlock, so be it. If we're still here when the dust settles, he can count on full pardons for himself and his crew, no questions asked. The same goes for anyone working with him. Is that clear, Admiral?"

Akaar nodded once. "Exceptionally clear, Madam President."

"Then let's all hope Picard has one more miracle up his sleeve. Because God knows we need it."

# 6

*"The truth, Captains, is that Starfleet no longer has a plan."*

Picard didn't remember Edward Jellico looking so old. In the scant months since Jellico had ascended to Starfleet's top flag office, he seemed to have aged a decade. His already white hair had thinned, and the lines in his face had deepened into gorges carved by the never-ending anxieties of command. More alarming to Picard was that he sympathized with how he imagined Jellico must feel. Standing in the ready room of a captain less than half his years, Picard felt like a relic of a bygone age.

Captain Dax replied, "Admiral, are you saying that Starfleet has no new orders for us?"

*"Not unless one of you has a bright idea,"* Jellico said.

The two captains traded apprehensive looks across Dax's desk. Picard looked back at Jellico's visage on the monitor and said, "We're still weighing our options."

Dax interjected, "Should we set a course for Earth, sir?"

Jellico shook his head. *"You won't make it in time. You're four days away. The Borg'll be here in twelve hours."*

"Actually, sir," Dax said, "my chief engineer tells me she can bring our prototype slipstream drive online within a few hours. There's a chance we could beat the Borg to Earth."

Holding up one hand, Jellico replied, *"One more ship won't turn the tide, Captain. We're past that now."*

Picard tried to mask his profound frustration, but hints of it slipped into his tone all the same. "Admiral, certainly Starfleet hasn't conceded the war already?"

*"Of course not, Jean-Luc. We've distributed the schematics for the transphasic torpedo to all ships and starbases, and we've given it to the Klingon Defense Force."* Dax glanced nervously at Picard as Jellico continued, *"It might be too little too late, but we're not going down without a fight."*

"Admiral," Dax said, "isn't it dangerous to send those schematics via subspace with so many Borg ships in the region? What if they've intercepted and decoded them?"

A frown thinned Jellico's lips almost to the point of making them vanish.

*"It was a calculated risk,"* he confessed. *"It's not what I wanted to do or the way I wanted to do it . . . but at this point,*

*not doing it is tantamount to surrender. I gave the order to over-ride Admiral Nechayev's security directive. If it turns out to be the wrong call, there's no one to blame but me."*

Hearing such humility from Jellico surprised Picard. He didn't know whether it was because Jellico, having reached the top of the Starfleet career ladder, had finally relaxed or because crisis brought out the most human facets of his persona.

"Admiral," he said, "with your permission, I'd like to take the *Enterprise* and the *Aventine* back into the nebula to search for survivors from the expeditionary group. We've confirmed that half of *Voyager*'s crew is still alive; there may be others."

Jellico nodded. *"By all means, Captain. Proceed at your discretion. But make certain you have an exit strategy."*

Again, the admiral's pessimistic turn of phrase captured Picard's attention. "An exit strategy?"

*"Jean-Luc, if Earth falls . . ."* Jellico choked on his words for a moment, and then he continued, *"If Earth falls, the war's pretty much over. The fighting might go on for a few more weeks, but the Federation as we know it will be gone. If it comes to that, take your ship and anyone you can carry, and try to get to safety. Don't launch some quixotic mission to liberate the Federation, because there'll be nothing left. Just save your ship and your crew."* A melancholy gloom settled in his eyes. *"Don't die for a lost cause, Jean-Luc."*

Then he blinked away the sentiment and added, *"Wish us luck, Captains. Godspeed to you both. Starfleet Command out."*

The Federation emblem replaced Jellico's face on the desktop monitor. Dax deactivated the screen and sighed. "Nothing like a pep talk from headquarters to boost morale." She stood and turned to her replicator. "I'm having a *raktajino.* Can I get you something?"

"Tea, Earl Grey, hot," Picard said.

She turned to the replicator and said, *"Raktajino,* hot and sweet, and an Earl Grey tea, hot." The drinks formed in a whorl of golden light and white noise. When the machine had finished, she took the drinks from the nook and handed the tea to Picard.

He took a sip and savored it. "Thank you."

"You're welcome," she said, easing back into her chair and taking a sip of her caffeinated Klingon beverage. "Sorry to hear about your ready room."

"Not as sorry as I am," Picard said. He enjoyed another sip of his tea, then added, "We should set course back to the nebula as soon as possible."

Dax said, "All right, but I don't think we're going to find many survivors beyond the *Voyager* crew."

"Perhaps not," Picard murmured, even as he was distracted by an awareness of something new—something different—shining in his thoughts like a beacon in the darkness of mere being. "But we need to get under way, soon. There's something there, and I need to know what it is."

Slowly shaking her head, Dax replied, "If you say so. I just hate feeling like we're running for cover when everyone else is fighting for their lives."

"Running for cover?" Picard said.

She called up a short-range starmap overlaid with tactical data about the Borg armada's deployment into the surrounding sectors. Pointing at the Azure Nebula, Dax said, "It's the eye of the storm, Jean-Luc. All Borg ships are moving away from it. It's the safest spot in known space."

He studied the star chart and nodded. "Indeed. Which makes it the ideal location from which to plan our next move."

"I wasn't aware that we *had* a next move," Dax said.

The sense that something was drawing him back to the nebula intensified. "We don't—at least, not yet. But I have a feeling that's about to change."

# 7

Walking through darkened corridors, Riker felt like a shade haunting his own ship. Two hours after returning to Federation space, most of *Titan* was still without main power. The bridge and the main computer were back online, but little else was.

He turned a corner into a small stampede of pressure-suited bodies and was forced to step clear of the team of damage-control engineers, who were quick-timing it to their next crisis du jour. All the way down from the bridge, from deck to deck and from one emergency ladder to another, Riker had seen similar frantic scrambles of activity by the ship's engineers.

*They're earning their pay today,* he mused.

"*Ra-Havreii to Captain Riker,*" said the chief engineer, the richness of his voice flattened by being filtered through Riker's combadge.

Riker stepped to the side of the passage and stopped. "Good to hear your voice. Are all comms back up?"

*"No, sir,"* Ra-Havreii replied. *"I'm talking to you from the shuttlecraft* Gillespie. *We're currently routing all shipboard comms through the shuttles' transceivers."*

"Good thinking," Riker said. "Can we use them to get a signal to Starfleet Command?"

Ra-Havreii said, *"Not yet, but soon. I'm interplexing their comm systems now to boost their range. I expect to have it ready in a few minutes. But that's not why I hailed you, sir."*

Stepping down a short, dead-end side passage for a bit of additional privacy, Riker said, "What's on your mind?"

*"We have some fairly systemic damage in a number of critical areas, Captain,"* Ra-Havreii said. *"Without main power, we can't replicate new parts—but without replacement parts, we can't restore main power. So I need your permission to acquire the necessary components, sir."*

It took Riker a moment to pierce Ra-Havreii's unusually subtle wording. "You want to salvage from the wrecked ships in the nebula," he said, nodding with grim understanding.

*"Aye, sir. I know it must seem a bit ghoulish, but we need those parts. We've opened the shuttlebay doors using manual controls, and the* Armstrong, *the* Holliday, *and the* Ellington *are ready to begin recovery ops—on your order, sir."*

As distasteful as Riker felt it would be to plunder a fresh starship graveyard, he knew that the chief engineer was right. It was an absolute necessity. "Proceed, Commander. Do what you have to do, and keep me posted."

*"Aye, sir. Ra-Havreii out."* A barely audible click signaled the closing of the comm channel.

Riker walked out of the dead end and back to the corridor, turned right, and continued toward his destination.

The two female security guards posted outside the door watched Riker as he approached. To the left of the door was Senior Petty Officer Antillea, a Gnalish Fejjimaera. Aside from resembling a human-sized bipedal iguana, her most noticeable physical characteristic was the prominent fin on the top of her scaly, olive-hued head.

On the other side of the door was Lieutenant Pava Ek'Noor

sh'Aqabaa, a statuesque and breathtaking Andorian *shen* who preferred to let her flowing white hair frame her blue face. The only parts of her that looked remotely fragile were her antennae, but Riker pitied the person who dared try to lay a finger on them without permission.

He looked to sh'Aqabaa as he arrived at the door. "Any trouble, Lieutenant?"

"None, sir," sh'Aqabaa said.

Riker nodded. "Good. I'm going in to talk to her." He keyed in a security code to unlock the door to the guest quarters. The portal slid open ahead of him, and he walked in.

Once he was a few meters inside the compartment, the door hushed closed behind him, and he heard the soft confirmation tone of it returning to its locked state. He remained still for a moment while his eyes adjusted to the dim illumination into which he'd stepped. Noting the cyanochrome hues that surrounded him, he realized that all of the artificial lighting was off. The only light came from the glow of the Azure Nebula outside the row of rounded-corner windows that sloped along one side of the living area. Silhouetted in front of them was *Titan*'s latest guest, Erika Hernandez.

She didn't look in his direction as she said with serene courtesy, "Don't bother to knock, Captain. Come right in."

He felt abashed at his faux pas and slightly wary of this peculiar stranger who had appeared without warning on his bridge. True, she had done him and his crew a great favor, but it still felt too soon to trust her. Feigning a casual demeanor, he sidled over to her in front of the windows. "Now that my crew is able to work on repairs, I thought it was time we talked."

"I figured as much," Hernandez said.

Outside the windows, in the middle distance, shuttlecraft from *Titan* maneuvered through the roiling cobalt mists and snared large hunks of starship debris in tractor beams. "We've been forced to scavenge, I'm afraid," Riker said.

"Don't feel you need to apologize," Hernandez said. "Out there, it's just wreckage. In here, it's survival. That's just the way it is. If this had happened to my ship, I'd have done the same thing."

Riker cleared his throat. "Since you've brought it up, let's talk about your ship," he said. Gesturing toward the sofa beneath the window, he asked, "Can we sit down?"

"Of course," she said. She settled in at one end of the couch, and Riker took a seat at the other end. She asked, "What do you want to know?"

"You said your ship was the *Columbia*," Riker said. "You were talking about the twenty-second-century Earth starship?"

Hernandez nodded. "Yes, the NX-02."

"That ship went missing more than two hundred years ago," Riker replied. "And according to our records, its captain was in her forties. You look a bit young for the part."

The youthful woman brightened the room with her laughter. "I've had some work done," she said with a playful lift of her brow.

"Apparently," Riker said, returning her smile with one of his own. "Starfleet also discovered the wreck of the *Columbia* in the Gamma Quadrant, more than seventy thousand light-years from here and even farther from where we found you."

She sighed. "Yes, I know. When Erigol's star went supernova and created this nebula in 2168, the Caeliar took off in their city-ships. Most of them didn't make it. I was in the capital, which did escape, but it wound up a few hundred years in the past. My ship stayed in the present and entered another passage; it got tossed across the galaxy, and my crew was probably incinerated by the radiation inside the subspace tunnel."

Riker was about to ask another question when she cut him off. "Why the third degree, Captain? Can't you just take a sample of my DNA and use that to see if I am who I say I am?"

"I did," he confessed. "My chief nurse recovered traces of your DNA from the bridge consoles you touched and from some of your hairs we found on the deck. I already know you're the real Erika Hernandez—and the way you turned Lieutenant Rri-arr's phaser into dust when you came aboard tells me you're also something more. What I want is to know more about your history, so I can understand why you helped us escape."

Her disarming smile returned. "You could have just asked."

"What fun would that be?"

They laughed for a few seconds, and then Hernandez looked away and became serious. "You really want to know why I helped you? The truth is, there's no one reason. I've wanted to get away from the Caeliar pretty much from the first moment they told me I couldn't leave. I also spent the last several hundred years feeling I let down all the people I was supposed to protect. The convoy the Romulans ambushed . . . my crew . . . Earth . . . my friends in exile." Hernandez became quietly introspective for several seconds, and Riker let her collect her thoughts.

She continued, "Anyway, when the Caeliar took your people on the planet prisoner, it was like seeing it happen to myself all over again. Then I saw those black cubes destroy your fleet, and I remembered how much I wanted to be there for Earth when the Romulans attacked. I figured you'd feel the same way about this." She looked up at him, and her expression conveyed a deep sadness. "I'm so sorry I couldn't save your landing party. Especially your wife. But there was no other way."

"It wasn't your fault," he said, and he meant it. "I made the decision. You have nothing to apologize for." He hesitated to ask what he really wanted to know, but his need was too great to be denied. "Can you just tell me . . . is Deanna all right?"

"She was pretending to be, but I noticed signs that she was in pain—and when I listened in on the Caeliar, I heard them say she was in some kind of medical distress."

Riker wrapped his left hand over his fist and clamped down, focusing his thoughts on remaining calm. Hernandez cast her eyes toward the floor, away from his obvious emotional turmoil. She said, "I'm sorry the news isn't better."

"I'm all right," he said, and he pressed his fist over his mouth for a second. It was an effort to lower and unclench his hand. "One more question: If you were able to open a passage and bring us here, why couldn't you take us back to Earth?"

"Because I didn't create the passage we traveled through," she said. "I only widened it, by amplifying the power to the machine that generated it. If I had tried to open a new passageway, the Caeliar would have detected it and shut it down. As it was, the gestalt was about to collapse the tunnel that pointed here. So it really was this or nothing."

"Good enough," Riker said. He stood. "Thank you for your patience, Captain."

"My pleasure," she said. He started to leave but turned back as she asked, "Now that you're home, what's your plan?"

He flashed a rueful smile. "I plan to call for help."

\* \* \*

Jean-Luc Picard stepped back onto the bridge of the *Enterprise*, expecting an update on the ship's repairs. Instead, Worf rose from the command chair and said, "Captain, we are being hailed."

"By the *Aventine*?" Picard wondered what could have happened in the minutes since he had left Captain Dax's ship.

Surrendering the center seat to Picard, Worf replied with an uncommon gleam, "No, sir, by the *Titan*."

The name of the ship was enough to provoke a double-take by Picard, who cast an incredulous stare at his first officer. *Titan* was supposed to be thousands of light-years away, months from Federation space. "What is the signal's point of origin, Number One?"

Worf said, "Directly ahead, sir. Inside the Azure Nebula."

"Do we have a visual?"

"Affirmative."

Picard stood tall and smoothed his uniform. "On-screen."

Sickly colors fluctuated on the main viewscreen, and an oscillating whine stutter-scratched through the speakers. Then the signal resolved into an unstable image with mildly garbled sound, and Picard recognized the haggard face of his old friend and former first officer, William Riker. *"Captain Picard?"*

"Yes, Captain," Picard said, unable to suppress his profound elation. "It's good to see you again."

*"Likewise, Captain. I wish it could have been under better circumstances."* He nodded to someone off-screen and continued, *"We're pretty banged up over here. My people are working a salvage mission in the nebula, but if there's any way you can lend us a hand, we'd be grateful."*

"I think something can be arranged," Picard said. Out of the corner of his eye, he caught Worf's confirming nod. "We're on our way back to the nebula with the *Aventine*. Have your people found any survivors during your salvage?"

Frowning, Riker replied, *"Only on* Voyager, *and they refused to abandon ship or be rescued. They're doing the same thing we are, scrounging for parts, except they have to rebuild an entire warp engine, one coil and bolt at a time."* He shook his head. *"You have to give them credit—they've got spirit."*

"Indeed," Picard said. "Will . . . don't think I'm not glad to see you, but your arrival is rather *unexpected*. How did *Titan* come to be in the Azure Nebula?"

The question pulled a tired sigh from Riker. *"It's kind of a long story,"* he said. *"Do you want the full explanation?"*

"I'm afraid we don't have time for that," Picard said. "Perhaps you could sum up?"

Riker nodded and lifted his eyebrows in mild amusement. *"Long story short: We followed energy pulses that we thought would lead us to a Borg installation. Instead, we found a species of powerful recluses called the Caeliar, who took us prisoner. A fellow prisoner helped my ship escape through a subspace tunnel, but I had to leave my away team behind."*

At the mention of a subspace tunnel, Picard's attention sharpened. His next question was driven not by logic but by a gut feeling, an intuition that the presence he'd sensed a short time earlier had to be connected in some way to *Titan*'s sudden arrival in the nebula. "Captain, by any chance, did the prisoner who aided your escape come with you aboard *Titan*?"

*"As a matter of fact, she did,"* Riker said.

For a moment, Picard broke eye contact with Riker and concluded that his feeling had been right. The timing of the two events was definitely not a coincidence. Riker pulled him back into the conversation by inquiring, *"Why do you ask?"*

"Simple curiosity," Picard lied. "We'll reach you in just over an hour. If possible, have your chief engineer advance us a list of any parts or personnel you need to effect repairs."

*"Will do, Captain,"* Riker said, looking utterly exhausted. *"We'll be looking forward to your arrival. Titan out."* The channel closed, and the nebula's distant blue stain on the starry heavens returned to the *Enterprise*'s main viewscreen.

Picard returned to his chair and sat down. Worf took his own seat at the captain's right. "Mister Worf," Picard said. "Please contact Captain Dax and let her know that I would like her and Commander Bowers to join us here on the *Enterprise* when we welcome Captain Riker aboard."

"Aye, sir," Worf said.

The captain added, "And instruct Commander Kadohata to coordinate with the *Aventine* in the creation of spare parts for *Titan* and the assignment of emergency crews."

"She has already done so, sir."

"Very good." From his chair, Picard had an all but unobstructed line of sight through the still-open door of his ready room, which remained a darkened, carbonized cave just off the bridge. Nodding to his scorched sanctum, he said to Worf, "I want that door closed, Mister Worf."

Worf scowled at the open portal. "We have tried, sir. A plasma fire warped the interior bulkhead. The door is stuck."

Unable to rein in a surge of irrational anger, Picard snapped, "No excuses, Worf! Get it done." Embarrassed by his own outburst, he got up and walked to the aft turbolift. "You have the bridge, Number One." He felt the eyes of the bridge crew on him as he made his exit. The lift doors closed, granting him sanctuary in the solitude of the turbolift car.

"Deck Eight," he said.

It took the turbolift less than ten seconds to descend seven decks. The doors parted with a soft hiss. Picard walked quickly and was grateful to return to the refuge of his quarters without encountering anyone else along the way.

He moved in light, careful steps through the living area and poked his head inside the bedroom. Beverly was asleep. Picard noted the time—just shy of 0500—and wished he had the luxury of slumber. *No time for that now,* he scolded himself. He undressed in the dark, kicked off his boots at the foot of the bed, and lobbed his perspiration-soaked, battle-soiled uniform into one corner, intending to put it in the reclamator later, when Beverly was no longer trying to rest.

Stripped naked, he padded into the bathroom and shut the door. The light faded up slowly, and he felt as if it were revealing him to himself, a figure taking shape in the shadows. There were fatigue circles under his eyes, darker than any he'd ever seen on his face before. Somewhere beneath the mask of years that stared back from the mirror, there lurked the younger man he'd remembered being not so long ago.

Keeping his voice down, he said to the computer, "Shower, forty-six degrees Celsius." Inside the stall, a fierce spray of hot water flooded the small compartment with water vapor. Overhead, the ventilators purred into action, drawing up the moist clouds to stabilize the humidity.

Picard stepped inside the shower and bowed his head under the pleasantly sultry mist. *If only I could just stay here,* he thought. But with his eyes closed, he continued to see the charred bulkheads and seared-bare deck of his ready room. He shook his head, trying to cast off the memory, which disturbed him for reasons he didn't dare to let himself name.

Instead, he focused his mind on the new presence. He didn't hear it the way he heard the Borg. Where the Collective spoke in a roar, this was but the faintest hush of a whisper, and it was all the more compelling for its subtlety.

As the *Enterprise* continued toward its rendezvous with *Titan*, Picard knew one thing for certain: Whatever this new intelligence was, every moment was bringing him closer to it.

And one word echoed unbidden in his thoughts.

*Destiny.*

# 4527 B.C.E.

## 8

"The wind's picking up," Pembleton said with a wary eye on the gunmetal gray sky. He and the rest of the survivors huddled around the campfire, all bundled tightly against the frigid gale. "Smells like more snow."

"God hates us," Crichlow muttered. "That's what it is."

A week had passed since they left the wreckage of Mantilis and encamped near the shoreline below. In that time, at least sixty centimeters of snow had fallen. Temperatures had plummeted daily, and the fjord, which had been crowded with pack ice, now was frozen solid. Adding to the group's misery was the fact that the days were growing shorter. Soon the sunrises would cease altogether, and several months of night would be upon them.

Flames crackled and danced around a tiny, gutted rodent carcass, which was impaled on a scrap-metal spit mounted on a pair of Y-shaped branches. Evaporating water inside the firewood hissed as it escaped, and one of the logs fissured along its length with a sharp *pop*. The aroma of cooking flesh had Pembleton's stomach craving sustenance, but it wasn't his turn to eat. Every other meal was reserved for Kiona Thayer, who needed to maintain her strength to fend off infection and promote the healing of her wounded foot, which would soon be strong enough for her to walk.

Mazzetti, who had become the group's de facto cook, gave the broiled rodent another quarter-turn on the spit. "Almost done," he said to Thayer, who nodded.

A chilling gust made the taut ropes of their shelter sing with vibration. Graylock eyed the ramshackle mass of metal, fabric, and microfiber rope. Then he turned with a glum expression back toward the fire and scratched at his stubbled face. "We need to reinforce before we get more snow," he said.

The three MACO privates groaned, and Steinhauer hung his

head in denial. The chief engineer had sent them on daily hikes back up the slope, to salvage everything they could carry back down from the debris of Mantilis. Between the thin air and the strain of fighting this planet's gravity, it would have been a miserable assignment even in good weather.

Crichlow sighed, frowned, and shook his head. "Right, lads. Time for another trip up Junk Mountain."

"Steinhauer, make sure you check the traps before we go," Pembleton said. To the two officers, he said, "It'll be faster work if I go with them to lend a hand. Will you two be all right here on your own for a few hours?"

Thayer harrumphed. "Sure," she said. "We'll have a grand ol' time. Maybe we'll go ice fishing."

Through chattering teeth, Mazzetti replied, "For what? More poisonous seaweed?"

"I think she was kidding, Nicky," Crichlow said.

Pembleton summoned all his willpower to stand and step away from the comfort of the fire. "On your feet, men, we need to move. We'll only have about nine hours of daylight today. Let's not waste them." Watching the privates lag and dawdle, he coaxed them. "Up, gents. With a purpose, let's go."

Getting his men in motion was always the hardest part of the day. Once they were walking, even uphill, they were fine. It was a simple matter of overcoming their inertia.

Two hours later, they had settled into a rhythm, trudging single-file up the easiest face of Junk Mountain. Their boots crunched through the thin, icy crust and sank almost knee-deep into the wet, heavy snow underneath. "We need snowshoes," said Pembleton. "Any of you know how to make snowshoes?"

Steinhauer replied, "I do, Sergeant."

"Consider yourself volunteered when we get back to camp."

"*Jawohl,* Sergeant."

Crichlow, walking point, lifted his fist and halted the squad. He looked back at Pembleton, made a V sign with two fingers under his eyes, and pointed to something several meters away, to the right of their position. Pembleton strained to pick out textural details in the vast swath of white.

Then he saw them: fresh footprints. Animal tracks.

Something big. Maybe even edible.

Graylock's infusion of parts and materials would have to wait. Their shelter wasn't perfect, but it would hold for another night. Food was a far more pressing concern, one that needed to be dealt with as soon as possible.

Pembleton eased his phase rifle off his shoulder and into his hands. The three privates unshouldered their weapons and mimicked Pembleton as he released his rifle's safety. With a series of quick gestures, he gave the order to move out and follow the animal tracks in the snow.

Crichlow remained on point, and the four MACOs remained in single-file formation as they stalked their prey. The trail led uphill, along a more treacherous section of the mountain's face. Within an hour, it was clear that the animal had taken refuge in a massive formation of jagged, coal-black crags.

"Steinhauer," whispered Pembleton. "Scanner."

The private, whose formerly severe crew cut had started to grow out into ragged shocks of fair hair, retrieved and activated his hand scanner. On Graylock's orders, the survivors had been sparing in their use of the devices, and also their weapons, because recharging them in the weak arctic sunlight was problematic. The team was supposed to resort to the powered equipment only as an emergency measure.

*Starvation counts as an emergency,* Pembleton decided.

Thrusting and slashing with his arm, Steinhauer directed the squad through a narrow pass in the crags. The men braced their weapons against their shoulders and hovered their fingers over the feather-touch triggers. Every step of the way, Steinhauer directed them toward the animal's life sign.

Then he held up a fist. The group halted.

He checked the scanner again. Looked up and around. Held up two fingers and pointed in one direction, then another. Two signals, diverging. Retreating deeper into the crags.

Pembleton gave the signal to advance in pairs, with each covering the other. Steinhauer and Mazzetti pushed ahead, while Crichlow remained at Pembleton's side.

The pass grew narrow as the four men worked their way past several irregular switchbacks, trading the point position at each one. Inching around another corner, Pembleton saw the narrow trail open into a small clearing. It was somewhere in the middle of the towering rock formation, which jutted up on all sides toward the ashen sky.

In the middle of the clearing was a mound of gnawed-rough bones, half buried in the bloodstained snow. It took him only a fraction of a second to realize that he and his team were not hunters here in this frozen wasteland but prey.

He turned to give the order to fall back. Then he heard Mazzetti scream. The crags filled with the shrill echoes of a phase rifle firing on automatic. He sprinted back through the pass, his muscles burning with fatigue as they fought the gravity, his lungs screaming for oxygen in the thin mountain air. Stumbling through a hairpin turn, he found Steinhauer standing with his back to a slab of rock, snapping off short bursts of charged plasma into random gaps between the sawtooth stones. The man's entire body was shaking with the effects of adrenaline overload.

A few meters farther down the pass, all around Mazzetti's dropped rifle, there were massive splatters of blood on the snow. Red chunks of viscera dangled from rough edges between the crags, along a steady crimson smear on the rocks—the kind of stain that would be made by dragging a mauled man over them.

"Cease-fire!" said Pembleton. He laid a hand on top of Steinhauer's rifle, and the private relented in his pointless barrage. "Lead us out of here, Private."

Steinhauer regarded him with a horrified stare. "We can't just leave Niccolo to those . . . those *things*," he said.

Pembleton took the hand scanner from Steinhauer's belt, powered it up, and made a quick sweep for life readings. Then he turned it off and handed it back to the private. "Mazzetti's dead," he said. "Move out, back to camp. That's an order."

With a keen awareness of now being the hunted, Pembleton retrieved the dead man's dropped rifle and herded his two shocked-silent enlisted men back the way they had come, out of the pass, and back down the mountainside. One man short, the squad retreated into the coming night.

*Graylock will have to make do without any more spare parts,* Pembleton decided. *Because if the predators on this planet are anything like the ones on Earth, this isn't over.*

He feared it wouldn't be long before he faced these creatures again. It would be dark soon.

\* \* \*

The line between existence and oblivion had become faded and permeable for the Caeliar exiles. Robbed of mass, Lerxst now recalled physical sensations only as abstractions. Texture and temperature were no longer comprehensible to him since he had given up his frame of reference in the material realm. Motion was all but imperceptible. Pressure had given way to an almost unbearable dispersion of his essential being.

All that remained real to him was the emotional landscape of the gestalt, his communion with the other eleven Caeliar.

"Time seems to move faster now," said Sedín, her thoughts instantly shared with the others.

Agreement resonated among them without words.

Ghyllac added, "I no longer sense a distinction between light and darkness. Everything has turned to twilight."

Assent came from Felef, Meddex, and Ashlok.

"I can't remember twilight," countered Denblas, drawing concurrence from Celank and Liaudi.

Ripples of concern came from their youngest, least resolute members—Dyrrem, Narus, and the trio's speaker, Yneth. "We three cannot remain coherent for much longer without an influx of new energy," she said. "Our thoughts are . . ." She submerged into a long pause. "Disordered," she added at last. "Entropic."

"Without the anchor of mass, we cannot risk traveling this world," Lerxst told her. "Outside Mantilis, we could become dispersed by natural phenomena such as wind or tides."

Sedín replied, "And if we remain in Mantilis, we will slide toward chaos without even trying to save ourselves." Cradling the psionic presences of Yneth, Dyrrem, and Narus in her gestalt projection, she continued, "We must act to save our own."

"There is nothing we can do," Ghyllac said. "Our grounding in the physical is now too fragile to tap this world's resources or to move toward stronger solar radiation at the equator."

Felef replied, "That is not strictly true. In the most extreme circumstances, there is always consolidation."

A mental shudder traveled through the gestalt.

Liaudi asked with pointed curiosity, "And how would we decide who was to surrender their energy to the gestalt? Would the strongest expire to sustain the weaker among us? Or would we claim the weakest to bolster the others?"

"It would be best if the selections were governed by dispassionate logic," said Meddex, "employing a calculation of how to achieve the greatest degree and duration of good from the least amount of sacrifice."

Ashlok said, "I have already made such an analysis. Despite the logic of it, the sacrifices it demands feel arbitrary. I think it might be best if we let ourselves be guided by our consciences rather than by a tyranny of numbers."

"Might that be because you find the verdict of the numbers troubling?" asked Celank. "Do they call for your divestment?"

"No, not at first," Ashlok said. "My concern is that, as Liaudi speculated, the physics of the situation suggest that the maximum survival rate is obtained by sacrificing the weakest for the benefit of those requiring the least aid."

"Regardless of whether we consolidate according to logic or to our charitable impulses, it still amounts to a slow death by dissolution," argued Dyrrem.

Narus added, "The humans sustain themselves by consuming the local fauna. Perhaps there is a biological solution to our dilemma as well. Symbiosis, perhaps, rather than consumption."

"Doubtful," Sedín said. "Except for trace molecules, we crossed the barrier from organic to synthetic aeons ago. It may not be possible to backtrack on the path of our evolution."

"Even if it was possible," Ghyllac said, "we would need a sentient life-form with which to bond, to guarantee sufficient neuro-electric activity to power our catoms. Such a fusion would be a delicate and dangerous undertaking. If it is mishandled, it might debase us or turn our hosts into automatons—or both."

Lerxst made it clear that his was to be the last word on the matter. "We have neither the strength nor the facilities to perform the necessary research for such a task," he said. "If we wish to propose it to the humans, we will need to have the ability to pursue it, and that will entail consolidation. If that is the consensus of the gestalt, then we should resolve now which few will donate their energy for the sake of the others."

The hesitation was brief. Dyrrem, Narus, and Yneth projected their intention to release their catoms' energy to the gestalt, condemning the last afterimages of their forms to chaos and expiration. Gratitude and sorrow came back to them threefold from those they were about to preserve.

It was a swift transition. Three minds withdrew from the gestalt, which diminished in richness but grew in strength as power flowed through it, restoring form to its remaining members. Dyrrem, Narus, and Yneth were gone.

Sedín asked, "Who will make our proposition to the humans?"

"I will," Lerxst said.

Ever the cynic, Ghyllac asked, "And if they refuse?"

Lerxst replied, "Then we have just seen the fate that awaits us all."

"Try bending it," Graylock said, over an atonal howl of wind that fluttered and snapped the fabric of the shelter's walls.

Kiona Thayer flexed her ankle backward and forward in slow, stiff movements. "It's still fighting me," she said, nodding at the motor-assist brace Graylock had fashioned to enable her to walk normally.

"I think it's just the cold," Graylock said. "Gumming up the lubricant. It'll be fine once it's been moving for a while." He nodded toward the glowing rock in the middle of the enclosure. "Keep it close to the heat, and we'll try it again in an hour."

The weight of snow on top of the shelter had caused an unsupported section to droop inward. Graylock ducked under it as he circled around the heated rock to look over Private Steinhauer's shoulder. The young German man worked with pale, calloused hands, twisting together lengths of separated wood fiber that had been soaked in hot water until they had become flexible enough to manipulate. Woven together into a tight grid, the fibers formed the walking surface of handmade snowshoes.

"Those are looking good, Thom," Graylock said.

Steinhauer shrugged. "They're all right."

"How many pairs do you have finished?"

The private leaned forward and pulled open a folded blanket that protected his finished work. "Two and a half pairs," he said. Holding up the unfinished, teardrop-shaped shoe frame in his hands, he added, "This will make three."

"Good, good," Graylock said with a satisfied nod.

He continued around the shelter's perimeter and kneeled

beside Crichlow, who lay almost on top of the heated rock. The young Liverpudlian was swaddled in blankets, sweating profusely, and shivering with enough force that he seemed to be suffering a seizure. Graylock removed the damp but fever-warmed cloth from Crichlow's forehead and used it to mop some of the sweat from the sick man's face and throat. Wringing it out over the dirt near the hot stone, he asked his patient, "Do you prefer it hot or cold, Eric?"

"Cold," Crichlow said through chattering teeth.

Graylock stepped over to a bowl set near the outer wall. He used a tin cup beside it to scoop out a small amount of cold water and pour it with care over the cloth. Then he brought the cloth back to Crichlow, folded it in thirds, and set it gently across the man's forehead. "Feel better," he said to him.

As much as he was tempted to crawl inside his own bedroll and retreat into slumber, Graylock knew when he checked his chrono that sleep would have to wait. He pulled extra layers of Caeliar-made fabric over himself, and he was careful to wrap his face, cover his nose and mouth, and shield his eyes with lightweight goggles he'd borrowed from Crichlow. Before he parted the overlapping folds of the shelter's entrance, he warned the others, "Bundle up, everyone. I'm heading out." When the others had draped themselves under covers, he made his exit.

Stepping outside had become an act requiring great willpower. In the fortnight since Mazzetti had been killed, the days had grown noticeably shorter on daylight, and the average temperature had gone from the kind of cold that could give someone frostbite to the kind that could kill a careless person in a matter of minutes.

Graylock watched his breath condense in front of him, filtered through three layers of fabric. Underneath his scarves, the moisture collected on his skin and chilled instantly, making his face feel clammy. He followed a narrow path that Steinhauer and Pembleton had excavated from the hip-deep snow that surrounded their camp. The footing was slick and icy, and the fact that he was trudging uphill to the lookout position made the short trip all the more difficult.

At the top of the rise, Pembleton paced in a circle around a stand of tall boulders. From there, in clear weather, a sentry could see anything that might approach within seventy to eighty meters of the shelter. Even at night, with only starlight for illumination, it was possible for one's eyes to adjust and pierce the darkness to keep watch for predators.

The sergeant nodded to Graylock as they met at the mound's peak. "Evening, Lieutenant," Pembleton said.

"I'm here to relieve you, Sergeant."

Pembleton replied, "I wanted Steinhauer to cover Crichlow's shift, sir."

"Too bad," Graylock said. "Steinhauer's making good progress on those snowshoes. I want him to rest and keep working. The sooner we have five pairs of shoes, the sooner we can move out."

Nodding, Pembleton said, "I understand, sir. But you're in command—we need to keep you safe in the shelter. Let me take the late watch."

"You've stood two watches today already," Graylock said. "It's a wonder you aren't frozen solid. Go inside. I can spot motion and shoot a rifle as well as anyone."

A larger-than-usual plume of breath betrayed Pembleton's frustrated sigh. "Yes, sir," he said. He removed the rifle that was slung over his shoulder and handed it to Graylock. "How's Crichlow doing?"

"Worse," Graylock said. "I don't know if it's a medical issue, like a congenital disease, or a virus or a parasite."

Pembleton asked, "Can't the hand scanner tell you that?"

It was Graylock's turn to sigh, this time in dismay. "The power cell ran out this morning."

"Can we transfer power from one of the rifles?"

Graylock shrugged. "Not efficiently, and most of the rifles are getting low, too. A few more weeks, and we're unarmed." He looked up at the alpine peaks high above them. "Unless we want to make another trip up Junk Mountain and ask the Caeliar for more batteries."

"And risk running into our friends with the fangs and claws again? No, thank you." Pembleton leaned sideways and looked past Graylock, surveying the rolling, snow-covered landscape that ringed the mountain's base. "Besides, I think the mountain's coming to us." He pointed, and Graylock turned his head.

A single Caeliar moved quickly toward them, its wide, three-toed feet bounding over the fresh-fallen snow without leaving so much as a mark. The alien's pale, mottled skin seemed made to catch the weak starlight. Its bulbous cranium and long, stretched-frown visage became distinct as it drew within a dozen meters of the sentries' peak.

Pembleton asked Graylock with politic courtesy, "Are you planning on challenging it, sir?"

Chastened, Graylock lifted the phase rifle, aimed it at the Caeliar, and shouted, "Halt! Identify yourself!"

The Caeliar stopped moving a few meters away. Its ridged air sacs puffed and deflated with the deep motions of respiration. "Karl, it is Lerxst."

Graylock demanded, "What do you want?"

"To talk with your people, Karl—all of them. I am not exaggerating when I say that our lives may depend on it."

# 2381

## 9

Dr. Shenti Yisec Eres Ree paced back and forth on the terrace outside the away team's shared residential suite. It wasn't easy for him to negotiate such narrow turns with his therapodian build—semirigid tail extended behind him for balance, head thrust forward, torso almost level to the ground.

All around him, the Caeliar city of Axion was lit from within and reflecting itself in its polished, vertical surfaces. Overhead, the sky was perfectly black, unblemished by stars; only a few low-running clouds bounced back the bluish-white glow of the metropolis. Natural scents from the planet below traveled on the breeze, but Ree couldn't dispel the sensation of being caught up in a half-formed illusion of a real world.

Footsteps drew closer. Ceasing his perambulations, Ree turned to find Commander Tuvok stepping through the open portal to the terrace. "Good evening, Doctor," said the Vulcan.

"Commander," Ree said, watching Tuvok with a wary eye.

Tuvok continued past him to the low barrier, stopped, and rested his hands on the wall's shallow ledge. To Ree's surprise, the tactical officer said nothing else; he seemed content to stare out at the cityscape in stoic silence.

Ree didn't buy it. "You're here to berate me, aren't you?"

"Quite the contrary," Tuvok said. "I feel that I owe you an apology. However, I was not certain whether this would be an appropriate time to express it."

With exaggerated swoops of his long head and sinewy neck, Ree scoped the entirety of their immediate vicinity. "No one here but us and the invisible Caeliar who spy on us," he said. "So speak freely, Mister Tuvok."

Turning about to face Ree, Tuvok said, "Very well. I should have arrived sooner to help you explain yourself to the others. I had been meditating and monitoring Commander Troi's mental state. Though I sensed her distress, I understood that you were trying to help her. Unfortunately, I did not realize that you were in danger because of the security team's misreading of your actions. By the time I extricated myself from my telepathic link with Counselor Troi, I was too late to corroborate your account of events before the matter got out of hand. So I ask your forgiveness."

Ree bowed his head. "Thank you, Tuvok. I don't think you owe me any such apology, but if you think it was called for, I accept it in the spirit in which it was given."

Tuvok nodded once, and then he pivoted again to face the needle-thin towers and the gossamerlike metal filaments that linked them. With the conversation apparently ended for the time being, Ree resumed pacing. He took care not to swat the Vulcan man with his tail while making his turn at the end of each lap. In the silence of the night, Ree's claws clicked with a sound like a low spark on the rough stone of the terrace.

He paused again when he heard more footsteps approaching. Commander Vale emerged from the main corridor, trailed by the loping figure of Inyx. Lieutenant Commander Keru followed them.

When the three were meters shy of the terrace, Ree flicked his tongue twice in quick succession to taste the pheromones in the air. Vale's biochemical emissions matched her demeanor: aggressive. Keru's scent suggested he was calmer than she was. As usual, the Caeliar scientist made no mark in the air, though Ree thought an odor of sulfur might have been appropriate.

Behind Ree, Tuvok faced the oncoming trio.

"Doctor," Vale said, "Inyx needs a sample of your venom."

Openly suspicious, Ree asked, "Why?"

Inyx stepped around Vale and walked a few steps forward. "I've had centuries to study human anatomy and biology in detail, but Deanna's heritage is of mixed ancestry. That made it more difficult for me to make a diagnosis and select a course of treatment. However, I am also unfamiliar with your species and its unusually complex venom. If I am to save your friend's life, I cannot afford to spend time separating your biotoxin from Deanna's bloodstream. A pure sample will enable me to sequence its properties more quickly and develop an antivenom."

"If you're treating her medically, I demand to monitor the process," Ree said.

Inyx straightened and took on an imperious mien. "Given the crudity of your methods, that is quite out of the question."

"She's my patient," Ree said.

Vale replied, "I'm pretty sure she fired you when she told you to keep your hands off her."

"That was hardly an enforceable dictate, Commander," Ree retorted. "The good counselor was clearly *non compos mentis*."

"Doctor, just give Inyx the venom," Vale said. Beside her, Inyx proffered a small sample jar with a cover of taut fabric.

Stalking forward, Ree said, "If you want a sample from me, you can draw it in whatever facility you're holding my patient."

"Deanna is not being held," Inyx said. "We are trying to help her, but her condition has become critical. Though your venom may have preserved her fragile status for a few minutes, it has complicated her treatment. Your patient's best interest is now best served by your cooperation, Doctor."

Ree paused and reflected that Inyx's position was actually reasonable. His reluctance to comply with the Caeliar's request was rooted in the simple fact that he didn't trust them.

His ruminations were interrupted by the firm squeeze of a hand near the nerve cluster above his shoulder. He swung his head back along his flank to see Commander Tuvok. The Vulcan was clamping his hand and scrunching a fistful of the Pahkwa-thanh's leathery hide in his grip. Ree flashed a toothy grin at the swarthy humanoid. "If you're trying to render me unconscious with a nerve pinch, Commander, don't bother." Tuvok released his grip on Ree and backed off, his expression neutral. Ree added, "I presume all that business about making an apology was a ruse to put you in position in case I refused Commander Vale's request?"

"No," Tuvok said. "My apology was sincere."

"And I'm not making a request, Doctor," Vale said. "I'm giving you an order: the venom sample, now."

Taking a more conciliatory tack, Inyx said, "Had it not been for your comrades' recent attempt at escape, I might have been persuaded to permit you to observe Deanna's treatment. Under the circumstances, however, I am under orders from the Quorum to restrict your access to all information about our technology and methods. So I will ask you again, as one healer to another, help me save Deanna's life. I beg of you."

"Give me the cup," Ree said, holding out one clawed hand.

Vale transferred the container from Inyx to Ree, who impaled its fabric cover with one incisor fang and released roughly fifty milliliters of colorless, odorless venom into the cup. Inyx stepped forward, and Ree handed him the sample. "Keep me apprised of Counselor Troi's progress, please."

"Of course," Inyx said. "And thank you."

As the Caeliar turned to depart, Ree asked, "Why didn't you send your errand girl Hernandez to collect the sample?"

"Because she is the one who enabled your ship to escape," Inyx said. He walked out onto the terrace and levitated away into the night.

Keru shambled away, back toward his quarters, followed closely by Tuvok. Vale lingered a moment and glared at Ree.

"Do you realize that every second you stood there arguing, Troi could be dying?" she asked once the others had gone. "Is that really a chance you wanted to take?"

"Not at all, Commander," said Ree. "But you know the details of her condition almost as well as I do, and you know what has to be done. But what will the Caeliar do after they assess the situation? What if their imponderable brand of moral calculus compels them to sacrifice Deanna to save her fetus?"

Vale rubbed her eyes, signaling that she was not only tired but also tired of their conversation. "Do you really think that if you were there, you'd be able to sway their judgment in the slightest?"

"Of course not," Ree admitted. "But at least I'd be in a position to bite one of *them*."

Rolling her eyes, Vale replied, "*Now* you tell me. If I'd known *that* was your plan, I would've taken *your* side."

# 10

Erika Hernandez felt queasy as she stumbled in a panic through her quarters on *Titan*. Screams echoed from the corridor, and she heard the sounds of energy weapons being discharged in the corridor outside her locked door.

Thunderclaps of impact shook *Titan,* knocking her to the deck. She scrambled to her feet and staggered across the heaving floor. Something had set upon the ship with such speed that there had seemed to be no time to react.

Through the windows, she glimpsed a fearsome black cube moving through the indigo fog of the nebula. It battered its way through the storm of starship debris, firing brilliant green beams at *Titan,* which pitched and lurched after every shot.

A direct hit rocked the ship. The lights stuttered out. Outside her quarters, the clamor of battle grew more intense. On a gamble, she dashed to the door, which opened ahead of her. One of the guards who had locked her in, an Andorian *shen,* lay dead on the deck, her nubile form butchered and bloodied. Hernandez grabbed the *shen's* rifle and prowled away, through the dark, smoke-filled corridors, following the din of combat.

Everywhere she looked, biomechanoid components seemed to have sprouted from the bulkheads, as if the ship were diseased.

She turned a corner and stepped into a cross fire.

Emerald streaks screamed over her shoulder and seared crackling wounds into the chests of two of *Titan's* security personnel. Hernandez hit the deck as two other security officers, of a species Hernandez had never seen before, returned fire at their opponents. Shimmering beams of phaser energy crisscrossed in the hazy darkness.

*I should get to cover,* Hernandez told herself, but she didn't dare stand to run, and her curiosity demanded to see who or what had boarded *Titan.*

She turned her head and saw the enemy. They were humanoid, clad in formfitting black bodysuits and festooned with cybernetic enhancements. Their optical grafts swept the corridor with red laser beams, and several of the boarders had one hand replaced with complex machinery, ranging from cutting implements to industrial tools.

They advanced into the phaser barrage at a quick march, moving with the kind of precision she had only ever seen from jackbooted thugs in old historical films. To her shock, the phaser beams had no effect on them—they simply deflected them with personal energy shields.

Mustering her strength, she coiled to spring to her feet and sprint toward the security team. Turning back, she saw that it was too late for that. They had been ambushed from behind by more of the cyborgs, who slashed and impaled with abandon. Cries of pain were swallowed by the cruel whirring of machinery.

She rolled and tried to turn back the way she had come. There was another squad of the malevolent invaders closing in from behind her. Pivoting in a panic, she realized she had nowhere to run. *Not without a fight,* she vowed, and she opened fire. None of her shots did any good.

The black throng surrounded her and pressed inward.

Then came the oppressive roar of a voice inside her mind. *We are the Borg. Resistance is futile. You will be exterminated.* It was as intimate to her thoughts as the gestalt once had been, but it was hostile, savage, and soulless.

A spinning saw blade cut away the front half of her rifle, and the weapon spat sparks as it tumbled from her grasp.

Hands closed around her arms and pulled her backward, off-balance. She flailed and kicked, lashing out with wild fury.

More hands seized her ankles, her calves. The sheer weight of bodies smothered her, and a sting like a needle jabbed her throat. Twisting, she saw that one of the Borg drones had extended from between its knuckles two slender tubules that had penetrated her carotid.

An icy sensation flooded into her like a poison and engulfed her consciousness in a sinking despair.

Pushed facedown as the Borg's infusion took root, she smelled the ferric tang of blood spreading across the deck under her face. Then a hand cupped her chin and lifted her head.

She looked into the eyes of a humanoid woman whose skin was the mottled gray of a cadaver. Hairless and glistening in the spectral light, the female Borg flashed a mirthless smile at Hernandez. "You are the one we have waited for," she said. "Surrender to the Collective . . . and become Logos of Borg."

The human part of Hernandez unleashed a defiant scream, a torrent of pure rage. But her body lay still and silent, submerging into the merciless grip of the Collective. Trapped inside herself, Hernandez was tortured by her memory's endless refrain of mute protest: *No!*

She awoke screaming. She covered her mouth with one hand.

The door signal was loud in the silence of her quarters. Lieutenant sh'Aqabaa asked via the comm, *"Captain Hernandez? Are you all right?"*

"Yes," Hernandez said. *"Just a bad dream." A dream,* she repeated to herself, unable to believe it. The padd by her side still displayed the file she had been reading—a declassified report about the Borg that Captain Riker had suggested she take a look at. *I must have drifted off while I was reading.*

It had been nearly eight hundred years since she had slept. After bonding with the Caeliar gestalt, her body had no longer required sleep, either for physical or mental rejuvenation. The catoms that infused her cells regulated her neurochemistry and biological processes. Axion's quantum field had been the only solace or sustenance she had needed since undergoing the Change.

*Until now, apparently.*

She recalled a threat the Caeliar had once made to Inyx, in order to coerce him into thwarting her attempts at communication with Earth. They had warned him that if he could not control her, they would exile her to a distant galaxy, where, without Axion's quantum field, she would age normally and die alone.

*I guess escaping from Axion has other consequences,* she reasoned, rubbing the itch of slumber from her eyes. *I wonder what other surprises I have to look forward to.*

As if on cue, her belly gurgled loudly, its acid-fueled yodel resonating inside her long-dormant stomach.

*Naturally.*

Hernandez got up and walked to a device that her Andorian guard had called a replicator. "You can get your meals from here, and it'll even do the dishes," sh'Aqabaa had said. It was time, Hernandez decided, to put that claim to the test.

Standing in front of the machine, which resembled little more than a polished-polymer nook in the wall, she muttered aloud, "How am I supposed to use this thing?"

A feminine computer voice replied, *"State your food or beverage request with as much specificity as you desire or are able to provide."*

"A quesadilla with Jack cheese and black beans, with sides of hot salsa, guacamole, and sour cream. And a mojito."

The machine responded with a flurry of glowing particles and a thrumming swell of white noise. When both had faded, a tray sat in the nook. On it was a plate covered by a piping-hot quesadilla, some small bowls with her condiments, and a glass with her minty-sweet rum beverage. She removed the tray from the replicator and carried it to a small table.

The aroma of food awakened memories she had thought long faded—of her childhood home and family dinners; the delicate texture of a flour tortilla fresh from a skillet; the sublime flavor of stone-ground guacamole made from ripe avocados, fresh cilantro, salsa, salt, garlic, and a touch of lime juice; the cool, refreshing decadence of a perfect mojito.

With great expectation, she sampled her replicator repast.

The quesadilla was rubbery, the salsa was bland, the guacamole was greasy, the sour cream tasted like paste, and there was something subtly but undeniably wrong with her mojito.

She pushed the tray away. *Food that's not food, booze that's not booze,* she fumed. *This is why I had a chef.*

Sleep eluded Will Riker.

All he'd wanted was a short nap. He turned from his right side to his left, flipped and punch-fluffed his pillow in search of a cool spot, and slowed his breathing in an effort to cajole his mind and body into letting go of consciousness. Closing his eyes, he focused on the white noise he had requested on a loop from the computer, of a low wind rustling the leaves of a tree.

It was all in vain. Rolling over, he let his arm splay across the empty half of the bed. Deanna's half.

Her absence had pierced him like a needle; his every thought was stitched with its doleful color. Worse still was the guilt. He kept picturing her expression when she learned that he and *Titan* had escaped from New Erigol, leaving her and the rest of the away team behind.

*I deserted them,* he accused himself.

In the hours since *Titan*'s return to Federation space, he had begun to second-guess himself. *What difference will one more ship make now? Especially one as beat-up as ours?*

Lying alone in the darkness, he examined his decision with an increasingly critical eye. On the face of it, it had seemed at first to be the one that served the greatest good: It had freed his ship and the hundreds of personnel still onboard. That was as far as his justifications could take him, however. He couldn't persuade himself that he had really done any good for Starfleet or the

Federation. In the end, all he could say was that he had saved the many by sacrificing the few.

By sacrificing his *Imzadi.*

*She would never have done that to me,* he told himself. Vivid recollections of his month of brutal captivity on Tezwa paraded through the theater of his memory. In those dark hours, when he had been beaten and broken, tortured and terrorized, only two things had kept him anchored in himself. One had been the indelible memories of music, of melodies and virtuoso performances by jazz master Junior Mance; the other had been the unshakable certainty that his *Imzadi* would never give up her search for him, that she would never abandon hope. Now he had repaid her devotion with a hollow appeal to duty.

He threw off the covers and sat up on the side of the bed. Leaning forward, he planted his face in his palms and imagined himself returned to the fateful moment, hours earlier, when Hernandez had made her proposition. Replaying it in his mind, he tried to conceive of how he could have answered differently, of some case that he could have made for not leaving the away team. There were no answers.

Every time he asked himself the question again, he was forced to admit that no matter how futile it might seem to hurl his ship into a war that was already all but lost, he was being driven by instinct—and drawn toward something.

"Computer, cease white noise," he said, and the breathy whisper of air through leaves came to an abrupt end. "Unshade the windows." The sloped, rounded-corner windows above his bed lost their dark tint and became transparent, revealing the backlit blue radiance of the nebula. Several of *Titan*'s shuttlecraft were on their way back, their tractor beams towing large sections of hull salvaged from demolished starships.

Watching the recovery operations in the nebula, he felt as if abandoning Deanna had blasted him to bits and that he was now struggling to piece himself back together from broken parts. He would do a fair job of presenting himself as functional and whole, but he knew that without Deanna, he would be like a phaser rifle field-stripped by a cadet and then misassembled, with one vital component left out, forgotten on the ground.

*In other words,* he castigated himself, *useless.*

A comm signal filtered down from the overhead speaker,

followed by the voice of Commander Hachesa. *"Bridge to Captain Riker,"* said the acting first officer.

"Go ahead."

*"Update from the* Enterprise, *sir,"* replied Hachesa. *"They and the* Aventine *will rendezvous with us in fifteen minutes."*

"Acknowledged," Riker said. "Tell Lieutenant Commander Pazlar and Commander Ra-Havreii to meet me in transporter room two in ten minutes."

*"Aye, sir. Bridge out."*

He stood and stretched. "Computer, fade up lights to one-half," he said, and the room slowly brightened. Shambling groggily toward the bathroom, he hoped that a shower would revive him before it was time to meet with his former captain. The chrono on his end table displayed the time as 0617 hours.

*Not bad,* he thought. *I almost got an hour of sleep. Except it wasn't quite an hour, and I never actually slept.* He tapped a padd next to the bathroom sink and turned on the cold water. He cupped his hands, filled them beneath the icy stream, and splashed his face, shocking himself to full alertness.

He blinked at his dripping-wet, frazzled reflection in the mirror. *Who needs sleep, anyway?*

"Energizing," said the transporter officer.

Jean-Luc Picard turned to face the raised platform. The system powered up with a resonant hum. To his left stood Beverly and Worf, and on his right were Captain Dax and Commander Bowers from the *Aventine.*

In front of them, three columns of sparkling bluish-white particles surged into existence and adopted humanoid shapes. Even before the radiance faded, Picard recognized the welcome sight of his old friend and former first officer, William Riker, standing at the front of the platform.

The transporter effect dissipated. Standing behind Riker were an Efrosian man with long white hair and a flowing mustache to match, and a slim, blond Elaysian woman who wore a motor-assist armature over her uniform, from neck to ankles.

Riker descended from the platform, and Picard stepped forward to greet him. "Welcome aboard, Captain," Picard said, shaking Riker's hand and flashing a wide, friendly smile.

"Thank you, Captain," Riker said, his own smile guarded and ephemeral. He let go of Picard's hand and gestured to the two officers who had beamed in with him. "Allow me to introduce my chief engineer, Commander Ra-Havreii. And I think you know my science officer, Lieutenant Commander Pazlar."

"Indeed, I do," Picard said, nodding to the duo. "Commander Ra-Havreii, it's a pleasure. Your reputation precedes you."

Ra-Havreii lifted his snowy brows. "That's what I'm afraid of," he said, with a weariness that belied his jesting tone.

Dax stepped forward and met Riker with a smile. "It's good to see you again, Will," she said. Nodding over her shoulder, she added, "This my first officer, Commander Sam Bowers."

Riker reached out and shook Bowers's hand. "A pleasure."

Pazlar stepped around Riker and offered her hand to Dax. "Nice to see you again, *Captain*."

"Likewise, Melora," Dax said with a friendly smile. "You look wonderful, as always."

"Says the woman who gets younger *every* time I see her," Pazlar said, with a teasing roll of her eyes.

Worf stepped forward and greeted Riker with a firm and enthusiastic handshake. "Welcome back, sir."

Clasping the Klingon's hand in both of his, Riker replied, "Thanks, Worf. How're you liking my old job?"

"Too much paperwork," Worf said.

"Try being a captain," Riker quipped. He released Worf's hand and accepted a quick, friendly embrace from Beverly.

"Welcome back, Will," she said. As they parted, she added, "I thought Chris and Deanna were coming. Are they all right?"

The stricken look that paled Riker's face warned Picard that something terrible had happened and that Beverly's innocent question had salted an open emotional wound. A sidelong glance at Dax's sympathetic expression made it clear to Picard that she, too, understood what was being left unsaid.

Riker turned his eyes toward the deck. "I had to leave them behind to save the ship. . . . It's a long story."

It was a terrible strain for Picard, in the aftermath of such losses and tragedies as he had recently endured, to mask his own pangs of loss and grief at this revelation. Deanna Troi was almost like a daughter to him—even more so after her long-overdue (in his opinion) wedding to Riker. He'd developed similarly paternal feelings for Christine Vale, with whom he had suffered and been tested in several crucibles that had claimed the lives of many *Enterprise* personnel—the bloody Dokaalan colony incident, the planetwide riots on Delta Sigma IV, and, worst of all, the protracted carnage of the Tezwa debacle.

*If it's this deep a wound for me, imagine how much worse it must be for him,* Picard thought, trying to impose some perspective on the matter. *To lose his wife and his first officer, both at the same time. How could anyone bear that?*

Bowers broke the uncomfortable silence. "I don't mean to be callous, but we have a lot to talk about and not much time. Maybe we should adjourn to a more appropriate setting."

"Wait a second," Riker said to Bowers, and then he looked to Picard. "The *Voyager* crew has more experience with the Borg than anyone. Shouldn't they be part of this?"

"I wish they could be," Picard said. "Unfortunately, Captain Chakotay is in critical condition, and many of his officers and crew were killed. *Voyager* won't be mobile for several days, and Commander Bowers is correct, we can't wait." He turned to Worf. "Are the arrangements made, Number One?"

"Yes, sir," Worf said. He stepped toward the door, which opened with a soft hiss. Turning back, he said to the group, "Everyone, please follow me."

Dax and Bowers were the first to act on Worf's invitation, and Picard gestured to Riker and his officers that they should go ahead of him. After the trio had stepped out of the transporter room, Picard and Beverly followed them and remained at the back of the group.

Beverly didn't say a word as she took Picard's hand. She didn't need to explain why; he understood. In a crisis, Riker had made a decision that would likely haunt him, no matter how the situation ultimately resolved itself. It was a dilemma that could only be fully appreciated by another captain whose wife served with him aboard the same starship. She gave his hand a brief squeeze and then let it slip from her grasp.

Picard wondered if he could possibly have the courage to make the choice that Riker had made—to desert his pregnant wife in the name of duty, in the service of the abstraction known as the greater good. Then he thought of how much time's merciless fires had already taken from him, and he knew that he couldn't.

He walked in somber silence with Beverly . . . and wished that decorum had let him hold her hand just a little bit longer.

Sequestered in the *Enterprise*'s crew lounge—a.k.a. the Happy Bottom Riding Club—the three captains and their officers helped themselves to hot and cold beverages that had been set out on the counter by the lounge's civilian barkeep, Jordan. He had ushered out the other patrons before the officers' arrival. Now that the VIP guests were inside, Dax saw Jordan exit through the main portal, leaving the officers to confer in privacy.

Dax filled a mug with fresh-brewed *raktajino*. She took a sip of her piping-hot beverage and admired the lounge's many decorative touches. Among them were dozens of portraits of *Enterprise* personnel who had been killed in the line of duty, with small bronze placards denoting their names, ranks, and KIA dates; a map of California, with a star denoting the location of the lounge's twentieth-century-Earth namesake; a replica of that bar's liquor license; and memorabilia of past starships that had borne the name *Enterprise*.

Worf stepped up to the bar on Dax's left and filled a tall glass with prune juice. Captain Riker sidled up on Dax's right and poured himself a mug of piping-hot coffee. Noticing her wandering gaze, he confided, "Jordan spruced the place up, but I was the one who named it."

As soon as he'd said it, Dax was certain she noted a glower from Worf that was aimed in Riker's direction.

*That's a story I'll have to ask Worf about later,* she decided, while nodding politely at Riker.

Captain Picard raised his voice for the room and said, "Could we all gather, please? We haven't much time." The officers convened and sat down on either side of a row of small tables that Jordan and his staff had pushed together at the forward end of the lounge, along a wall of windows with a spectacular view of the nebula.

Dax only half listened as Picard summarized for Riker how the *Enterprise*'s efforts to halt the Borg's access to Federation space had led him and his crew to the Azure Nebula.

After Picard finished, Dax quickly apprised Riker of the link between her crew's investigation of the downed Earth *Starship*

*Columbia* NX-02 in the Gamma Quadrant and the subspace passage that brought them to the nebula.

Then came Riker's brief but gripping account of *Titan*'s detection of energy pulses in a remote sector of the Beta Quadrant and the trap into which he and his crew had been led as a result. Dax saw the anguish in Riker's eyes as he related in detail the circumstances that had compelled him to abandon his wife and his away team. "I had to make a snap decision, so I chose to bring my ship home," he said. "But it was a rough trip, and if what Captain Hernandez tells me is true, the Caeliar gestalt put up a hell of a fight to keep us there."

Two words leaped out at Dax, who interrupted, "Did you say 'Caeliar gestalt'?"

Riker did a surprised double-take. "Yes. Why?"

"The alien that stole the runabout from my ship," Dax said. "The one who led us here. He identified himself as Arithon of the Caeliar. He was looking for something called the gestalt."

"Well, I'd say we found it," Riker said. "And the Caeliar."

Pazlar interjected, "Captain Hernandez's account of the destruction of Erigol and the recorded date of the supernova that made this nebula are a match. If the Caeliar created those subspace passages, it would explain why this was their nexus."

Bowers, whose body language telegraphed his impatience, replied, "I'll admit that's all fascinating, but is any of it relevant to stopping the Borg armada?" Unfazed by the group's many stares of reproach, he continued, "Seriously, what's the plan here? What's our next step?"

Captain Picard frowned but salvaged Bowers's pride by answering, "The commander has a point. We need to focus on the future, not dwell on the past. I'll open the floor to ideas."

"Part of the problem," Ra-Havreii said, "is that there's little chance we could reach any of the threatened worlds in time to make a difference. The Borg outpace us by a wide margin. By the time we reach Earth or Vulcan or any of the other core systems, the battles for their fates will be long over."

"Maybe not," Dax said. "The *Aventine*'s carrying a prototype quantum slipstream drive. We weren't scheduled to start testing it until next month, but I think we can bring it online now, with a few hours' notice. If it works, we could leapfrog past the Borg, maybe even beat them to Earth by a few hours."

With casual skepticism, Picard replied, "To what end? With all respect, Captain, that's not a plan—it's just a tactic."

"I was simply refuting Commander Ra-Havreii's assertion that we're too slow to make a difference," Dax said.

"I see," Picard said. "You're right. It's important to know what capabilities we have at our command. But before we deploy them, we owe it to ourselves to be certain of our objectives."

Dax summoned the calm confidence that her symbiont's lifetimes of experience granted to her. She quashed her initial defensive reaction and let herself hear the wisdom in what Picard had said. "You're absolutely right," she replied. "Before we make any plans, we need to take stock of our strengths and resources." Looking at Riker, she added, "Starting with Captain Hernandez. After eight centuries among the Caeliar, she might have knowledge of advanced technologies that could help us fight the Borg. Before we do anything or set any plans in stone, we should see if she's able and willing to help us."

Picard nodded. "An excellent point, Captain." He pushed away his mug of Earl Grey and stood up. "I think it's time you and I met Captain Hernandez." Then he asked Riker, "Can I impose on you to make the introductions?"

Riker nodded and said, "My pleasure."

"Very well. Meeting adjourned."

Everyone stood and moved in a loose group toward the exit. Bowers fell into step close beside Dax and said confidentially, "What if she can't or won't help us?"

Dax frowned as she pondered that scenario. "In that case," she replied, "I wouldn't make any long-term plans if I were you."

# 11

The shortest battle of Martok's life was rapidly becoming the costliest. In the few minutes since his fleet had uncloaked and engaged the Borg armada with a barrage of transphasic torpedoes, more than seventy percent of both forces had been annihilated.

"Keep firing!" barked Captain G'mtor, over the rumbling of shockfronts and debris buffeting the *Sword of Kahless*. "Set course, bearing two-six-one! Don't let that cube get away!"

Already, several Borg ships had broken through the line and

were accelerating deeper into Klingon space, their trajectories gradually diverging as they zeroed in on different star systems. Just as they had in the Azure Nebula, they had rammed their way through the Klingon blockade, sacrificing a few cubes for the sake of the overall invasion effort. *Once they pass out of range, we'll never catch them again,* Martok knew.

He watched the image of the receding Borg vessel shrink on the main viewscreen. Then the tactical officer called out, "Weapons locked!"

"Fire!" snapped G'mtor. Six transphasic torpedoes slashed in blue streaks up the center of the viewscreen and converged with lethal alacrity on the cube. A sunflash blanched the viewer. When it faded, it showed a cloud of smoldering black wreckage being dispersed by the navigational deflector of the victorious *Sword of Kahless.* "Hard about!" bellowed the captain. "Tactical, acquire a new target!"

Fire and fury blasted through the bridge's starboard stations. A slab of metal struck Martok's chair and knocked it off its pedestal. The impact hurled him from the rushing jaws of spreading flame and slammed him brutally across the deck, where the bulkhead fragment pinned him and shielded him at the same time. Soldiers and parts of soldiers ricocheted off the port consoles and collapsed in smoking heaps on either side of him.

The bright white battle-stations lighting went dark, and the ruddy glow of standard illumination took its place. Gray static flurried on the main viewscreen, and the air was bitter with smoke from overloaded circuits and the stench of burnt hair. Martok spat out a mouthful of his own blood and tried to drag himself out from under the metal slab. Knifing pains alerted him to broken bones in his rib cage and left leg.

General Goluk stumbled over the rubble-strewn deck to Martok and yelled to a pair of nearby warriors, "Help me lift this bulkhead plate off the chancellor!" The tall, broad-shouldered duo did as the general ordered. With three pairs of hands and deep grunts of pained effort, they raised the slab high enough for Martok to free himself. Once he was clear, they let it fall to the deck with a resonant peal of metal on metal.

Martok reached up and took Goluk's offered hand. The general pulled Martok upright and steadied him until he could balance himself on his unbroken leg. To the two warriors, Martok said, "Get me damage reports and a battle update." Once they had stepped away, Martok asked Goluk in a confidential tone, "G'mtor?" The general nodded at the smoking heap of rubble and bodies from which Martok had been extricated.

Around the bridge, bloodied and scorched soldiers of the Empire struggled to wrest data or responses from their consoles. A faint crackle of comm chatter permeated the hazy compartment like an undercurrent. The minute Martok spent waiting for reports from his crew felt like an eternity.

One of the soldiers who had aided him returned. "Engines, shields, sensors, and weapons are offline, Chancellor," he said. "Life support is failing."

"What of the rest of the fleet?"

The warrior's jaw tensed, as if he refused to let the words escape his mouth. Then he bowed his head and said, "Broken."

Goluk asked, "Do we have communications?"

"Yes, sir," the soldier replied. "General Klag reports the *Gorkon* has been crippled and is unable to continue pursuit of the escaping Borg vessels."

Martok heaved an angry sigh. "How many broke through?"

"Sixty-one," said the soldier. "Ten heading to Qo'noS, two to Gorath, and the others to targets not yet identified. Also, another wave of Borg ships has been reported in the Mempa Sector, on course for more remote parts of the Empire."

Grim stares passed between Goluk and Martok. The general placed a hand on Martok's shoulder. "It was a glorious battle."

"Yes," Martok said. "But what will that matter if no Klingon remains to sing of it?" Nodding to the soldier, he said, "Open a channel to Qo'noS. We need to alert the home guard."

The warrior moved briskly to one of the bridge's few operational panels and tapped in a series of commands. "Channel open, Chancellor," he reported.

"On-screen," Martok said.

The gunmetal hash of electronic snow on the viewscreen gave way to a murky, unsteady signal from the High Council chamber in the Great Hall of the First City. Looking back at Martok was his political nemesis, Councillor Kopek. *"What news, Chancellor?"*

"Our fleet has fallen," Martok said. "The enemy is en route to worlds across the Empire. I trust you know where duty lies, Councillor."

Kopek nodded. *"Of course. We will defend Qo'noS, my lord."*

"Summon every ship that can reach you in time," Martok said. "The fate of our homeworld is now in your hands."

*"The Borg will not come to Qo'noS and live, Chancellor. When your fleet returns home, your throne will await you."*

"With you sitting on it, I presume?"

With no trace of mockery, Kopek replied, *"Today is not a day for politics, Chancellor. Today is a good day to die."*

*Perhaps he longs for his place in* Sto-Vo-Kor *like the rest of us, after all,* Martok thought. He didn't know whether *Fek'lhr* would permit such a vile spirit as Kopek to redeem himself with a single hour of heroism, but part of him wanted to believe that it was possible—and that every warrior deserved such a chance.

He saluted him. *"Qapla',* Kopek, son of Nargor."

*"Die with honor, Martok, son of Urthog. Qo'noS out."*

The signal ended, and the screen went dark.

*I have fought the good fight,* Martok told himself, but he found no solace in the thought. With his leg broken and his ship adrift, there was nothing more for him to do but stand and wait to see if the Empire's final hour had come around at last.

"Someone bring me a drink," he said.

# 12

Erika Hernandez sat alone at a dressing table in her quarters on *Titan.* She stared at her reflection in the large oval mirror. With her hands resting in her lap, she concentrated on her hair and felt the energy demands of her catoms as she altered her coiffure to match her fickle whims.

Her wild mane of thick, curly black hair retreated toward her head and turned an intense shade of indigo. Eyeing the more conservative spill of deep blue hair over her shoulders, Hernandez frowned. "I don't think so," she muttered to herself.

It took great effort to rein it back to a compact bob and shift its color to an auburn hue that matched her memories of cinnamon, fresh from the jar in her mother's kitchen. A fleeting whimsy drove her to go blond for all of eleven seconds.

She halted her hairstyling experiments as the door signal softly disturbed her privacy. "Come in," she said.

The door opened. Captain Riker entered, followed by two other officers—a bald human man and a young Trill woman—who wore the same rank insignia that he did. The trio was barely inside the room before Hernandez had used her catoms to restore her hair to its previous state, a mass of black waves that covered her back.

"Captain," Riker said. "I hope we're not interrupting."

"Not at all," she said. She added with teasing sweetness, "And thanks for knocking this time."

The Trill woman gleamed with fascination. "How do you do that with your hair?"

"Catoms," Hernandez said. "Sophisticated nanomachines made and infused into my body by the Caeliar. The catoms can direct energy and reshape matter in remarkable ways, if they have enough power. Unfortunately, this little parlor trick's about all I have left in me—and to be honest, it's tiring me out."

Folding his arms, Riker said to the other two captains, "She's being modest. When she showed up on my bridge a few hours ago, she turned Ensign Rriarr's phaser to dust with a glance."

Hernandez shook her head to deflect his praise. "Captain Riker's giving me a bit too much credit," she explained. "When I did that, we were still in orbit of New Erigol, where I had access to the Caeliar gestalt. Without that power to draw from, I can barely curl my hair."

The Trill cracked a smile, but the older man had the stern carriage of one who had seen too many days of war. Hernandez wondered if he saw her as clearly as she saw him.

He cleared his throat and threw a look at Riker, who dipped his chin at the reproach and gestured at his colleagues.

"Captain Hernandez," Riker said, "permit me to introduce Captain Ezri Dax of the Federation *Starship Aventine* and Captain Jean-Luc Picard of the *Enterprise*."

Unable to mask her confusion, Hernandez cocked her head and eyed Picard with suspicion. "But . . . you're the one the voice calls *Locutus*," she said.

Dax's and Riker's eyes widened in horror and surprise, and Picard froze as they looked at him. His face became pale, and he looked lifeless, Gorgonized. At last, he replied in a shocked whisper, "You heard a voice . . . call me . . . *Locutus*?"

"Yes," she said, listening to the inhuman chorus of distant

voices that filled every empty space in her thoughts. "Are you telling me the rest of you don't *hear* that?" She looked from one captain to another in an effort to gauge their reactions. Their obvious dismay and withdrawn body language told Hernandez that her revelation had left them ill at ease. "Great," she said. "You think I'm crazy, right? Think I'm hearing things?"

Picard stepped toward her. His voice was cautious and gentle. "Do you know what you've been hearing? Its name?"

Anticipating the direction of his questions, she replied, "Yes. Do you?"

As if he were reading her thoughts, he said under his breath, "The Collective." He looked at Riker and seemed to draw strength from the younger man's quiet fortitude. Turning back toward Hernandez, he continued, "When I hear the Borg, it sounds like a roar of voices, more like a noise than a chorus. Then the strongest voice overpowers the others. Is that what you hear?"

She shook her head. "No." She closed her eyes and let the ever-changing chaos of the Collective cascade inside her mind. "I hear all of them," she explained. "Every voice adding to the others, like a conversation. But I also hear the unifying voice, both on its own and when it speaks through the Queen."

"I hear only the many," Picard said.

"I hear what I choose to hear," Hernandez said. "I can isolate lone voices, if I try hard enough."

Riker swapped excited glances with Dax and asked Hernandez, "Can you communicate with them? Talk to them?"

"No," Hernandez said. "I can eavesdrop on their party, but I'm definitely not invited, if you know what I mean."

Picard paced slowly. "Captain, have you ever encountered the Borg before now?"

"Never even heard of them before today," she said.

"But you can hear the Collective in your thoughts," Picard said, lost in his own musings as he reversed direction and kept pacing. "Even though you've never been assimilated."

Hernandez hadn't encountered the term *assimilated* in the brief and heavily redacted file that Riker had let her read, and she wasn't certain she wanted to find out what it meant.

Captain Dax interrupted Picard's pensive perambulations. "It's probably related to the catoms the Caeliar put into her body. Somehow those nanomachines let her tap in to the Borg

Collective's frequency, and—no offense, sir—with greater precision than you can." The sharp-eyed young woman focused on Hernandez. "You mentioned that you can tell one voice from another in the Collective. You also mentioned the Queen. Does that mean you can tell if the Queen's leading the attack on the Federation right now?"

"Yes," Hernandez said. "The armada's under her direct control." Closing her eyes again, she attuned herself to the thought-waves of the Borg monarch. "She's young, newly installed," Hernandez continued, even as she struggled to glean more details. "Full of fury. She . . . she even thinks of herself as being expendable—as long as Earth is destroyed."

Desperate, Picard asked, "Why? What's driving them?"

"I can't tell," Hernandez said. "It's all too muddled."

Riker and Dax pressed in closer, and Dax asked, "Can you tell us where the Borg Queen's ship is?"

Clearing her mind of all other questions, Hernandez sought that detail and found it. "I know where she is," she said. Then she opened her eyes and let her tears fall. "She's leading a phalanx of several dozen Borg vessels."

Riker's voice was taut with urgency. "But where *are* they?"

Hernandez palmed tears from her face. "Destroying Deneva."

# 13

The Queen had emerged from her chrysalis with two mandates coded into her being: Destroy Earth, and crush the Federation.

*For too long, we have obsessed over Earth,* she had directed her trillions of drones, attuning the Collective's will to her own. *It has lured us, tempted us, thwarted us. No longer.*

She had projected her murderous fury to the drones and adapted them to the lightning pace that she and the Collective now demanded of them. *We offered them union. Perfection. They responded with feeble attempts at genocide. Earth and its Federation are not worthy of assimilation. They would add only imperfection. Since they offer nothing and obstruct our quest for perfection, they will be exterminated.*

It was all coldly logical and mechanically precise, but none of that mattered to the drones. They would follow the will of the

Collective and execute the Queen's dictates without question or hesitation. No justification had to be given to drones. The Queen, however . . . she made different demands.

She was a conduit, a voice for something that no longer had one. Its will existed outside her, and it *was* her, all at once. It was the Collective—not a chorus of voices but one voice speaking through those bound into its service.

The drones, the cubes, the Unimatrix, and even the Queen all were nothing more than the trappings of the Collective's true nature. *It* was the authentic essence of the Borg, and *It* told the Queen that the time had come for worlds to burn.

From her attack force, she dispatched six cubes toward the next inhabited planet that lay along their course to Earth.

*Leave nothing alive,* she commanded her drones.

And she knew that they would obey, without question.

Captain Alex Terapane bolted from his command chair to point at his preferred target on the main screen. "All ships, fire on the flanking cube! Clear a path for the escaping transports!"

The bridge crew of the *U.S.S. Musashi* scrambled to carry out his order as the ship bucked and shuddered under a fierce barrage by the Borg. His first and second officers had both been killed in the opening minutes of the battle, and there was no turning back now. With five other Starfleet vessels—the starships *Forrestal, Ajax, Tirpitz, Potemkin,* and *Baliste*—the *Musashi* was struggling to fend off an equal number of Borg cubes. The enemy vessels had approached at such high speeds that there had been almost no time to brace for the attack.

The *Musashi* slipped through a gap in the Borg's firing solution as the security chief, Lieutenant Commander Ideene, called out, "Torpedoes away!"

Terapane tensed to sound a victory cry. Then he watched the three transphasic torpedoes slam into the Borg cube's shields, which flared and then retracted but didn't fall. He snapped, "Hit them again!"

A thundering impact snuffed the lights and pitched the deck violently. Terapane fell and landed hard on his left hip. White jolts of pain shot through his torso. He forced his eyes to relax from their agonized squint just in time to see the *U.S.S. Tirpitz* vaporized on the main viewer. Seconds later, the *Ajax* suffered the same fate and vanished in a flash of golden fire. Then came the *Baliste*'s blaze of glory, as it followed the others into oblivion.

"Strigl," Terapane shouted to his ops officer. "Tell *Forrestal* and *Potemkin* to regroup—protect the transports!"

"Comms are jammed," Strigl replied. "All frequencies."

Pulling his brawny form back into his chair, Terapane snarled at his security chief, "Ideene! Report!"

"Targeting scanners are gone, I have to aim manually," said the square-jawed Orion woman. "Firing!"

Another volley of transphasic torpedoes soared from the *Musashi,* slammed through the nearest Borg cube, and pulverized it in a bluish-white fireball. As the burning cloud dissipated, Terapane saw another cube struck by a double volley from the *Potemkin* and the *Forrestal.* The black hexahedron erupted and disintegrated. Spontaneous whoops of celebration filled the *Musashi*'s dim, smoky bridge.

Then a scissoring crisscross of green energy blasts from the four remaining Borg cubes slashed through the *Potemkin* and the *Forrestal* and transformed both ships into chaotic tumbles of fiery wreckage. Dozens more beams lanced through the hundreds of fleeing civilian transports, reducing them to glowing debris.

With Starfleet's defense forces shattered, the four remaining Borg cubes accelerated away from the *Musashi,* into orbit of Deneva, millions of kilometers away.

*We're all that's left,* Terapane realized. His ship was Deneva's last defender, and it was outnumbered and outgunned. "Arm all transphasic warheads," he said to Ideene.

"But I don't have a target," Ideene protested.

Terapane shot back, "Arm every warhead we have, right now, wherever they are—in the tubes, in the munitions bay, I don't care. Do it now." He took a deep breath. "Helm, put us smack in the middle of those cubes, best possible speed, on my mark." Throwing a look back at Ideene, he snapped, "Well?"

"Warheads armed," she replied.

On the main viewer, the four cubes were demolishing Deneva's orbital defense platforms, which had been heavily upgraded after the Dominion War. *Not upgraded enough,* Terapane brooded, as he watched the Borg turn them to scrap. Then the cubes spread apart in high orbit and turned their formidable weaponry against the planet's surface.

"Captain," Ideene said, "because of the Borg's deployment pattern, at best we might be able to take out two of them." She started to say something, but she stopped and averted her eyes toward her console. She swallowed. "Even in a best-case scenario, we can't save Deneva, sir."

"No, we can't," Terapane acknowledged. "But I won't just hand the Borg their victory. I plan on making them pay for it." He used the controls on his chair's armrest to open a shipwide comm channel. "All decks, this is the captain. All noncombat personnel, abandon ship. Medical teams, evacuate sickbay, and split up to provide support for as many manned escape pods as possible. All pods will be ejected in two minutes." He closed the comm channel. "Mister Strigl, prep the log buoy."

Terapane sat and passed the final two minutes of his life in quiet reflection while his crew readied the *Musashi* to make its futile sacrifice. He thought of his wife and sons on Rigel IV, of the countless lives being extinguished on Deneva, of the grim fate that seemed to lie in store for all of the Federation. Watching the Borg cubes bombard the world that he had been tasked to defend, he seethed. *Every second you wait, more die,* his conscience scolded. His reason countered, *They're all going to die today, anyway. Two minutes won't make any difference.*

The hull resounded with the metallic thumps of magnetic clamps opening. Lieutenant Strigl swiveled his chair around from the ops console to report, "All escape pods away, Captain."

"Release the log buoy, Mark," Terapane said.

Strigl keyed in the command. "Buoy's away," he said.

Terapane stared at the carnage on the viewscreen and saw no point in lying to himself. He wasn't about to work a miracle or save the day; nothing would be gained by what he did next. But his ship had been named for the famous samurai Miyamoto Musashi, and it seemed only right and proper, in the aftermath of such a colossal failure, to fall on his sword.

If his figurative seppuku also happened to claim the lives of a few more of his foes, so much the better.

"Helm, is the course plotted?" he asked.

"Aye, Captain," replied the young Vulcan pilot.

He looked at Ideene. "Tactical?"

"Armed and ready, sir. Just say go."

The atmosphere of preternatural calm on his bridge filled Terapane with pride in his crew. "It's been an honor, friends," Terapane said. "Helm . . . engage."

In a flash of warp-distorted light, the pinpoint of Deneva became the shallow curve of its northern pole, which sprawled beneath two Borg cubes unleashing a cataclysm of emerald fire. The *Musashi* had dropped to impulse directly between them.

In one word, Captain Alex Terapane fell on his sword.

"Go."

Ione Kitain's whole world was on fire.

Great peals of thunder overpowered the screaming that seemed to fill every corner of Lacon City. The street outside her residential tower heaved like a chest expanding with breath, and then it cracked and collapsed into itself, swallowing dozens of people who had been fleeing without direction.

Millions of people all around her, throughout Deneva's lush Summer Islands, were panicking, descending into a communal terror that assailed her keen Betazoid senses like a tsunami.

Every animal impulse in her brain told her to run, to seek shelter, but she knew there was no point. There were no hiding places to be found. So she huddled in the arched entryway of her apartment complex and focused her psionic senses through the maelstrom of fear to find her husband's mind amid the mayhem.

Sickly green pulses of energy fell from the heavens. Titanic mushroom clouds billowed skyward at multiple points around the horizon, turning the dusk to darkness. Every detonation rocked the city with the force of an earthquake.

From high overhead, Ione heard the mournful whine of a failing engine. She looked up in time to see a damaged personnel transport spiral out of control and slam into a commercial tower, several blocks from her home. Its impact shattered the entire façade of the building, and the transport exploded in a flash, followed by gouts of flame. With the tower's center all but obliterated, its upper portion swayed like a wounded giant before it plunged at an angle, crushed the lower half, and toppled into the streets. A toxic cloud of pulverized debris, atomized bodies, and glass and metal shards spread through the artificial canyons of the urban center.

Lacon City reeked of smoke, death, and sewage.

The buzz of emergency-service aircars and other antigrav vehicles ceased all at once. At first, Ione thought they had gone—and then she heard the dull thuds and crunches of hundreds of vehicles falling to Earth and caroming off buildings and the elevated pedestrian walkways above the streets. Her best guess was that an energy-dampening field had blanketed the city.

*That means our shield's completely gone,* Ione realized. *It won't be long now.* Fear began to cloud her thoughts and dull her telepathic senses. Then her husband's thoughts touched her own.

*I am near, wife. I am at the fountain.*

She bolted from the archway and sprinted through streets littered with broken, burning vehicles and mounds of smoldering debris. *I'm coming, my love,* she projected to her *Imzadi.*

Another blast, closer than all the others. A deathly silence washed over the street. Ione flattened herself against a pile of shattered asphalt and covered her head with her arms as the shockwave hit. It ripped through the upper sections of the buildings on either side of her. A delicate music of destruction lingered behind it and deluged the boulevard with a storm of broken glass. Most of it was sandlike, tiny abrasive granules, but a few substantial chunks gouged her back and thighs.

She tried to be stoic, to contain the sharp agony of her wounds rather than accost her husband's own telepathic mind with them, but her control was compromised by anguish and fear. Minuscule fragments of glass bit into her palms as she forced herself up from the ground. Then a pair of strong brown hands gripped her forearms and lifted her to her feet.

He'd found her.

"Elieth," she said, smiling sadly at her husband.

He responded with typical Vulcan stoicism. "We must move," he said, pulling her into motion beside him. He ushered her out of the street and toward the space beneath the overhang of an elevated promenade. His peace officer's uniform was ripped and stained with dust and blood. One of his ears was mauled and bloodied. She reached toward it in sympathy. "You're hurt."

"Quickly," he said, applying gentle pressure with one arm on her back, until they were sheltered under the promenade. A moment later, she understood the reason for his urgency.

Bodies began falling into the street.

The sounds were more horrible than anything Ione had ever imagined. Her stomach heaved in disgust with every wet, muffled impact, every dull slap of flesh meeting stone. Just meters from where she stood, the street became an abattoir.

When the grotesque percussion ceased, Ione realized she was weeping into Elieth's shoulder. At any other time, he would have radiated intense disapproval for such an overt exhibition of emotion. Instead, he imparted comforting thoughts.

*Don't be afraid. The worst is over.*

Staring out at the apocalyptic cityscape, Ione replied, *I sincerely doubt that, my love.*

Despite all the times that Elieth had argued to her that regret was a worthless emotion, Ione wished that they had been on the last transport out of Lacon City.

When the order had come from Deneva's president to evacuate the planet, however, she and Elieth had stayed behind to lend their expertise to the Civil Defense Corps. She had applied her skills as a particle physicist to improve the city's defensive shields, to buy more time for the transports to be loaded and launched. Elieth's job had been to maintain order at the launch site and make certain that the most vulnerable citizens had been given priority, especially families with young children.

The plan had been to meet back at home after the last transport was away. Looking back, she saw their apartment tower being consumed from within by a raging blaze.

"We could have left," she said, knowing it wasn't true.

"There was insufficient room on the transports," Elieth said, calm in the face of calamity. "We also did not fit the criteria for prioritized rescue."

Spite and selfishness surged inside her. "I'm a daughter of the Fourth House of Betazed, and you have a badge. We *could* have left." As soon as she'd said it, she felt ashamed.

Elieth let her remarks pass.

A deep rumbling resonated in every solid surface, and the city was bathed in a terrifying monochromatic green radiance.

Ione trembled, and her heart pounded furiously. Adrenaline

coursed through her, but she had no use for it. Embracing her *Imzadi,* she opened her mind to his. *What will you miss most?*

*I will not be aware of any loss after I have ceased to exist,* Elieth responded. *So I will miss nothing.*

Unswayed by his resolute devotion to logic, Ione shared, *I'll miss music. And you.*

It was only a blink, a micro-expression that vanished almost as soon as it manifested, but Ione saw the crack in Elieth's façade. Beneath his carefully trained discipline, he was grieving just as deeply as she was—and perhaps far more. He made a silent confession: *If it were possible for one with no awareness to miss something . . . I would miss you most of all.*

He tightened his embrace, and Ione shed grateful tears for that one last moment of proof that Elieth, youngest son of Tuvok and T'Pel, truly loved her.

Her tears cut trails across her grime-covered face. Then the viridian glow from above brightened, and she cringed. "I didn't think it would end like this."

*Nor did I.*

A pulse of light and heat penetrated every atom of the city, and then there were no more tears.

The sun was sinking below the horizon and painting all of Paris with a single shade of salmon-pink light, when President Nan Bacco heard her office door open behind her.

She turned to face her lone visitor, Esperanza Piñiero. Tears ran in streaks from Piñiero's dark brown eyes. The chief of staff crossed the room to the president's desk. Agent Wexler remained outside and closed the door behind her. By the time Piñiero reached the desk, she looked too distraught to speak. She bowed her head and struggled to control her breathing.

Bacco anticipated Piñiero's news with deep anxiety. She didn't want to know the truth; she didn't want to make the disaster real by allowing its tragedies to be spoken. But what she wanted didn't really matter anymore.

"Esperanza," she said. "Tell me. In simple words."

Piñiero palmed her eyes dry and forced herself into a ragged facsimile of composure. "We've lost Deneva," she said.

A churning tide of sickness and a destabilizing feeling of

emptiness struck Bacco at the same time. Overwhelmed, she sank into her chair, faltering like an invalid. There had been no surprise in Piñiero's report, but it was still devastating to confront it as a hard truth. Billions more dead. *Billions.*

"What's coming next?" Bacco said.

"Regulus is under siege now, and an attack on Qo'noS is imminent," Piñiero said. "Martok's fleet is gone. All he has left is a rear guard at the Klingon homeworld."

Even if it would amount to merely going through the motions, Bacco was determined to serve a purpose until the bitter end. "Do we have any forces close enough to help them?"

"Admiral Jellico redeployed the *Tempest* and its battle group from Ajilon to Qo'noS six hours ago. Admiral Akaar can't guarantee they'll get there in time to make a difference."

Bacco felt like a chess player who knew she had already been checkmated but was obliged to continue until the endgame. "Which worlds are getting hit next?"

"Elas and Troyius are both facing attacks in two hours," Piñiero said. "So are Ajilon, Archanis, Castor, and Risa."

*I feel like I'm drowning.* Bacco closed her eyes for a moment. "What about the core systems?"

"Borg attack groups are on course for Vulcan, Andor, Coridan, and Beta Rigel. ETA five hours."

*It would be negligent of me not to ask,* Bacco reminded herself. "And Earth?"

"Eight hours, Madam President." Despair loomed over Piñiero like a black halo. "Ma'am, this might be a good time to consider moving your office into the secure bunker at Starfleet Command."

Bacco sighed. "I think it's a bit late for *that.*" She reached forward and activated the comm to signal her assistant. "Sivak, round up the cabinet members and the senior staff, and have them meet me in the Roth Dining Room in one hour."

*"Certainly, Madam President. Should your guests inquire, shall I tell them that formal dress is demanded or optional?"*

"They can show up naked, for all I care. And tell the chefs I want to see the best of everything they've got. If they've been waiting for a chance to impress me, this is it."

*"Yes, Madam President. I'm sure the kitchen staff will find your enthusiasm for their work deeply inspiring."*

"And have them set a place for you as well, Sivak."

She savored the moment of stunned silence that followed. It was rare that Sivak spoke without sarcasm or a subtle jab of wit, so hearing him reply with courtesy was a rare delight. *"Thank you, Madam President,"* he said. *"The dining room will be ready to receive you and your guests in one hour."*

"Thanks, Sivak," Bacco said, and she closed the channel.

Piñiero planted one hand on her hip and gesticulated with the other. "Ma'am, what was *that* about?"

"Dinner," Bacco said. "If you have a special request, I suggest you send it to the kitchen sooner rather than later."

The chief of staff blinked. She looked as if Bacco had just swatted her in the back of the head with a baseball bat. "Do you really think an impromptu state dinner is what we need right now? We're eight hours away from seeing Earth get turned into a glowing ball of molten glass."

"Exactly," Bacco replied. "It's an old Earth tradition. The condemned get to enjoy a final meal, so they can savor what it means to be alive one last time before they die." She stood and circled around her desk to join Piñiero. "This might be our last supper, Esperanza—so let's dine with style."

A bittersweet smile broke through Piñiero's veil of gloom. "I like the way you think, ma'am."

Bacco shrugged. "It's my job."

# 4527 B.C.E.

## 14

Pembleton and the other human survivors pushed into the middle of their shelter, closer to the pile of fire-heated rocks, and listened with unease and suspicion as Lerxst answered their questions about the Caeliar's bizarre proposal.

"Help me understand," Graylock said, holding out his empty palms. "You want to use us as batteries?"

Lerxst replied, "Engines would be a better analogy. Even that falls short of the mark, however. What we are suggesting is a fusion of our strengths, for our mutual survival."

Thayer narrowed her eyes at Lerxst. "But you did say that you'd be using our bodies as a source of power."

"In the short term, yes," Lerxst said.

Steinhauer, who kept his hands busy threading fibers into the loop of a snowshoe, looked up and said, "Why not use one of those creatures that killed our man Niccolo?"

"It is not merely biochemical reactions that we require," Lerxst said. "The interaction of our catoms is similar in many respects to the synapses of your brains. To sustain ourselves and maintain the integrity of our consciousness, we would need to bond with a sentient being, one with enough neuroelectric activity to power our catoms. Mere animals will not suffice."

Pembleton said, "So we've established why you need us. Why do we need you?"

The Caeliar lifted his arm and made a sweeping gesture at the confines of the shelter. "Your current situation appears to speak for itself," he said. Directing their attention to the ailing Crichlow, he added, "Our catoms could enhance your immune systems and enable you to adapt to this world's aggressive pathogens." He pointed at Thayer's mechanically augmented foot. "They would also speed your recovery from injuries and prolong your ability to survive a famine."

"I presume that's a best-case scenario," Graylock said.

Lerxst bowed slightly to the engineer. "Yes, it is."

Graylock shook his head slowly. "Now let's hear the worst-case scenario."

"The fusion of our catoms and gestalt with your organic bodies does carry significant risks," Lerxst said. "Normally, we would not attempt anything so complex without first conducting extensive research and testing. Given the primitive nature of our surroundings and the urgency of our respective crises, we would have to attempt this bonding without such preparations."

Thayer's anger put an edge on her voice. "Get to the point. What happens if it goes wrong?"

Tense silence followed her question. Lerxst's demeanor was subdued as he replied, "An unsuccessful fusion could result in the death of the intended host, the dispersal of the Caeliar consciousness, or both. It could also inflict brain damage on the host, turning him or her into an automaton under the control of the bonded intelligence; or the bonded entity might prove incompatible with the host and would become corrupted. It is also remotely possible that your bodies' immune systems might reject the catoms as foreign tissue and treat the fusion as a form of infection. Any or all of these outcomes might occur."

"Great," Steinhauer said. "Just great."

Graylock scowled at the grousing private before saying to Lerxst, "Brain damage? Death? It sounds as if the risks of this 'fusion' far outweigh the benefits."

"The alternative is death," Lerxst said.

"For you, maybe," Pembleton replied. "As soon as we have enough snowshoes to go around, we're going south."

"Or north," Graylock said. "Whichever way the equator is."

The Caeliar turned his inscrutable visage toward Pembleton. "How far do you think you'll get? Shall I draw you a map of what lies ahead?" Lerxst hadn't raised his voice, but there was something smug and angry in his manner. "This is an *island,* Gage, more than a hundred kilometers from the nearest major continent. You and your friends can no more flee from your predicament than we can from ours."

Pembleton looked at Graylock. "Your call, sir."

The lieutenant's brow tensed, and a V-shaped wrinkle formed between his thick eyebrows. He pinched the bridge of his nose.

"To hell with rank for a minute," he said. "This is all of our lives on the line. We'll put it to a vote, a show of hands. Who wants to risk becoming a Caeliar meat puppet?"

A look around the room revealed not a single raised hand.

"All right," Pembleton said. "Who votes to look for a way off this island?" He lifted his own arm, and four others reached for the drooping fabric ceiling.

Graylock nodded, and they put their arms down. "The ayes have it," he said to Lerxst. "Escape, five; meat puppets, zero."

"Please reconsider, Karl," Lerxst said. "If we don't join together now, while my people still have the strength to control the process of the fusion, we might never have another chance."

"Sorry," Graylock said. "We've made our decision."

"Then both our peoples will die," Lerxst said.

The Caeliar envoy stood and walked out of the shelter. As he exited through the overlapping flaps of the shelter's portal, a gust of subfreezing air slipped past him and momentarily cut through the pungent miasma of body odor, bad breath, and mildew.

Graylock got up, tied the flaps closed, and returned to the heated rocks with the other survivors. He reached forward, picked up the makeshift cooking pot, and poured himself a bowl of bitter bark soup. He had a worried look on his face as he confided to Pembleton, "If Lerxst is telling the truth about this being an island, we're in big trouble."

"Relax, sir," Pembleton said, pretending to be confident. "We'll be fine. After all, you're an engineer, aren't you?"

Exhausted and perplexed, Graylock replied, "What does that have to do with anything?"

Pembleton shrugged. "So there's an ocean. How hard can it be to make a raft?"

The lieutenant sipped his soup and winced. "Harder than you think, Sergeant. A lot harder."

"Didn't Thor Heyerdahl cross an ocean on a raft?"

"Yes, he did," Graylock said. "But that was the Pacific in high summer, not an arctic sea in deep winter. Also, Heyerdahl built his raft in Peru, where he had access to the right kinds of wood and fabric. At the rate we're going, we'll probably end up drifting out to sea on ice floes, like dying Inuit."

Pointing in the direction of Junk Mountain, Pembleton said, "Do you want me to go get Lerxst and bring him back? Should we just give up now and ask the Caeliar to mulch our brains and put us out of our misery?"

Graylock sighed. "No."

"Then we'd better start thinking of ways to stay warm, dry, and afloat," Pembleton said, "because the only way we'll survive until spring is if we get *off this island*."

"Let the inner edges slide over each other as you step," Steinhauer said, coaching Graylock. "And roll your foot a bit when you lift it. Exaggerate your stride a little."

Graylock did his best to turn the young MACO's directions into actions, but he continued to stumble and teeter as he trudged across the snow-covered plain by the fjord. "*Scheisse*," he said under his breath. "I feel like I'm drunk."

"It takes some getting used to," Steinhauer said. "Of course, if you think going forward is hard, wait until it's time to learn how to turn around."

Glaring in frustration, Graylock muttered, "I can hardly wait." He took another halting step forward, supporting his weight with two walking poles. The snow settled under his feet.

"Right now, it's harder because you're breaking a trail," Steinhauer said. "It'll be easier when you're following." He watched Graylock make a few more clumsy lunges and said, "Sir, stop a second. Watch me." Graylock halted and turned his head to observe the private, who moved in gliding strides. "As you finish each step," Steinhauer said, "pause a bit before you put your full weight on the shoe. It helps smooth the snow and pack it better for the person behind you."

Nodding, Graylock said, "Okay. Noted."

"Give it a try," the MACO said.

The engineer did as Steinhauer had said, easing into each step, keeping his eyes on the terrain ahead so that he could train his muscle memory to feel when his stride was correct. After a few minutes of exhausting pushing against the wet snow, his movements became more graceful, though still tiring.

"Now you're getting it," Steinhauer said. "Hold a second. It's time to learn how to turn."

Graylock was grateful for a chance to stop, even if only for a minute. He was the only one of the survivors with no previous experience at snowshoeing, so he had committed himself to an intensive training regimen. Once he mastered the basics of the skill, the only barrier to the team's departure would be Crichlow's fever.

Steinhauer shuffle-stepped alongside Graylock. "When you have a lot of room to turn around, like we do here, the easiest thing is to walk a wide semicircle," he said. "But in a forest or on a slope or narrow trail, that might not be possible. In those situations, you'll have to do a kick turn, like so." He lifted one of his snowshoes high off the ground while keeping the other firmly planted. Then he set his lifted shoe down at a right angle to the other, and brought the second one up and set it down parallel to the first. In a few kicks, he had done an about-face. "It's hard on the hips," he said. "And it's easier with poles than without. Use them to keep yourself steady."

As Graylock emulated the MACO's athletic leg lifts and turns, he strained a muscle in his groin, stopped, and doubled over. Through gritted teeth, he said, "I hate you."

"Wait till tomorrow, when your whole body starts aching," Steinhauer said. "Then you'll *really* hate me. Breathe a minute, then we'll head back to the slope near the shelter, and I'll teach you how to use kick steps to make climbing easier."

Graylock squatted and watched his breath form white clouds while he waited for his pain and nausea to subside. He had almost recovered his equilibrium when he saw someone in the distance, standing outside the shelter and frantically beckoning him and Steinhauer to return.

Steinhauer made a few comical hop steps sideways and placed himself directly in front of Graylock. "I'll break the trail back, sir," he said. "Are you ready to move?"

"I'm fine," Graylock said, masking his lingering discomfort. "Move out. I'll be right behind you."

The MACO cut a fast path across the open snow, and Graylock did his best to keep his eyes on the man's back and his feet in the smooth rut Steinhauer's snowshoes had carved. Just as the private had said minutes earlier, following a trail was far less taxing than breaking one. Less than two minutes later, he aped the young German's sidesteps up the slope to the camp. Once they were in the cleared area around the fire pit, they unwrapped the snowshoes' crude bindings from their boots and hurried inside the weather-beaten, ice-covered shelter.

As soon as Graylock was inside, he saw Pembleton and Thayer hovering over Crichlow, who was deathly pale and breathing in short, weak gasps. Graylock freed himself from the bulky layers of fabric in which he had wrapped himself for the afternoon of outdoor training. Wiping cold sweat from his beard, he said, "Sergeant. Report."

"He's dying," Pembleton said. "We tried keeping him warm and cooling him off. Nothing works."

Graylock frowned. He'd feared the worst a few days earlier, the morning after Lerxst had left their camp. Crichlow's symptoms had been steadily worsening, and without a doctor or the hand scanners, they'd had no idea what was wrong or how to help him. They'd fallen back on the basics: keep him warm, dry, and hydrated, and let him rest. It hadn't helped.

Crichlow had always been pale, and his face had always had a gaunt and awkward quality. Now, despite the wiry scraggle of beard whiskers on his chin and upper lip, he looked almost skeletal. Lying on his back, partly mummified in his bedroll, he stared up at his comrades with dull eyes that lay deep in their sockets. His lips parted, and a weak tremor shook his jaw as air hissed from his mouth. Everyone leaned closer to hear him as he said in a hoarse whisper, "Kiona . . ."

Thayer reached out and pressed her palm to his face. "I'm here, Eric," she said.

"Sorry, love," Crichlow said.

She shook her head. "For what?"

He was looking in Thayer's direction, but his eyes didn't seem to be focusing on her, or on anything else. "For my part," he rasped. "For what . . . we did to you."

His apology made Thayer wince. She hadn't spoken to any of the MACOs since the failed attempt to commandeer the control center of Mantilis, but she had confided to Graylock her fear and her resentment of them—Pembleton in particular, since he had been the one who'd pulled the trigger and maimed her.

"Not your fault, Eric," she said. "You're the only one who *didn't* point a weapon at me."

"Still . . . sorry."

She leaned down and kissed his forehead. "No worries."

A reedy breath passed from his lips, and then he was perfectly still. For a moment, the only sound was the low cry of the wind and the snapping of loose fabric on the outside of the shelter. Steinhauer and Pembleton both touched forehead, chest, and each shoulder with their right hands. Thayer reached over and nudged Crichlow's eyelids closed.

Pembleton wasted no time on sentiment. "Steinhauer," he said, "sanitize Crichlow's gear, and parcel it out to the rest of the team. When you're done, we'll take him up by the rocks and bury him in the snow."

"That's it?" asked Graylock. "We're just going to toss his naked body in a drift?"

Steinhauer and Thayer both turned away and pretended to be busy with other tasks as Pembleton replied, "What would you prefer, Lieutenant? Should I dump him in the fjord?"

"He deserves a proper burial," Graylock said.

"I agree," Pembleton said, "but the ground is frozen solid, and we're short of food. We need to save our strength for the trip, not waste it digging a hole."

"What about a funeral pyre?" asked Graylock.

"We're low on firewood, too, remember?"

Graylock sighed and nodded. "I know. It just feels heartless to throw him aside like this."

Pembleton replied, "Heartless would be carving him up as food. But since we don't know what killed him, we can't risk it." He pulled the flap of Crichlow's bedroll over the dead man's face. "After we put him outside, we should break down everything but the main shelter and get ready to travel. We need to be on the move by daybreak tomorrow."

"So soon?" asked Graylock.

"We're losing light every day, sir," Pembleton said. "At this rate, we're looking at God only knows how many months of night, starting in just a couple of weeks. If we aren't floating to warmer climes by then . . . we're finished."

A few days later, during their journey south, the survivors passed another interminable night huddled for warmth inside a crude shelter, which they had insulated from the wind by burying it inside a snow drift.

Rows of metal poles and sheets of taut fabric lashed together kept their fresh excavation from imploding on them while they slept. It didn't keep the cold out, though. Drafts of air so frigid that they felt like razors slipped through gaps in the shelter and always seemed to find Kiona Thayer, no matter how deep in the huddle she hid herself.

Tucked in that cluster of bodies, hidden in the dark, she stayed close to Karl Graylock, her fellow officer. She relied on him not just for heat but to act as a barrier between her and the MACOs, whom she still viewed with anger and anxiety.

Though she had never been attracted to Graylock, the tickle of his beard on her shoulder was a comfort as he wrapped himself around her. She dreaded awakening each morning to another day in exile with Pembleton and Steinhauer. At night, she dreamed of the only thing she truly cared about any longer: Earth, home soil, so far away now, farther than she'd ever imagined it would be.

Memories of Earth haunted Thayer's every waking moment, so she tried to spend as much of her time as possible asleep. Growing up in Québec, she had often thought of herself as being acclimated to the cold, perhaps even impervious to it. This world's arctic circle had taught her differently. Now the bitter wind was the enemy, and sleep's gray realm was her only haven from the constant discomfort of numb fingers and toes.

Some of her dreams took her to tropical locales; others put her fireside in her father's home, outside Montréal. She often dreamed of being back aboard the *Columbia* or in training on Earth or reliving her first day on campus at Dartmouth. Sometimes she was young again, and sometimes she was her current age but revisiting a past chapter of her life, like a tourist.

The one detail that was consistent in all her dreams, however, was that her left foot was whole. And that made it all the more terrible to awaken to her scarred, mangled extremity, which now required mechanical reinforcement.

She was running through tall grass in a Vermont apple orchard with her older sister, Winona, when a hated voice shattered the moment. "Up and at 'em," Pembleton barked, his baritone voice filling the tent. "Only five hours of light today! We can't waste a second of it. Everybody up! Let's go!"

Québécois epithets flew to her lips and no further.

Breakfast barely qualified as a meal. Steinhauer lit a small fire to reheat some weak broth they had saved from their last boiled rodent of several days earlier. They also drank as much wretched bark tea as they could swallow, because Graylock had noted that Crichlow, who had made a point of spurning the foul-tasting beverage, had been the one to grow sick and die.

"No more," Steinhauer said after half a cup. "One more drop, and I swear I'll vomit."

"Drink it," the engineer said. "Quinine tastes terrible, too, but it helped people fend off malaria."

"I think you only make us drink this piss to take our minds off the cold," Thayer said between lip-pursing sips.

Graylock smiled at that. "Is it working?"

"No," she said.

Minutes later, all traces of their camp had been cleaned up, stowed away, and hefted onto their backs for the continuing march toward the equator. Steinhauer returned from checking and collecting the traps, which he put out each night in the hope of snaring a few more small rodents to sustain them another day. That morning, unfortunately, he returned empty-handed. He packed away the traps, and Pembleton led the team onward, into a landscape concealed by dense, spinning flurries of falling snow.

The quartet moved in single file, with the three men taking turns as trail breakers, sometimes in shifts as short as five minutes. Thayer slogged along behind them, doing her best to keep up but knowing full well that she was slowing them down.

The survivors hugged the coastline rather than try to scale the rugged slopes and peaks of the barren arctic landscape. As a result, their journey often seemed to entail long periods of little to no forward progress, as they trekked parallel to their course, and occasional periods of backtracking, when the shoreline switched back around one body of water or another.

A few hours out of camp and less than two hours shy of nightfall, they found themselves circumnavigating a frozen, narrow fjord. When it was Graylock's turn to take the lead, he started breaking a trail across the ice sheet.

Pembleton shouted ahead, "Lieutenant! What the hell are you doing? Trying to get us killed?"

"It's less than a kilometer across," Graylock said. "But it's got to be at least nine kilometers long. It'll take hours to go the long way around, but if we take the shortcut, we can reach those trees and still have time to set traps before dark."

Despite the fact that Pembleton was swaddled in layers of fabric that looked like a portable tent, his contemptuous slouch was easy to detect. "That's a saltwater fjord, Lieutenant," he said. "There's no guarantee it's frozen solid all the way across or that the ice is thick enough to hold your weight. If you feel like taking a bath in water that'll shock you dead in less than thirty seconds, be my guest, sir."

Graylock reversed course with a series of kick turns and waved Pembleton ahead on the original trail around the fjord. "Lead on, Sergeant."

"Yes, sir," Pembleton replied, moving down the desolate shoreline, breaking a trail through the snow with smooth but flagging strides. On either side of the fjord, high cliffs of bare, black rock ascended into the violet sky.

From the back of the line, Steinhauer said, "I would give anything to be on Earth right now."

"Right now, it's around 4500 B.C.," Pembleton replied as he fell back behind Thayer and let Graylock take the lead again. "You'd be living in the Neolithic period."

"That'd be fine," said Steinhauer. "Someone in Sumer is inventing beer about now."

"That's right!" Graylock hollered back from the point position. "*Mein Gott,* I could use a beer."

Trying to distract herself from the acidic churning and pathetic growling of her empty stomach, Thayer asked, "What about agriculture and written language? The Sumerians are inventing those about now, too."

Her observation drew a few moments of thoughtful silence from the three men.

Then Steinhauer replied, "I'd rather have the beer."

"And some barbecue," Pembleton said.

Graylock added, "With a side of beer."

"Well," Thayer said, rolling her eyes, "I'm happy to see we at least have our priorities straight."

Lerxst had sacrificed the corporeal bonds of his body to preserve the integrity of his memory and awareness—and now those, too, were starting to slip forever from his grasp.

*I'm losing myself,* he shared with the gestalt.

Their communion had been winnowed to four voices. Of these, Lerxst was the strongest, with only Sedín as his close equal. Ghyllac and Denblas clung to vestiges of coherence, but their thoughts had become increasingly disjointed as they faded.

All four knew that they were dim shadows of their former selves, but the quality of their past lives now eluded them. They wandered together through lightless catacombs of twisted metal and shattered stone, always near one another, like bodies united in deep space by a weak but undeniable gravity.

*This place had a name,* Denblas thought, disguising his plea for information in the form of a declaration.

His query lingered in the gestalt, but none of the four minds submerged into the bond could produce the answer. Denblas repeated himself. *This place had a name.*

*So did we, once,* replied Ghyllac. *It's lost now, like us.*

All of them felt the depths of history yawning below them, but not one of them could recall the events that had delivered them to this gray purgatory. They were simultaneously one in the gestalt and four in the world but only to the extent that they still sensed themselves as separate beings. Lerxst tried to mask his shame as he realized that although he remembered his name, the specifics of what he had considered his identity had become fragmented and opaque in his memory.

He wondered with naked confusion, *Who are we?*

Sedín answered his question with a question: *What are we?*

*We are those who are and that which is,* Denblas added.

It was an evasion. The four knew that they were the same, but none could name their species. They defined themselves now in the hollow context of knowing what they weren't.

A swift current of images and sounds surged through the gestalt. Lerxst couldn't tell if they were real memories or delusions, snippets of history or the products of a deranged imagination. They all were rooted in the physical and tangible, the empire of crude matter and the illusion of solidity, and they ran like a river flowing into a canyon, like vast jets of energy sinking into the insatiable maw of a singularity.

Light and sounds, artifacts of the tangible, passed from the grasp of the gestalt and vanished into the darkness.

Then came a terrible moment of clarity, as one cluster of catoms and then another released their energy reserves to bolster the gestalt. *Our core catom groups are breaking down,* Lerxst realized. *Our memories are collapsing into entropy.*

*We're really dying,* Sedín replied.

Deep, flat notes of dismay droned in the gestalt, and Lerxst extended himself to call for harmony's return. Then he sensed the diminished scale of the gestalt, and he understood the cost at which his clarity had been purchased.

Denblas was gone.

Lerxst and Sedín both seemed to have been fortified by their consolidation with their lost colleague, but Ghyllac appeared to have reaped no benefit from Denblas's demise.

Worse still, Ghyllac was no longer Ghyllac.

Where the essence of Ghyllac once had blazed, there was now a dark spiral of confusion, a mind trapped in the endless discovery of the present moment, with no sense of its past and no anticipation of its future. The echo of Ghyllac would spend the rest of its existence imprisoned in a limbo of the now.

*Without thought, without memory, his catoms serve no true purpose,* Sedín lamented. *They are expending energy without gain.*

The implications of her statement troubled Lerxst. *Is it our right to decide when his existence no longer has meaning?*

*He doesn't even have existence,* Sedín argued. *Without the mind, his catoms are an empty machine. A waste of resources. If you won't take your share of their reserves, I'll take them all.*

Lerxst understood the deeper threat implicit in her words. If she absorbed all of the residual energy from Ghyllac's catoms, it would reinforce hers to a level of stability much greater than his own. Inevitably, he would find his catoms depleted far ahead of hers, and the only logical choice would be for her to consolidate his remaining energy into herself. He could either hasten Ghyllac's premature demise or else guarantee his own.

*Very well. We'll consolidate his energy reserves into our catoms.* There was no masking the deep regret he felt at his decision. They weren't killing Ghyllac, whose essence had already been lost, but taking the last of his catoms' power made Lerxst feel as if he had crossed a moral line.

*Were we ever friends, Sedín?*

*I don't remember. Why do you ask?*

Lerxst hesitated to continue his inquiry. *When you and I begin to fade . . . will you consolidate me as you did Ghyllac?*

*As* we *did Ghyllac.*

*I will concede your semantic point if you'll answer my question. Are we mere fodder to each other? Will we meet our end united or as mutual predators?*

*We'll improvise,* Sedín said. *It's how we survive.*

*But what of the moral considerations?*

*They need to be secondary,* Sedín replied. *All that matters is that we survive until the humans return. Then we shall bond with them, for their own good. Their synaptic pathways can be easily mapped and made compatible with our needs. As soon as it becomes practical, we will facilitate their journey toward this planet's populated middle latitudes.*

*You underestimate the humans' natural antipathy for enslavement,* Lerxst warned.

*And you overestimate the strength of their free will.*

He suspected that only bitter experience would disabuse Sedín of her illusion of omnipotence. *Heed me,* he told her. *If you try to yoke them, they will fight back.*

*Let them,* Sedín replied. *They will lose.*


It had been hours since Karl Graylock had been able to feel his toes. For a long time, they had been painfully cold, and then for a while, he had been aware of their being numb. Now they felt like nothing at all. The harder he tried not to think about frostbite, the more he dwelled on it.

Pembleton fell back from the trail-breaker position and slipped into the line behind Graylock, who now had Steinhauer's back to focus on. One shuffling, ankle-rolling step followed another. Graylock's stride was well practiced after only five short days of snowshoeing along the island's coast. He no longer needed to look at his feet while he was slogging forward against the ice pick wind and through hypnotic veils of falling snowflakes.

He had started the journey with an appreciation for the austere beauty of the empty arctic landscape, but he had since come to think of it as the proscenium to his traveling misery show. To one side lay low hills blanketed in snow, stretching away in gentle white knolls toward the distant mountains. On the other side was a sheer drop down fearsome cliffs of black rock, to a relentless assault of surf against the sawtoothed, obsidian boulders that jabbed up from a sea as black as the night sky.

Steinhauer led the foursome up a gradual rise. He kicked with the sides of his snowshoes and made a diagonal stair in the snow. After a few minutes, he began to fall backward. Graylock caught him and heard the labored gasps of the younger man's breathing. "It's all right, Thom," he told the private. "It's my turn to break. Fall back a while." Graylock handed the man into Pembleton's grasp and then stepped forward.

Each sideways chop at the hillside buried Graylock's feet in snow, which he carefully stamped down to make solid steps for the others. It was harder than regular snowshoeing, and for much of their journey they had avoided it when possible, opting for the most level paths they could find. As they'd neared the far southern end of the island, however, they had been forced to climb several shallow inclines to avoid plunging over sheer cliffs and to detour around impassable formations of rock that cut across the beaches and extended out into the turbulent sea.

Each step brought Graylock closer to the top of the hill and revealed more of the vast seascape that lay beyond. The ocean at night was pitch dark. The jagged cliffs on his right became more gradual, and ahead of him they descended in a steep but no longer vertical drop to the water.

Then he stepped over the crest and beheld the easy slope down to the rocky beach. The snow thinned and then ended roughly sixty meters before reaching the water, revealing miles of black sand. Majestic rock formations knifed up from the sea less than a hundred meters from shore. Great swells of black water curled around the rocks like ripples in a gown.

The vista possessed a stark beauty—but it was a wasteland.

And, as Graylock had feared, there wasn't a tree in sight.

He felt light-headed. Was it from not having eaten for three days? Or was it the result of six days of forced march over snow and ice, through an unforgiving wilderness? He reasoned it was probably both, colliding inside his frostbitten body and overwhelming his already sapped will.

The rest of the team huddled close beside him. They all stared at the wind-blasted shoreline. Coal-black sand and stones were lapped by inky waves, which broke into gray rolls of foam. Then a fierce wind blasted stinging particles of sand and ice into their faces, and the survivors shuffled clumsily about-face to protect themselves from the scouring gales.

Graylock said, "We have to go back."

"We're not going back," Pembleton said. "We have to go forward, across the water, or we'll die."

With a sweep of his arm toward the beach, Graylock snapped, "What am I supposed to build a raft from, Gage? Rocks? At least when we were on the mountainside, there were trees."

Thayer snapped, "Then why didn't we build the raft there?"

"Because the goddamned fjords are frozen!" Graylock stopped himself. He took a breath and said to Pembleton, "Even if we make it back to Junk Mountain, we're stuck until spring."

Pembleton's voice started out soft and grew louder as he repeated, "No . . . no . . . No . . . NO!" Overcome by frustration, he spun away from the group, then pivoted back. "Don't you get it?" He made wild gestures with his outstretched hands. "We have to go forward! It's our only chance. We *won't make it* to spring—not here and not on the mountain."

"Not without help," Graylock said.

"Tell me you're not saying what I think you're saying," Pembleton said. "Are you suggesting we bond with the Caeliar?"

Graylock hunched his shoulders and lifted his hands in a plaintive gesture. "What choice do we have, Gage? You said it yourself, we won't make it to spring. And I'm telling you, we can't sail until the ice thaws. Remember what Lerxst said. The catoms would help us survive famine and fight off disease."

"Only if we're lucky," Thayer cut in. "If we're not, we'll either end up dead or brain-fried. Is *that* what you want, Karl?"

"Dammit, be logical about this," Graylock said. "If we don't bond with the Caeliar, we'll die for certain. If we do, we might die anyway, just differently. But there's also a chance we could live. We'd be changed, but at least we'd be *alive*. Don't you think that it's at least worth taking the risk?"

Pembleton and Thayer exchanged dubious glances, and then each gave Graylock a grudging nod of agreement. The engineer looked around for Steinhauer, to confirm his assent to the plan.

The first things Graylock saw were Steinhauer's abandoned snowshoes. His eyes followed the deep, ragged bootprints that led away from them down the slope. One discarded layer of Caeliar fabric after another lay beside Steinhauer's trail. Then he saw Steinhauer, who was halfway to the water's edge, peeling off his protective layers of clothing as he went.

"*Scheisse*," Graylock muttered. "Steinhauer's losing it." He stumbled over his own feet in his haste to turn around, and Pembleton and Thayer did little better. By the time they began breaking their own haphazard trails down the slope, Steinhauer had almost reached the water. He had stripped to his jumpsuit and boots, and he carried his phase rifle in one hand.

"Thom, stop!" called Pembleton as he charged downhill. "Put your gear back on, Private! That's an order!"

Steinhauer ignored them and kept walking toward the sea.

The trio in pursuit kicked free of their snowshoes when the snow became too shallow to hold a trail. Graylock and Pembleton sprinted the rest of the way to catch up to Steinhauer, while Thayer limped awkwardly far behind them.

The two men were still several meters away from catching Steinhauer when the private turned and aimed his rifle at them. "Don't come any closer," he said.

Pembleton and Graylock slowed to a careful walk. "Calm down, Thom," the sergeant said. "We just—"

The phase rifle blast struck the ground at their feet with a deafening shriek. Both men recoiled and halted. Behind them, Kiona slowed her own approach and then stopped at a distance.

Standing ankle-deep in the frothing surf, Steinhauer looked like an emaciated wild animal dressed in human clothing. His face was gaunt, and his eyes, though sunken in their sockets, burned with feral desperation. Spittle had turned to ice in his ragged beard whiskers. Behind massive clouds of exhaled breath, he shivered violently, and his jaw chattered loudly. The tips of most of his fingers were black and blistered with frostbite almost to the first knuckle. Graylock was amazed the man could still hold a rifle in his condition, never mind fire it.

"I won't go back," he said, his voice breaking into a near-hysterical pitch. "I can't. Too far. Too cold." He shook his head from side to side with mounting anxiety. "Can't do it. Won't."

With slow, cautious movements, Graylock extended his open hand to Steinhauer. "Thom, please. Put down the rifle, get dressed, and come with us. We have to go back to the Caeliar. It's the only way."

"Not for me," Steinhauer said.

In a fluid motion, he flipped the barrel of his phase rifle up and back, held its muzzle inside his mouth with his right hand, and pressed down on its trigger with his left thumb.

A flash of light and heat disintegrated most of his head.

The weapon fell from his hands. His decapitated body collapsed and fell backward into the pounding surf.

Graylock and Pembleton stood in silence for a minute and watched the waves wash over Steinhauer's corpse. Then Pembleton waded out to the body, retrieved the phase rifle and a few items from the dead man's jumpsuit, and returned. "We'll collect the fabric he left behind on the way down," he said. "A few more layers might make the trip back a bit less miserable."

As he followed the sergeant back up the beach to their snowshoes, Graylock felt a pang of regret at leaving Steinhauer unburied. He interred his guilty feelings instead. With no food left and temperatures dropping daily, he and the others could no longer afford to be sentimental; death was a simple reality in the hard land of the winter.

Thayer picked up Steinhauer's cast-off snowshoes. "These'll make good firewood," she said. "Where should we make camp?"

"We should get moving," Graylock said. "Right now."

Thayer looked askance at him. "In the dark?"

"Might as well," he said. "Because if my math is right . . . for the next five months, dark is all we're going to have."

# 2381

## 15

Riker and Picard stood behind the desk in *Titan*'s ready room and watched Admiral Alynna Nechayev on the desktop monitor. *"We just broke through the Borg's jamming frequencies,"* she said, her lean and angular features now drawn and pale. *"It's confirmed. Deneva's been wiped out. It's gone."*

*Maybe I did Deanna a favor by leaving her with the Caeliar. At least she's safe from all of this.*

"How much time until the Borg reach Earth?" asked Picard.

Nechayev replied, *"About seven hours. Maybe less. Why? Have something up your sleeve, Captain?"*

"That remains to be seen," Picard said. "But Captain Dax informs us she has an idea in the works."

*"Say no more,"* Nechayev said. *"Unless you need us to play a part, maintain operational security. You've all been given full presidential authority to do whatever it takes. I'm counting on you two and Captain Dax to make the most of it."*

Riker nodded. "Understood." His door signal chimed softly. "If you'll excuse us, Admiral, Captain Dax has arrived."

*"By all means,"* Nechayev said. *"Nechayev out."*

Riker turned off his desktop monitor and said, "Come."

The door sighed open. Dax entered, followed by Hernandez. The two women seemed to project an aura of excitement mixed with apprehension. They stopped in front of Riker's desk. "We have something," Dax said. "As always, it's a long shot."

"Naturally," Picard said. "What is it?"

Hernandez replied with confidence and élan, "Supersedure."

The term meant nothing to Riker. He threw a confused glance at Picard, who looked similarly befuddled, then said to Hernandez, "I'm afraid you'll have to explain that to me."

"I was telling Erika about some of the oddities of Borg social structures," Dax said. "And she immediately drew the comparison to a bees' nest."

Picard reacted with a dubious frown and said to Hernandez, "I trust Captain Dax also explained that you're not the first person to apply that flawed analogy to the Borg."

"Yes, she did," Hernandez said. "But I still think you ought to hear the details of our plan."

"Hell," Riker cut in, "I just want to find out what 'supersedure' means."

Making small gestures as she spoke, Hernandez replied, "It's a technical term for the process by which bees replace old queens with new ones."

"I got the idea when Erika mentioned her ability to hear the individual drones," Dax said. "That suggests that her link with the Borg is precise and deep. If we could give her a way to talk to the Borg, maybe we could use that ability to introduce her to the Collective as a new queen."

Picard walked out from behind the desk to face the two female captains more directly. "I'm hardly an expert on the subject of bees," he said. "But I seem to recall learning in elementary school that most beehives react to the arrival of a strange queen by killing the intruder."

"That's why I won't be presenting myself as a stranger," Hernandez said. "I'll use my catoms to impersonate the Queen's presence inside the Collective."

Riker replied, "Forgive me, but that sounds a bit vague. You said you'd never encountered the Borg before. What makes you so sure you can trick them into thinking you're their queen?"

"Her voice," Hernandez said. "It's unique within the Collective, much like the piping a queen bee uses to direct her hive. My catoms can resonate on an identical frequency and make my thought patterns a dead ringer for the Queen's."

Dax added, "There are two stumbling blocks to linking Erika to the Collective without losing her to it. First, we'll need to physically patch her into a vinculum. Second, she'll need a lot of raw power to help her drown out the Queen's voice."

Hernandez continued, "The *Aventine* has more than enough power to help me pump up the volume, so to speak."

"Once she does, she can take control of the Borg armada, or

part of it, at least. Then she turns the Borg against themselves. It'd be like someone with multiple personality disorder whose personas start attacking each other."

Riker grinned. "Leave it to a joined Trill with psychiatric training to make that comparison."

Dax said, "Go with your strengths—that's what my mom always said."

Picard paced past the two women, stopped, and turned back. "I admire your proposal for its audacity, Captains, but I can't endorse it." He looked Hernandez in the eye. "The technology you carry within your body is too advanced, too potent, to risk letting it be assimilated by the Borg."

The youthful woman blinked with confusion. "Assimilated?"

Captain Picard cast an accusing stare at Dax. "Didn't you tell her what the Borg do when they encounter new species and technologies?"

Dax averted her eyes and replied in a humbled tone, "I may have skipped that part of Borg 101."

Riker could see the strain on Picard's face. Clearly, in the course of trying to formulate an explanation of assimilation for Hernandez, Picard was reliving the various ordeals he had suffered at the Borg's hands. To spare his former commanding officer that effort, Riker spoke up instead.

"With organic beings, it's a physical process," he said. "A Borg drone, queen, or sometimes even one of their ships, injects its victims with nanoprobes. These nanomachines bind with the subjects' RNA and effect a number of biological changes. More important, they suppress the subjects' free will and make them extensions of the Borg Collective, which gains access to its drones' memories and experiences. On a more practical level, the Borg assimilate technologies and concepts by stealing them."

Hernandez nodded and looked somber. "In other words, the Borg take all your best toys and make you a zombie."

"Basically, yes," Dax said.

Picard's countenance was haunted by his memories. "It's far more terrible than anything you can imagine," he said, though not to anyone in particular. "Part of you remains trapped inside yourself. You become a spectator to the hijacking of your mind and body. It's like a nightmare from which there's no awakening. You see everything, and you can't even shut your eyes."

A grim silence descended on the room.

Dax coughed to clear her throat. "Well, we weren't planning on risking Erika, for whatever that's worth."

"Any time you enter a Borg ship, it's a risk," Riker said. "And unless the *Aventine* has another amazing innovation we don't know about, I'm guessing you'll need to board a Borg ship to gain access to a vinculum for Captain Hernandez."

"You're right," Dax said. "I do plan on boarding a Borg ship to use its vinculum. But first, I plan to have my people eliminate every drone on the ship and neutralize its defenses. Erika won't set foot on it till it's been secured."

With his composure recovered, Picard replied, "That's a tall order, Captains. How do you intend to carry it out?"

Nodding toward Hernandez, Dax said, "Erika has a very keen sense for where the Borg are. If we give her natural gifts a boost, she can help us pinpoint a small scout cube or some other smaller Borg vessel traveling alone."

"I'd need energy and equipment to extend my range and enhance my precision," Hernandez said. "If I could make a direct interface with *Titan*'s sensor module, it'd be a big help."

Riker nodded. "All right. I'll have my science officer help you set it up."

Picard sounded doubtful and dismissive. "Even a brief infiltration of a Borg cube is dangerous," he said to Dax. "What, may I ask, is your plan for *capturing* such a vessel?"

Dax's voice took on an aggressive edge. "We'll fight them with the same tactics the Hirogen used on us," she said. "Erika picks a target, and the *Aventine* uses its slipstream drive to catch it. We fire a few low-yield transphasic torpedoes to knock out their shields. Then our strike teams beam in with projectile weapons, chemical explosives, and energy dampeners replicated from the ones we captured. The *Aventine* emits an energy-dampening field to suppress the Borg ship's regenerative capacity and defensive systems. Then my people go deck by deck, section by section, and secure the cube. Once we eliminate all the drones and access the vinculum, we send over Erika to do her thing— and coronate a new queen for the Borg."

The grimace on Picard's face was sterner than any Riker had ever seen. Picard heaved a deep sigh. "I can't fault you for a lack of ambition," he said, "but I remain unconvinced. Your plan is beyond dangerous; it runs the risk of granting the Borg access to a staggering new level of technology. Furthermore, you grossly underestimate their speed and ferocity."

Riker thought he heard an undercurrent of fear in Picard's voice, and he wondered if perhaps the captain's recent brief reassimilation had inflicted deeper wounds than Picard let on.

Picard continued, "Put simply, Captain Dax, your plan is foolhardy."

Undaunted, Dax replied, "It's also our only chance."

From the first moment Hernandez stepped inside *Titan*'s stellar cartography lab, she was overwhelmed by a sense of déjà vu. Standing beside Melora Pazlar at the end of the widow's-walk platform, she watched the galaxy appear from the darkness and take shape in reduced form all around them.

Pazlar freed herself from her metal motor-assist armature and said with a smile, "When you're ready, just give a push to come up and join me." Then she vaulted straight up, off the platform, with the same ease that Hernandez herself had once taken for granted in Axion.

Hernandez hesitated to follow the science officer, unsure of how much freedom of movement she would have in her new clothing. At Captain Riker's request, Hernandez had exchanged her Caeliar-made attire for the current Starfleet duty uniform. The black jumpsuit with gray shoulder padding and a burgundy-colored undershirt had appeared in her quarters' replicator, complete with the rank insignia for a captain.

She took a breath, bent her knees a bit, and sprang with grace into the open space above. It felt strange, she thought, to be back in a uniform after eight centuries of wearing gossamer. She added it to the other aspects of her past—sleep and hunger—that had caught up with her since she'd fled her captivity in Axion. A lifetime of sensations had come back to her in a matter of hours.

Within moments, she was beside Pazlar, who reached out and manipulated elements of the simulation in much the same way that Inyx had plucked stars from the darkness in the Star Chamber, during the century that Hernandez had helped him seek a new homeworld for the Caeliar. *I hope he's all right,* she thought. *The Quorum must've been furious at him for letting me get away.*

"It's easy to configure," Pazlar said. She raised an open palm and extended it. As she drew her hand back, a low-opacity holographic interface appeared. "You can alter any of the simulation parameters with this. Just be careful if you start messing with the gravity." She cocked her head and gestured at the lower part of her body. "I'm a bit fragile, you see."

"Understood," Hernandez said. She reached forward and expected to find herself miming physical interaction with the projected controls. Instead, when she pushed her fingers on the various padds and slider panels, they met with the same resistance she would have expected of a physical console. Muted feedback tones followed each of her inputs. "It's very intuitive," she said.

"I know," Pazlar said. "Xin—I mean, Commander Ra-Havreii—designed the interface himself." The slender blond Elaysian averted her eyes when Hernandez glanced over at her.

"All right," Hernandez said. "I've set up a signal feed on the same frequency as my catoms. How do I activate the sensors?"

Pazlar pointed at a radiant blue panel on the interface. "Press that, and the sensor module switches into high gear. You'll be able to pull up high-resolution scans on anything within a hundred light-years."

"Then the only thing I still need is a simulated quantum field to power my catoms."

Nodding, Pazlar said, "We can't generate even a fraction of the energy that the Caeliar were making at New Erigol, but we'll give you everything we can."

"It'll be enough," Hernandez said. "Axion had to sustain itself, millions of Caeliar, and who knows what else. I just need enough to boost my catoms back to full strength. A fraction ought to do the trick, I'd think."

The science officer tapped her combadge. "Pazlar to Ra-Havreii," she said, and Hernandez noted a subtle shift in the woman's vocal inflection—it became gentler and a bit higher. "We're ready for the simulated quantum field."

*"Perfect timing, Melora,"* Ra-Havreii replied. *"Stand by while I bring it online. . . . Charging the deflector."* The channel closed with a soft double beep a few seconds later.

Hernandez waited to feel the infusion of new strength. Several seconds passed with no change. Pazlar filled the silence by explaining, "It might take a few minutes to bring the main deflector up to full power as a quantum-field generator."

"I know," Hernandez said. "I was the one who wrote the plan for the reconfiguration."

"Right," Pazlar said, embarrassed. After another awkward moment, she added, "I'm sure Commander Ra-Havreii was able to make the changes. You can count on him."

Overcoming her aversion to meddling in others' business, Hernandez said, "Commander, may I make an observation?"

"Of course," Pazlar said.

"I've noticed that you and Commander Ra-Havreii seem to have a very cordial working relationship."

Immediately, Pazlar became tense and defensive. "So?"

"Don't misunderstand," Hernandez said. "I'm not making any assumptions about your relationship with—"

"Xin and I don't *have* a relationship," Pazlar said. "We're just friends."

Unable to suppress a knowing smile, Hernandez replied, "If you say so, Commander."

Pazlar crossed her arms and spent a moment looking flustered. "All right, there was one time when he tried to kiss me, but it didn't happen, and it was all a big misunderstanding—just crossed wires, you know? It didn't mean anything."

"Forget I mentioned it," Hernandez said. "It's none of my business, anyway. Sorry I pried."

Apparently unwilling to drop the subject, Pazlar added, "I made it very clear that I don't feel that way about him."

"No doubt," Hernandez said.

A fresh silence yawned between them. Then came Ra-Havreii's voice, filtered through the overhead comm. *"Engineering to Pazlar. Quantum field stabilizing at full strength . . . now."*

Again, Hernandez opened her senses to the state of the local ambient energy potential. She was rewarded by a flood of strength and focus as her catoms pulsed with renewed vigor. Nodding to Pazlar, she said, "I'm ready."

"Sensors online and ready," Pazlar said. "The system's all yours now, Captain."

Hernandez closed her eyes and felt a rush of raw data from

*Titan*'s sensors being transmitted directly to her catoms, which processed all of it and accelerated her synapses to keep pace. Then she extended the range of her senses and let herself hear the intimidating chorus of the Borg Collective.

Millions of voices—some near, some distant. Clustered in groups as small as three or as large as thousands, a roar of minds yoked to the will of something that included them all and yet remained apart from them, aloof and domineering. She fought to parse their cacophony and subdivide it into manageable blocs. With effort, she began to separate them by sectors, and then by subsectors, and then by individual ships.

"I hear them," she said to Pazlar. "I see them."

Holding the snapshot of the Borg armada in her mind, she began to search it; she combed it for lone vessels, stragglers, outriders, or scouts. Her mind raced from one target to the next, flitted from sector to sector at the speed of thought.

Each time she found a promising lead, she targeted *Titan*'s sensor module on the coordinates that she heard echoing from that link in the Collective. Her first effort found a trio of small Borg vessels—ostensibly a light attack group but still too formidable for the *Aventine* to challenge alone. Several subsequent leads proved to be massive assault cubes en route to major star systems; such targets would be too heavily manned by drones for the *Aventine*'s limited strike forces to overcome.

Then she found it. The ideal target.

Zeroing in with *Titan*'s sensors, she said to Pazlar, "Have a look at this." The simulated galaxy expanded and flew away as the holographic projection enlarged a detailed sensor scan of a small Borg probe, traveling alone. "I'm not reading any major targets along their trajectory," Hernandez said. "They might be a long-range recon vessel."

Pazlar summoned a new command interface and made a quick evaluation of the ship. "Definitely a scout of some kind," she said. "Probably no more than fifty to a hundred drones onboard. What are their coordinates?"

"Bearing zero-one-three, approximately ten-point-five light-years from Devoras." She felt a profound trepidation as she added, "Inside Romulan space."

Pazlar replied, "Good thing they're on our side in this fight."

*That's right,* Hernandez reminded herself, ashamed that she had succumbed so easily to old fears. *Things changed while I was gone. The Romulans aren't the biggest problem anymore.*

Pazlar tapped in more commands. "Target locked in," she said. "Sending its coordinates to the *Aventine*." A moment later, she added, "*Aventine* confirms: target acquired."

"Now all we have to do is go get them," Hernandez said, with a bit more brio than she had intended.

Throwing a cautionary look in her direction, Pazlar said, "I wouldn't be in such a hurry to meet the Borg if I were you. Finding them was easy." She eyed the image of the black ship in front of them and frowned. "What comes next won't be."

The transporter beam released Hernandez as her new surroundings took shape around her. The transition felt smoother than it had in her days aboard the *Columbia*. It helped that the process was faster, but she was certain that the confinement beam had been made less oppressive—a change for which she was grateful.

Freed from its paralyzing hold, she found herself in a transporter room aboard the *Aventine*. Several security personnel from *Titan* had beamed over with her. Lieutenant sh'Aqabaa and Senior Petty Officer Antillea flanked Hernandez, and Lieutenant Shelley Hutchinson stood behind her. The Andorian and the reptilian female, whom Hernandez had been told was of a species known as the Gnalish, stepped off the padds. Hutchinson, a trim woman with short brown hair, walked around Hernandez and followed her colleagues out of the transporter room.

Waiting to greet Hernandez were Captain Dax and a lean man with short black hair whose face was defined by parallel drooping ridges on his cheeks. "Captain Hernandez," Dax said. "Welcome aboard the *Aventine*. This is my second officer and senior science officer, Lieutenant Commander Gruhn Helkara."

"Thank you, Captain," said Hernandez, stepping down from the platform. She offered her hand to Helkara, who shook it. "Pleasure to meet you, Mister Helkara."

"Likewise, Captain," Helkara said with a polite nod.

"Well," Dax said, "I hate to beam and run, but I need to get back to the bridge. Mister Helkara will escort you to main engineering, where you can offer Chief Engineer Leishman the benefit of your technical expertise."

Hernandez nodded. "I understand, Captain. Thank you."

Dax smiled, turned, and left the transporter room. Hernandez reflected on how much Dax reminded her of herself at that age, as a young starship captain, brimming with confidence and as-yet-unrealized potential.

Behind Hernandez, the transporter's energizer coils came alive with a deep hum. She pivoted on her heel and saw five more shapes materialize: two human men, a Vulcan woman, and a male and a female of different species that she didn't recognize. All carried imposing-looking rifles and other combat equipment.

Helkara touched Hernandez's elbow to guide her. "Captain," he said. "We should go. Lieutenant Leishman is waiting for us."

"Of course," Hernandez said. She followed him out of the transporter room into the corridor. Security personnel, attired in padded and reinforced all-black uniforms, moved past her and Helkara in groups. Most of them were armed with the same rifles that she had seen in the hands of the officers who had beamed in after her. A few carried stockier weapons with wide barrels. As she and Helkara turned a corner, they passed a squad of security personnel who were field-stripping their weapons, making modifications to them, and reassembling them.

She and Helkara stepped inside a turbolift. "Main engineering," he said as the doors closed. A high-pitched pulsing hum accompanied their descent.

"Your people look pretty confident with those rifles," she said. "But how're they going to fire them once they're inside a dampening field?"

"TR-116s fire chemical-propellant projectiles ignited by a mechanical firing pin," Helkara said. "Gas-capture recoil drives the reloader at a rate of nine hundred rounds per minute. No power needed except a pull on the trigger."

"In other words, they're primitive firearms."

"I wouldn't call them primitive. More like a modern update of a classic idea. They were designed during the Dominion War for use against the Jem'Hadar, but they didn't make it much past the testing phase until the Tezwa conflict." He caught her quizzical glance and reacted sheepishly. "None of what I'm saying means anything to you, does it?"

Hernandez shook her head. "Not really, no."

"Sorry," he said. "Maybe when this mess is over, we can hook you up with some light reading to bring you up to speed."

"I'd appreciate that," she said.

The turbolift stopped, and the doors opened on the manic activity of the *Aventine*'s main engineering deck. Helkara led Hernandez into the middle of the commotion. Sparks fell from upper levels around the warp core as critical components were welded back into place, and the bulkheads were lit by infrequent flashes of acetylene light. A dozen discussions—some between people in the compartment, some over the comms—overlapped beneath the low-frequency throbbing of the antimatter reactor.

In an alcove opposite the warp core, a group of engineers were gathered around a hip-height table of control consoles. At the far end was a young, brown-haired human woman doling out assignments. "Selidok, tell your team they have ten minutes to finish adjusting the yields on the warheads," she said to an alien who wore a mist-producing apparatus in front of his nostrils. To a diminutive lieutenant who resembled an upright pill bug, she continued, "P7-Red, we need at least twenty more of those energy dampeners replicated and distributed, on the double." Turning toward a looming Vulcan man—Hernandez guessed the ensign was at least 193 centimeters tall—the chief engineer said, "Navok, what's the status of the slipstream drive?"

"All components are operating within expected parameters," Navok said. "However, we continue to have difficulty predicting the phase variances."

Hernandez blurted out, "You can control the pattern of the phase variance by projecting soliton pulses ahead of you, inside the slipstream."

Everyone at the table looked in Hernandez's direction, and Helkara said to the woman at the end of the table, "Lieutenant Leishman, allow me to introduce Captain Erika Hernandez, our new technical adviser."

Leishman's reaction was barely noticeable. "All right," she said to her team. "You have your assignments. Navok, see if you can apply Captain Hernandez's suggestion for a soliton pulse."

"Aye, sir," Navok replied.

"Meeting adjourned," Leishman said. The junior officers split up and left the compartment. The chief engineer circled around the table to greet Hernandez. "Captain. A pleasure."

"Glad to be of service, Lieutenant." Hernandez motioned toward the table of consoles. "Care to show me your biggest technical hurdles?"

"Sure," Leishman said. She turned to the console and called up several sets of schematics on adjacent displays. "We have two small problems to deal with. The first is that we need to shore up our transphasic shielding to keep the Borg from slicing us in half before we hit them with the energy dampener."

Hernandez reached forward to input some commands. She paused before touching the interface. "May I?"

"Be my guest," Leishman said.

After centuries of dissecting and trying to improve on Caeliar technology, Hernandez found it easy to analyze and reconfigure twenty-fourth-century Starfleet software and hardware, which was much simpler by comparison. She rewrote power-distribution algorithms and adaptive shield-harmonic subroutines as if by instinct. By her reckoning, she had, in a matter of seconds, advanced Starfleet defensive technology by at least a decade.

She turned to the wide-eyed chief engineer and asked, "What's your second problem?"

Neither Leishman nor Helkara responded right away. They were both mesmerized by the designs and formulas that Hernandez had crafted in front of them.

After a few seconds, Leishman snorted with amusement. "Something tells me you're gonna have a bright future at Starfleet Research and Development, Captain."

"We'll see," Hernandez said. Then she prompted Leishman, "Your second 'small problem,' Lieutenant?"

"Right," Leishman said, calling up a new array of complex computations on the tabletop's assorted display screens. "We're tracking the Borg ship you located, but it's pretty far away from here." She directed Hernandez's attention to a specific equation. "The problem is one of control. Once we engage the slipstream drive, we'll catch up to the Borg in a matter of minutes. But if we come out of slipstream too soon or too late, we'll be too far away to make a sneak attack. They'll have time to raise their defenses, and we might end up the hunted instead of the hunter. Unfortunately, our sensors and conn weren't made to drop in and out of slipstream with that degree of precision."

Hernandez studied the data on the screens and considered what Leishman had said. "Yes," she replied. "I see the problem."

Leishman said, "Does that mean you can help us?"

"That depends," Hernandez said. "Do you think you can persuade Captain Dax to let me fly her ship into combat?"

The chief engineer threw a questioning look at Helkara, who replied, "I think that can be arranged."

Dax emerged from her ready room feeling charged and impatient. Captain Picard had told her to have a plan before taking her ship into action; with her plan in place, she wanted to be in motion, tearing through a quantum slipstream for a rendezvous with a Borg ship whose minutes now were numbered.

Taking her seat beside her first officer, she asked, "How much longer, Mister Bowers?"

"Ten minutes at the most, Captain," Bowers said. "We're beaming over the last of the reinforcements from *Enterprise* and *Titan* right now."

She leaned closer to him and lifted her chin toward Erika Hernandez, who was seated at the conn. In a whisper, she inquired, "How's our new pilot doing?"

"Fine, so far," came Bowers's hushed reply.

"Good," Dax said. She swiveled her chair toward the tactical station, where Lieutenant Lonnoc Kedair was working with an intense focus on her console. "Tactical, report."

The Takaran security chief snapped her head up and answered with poise and calm, "Transphasic warhead yields adjusted for shield collapse only. Our own shields have been updated to stay a few steps ahead of the Borg's weapons"—she nodded toward Hernandez—"courtesy of our guest."

Dax shot an appreciative look at Hernandez. "Sounds like you've had a busy morning, Captain."

"Haven't we all?" replied Hernandez.

Looking to ops, where Ensign Svetlana Gredenko was filling in for the critically wounded Lieutenant Mirren, Dax asked, "Ops, do we still have a solid lock on the Borg scout vessel?"

"Aye, Captain," Gredenko said.

"Helm," Dax said, "is the slipstream drive online yet?"

"Affirmative, Captain," said Hernandez. "Main deflector is fully charged, and chroniton integrator is online. Ready to engage on your order."

A signal chirruped on Bowers's armrest display. He silenced it with a tap of his index finger and said to Dax, "The last of the strike-team members are aboard, sir." Something on his screen made him do a double-take. "And you have a visitor."

"A what?"

Bowers relayed the message to her command display, at the end of her chair's right armrest. He lowered his voice. "It's Commander Worf from the *Enterprise*, sir. He beamed aboard with the last squad of reinforcements, and he's waiting for you in transporter room one. Says he won't leave till he sees you."

Dax stood from her chair. "Tell him I'll be there in a minute. Until then, hold the attack."

"Understood," Bowers said.

"You have the bridge, Commander," Dax said.

She strode to the turbolift as quickly as she could without looking as if she was in a hurry. The ride to Deck Three took only a matter of seconds, and then she walk-jogged to Transporter Room One. The door slid open ahead of her, and she entered to see Worf standing alone in front of the transporter platform. In one hand he held his *bat'leth,* in the other his *mek'leth.* He regarded her with quiet resolve. "I request permission to join your attack on the Borg, Captain."

Dax looked at the transporter operator, an imposing male Selay whose cobralike cranial hood was marked by a colorful pattern that reminded Dax of hourglasses. "Dismissed," she said.

"Aye, Captain," the Selay replied. He put the transporter console into standby mode and made a quick exit. The door closed with a muffled hiss behind him.

Dax walked slowly toward Worf as she asked, "Does Captain Picard know you're here?"

"Yes," Worf replied. "He granted my request to volunteer for this mission."

"I find that hard to believe," Dax said. "Captain Picard doesn't think we should even *attempt* this mission. So why would he loan me his first officer?"

Bristling at the naked suspicion in her tone, Worf broke eye contact and lifted his chin in a display of defiant pride. "When it comes to fighting the Borg, I am one of the most experienced tacticians in Starfleet. Even if the captain does not approve of your plan, he wants you to have the best possible chance of success."

"Can I let you in on a little secret, Worf?" Dax leaned closer as he looked back. "The way you lifted your chin and looked away just then? That's one of your tells. Every time you do that, I know you're hiding something." The abashed look on Worf's face—and the speed with which he averted his fuming stare—told Dax she had scored a verbal direct hit. "Why don't you try telling me what you're really doing here?"

Worf sighed and set his weapons on the transporter platform behind him. "Captain Picard did ask me to try to change your mind about the attack. He considers it a foolhardy effort."

"And what do you think of it, Worf?" She tried to look into his eyes, but he turned his head to show her his stern profile.

"What I think is not important," he said.

"In other words, you agree with me, but you don't want to dishonor your captain by second-guessing his orders." His silence told her more than anything he might have said in response. "Let me ask you a question," she continued. "If we don't take the offensive in this battle, what are we supposed to do? If Captain Picard objects to my plan, what's his?"

The Klingon's prodigious eyebrows knitted together above the bridge of his nose as he frowned in irritation. "The captain has not yet presented his plan," he said.

Dax reached out and placed her hand on his arm. "Let me save us both a lot of talking, Worf. I'm sure that if you tried, you could give me a dozen good reasons not to go forward with the attack, and I could give you a dozen good reasons why I should. But in the end, it'll all come down to one simple fact: This is my command; I call the shots here. Starfleet protocol demands that I show Captain Picard deference because of his seniority, but if push comes to shove, he doesn't outrank me, Worf. I'm a captain, the same rank as him. This is my ship, and I am taking her, and her crew, into battle. And that's final."

He looked at her with both respect and pride. "That is exactly as it should be," he said. "And I will be proud to serve under your command."

"That's kind of you to say, but you're not coming with us," Dax said. "The *Enterprise* needs you more."

Worf became bellicose. "Do not be foolish, Ezri. You will need every advantage you can get against the Borg."

"I already have an advantage," she said with a broad smile. "I'm a Dax, remember?"

A proud gleaming broke through his wall of gloom. "It is at times like this that I see Jadzia in you," he said. "Are you certain you will not reconsider my petition?"

"Positive," Dax said.

He stood. "Then I wish you success and glory in the battle to come. *Qapla'*, Ezri, daughter of Yanas, House of Martok."

She got up and stood in front of him. "*Qapla'*, Worf, son of Mogh." Then she wrapped her arms around his barrel-thick torso and hugged him with all the strength she could muster. He returned her embrace for several seconds, and then they parted.

He picked up his weapons from the platform, climbed the stairs, and stepped onto a transport pad. Turning back, he said, "Victory against these odds will be almost impossible."

Dax narrowed her eyes. "I wouldn't say impossible."

Worf replied, "I meant for the Borg."

There were a thousand potential distractions on the bridge of the *Enterprise,* but every time Captain Picard looked up from the padd in his hands, his eyes found the blackened cavity of his ready room. Engineers and mechanics carried out scorched bulkhead panels and the charred remains of his chair and a crate's worth of his personal effects, all incinerated.

He fixed his eyes once more on the padd, which felt cold in his palm. Updates from the *Aventine* confirmed that Captain Dax and her crew would be ready to launch their bold—and possibly suicidal—attack on the Borg within a matter of minutes.

*It's an audacious plan,* he admitted to himself. *I only wish it didn't seem so . . . futile.* Perusing its details, he feared all the ways that it could fail. *If the Borg adapt to the transphasic torpedo, the* Aventine *will be an exposed target. Even if the strike teams board the probe, there's no guarantee they'll prevail. And those crude weapons are bound to produce friendly-fire casualties.* He frowned as he scrolled through a summary of the plan's later phases. *Worst of all, it could backfire beyond our worst nightmares. If the Borg assimilate Captain Hernandez, there's no telling what kind of evil we might unleash on the galaxy.*

A female voice with a vaguely British accent interrupted his pessimistic musings. "Excuse me, Captain."

He looked up to see Miranda Kadohata, the ship's second officer, standing in front of him. "Yes, Commander?"

"The final roster of personnel who've transferred to the *Aventine* is ready, sir," she said. "I routed the report to your command screen."

He nodded and started calling up the file. "Thank you." After a few moments, he realized Kadohata was still there, as if she was waiting for something. He looked up at her. "Something else, Commander?"

She raised her eyebrows as she glanced away. The gesture accentuated the normally subtle epicanthic folding around her eyes, emphasizing her mixed European-Asian human ancestry. "Starfleet Command passed along a suggestion from Seven of Nine, but I'm not sure you'd approve of it, sir."

Her apprehensiveness piqued his curiosity. "Go on."

"There is one weapon we haven't considered using on the Borg," she said, "and maybe we should."

"And that would be . . . ?"

"A thalaron projector," Kadohata said. "Like the one Shinzon had aboard the *Scimitar*."

Picard recoiled slightly. "A thalaron weapon," he muttered. "Rebuilding such a device would antagonize every power in the quadrant—an outcome your predecessor died to prevent."

"I'm aware of that, sir," Kadohata said. "However, a cascading biogenic pulse powered by thalaron radiation would, in theory, be able to destroy the Borg's organic components. Without their drones or the organic portions of their ships—"

Picard cut her off with his raised hand. "Point taken, Commander," he said. Then the port turbolift door opened, and he saw Worf step onto the bridge. "We'll continue this another time."

"Aye, sir," Kadohata said, and she turned and walked back to ops. As Kadohata settled in at her post, Worf offered a discreet nod of greeting to Lieutenant Choudhury at tactical, then sat down in his chair beside the captain.

"I talked to Captain Dax," Worf said.

"And . . . ?"

"She declined to approve my transfer," Worf said. "And she is proceeding with the attack."

Picard breathed a disappointed sigh. "Of course she is."

"You do not approve of her plan," Worf said.

"It's not up to me to approve or disapprove, Mister Worf," Picard said. "I simply lack Captain Dax's confidence in her odds of success."

Worf shifted his posture, straightening his back. "I reviewed her attack profile," he said. "It is bold, but I believe it has a reasonable chance of securing the Borg probe."

"Yes, but what then, Number One? Does pitting Captain Hernandez in mortal psychic combat with the Borg Queen strike you as a viable strategy? Or as yet another in a long line of hopeless delaying tactics?"

Undaunted by the captain's pessimism, Worf replied, "I will not know until I see how the fight ends."

"That's what I'm afraid of, Mister Worf." Picard frowned. "Are you certain you tried every argument to dissuade Captain Dax from going forward with this?"

"She did not give me the chance," Worf said. In a more diplomatic tone, he asked, "May I offer some advice, Captain?"

"By all means, Commander."

"A lesson I learned while I was married to Jadzia remains just as true today about Ezri: She is a Dax. Sometimes they do not think—they just *do*."

# 16

Ezri Dax took a breath and settled her thoughts. Within moments, she and her ship would plunge headlong into the chaos of battle. She was determined to take one brief moment of quiet before the storm in order to steel herself for whatever followed.

Months earlier, when Captain Dexar and Commander Tovak had been killed, Dax had stepped up to fill the void at the top of the *Aventine*'s chain of command. That moment had inaugurated her captaincy. The one that was about to unfold—an arguably insane, all-or-nothing assault on which depended the survival of everything she had ever known—would *define* her captaincy.

On the main viewer, stars stretched past, pulled taut by the photonic distortions of high-warp travel.

She wiped the sweat from her cold palms across her pant legs and set her face in a mask of resolve. It was time.

"Helm," Dax said, "engage slipstream drive on my mark."

Erika Hernandez keyed the commands into the conn and answered, "Ready, Captain."

Dax looked at Bowers. "Sam, tell the transporter rooms and

strike teams to stand ready. Tactical, raise shields and arm torpedoes." She lifted her voice. "Three. Two. One. *Mark.*"

Hernandez patched in the slipstream drive.

It was like being shot through a cannon of blue and white light or a faster-than-light patch of whitewater rapids. A peculiar, quasi-musical resonance filled the ship, like the long-sustained peal of a great iron bell but without the note that started it ringing. Dax detected no real difference in the sensations vibrating the deck under her feet, but adrenaline and anxiety were enough to crush her back against her chair.

Then the rush of light became the black tableau of space, and at point-blank range in front of the *Aventine* was the Borg reconnaissance probe. As promised, Hernandez had guided them out of their slipstream jaunt with surgical precision, into a perfect ambush position against the Borg.

Dax sprang to her feet. "Fire!"

"Torpedoes away," replied tactical officer Kandel.

Three electric-blue streaks arced toward the Borg ship and flared against its shields, and a fourth sailed through with no resistance and hammered the long, dark vessel amidships.

Kandel reported, "Direct hits! Their warp field's collapsing!"

"Stay with them, helm," Dax said, before she realized that Hernandez was already compensating for the changes in the Borg ship's velocity. *Not bad for a person who learned to fly starships in a different century,* Dax mused.

Hernandez matched the Borg's course and speed almost perfectly, then said, "We're at impulse, Captain."

"Strike teams, go," Dax said.

Gredenko relayed the order from ops to the *Aventine*'s twenty transporter sites, which included four upgraded cargo transporters and six emergency-evacuation transporters. More than two hundred Starfleet security personnel were, at that moment, being beamed inside the Borg probe. If the estimate of the ship's drone complement was accurate, her people could expect to outnumber the enemy by a ratio of four to one.

Dax hoped that it would be enough, because once they were deployed, there would be no reinforcements—and no turning back.

"Transports complete," Gredenko said.

"Helkara, activate the dampener field," Dax said.

The Zakdorn science officer keyed in the command and replied, "Field is up and stable, Captain."

She nodded. "Good work, everyone."

Bowers watched Dax as she returned to her seat. Once she had settled, he said, "Now comes the hard part: the waiting."

The single drawback to Dax's plan lay in the dampening field that the *Aventine* was projecting toward the probe. By using the Hirogen's tactics, her crew had neutralized the Borg ship's weapons, shields, communications, and ability to repair itself. However, the field also prevented contact with the strike teams inside the vessel, and it made it impossible to beam them out or to send reinforcements. Unless and until the strike teams gained control of the ship and established visual contact with the *Aventine,* there would be nothing for Dax to do but sit and wait—and keep a volley of transphasic torpedoes armed and ready to fire, in case her captaincy's defining moment turned out to be a historic blunder.

The shimmering haze of the transporter beam dissolved into the darkness of the Borg ship's interior, and Lieutenant Pava Ek'Noor sh'Aqabaa felt her antennae twitch with anticipation.

Heat and humidity washed over her. "Flares!" she ordered, bracing her rifle against her shoulder. "Arm dampeners!"

Ensign Rriarr moved half a step ahead of sh'Aqabaa and snapped off several quick shots from the flare launcher mounted beneath the barrel of his T-116 rifle. Pellets of compressed, oxygen-reactive illumination gel made glowing green streaks across the deck, bulkheads, and overhead of the Borg vessel's frighteningly uniform black interior.

Clanging footsteps echoed around the strike team of *Titan* security personnel, and the ominous footfalls grew closer. Through tiny gaps in the ship's interior machinery, sh'Aqabaa caught sight of drones advancing on their position at a quick step. Red beams from Borg ocular implants sliced through the dim and sultry haze. "Activate dampeners," sh'Aqabaa said.

She and the rest of her strike team keyed the replicated dampeners attached to their uniform equipment belts. Senior Petty Officer Antillea switched on several more of the small spheres and lobbed them down the passageways and around corners. All around them, and everywhere one of the spheres rolled, the faint lighting inside the scout ship faltered and went black, along with any powered machinery or data relays.

The intimidating thunder of converging footsteps slowed. Looking out through the vast empty space in the middle of the probe's hull, toward sections along its opposite side, sh'Aqabaa saw dozens more sites going dark. Then the entire probe shuddered, and darkness descended like a curtain drop.

"Seek and destroy," sh'Aqabaa said, advancing toward the enemy, her finger poised in front of her rifle's trigger.

Then the Borg drones quickened their pace. In the uneven light of the flare plasma, shadows both massive and misshapen crowded in her direction. As she turned the corner to her right, Antillea was at her left shoulder, while Rriarr and Hutchinson broke down the left corridor. In unison, they opened fire.

Muzzle flashes lit the passageway like strobes, and the explosive chatter of the rifles was deafening. High-velocity monotanium rounds tore through the oncoming wall of Borg drones, spraying blood across the ones advancing behind them.

Gunfire echoed from every deck of the ship.

Another rank of drones fell, holes blasted through their centers of mass, vital organs liquefied by brutal projectiles. And still the next waves never faltered, never hesitated. Not a glimmer of fear or hesitation crossed their pale, mottled faces, and sh'Aqabaa knew they would never retreat or surrender. This was a battle to the death.

Her rifle clicked empty. A push of her left thumb against a button ejected the empty magazine as her right hand plucked a fresh clip from her belt and slapped it into place.

In the fraction of a second it took her to reload, the drone in front of her charged, grabbed the barrel of her rifle with one hand, and forced it toward the overhead. His other hand shot forward, and sh'Aqabaa caught the glint of emerald light off a metallic blade. She twisted from the waist and pivoted, dodging a potentially fatal stab.

A staccato burst of gunfire flew past her and perforated the drone, who let go of her rifle as he collapsed backward.

Sh'Aqabaa nodded her appreciation to the Bolian officer who had fired the rescuing shot, then leveled her weapon and felled another rank of drones.

Lines of tracer rounds overlapped in the deep green twilight.

Drowned in the buzzing clamor of the assault rifles were the distant alarums of struggle and flight from other sections of the ship. *Can't let ourselves get pinned down,* sh'Aqabaa reminded herself. *Have to keep moving.*

She shouted over the buzz-roar of her rifle. "Second Squad! Advance, cover formation, double-quick time!"

Behind her, the second six-person team that had beamed in with hers hurried down a corridor perpendicular to the one in which she and the rest of First Squad were fighting. Within seconds, the rapid clatter of weapons fire reverberated from Second Squad's new position.

Then came an agonized caterwauling from behind her. She glanced over her shoulder. Rriarr had been impaled by a drone's deactivated drill, which had penetrated the Caitian's armored combat-operations uniform by sheer force.

A scaly hand shoved her to the right. "Move, sir!"

As she slammed against the bulkhead, sh'Aqabaa saw Antillea suffer a killing jab that had been meant for sh'Aqabaa herself. A drone plunged a stationary but still razor-sharp rotary saw blade attached to the end of his arm into the Gnalish's throat. Antillea twitched and gurgled as blood sheeted from her rent carotid, but she still managed to squeeze off a final burst of weapons fire into the drone. Then the reptilian noncom and her killer fell dead at sh'Aqabaa's feet.

The Bolian ensign tried to provide sh'Aqabaa with covering fire, but she could see that he was beginning to panic.

Feeling the battle rage of her Andorian ancestry, sh'Aqabaa screamed a war cry and resumed firing, eschewing safe center-of-mass shots for single-round head shots. Each sharp crack of her rifle sent another bullet through another optical implant, terminated another drone, dropped another black-suited killing machine to the deck missing half its head. Then her rifle clicked empty again. She ejected the exhausted clip and jabbed the butt of her rifle into the face of the drone charging at her, knocking him backward. Then she fired a round of flare gel into the face of the next-closest drone.

It bought her only half a second, but that was all she needed. She slammed a fresh magazine into her weapon and unloaded in three-round bursts on the remaining drones in front of her. When her third clip was empty, so was the corridor.

"Tane, collect Antillea's belt," sh'Aqabaa told the Bolian, who nodded, despite his face being frozen in an expression of shock. Without a word, he kneeled beside the slain Gnalish, removed her equipment belt, and strapped it diagonally across his chest as if it were a bandolier.

On the other side of the intersection, Lieutenant Hutchinson was doing the same for Rriarr. Her backup, a Zaldan enlisted man, stood sentry, checking up and down the various passageways for any sign of new attackers. The probe resounded with far-off gunfire.

Loading a fresh clip into her TR-116, sh'Aqabaa stepped beside Hutchinson. "Ready?"

"Yes, sir," Hutchinson said. "Now what?"

"Reload, regroup, and go forward," said sh'Aqabaa.

Hutchinson and the others fell into step behind sh'Aqabaa, who led them back up the main passage. Second Squad was several intersections ahead of them, apparently having made quick work of whatever they'd encountered along the way. "Check all corners," sh'Aqabaa said to her team. "Take no chances."

Around the first few corners, they found only dead drones. As they got closer to Second Squad, the area looked clear. The passage was open on their left to a wide, yawning space in the middle of the probe. In its center, on an elevated structure, was the secure area where the cube's vinculum was housed.

Ahead of sh'Aqabaa and First Squad, a spark flashed off the edge of the partial left wall. She and the others pressed against the bulkhead to their right and crouched for cover.

"Stray shot?" Hutchinson speculated.

"Maybe," sh'Aqabaa said, peering into the shadows on the far side of the ship. "Be careful, and watch the flanks." She stood and led her team forward to catch up with Second Squad.

A burning sledgehammer impact in sh'Aqabaa's gut knocked her backward before she heard the crack of gunfire or saw the flash of tracer rounds slamming into her and her team.

Then she was on the deck, doubled over and struggling to hold her abdomen together. A sticky blue mess like the core of a smashed *kolu* fruit spilled between her fingers.

She heard heavy footfalls drawing closer, and she wondered if it was the Borg coming to finish them off.

*I won't be assimilated,* she promised herself. She fumbled

with one blood-slicked hand to pry a chemical grenade from her belt. She barely had the strength to pull it free.

Dark shapes hove into view above her.

Sinking into a dark and silent haze, she decided it didn't matter anymore. *It's over,* she thought. Her strength faded, and the grenade slipped from her grasp, along with consciousness.

The oppressive monotony of the Borg probe's interior was one of the most disorienting environments Lonnoc Kedair had ever seen, and the near-total darkness enforced by the energy dampeners only made it more so. Every time her eyes began to adjust to the shadows, another blinding flash of rifle shots or another stream of tracers made her wince and turned the scene black again.

Marching footsteps echoed from a few sections ahead of her and her squad from the *Aventine*. Red targeting beams from Borg ocular implants crisscrossed erratically in the dark.

Kedair waved her squad to a halt with raised fist. At her back was T'Prel, and across from them were Englehorn and Darrow. With quick, silent hand gestures, Kedair directed Darrow and Englehorn to alternate fire with her and T'Prel. Then she looked back and signaled ch'Maras and Malaya to guard the rear flank.

She detached an energy dampener from her belt and primed it. Twenty-odd meters away, at the intersection, a platoon of Borg drones rounded the corner, spotted her and the rest of her team, and sprinted toward them, firing green pulses of charged plasma from wrist-mounted weapons.

Their flurry of bolts dissipated into sparks as it made contact with the outer edge of the squad's dampening field. Then Kedair lobbed her spare dampener at the drones, aimed her rifle, and waited for the Borg's roving ocular beams to go dark. They all went out at once, like snuffed candles.

With a tap of her finger against the trigger, a stutter-crack of semiautomatic fire dropped two drones to the deck.

T'Prel crouched beside Kedair and snapped off a fast series of single shots, and each one found its mark at a drone's throat, just above the sternum.

The rear ranks of drones hurdled over their dead, in a frenzy to reach the intruders.

*Whoever said this ship would have only fifty drones was either lying or out of their mind,* Kedair decided as she fired the last few rounds in her clip. There was no break in the buzz of weapons fire while she and T'Prel reloaded; Englehorn and Darrow had started firing just in time to overlap them.

Two more drones down. Four. Six. They kept getting closer.

Darrow set her weapon to full auto and strobed the corridor with a steady stream of tracers. Then her clip ran dry.

Kedair and T'Prel snapped fresh clips into place. Able to count the rear rank of drones in a glance, the Takaran security chief switched over to full automatic and mowed down the final handful of Borg in the corridor. She released the trigger as the last drone fell in a bloody, shredded heap. The tang of blood and the acrid bite of sulfur hung heavily in the sweltering darkness.

"Like clockwork," Kedair said to her team. "Nice work. Let's keep moving. Malaya, ch'Maras, on point."

The rear guard moved past Kedair and the others and advanced through the passage, occasionally peppering the overhead or the bulkheads with streaks of flare gel. As she followed them, Kedair retrieved her spare dampener from the deck, deactivated it, and put it back on her belt.

At the end of a long corridor, they arrived at a T-shaped intersection. The perpendicular passage was open on one side into the great empty space that surrounded the vinculum, which was housed in an hourglass-shaped structure at the probe's center. Kedair stared out at the other sections of the ship. From the highest deck to the lowest, the interior of the probe was almost as dark as space, except where weapons fire flashed white, explosions blossomed in crimson, or flares bathed their surroundings in lime green. The constant, echoing rattles of rifle fire reminded Kedair of the sound of construction work.

Movement caught her eye from the opposite side of the ship. A group of black shapes moved in quick steps through the murky shadows, heading straight toward a Starfleet strike team that had its back turned to the ambush. Out of force of habit, Kedair reached toward her combadge before she remembered that the energy dampeners had cut off all communications. She considered shouting a warning to the other strike team, but then she thought better of advertising her squad's position, and she doubted that her voice would carry all that distance with enough volume to pierce the din of the ongoing battle.

*There's more than one way to get someone's attention,* she realized, and she lifted her rifle, put her eye to the scope, and targeted a bulkhead support beam near the Starfleet team. Her single shot pinged off the metal beam, startling the other Starfleet team, whose sharpshooter immediately turned his weapon toward her. Kedair looked up from behind her scope and pointed emphatically in the direction of the coming ambush.

The sharpshooter and his fellows dropped into covered positions and took aim at the approaching pack of drones. From a distance, all Kedair saw was a blaze of tracers and the violent, twitching dance of the mortally wounded. Then the Starfleet squad's commander was up and shouting, but Kedair couldn't hear what the man was saying. The shooting came to an abrupt stop, and the squad fired some flare rounds down the passageway.

As soon as the corridor brightened, Kedair saw what she'd done. A bullet-riddled Starfleet strike team lay on the deck in a spreading pool of its own blood. Four of her brothers and sisters in arms had been shot down on her command.

Kedair wanted to scream as if she had been the one who was shot. Denial and guilt collided in her thoughts while she stared wide-eyed at the carnage she'd carelessly provoked.

"Sir," T'Prel said, "we need to keep moving and clear this deck." The Vulcan woman's flat, uninflected manner of speaking conveyed no sympathy or pity for Kedair's tragic mistake, and that suited Kedair perfectly.

"All right," Kedair said. "Take point with Englehorn."

T'Prel and the human man stepped away and continued the sweep through the Borg probe. Kedair turned her back on the bloody consequence of a moment's error, already knowing she would bear its memory with shame until the day she died.

*Enterprise* security officers Randolph Giudice, Peter Davila, Kirsten Cruzen, and Bryan Regnis stood guard beside an opening that led to the probe's center. Two of their shipmates—an acerbic Vulcan woman named T'Sona, and Jarata Beyn, a hulking Bajoran man whom Giudice had nicknamed "Moose"—used compressed-gas tools to sink self-sealing anchor bolts into a bulkhead opposite the gap.

Giudice winced at the series of sharp pneumatic hisses and reverberating *thunk*s of metal piercing metal. "Hurry up," he said, impatient to be on the move again.

He tried not to think about the fact that Dr. Crusher had told him he shouldn't be moving around at all for a few more days; it had been less than ten hours since she and the rest of the *Enterprise*'s medical staff had spliced him, Davila, and Regnis back together after their harrowing fight with the Hirogen boarding party.

*Hiss-thunk. Hiss-thunk.* "Anchors secure," T'Sona said.

Jarata threaded four thin but resilient cables through the eyes of the anchor bolts, then affixed the cables to grapples cocked in the barrels of four handheld launchers. "Ready to go," he said to Giudice.

"Nice work, Moose," Giudice replied. He slung his TR-116 across his back and picked up one of the grapple guns. Davila, Regnis, and Cruzen did likewise. "Time to go to work," he said, bracing the device against his shoulder. He shut one eye and peered with the other through the launcher's targeting scope. "On count of three. One . . . two . . . *three*."

Four grappling hooks soared away through the bulkhead gap, down toward the hourglass-shaped vinculum tower at the heart of the Borg ship. Each grappling hook penetrated the black tower's chaotic twists of exterior machinery and stuck fast, directly above an entrance passage whose access walkway had been retracted into the tower's foundation.

Working quickly, Giudice and his team took up the slack from the cables and secured them as tightly as they were able. "Moose, T'Sona, watch our backs. We're going in." He locked a handheld pulley over his cable and then attached himself to it with a safety line that was looped through a carabiner on his belt. In a few seconds, the other three humans had also hooked up their pulleys and safety loops to their zip lines.

"Now the fun part," Giudice said. Gripping his pulley with both hands, he pulled himself up onto the ledge of the barrier that stood between him and the great emptiness on the other side. He waited until Davila, Cruzen, and Regnis were perched beside him atop the barrier. "Three . . . two . . . one."

They tucked their knees toward their chests and let gravity do the rest. The incline was fairly shallow, less than fifteen degrees, but within seconds, they were hurtling through open air at an exhilarating speed. Deep aches and sharp pangs—aggravated by his sudden, extreme exertion—reminded Giudice of the impaling wound he'd suffered hours earlier.

He stole a glance at Davila and saw that the older man, who had been slashed across his chest, was also in considerable pain. *I guess even Starfleet medicine has its limits,* Giudice mused. Only Regnis had recovered fully from the Hirogen attack, despite having been garroted nearly to death. Giudice scowled. *Some guys have all the luck.*

The vinculum tower loomed ahead of them. Giudice clutched the braking clamp on his pulley and slowed his descent. On either side of him, the rest of his team decelerated. Moments later, their feet made contact with the tower, and they braked to a halt as they bent at the knees to absorb the impact. With practiced ease, they detached their safety lines and dropped down onto the platform in front of its recessed entrance.

Davila nodded at the bulkhead which had sealed the tower's entrance. "Looks like they were expecting us."

"I guess we'll have to knock," Giudice said. "Cruzen, want to do the honors?"

While her comrades took cover around the corners from the entrance alcove, Cruzen moved forward. The petite, innocent-looking brunette removed her backpack, opened it, and retrieved a peculiar demolition charge. It was a malleable chemical explosive with a binary chemical detonator. Though less powerful than Starfleet's most advanced photonic charges, it would suffice to open the passage—and it had the advantage of being able to function despite the energy-dampening fields being generated by the *Aventine* and its strike teams.

Cruzen primed the detonator and fixed the charge in place against the barricade. She made a final tap of adjustment and then sprinted back toward Giudice and the others. "Fire in the hole!"

She ducked around the corner with Giudice half a second before a massive explosion spouted orange fire out of the alcove and rocked the entire Borg probe. The cloud of fire and oily, dark smoke persisted for several seconds. Aftershocks trembled the vinculum tower as the blast effects dissipated.

"Hell of a boom, Cruzen," Giudice said. "I hope the vinculum's still in one piece."

"Should be," she said. "I used a shaped charge." She peeked around the corner. "Looks okay from here."

He heard the heavy percussion of approaching footsteps. "And what about the drones guarding it?"

"They're fine, too," she said.

"Great." He unslung his rifle and thumbed off the safety. In a smooth pivot step, he rounded the corner and fired several controlled bursts directly into the advancing company of Borg. There were so many, in so dense a formation, that he didn't need to aim. All he had to worry about was running dry on ammo. Glaring left and right at his teammates, he snapped, "What're you waiting for? Invitations?"

As if suddenly remembering why they'd come, Davila, Regnis, and Cruzen stepped out on either side of Giudice and formed a skirmish line. Davila and Cruzen fired while Giudice reloaded, and Regnis held his fire until he and Giudice could cover for the others. Working together, they cut down rank after rank of drones. For a moment, Giudice almost felt guilty about it, as if he and the others were shooting defenseless foes. Then he remembered what any one of those drones would do if it laid hands on him or any member of his team, and he resumed firing.

Regnis said to Giudice between blazing salvos, "Lieutenant? You know we're all down to our last two clips, right?"

Giudice shouted back, "Yes, Bryan, I see that."

"Well, I still see a lot of drones coming, sir."

"I see that, too, Bryan. Everyone, aim for effect!"

The team's shots became more precise, but the attacking drones drew inexorably closer. Then, all at once, there seemed to be only a half-dozen of them left standing. Unfortunately, that was when all four of the team's rifles clicked empty.

The drones prowled forward, pale revenants of malice.

"Crap," Giudice muttered.

Davila said, "We were close, too."

"Too bad the Borg don't give mulligans," Regnis said.

Reaching toward her belt, Cruzen asked, "Grenades?"

"No," Giudice said. "It might damage the vinculum."

The six Borg were only a few meters away. Giudice and his

team had retreated to the edge of the platform and had nowhere left to go. Giudice wished he could just shimmy back up the zip line. He glanced upward and had an idea. "Everybody down!"

He used his weapon's gel-flare attachment to paint all six advancing drones with radiant green splatters, and then he hit the deck beside his team.

Less than two seconds later, an overpowering barrage of sniper fire from the distant sides of the probe tore through the six drones. As Giudice had guessed, sharpshooters from other strike teams had wanted to help him take the vinculum—they just hadn't been able to identify their targets in the dark.

"That's what I'm talking about," Giudice said as he and the others stood and eyed the captured vinculum. "Teamwork."

Erika Hernandez manned the *Aventine*'s conn and eyed the black, oblong vessel on the main viewer with dread and enmity.

Her hatred was fueled by what the probe and the other Borg vessels had done at the Azure Nebula. She was beginning to understand the threat that the Borg Collective posed to Earth and its Federation. She could only hope that her wrath would be strong enough to overcome her fear when the time came to add her voice to the Collective's dissonant chorus, in an effort to bring at least part of it under her control.

At the aft stations of the bridge, Captain Dax and her first officer, Bowers, conferred in muted tones with the *Aventine*'s science officer, Helkara. They and the other officers on the bridge all presented calm appearances, but there remained a palpable undercurrent of tension. No one wanted to speculate about what might be happening inside the Borg ship. *We're all hoping for the best and expecting the worst.*

An alert beeped on the ops console. Ensign Gredenko silenced it with a feather touch and said, "The Borg ship just vented a small amount of plasma."

Dax and Bowers hurried back to the center of the bridge. "Magnify," Dax said.

The image on the viewscreen snapped to a close-up view of a small exhaust portal low on the Borg ship's aft surface. Another brief jet of rapidly dissipating plasma appeared. Moments later, two short plumes occurred in quick succession. "The delay between ventings has been exactly five seconds," Gredenko reported. The bridge crew watched with anticipation. Then came three rapid spurts of plasma. "Five-second delay," Gredenko repeated. "Counting down to next venting. Three . . . two . . . one." Right on cue, a series of five fast plasma ejections sprayed from the port. "Fibonacci pattern and timing confirmed."

"All right," Bowers said. "Mister Helkara, lower the dampening field. Kandel, keep the shields up and the weapons on standby, just in case it's a trap."

Helkara tapped at his console and replied, "Dampening field is down, sir."

Immediately, Hernandez heard a few lonely Borg voices from aboard the probe. They had been cut off from the roar of the Collective, and they sounded disoriented and afraid. She stole nervous glances at the rest of the bridge crew and quickly realized she was the only one who heard the panicked drones.

"Lieutenant Kedair is hailing us from the Borg ship," Kandel reported.

"On speakers," Dax said.

Kandel replied, "Channel open."

"Lieutenant," Dax said, speaking up toward the comm, "this is *Aventine*. Go ahead."

*"The Borg probe is ours, Captain,"* Kedair replied. *"The vinculum is intact, and we've taken it offline while we make our modifications for Captain Hernandez."*

Dax nodded. "Good work. Is it safe for her to beam over?"

*"Not yet,"* Kedair said. *"There are still a few drones kicking around in here, but we have them cornered. Once we finish them off, we'll be ready to proceed to phase two."*

"Well done," Dax said. "Keep us posted. *Aventine* out."

The channel closed with a barely audible click from the overhead speaker. Hernandez's thoughts drifted as she tuned out the bridge's muffled ambience of urgent business. Her mind reached out as if to the Caeliar gestalt, the way it had in Axion when she'd eavesdropped on her captors. Now, however, she was listening to the Borg drones on the probe ship.

A bond was formed, a communion of sorts . . . and then she was seeing through the drone's eyes.

It was wounded and immobilized, lying on a deck inside the Borg ship. To her eyes, the interior of the probe vessel looked more like an automated factory than a starship. A celadon glow suffused its vast, deceptively open-looking architecture.

She felt the drone's labored breathing, the dull pain throbbing in its abdomen, the quickened beating of its heart. Its thoughts were chaotic and wordless, little more than surges of emotion and confusion. Then it reacted to the presence of Hernandez's mind with a desperate attempt to merge. It reminded her of the way a hungry infant might reach for its mother.

Its vulnerability and fear took hold of her, and she felt a deep swell of compassion for the mortally wounded drone. *Don't be afraid,* she assured the drone, acting on a reflexive desire to provide comfort. The drone relaxed; its pulse slowed. As its breaths became deep and long, it began to feel to Hernandez like a psychic mirror that reflected her will and desires.

Then a pair of Starfleet personnel turned the corner a few meters away. They had weapons braced at their shoulders as they advanced on the fallen drone.

Hernandez lost sight of the difference between herself and the drone. Its fear became hers as it stared into the barrels of two rifles, pointed at its face from point-blank range.

A shocked half-whisper passed her lips, and she felt the drone speaking with her, as if they shared a voice: "No . . ."

The bond was broken in a crack of gunfire.

Slammed back into the solitude of her own consciousness, Hernandez recoiled with a violent shudder. She gripped the sides of the console to steady herself. Her eyes glistened with tears of anguish and fury, as if she had just witnessed the slaughter of her own flesh and blood. She knew that the Borg were still the enemy of humanity and its allies and that the Collective had to be stopped, but now she was also convinced that there was more to this implacable foe than she had been told—and perhaps more than Starfleet and its allies realized.

A brown hand settled gently on her shoulder. Bowers leaned down and asked quietly, "Are you all right, Captain?"

For a second, she considered telling him about her vision of the drone, but then she thought better of it. *These people are terrified of the Borg,* she realized. *If they think I'm bonding with the enemy or sympathizing with them, there's no telling what they might do to me.*

"I'm fine," she lied. "Just nerves, I guess."

Bowers nodded. "It'll be a while before they're ready for you on the Borg ship," he said. "Maybe you should go back to your quarters and rest a bit before we start phase two."

Hernandez forced herself to muster a grateful smile. "Sounds like a good idea," she said. She got up and walked to the turbolift as Bowers summoned a relief officer to the conn.

Before she stepped inside the lift, Dax intercepted her. "I just wanted to thank you for all your help today," Dax said. "I doubt we'd have succeeded without you at the conn."

"You're welcome, Captain," Hernandez said. "Could I ask a favor in return?"

Dax's eyebrows peaked with curiosity. "Depends. What'd you have in mind?"

"Seeing as you mean for me to pose as the Borg Queen in an hour or two, it would help if I knew as much about the Borg as possible," Hernandez said. "Can you give me clearance to review all your files about them? Including the classified ones?"

"Consider it done," Dax said. "But be warned—there's a lot of it. I doubt you'll get through it all in an hour."

Hernandez knew she could absorb the data in minutes, but chose to err on the side of modesty.

"Don't worry. I'm a fast reader."

Lonnoc Kedair's first order after the *Aventine* deactivated its dampening field had been to have wounded personnel beamed back to the ship for emergency medical treatment.

Her second order had been to make sure every drone on the probe vessel was "one-hundred-percent dead."

"As opposed to mostly dead?" T'Prel had inquired with her trademark arid sarcasm. Kedair had responded with a withering glare that made it clear she was in no mood for witty repartee.

She stood in front of the vinculum, which a team from the *Enterprise* had captured and taken offline. The vertical shaft was capped at its top and bottom by diamond-shaped, emerald-hued polyhedrons. An intricate cage of protective black metal surrounded each major component, and the core shaft was surrounded by several rows of horizontal bands. It vaguely reminded Kedair of a warp core on a Federation starship.

Irregular impacts echoed in the cavernous space outside the

vinculum's tower. Kedair looked down the passage and through the blasted-open entrance to see her people clearing the corpses of Borg drones from the tower by tossing them over the edge of the entrance's exterior platform, into the belly of the ship, which was a random-looking pit of snaking pipes and jutting machinery.

Kedair fought the urge to contact sickbay on the *Aventine* and pester Dr. Tarses for an update on the wounded personnel. *Just let the medics work,* she told herself. She dreaded going back to the ship. Sooner or later, she would have to write and submit her after-action report for this mission, and she was torn over whether to describe her blunder as the result of incompetence or of negligence. All that really mattered to her was that the officers who had obeyed her order to fire not face a court-martial; as far as Kedair was concerned, they were as much victims as the people they'd shot.

"All squad leaders have checked in, Lieutenant," T'Prel said, interrupting Kedair's guilty ruminations. "All drones have been neutralized, and all decks have been secured."

"Good," Kedair said. She stepped away and tapped her combadge. "Kedair to *Aventine.* We're ready for the engineers."

*"Acknowledged,"* Commander Bowers replied over the comm. *"They're beaming in now."*

There was a faintly electric tingle in the air before the first sparkle of a transporter beam appeared in the darkness. Then six figures took shape in a flurry of particles and a euphonic wash of sound. The effect brightened the entire vinculum chamber for several seconds. When it faded, Lieutenant Leishman and five of her engineers stood before the mysterious Borg device, holding toolkits and eyeing their surroundings with equal parts apprehension and professional curiosity.

"This ought to be interesting," Leishman said, gazing at the vinculum. "Assuming *Voyager*'s technical specs are accurate."

Unable to stomach Leishman's good mood, Kedair extinguished it with a glower as she said, "Whatever you're gonna do, Mikaela, do it fast. It's time to give the Borg a new queen."

# 17

*A flash of movement and a snap of jaws, the sting of fangs breaking flesh, a rush of terror—*

Deanna Troi awoke with a shudder and pulled her arms up and in, striking a defensive pose. Her hands and feet were stiff and cold, and a tingling of chilled gooseflesh traveled up her legs. Exhaled breaths became white clouds above her. Shaking off her disorientation, she realized she was no longer in her quarters.

The room was narrow, but its ceiling was far above, at a dizzying height. A clamshell-shaped skylight was directly over Troi, who tucked her chin to her chest and examined her own situation. She was lying on a dull metal slab and surrounded by bizarre machines, which pulsed with violet light and whose purposes she couldn't begin to divine. An especially large and fearsome-looking contraption hovered near the ceiling, above a point several meters past the foot of what Troi surmised was an operating platform. Along the top of one wall, in the only area uncluttered by machines and unobstructed by crisscrosses of drooping cables, was a broad observation window.

Inyx stood behind a transparent barrier to her right. He appeared to be engrossed in a complex task and did not yet seem to be aware that Troi had regained consciousness.

She reached slowly toward her chest and gingerly touched where Ree had bitten her. Searching with her fingertips, she found the rips in her uniform but no corresponding wounds in her flesh. Though the air in the laboratory felt cold to her, she wasn't in any real discomfort. Closing her eyes, she focused on the sensations from within her body, in an effort to assess her own condition. *No pain,* she realized. *That's good . . . I hope.*

Troi opened her eyes to find Inyx looming over her.

"You're awake," he said in his mellow baritone. "Good."

Inyx, like the other Caeliar, projected no emotional aura that Troi's empathy could detect. If his intentions were sinister or duplicitous, she had no way of knowing beforehand. She propped herself up on her elbows and asked, "Where are we?"

"In my lab," Inyx said. "It was the only sterile facility in Axion that was properly equipped to assist you."

She tried to swallow, but her mouth felt too dry. "The last thing I remember, Ree attacked me."

"A misunderstanding, apparently," Inyx replied. "He used his species' natural venom to place you temporarily in a suspended state. It was a crude solution to your dilemma, but it did briefly stave off the immediate crisis."

Panic quickened her pulse. "Venom?"

"There is no danger, Deanna," Inyx said. "I've purged the toxins from your system and stabilized you—for the moment. I didn't wish to take any further steps without your informed consent, however. That's why I've revived you."

Pondering the degree to which Inyx must have examined her to be able to cleanse her system of Pahkwa-thanh venom, Troi surmised that he had likely become privy to all of her extant medical issues. "You know that I'm pregnant . . . don't you?"

"Yes, Deanna."

After days of running from the heartbreaking truth of her situation, confessing it almost felt like a relief. "Do you also know that it's not going well?"

"That much was clear when I saw that its mutation had threatened your life," Inyx said. "I would like to help you."

Tears rolled from her eyes and blazed fiery trails across her cold cheeks and over the edge of her jaw. "The captain of *Titan* is my husband and the father of my child," she said. "I want to go back to my ship and be with him."

"I'm sorry, Deanna, that won't be possible." Before Troi could protest, Inyx added, "*Titan* escaped orbit and returned to your Federation approximately ten hours ago."

The news cut through her like a blade. Shock dominated her thoughts. *My* Imzadi *left me? He's gone?* Denial took hold. "How could *Titan* be back in the Federation already?"

"It repurposed a subspace passage that we had created for reconnaissance purposes," Inyx said. "With assistance from Erika Hernandez, *Titan*'s crew enlarged the subspace aperture and used it to make a near-instantaneous journey home. As I'm sure you can imagine, the Quorum is feeling rather vexed."

Troi lay back on the slab and covered her face with her hands. "I can't believe he left me," she muttered.

The part of her that was an officer understood Riker's actions perfectly. No doubt, he'd been forced to choose between saving the ship and the majority of its crew or risking their freedom for the sake of the already captured away team. Viewed in that light, Troi knew that her captain's decision had been logical. But the part of her that was a wife shrank beneath the crushing emotional blow of Will's abandonment.

Inyx said, "Deanna, we really can't afford to wait any longer.

I am ready to assist you medically, but I require your permission to proceed."

She lowered her hands and folded them protectively across her abdomen. "Dr. Ree wanted to do this days ago," she said. "I wouldn't let him. I don't know why not. Maybe I was hoping for a miracle." A surge of emotion constricted her throat. It took her a few tries before she could continue. "But I guess it's time to accept that maybe some things weren't meant to be."

"I don't understand," Inyx said.

Troi replied, "I'm giving you permission to proceed. To terminate my pregnancy."

The imposing Caeliar scientist recoiled from her, as if in horror. "Deanna, I think you've mistaken my intentions." He recovered a small measure of his composure and continued, "As I've explained to you before, the Caeliar abhor violence and will not terminate sentient life for any reason. Likewise, for us to abandon a life in peril that could be saved is also anathema." Resuming his proud bearing, he finished, "I was not asking to end your pregnancy, Deanna, but to repair it."

"You could do that?" she asked, amazed at the very idea.

"And more," Inyx said. "I have spent a considerable fraction of the past several centuries learning about humanoid biology, mostly for Erika's benefit. However, I am certain that I possess the knowledge and expertise to restore the proper, natural genetic pattern of your fetus and to repair the damage in the unfertilized ova of your uterus. While I won't impose my cures on you or your child without consent, I am not too proud to beg you to accept my help." He transformed the waggling cilia at the end of one of his arms into a semblance of a long, bony humanoid hand, and he extended it in invitation toward Troi.

"Grant me your permission, Deanna," he said, "and I will heal you—and your child."

The passage through the catacombs of Axion grew narrower with every step Keru and Torvig took. "Where are we going, Vig?"

"Just a bit farther, Ranul," Torvig said. "If my senses are accurate, there should be an opening twenty-two meters ahead."

Their voices and scuffling steps echoed and carried in the pitch-dark tunnel. "I wish you'd told me we were going spelunking," he said to the Choblik engineer, his voice echoing off the close walls. "I'd have brought one of the palm beacons."

"Not necessary," Torvig said. "There is an increase in the ambient light ahead, at the tunnel's terminus."

Keru's eyes saw nothing but the same pools of darkness broken by occasional patches of deep shadow. "I'll take your word for it, Vig." He looked back over his shoulder and found the path back just as dark as the path forward. "I wonder which one of our Caeliar observers is trailing us right now."

"You could simply ask them," Torvig said.

"I don't really care that much," Keru replied.

They continued walking without speaking for thirty seconds, the two of them shades barely visible to Keru's eyes, and then Torvig said, "The passage slopes downward here. Mind your step."

Keru slowed his pace just enough to adjust his stride to the new descending grade. He noticed the sharpness of Torvig's silhouette in front of him, and he realized that he, too, could now see the growing illumination ahead. The air was getting warmer as they advanced toward the pale blue flicker.

"Vig, how'd you even find this passage?" he asked.

"I would rather not answer with too much specificity, since we are being monitored," Torvig said. "Let it suffice to say that the senses I was granted by the grace of the Great Builders enabled me to perceive a shift in Axion's quantum field. I attuned my senses to its particular properties and traced the field to its source point. Which is six-point-two meters ahead."

The ensign's explanation drew a smile from Keru. It hadn't occurred to the Trill security chief until that moment that though the Caeliar had destroyed the away team's tricorders, Torvig's bionic enhancements—including his cybernetic eyes and his assortment of advanced computing and sensory devices—made him an ideal, self-mobile substitute for the lost equipment. Only a few months earlier, Torvig had put his implanted systems to good use saving *Titan* after an ill-fated encounter at Orisha with the Eye of Erykron. *After a feat like that,* Keru mused, *filling in for a tricorder must seem like child's play.*

The duo reached the bottom of the sloped passage and made a hard switchback turn. Then they moved from the shadows into twilight and into the heart of a blue sun in a few short steps.

Keru lifted his arm to shield his eyes. The duo stood on a

ledge overlooking a vast, hollow sphere of a chamber. Hovering at its center was a huge, brilliant orb of electric-blue fire. Its deafening roar, like an endless thunder of crashing waves and the angry buzz of a hundred billion bees, overpowered him.

Averting his gaze, Keru looked at Torvig, whose metallic eyes blazed with reflections of majestic azure lightning. "Vig!" Keru shouted over the sonic assault of the hidden sun. "What is that thing? Is it the Caeliar's power source?"

"I believe so, Ranul," Torvig said, his normally quiet voice cybernetically amplified and frequency-shifted to cut through the noise. "Its output exceeds my ability to measure."

Another squinting look around convinced Keru that sabotage was out of the question. The distance from their ledge to the burning orb was at least a hundred meters, and if the scorching tingle on his skin was any kind of warning, he was certain he didn't want to get any closer to the object than he already was. There appeared to be no other vulnerable points or exposed systems inside the polished silver-gray chamber. He also suspected that whatever the orb proved to be, destroying it would no doubt prove to be a death sentence for every living thing on New Erigol, starting with himself and Torvig.

He patted Torvig on the back and nodded for the ensign to follow him. They returned the way they had come, and after gazing into such intense light, the darkness seemed much deeper to Keru's eyes. "I don't get it," Keru said, his ears still ringing from exposure to the bone-shaking wall of sound. "If the Caeliar have that much power at their command, why go to the trouble of harnessing a sun and a planet?"

Torvig replied, "I suspect that the planet and the star were shelled in order to mask this source, sir. If it were possible to study the link between the two shells, I might hypothesize that the harnessed star provides the energy to support the shell around the planet, whose purpose is to contain the emissions of this exotic-particle generator."

"Exotic particles?" echoed Keru. "What kind of particles?"

"I have not yet identified them," Torvig said. "They are more energetic than anything I have observed before now."

Keru wished that he and Torvig had access to *Titan*'s main computer and sensor module. He asked, "If the planet wasn't covered up, how detectable would those particles be?"

"To anyone with the ability to scan that frequency, they would be the brightest energy source in the galaxy."

It took a moment for Keru to process Torvig's report, and when he did, he began chuckling at the irony of it.

The engineer seemed perturbed by Keru's reaction. "I was not aware that I had committed a faux pas or spoken in jest."

Regaining control of himself, Keru stifled his chortling and said, "I'm not laughing at you, Vig. I'm laughing at the Caeliar." He imagined his friend's bemused reaction concealed by the darkness. "I just think it's funny that a species that puts such a premium on going incognito uses a power source that can be seen from across the universe."

# 18

Beverly Crusher stepped inside the holodeck and found herself surrounded by green leaves, blue sky . . . and mud.

The portal closed behind her with a deep, soft rumble of servomotors and a muffled thud of contact. Then all she heard was blissful quiet. A mild breeze susurrated through the thick walls of leaves and grapes and rippled the shallow puddles in the muddy lanes between the vineyard's rows. The rich aroma of turned earth mingled with the sweet scent of country air after a night of spring rain. Tattered clouds sped by, high overhead.

Verdant hills rolled one beyond another, along the horizon, past the far end of the straight lane between looming stands of grapevines. The only signs of technology in the otherwise pastoral landscape of La Barre, France, were a handful of metallic towers linked to Earth's weather-control grid.

She turned in the other direction, toward the closer end of the row. Her small, pivoting steps squished and slipped in the slick, peaty muck. As far as Crusher could see, she was alone in the vineyard. There was no sign of workers, and no robotic tenders or harvesters were in use. The vineyard looked deserted.

But she knew better.

Walking slowly and taking care to plant her steps on tiny islands of dry ground scattered along the path, she skulked down the dirt lane until she spied Jean-Luc, two rows over, through a tiny gap in the leafy vines. Her vantage point came and went from view as the breeze rustled the greenery, by turns momentarily revealing him and concealing him with foliage.

Crusher tried to keep her voice down as she said, "Computer, modify program. Give me a temporary passage through the vines, to the row where Captain Picard is standing."

A two-meter-wide path appeared without a sound through the two rows of vines that separated her from her husband. She moved in gingerly steps through the passage. As soon as she reached her desired row, the holodeck closed the route behind her, silently knitting shut the walls of branches.

The suction of mud on her boots made it impossible for Crusher to sneak up on Jean-Luc, so she didn't try. Still, she approached him slowly, with caution, to gauge his reaction. When she was a few meters away, he turned his head and acknowledged her with a melancholy look. "Beverly."

"What are you doing here?" she asked, stepping beside him.

He gazed into the foliage. "I needed a place to think."

She rested her left hand against his lower back and took a few seconds to look around at the bucolic simulation of his childhood home. "Why here, Jean-Luc? Why now?"

"Because it might soon be gone forever," he said.

"Not without a fight," she said. "The war's not over yet."

Jean-Luc inhaled sharply and stepped away from her. "Are you certain of that?" He walked slowly along the muddy trail, his hands brushing through the leaves and vines, his fingertips lingering delicately over the fragile Pinot Noir grapes. "Why should I believe that Captain Dax's plan will amount to anything more than another postponement of the inevitable?" He stopped and pulled a small bunch of grapes toward him. "At this point, I suspect it's all a matter of too little, too late." Pinching one tiny, violet fruit between his thumb and forefinger, he continued, "No one heeded my warnings when it might have made a difference. Not the admiralty, not the president, not the council. I told them this day would come, but no one listened." He crushed the grape into skin and juice, and dropped it on the ground. Then he looked away, past the end of the row. "Now all of this . . . history . . . will be lost. Trampled underfoot."

He resumed walking, moving in quick strides. Beverly stayed close beside him, refusing to let him leave her behind. "So, is that it?" she asked. "You've already lost, so why finish the battle? What happened to the man who demanded we draw a line in the sand and say 'no further'? Is this all that's left of him?"

Near the end of the lane, Jean-Luc stopped and frowned as he gazed toward the distant hills. Avoiding eye contact with Crusher, he reached over and pulled toward him a length of the vine that was thick with leaves and heavy with fruit. Rolling its rough skin between his fingers, he sighed. "A vine is like a person, Beverly," he said, his voice somber. "Some of its nature is the product of heritage, but its personality also reflects its experiences. A gentle season can give it a mellow quality, and adversity can add depth to its character"—he looked up at her—"but only up to a point. There's a limit to how much damage and pain one vine can absorb before it turns bitter and brittle . . . and before it withers and dies."

He let the vine snap back into the embrace of its mother plant and continued walking, though much more slowly this time. Beverly was certain now that the dark mood that traveled with Jean-Luc was more than just anxiety about the apparent unstoppability of the Borg invasion. Her suspicion was confirmed as they emerged from the narrowed field of vision enforced by the vineyard row, to behold the sight on the nearest hill.

Where she had expected to see Château Picard, there stood only the scorched ruin of a house, a pile of charred timbers toppled at oblique angles over the pit of a black and broken foundation. Its interior was nothing but mounds of ash and rubble, cinders and shattered stone—exactly as it had been nearly ten years ago, the morning after the fire that had killed Jean-Luc's older brother, Robert, and his young nephew, René.

She took his arm. "You shouldn't do this to yourself."

There were tears in his eyes, and his face looked stricken as he placed his hand over hers. "I'm all that's left."

"No," she said sternly, commanding his attention. "*We're* all that's left." She touched her belly, where their son grew. "*Us,* Jean-Luc. *Us.*"

He shut his eyes as tightly as he could to stanch the flow of his tears, and he clenched his jaw to hold back the flood of bitter grief and fear that Beverly knew raged inside him.

She pulled him to her and forced him to turn away from the grim vision of his sundered home. He embraced her as he buried his face between her neck and shoulder, but Beverly still felt as if she were standing outside the wall of his despair, making futile efforts to peek inside.

There wasn't a millimeter of space between them, but it felt to her as if the man she loved were light-years away—and growing more distant by the day. And the Borg were to blame.

"I won't let them take you from us," she said.

"Neither will I," he said.

It wasn't what he'd said but how he'd said it that made Beverly tremble and fear that the worst was yet to come.

Worf pressed the door signal outside Jasminder Choudhury's quarters and waited patiently. Seconds later, he heard her invitation, shaken by grief's vibrato: "Come in."

He stepped forward, and the door opened. Jasminder stood in front of the sloped windows of her quarters, one arm across her chest, the other hand half hiding her face. Worf took slow, cautious steps toward her. Behind him, the door sighed closed.

Exorcising all edge and aggression from his voice, he asked, "Are you all right?"

"Yes," she said. "Why do you ask?"

"It is unlike you to leave your post, even with permission," he said. "I was concerned."

She brushed a tear from her cheek and looked at him. "What about you? I thought you had the bridge?"

"I gave the seat to Kadohata," he said.

Turning back toward the windows and the nebula beyond, she said, "I just needed a few moments. No telling when we'll get another lull, right?"

"True," he said. He stepped closer to her as she folded her arms together in front of her and lowered her head. On the coffee table in front of her, a small hologram projector displayed a miniature, ghostly image of a majestic, multilimbed oak tree in front of a quaint rural home. Settling in beside Jasminder, Worf noticed that she was staring at the hologram.

He didn't need to ask where the image had been recorded. It was easy enough to guess. "It is possible your family escaped Deneva before the attack," he said.

"Possible," she said, choking back a hacking sob. "Not likely."

Her eyes were red from crying. "But that's not what's killing me." She nodded at the hologram. "It's the tree."

"I do not understand," he said.

Her jaw trembled, and she covered her mouth with her hand for a moment until she was steady enough to talk. "Thirty-two years ago, my father and I planted that tree in front of our house. My mother used to have a picture from that day in our family album—my dad with his shirt off and a shovel in his hand, me holding up the new tree while he filled in the dirt. Dad used to joke that he couldn't remember which was skinnier that day, me or the sapling." Her face brightened behind a bittersweet burst of laughter. "I don't remember, either. It was barely a tree, not even as thick as my arm." Sorrow overtook her face again. "See those two figures under the tree in the hologram? That's me and my dad, last year, when I was home on leave. Look how big that tree is: almost sixteen meters tall, nearly two and a half meters around at the base. It's just amazing . . . or it was. Now it's gone, and I'll never see it again."

Fresh tears rolled from her eyes, but the emotion flowing behind them was anger. "I just feel so damned stupid," she said. "I should be crying for my mother or my father or my sisters, all my cousins, my nieces and nephews . . . and what am I crying over? A tree. I'm going to pieces over a *tree*."

She was shaking, and Worf saw then that Jasminder's aura of serene detachment and dispassionate resolve had been shattered. The sudden loss of her home and family and the violent rending of every tangible connection to her past were pains he knew well. The murders of Jadzia and K'Ehleyr were old wounds for him, but the pain they brought him had never diminished.

"You do not mourn the tree," he said.

She shot a defensive glare at him. "Then why am I crying?"

"You weep for what it represents."

Jasminder regarded him with a stunned look for a few seconds, then turned her searching gaze at the hologram. "Myself?" she wondered aloud, and shook her head. "My home?"

"I see many trees on your family's property," Worf said.

"But this is the one I . . ." Her voice trailed off as she followed his leading question to her own understanding. "It's my father," she whispered, her eyes fixed on the spectral image. "A symbol of our bond, our relationship."

Worf nodded. "For a Klingon warrior, there are few things more important than one's father and how one honors him."

She turned toward him, and he saw the dawning of a terrible understanding in her eyes. "My father's gone, Worf."

The outpouring of her grief was incremental for a few seconds, and then it cascaded out of her, like an avalanche exploding without warning from a fractured mountainside.

He pulled her toward him as she howled with rage and sorrow. Her guttural wails made him think of the Klingon warriors who were storming the fields of *Sto-Vo-Kor* that day.

Her cries subsided, but still she lingered in his embrace, as deathly still as someone in deep shock. In a voice hoarse and raw, she said, "I just can't believe it, Worf. Everything I ever called home is gone." She looked up at him with tearstained eyes. "Do you have any idea what that's like? To have your whole world blown away? Your whole family taken from you?"

His early childhood came back to him in bitter flashes. Memories of fire and fear on Khitomer. Bodies and blood.

"Yes," he said in a sympathetic whisper. "I do."

# 19

Dr. Simon Tarses felt his feet slip-slide for the third time in a minute while he struggled to close Lieutenant sh'Aqabaa's shredded torso. He shouted over his shoulder, "Somebody mop up this blood before I break my neck over here!"

Turning back toward Nurse Maria Takagi, who was assisting him, he snapped, "Clamp the aorta, dammit!"

His temper was flaring, but he couldn't afford to waste precious seconds reining it in. There were five different colors of blood pooling on the deck between the biobeds, and the air was filled with pained cries, delirious groans, and panicked screams. Then the main doors gasped open, and a troop of medics carried in four more security personnel who were broken and saturated with their own blood.

A triage team led by the *Aventine*'s assistant chief medical officer, Dr. Lena Glau, descended on the new arrivals. They worked in rapid whispers and grim, meaningful glances. At the end of several seconds' review, Glau pushed a lock of her sweat-stringy dark hair from her face and called out directions to her gathering flock of nurses and medical technicians. "Move the chest wound to the O.R., stage the bleeders in pre-op, and call the time on the head wound."

Sealing off a major tear in sh'Aqabaa's vena cava while dark blue ichor oozed over his gloved fingers, Tarses called over to Glau, "Lena, what've you got?"

"More friendly-fire victims," she said, following her patient with the chest wound as he was moved on his antigrav stretcher toward the O.R. "I have two minutes to save this guy."

"Let me know if you need a hand," Tarses said, and then he gritted his teeth while he struggled to work around the tattered remains of his Andorian patient's traumatized pericardium.

Glau replied, "Looks like you've already got your hands full, but thanks, anyway." She, her patient, and her surgical-support team vanished inside the O.R.

He grimaced at the critically wounded Andorian *shen* on the biobed between himself and Takagi. Ideally, he'd have performed her operation in the *Aventine*'s main surgical suite, but sh'Aqabaa's vitals had crashed too quickly. There hadn't been time to move her to O.R. before the need to operate had become imperative. He didn't know who was to blame for the shortage of surgical arches, but as Tarses rebuilt sh'Aqabaa's chest cavity by hand, he promised himself that someone at Starfleet Medical would get an earful about this.

*Assuming Starfleet Medical still exists tomorrow,* he reminded himself. *Or, for that matter, assuming* we *still exist tomorrow.*

The other three members of sh'Aqabaa's squad were in the hands of the *Aventine*'s chief resident physician, Dr. Ilar Prem, and its surgical fellow, Dr. Nexa Ko Tor. Dr. Ilar was a Bajoran man with a slight build, finely molded features, and dark eyes capable of snaring one with a sudden, shockingly direct stare. Dr. Nexa was a female Triexian with ruddy skin and deep-set eyes that seemed custom-made for keeping secrets. Her most impressive quality as a surgeon was the ability to use her three arms to operate on two patients with equal efficacy at once.

Prem's patient was a human woman, and Nexa was working on two men, a Zaldan and a Bolian. Even from across the room, Tarses could tell that none of the three surgeries was going well. The vital-signs displays above the biobeds fluctuated wildly, and then they began to go flat.

"Cortical failure!" called Ilar's nurse.

A medical technician who was assisting Nexa with the Bolian patient scrambled for resuscitation gear as he declared, "Cardiac arrest!" Meanwhile, Dr. Nexa and Nurse L'Kem were turning all their attention to the Zaldan, whose body was twisted by a series of gruesome convulsions while he gagged on an overflowing mouthful of maroon blood.

Tarses wanted to sprint across the room to intervene, to take charge, to try to save three lives at once, but he knew there wasn't anything he could do for those patients that his fellow physicians weren't already doing. Instead, he kept his eyes trained on the bits of shattered bone, the ragged flaps of rent skin, and the semiliquefied jumble of damaged organs that he and Takagi were racing to reassemble inside sh'Aqabaa.

Minutes passed while he blocked out the tense, barked orders and the rising tide of desperation that surrounded him. Then the sharp clanging of a medical instrument ricocheting off the bulkhead and the clatter of it bouncing across the deck made him look up. Dr. Ilar tore the bloody gloves from his hands and hurled them to the floor, cursing under his breath. He stormed out of the main sickbay and into the triage center.

Dr. Nexa accepted her forced surrender to the inevitable with a greater modicum of grace. She looked at Nurse L'Kem and said, pointing to the human, the Bolian, and then the Zaldan, "Time of death for Lieutenant Hutchinson, 1307 hours; for Lieutenant Tane, 1309 hours; and for Crewman Doron, 1311 hours." L'Kem noted the times in the charts and gave the padd to Nexa, who reviewed it, signed it, and handed it back to the Vulcan nurse.

Tarses had just finished stabilizing sh'Aqabaa and was making some temporary closures to the incisions as a precaution before moving the Andorian lieutenant to the O.R. He looked up as Dr. Nexa sidled up to the biobed beside Nurse Takagi and asked, "Is there anything I can do to help, Doctor?"

"No," Tarses said, surprised at how cold and unfeeling his own voice sounded. "She's stable. Go help Ilar with those two bleeders who came in."

The slender Triexian nodded and ambled silently away. It still amazed Tarses that for a person with three legs, Nexa made so little sound when she walked.

"Okay," he said to Takagi. "She's ready. Have the medtechs

come move her to the O.R., and tell them to find me another surgical arch, stat."

"Yes, Doctor," Takagi said, stepping away to summon help.

He stood beside the biobed as he peeled the gloves off his hands, and he thought of Ilar's outburst minutes earlier. *A stickler for regulations would put Prem on report for that,* Tarses thought. He looked down at sh'Aqabaa and brooded on how hard he'd already fought to save her; then he pondered how he might react if she didn't make it out of surgery.

*If she dies, I'll probably start throwing things, too.*

Tuning her mind to the frequency of the Borg Collective was proving more difficult than Erika Hernandez had expected. She felt she was close to being able to link with it, as she had with the Caeliar gestalt centuries earlier, but the closer she got, the more elusive the Borg's voice became.

She stared at her access to the vinculum and asked engineer Mikaela Leishman, "Are you sure this thing is set up correctly?"

"Positive," Leishman said. "It's responding to your own bio-feedback, just like you asked."

Beside the *Aventine*'s chief engineer was its second officer and science department head, Gruhn Helkara. The Zakdorn clenched his jaw, pushing up his facial ridges. "If you don't feel up to this, we should scrub the mission now."

"I'm fine," Hernandez said. "Just let me concentrate."

She closed her eyes and focused on aligning her brainwaves with those of the Collective. She blocked out the muggy climate inside the Borg ship, the discomfort of her semi-invasive neural interface with the vinculum, and her own fear.

Two oscillating tones, slightly mismatched, served as her guide. Hers was the shorter, faster wave of sound; the more she relaxed, the closer her alpha-wave tone matched that of the Borg.

Perfectly measured, crisp footfalls approached. She knew before she heard the voice that it was Lonnoc Kedair, the security chief. "The transphasic mine is armed," she said to Leishman and Helkara. "How's our royal infiltrator doing?"

"She's working on it," Leishman said.

Hernandez was very close to bringing her psionic frequency into synch with the Collective's when Helkara's combadge beeped and broke her concentration. Dax's comm-filtered voice sliced through the low thrumming and anxiety-filled silence inside the vinculum. *"Commander Helkara, report,"* she said.

Opening her eyes to glare at Dax's three officers, Hernandez noted the abashed look on Helkara's face.

"We're almost there, Captain," he said.

*"Well, get there faster,"* Dax said. *"The Borg are minutes away from hitting five major targets, including Andor, Vulcan, and Qo'noS. If this plan's gonna work, it has to happen now."*

Leishman and Helkara traded glances of dismay. Kedair stared intently at the pair, awaiting their reaction. Helkara replied to Dax, "We need a few more minutes, Captain."

*"We're out of time,"* Dax said. *"What do you have now?"*

Hernandez beckoned to Leishman. "I have an idea."

The engineer arched her eyebrows. "I'm listening."

"I'll be able to adjust my modulation faster if you remove the feedback buffer from my interface," Hernandez said.

Helkara dismissed the suggestion with the energetic waving of both hands. "Absolutely not," he said. "Without that, you'll run the risk of a counterattack by the Borg."

"I'm a big girl, I can handle it," Hernandez said. "Look, the buffer is most of what's slowing me down. If I don't get inside the Collective's head right now, billions of people are going to die. Risking my life to save all of theirs makes sense, at least to me." She raised her voice. "Captain Dax, I'm asking permission to remove the buffer and face the Borg head-on."

*"Granted,"* Dax said. *"Gruhn, Mikaela, get it done."*

"Aye, Captain," Helkara said, acquiescing with reluctance.

*"Aventine out,"* Dax said, closing the channel.

The wiry Zakdorn frowned and ran a hand through his thatch of black hair. He pointed at the interface jury-rigged to the vinculum and said to Leishman, "Remove the buffer, Lieutenant."

Leishman stepped forward, tapped a few buttons on the control panel, and reached under the console to pull free a sheet of isolinear circuits, from which dangled a bundle of optronic cables. Holding the deactivated component in one hand and leaning on the other, Leishman shook her head at Hernandez. "I hope you know what you're doing, Captain," she said.

"So do I, Lieutenant," Hernandez said.

Then she turned her thoughts to fusing with the Borg.

\* \* \*

A crowd of frazzled bodies and fearful faces had gathered in the combat operations center in the secure bunker below Starfleet Command.

Towering screens high on every wall showed images from orbital platforms above five different worlds, and a sixth hard-line feed showed President Bacco and her cabinet gathered in the Monet Room at the Palais de la Concorde in Paris.

Admiral Edward Jellico leaned against the room's enormous central strategy table, flanked by his colleagues, Admiral Alynna Nechayev and Admiral Tujiro Nakamura. Together, they watched the majestic displays that surrounded them and awaited a catastrophe. An undercurrent of comm chatter and muted voices droned beneath the pall of fear that filled the room. For the junior officers working in the command center, there was still work to be done, something to focus on, tasks to distract them from the terror of speculating about what would happen next.

For Jellico and the other admirals assembled in the command center, there was nothing left to do but wait. They had drafted their plans and moved thousands of starships and hundreds of thousands of people like pieces on a chessboard—all in what felt to Jellico like an increasingly pointless effort to escape what they all knew was really checkmate.

Quietly, he said to Nechayev, "We've done all we could."

"Yes, Ed, we did." She smiled sadly in his direction and then, with tremendous subtlety and discretion, placed her hand on top of his. It was a small gesture of friendship and comfort, but in the pressure of the moment, it touched Jellico profoundly.

And for just a few seconds, he almost smiled, too.

Then a masculine voice boomed from the overhead comm, *"Borg attack fleets are within two minutes of Vulcan, Andor, Coridan, Rigel, and Qo'noS."* The subspace feeds switched to show nearly identical images, of five groups of eight to ten Borg cubes. An electric prickling raised every hair on Jellico's body, and fear washed through him like a surge of ice water in his veins.

"Order all ships to intercept and engage," he said.

*History will say we tried,* he lamented, as his order was relayed to the fleets above five distant worlds. *Assuming that history remembers us at all after the Borg get done with us.*

\* \* \*

The coming battles all were light-years away, but watching them unfold on the desktop monitor in his ready room on *Titan,* William Riker felt as if he were in the thick of the melee.

Less than a few light-minutes from four Federation member worlds, fleets of allied ships rallied in formation and raced to meet the enemy. Riker watched them speed toward the Borg cubes and was both grateful and enraged that he and his ship weren't there to do their part.

*I should be watching this on the bridge,* he told himself. He got up from his chair, took a few steps toward the door, and stopped. *What if the battle goes against us? Morale's bad enough as it is. Do I really want to make my crew watch the end of Vulcan or Andor?*

Then he imagined what Troi would say: *They're strong, Will. They can handle it. Trust them—and let them see your trust.*

He forced himself back into motion and out the door, onto the bridge. Lieutenant Commander Fo Hachesa vacated the center seat as Riker approached. "Repairs are continuing on schedule, Captain," said the Kobliad acting XO.

"Very good," Riker said, taking his seat. "Patch in the feed from Starfleet Command on the main viewer."

Hachesa pulled his hands to his chest as a nervous frown creased his brow. "The battle in the core systems, sir?"

"Yes, Commander," Riker said. Noting the man's discomfort, he continued, "Is there a problem with that?"

Spreading his hands, Hachesa said, "Lieutenant T'Kel suggested that earlier, but I disagreed."

Riker glanced toward the tactical console, where T'Kel was directing an icy stare at Hachesa. Looking back at Hachesa, Riker asked him, "On what grounds?"

"I did not want to jinx it," Hachesa said.

It took a few seconds for Riker to be certain that Hachesa was, in fact, utterly serious. "Overruled," Riker said. "This isn't like quantum mechanics, Fo. We won't affect the outcome by observing it." He nodded to T'Kel. "Put it on-screen."

While the Vulcan woman carried out the order, Hachesa confided to Riker, "I also feared it might be bad for morale."

"Thousands of Starfleet personnel are about to put their lives on the line," Riker said, loudly enough for all on the bridge to hear. "Many of them are about to make the ultimate sacrifice. Since we can't be there to fight beside them, we owe it to them to bear witness—and to remember their courage."

Images of the five battles appeared on *Titan's* multi-section main viewer.

That was when Riker realized that maybe Hachesa's instincts had been right after all.


Picard stood at the center of the *Enterprise's* bridge, his posture erect, his bearing proud, and his soul mired in despair.

On the main viewer, enormous Borg cubes moved in clusters. The sheer mass of each attack group was more daunting than Picard had ever dared to imagine.

The sight of even a single cube was enough to set his pulse racing and fill his stomach with acid. Instantly, he was back in the hands of the Collective, being absorbed, erased, violated, and entombed inside himself. He was lording over the slaughter of Wolf 359. He was hearing the voices whispering below the fray at the Battle of Sector 001. He was alone.

Lieutenant Choudhury's voice pulled him back into the moment. "Klingon and allied forces have engaged the Borg at Qo'noS and Beta Rigel," she said. "Allied battle groups moving into attack formations at Andor, Vulcan, and Coridan."

Worf stepped forward to stand on Picard's right side. Out of the corner of his eye, Picard saw that his first officer was emulating his stance, in a show of solidarity and dignity. It was to Worf's credit, Picard thought, that he saw no need to sully the moment with words, and Picard showed Worf the same stoic courtesy in return.

The images of battles far removed blazed with the cold fire of transphasic torpedoes.

Picard wanted to believe that Starfleet was ready for this fight. He wanted to believe that the Federation would endure this crisis, as it had so many others before it.

Then the torpedoes found their marks . . . and he knew that the only truth left to believe was the one promised by the Borg.

*Resistance is futile.*

\* \* \*

"Torpedoes are away," announced the tactical officer of the *U.S.S. Atlas,* and Captain Morgan Bateson clenched the armrests of his chair as he watched the missiles on the main viewer spiral toward their targets.

"Reload and keep firing, Reese," Bateson said. "Don't give them time to regroup." He stole a quick look at his fleet's deployment pattern on his command monitor. "Kedam, tell the ships on our port flank to spread out. They're too close."

The Antican operations officer replied, "Yes, sir," as he relayed the order to the other ship's commanding officers.

"Five seconds to impact," said Lieutenant Reese.

Bateson's hands were coated in cold sweat. He'd fought at the Battle of Sector 001, which had taught him a costly lesson about how devastating a single Borg cube could be in battle. Now he was leading an attack against ten cubes.

*We outnumber them four to one,* he reminded himself as the transphasic torpedoes detonated against the Borg ships with a blinding flash. *Please, God, let it be enough.*

He didn't expect more than a handful of the cubes to emerge intact from the blistering blue firestorm that engulfed them. Then a black corner pierced the dissipating fog, followed by another . . . and then by six more.

"Two cubes destroyed," reported Lieutenant Kedam. "The remaining eight cubes are still on course for Vulcan."

Commander Sophie Fawkes, the *Atlas*'s first officer, said, "Helm, attack pattern Foxtrot Blue!"

"Second salvo's away," Reese declared from tactical.

Fearing the worst, Bateson said, "Ready another."

On the main viewer, he saw the fleet's second barrage of transphasic warheads flare like a blue sun . . .

. . . and all eight cubes burst from its flames unscathed.

*Dear God.* "All ships, break off!" Bateson ordered. "Fall back to Vulcan orbit and regroup!"

"Sir," Kedam said. "The *Billings* is leading the reserve wing on a collision course with the Borg ships."

Bateson looked to his XO. "Fawkes, hail them! Tell them to break off!" She tried to do as he asked, but Bateson knew it was too late. He watched in horror as the *U.S.S. Billings* and more than a dozen Federation starships were blasted into scrap and vapor by the Borg cubes, which rammed their way through the spreading cloud of smoldering debris.

Reese cried out, "The Borg are locking weapons!"

"Helm, evasive!" Fawkes shouted.

The young Andorian *chan* at the conn struggled to guide the *Sovereign*-class vessel through a series of rapid and seemingly random changes in speed and direction, but the hull rang under a succession of crushing blows from the passing Borg cubes. A brutal impact sent the *Atlas* spinning and rolling and plunged its bridge into darkness for several seconds.

When the overhead lights and bridge systems came back on, Bateson was crestfallen as he confronted the grim scene on the main viewer. Only a handful of ships from his attack fleet were intact, and even fewer appeared to be operational.

"Kedam, open a channel," Bateson said, fuming mad at his failure to halt the Borg's genocidal march. "Warn the Vulcans: The Borg will reach orbit in one minute."

President Bacco, her cabinet, and her advisers stood and traded nervous whispers around the conference table in the Monet Room, sequestered below the Palais de la Concorde. Esperanza Piñiero positioned herself to monopolize access to the president.

"We still have time to get you to safety, ma'am," she said, her tone more insistent than it had been the last three times she had made this suggestion. "There's a high-warp transport standing by. We can have you halfway to Rhaandar by the time the Borg reach Earth."

"Enough," Bacco said. "One more word about this, and I'll have Agent Wexler put *you* on that transport by yourself."

Piñiero scowled. "You say that like you think it'd be a punishment, ma'am."

"Hush," Bacco said. "There's nowhere to retreat to, anyway. We're making our stand here, Esperanza. Besides, if the Federation falls, I don't want to live to see it. Now, step aside. You're blocking my view."

She didn't really want to see any more of the developing calamity, but it was as good an excuse as any to end their conversation. The room's multiple display screens all showed similar images, telling the same story. Starfleet vessels were broken and burning or scattering in confused retreat. A Klingon fleet was making one valiant sacrifice after another to defend Qo'noS. Borg cubes advanced all but unopposed on the strongholds of the

Federation and its allies. And volley after volley of transphasic torpedoes made not one blessed bit of difference.

The Borg were winning the war.

Off to one side, Admirals Akaar and Batanides conferred with Seven of Nine, who had joined them to review the latest dispatches from Starfleet Command. The admirals' faces were easy to read: naked fear. Seven, as usual, maintained an inscrutable mien as she whispered to the two flag officers. The statuesque former Borg drone turned, took a few steps toward the table, and faced Bacco. "Madam President," she said, snaring everyone's attention. "The Borg have adapted to the transphasic torpedo."

The admirals joined Seven, and Akaar said, "We've confirmed it, Madam President. As of this moment, the Federation no longer has a defense against the Borg."

Energy and signals from the Borg Collective coursed through the catoms that infused Erika Hernandez's body and mind. A surge of raw power flooded her senses, giving flavor to colors and sounds to the cold touch of wires against her flesh. It was narcotic and addictive, and the ocean of tiny voices that was swept up in the psychic wave of the Collective's imperial will was both suffocating and awe-inspiring.

She had expected it to be more like the gestalt, but its similarity was only superficial. Many voices had been fused into a single consciousness, but not willingly. Unlike the Caeliar, who had united their minds for the elevation of their society as a whole, the Borg Collective subjugated sentient minds and then yoked their hijacked bodies to serve its own aims.

The deeper she delved into the Collective, the more she realized that it was nothing like the gestalt. It was darker, almost primordial in its aggression, brutally authoritarian, and utterly domineering. She hadn't realized how much she had taken for granted the benign nature of the Caeliar gestalt; where it had linked individuals with a warm bond of common purpose that respected its individuals' right to free will, the Collective hammered disparate entities together with cold force, like a blacksmith crafting a sword in a forge of ice.

Hernandez wanted to flee from its casual cruelty, free herself from its oppressive embrace, but there was too much at stake. *I have to keep going,* she told herself. Pushing her mind into deeper levels of connection with the Collective, she felt her thoughts taking on its primal hues. *I have to surrender myself to the Collective and experience it the way the drones do. I need to hear the Queen and know what she sounds like.*

Surrendering to the gestalt had been like returning to the womb and becoming a fluid in an endless stream of consciousness. Submitting to the Collective felt more like being swallowed in a tar pit, enclosed in oily darkness, smothered, and silenced.

Then, alone in the dark, Hernandez heard it.

The voice of the Borg Queen.

Harsh and autocratic, it was a psychic whip of fire on the backs of the drones. Even the cube-shaped ships answered to its unswerving command. Hernandez let herself see what the Queen wanted her to see: fleets of Starfleet and Klingon starships being crushed without mercy or regret, orbital defense platforms above five worlds being obliterated with ease, and the cubes' preparations for surface bombardments that would turn those worlds into lifeless slag.

Vulcan. Andor. Coridan. Beta Rigel. Qo'noS.

In moments, they would all be gone.

Erika Hernandez directed her catoms to vibrate in harmony with the essential frequency of the Borg Queen and steeled herself to speak to the Collective.

Only then did she realize she had no idea what to say.


Charivretha zh'Thane watched green bolts fall from the sky above Therin Park on Andor. As the matron of her clan, she had refused to abandon her home. It would have served no purpose, she'd decided. There was nowhere safe to go, and her *chei,* Thirishar, and his bondmates and their offspring all were long gone from Andor. There was nothing left here for her to protect.

She'd still hoped it wouldn't end like this, that Starfleet would devise some brilliant tactic to repel or thwart the Borg's latest incursion. During her years as Andor's representative on the Federation Council, she had often been amazed by Starfleet's seemingly endless resourcefulness.

*Not endless after all,* she admitted, as a viridescent fireball descended toward the park. Strikes beyond the city's perimeter trembled the ground under her feet.

Too jaded to mourn the loss of her own life, zh'Thane felt a profound sorrow for the doomed beauty that surrounded her and the several thousand other Andorians who had chosen to await their end in Therin Park. Cloistered in the heart of the capital city, it was a place of great natural beauty. Its aquatecture filled the air with the gentle burbling of flowing water, and its sprawling gardens and terraced waterfalls were designed to create secluded enclosures. Exotic, colorful fish in its ponds nipped and leaped at floating transparent spheres that housed dancing flames. Though portions of the park had been damaged by terrorist bombings years earlier, it had been rebuilt into something even more beautiful than what had been lost.

Vretha doubted that would be the case this time.

She drew her last breath of cool, floral-scented night air.

Then she and the park, along with the fish and the flowers and the soft music of flowing water, were gone.

All that remained was fire.


The skies of Vulcan wore many colors. At daybreak, brilliant shades of pink and vermillion ruled the lower degrees of the heavens. At midday, faded hues of amber and cinnamon set the tone. Come sunset, gold and crimson owned the horizon.

At every longitude of Vulcan, the red and bronze dome of the sky was split by jade-colored thunderbolts from orbit.

T'Lana had ventured alone into the vast wasteland of the Forge in search of solitude and healing. Her judgment as a counselor and as a Starfleet officer had been compromised by her ego and by her own surety that she'd known better than everyone around her, about everything. It had taken a failed—and, in retrospect, disastrously misguided—mutiny against her commanding officer to make clear to her just how skewed her reasoning had become. Faced with the inexcusable nature of her actions, she had done the only logical thing: She had transferred off the *Enterprise,* requested an indefinite leave of absence, and returned to Vulcan to place herself in the care of experts who could guide her back to the path of selfless reason and logic.

She saw the death stroke falling and wondered, *Did I play*

*some part in this tragedy? Were my actions part of a series of errors that led the Federation to this moment?*

Logic suggested that she was succumbing to egotism again. In any reasonable evaluation of the matter, her own role would likely prove to be so small as to be inconsequential. *Only a rank egotist would seek to accept solitary blame for an event of such epic proportions,* she assured herself.

Her inner eyelids blinked shut as the blast of burning emerald plasma slammed down into the heart of ShiKahr and turned the city to slag, vapor, and rubble. The shockfront from the detonation raced from the vanished metropolis as a kilometers-tall mushroom cloud reached into the soot-blackened sky.

T'Lana watched the tsunami of pyroclastic ash, displaced sand, and toxic fallout surge across the flatlands, toward the rocky peaks and canyons of the Forge. *At its current rate of speed, the blast wave will reach me in six-point-two seconds,* she deduced. *I will not reach sufficient cover in time.*

She had come home to complete the *Kolinahr* and purge herself of emotions and prejudice. It therefore struck her as ironic that her final musings were so deeply emotional. She was filled with regrets for her life's unrealized possibilities.

*I can never make amends for betraying Captain Picard.*

*I can never apologize for insulting Ambassador Spock.*

A blast of heat kicked up the sand and seared her skin, a stinging harbinger of the lethal onslaught to come.

*I will never be able to tell Worf how I desired him.*

The roar of the explosion struck with stunning force. T'Lana shut her eyes . . . and accepted what she could not change.


Erika Hernandez gave orders without speaking, in a voice that wasn't hers, to an army that had no choice but to obey.

*Cease-fire.*

It was like opening the clamshell skylight in Inyx's lab. She pictured an event, an outcome that she desired, and the Collective turned itself to fashioning her wishes into reality.

The barrages against the planets stopped. She was anguished to see how much damage had already been wrought. Great glowing scars on the surfaces of five worlds spread horrid, ash-packed clouds through their atmospheres.

The symptom addressed, Hernandez looked to the cause. The cubes. The hostile drones. The Queen.

*Destroy them,* she commanded, and throughout the Collective, her legions of followers complied without question, oblivious of the fact that they were the targets in their own crosshairs.

Firefights erupted inside Borg ships throughout known space. Drones cut one another down, pummeled one another with ruthless efficiency, slashed and shattered and impaled one another with mindless abandon. The cubes turned their awesome batteries against one another and blasted themselves to pieces.

Borg attack fleets in deep space dropped from warp as they hammered one another with weapons fire. The Collective stood divided, every cube a battlefield in an instant civil war.

Aftershocks rocked the Collective. So many drones being extinguished at once was an excruciating jolt, and Hernandez felt her mind recoil and shrink from the horror of it. Without the feedback buffer, she was forced to experience every Borg drone's death, every violent end, every lonely submersion into darkness. With each passing second, a thousand more voices cried out in the night, and her guilt felt like knives in her heart.

Then one voice rose above the carnage, that of a presence unlike any other Hernandez had encountered.

It was indomitable. Amoral.

Seductive and insidious.

The Queen answered Hernandez's challenge.

In a blinding flash of agony, Hernandez understood the true nature of the Borg . . . and for the first time in more than eight centuries, she was afraid.


A second queen. In all its millennia of expansion, assimilation, and steady progress toward perfection, the Collective had never before found itself torn between two monarchs.

Even when the Borg Queen had been forced in times past to manifest in multiple bodies at once, all her avatars had represented the same will, the same mind, the same purpose. The guiding voice had always been unique and inimitable.

Now, on the cusp of the Collective's latest triumph, an impostor had risen. Harmony became discord; unity turned to conflict. Perfection had been tainted.

The Borg Queen quelled the millions of confused plaints and imposed order.

*Sleep,* she decreed. *Regenerate.*

These were the most basic directives the drones knew. They were among the first to be written, the building blocks for all that had come afterward. Willed by the Queen, they were irresistible fiats that overrode all other directives.

Throughout the enemy's territory, her drones halted their self-destructive struggles and sought out alcoves in which to replenish themselves and aid the restoration of their vessels. As the drones dropped out of the Collective, the Queen searched the still-waking minds for her rival.

Cube after cube went dark, slowed, and stopped in space, as the drones hibernated. The Queen pushed the blank spots in the Collective from her mind and raced among the swiftly dwindling points of consciousness. Then there was but one besides herself.

Not human, not Borg. Something familiar but still alien.

*Designation is irrelevant,* the Queen decided. *The intruder must be removed.* She searched the isolated scout vessel for any remaining drones to serve her, but she found none. There were many humanoid interlopers on the ship, however. She decided they would suffice as replacements.

The ship awakened slowly to the Queen's will. It had not been engineered to play such a singular role, but it had been designed to support and create new drones—and to destroy all that opposed it, within and without.

More important, as with all creations of the Borg, it had been made to do one thing above all else: adapt.


Everyone in the combat operations center was talking at once, and Admiral Jellico could barely hear what Admiral Nechayev was saying from across the room. "Speak up, dammit!" he shouted.

"It's confirmed, sir," Nechayev hollered back. "The Borg cubes fired on each other, and now they've all stopped, dead in space." She turned away as a harried-looking Arcturian captain thrust his padd into her hands. Turning back toward Jellico, Nechayev lifted her voice to add, "All the Borg cubes are showing heavy damage—most of their cores are exposed."

*We might never get another chance,* Jellico realized. "All ships, reengage! Press the attack while we can!"

His legion of officers snapped into action, rallying the fleet and directing an immediate counterattack. Watching the massive screens full of tactical diagrams shift to represent the recommitted battle forces, Jellico dared to hope.

*If we're fast enough, we might just survive this.*

"Fawkes, we need to strike now!" Captain Bateson bellowed, as the *Atlas* accelerated on an attack heading. "Who's left?"

His first officer studied her tactical monitor and frowned. "*Exeter, Prometheus,* and *Kearsarge.*"

"Well, tell *Prometheus* to do its three-way-split trick. We need to hit as many of those cubes over Vulcan as fast as we can." Too energized to stay seated, he sprang to his feet and prowled forward. "Helm, attack pattern Theta-Red. Weapons, hit the Borg with everything we've got: transphasic torpedoes, phasers, bad grammar—whatever it takes!"

The reddish orb of Vulcan grew swiftly larger in the frame of the *Atlas*'s main viewscreen, and within seconds, the mangled and immobilized Borg cubes lingering in orbit became visible.

At tactical, Lieutenant Reese's youthful and delicately feminine features hardened with resolve. "Targets locked, sir."

Lieutenant Kedam at ops added, "*Kearsarge* and *Exeter* have their targets, and *Prometheus* has initiated multivector assault mode." A signal beeped on Kedam's console. He eyed the display and glanced back at Bateson. "New orders from Starfleet Command, sir: Reengage the Borg."

"Typical brass," Bateson said, rolling his eyes.

"*Prometheus* has its targets, sir," Kedam said.

Bateson decided that if ever a moment had called for the invocation of Shakespeare, this was it. "Once more unto the breach, dear friends, once more! *Fire at will!*"

His blood was hot in his veins and his pulse heavy in his temples, almost to the point of vertigo, as he gazed in awe at the staggering volume of sheer firepower that the *Atlas* and its allies loosed upon the Borg cubes. Great clusters of blazing warheads and brilliant slashes of phaser energy lanced through the black monstrosities in orbit of Vulcan and pummeled them into wreckage and dust. Any piece large enough to be detected by a scanner was targeted and shot again, until every hunk of bulkhead and every vacuum-exiled drone had been disintegrated.

"All targets eliminated," reported Lieutenant Reese.

"Secure from Red Alert," Bateson said, cracking his first smile in weeks. He gleamed with satisfaction at his first officer. "Thank Starfleet Command for their permission to engage—and tell them the attack on Vulcan is over."

Erika Hernandez gasped for breath and couldn't fill her lungs. Her mind was empty of thoughts but filled with white agony. All at once, dozens of cubes and countless thousands of drones had been annihilated, and their savagely curtailed suffering was too much for her to shut out or shunt aside.

Then came the real pain.

Psionic attacks pierced her memories like spears of fire, searing her to the core of her soul. Every engram jolted into action was transformed, bastardized, tainted into a memory of torment and violation.

She was a child again, screaming for rescue as her family's home went up in flames, and blistering licks of orange heat consumed her beloved stuffed-animal companions . . .

*No, our house never burned . . .*

A dank basement, a dust-revealed shaft of dull gray light through a narrow window, her uncle sitting beside her on a sofa with torn upholstery and old stains, his hand resting somewhere that it shouldn't have been . . .

*He never did that! It's a lie!*

She was sixteen and on her back in the snow, on a slope in the Rocky Mountains. Kevin, the boy she'd adored since eighth grade, was on top of her—with his hands at her throat and a narcotic haze clouding his crazed countenance. Her flailing and kicking and twisting bought her no freedom, not even one more tiny breath. She scratched at his wrists but couldn't reach his face. He was exerting himself, and clouds of exhaled breath lingered around his head, which was backlit by a full moon, giving him an undeserved halo as he throttled her.

*That's not what happened! He was my first love!*

None of her protests mattered. Each stab into her psyche

twisted another cherished moment of her life into something sick and shameful. Every milestone of achievement, every fleeting moment of tenderness and connection, was trampled. It was the psionic warfare equivalent of a scorched-earth policy. Her foe intended to leave her no safe haven, no place to retreat, nowhere she could go to ground.

Hernandez didn't know how to fight something like this. It was too powerful, too ancient, too cruel. It had no mercy, and it possessed aeons of experience with shattering minds and devouring souls. A destroyer of worlds, an omen of the end of history, it was not merely the Borg Queen—it was the singular entity beyond the Queen, the very essence of the Collective.

A cold darkness enveloped her, and she felt her fear being leached from her, along with joy and sorrow, pride and shame. *This is assimilation,* she realized. *It's even worse than Jean-Luc said. All you can do is surrender.*

Physical sensations returned with an excruciating spasm.

Hernandez's back arched off the deck, and fiery needles shot through her arms and along her spine. A scream caught in her constricted throat, behind her clenched jaw. Sickly green light was all she saw in the dark blur that surrounded her.

Helkara shouted, "Pull the rest of the leads! Now!"

"Not yet!" Leishman said. "Too much residual charge!"

Hands pulled at cables that snaked under Hernandez's skin, and she heard the hiss and felt the tingle of a hypospray at her throat. "We're losing her," Helkara fumed. "Somebody get a medic! Chief, get that first-aid kit over here!"

The convulsions ceased, and Hernandez let her body relax on the deck. Her vision started to clear and sharpen, but she felt utterly drained, and she began shivering intensely.

"Bring blankets," Leishman said to someone running past.

Hernandez reached out and took Leishman's forearm in a weak grasp. "Queen," she croaked, surprised at how difficult it was for her to form words. When she tried to speak again, all that issued from her lips were reedy gasps.

Helkara leaned in and asked Leishman, "What'd she say?"

"She said, 'Queen.' I guess the Borg Queen shook her up."

"No kidding," the Zakdorn science officer said.

Vexed by their obtuseness and quickly losing consciousness, Hernandez let go of Leishman's arm and grabbed Helkara's collar.

She yanked his face down to her own and stammered in a brittle whisper, "The Qu . . . Queen . . ."

Helkara pried her hand from his uniform and straightened his posture. "Is on her way to Earth—we know, Captain," he said, placing her weakening hand on her chest and patting it in a patronizing manner. "We'll deal with her next. Right now, you need to rest. Just hang tight till the medics get here."

The sedatives they had given her were kicking in, and the edges of her world were growing soft and fading away.

*Morons!* she raged, imprisoned inside her tranquilized body. She wanted to warn them, but then she sank into the smothering arms of dark bliss, unable to convey a simple report:

*The Queen is here.*

The news was almost too good for Nan Bacco to believe it. She kept waiting for the correction, the retraction, the nuanced clarification that would negate what she and her people had just witnessed on the subspace-feed monitors in the Monet Room.

A hushed conference between Seven of Nine and Admirals Batanides and Akaar ended, and Akaar strode to the head of the conference table. He lifted his large hands and silenced the nervous chatter that had filled the room.

"We've just received confirmation from Starfleet Command," he said, lifting his chin and letting his long gray hair frame his squarish features. "The Borg attack fleets at Vulcan, Andor, Coridan, Beta Rigel, and Qo'noS have been routed."

He had more to say but was cut off by the room's thunderous applause and whooping cheers of jubilant relief. Bacco permitted herself only a tight, grateful smile, for fear of tempting the Fates with premature celebration. She caught sight of a deep frown on Piñiero's face, and then she noticed that similarly grave expressions were worn by Batanides, Akaar, and Seven.

Akaar lifted his palms again and hushed the assembled cabinet members and advisers. "There were reports of infighting among several other Borg battle groups, but those have now ceased—and all remaining Borg attack fleets are once again on the move." He met Bacco's questioning look and added, "Including the one on its way to Earth."

# 4527 B.C.E.

## 20

Karl Graylock, Kiona Thayer, and Gage Pembleton were desperate and dazed with hunger after eight days of exhausting snowshoeing in a brutal deep freeze. Walking on unraveling snowshoes, they trudged through the endless night, up the side of Junk Mountain, their every step resisted by frigid knives of screaming wind and pelting sleet.

Less than two hundred meters up the slope of Junk Mountain, Graylock's snowshoes finally came apart beneath him. First his left foot plunged through the sagged webbing, and then his right foot tore free of its rotted binding. "*Scheisse,*" he cursed under his breath, fearful of triggering an avalanche.

Pembleton poked at the snow with his walking stick. "It's pretty hard-packed," he gasped in the thin air. "You didn't sink much past your ankles." He tapped the side of his snowshoe with the stick. "We probably don't need these anymore."

"Probably not," Graylock said. Thayer and Pembleton pulled off their snowshoes. Graylock gathered up the broken pieces of his footwear and stuffed the fragments into folds and under flaps on his backpack; they'd make decent kindling once they dried. Looking up the slope, directly into the path of the gale-driven sleet, he winced and said, "Let's keep going."

Graylock remembered the way to the Caeliar's redoubt as well as Pembleton did, so he took the lead as they ascended into the lashing gusts of the storm. It was up to Pembleton to keep watch for the local predator that had slain Mazzetti weeks earlier. All Thayer had to do was keep herself upright while hiking uphill over ice and snow with her braced foot.

From a distance, the three survivors would have looked all but identical. Mummified in multiple layers of the now-sullied silver-gray Caeliar fabric, only their heights distinguished them; Pembleton was the tallest, followed by Graylock, and then Thayer. It occurred to Graylock that they had not seen one another's face in more than a week. As the temperatures had plummeted, they had resisted removing any but the tiniest strips of their swaddling, and then only for absolute necessities.

In the mad swirls of sleet that surrounded him, his view of the path ahead was limited to its next few meters. Fighting gravity to push his weakened body up the mountainside left his head spinning. The next thing he knew, he was on his hands and knees, dry-heaving through his face wrappings.

Hands closed tentatively around his arms. Thayer and Pembleton labored to pull Graylock back to his feet.

"Don't quit on us now, you Austrian clod," Thayer said.

He wobbled as he found his footing. "Well, since you asked so nicely," he mumbled to her. "Gage, can you . . . ?"

"Take point? Sure." Pembleton stepped past Graylock and led the trio up the slope, past icicle-draped rock formations. Towering snowdrifts had formed against the windward side of the huge black crags that jutted from the pristine slope.

Concealed beneath a deep blanket of snow, the shape of the terrain had become unfamiliar to Graylock's eyes. He hoped that Pembleton's wilderness combat training would enable him to find the entrance to the Caeliar's buried laboratory.

The effort and the exhaustion, the hunger and the pain . . . they all blurred together as Graylock forced his aching muscles to go through the motions: taking one step and then another, walking where Pembleton had walked, never looking back.

His eyes felt leaden, and an overpowering desire for rest sapped his will to continue. *So cold I can't even feel it anymore,* he mused, poised on the edge of a hallucination. He was all but ready to collapse face-first into the snow when a mitten-wrapped hand yanked him forward.

"I found it," Pembleton said. "The tunnel's pretty slick, but I think we can make it down. Come on!"

The three survivors doffed their backpacks and huddled around a cave in the snow. It looked like an enlarged version of a trapdoor spider's lair. The sides of the opening were sheathed in ice and dusted with clinging snow that had gathered in a long, shallow slope at the bottom. Graylock peered cautiously over the edge and down the icy incline. "It's mostly clear," he said. "But how—"

A quick push sent him headfirst over the edge. He put out his hands by reflex. They slipped over the ice and did nothing to slow him down as he caromed off the sides, but the snow piled at the end broke his fall, and he was able to use his arms to guide himself down the slope on his chest. Then he slid to a stop in the pitch-dark corridor that led to the shielded lab.

He got up, dusted himself off, and walked back to the opening. When he glared up at his two comrades, Kiona said, "Sorry. Impulse."

"I'm fine, thanks for asking," he said, projecting wrathful sarcasm. "Get down here."

Graylock stepped back and waited. Seconds later, Thayer slid feetfirst onto the snow and glided on her buttocks into the corridor. He helped her up, and she called back up to Pembleton, "Clear!" Next, the trio's backpacks were dropped, and Thayer helped Graylock recover them and move them to one side. After the third one, Thayer again yelled back, "Clear!"

Then Pembleton joined them, landing and sliding as Thayer had. Graylock and Thayer pulled him to his feet. He brushed the snow off the backs of his legs as he asked, "Where do you think the Caeliar would be?"

"Probably near whatever energy-storage system they were living from," Graylock said. "We should probably start looking in the lab." The engineer opened his pack and removed the fire-making kit. They quickly fashioned small torches from their remaining thick branches of firewood and some strips of their old uniforms soaked in salvaged machine oil. Pembleton lit two torches with a flint and steel, passed them to Thayer and Graylock, then lit his own. Weak firelight and massive shadows danced on the metallic walls.

Graylock started down the corridor, and the others followed him. It felt strange to him to be back inside an artificial structure again. Their footsteps were loud and crisp on the hard floors, and they reverberated in the empty passages. The wind sang mournful songs in the dead city's empty spaces.

Away from the ice chute and the brunt of the wind, Graylock peeled off the layers of fabric wrapped around his head. The final layers felt glued to the front of his face, and he teased the fabric loose with gingerly tugs. As it came free, he saw why it had held fast. It was crusted with dried blood. Exposed for two weeks to extreme cold and aridity, his sinuses and lips had cracked like salt flats in the desert.

Thayer and Pembleton coaxed off their own bandages, revealing the same kind of cold-weather damage to their faces. What alarmed Graylock, however, wasn't the blood but the bones. Their cheekbones looked as if they might pierce their skin at any moment. Touching his own face, Graylock realized with horror how gaunt they all had become. *We look like walking corpses.*

They turned a corner, entered the lab, and found the cavernous space deserted. Every corridor and chamber they had explored had deepened Graylock's profound unease; as they wandered through the open space, he felt as if he were lurking in a crypt. "I think we're too late," he said. "They're gone."

"Maybe if you tried calling for them," Thayer said. "What was the name of the one you knew?"

"Lerxst," Graylock said. He looked to Pembleton for an opinion. The man shrugged as if to say, *Why not?* Raising his voice, Graylock called out for the Caeliar scientist. "Lerxst?"

There was no answer but the keening of the wind.

He tried again: "Lerxst?"

His voice echoed several times.

Then a sepulchral groan shook the ruined city.

"Maybe we should leave," Pembleton said, turning a wary eye toward the ceiling, while Thayer threw frightened glances in every other direction.

"Not the worst plan I've ever heard," Graylock said.

They turned to retreat from the lab—and saw a specter looking back at them. It was barely there at all, a ghostly approximation of a Caeliar's shape, as if made of steam.

Unable to mask the fear choking his voice, Graylock squeaked out, "Lerxst?"

An electric jolt spiked through Graylock's mind and rooted him to the floor. Thayer and Pembleton stood shaking beside him. Then a voice—at once feminine, malevolent, and invincible—whispered inside his thoughts as a chill like death crusted the trio's bodies and faces with a delicate layer of frost.

*Sedín.*

Pinpricks of cold fire became unbearable stabs of pain across every square centimeter of Graylock's body. He wanted to scream and run, but he couldn't move. There was nowhere for his agony to go, so it rebounded on itself, creating a feedback loop of suffering that drowned out every other sensation. He kept expecting to pass out, to implode under the strain, but Sedín wouldn't let his mind shut down. She wouldn't let him escape; she just hammered and hammered.

*No!* he raged. *I won't be . . . won't become . . . a . . . cy—*

*—borg.*

The hunger had found new strength. Three drones, easily controlled. Two males, one female. Properly replenished, they would serve. But these were nearly depleted. *The female must be preserved to produce more vessels,* decided the hunger. *One of the males must be consolidated for the collective good.*

It read the chemical engrams of the males' minds. One was a warrior, the other an engineer. *The engineer's knowledge is more valuable,* the hunger concluded.

The drones' tools were crude and clumsy, but they would suffice. Organic nourishment, though inefficient, also would have to do until a more efficacious means of sustenance and maintenance could be devised. Until then, adjustments to these beings' simple genetic code would maximize their longevity and facilitate needed energy-saving biological processes.

Operating the drones as though they were limbs, the hunger used the female and the engineer to terminate the warrior. Its loss was regrettable but necessary. With care and precision, its body was cut apart, meat and fat separated from bone, the edible from the inedible. When all of the warrior's digestible fuels had been isolated, the hunger recharged her two remaining drones with the resources liberated from the third.

When warmer weather returned, the search could begin for a new source of energy. Until then, these vessels of the hunger had to be protected and their energy conserved.

Survival would depend on patience.

*Sleep,* the hunger bade its drones. *Sleep.*

Icy seawater crashed over the gunwales of the launch as it neared the shore. Sedath, the second-in-command of the private icebreaker *Demial,* took the brunt of the chilling spray but turned his head and shut his eyes until the stinging mist abated. He opened his eyes and saw the rowers laughing at him.

"Pick up the pace, men," he said, his voice as level and professional as ever. He didn't begrudge his men a bit of amusement at his expense, but discipline had to be maintained.

At the rear of the launch sat Jestem, the *Demial*'s athletic and weathered commanding officer, and Karai, a nervous and evasive young executive from the consortium that owned the icebreaker and employed its officers and crew. Both men were eager to be ashore, though for different reasons. Jestem was a glory seeker, always on the lookout for another chance to grab a measure of fame and acclaim. Karai's ambition was more prosaic: He was in it for the money.

Sedath looked up at the pale sky. The sun had just peeked over the horizon, casting a golden glow on the arctic mountains. The landing party would have barely enough time to climb the slope to the lowest edge of the astounding scar that *something* had gouged into the primeval rock.

The scar fascinated Sedath. He had studied dozens of old topographical maps and surveyors' drawings of this peak on the *Demial*'s months-long sea journey, and he was certain that the multitude of jagged, semivertical rock formations that dotted the lower slope had not been there just a few decades earlier.

*It's a meteorite,* he surmised. *Has to be. The distribution of the debris on the slope suggests an oblique impact from above.* Although the *Demial*'s principal mission was to search the seabed for carbon fuel deposits, Sedath had always viewed his work aboard the arctic explorer as an opportunity to conduct scientific research far away from the meddling of the company's sponsored labs or the ideologically extreme halls of academia.

*Let the commander have the glory,* he mused. *Karai can keep the money. I just want to run some tests on those meteorites.*

The hollow scrape of aluminum over pebbles and sand told Sedath that the launch had reached the shore of the fjord. Malfomn, the ship's graying, square-jawed gendarme, got up from his seat next to Sedath and vaulted over the side of the launch. The older man landed with a splash in the frigid, knee-deep water, grabbed the prow of the launch, and towed it farther onto the shore. Sedath stood, laid a plank from the front benchboard to the bow, walked across it, and made a short hop to dry land.

Jestem and Karai were the next out of the launch, followed in short order by the rowers and the ship's surgeon, Dr. Marasa. To the same degree that Karai, Jestem, and Sedath himself were over-come with enthusiasm for the consortium-ordered fact-finding mission, Marasa had wanted no part of it. The weary-looking physician shivered as he took in his surroundings. "Okay, we've seen it," he grumped. "Can we go back now?"

"Quit complaining, Doctor," Jestem said. "We're heading up the slope for a closer look at whatever hit this mountain."

Marasa narrowed his eyes. "I bet it was a rock."

Jestem replied, "Just put your snowshoes on, Doctor."

Malfomn, Karai, Sedath, Jestem, and Marasa set down their backpacks, unstrapped their snowshoes, and started putting them on. Jestem was the first to finish securing his bindings. He began slide-stepping away, heading for the incline. "Come on," he called back. "We're losing the light, gentlemen!"

The rest of the group was about to set out after him when Mal-fomn called out, "Hold up! Everybody, stop!" All eyes turned to-ward the gendarme, who pointed at a nearby rocky outcropping. "What's that, between the rocks?"

It was difficult at first for Sedath to see what Malfomn was talking about. Then he began to discern artificial-looking shapes and angles lurking beneath the deep, driven snow. "Malfomn, come with me, we'll check it out."

Sedath and Malfomn split away from the group and side-stepped up a gradual hillside to the rock formation. As they got closer to it, he saw pieces of metal jutting up out of the snow and catching the morning sunlight. As soon as he was close enough, Sedath reached out with one gloved hand and tugged on the nar-row beam. It shifted a bit in the snow. "Help me pull this up," he said to the gendarme.

Together they took hold of the metal bar and pulled it free of the snow. It was half again as long as Sedath was tall, and its edges were twisted and jagged, as if from shearing stress.

"Do you recognize this alloy?" he asked Malfomn.

The older man shook his head. "Never seen anything like it." Nodding at the snow where they'd found it, he added, "Maybe we ought to do a little digging here, see what we find."

"Good idea," Sedath said. They retrieved their entrenching tools from the back of their packs and started shoveling away the snow and ice. Within a few minutes, beneath only a thin layer of the snow cover, they had exposed more metal pieces and a large patch of tattered, metallic-looking fabric. Lifting it and eyeing it in the sunlight, Sedath speculated, "Part of a shelter, you think?"

"Maybe," Malfomn said. "But I don't know anybody anywhere who makes shelters with materials like this—do you?"

Sedath bunched the shredded fabric and stuffed it into his pocket. "No, I don't," he said. He cast an apprehensive look up the mountainside at the raw wound in the stone and turned back to Malfomn. "We should get back to the others," he said. "Jestem wants to climb that slope and make it back to the *Demial* before sundown." Stepping closer to the gendarme, Sedath added in a confidential tone of voice, "Have the rowers come up here and finish digging this out while we're gone. Whatever they find, I want it wrapped in a tarp and stowed in the launch."

"Yes, sir," Malfomn said. "It'll be good for them to have work to do while we're up on the mountain."

"My thoughts, exactly," Sedath said.

The two men kick-stepped back down the hillside. Back on level ground, they split up; Sedath cut across the plain to rejoin the commander, and Malfomn detoured to the shore and relayed Sedath's orders to the rowers before regrouping with the climbing expedition at the base of the mountain.

"What'd you find?" Jestem asked Sedath.

"I'm not sure yet," Sedath said, and it was an honest, if evasive, answer. "Some metal and some fabric."

Jestem frowned inside his fur-lined parka hood. "Metal and fabric? Like you might find in a hastily concealed base camp?"

"Possibly," Sedath said, not refuting the commander's hypothesis, even though he had a more exotic idea of his own.

Karai shot a worried glance at Jestem. "Commander, the consortium has to defend its rights to all claims in this territory, mineral or chemical, or else we'll lose them."

"I know that," Jestem said.

"If another landing party has arrived ahead of us, we can't let them seize any materials or stake any—"

Jestem cut in, "I get it!" He nodded to Malfomn. "Keep your weapon handy, Mal. Seems like we might not be alone up here." To the rest of the group, he declared, "Let's go! Follow me."

As the climb began, Sedath pulled a corner of the fabric from his pocket and stole another look at it. It was lightweight but substantial enough that no light penetrated its weave; it slipped easily between his gloved fingertips, like gear oil. Its metallic threads reflected a rainbow of colors as they caught the light. He truly had never seen anything like it before, and he had no idea how it had been made. But if his hypothesis about its origin proved to be correct, then Sedath was about to make a great discovery for science.

*Of course, if we actually find an alien spaceship,* he admitted to himself, *the commander will be the one who gets famous, and Karai'll probably end up the world's richest man. The best I can hope for is to get the first look at the thing before it gets shut away in some company lab.*

He smiled beneath his balaclava. *I can live with that.*

"Over here!" Jestem was far ahead of the rest of the group, standing near an ice fissure at the bottom of a steep cliff patched with snow. Sedath and the others hurried their pace, but only with difficulty. None of them had snowshoed in a long time, and the hike up the slope had proved exhausting for everyone—except the commander, apparently.

Malfomn and Sedath reached the fissure, where Jestem stood at the mouth of a narrow ice cave, staring into its depths. Sedath looked back and admired the view of the fjord. At its far end, near the channel, the *Demial* lay at anchor, silhouetted on quiet waters that reflected the dusky afternoon sky. A whistling gale sparkled the air with a dusting of ice crystals lifted from the slope around the landing party.

Karai and Marasa arrived looking wilted and sounding out of breath. The doctor said, "I promise to rig a clean drug test for anyone willing to carry me back down."

Before anyone could take Marasa up on his offer, Jestem turned and said to Sedath, "Give me your palmlight, will you?"

Sedath undid the loop that held his portable light on his belt and handed the device to Jestem—who, as a privilege of his rank, usually traveled light and expected everyone else to come prepared with whatever he might need. The commander switched on the palmlight and aimed its narrow beam down the ice shaft. He squinted and said, "Sedath, do you see that surface down there?"

Peering into the foggy gloom, Sedath replied, "I think so."

"What does that look like to you?"

He watched the way the light reflected off a bare patch of the cave's floor, and he nodded. "Metal," he said.

Jestem turned off the light, tucked it into his own belt, and said, "We're going down there. Secure some safety lines in the cliff face, and relay our coordinates to the *Demial*."

"Yes, sir," Sedath said. He nodded to Malfomn, who set himself to work hammering spikes into the stone cliff face and securing sturdy ropes to them. Sedath removed his pack and dug out the radio. He turned it on, set it to the ship's frequency, and pressed the transmit button. "Landing party to *Demial*, acknowledge."

The watch officer's voice squawked and crackled over the barely reliable portable transceiver, "Demial *here. Go ahead.*"

"Our coordinates are grid *teskol* seventeen, azimuth three-fifty-six-point-two, elevation one thousand three hundred nine."

*"Noted,"* said the watch officer. *"Any details for the log?"*

"We've found an opening in a cliff wall," Sedath said, and then he paused as Jestem snapped around and glared at him, as if to say, *Not another word—not yet.* Composing himself, Sedath continued, "We're going underground to see where it leads, so we'll be out of touch for a bit."

*"Got it. Watch your step down there."*

"Count on it. Landing party out." He switched off the radio and tucked it back inside his pack. He walked back to the others and saw that Malfomn had finished securing two safety lines and was hurling their coils of slack down the ice shaft. Sedath sidled up to Jestem, who was still gazing down into the subterranean darkness. "Sir," Sedath said, "maybe I should go first, just this once."

"Nonsense," Jestem said, slipping back into his practiced persona of nonchalant bravery. "I was just getting my bearings, that's all. Let's get down there before we lose the light."

There was no time for Sedath to protest. Jestem locked his jacket's climbing loop around the safety line and started down the shaft, his boots slipping clumsily across the snow-dusted ice as he worked his way down the rope, using his hands as a brake. Half a minute later, the commander was at the bottom, shining his borrowed palmlight down the tunnel.

Sedath directed and supervised the descents, and he was the last person down. After a few strides away from the ice, his footsteps echoed against metal, much as they did aboard the

*Demial.* He halted in mid-step as Jestem, Karai, and Malfomn spun around and shushed him. As soon as he stopped, they turned away and seemed to be listening intently, so Sedath did the same.

Faint sounds reechoed in the darkness, so softly that they almost became lost in the melancholy moaning of the wind through the passages. Then the sounds became closer and clearer: a soft scrape and several light footfalls.

"Lights," Jestem said, switching on his palmlight. Karai, Malfomn, and Marasa did the same. Empty-handed, all that Sedath could do was stand to one side and try to gaze past the crisscrossed beams to see what might emerge from the darkness.

Two shapes shuffled into the penumbra of the palmlights. At first, all Sedath could see were their dark outlines, but even from those, he was certain that he was looking at a man and a woman. They were emaciated and garbed in tattered, loose-hanging bits of fabric, which fluttered in the chilly breeze that never seemed to cease. The beams from the palmlights were reflected in the pair's eyes, which even from a distance had a disconcerting emptiness that sent a shiver of fear down Sedath's spine.

"Identify yourselves," Jestem called out.

Karai said with venomous anger, "We know who they are—corporate spies." Sneering at the disheveled figures limping and walking stiffly out of the darkness, he added, "Looks like they already got what they deserve, too."

Then the mysterious duo stepped fully into the harsh glare of the palmlights. They were definitely a male and a female, but Sedath was certain they weren't Kindir. For one thing, their hands each had only a single opposable thumb instead of the normal two. Even more shocking to him were their pallid, mottled-gray complexions. Kindir skin varied in pigmentation from golden brown to ebony, and no one in the history of the world had ever had eyes the color of the sky—but this woman did.

The landing party was still and silent, dumbfounded by the significance of this encounter: They were face-to-face with living, intelligent beings not of their world.

The alien woman spoke in a monotonal voice. Her words didn't sound like any of the dozens of major languages on Arehaz. She repeated herself as she and her companion advanced on the landing party.

Jestem muttered to Sedath, "Any idea what she said?"

"No clue," Sedath said.

The aliens stopped at arm's length from the landing party. The woman spoke again, repeating her monotonal declaration. Then she and the man each extended one hand to the landing party.

"I think it's some kind of greeting," Sedath said.

He stepped forward to take the man's hand, but Jestem grabbed his shoulder and stopped him. "Looks like she does the talking around here. Let me handle this." Jestem took half a step forward and offered his hand to the woman. "I am Salaz Jestem of the icebreaker *Demial*," he said. "On behalf of Kindir around the world, welcome to Arehaz."

The woman grasped the commander's extended hand. Slender metallic tubules broke through the skin between her knuckles and leaped like serpents into the fleshy part of Jestem's wrist. He convulsed and then became rigid. The light left his eyes.

Sedath and Malfomn sprang to Jestem's aid. The male alien's hand struck in a blur, locked around Sedath's throat, and lifted him off the ground. The female let go of Jestem and snared Malfomn's arm before he could land his punch.

The two men struggled in vain to free themselves. Despite the aliens' gaunt appearances, they were amazingly strong. Out of the corner of his eye, Sedath saw Dr. Marasa spring to catch Jestem, who had staggered away from the melee in a daze.

Marasa shook Jestem by his shoulders. "Commander? Are you all right? Are you hurt?"

Jestem looked up at Marasa—and then he lifted one hand to the doctor's throat and skewered it with two silver tubules from his own knuckles. Marasa twitched in Jestem's clutches, and next to Sedath, Malfomn was quaking and wearing a glazed look as the female alien withdrew her tubules from his wrist.

Then Sedath felt a bite on his own neck, like a pair of tiny fangs piercing his carotid. A dark, muffling curtain of terror descended on his thoughts as the female spoke again. This time, hearing her inside his mind, he understood her perfectly.

*You will be assimilated.*

# 2381

## 21

Gredenko looked back from ops and said, "Starfleet Command is confirming all reports, Captain."

Dax smiled and heaved a deep, relieved sigh. Applause and cheering filled the *Aventine*'s bridge, and even Bowers let down his guard for a moment to pump his fist and shout, "Yes!"

*It really worked.* Dax could barely believe it. Assaulting the Borg probe ship had been a terrible risk and the wildest of long shots, but they had done it—and played a decisive role in saving five allied worlds from annihilation.

As the applause tapered off, Dax joined Lieutenant Kandel at tactical and asked, "How long before Captain Hernandez can tap into the Borg vinculum again?"

The Deltan woman replied, "We don't know yet, Captain. The last report from Lieutenant Kedair said that Captain Hernandez had to be disconnected from the vinculum for her own good."

"Has the captain regained consciousness?"

"Yes, a few moments ago," Kandel said.

"Then I want her patched back into the vinc—" A thunderclap and a jarring impact knocked the bridge into a confused jumble of bodies falling and tumbling in the dark.

Bowers shouted, "Shields! Tactical, report!"

Several more blasts shook the *Aventine* in rapid succession. "Taking fire from the Borg ship," Kandel called back over the din of explosions.

"Return fire!" Dax said. "Target their weapons!"

"Firing," Kandel said. On the main viewer, blue streams of phaser energy skewered the Borg scout's hull, vaporizing its primary and secondary armaments. Dax hoped she wasn't inflicting more friendly-fire casualties on her boarding teams.

The lights flickered back to full strength as Bowers said, "Helm, evasive pattern sigma. Give tactical a clear shot at the other side of the Borg ship."

"Aye, sir," replied Lieutenant Tharp. The Bolian guided the ship through a series of rolling maneuvers that dodged the Borg's next barrage. Then a fresh wave of phaser and torpedo hits from the *Aventine* halted the Borg's attack.

"Cease-fire," Bowers ordered. "Gredenko, damage report."

The ops officer's hands moved lightly and quickly over her console as she compiled data flooding in from several decks and departments. "Weapons grid overload," she said. "Shields offline. Direct hit to the main deflector—minor damage, but we've lost the ability to generate a dampening field."

"I'll bet that was the Borg's intention," Dax said.

Gredenko added, "There's more, Captain. We've also lost our long-range comms. Complete system failure."

"Sam, start beaming our people back," Dax said. "I want them off that ship, on the double. Then I want it fragged."

"Aye, Captain," said Bowers, relaying the order to Kandel with an urgent nod.

A moment later, Kandel looked up from the tactical station and said, "Scattering fields are going up in the core of the Borg ship—and the boarding parties report they're under attack!"

Bowers snapped, "By whom?"

Kandel's reply confirmed Dax's fear: "By the ship, sir."


The walls were alive, and the floors couldn't be trusted. Hungry maws filled with shining cables writhing in viscous black fluids had started to appear in the middle of bulkheads and corridors, as if invisible knives were slashing wounds into the ship's metal flesh and revealing its biomechanoid innards.

Helkara looked around the transforming vinculum tower in shock. Over the deafening screeches of wrenching metal, he shouted, "What the hell is going on?"

"The ship's adapting," Kedair said, looking around in terror at the collapsing catwalks and wildly undulating wires that whipped like angry serpents in the space around the ship's hollow core. "That means it's about to start either killing us or assimilating us. Either way, I'd rather not stick around to find out." A booming groan from the ship seemed to answer her.

Leishman and a Mizarian paramedic named Ravosus strained to lift Erika Hernandez to her feet. "C'mon, Captain," Leishman said, grimacing under the effort of lifting the semiconscious woman. "We have to get you out of here."

As they carried her toward the exit, Hernandez's eyes snapped open, and her hand lashed out and snared Kedair's sleeve. "The Queen," she said. "She's here. On this ship."

Kedair tapped her combadge, intending to order the rest of the boarding teams to evacuate the Borg ship. Her metallic insignia returned a dysfunctional-sounding chirp that signaled an error. "Must be a scrambling field," she said, thinking out loud. She pried Hernandez's fingers off her arm, then pointed across the narrow causeway that had been extended to link the vinculum tower to the interior structure of the Borg vessel. "You three, get Hernandez to a beam-out point. Go!"

Helkara blocked the exit and protested, "What about you?"

"I have to set the detonator on the transphasic mine," she said. Then she added a lie: "I'll be right behind you. Go!" A hard slap on the Zakdorn's back impelled him into motion. Leishman and the medic hurried along behind him, supporting the dazed but now weakly ambulatory Hernandez between them.

*One minute for them to cross the bridge,* Kedair calculated, *two minutes to the nearest enhanced transport site. Add a minute for insurance.* She turned back and faced the dark heart at the center of the Borg vessel. The inside of the vinculum tower was now a horror show of biomechanical viscera spreading like a cancer, metastasizing into every open space. To reach the transphasic mine and set its detonator, she would have to fight her way through that snaking mass of lethal, merciless pseudo-flesh and hold her ground for at least four minutes.

There was no point sending anyone else to do it; she was the only one likely to have a chance of success . . . and she decided that she'd gotten enough of her people killed for one day.

From a sheath on the back of one of her slain comrades, she drew a sword with a monomolecular edge. Alone and resolved, she gazed into the yawning cavity of steel teeth, slithering sinew, and oily black death. It taunted her with evil whispers, as if daring her to rush in where all others feared to tread.

She lifted her blade and charged.

Every turn seemed to lead to a dead end. Dark chords of panic rang out from all directions, echoing and vanishing into the shadowy recesses. The inside of the Borg probe was a maze of snaking conduits and sliding walls. Great slabs of machinery moved of their own volition behind the façades, traveling with deep rumbles and ear-splitting screeches.

Erika Hernandez had recovered most of her strength and was sprinting behind Leishman and Helkara, with Ravosus close behind her. She wished they could run faster. In theory, Helkara was leading them out of the industrial-style labyrinth, back to one of many secured platforms where a quartet of transporter-pattern enhancers had been set up to facilitate a rapid evacuation of the ship. In practice, he was steering them down passages to nowhere.

They rounded a corner, and Helkara slammed into a solid wall of layered metal plating and overlapping conduits. Leishman ran into him, and Ravosus collided with Hernandez and then awkwardly backed away, into the corridor from which they'd come.

Helkara stumbled backward and squinted in pained confusion at the barrier. "What the . . . ?" Staring in dismay at his tricorder screen, he said, "There should be a passage here."

"We were warned about this," Leishman said, pulling Helkara back the way they'd come, past Hernandez, around the corner. "The ship's reshaping itself, corralling us." As soon as she had turned the corner, she stopped, looked around, and asked with obvious alarm, "Where's Ravosus?"

Hernandez opened her catom senses to the energies that dwelled inside the Borg vessel's vast machinery, all of it guided by a sophisticated inorganic intelligence. She saw the patterns in its alterations of form, and she felt it focusing itself to strike. Behind all of it, she heard the voice of the Queen.

"He's gone," Hernandez said. "Follow me."

She led her two remaining comrades down a narrow pass between two bulkheads. It was barely wide enough for Leishman to pass; her shoulders scraped the sides, and Helkara had to shuffle-step at an angle to follow. Several meters away, at the end of the sliver-thin passage, the sickly green glow of the ship's energy-transfer systems lit the way.

Leishman called out in alarm, "I'm snagged on something!"

Hernandez stopped and looked back. Black tendrils squirmed up through holes in the waffle-grid deck plates and snaked around Leishman's ankles and up her legs. Hurrying back to the trapped engineer, Hernandez saw Helkara reaching for his phaser. "Stop," she said, holding out one hand. "You could hit Mikaela!"

Helkara stared past her, and his jaw went slack as a shadow fell over him. "I think we have bigger problems," he said.

Her catom senses had already told her what was happening, but she needed to see it for herself.

She looked over her shoulder.

The path ahead went black. The passage was closing on them.

*Resistance is futile,* hissed the Queen, invading the sanctum of Hernandez's thoughts.

*We'll see about that,* Hernandez projected in reply.

"Take my hand, Mikaela!" she shouted. "Gruhn—you, too!"

The two officers reached out for Hernandez's outstretched hands. She grasped their wrists.

The walls pressed inward and reached for the trio with eager tentacles. The deck fell away beneath them.

And another took its place.

She had found the royal frequency and made it her own.

For every trap the Borg Queen triggered, Hernandez improvised a defense. Rebuilding the lost deck behind her, she pulled Leishman and Helkara with her as she fought for each step. Prehensile twists of tubing as thick as her arms wrapped around her throat, Leishman's waist, Helkara's legs. Hernandez answered each attack with a focused mental image of its opposite. The physical reality of the Borg ship, for aeons the solitary domain of the Borg Queen, now bowed to her imagination. Tentacles withdrew or broke apart. Vanished decks rebuilt themselves. The lethal pressure of closing bulkheads became the freedom of open space. Then her back struck the final barrier, and at her command, it turned to coal-black dust.

The trio collapsed onto the secured platform, which had been partitioned from the rest of the Borg ship by directional dampening field projectors. Arranged in a large square formation were four transport-pattern enhancers, all blinking in their ready standby mode.

Hernandez dropped Leishman and Helkara into the middle of the enhancers, tapped the combadge on Helkara's chest, and said, "Boarding party to *Aventine.* Two for emergency beam-out!"

*"Acknowledged,"* said a voice made small by being filtered through the combadge. *"Stand by for transport."*

Leishman and Helkara were still staggering weakly to their feet as Hernandez bounded away, clear of the pattern enhancers, and landed with preternatural grace atop a centimeters-thin railing. Perched on it, she felt the same rush of power that she'd had in Axion. Having attuned the catoms in her body to the Borg's unique wavelength, she had usurped their strength.

The images in Hernandez's mind were absolutely clear.

She saw Kedair being smothered inside the vinculum tower, her life fading, her mission to trigger the transphasic mine on the verge of failure. There was no direct route to the transport-shielded tower, no way for anyone to come to Kedair's aid . . . no one except Hernandez.

She coiled and tensed to leap off the railing into the moving parts of the Borg ship, already visualizing herself negotiating its lethal gears with impunity.

The whine of a transporter beam began to fill the air.

"Where are you going?" Leishman asked over the eerie wails and mechanical clankings of the ship's infernal works.

Hernandez looked over her shoulder. "To save Kedair."

Helkara and Leishman became pillars of swirling particles as the transporter beam took hold, and Hernandez leaped off the railing and fell willingly into the belly of the beast.


Lonnoc Kedair knew that she was close to the detonator controls for the transphasic mine, but she couldn't see it. Entombed in the squirming black tangle that surrounded the Borg vinculum, all she saw was darkness, as if she'd drowned in tar.

There was no air to breathe, nowhere to move, no way to get any leverage for a counterattack. Her feet had been pulled from under her, and stinger-tipped tentacles began impaling her from the front and from behind.

Horrendous grinding sensations filled her torso as the Borg ship's mechanical limbs pierced her body in several places at once. Almost as quickly as the wounds were inflicted, her body fought to heal them, but it was a losing battle. Several centimeters thick, the tentacles battered her with blunt force, snapping her bones, rending her skin, and pummeling her last hoarded breaths from her lungs.

She cried out in agony and felt her scream buried in the

smothering, oily lubricant of the Borg machine. The foul liquid seeped into her nostrils and poured into her mouth. Reflex and instinct told her to spit it out, but she had no more breath left to push with.

Needling jabs pricked her skin with sharp, icy twinges. *Assimilation nanoprobes,* she realized. For a moment, she regretted the aggressive combination of antiassimilation implants and injections she and the other boarders had received. Although the Borg's nanoprobes had faced and overcome some of these prophylactic measures in the past, they had never encountered this precise amalgam of genetic and neurological blockades. *Lucky me,* Kedair realized. *Since I can't be assimilated, I get to spend more time being chewed up. Great.*

Tentacles at either end of her torso pulled in opposite directions, and she realized only then that it meant to rip her in half. Then the shearing tension began, and excruciating pain expelled everything from her mind except agony.

No amount of rapid-healing possessed by any Takaran could keep pace with what was being done to her; the Borg ship was breaking down her resilient body by degrees. Kedair's mouth contorted as the pressure intensified, and the dark, metallic-smelling fluid found its way inside her ears. Then, fully submerged inside the horror, she heard it.

Beneath the frantic pounding of her pulse, a malevolent whisper lurked in the suffocating fluid of this dark womb. Its message penetrated her thoughts, and she knew that it couldn't be debated or bargained with. *Strength is irrelevant,* it told her. *You are small, and we are endless. You are one, and we are legion. You will become as we are. You will become part of us.*

Kedair was ready to surrender to the darkness.

Then there was light.

The vile tentacles pulled out of her flesh and retreated into the walls. The crushing press of machines and needles and saws fell away, and some of the contraptions that turned humanoids into drones fell to pieces and scattered across the deck. Kedair's body fell free, and she landed in a twisted, mutilated heap on the floor. Through the cloudy stains in her vision, she saw that her left arm was partially severed and dangled by a tendon just below the elbow. Everything had a flat, distorted quality, and when she tried to blink away the slime, she realized she had only one working eye. The other had been gouged out to make way for some monstrous implant.

She heard footsteps approaching.

Turning her head, she saw Erika Hernandez striding back into the vinculum tower, heading directly toward her. The woman's uniform had become stained and tattered, but Hernandez herself looked none the worse for whatever she'd endured. She asked Kedair, "Can you walk?"

Kedair sputtered through a mouthful of filth, "Both my legs are broken." She jerked her head toward the transphasic mine, which had been securely affixed to the Borg ship's central plexus—essentially, its nerve center. "Set the detonator. We—" She paused to hack up a mouthful of viscous black oil and spat several times to clear her mouth. "We have to frag this ship."

Hernandez walked toward the mine. "Tell me what to do."

"It's already armed," Kedair said, wincing as her back and chest muscles began pulling shattered bones back into place before mending them. "Enter a delay in seconds using the touch-pad, then press 'Enable' to start the countdown."

Standing at the detonator, Hernandez keyed in the data. She hurried back to Kedair. "It's running," she said, kneeling beside Kedair's mangled body.

Kedair asked, "How long?"

"Seventy-five seconds," Hernandez said.

"Are you crazy?" Kedair snapped. "That's not—"

A three-clawed biomechanoid tentacle lunged at Hernandez from behind. Kedair meant to shout or point or give a warning—then, without seeming to notice or care, Hernandez lifted a hand in a dismissive gesture, and the tentacle shredded into scrap metal. Hernandez straightened Kedair's mauled limbs and prompted her, "You were saying?"

It took Kedair a second to recover her wits. "It's not enough time to reach a transport site," she said.

"Yes, it is," Hernandez replied. She slid her hands under Kedair, who at first felt no contact—and then she realized that she was floating a few centimeters above the deck. She was in Hernandez's arms and being lifted gently over the woman's shoulder. "Hang on," added Hernandez. "This part won't be fun."

Kedair's full weight rested on Hernandez's shoulder, and the youthful woman carried Kedair out of the vinculum tower at a brisk pace. The bobbing cadence of Hernandez's stride and the pressure on Kedair's abdomen made the Takaran cough up more of the bitter, toxic black fluid she'd inhaled while snared in the Borg ship's grasp.

Between hacking coughs, she saw more serpentine appendages lash out at Hernandez, who deflected each attack with the slightest motions of her fingers, like a sorcerer cowing demons. Passages and exits closed themselves with piping and components that spread like black metallic ivy, but the hastily risen barriers retreated ahead of Hernandez, who parted them with broad waves of her hand.

They passed through the last portal and reached the platform outside the tower. The bridge back to the ship's outer superstructure had been retracted. The space above them, which only minutes earlier had been empty, now was alive with moving metal and blue-black clouds of some primordial matter that flashed with static electricity.

"Are you afraid of heights?" Hernandez asked.

"No," Kedair said.

"Good."

She stretched one hand toward the distant top of the ship's interior, and then they were aloft, rising away from the platform and accelerating toward the shadowy maelstrom overhead.

Kedair, still draped over Hernandez's shoulder, watched the vinculum tower shrink beneath them. "How in the name of Yaltakh are you doing this?"

"Easy," Hernandez said. "I imagine I've already done it."

They arrowed through the center of the ship's brewing thunderhead, and an eye of calm swirled around them as they passed. Then they were near the top deck of the ship, and a dampener-secured platform equipped with transporter-pattern enhancers hove into view.

"Ten seconds," Kedair said. "No pressure."

Hernandez alighted on the platform, leaned forward, and shrugged Kedair off her shoulder. Catching the wounded woman with one arm, she tapped her combadge with her free hand. "Hernandez to *Aventine*! Two to beam up!"

"*Energizing,*" replied a transporter chief over the comm.

Kedair clasped Hernandez's arm. "In case we don't make it," she said, "nice try."

The paralyzing embrace of the transporter's annular confinement beam found them, and the tenebrous steelscape of the Borg ship began to fade behind a glittering veil—then a flash turned everything white.

The Borg scout ship vanished from the *Aventine*'s main viewer in a fiery blue detonation.

Dax paced in quick steps behind Lieutenant Kandel, manic with anxiety. "Tell me we got them," she said, pestering the tactical officer for the third time in fifteen seconds.

From the other side of the console, Bowers tossed a sidelong frown in Dax's direction. "And you wonder why I don't let you go on away missions."

Pressing herself against the tactical panel beside Kandel, Dax said to Kandel, "Report, Lieutenant."

The Deltan woman finished reviewing the data on her screen in a calm, unhurried manner, looked up at Dax, and said, "Transporter Room Two confirms Captain Hernandez and Lieutenant Kedair are aboard. The lieutenant is being rushed to sickbay."

"Where's Captain Hernandez now?"

Kandel nodded at her companel. "In the transporter room."

"Patch me through to her," Dax said. She waited for Kandel to confirm that she had opened a channel, and then she said, "Captain Hernandez, this is Captain Dax. Are you all right?"

*"I'm fine, but I need to meet with you, alone, right now."*

Bowers glanced at Dax, as if she needed reminding of the damage her ship had just taken and the dire need for repairs and a new plan. "Can this wait an hour, Captain? We have a lot—"

*"Right. Now. In my quarters."*

The vehemence of Hernandez's demand left Dax taken aback. She twitched her eyebrows at Bowers, who shrugged in return.

"All right, then," Dax said. "I'm on my way."

The door to the VIP guest quarters opened at Dax's approach, and she entered unannounced. A few paces into the compartment, she saw Hernandez leaning against the bulkhead.

Hernandez regarded Dax with a dour frown. "You're the second captain to barge into my quarters without knocking today," she said. "Doesn't Starfleet teach courtesy anymore?"

"My ship, my rules," Dax said. "Besides, you made it pretty

clear—on an open channel—that you were in a hurry to see me."
Spreading her arms in a sarcastic pantomime of openness, she
added, "Well, here I am. Talk." She folded her arms across her
chest while she waited for the other woman's reply.

As she meandered toward Dax, Hernandez wore a troubled
look. "Bear with me, Captain," she said, her voice quieter than
it had been. Her shredded uniform hung loosely on her slender
frame. "What I need to tell you is vital, but it's hard for me to
come at a problem straight. After eight hundred years with the
Caeliar, keeping secrets becomes a virtue."

"I understand," Dax said. Hernandez stopped a mere arm's
length in front of her. Looking more closely at her, Dax saw that
despite the youthful appearance of her face and physique, Hernandez's eyes possessed an ancient light. It was a curious trait
Dax had seen in joined Trills with very old symbionts.

Rubbing her palms slowly against each other, Hernandez said,
"I read everything in your files about the Borg before I went to that
ship. I thought I was ready for whatever I'd find. I was wrong."

"If you're blaming yourself over what happened during the
counterattack, don't," Dax said. "As far as I'm concerned, you
deserve a medal for saving three of my officers—especially going
back for Kedair like you did."

Hernandez averted her eyes and stepped away from Dax,
toward the windows that looked out on the deceptively placid
starfield. "I'm not talking about what the Borg do," she said. "I'm
talking about what they *are*. I wasn't ready to believe it." Her
voice fell to a hush, and Dax inched closer behind her to listen
as she continued. "I was expecting a group mind, but that's not
really what the Borg is. It's *one* mind, one tyrant consciousness
enslaving all the others. What it does to individuals is beyond
cruel—it's sadistic, barbaric. And it's so . . . empty. It's a hunger
void of form, a frozen pit that can never be filled, no matter how
much it eats—and the larger it gets, the more it wants."

She looked at Dax. "It was like a melody I'd heard before, but
now it was changed—darker, more dissonant. Instead of uniting
the minds, the way a conductor guides the musicians in a symphony, it buries them, makes them into mute spectators, while it
uses their bodies as tools. It's like a prison of lost souls, with trillions of beings chained to the will of something that doesn't even
know what the hell it wants."

"Sounds like a bad Joining," Dax said. Noting Hernandez's uncomprehending head shake, she added, "Sometimes, when a Trill symbiont is incompatible with its new host, it creates a persona so terrible that the only proper response is forced separation."

"That about sums it up," Hernandez said. Sorrow darkened her expression. "The worst part is how familiar it felt."

Suspicion percolated in Dax's gut. "Familiar?"

Stepping away, perhaps hoping to insulate herself from Dax with a bit of distance, Hernandez said, "I first noticed it a few hours ago, after the boarding teams contacted us. When we lowered the dampening field, I was able to sense one of the dying drones on the Borg ship in the same way that I used to be able to sense the Caeliar. And when I was inside the Borg ship and it regained full power, it was like I was back in Axion."

Dax kept a wary eye on Hernandez. "Is that all?"

"It's just the beginning," Hernandez said, stopping at her quarters' wall-mounted companel. She activated the screen with a gentle tap. It was crowded with multiple side-by-side windows of information—starmaps, ships' logs, and more.

"Records from *Voyager* and the *Enterprise*-D both suggest the origin of the Borg is somewhere deep in the Delta Quadrant," Hernandez said. Swapping one starmap for another, she continued, "When the Caeliar homeworld was destroyed, the event created a number of passages through subspace—the tunnels you and your people were trying to shut down. Those were the stable ones."

A diagram of a subspace passage took on a distorted twist. Hernandez explained, "Some of the tunnels cut through time as well as space; that made them unstable, and they collapsed shortly after the Erigol cataclysm, from which only three Caeliar city-ships escaped." She drew bright, straight-line paths across the starmap with her fingertip. "One of those passages tossed the city of Axion deep into the Beta Quadrant, about eight hundred and sixty-odd years ago. A second one threw the city of Kintana into another galaxy at the dawn of time."

"And the third city . . . ?"

"Mantilis," Hernandez said, inscribing another line across the map, from the Azure Nebula to the Delta Quadrant. "Several members of my landing party were trapped in that city when it vanished. Until now, the Caeliar believed that Mantilis was lost or destroyed in some distant past. Now, based on my analysis of Borg nanoprobes and my own experiences with the Collective, I have a new theory. Through some kind of botched version of the process that made me what I am . . . they became the Borg."

Dax approached the companel to study the data up close. She imagined the horrified reaction it would provoke in Captains Riker and Picard—and likely in any human who was made aware of it. The origin of the Borg was a tragic confluence of long-past human actions and errors. "Are you sure about this?"

"Positive," Hernandez said.

Shaking her head as a frown creased her brow, Dax said, "According to Captain Riker, we wouldn't stand a chance against the Caeliar, so why are you acting like this is good news?"

"Because now I know which of the Borg's weaknesses we can exploit," Hernandez said. "And if Caeliar technology made the Borg, maybe it can *un*-make them, too."

# 22

Riker was waiting for the punch line. Still grappling with disbelief, he said, "The Caeliar created the Borg?"

"I don't think it was intentional," Hernandez said. She stood, attired in a new Starfleet duty uniform, in front of the companel in the *Enterprise*'s observation lounge and faced Riker, Dax, and Picard. Nodding at the side-by-side images displayed on the screen behind her, she said, "The similarities between Borg nanoprobes and Caeliar catoms are too profound to be coincidence. But they're not obvious, because their exterior configurations are completely different, and inside, in their cores, the nanoprobes have been badly corrupted."

Picard sat at the head of the curved table on Riker's left, his countenance stern as he listened to Hernandez. "Your evidence is compelling, Captain," he said. "But how does this knowledge help us or the Federation in the time we have left?"

Across the table from Riker, Dax folded her hands on the table in front of her and said, "We have a plan."

"You had a plan several hours ago," Picard replied. "It nearly cost Captain Hernandez her life."

Dax bristled. "It also saved five planets and cut the Borg invasion force in half."

"But if the Borg had assimilated her Caeliar technology—"

Riker interrupted, "They didn't, and there's no point arguing about something that *didn't* go wrong. We need to plan our next move, not dissect our last one." Realizing that he had only added to Dax's smug air, he looked at her and continued, "But the limited success of one reckless plan doesn't mean we should embrace another." With the room's tensions balanced, he added, "That said, we should at least hear what they have in mind."

"Very well," Picard said. He looked at Dax and waited.

Dax volleyed the expectant look toward Hernandez and said, "It was your idea."

"It's simple," Hernandez said to Picard and Riker. "We need to prevent the Borg from attacking any more planets and put them in a position where we can deal with all of them at once. I'm proposing that we end their invasion by luring them all back here to us, in deep space."

Picard telegraphed his skepticism with one arched eyebrow. "And how, precisely, do you propose that we do so?"

Dax interjected, "By tempting them with the one kind of bait they can't resist: the Omega Molecule."

Riker asked, "How are we supposed to create one without any boronite? Replicators can't make it, and the nearest source is over two hundred light-years away."

Hernandez said, "We're not going to make Omega Molecules, we're going to bring them to us. More precisely, we're going to make the Caeliar bring them to us, by persuading them to move their city-ship here from New Erigol." She reached over to the companel and keyed in some new commands. An image of an Omega Molecule appeared on the screen. "After I came back from the Borg ship, I remembered reading in your files that the Borg worship 'Particle 010' as a symbol of perfection. I knew there was something familiar about it, so I bypassed your security protocols and accessed your data on the molecule. When I did, I knew where I'd seen it before, and it all made sense.

"The Caeliar power their city with an Omega Molecule generator," Hernandez continued. "All the energy they harness from the shells around their planet and its star is used to mask the OMG's emissions. If I can get them to bring Axion here, free of that shielding, it'll be like a beacon for the Borg. They won't be able to resist it."

Grim-faced, Picard replied, "And once the Borg armada converges on us . . . what then?"

"We let the Caeliar deal with them," Hernandez said.

Picard got up from the table and paced away, visibly agitated. "Your last plan was reckless," he said to Dax. "This one is insane. Have you considered the risks? Never mind the damage the Borg could do if they assimilate Caeliar catoms. What if they gain control of an Omega Molecule generator? They'd have unlimited power to wreak havoc throughout the galaxy—and beyond. And if they were to lose control of the generator, an Omega Molecule explosion of that magnitude would destroy subspace for millions of light-years in every direction. Warp flight as we know it would cease to exist in this galaxy and several others."

Dax replied, "Yes, it's dangerous. We know that. But it's not like we have any better options. It's the best chance we have of stopping the Borg while there's still something left of the Federation to save."

"There are other options," Picard said. "We haven't tried using thalaron weapons against the Borg, and there's every reason to think thalaron radiation will affect the drones the same way it affects all other organic matter. If Commander La Forge can rig our deflector to emit a large enough thalaron pulse, we could wipe out the entire Borg armada."

Riker shot a dubious look at his former captain. "That's what Starfleet said about the transphasic torpedo, and the Borg have already adapted to that. Hell, for all we know, the Borg already have a defense against thalaron radiation."

"Perhaps," Picard said. "But we have to try, and it might buy us the time we need to organize and fight back."

"It's too late for that," Hernandez retorted. "We're long past settling for half-measures and stopgaps. We need to *end* the war with the Borg, Captain—and we need to end it now."

Leaning forward, Riker said, "I'm not convinced thalaron weapons are the best choice. Once that technology's unleashed, it'll be impossible to contain ever again." Looking at Dax and Hernandez, he continued, "But I also think we're forgetting one important fact about the Caeliar. First and foremost, they're isolationists, and just as important, they're pacifists. Not only will they not use force against the Borg, they might prevent us from defending ourselves."

Hernandez shook her head. "No, you're misreading them. They may be pacifists, but they're not suicidal. They won't let the Borg assimilate them or hijack their technology."

"What makes you so certain they could stop them?" asked Picard, his voice rich with cynicism. "I read the report you gave to Captain Riker. A squad of MACOs from your ship got the better of the Caeliar in 2168 and destroyed one of their cities. I guarantee you, the Borg will pose a far deadlier threat than your ship's military company."

"The MACOs took the Caeliar by surprise," Hernandez said, a deep bitterness infusing her words. "The Borg won't."

With sharp suspicion, Picard said, "What if they sympathize with the Borg?"

"I think that's unlikely," Hernandez said.

"But not impossible," Picard countered. "You said yourself that Caeliar technology was the likely foundation of the Borg's nanoprobes. What if the Caeliar see the Borg as a kindred race?"

"Actually," Dax said, "we're counting on it."

Riker and Picard exchanged befuddled stares. Then Riker said to Dax, "Come again?"

"No offense, Captains," Dax said, "but we—and Starfleet—have been pursuing the wrong strategy against the Borg. We've tried to match strength with strength, violence with violence. We keep getting suckered into battles of attrition we can't win."

Hernandez added, "The key to securing the Caeliar's help is to change our mission. Instead of destroying the Collective, we should liberate it. The Borg don't need to be wiped out, they need to be saved. The Caeliar can help us do that."

"Are you mad?" Picard said. "The Borg are laying waste to worlds, and we need to *save* them?"

"I'm disappointed," Hernandez said. "You, of all people, should know this. You were assimilated and came back; you know from experience what it's like to be smothered in that nightmare. Now imagine trillions of beings like yourself, all trapped in that hell. They're *slaves,* Jean-Luc, and we might have the power to release them."

Dax added, "I think that as Starfleet officers—as *sentient beings*—we owe it to them, and to ourselves, to at least try."

Picard turned away and stared out a window at the stars. "As you pointed out so eloquently, Captain Dax, we hold the same rank. I can't compel you not to pursue this course of action." He looked over his shoulder at her and Hernandez. "You ignored my advice before, and I expect you'll do so again. So be it."

"If only it were that simple," Dax said. "Unfortunately, this time, I actually need your consent."

Picard turned back to face the other captains. "Why?"

"Because we need your help," Dax said. "The *Aventine*'s subspace transmitter got fried when the Borg hit us with our shields down, and *Titan*'s transmitter is too badly damaged to be repaired in time." She traded dismayed looks with Hernandez and added, "Our only hope of contacting the Caeliar is to reconfigure the *Enterprise*'s transmitter to create a subspace microtunnel, through which Erika can link with their gestalt."

Frowning, Picard returned to the table and rested his hands on the top of his chair. "So . . . if I refuse, this plan cannot proceed?" Dax and Hernandez nodded. "Then consider it vetoed."

The two women looked dejected, and Riker knew how they felt. He was certain something was wrong with Picard. In as diplomatic a tone as he could muster, he said "Captain Dax, Captain Hernandez, would you give us the room, please?"

Dax got up from her chair as Hernandez switched the companel screen back to its standby mode. The two women left the observation lounge. After the door hushed closed behind them, Riker reclined his chair a bit and let the silence weigh on himself and Picard, to see if his old friend and former commander had any desire to elaborate.

Finally, Picard said, "I take it you disagree with my decision, Will."

"Frankly, yes," Riker said.

Picard pulled back his chair and settled into it. "We can't take that kind of risk with the Borg," he said. "This is bigger than the Federation. If we give the Borg a chance to acquire the kind of technology the Caeliar possess, we might condemn the entire galaxy to suffer our fate—and maybe others, as well."

"If we don't stop the Borg now, that's all pretty much guaranteed," Riker said. "Besides, you're talking like the Federation's already gone. If the Caeliar can help unmake the Borg, we can end this without more bloodshed *and* save the Federation. Isn't that what we ought to be aiming for?"

Hatred hardened Picard's frown. "I'm not sure the Borg deserve such mercy," he said.

"Maybe not," Riker said. "But what about the individuals trapped inside the Collective? Do they deserve it?"

Swiveling his chair away from Riker, Picard mumbled, "Perhaps. I don't know."

"Captain Hernandez seems to think they do. And given a choice, I'd rather try to save lives than destroy them."

"It's not so simple a calculus," Picard said. "How can I commit myself to aiding the enemy when my people are poised on the brink of destruction?" He turned and looked Riker in the eye. "Maybe *you* can explain that to me."

An unspoken accusation seemed to lurk in Picard's words, and it struck an uneasy chord in Riker. "What's really bothering you, Jean-Luc?"

"Aside from Borg invasion fleets marauding through Federation space?"

Riker replied, "Yes, besides that. You sounded as if you were blaming me for something. More than that, you don't sound like yourself—not like the man I served with for fifteen years. Where's *that* Jean-Luc Picard?"

"*Et tu?*" Picard breathed a heavy, defeated sigh. "First Beverly, now you. Who was this other man you all claim to have known? I thought it was me, but I keep hearing otherwise."

"The man I know isn't afraid to risk taking the high road," Riker said. "He wouldn't let fear make him choose certain defeat instead of a shot at victory, just because success might mean mercy for an enemy that had hurt him."

"Is that what you think this is about? A vendetta? Or some simple phobia? I wonder, then, whether you ever knew me at all."

"You keep pushing me away," Riker said. "Did I do something to offend you? Was it something I said?"

Picard shook his head. "Of course not."

"But there is something that's bothering you, isn't there?"

"It's not my place to interfere," Picard said.

"It's not interference if your advice is invited."

Wound up with tension, Picard turned his chair away from Riker, stood, and paced along the bulkhead opposite the windows. He folded his hands together in front of him as he walked the length of the observation lounge, turned back, and retraced his steps. He stopped in front of the companel. "I don't really have advice, Will. Just confusion."

"About what?"

"How could you abandon Deanna?" Picard fixed Riker with a forlorn stare. "You left her behind, Will, and your away team."

"I did what I had to do," Riker said, pushing back against the rising tide of his guilt.

Picard moved in slow steps toward the windows. "Had I been in your place," he said pensively, "I'm not sure I could have chosen duty over Beverly so easily."

"I never said it was easy," Riker replied. "But I've seen you make decisions like that before. With Nella Daren, for one."

Holding up one hand, Picard replied, "That was different. For one thing, I wasn't married to Nella." He folded his arms. "For another, Nella wasn't pregnant. Beverly is."

A surge of grief and anger clenched Riker's jaw. All the feelings he had suppressed since Deanna left *Titan* rushed back in force, crowding his thoughts. He pressed his fist to his mouth as he fought to master his bitter, desperate emotions.

Picard took note of Riker's reaction and froze, his face a mask of embarrassment and sympathy. "What have I said, Will?"

The last thing Riker had wanted was to make this conversation about him. He inhaled sharply and set his still-clenched fist on the tabletop. "Deanna and I . . . ," he began, before his voice trailed off, swallowed up in his sorrow. He composed himself and continued in a clipped, strained voice. "We—we've been trying to start a family. It was hard. Hormone injections. Fertility treatments. Gene therapy." Finding a dispassionate frame of mind from which to continue was difficult. "We thought we'd done it," he said. "About half a year ago. But it . . . Deanna . . . we had a miscarriage."

"*Mon dieu,*" Picard whispered, and he seemed to deflate as he let go of a deep breath. He looked stricken by the news as he settled back into his chair. "I'm so sorry, Will."

"It's been a wedge, forcing us apart," Riker confessed. "After she recovered, we tried again. We thought this time it would all be okay, but it wasn't. The new embryo was deformed, and it'll miscarry, too—it's only a matter of time. But Deanna won't terminate the pregnancy, even though this one could kill her. And I think it's my fault."

"How is *any* of that your fault?" asked Picard.

"I was supposed to be the voice of reason," Riker said. "After the first miscarriage, I should have said enough and put an end to the whole thing. But the empathic bond between me and Deanna makes it hard to say no to her. I don't even remember anymore which one of us wanted a family. All I know is that I'm supposed to protect her." He slammed his fist on the table. "And when she needed me most, I left her behind! Alone, on the other side of the goddamn galaxy!" He finally unclenched his hand, but only so he could use it to cover his closed eyes.

Sotto voce, Picard asked, "Have you tried talking with anyone about this?"

"Yeah," Riker said. "I talked to Chris. What a mistake."

"Not an easy subject for a captain to discuss with a member of his crew," Picard said, acknowledging Riker's dilemma. "Not even with a trusted first officer."

Lowering his hand, Riker opened his eyes and nodded at Picard. "Exactly," he said. "Until now, I didn't really get how vital it is to keep some things from my crew—how valuable personal privacy is."

"I understand," Picard said. "Believe me."

"So, now you know what's eating me alive," Riker said. "Are you ready to tell me what's bothering *you*?"

Picard grimaced and drummed his fingertips on the table for a few seconds. "Our problems are similar but not the same," he said. "What they have in common . . . is fatherhood." He turned himself a few degrees closer to facing Riker and spoke in a measured hush. "For a long time, I told myself that I didn't want a family, that I didn't need one. Certainly, there were fleeting moments, days when I'd wonder, 'What if . . . ?' But I never took them seriously. Not until Robert and René died."

Riker recalled the day when Picard had received the news that his brother and nephew had perished in a fire on Earth. He saw in his friend's eyes that the pain of that tragedy still lingered in Picard's psyche, an open emotional wound.

"I even told myself I didn't need love," Picard continued. "Part of me actually believed it. Then I met Anij . . ." Mentioning the Bak'u woman's name brought a wistful, fleeting smile to Picard's face. "She showed me what I had given up and how much I really needed it. But I was still afraid. I should have just reached out to Beverly right then and made up for lost time, but

I hesitated—and I almost lost her. That's what it took for me to see what she really meant to me." Powerful emotions threatened to crack Picard's stoic façade, and Riker grasped how traumatic this discussion had to be for him. Picard's eyes gleamed with the threat of tears. "So I let her into my life. And it's been a wonder and a joy, Will. I curse myself daily for not having invited her in sooner. But when she suggested we have a child together, I panicked. The idea terrified me."

With gentle curiosity, Riker asked, "Why?"

"I concocted so many arbitrary reasons that you'd laugh if I told you half of them," Picard said. "But the truth is, I was afraid it would be like tempting fate." A haunted expression settled on him like a mask. "After all these years and excuses, for me to start a family . . . it seemed like a portent of doom. And no sooner did Beverly and I conceive our son than the Borg began their invasion." He shook his head and permitted himself a bitter chuckle. "I feel like Coleridge's Ancient Mariner, after he shot the albatross. I indulged myself with one selfish act, and in the process, I've condemned countless others to suffer and die for my mistake."

Shaking his head in denial, Riker replied, "You can't be serious. You don't really believe the Borg invaded because you and Beverly conceived a child?"

"No, of course not," Picard said, his tone sharp with frustration. "It's not about logic, or reason, or causality. It's about creating new life and then being afraid you'll have to watch it die." He lifted his hands and covered his face for several seconds while he slowed and deepened his breathing. Then he lowered his hands and said, "It took me so long to let something real into my life, and now all I can think about is the Borg taking it away. Even if we stop this invasion, what then? What of the next one, Will? Must my family, must *my son,* live in the shadow of this menace every day of his life?" The anger left Picard's voice; in its place was nothing but quiet desperation. "When will it end?"

"It will end when we end it." Riker leaned forward and stared at Picard until his old friend looked back at him. "I've seen what the Caeliar can do, Jean-Luc, and I think Hernandez is right. If anyone can stand up to the Borg, they can. I also agree with Dax. If we can end this war *and* save the people assimilated by the Collective, we have a duty as Starfleet officers to try."

Picard frowned. "And if Dax and Hernandez are wrong, we'll unleash the greatest horror the galaxy has ever seen."

"So, we hasten the inevitable," Riker said, fed up with Picard's impenetrable pessimism. "The Borg are less than two hours from Earth. Could our plan backfire? Yes, but we can't let that paralyze us. It's time for a leap of faith."

The older man shook his head dismissively and said, "You're talking about hope."

"Yes, I am."

"We'll need more than hope to fight the Borg."

"True," Riker said. "But without it, we might as well just give up." He got up and walked to the door, which hissed open ahead of him. Standing in the doorway, he looked back at Picard. "We can fight for hope, or we can give in to despair. The choice is yours, Jean-Luc. Let me know what you decide."

# 23

Deanna Troi felt as light as air and more fully alive than she had in months. She stood on the center of the silver disk, behind Inyx, who guided it through the breathtaking vertical spaces between Axion's grandiose platinum towers. A firm breeze whipped her hair behind her. Tossing her head back and basking in the soothing warmth of New Erigol's artificial sun, it was all she could do to contain herself and not laugh out loud.

The disk neared the tower where the away team had been housed. As she and Inyx began their gentle descent toward the penthouse's open terrace, she saw someone approaching from the main room. A familiar psionic presence brushed against her mind, and she knew with her empathic senses before she saw with her eyes that it was Tuvok. He looked up and saw her, and then he called back inside the suite to summon the others.

By the time she and Inyx touched down on the terrace, the entire away team had gathered to meet her. Vale, Keru, and Tuvok were at the front of the group, and Ree was close behind them. Dennisar and Sortollo flanked the doctor, and Torvig, as usual, lingered at the rear of the group, curious but also cautious.

"Hello, everyone," Troi said with a beaming smile.

Keru stepped forward and bear-hugged her. "To hell with protocol," he said. "I'm so glad you're all right."

It was as if he'd opened a floodgate. Within moments, Troi found herself in the center of a group embrace with the broadshouldered Trill, Vale, and the two security guards. Torvig kept his distance, however, and Tuvok remained aloof, as usual.

Ree sidled over to Inyx. "What is her current condition?"

"She is in perfect health, Doctor," Inyx said.

The Pahkwa-thanh physician replied, "I'd be grateful if you could show me her internal scans and serum profile."

Inyx looked at Troi, who was extricating herself from her friends' arms. She nodded to the Caeliar. "It's okay."

"Very well," Inyx said. He gestured with an outstretched arm toward the far end of the terrace. "Doctor, if you'll join me over here, I'll brief you in full." The scientist and the surgeon stepped away to confer.

"How long was I gone?" Troi asked.

Vale shrugged. "About thirteen hours."

Tuvok added, "And twenty-one minutes."

"Nice to know I was missed," Troi said. "What have you been doing since I left?"

"Keru and Torvig went sightseeing," Vale said. "The good doctor's been working on his tan, Dennisar and Sortollo played about three hundred games of checkers, and I've been catching up on my reading."

"Anything good?"

"Believe it or not, a former 'guest' of the Caeliar wrote a bunch of new *Captain Proton* novels," Vale said. She chortled softly. "I feel like I found a latinum mine."

"I'll bet," Troi said. She looked up as Inyx and Ree returned to the group. "Everything all right, Doctor?"

Ree tasted the air with a flick of his tongue and said, "To my amazement, everything appears to be perfect."

Vale discreetly rested her hand on Troi's shoulder and gave it a congratulatory squeeze. "Finally, some good news."

Inyx made a rattling rasp of a sound and commanded the team's attention. "I apologize in advance for ruining your jubilant mood," he said, "but now that Deanna's medical crisis is resolved, I think it might be time to share news of a less celebratory nature."

Keru asked, "About what?"

"About your home, the Federation," Inyx said. He conjured an oval surface of liquid metal that immediately came alive with sharp, clear images of distant worlds being assaulted by Borg cubes. "It appears that an enemy is waging a successful attack on your nation. Many of your worlds have been destroyed, including some known as Regulus, Lorillia, and Deneva."

At the mention of Deneva, Troi felt a pang of psionic alarm from Tuvok. It was acute enough to pierce the veil of the group's shared anxiety as they watched the images of destruction unfold on the hovering screen before them. The scene shifted to a starship graveyard in a blue-gas nebula. Hundreds of smashed, blackened vessels tumbled erratically on the screen.

"I thought you should know," Inyx continued, "that this information was what compelled your captain to take his ship home and leave you in our custody. In the past, the Quorum has restricted our guests' access to this kind of information. However, I found that Erika placed a great deal of importance on staying informed about events affecting her home, and I thought you might share her interest in such matters."

Vale stepped forward and interposed herself between the away team and the oval screen. "All right, that's enough. Everyone, fall out, find something else to do. Commander Troi and I will brief you all later." The others looked at her and were reluctant to leave. "That's an order. *Dismissed*."

Torvig turned and gamboled off at a quick step, while Dennisar and Sortollo glowered and slunk away from the terrace. Ree, Keru, and Tuvok made grudging exits, leaving Vale and Troi alone with Inyx. Vale sighed and said to him, "It's not that I don't appreciate the gesture, but that kind of news can be bad for morale. It would be better if the counselor and I could discuss it with you and ascertain what the facts are before we decide what to share with the rest of the team."

"As you wish," Inyx said. "I didn't mean to upset you." He looked at the images flashing across the screen. "I should have realized how distressing this would be."

Troi noted a melancholy undertone in his voice. "Are you also concerned by this news?"

"Yes, a great deal," he said.

Touching Inyx's arm in what she hoped would be construed

as a gesture of compassion, Troi said, "You're worried about Captain Hernandez."

"I am. That far from Axion, Erika's vulnerable." Inyx's voice resonated with sadness. "She could be harmed . . . or killed." He looked away from the screen, at Troi and Vale. "It would be such a waste. Erika is the most vital, vibrant being I've met in dozens of millennia."

A knowing look passed between Vale and Troi, and the first officer sounded surprised as she asked, "Inyx, are you *in love* with Captain Hernandez?"

The looming alien bowed at the waist and half turned away, as if to conceal his ever-dour visage. "I don't know if our species experience love the same way," he said. "All I can say is that for me, she made eternity worth contemplating."

Vale threw a wry look at Troi and said, "That's about as good a definition of love as I've ever heard. Counselor?"

"Yes," Troi said. "I'd have to agree."

Nanietta Bacco's office was dark except for the pale light of a waning gibbous moon and the amber glow of Paris at midnight.

Bacco stood at the far western end of the spacious, crescent-shaped room and leaned her shoulder into the nook between the wall and the floor-to-ceiling window.

The cityscape looked serene, partly because the night sky was unusually empty of air traffic. Most of the people who had some other place to go were there already.

The last report from Secretary of Transportation Iliop had indicated that nearly six hundred million people had fled Earth in the past six days. Some of the planet's smaller cities reportedly had taken on the airs of ghost towns. Paris was no exception, and neither were London, New York, Tokyo, and Mumbai.

On Bacco's order, most of the Federation Council had been ferried offworld, along with the majority of her cabinet, as part of the official continuity-of-government plan. Scattered to dozens of remote sites throughout—and, in a few cases, just beyond—Federation territory, dozens of elected and appointed officials awaited the final signal from Earth that would begin the process of presidential and legislative succession.

The interoffice comm on her desk buzzed. Bacco sighed,

plodded back to the desk, and opened the channel with a poke of her index finger. "What is it, Sivak?"

*"Admiral Akaar and Ms. Piñiero are here, Madam President,"* replied her elderly Vulcan executive assistant. *"They insist on presenting your midnight briefing."*

"Fine," Bacco said. "It might be the last one they ever make, so we might as well get it over with. Show them in."

She jabbed at the switch and closed the comm. A moment later, the east door of her office slid open. Agent Wexler stepped in ahead of Fleet Admiral Akaar and Esperanza Piñiero, and the door closed behind them.

"Computer," Bacco said. "Lights, one-third." The recessed light fixtures in the room slowly brightened to a lower-than-normal level, allowing her to see her guests with a bit more clarity and without having to squint like a blind woman.

As soon as her eyes adjusted, she got a good look at Akaar and couldn't suppress a resentful frown. She gestured at his crisp, perfect-looking uniform and salon-perfect mane of pale gray hair. "How do you do it?"

"Madam President?"

"You've been awake the past two days, just like the rest of us," Bacco said. She nodded at Piñiero. "But Esperanza and I look like we've been chasing a fart through a bag of nails, and you look like you just stepped out of a replicator. What gives?"

Akaar shrugged. "Good genes?"

"You're not endearing yourself to me, Leonard."

"My apologies, Madam President."

Circling behind her desk, Bacco replied, "Bring me some good news, and maybe we'll call it even."

"We have some," he said, "but not much. Thirty-six minutes ago, the Imperial Romulan warbird *Verithrax* sacrificed itself to halt the Borg attack on Ardana. Casualties on the surface are still disastrously high, but if not for the heroism of the *Verithrax*'s crew, our losses there would have been total."

"Which Romulan fleet was the *Verithrax* loyal to?"

"Donatra's," Piñiero said.

Bacco nodded, as if it were all perfectly normal, but she knew that it was nothing shy of extraordinary. If the Federation and the Imperial Romulan State both survived this war with the Borg, there would be no denying that Donatra and those loyal to her had committed fully to an alliance, in both word and deed. "Has there been any reaction from the Romulan Star Empire?"

"No," Piñiero said. "Praetor Tal'Aura probably hasn't heard the news yet. For that matter, Donatra might not even know."

"Then make sure we're the ones who tell her," Bacco said. "Send an official expression of gratitude on behalf of myself and the Federation to Empress Donatra."

Piñiero nodded and made a note on a small data padd she kept handy in her jacket pocket.

Looking back at Akaar, Bacco asked, "Anything else?"

He blinked once, slowly, and cocked his head at a slight angle. "We have received a credible if not entirely corroborated report that the planet Troyius was spared from a Borg attack, thanks to an intervention by the Corps of Engineers."

Bacco's eyes widened; her curiosity was piqued. "How?"

"According to preliminary reports," Akaar said, "the *U.S.S. da Vinci* made the planet disappear."

"Forgive me for repeating myself," Bacco said. "*How?*"

A perplexed glance was volleyed between Akaar and Piñiero, and then Bacco's chief of staff replied, "No one knows, ma'am. But as soon as Captain Gomez and her crew bring the planet back, we'll be sure to ask her."

"Unfortunately, that is the end of the good news, Madam President," Akaar said. "A Borg attack fleet is eighty-four minutes from Earth, and our perimeter defense groups have been unable to slow its approach. As we feared earlier, the Borg have completely adapted to the transphasic torpedo. And whatever had them shooting at one another has stopped."

An imaginary but still unbearable weight pressed down on Bacco's shoulders, and she sank into her chair. "Admiral, is there any reasonable possibility that Starfleet can halt the incoming Borg fleet?"

The question left Akaar's face reddened with shame. "No."

"Then order all remaining vessels in Sector 001 to break off and disperse," Bacco said. "Stop wasting ships and lives. Redeploy your forces to protect refugees and outlying systems."

Akaar clenched his jaw, and Bacco suspected the hulking flag officer was struggling not to protest a direct order. A few seconds passed. He relaxed with a deep breath, and then he answered, "Yes, Madam President."

Bacco sighed. "Esperanza, do the people of Earth, Luna, and Mars know what's happening right now?"

"Yes, ma'am," Piñiero said.

Propping her elbows on the desk and steepling her fingers, Bacco asked, "How are they coping with it? Panic? Riots?"

A soft huff of amusement brought a bittersweet smile to Piñiero's face. "Nope, not a one. There are silent, candlelight vigils on the Champs-Élysées, in Aldrin Park on Luna, and at the Settlers' Monument in Cydonia on Mars. Some people are gathering in the wilderness parks or attending impromptu concerts." Her voice broke, and she looked hastily at the floor. "Families are having reunions," she continued, her voice unsteadied by grief and fear. "Outgoing data traffic is spiking as people send farewell messages to friends and family offworld." She sniffled loudly, and then she looked up and wiped the side of her hand under her nose. Her eyes shone with tears. "I guess the world is ending with a bang *and* a whimper."

Shaking her head, Bacco said, "Not a whimper, Esperanza, with dignity."

Feeling her own emotions rising, Bacco swiveled her chair around to look out upon Paris. She stared through her ghostly reflection into the night. An entire world stretched out before her, facing its imminent annihilation and displaying more grace under pressure than she could ever have imagined possible.

In that moment, she was as proud as she had ever been to call herself a citizen of the Federation.

Akaar broke the silence. "I should excuse myself and relay your orders to Starfleet Command, Madam President."

"Of course, Admiral," said Bacco. "Thank you."

He turned on his heel and made a quick exit. Agent Wexler, lurking in the shadows as always, opened the door ahead of Akaar and closed it behind him. Then the compact protection specialist faded back into the dim spaces along the periphery of the room.

Piñiero palmed her tear-stained eyes dry and stiffened her posture. "We still have eighty minutes before the Borg arrive, ma'am," she said. "Would you like to make a final address to Earth or the Federation?"

Bacco admired the nightscape outside her office window and found at last a place of serenity within herself. "No," she said. "Why ruin a perfectly good apocalypse?"

# 24

Picard stood in the open doorway of his ready room, with his back to the bridge. The interior of his office had been gutted to the bare bulkheads and deck plates. All traces of the fire had been meticulously scoured away, leaving the antiseptic shell of the compartment harshly lit by new, uncovered lighting fixtures. It was utterly devoid of any trace of the mementos he'd stored there before the blaze. New carpeting and furniture were scheduled to be installed in a day's time, after the ship's engineers and technicians had attended to mission-critical repairs elsewhere throughout the *Enterprise*.

His thoughts remained fixated on Captain Hernandez's revelation of the Borg's true origin. Learning of humanity's complicity in the Collective's creation only made it harder for him to accept the staggering devastation the Borg had wrought throughout the galaxy.

He remembered succumbing to the hive mind when it had made him into Locutus. His secret shame in all the years since then had been how easy it had felt to give himself over to it. He had thought it was proof of some vile defect in his character, some classically tragic flaw. Now he understood why it had been so easy, why it had felt so familiar: The heart of the Collective was just the dark side of humanity itself. Even then, his subconscious mind had understood what he had been too ashamed to admit: Despite its pitiless, remorseless drive to crush and possess and devour, the Collective had a human soul.

He heard the soft tread of footfalls on carpeting behind him. Turning his head just a bit, he saw, on the edge of his vision, Worf approaching with a padd in his hand. "Yes, Worf?"

Worf stopped a respectful distance from Picard and said, "La Forge and Kadohata are completing their modifications to the subspace transmitter and the main deflector."

"How much longer?"

Worf said, "Both systems will be online in two minutes."

"Excellent," Picard said. He looked at the indentation in the ready room's bulkhead where a replicator once had been. The sight of the empty space made him want a cup of Earl Grey tea.

Refocusing his mind on work, he asked, "Have we heard from *Titan* or the *Aventine*?"

"*Titan* has locked in the coordinates of the Caeliar's home system," Worf said. "The *Aventine* has given us the software to generate and maintain a subspace microtunnel stable enough for a high-complexity signal."

Turning away from the hollowed memory of his ready room to face Worf, Picard asked, "Is Captain Hernandez ready?"

"Almost," Worf said. "Lieutenant Chen will help Lieutenant Commander Pazlar monitor the link to the Caeliar from *Titan*. When they signal ready, we can initiate the soliton pulse."

Picard nodded and walked to his chair. Worf followed, always close at his shoulder. They settled into their chairs, and Picard regarded the battle-scarred hull of the *Aventine*; every scorch and breach was rendered with perfect clarity on the main viewscreen. "Any news from Starfleet Command?"

"No change," Worf said. "The Borg attack fleet is thirty minutes from Earth and Mars." He took a cautious look around the bridge, where everyone was working with quiet determination. Lowering his voice, he continued, "I have a question, sir."

In the same confidential tone, Picard replied, "About?"

"Admiral Jellico's orders."

"How did you . . . ?" It took Picard a moment to reason it out. "Captain Dax told you."

"Yes, sir," Worf said. "A few minutes ago."

Picard frowned and nodded. "I take it you don't approve."

The semirhetorical statement provoked a scowl from Worf. "Running away would *not* be my first choice."

"We're long past first choices, Worf," Picard said. "The idea of surrender doesn't sit well with me, either, but the admiral may be right this time. When Earth falls, the war's over." Sensing Worf's protest, he held up a hand and continued, "Naturally, there's a plan for the continuity of government, but once the core worlds are gone, there'll be little holding the Federation together. Betazed and Trill will try, as will Bajor, but only until the Borg reach them, a few days from now."

Worf looked away from Picard and directed his intense stare at the forward viewscreen. "And what will become of us?"

"You mean the *Enterprise*?"

"And the *Aventine* and *Titan*," Worf replied.

"That's a very good question," Picard said. "To be truthful, I haven't really thought that far ahead."

Grim anticipation mingled with dark amusement in Worf's expression. "Then it might interest you to know that we are surrounded." He pointed at the tactical display on the armrest of Picard's command chair. "The Borg armada dispersed in a radial deployment from the Azure Nebula. At present, all sectors adjacent to this one are under Borg control."

Seeing the situation rendered as a simple graphic made Worf's point clear to Picard. "We have nowhere to run."

"Precisely," Worf replied. "Neither can we remain here. The Borg will seek us out. So . . . if we cannot flee, and we cannot hide, logic dictates that we should attack."

Picard needled his XO. "Channeling Spock again, are we?"

"I am merely stating the facts," Worf said.

Tugging his tunic smooth, Picard replied, "Be that as it may, we won't be doing any of those things just yet—not until we see the results of our current undertaking."

A muted tone beeped from the ops console. Commander Kadohata silenced it and swiveled her chair around to report to Worf and Picard, "Commander La Forge confirms the subspace transmitter and the deflector are online and ready to go, sir."

"Very good," Picard said. He looked left, toward Choudhury at tactical. "Lieutenant, hail Captain Hernandez on the *Titan*. See if she's ready to proceed."

"Aye, sir," Choudhury replied. She keyed the message into her station's companel, and a few moments later she was answered by a bright synthetic tone. "Captain Hernandez and Lieutenant Commander Paz-lar both confirm they're ready to go."

Standing up, Picard said, "Then it's time. Commander Kadohata, power up the transmitter and the main deflector. Lieutenant Elfiki, prepare to generate the soliton pulse. Lieutenant Choudhury, signal the *Aventine* and *Titan,* and give them the countdown."

As his officers snapped into hushed, efficient action around the bridge, Picard noticed that Worf, as usual, had followed his lead and risen from his chair to stand at Picard's right shoulder. "Captain," said Worf, "I have another question."

"Speak freely, Commander."

"It is my understanding that we are not, in fact, sending a message through the subspace microtunnel."

Picard nodded. "Correct."

Worf went on, "However, the mission profile requires us to provide Captain Hernandez with a high-bandwidth channel, on a frequency very much like the one used by the Borg."

"Also correct," Picard said, his manner dry and matter-of-fact. "What's your question?"

"What, exactly, are we doing?"

A wry, crooked smile pulled at Picard's mouth. *I've asked myself the same question a hundred times in the last hour.* He threw a sidelong look at Worf. "We're making a leap of faith."


Melora Pazlar moved in slow, graceful turns through the zero-gravity sanctuary of *Titan*'s stellar cartography hololab. She reconfigured the lab's holographic interfaces on the fly, to take direct control of the subspace transmitter hardware on the *Enterprise* while regulating an influx of beamed power from the *Aventine*. At the same time, she had to coordinate with several officers on all three vessels to maintain a real-time FTL datalink, in order to multiply their shared computing power.

A few meters away, between her and the microgravity catwalk that led to the corridor portal, Captain Erika Hernandez and Lieutenant T'Ryssa Chen floated in the weightless space. Chen, a cultural-contact specialist from the *Enterprise,* was supposed to be helping Hernandez set up her own interface with the hololab, but the half-human, half-Vulcan young woman seemed more focused on floating upside-down while talking Hernandez into a stupor.

"Eight hundred sixty years," Chen gushed, staring wide-eyed at Hernandez. "Wow! You must've learned so much about the Caeliar living among them for so long."

"Sometimes I think I've barely scratched the surface," Hernandez said. The youthful-looking octocentarian shot a pleading glance at Pazlar. "Commander, are we ready to send the soliton pulse yet?"

Pazlar gave an apologetic shrug. "A few more minutes, Captain. Sorry—we're working as fast as we can." In an effort to keep Chen distracted, Pazlar added, "Lieutenant, have you calibrated the alpha-wave receiver to the captain's brainwave frequency yet?"

"Yup, did it," Chen replied, before turning her intense focus back toward Hernandez. "I read a sanitized report of your time with the Caeliar, and I really need to ask, if their bodies are composed of programmable matter—"

"Catoms," Hernandez interrupted.

"Right, catoms—but they told you they made replicas of their old organic bodies and that they perceive the physical world the same way *after* their transition to synthetic bodies as they did before—but is that really possible? I mean, okay, they can defy gravity and become noncorporeal, and that's cool—but could they do that before?"

An exasperated reaction fleeted across Hernandez's face. "I don't know," she said.

"But what does it feel like, to be able to do that?"

Hernandez sighed. "Slipping free of gravity is like being one with the wind," she said. "I don't know a better way to explain it. As for their little trick of actually *becoming* one with the wind, I have no idea what that's like. I can't do that."

Before Chen could ask a follow-up question, Pazlar cut in, "Lieutenant, synchronize the delta-wave receiver frequency with the operating frequency of the captain's catoms."

"Already done," Chen said, doing an inverted zero-*g* pirouette, and then she continued to Hernandez, "If the Caeliar have a steady stream of—no, wait, that's not what I mean. If they have a . . . an unbroken—a *continuity* of memory dating back to their organic selves, but their bodies are completely synthetic now, how did they keep their memories? Was each memory engram individually copied and replaced? Did the old Caeliar brain even *use* engrams to record memories, like most humanoid brains, or did it use a . . . um . . . a cranial-fluid medium, like the Sogstalabians? Or something else, like a crystalline matrix?"

"Honestly, Lieutenant, it never came up."

"Never?"

"Well, I was only with them for about eight centuries."

Chen frowned for just a moment at the derailment of that line of inquiry, but then she soldiered on with her enthusiasm undiminished. "What about making little Caeliar? After they became synthetic, did they stop having kids, or did they find a way to simulate that, too? If their population is zero-growth, is it by choice, or was it a trade-off for going synthetic? Do they still have sex for pleasure?" At Hernandez's pointed stare, Chen added, "Not that you'd have any reason to know."

"I'll answer that," said Hernandez, "except for the last few parts—on one condition."

"Name it," Chen said, floating perpendicular to Hernandez.

"That you won't ask me any more questions about the Caeliar until after I'm finished in here."

The perky young human-Vulcan hybrid nodded. "Deal."

Pazlar caught Hernandez's eye and nodded at the interface controls while holding up an index finger to convey the idea *We'll be ready in a minute.* Hernandez noted the signal with an almost imperceptible glance and then said to Chen, "I asked my Caeliar friend Inyx about this, after the city of Axion went into exile. I wanted to know how long he thought it would take his people to repopulate. He said they wouldn't, that the fifty-two million Caeliar in Axion were all that was left. They'd stopped reproducing after making the shift to synthetic bodies. As you guessed, it was a side effect of the Change. Since they weren't really worried about dying, they'd figured a population of about a billion people could keep their civilization going indefinitely. But when the cataclysm destroyed Erigol, ninety-eight percent of their species was killed."

Chen blinked a few times, as if doing so would erase her stunned reaction. "Wow," she said. "Would you happen to know what their peak population was prior to—"

"We had a deal, Lieutenant," Hernandez said.

Hanging her head, Chen replied, "Right, sorry."

Pazlar finished the last of her modifications to the hololab's systems. Twisting and turning in a balletic inversion of her body relative to her guests, she locked in the power feed from the *Aventine* and confirmed that its computers were in synch with its counterparts on *Titan* and the *Enterprise.* "We're ready," she declared. "Captain, would you care to test your connection to the interface?"

Hernandez nodded, closed her eyes, and became very still. Then, as if moving of their own accord, multiple elements of the lab's holographic interface reorganized their layout; some faded out and were replaced by others, and some became flurried with data. After a few seconds, all of the changes reversed themselves, and the interfaces returned to Pazlar's final configuration. Hernandez opened her eyes. "Feels good."

"All right," Pazlar said. "I'm signaling the *Enterprise* and letting them know we're ready to do this thing."

Chen held up a hand to show her entwined index and middle digits. "Fingers crossed."

"Do you make a special effort to confound expectations about your Vulcan heritage?" Hernandez asked.

"Yes, actually," Chen said.

"Don't try so hard."

Suppressing a laugh at Chen's expense, Pazlar said, "Stand by, Captain. *Enterprise* is generating the soliton pulse now."

The semitransparent gauges around Pazlar peaked with massive surges of energy and torrents of data. The Elaysian science officer marveled at the complexity and sheer power of the signal the three vessels had united to create—chiefly because the most robust part of the outgoing stream was flowing directly through the mind of Captain Erika Hernandez.

Reaching across darkness and distance, Erika Hernandez felt the transmission systems of *Titan* and the *Enterprise* harmonizing with her catoms, vibrating in sympathy, reacting to her will like old limbs finally set free to move.

Safe in the redoubt of her own psyche, she opened her psionic senses. The gestalt was barely audible to her. A tremolo infused its every nuance and lent it a quality of dread. Though she was tempted to renew her contact with the Caeliar's shared mindspace, she regretted the need to surrender control again. Accepting the Change had meant letting go of her autonomy. At the time, she had felt broken, defeated, and diminished. Only with the benefit of centuries of hindsight did she appreciate the riches with which she'd been blessed in return, out of all proportion to her sacrifice. All the same, having once more tasted freedom, she savored it and was loath to give it up.

She guided her consciousness past the elaborate defenses of the gestalt and heard its voices. They were in disarray, a tumult of anger and anxiety. It felt to Hernandez like a surreal nightmare, as if she were one of the victims at the mythical sundering of the Tower of Babel, one of thousands milling about in confusion, each unable to understand any of the others.

Then the Caeliar sensed her mental presence among them, and the pandemonium was silenced. Their minds pulled away from hers as if by reflex, like a layer of grease on dishwater retreating from a drop of detergent.

Surges of shock and bitterness came in waves from the Caeliar. Bright anger emanated from Ordemo Nordal, their *tanwa-seynorral,* or "first among equals." Counterpointing his dudgeon was Inyx's conflicted mix of emotions—his resentment at her deception, his relief to be back in contact with her, and his amused pride at the true scope of her abilities.

Hernandez's thoughts took shape in the gestalt with the clarity of spoken words. "As long as I have your attention," she projected with obvious disdain, "let me apologize for my fly-by-night exit. I would have left a note, but there wasn't time."

Ordemo replied, "Your sarcasm remains as blunt as ever. No matter. Even if you had been sincere, mere words would hardly repair the damage you've inflicted."

"Still exaggerating for effect, I see," she shot back.

"For once, Ordemo has understated the matter," Inyx answered. "The feedback pulse you and *Titan*'s crew created caused significant harm to much of the apparatus we use for the Great Work. However, I suspect he and the majority of the Quorum are more aggrieved by your irreparable violation of our privacy." Though his words were chastising her, the aura of his emotions betrayed his lack of animosity.

The rest of the Quorum, however, blazed with indignation, and they were the ones she would have to persuade if humanity was to be saved from annihilation. "I won't pretend to seek your forgiveness," she said, addressing the whole of the gestalt. "That's not why I've come. I'm contacting you to ask for your help—and to tell you why you should give it."

"You're referring to the hostilities that currently threaten your homeworld, we presume," Ordemo responded.

"That's part of it."

The *tanwa-seynorral* channeled the Quorum's chilly reproof. "Then you're wasting your time and ours, Erika. We don't meddle in the affairs of others—you know that."

"Yes, I do," Hernandez said. "But I'm not asking you to help Earth—not directly. I'm asking you to help the Borg."

She started sharing images with the gestalt, aeons of memories she'd obtained from her union with the Borg Collective. Worlds plundered, technologies taken by force, all homogenized without mercy. Entire species and cultures violently adapted to service the Borg's single-minded pursuit of perfection, which its guiding intelligence defined as unfettered power.

Her plea was met with silent rejection. The gestalt recoiled en masse from her request. Even Inyx sounded perplexed by her entreaty. "Erika, the Borg are a brutal, rapacious culture. Why would you ask us to aid them?"

"Because you created them," she said. "And in a way, so did we. Look closer." She painted a mental image of the Borg's nanoprobe technology, and then she pushed past its cluttered outer shell to reveal its core components. "Their Collective operates on a frequency that is so close to the gestalt that I heard it from light-years away. It's not as sophisticated as your little psychic commune, but it's a lot more powerful."

She presented them with visions of sentient beings being assimilated. "Watch how that technology alters organic beings. Does that look familiar? It should. That was one of the outcomes Inyx warned me about before he Changed me—the suppression of higher brain functions, a mindless existence as an automaton. But the worst part of it is that they aren't really mindless. All those individual minds are still in there, each one a prisoner."

A pall of horror swept through the gestalt, and Hernandez realized with grim satisfaction that the Caeliar finally understood the truth.

"Mantilis," Inyx said, his telepathic voice muted by shock. "It must have survived its journey through the temporal disruption."

"With both human and Caeliar survivors aboard," Hernandez said, completing her mentor's thought. "Something happened that drove them to try to unite for survival, but instead of fusing their strengths, it amplified the ugliest parts of both species, made them into a diseased reflection of us. Your paranoia and fanatical desire for conformity got tangled up with human barbarism and aggression. It was a recipe for disaster."

Inyx replied with dark melancholy, "No, Erika, it's nothing less than a complete abomination."

"Call it what you want," she said. "The Borg Collective has abducted trillions of sentient beings over the past several thousand years and laid waste to vast swaths of the galaxy. But I can guarantee you, the drones aren't to blame. Every last one of them is a slave, living in perpetual suffering. The *real* culprit is whatever's controlling the Collective and speaking through its Queen. That's the root of the problem, and to deal with it, I'm going to need your help."

Ordemo's stubborn refusal to accede to her request held the Quorum's reaction in abeyance. "Though it seems likely that an unfortunate accident created this atrocity you call the Borg, that doesn't compel us to interfere. The timeline is as it was; if the Borg were meant to exist, then the natural order of events must be respected."

"Let me tell you two things you ought to consider," she said. "First, think about the threat the Borg will pose to you and your Great Work if they assimilate my catoms and my memories of your technology. Second, I'm not asking you to tamper with the timeline. As you might say, what's done is done. We can't change the past, but we still have a chance to shape the future."

Hernandez felt the mood of the gestalt shifting into alignment with her, but the *tanwa-seynorral* continued to resist her arguments. He said, "What, precisely, would you ask of us?"

"Bring Axion here, to my coordinates in Federation space, and I'll explain everything in person."

"And if we refuse?"

"Then you can stay hidden and afraid, until the Collective finds you. And mark my words, Ordemo, it *will* find you."

# 25

"The Borg attack fleet has passed Jupiter," said Fleet Admiral Akaar, his sonorous voice filling the cold, anxious silence in the Monet Room. "Four minutes to Earth."

President Bacco sat at the end of the conference table. She stared down its length at the faces of the few members of her cabinet and staff who had stayed behind to face the end with her. Jas Abrik, her top security adviser, occupied the chair to her left. Clockwise around the table from Abrik, with several empty chairs between each guest, were transportation secretary Iliop, press liaison Kant Jorel, special security adviser Seven of Nine, and Esperanza Piñiero, who was close at Bacco's right.

Sivak lingered a few paces behind Bacco's shoulder, and Agents Wexler and Kistler remained nearby, along the wall, trying without much success to be inconspicuous.

Bacco stared at the famous Impressionist painting on the room's north wall. *Bridge over a Pool of Water Lilies* was one of Claude Monet's masterpieces, a gently arcing bridge of spare blue beams over a pond crowded with pastel splashes of floral colors. The artist had painted the scene late in his career, when he had gone almost completely blind. Its complex but gentle beauty fascinated Bacco, and she lamented that it would soon pass into oblivion, with almost every other significant artifact of Earth's rich, troubled history.

"Why do you think Zife left that painting in here?" Bacco asked, startling the room's other occupants out of their own melancholy reflections.

Piñiero looked at the painting and then back at Bacco. "Are you serious, ma'am? Earth is three minutes away from being blown to bits, and you want to critique Min Zife's interior-decorating choices? With all respect, I don't think now is the best time."

"Relax, it's only a question," Bacco said. "This used to be just another meeting room before the Dominion War. Then Zife came along and had it rebuilt with every fancy gizmo he could find. The whole room got a makeover, top to bottom, but he left that painting right there. I'm just curious why."

Everyone in the room fixated on the painting—all except Seven of Nine, who afforded it a fleeting glance and no more. Bacco noticed the former Borg drone staring at the tabletop, her face a grim cipher, as usual.

"Seven?" Bacco prodded. "Any opinion on the matter?"

Looking up with stern formality, Seven replied, "The rationale for its continued display seems quite apparent."

"Really? Would you mind letting the rest of us in on it?"

The statuesque woman sighed. "Its placement opposite the chair of the president suggests that it was retained for his benefit. I suspect he found its muted palette and soft details helpful as a point of focus when attempting to concentrate."

Her answer provoked a frown from Admiral Akaar. Bacco noted his reaction and said, "You disagree, Admiral?"

"I served under President Zife, and I know exactly why it's there," Akaar said. "He loved that painting, and he wanted it displayed in this room as a reminder to himself, and the rest of us, that this is what's at stake if we fail—art, history, beauty, and everything we think of as our legacy." Lowering his gaze, he added, "It was one of his first decrees as president, at a time when everyone else in this building was obsessed with numbers and strategies and casualty reports. Our job was, and still is, to decide how to fight our enemies. But he left that painting there so we wouldn't forget *why* we fight."

Bacco regarded the nineteenth-century painting with a new, deeper appreciation. Though she had never been impressed with Zife as a president, she felt a pang of sympathy for him. Clearly, he had been more than the popular caricatures of his faults. After succeeding him in the presidency, she had learned the truth of how Zife had been removed from office, in a coup abetted by Admiral William Ross. Speaking privately with Bacco, Ross had implicated himself in the ouster of Zife, chief of staff Koll Azernal, and the Federation's secretary of military intelligence, Nelino Quafina, there in the Monet Room.

*How fitting. Zife's presidency ended here, and so will mine. There's a certain perverse symmetry in that.*

A rapid series of changes flickered across a wall of screens, updating the Palais de la Concorde on Starfleet's current status. Admiral Akaar reviewed the new information with a cursory look and then turned to face Bacco.

"Ninety seconds until the Borg fleet is within firing distance of Earth, Madam President," Akaar said. "The attack force is beginning to split into two groups, with one adjusting course and accelerating toward Mars."

Clammy sweat coated Bacco's hands. She dried them against the tops of her thighs. Her pulse quickened, throbbed in her temples, and left her dizzy and overheated. It was a battle to comport herself with the dignity befitting her office when an event of such unutterable gravity was imminent. For a moment, she regretted not having chosen to flee Earth when her advisers had suggested it, but then she resolved herself. *This is what I chose. No turning back now. Besides, if Earth falls, I wouldn't want to live past today, anyway—because whoever takes this job next is gonna have a lousy first press conference.*

Another fast shift in the tactical situation cascaded across the west wall's bank of situation monitors. Akaar studied them. Then he made a stunned double-take and froze.

Unable to imagine how the news could get any worse, Bacco called to Akaar, "What's happening, Admiral?"

He looked over his shoulder with his mouth agape and eyes

wide with shock. "We're not sure, Madam President. All Borg ships in this system have stopped, and we're getting reports that all Borg vessels we've been tracking have halted as well."

She asked, "Well, do we—" A shrill alert on the tactical console stole Akaar's attention from her, and she let her unfinished query trail off as the admiral raced to assemble a deluge of tactical information and situation maps into a concise report.

Then she heard him mumble, "I don't believe it."

"Admiral, I don't mean to be pushy, but I'd really like to know what the hell is happening, if you don't mind."

Akaar straightened his posture and walked back to the conference table. His voice was pitched with surprise. "Madam President . . . our scans at this time indicate that all ships in the Borg armada have reversed course and are heading at maximum speed toward the Azure Nebula."

Only one obsession held greater sway over the Borg Collective than its perverse fixation on Earth. Nothing less than the promise of perfection could eclipse the impulse to eradicate an enemy that had hobbled the Collective's quest too many times.

Now that exquisite lure blazed in the cold void between the stars. Its siren call was unmistakable. For ages the Collective had listened for it, patiently forded millennia of silence, tuned out the random noise of the universe's abandoned creations, anticipated the call of something whose power and beauty beckoned from across space and time.

It was tantalizingly close. In centuries past, the detection of even a single molecule of Particle 010 would have been enough to divert any and all cubes to its acquisition and assimilation. No matter how many permutations of adaptation the Collective endured, that essential fact of its nature had never changed. The devotion to one cause above all remained inviolate.

Reports from thousands of cubes dispersed throughout local space all relayed the same urgent message to the Borg Queen. A harnessed source of the revered particles had been pinpointed, its mass estimated at several million times greater than the largest previously known sample of Particle 010. A source of almost incalculable power, its potential output dwarfed that of the entire Borg Collective by several orders of magnitude.

The end of the Federation would have to be postponed.

*Converge on the energy source,* the Borg Queen commanded. *All other priorities and directives are rescinded.* She felt the far-flung vessels and drones snap into obedient action. *Assimilate Particle 010 at any cost.*


The heavens had twisted open in front of the *Enterprise,* and a storm of light had burst forth and enveloped the ship, whiting out the main viewer and momentarily blinding Picard. He'd raised his hand to block the glare, and he'd lowered it a few seconds later, as the prismatic eruption withdrew into the spiraling-shut aperture of the massive subspace tunnel.

The bridge crew was quiet as the majestic city-ship hovered in space, dwarfing the *Sovereign*-class starship and its two companion vessels. Picard found it difficult to estimate its size, because it more than filled the viewscreen. All he saw was a narrow slice of its middle, which was packed with shining metallic towers blessed with a graceful, fluid architectural style. Delicate walkways linked many of them, and the façades of the metropolis reflected the jet black of the void and the crisp, steady light of the stars with equal and perfect clarity.

Worf eyed the alien megalopolis with alarmed suspicion. "Should we raise shields, Captain?"

"No, Mister Worf," Picard said, still somewhat awestruck by the spectacle of the great city, which had traversed thousands of light-years with apparent ease. "They've come at our invitation. I think we owe them a measure of hospitality." He looked left toward Choudhury. "Hail them, Lieutenant."

"Aye, sir," Choudhury said.

Picard admired the aesthetic sophistication of the Caeliar city, and he found himself wondering whether Riker might be right, whether the Caeliar might, in fact, be able to stand firm in a confrontation with the Borg. He stepped forward and stood behind Kadohata at ops. "Commander," he said to her, "are we picking up any . . . *unusual* energy readings from the city-ship?"

"Affirmative," Kadohata said, working with haste to keep pace with the information appearing on her console. "Massive readings, of a kind the computer can't identify."

"All scans of the Caeliar ship are to be treated as classified information," Picard said, "to be reviewed only on my authority. Understood?"

"Yes, sir," Kadohata said, entering the appropriate command-level encryptions, which, once engaged, even she would be unable to deactivate.

*So far, so good,* he concluded. He had taken the precaution of bypassing the main computer's automatic Omega Directive protocol, which normally would have frozen command systems and duty stations throughout the ship the moment the Omega Molecule was detected by the sensors. It was a heavy-handed safeguard against anyone other than the ship's commanding officer having access to the potentially calamitous knowledge of the dangerous and notoriously unstable high-energy particle. In this case, such a measure would have drawn unnecessary attention—and since the presence of the Omega Molecule was integral to Captain Hernandez's plan to halt the Borg assault, being saddled with the Omega Directive was a distraction Picard wished to avoid.

Choudhury looked up from her station. "Sir, the Caeliar have acknowledged our hail but are refusing audible or visual contact. They've asked Captain Hernandez to return to the city."

"Dare I ask how she responded?"

"She agreed—on the condition that the Caeliar release *Titan's* away team. They've accepted her terms."

He nodded. "Understood. Keep me informed of any developments in the situation."

"Aye, sir."

Worf took a small step to stand closer to Picard, and he dropped his voice to a confidential level. "Once the Caeliar have Captain Hernandez back in their custody, they might go back where they came from—and abandon us to the Borg."

"Possibly," Picard said. "Though the departure of the Caeliar is hardly the worst outcome in this scenario. I'm more concerned about the risk of the Borg assimilating the Caeliar's technology, which appears to be formidable."

A muted tone from the tactical console signaled an incoming transmission. Choudhury silenced the alert with a brush of her fingertip and said, "New reports from Starfleet Command, sir. The entire Borg armada has reversed course."

"In other words," Worf said, "they are converging on us."

"Correct," Choudhury said, her tone dry but droll.

Picard asked, "How long until they reach us?"

"Fourteen hours," the security chief said.

The captain frowned. As powerful as the Caeliar appeared to be, Picard was unable to let go of his doubt that anything could truly stop the Borg. Worse, if the Caeliar either refused or proved unable to help, fourteen hours didn't leave him or his crew much time to formulate a backup plan.

He saw only one remaining alternative: to build a thalaron projector. The biogenic weapon might prove futile, but he doubted he would ever again be in a position to strike so many Borg cubes at the same time. He judged the risk worthwhile.

If it failed, then he, his crew, and the rest of the Federation were already as good as dead, anyway.

And if it worked . . . all it would cost him was his soul.

# 26

The shuttlecraft *Mance* ascended from Axion and passed through the city-ship's protective force field with hardly a bump.

Christine Vale sat at the aft end of the shuttlecraft's passenger cabin, across from Deanna Troi. Chief Dennisar and Lieutenant Sortollo from security sat at the forward end, and Dr. Ree and Ensign Torvig stood and awkwardly filled the space in the compartment's center. In the cockpit, Tuvok was at the controls, and Ranul Keru occupied the mission commander's seat.

Inyx had delivered the news of the away team's release from Axion with as little preamble as when, days earlier, he'd told them of their incarceration. One moment, they had thought of themselves as prisoners, and the next, their shuttlecraft was hovering beside their terrace, its boarding ramp extended.

At the urging of the Caeliar, they'd remained inside the *Mance* and had kept it landed inside Axion's shield perimeter while the city had risen from the surface of New Erigol. The sky had opened above them. At first, it had looked like a mere dark sliver, and then it had widened. The complex details of its inner mechanisms had become visible. Within moments, Axion had climbed into orbit, and then space-time itself had been torn asunder and sent pinwheeling into a blinding vortex.

The twist of light and color that had raged around Axion was unlike anything else Vale had ever seen. The vortex had exhibited a fluid quality, but it also had shimmered and pulsed. Before her eyes had been given an opportunity to adjust, Axion had sped free of the passage, back into normal space-time.

Waiting there, brilliant and still against the backdrop of stars, had been *Titan,* accompanied by two other vessels. The first was a *Sovereign*-class starship that Vale had recognized as her previous billet, the *Enterprise*-E; the other was a new *Vesta*-class explorer, a ship class she'd heard about but until that moment hadn't actually seen with her own eyes.

Via the shuttlecraft's comm, Inyx had delivered his terse valediction: *"You may go now."* Tuvok had wasted no time accepting the invitation. As soon as the channel had clicked off, the *Mance* had been airborne and on its way home.

Seeing *Titan* growing larger and sharper in front of the shuttlecraft brought a smile of relief to Vale's face. "I don't know how Will did it, but I'm glad he didn't make a liar out of me," she said to Troi. "I knew he wouldn't give up on us."

"So did I," Troi said, through her own bittersweet smile.

Vale leaned forward to keep their conversation discreet. "Are you sure you're okay?"

"Yes, Chris," Troi said, matching Vale's posture. "Better than okay."

"Good," Vale said, sincere in her concern. "You had us all pretty worried there—especially Will."

"I know," Troi said, lowering her eyes for a moment. "It's been hard on all of us. And I made it even worse for him. But it'll be all right now. I'm sure of it. I can hear him in my thoughts, and I know he's waiting for me to come home."

Unable to bury her envy, Vale blinked and looked away aft. She felt Troi's inquiring stare. Turning back to face her, she said, "Sorry. I'm happy for you, really. It's just hard for me to hear about your amazing bond with Will when I . . ." She hesitated, at a loss for words. "When I'm . . ."

"When you're still mourning Jaza?"

Vale's emotional barrier faltered enough for a single tear to escape from her eye. She palmed it away and laughed once, softly, because the alternative was to weep like a child. "Right to the heart of it, as always," she said. "Brava, Deanna."

"It's kind of my job," Troi said. "I know you've been under a lot of stress since we lost Jaza. The troubles Will and I have been going through left him . . ." She rolled her eyes toward the overhead, apparently searching for the most diplomatic word. "Not at his best," she finished. "And that left you to pick up the slack, for a lot longer than you should have. You had to do most of his job as well as your own. I'm sorry for that."

Shaking her head, Vale replied, "Not your fault."

"In a way, it was," Troi said. "I sensed what you were going through, but I was so caught up in my own pain and problems that I didn't get you the help that I should have."

"Apology completely unnecessary but accepted all the same," Vale said. A recent memory nipped at the edge of her thoughts: the moment, a few days earlier, when she had tried to comfort the distraught Will Riker in his ready room, only to come within millimeters (and a momentary lapse of reason) of kissing him. She balked at the idea of confessing her near-miss indiscretion to Troi. Then she considered the possible consequences if she tried to hide it and it came out in a less candid manner—or, even worse, if at some point she did something as monumentally stupid as to make out with her married commanding officer.

"Deanna," Vale said, "there's something I should probably get off my chest. It was nothing, really, but I feel kind of strange about it, and even stranger about feeling like I should hide it, and I—"

"You mean when you almost kissed Will a few days ago," Troi said, as if it were some mundane detail of ship's business.

"Um, well, yeah." It took a moment to push through the shock and realize how transparent she must seem to the half-Betazoid counselor. "How did you know?"

A broad grin lit up Deanna's face. "I haven't felt Will panic like that since he met my mother."

Troi laughed, and Vale found her friend's mirth contagious. Their self-conscious chortles drew curious stares from the rest of the away team and a disapproving arch of one eyebrow from Tuvok. The muscles in Vale's face hurt from the effort of reining in her laughter. "So, you're not angry with me?"

"Of course not. You were still missing Jaza, and I'd been pushing Will away for months. It's an almost textbook example of transference, with a touch of displacement."

Vale nodded and flashed an abashed smile. "I'm glad to hear you say that. I have to admit, I was worried there for a while."

"Don't worry about it," Troi said. "It's all in the past." Then she narrowed her eyes and added in a joking caricature of a threat, "But if you ever make a pass at him again, I will have to kill you. Nothing personal."

Answering Troi's stare with a knowing look, Vale felt an almost sisterly bond with her. "Understood," she said.


Geordi La Forge stopped at the door to Captain Picard's quarters. He looked at the padd in his hand. He'd been driven by a righteous indignation to come this far, but standing on the precipice of action, he considered turning back, surrendering in silence, and chalking it up to the cruel compromises of war.

*Not this time.* He pressed the visitor signal by the door.

A moment later, he heard Picard's voice call out from behind the door, "Come."

The portal sighed open, and La Forge stepped inside the captain's quarters. Everything was clean and well ordered, as usual. Picard stood in front of a set of shelves. He was holding his Ressikan flute; its burnished metal surfaces caught the light as it shifted slightly in his grasp. The captain looked up from the instrument in his hands and seemed pleasantly surprised to see La Forge. "Geordi," he said. "What can I do for you?"

La Forge took a few steps farther inside, and the door hushed closed behind him. "We need to talk," he said.

"Of course," Picard said, setting down the flute inside its protective felt-and-foam-lined box. He gestured toward the sofa and some chairs. "Please, come in, sit down."

Picard took a step toward the sofa before La Forge stopped him by saying in a firm tone, "I'd rather stand, sir."

Sensing the grave nature of La Forge's visit, Picard put on a wary mien. "Is something wrong, Mister La Forge?"

"Yes, sir," La Forge said. He held up the padd in his hand. "These orders you sent me a few minutes ago."

The captain hardened his countenance. "What of them?"

"You ordered me to turn the main deflector into a thalaron radiation projector, like the one Shinzon had on the *Scimitar.*"

"I know what I told you to do, Commander."

Frustration made La Forge clench his jaw and his fist as he fought to find words for his outrage. "How could you give me an order like that? How can you possibly expect me to obey it?"

Picard slammed the lid of the flute box shut with an earsplitting crack. "I am not in the custom of explaining my orders, Mister La Forge! And I expect you to obey them because you're a Starfleet officer."

La Forge shook his head. "Sorry, Captain. Not good enough. Not for this." He tossed the padd at Picard's feet. "I won't insult you by pretending I have any standing to question your order. I'll just say it to your face: I refuse to obey it."

With quiet menace, Picard replied, "You're treading on dangerous ground here, Mister La Forge."

"You want to talk about dangerous? Unleashing a metagenic superweapon—*that's* dangerous." The captain glared at La Forge, who continued, "Consider this. We're developing shields against thalaron radiation, and it's a good bet the Borg can, too. And the moment they do, this weapon becomes useless."

"But not until then," Picard snapped. "And when their armada surrounds us, we'll be able to eradicate them."

The thought of such a tactic horrified La Forge. "You're talking about mass murder."

Picard bellowed, "I'm talking about survival, Geordi! You can't negotiate with the Borg. You can't bargain with them, or seek a truce, or a cease-fire. There's no other way."

"I refuse to believe that," La Forge said. "After all we've done and all we've seen, if I've learned anything, it's that there are always alternatives to killing." He felt the captain's silent resistance and knew that he would never get him to concede the point, so he moved on. "Say you're right, and we wipe out the Borg with a thalaron weapon. What then? You know you can't put that genie back in the bottle. Once the Klingons and the Romulans find out about it, we'll be back at war."

Walking past La Forge on his way to the replicator, Picard replied, "That's a problem for the diplomats and the politicians."

"I'd say the politicians *are* the problem. Access to a weapon like that would give them ideas. Power corrupts, and a thalaron weapon that can fry a planet is a *lot* of power."

The captain seemed to ignore La Forge's remark as he stood in front of the replicator and said, "Tea, Earl Grey, hot." His drink appeared from a singsong flurry of particles, and he picked it up and took a sip. He carried the cup to a table and set it down. "Your concerns and objections are noted for the log, Mister La Forge, but we don't have time to debate this. I need that weapon operational immediately."

"Maybe I didn't make myself clear, Captain. I didn't come up here just to register a complaint so I could work with a clean conscience. When I say I won't do it, I mean it."

Incensed, Picard shot back, "The Federation is a democracy, Mister La Forge, but this starship is not. I gave you a direct order, and I'll repeat it for the last time: Turn the main deflector into a thalaron projector before the Borg arrive."

"No," La Forge said. "Repeat it as many times as you want, it won't make any difference. I will not resurrect that . . . that *abomination*. I won't be party to whatever atrocities it winds up being used for." He stepped closer to the captain and gestured emphatically as he continued, "When Shinzon had one, you were ready to die to stop it. Data gave his life to destroy it. For me to rebuild it now would be an insult to his memory and a betrayal of his sacrifice. I can't do that. I won't.

"You want to put me in the brig? Fine. I'll walk down there and turn myself in. But I absolutely will not follow that order. It's immoral. It's illegal—and since no illegal order is valid, it's my *duty* to refuse to obey it. And yes, I know that you'll just get someone else to do it, someone who won't put up a fuss, who won't question orders, who'll just get it done.

"But it won't be me."

La Forge didn't wait for the captain's response. He turned and walked out, and he kept walking, down the corridor and into the turbolift, which he directed to main engineering. Reflecting on his outburst toward the captain, he half expected to find armed security personnel waiting there to take him into custody.

*Assuming we live till tomorrow, I may have just ended my career,* he realized. He was surprised to find the thought didn't scare him as much as he had thought it would. *If that's how it has to go,* he decided, *so be it.*

Then his bravado faded, and he felt an overpowering desire to hide someplace dark and have a drink . . . or two . . . or six.

"Computer, halt turbolift," he said. "New destination: the Riding Club, on the double."

* * *

Riker was about to walk into Erika Hernandez's guest quarters unannounced, until he remembered his earlier faux pas and stopped at the private comm panel. He pressed the visitor signal and waited until Hernandez responded from inside, "Come in."

The door shushed open, and he walked in to find Hernandez sitting on the floor behind her living area's coffee table, whose top was covered from edge to edge with nearly a dozen plates of food and several beverages both hot and cold.

He admired her one-woman feast. "I'm glad to see *someone* likes the food on this ship."

She returned his jovial look and said, "It took a while, but I found a few things your replicator actually makes well. Since the Caeliar won't make any of these in Axion, I figured I'd better enjoy them while I can." She speared a hearty chunk of light-colored meat dressed with rich brown gravy. "Care for a bite of the milk-braised pork loin? The sauce is fantastic."

"No, thanks," he said, watching her devour the forkful and then swoon with gustatory ecstasy. "I'm saving my appetite for dinner with Deanna." Lifting his chin toward her expansive repast, he added, "Do you want to take some of that to go?"

She swallowed and said, "I guess that means your away team is on its way back?"

Riker nodded. "Commander Hachesa just confirmed the *Mance* is on its final approach."

"Then I'd better get ready to go," Hernandez said. She grabbed a glass with a wide, shallow body atop a narrow stem and downed half its pale chartreuse contents in a long draught. She smacked her lips and let out a satisfied gasp. "It's not quite right with synthehol, but it's still the best margarita I've had in eight hundred years." She set down the glass and stood up.

"Before you go, I want to thank you," Riker said. "I don't know what you told the Caeliar or what you promised them, but however you did it, thank you for helping free my people."

She looked embarrassed by his gratitude. "It was the least I could do," she said. "It's what I wished someone could have done for my crew." Turning her gaze toward the floor, she added, "But what's done is done, I guess."

He empathized with her sense of loss and her guilt, and

his gut impulse was to change the topic. "Will you be coming back?"

"I don't know," she said, stepping out from behind the coffee table to join him in the middle of the room. "There's a lot to do once I get back to Axion. Convincing them to come out of hiding was only the first step. Now that they're here, they might not like what I have to say."

The apprehension in her voice stoked his concern for her. "Is it safe for you to go back?"

"Of course," she said. "They won't hurt me."

"But will they take you prisoner again? If you go back, will they ever let you leave?"

A shadow of melancholy settled upon her. "I don't know," she said. "But to be honest, that's the least of our worries."

"True," Riker said. "Can you even guess at what the Caeliar will say about helping us stop the Borg?"

"No, I can't. I know they won't help the Borg hurt us, but beyond that, it gets complicated. The Caeliar prefer to stay out of other people's business, but now that I've shown them their own link to this mess, they might take responsibility for it. Or they might not. For all I know, they might hear me out and choose to stay neutral."

Riker frowned. "In which case, we're all pretty much dead."

"Pretty much, yeah."

A few meters behind Hernandez, there was a rippling effect in the air, like heat distortion. It blurred the image of the bedroom behind it, and within seconds, it was like looking at something through a deep pool of water. The shimmer took on a metallic quality, like a hovering vertical puddle of mercury. Then the effect stabilized, and Riker saw himself and Hernandez reflected on its serene, silvery surface.

Hernandez looked over her shoulder as if she were being called by a voice that only she could hear. She sighed and looked back at Riker. "Time for me to go," she said, favoring him with a coy glance. She turned and walked toward the liquid-metal oval that hovered a few centimeters above the deck, and she stopped in front of it and looked back. "Before I leave, I ought to thank you, too," she said. "Fifteen hours ago, you didn't know me, and you had no reason to trust me. But you did. Because of you, I got to be free again, even if just for a moment. Thank you for taking a chance on me."

He smiled with sincere admiration and affection. "You're welcome," he said.

She lingered a moment, and then she turned and stepped forward, passing through the quicksilver membrane without so much as a ripple. As soon as she had vanished into it, the liquid portal faded into vapor.

Riker stood and stared at the empty space in front of him, and he was startled as Commander Hachesa's voice crackled over the comm, *"Bridge to Captain Riker."*

"Go ahead."

*"The deck officer in Shuttlebay One reports the* Mance *is aboard, and all away team personnel are safe and accounted for."*

"Acknowledged," Riker said, jogging toward the door to the corridor. "Riker out!" He was through the door, and as soon as he was in the corridor, he broke into a full-out sprint for the turbolift. Enlisted crewmembers and junior officers froze in his path ahead of him, caught by surprise. "Make a hole!" he shouted, and everyone reacted by reflex, pressing their backs to the bulkheads as he tore down the middle of the passageway.

He knew that it was unseemly for him to be seen running like this, to be so loud and so frantic in front of his crew, but he didn't care. His *Imzadi* was home, and she was safe—he could feel it.

*Decorum be damned,* he decided, and surrendered to his joy.


La Forge stood in front of the forward-facing windows in the *Enterprise*'s crew lounge, which Will Riker had named the Happy Bottom Riding Club before he left to take command of *Titan*. Riker had said he'd chosen the name as an homage to a famous social club for aviators and early Earth astronauts, but La Forge suspected his real intention had been to annoy Worf.

The vodka tonic in La Forge's hand had become diluted as its ice cubes melted, but it hardly mattered, since the beverage had been made with synthehol.

He'd taken only a few sips from it in the half hour since he'd come from the captain's quarters, because his attention had been fixed on the massive Caeliar city-ship looming in space before the *Enterprise,* the *Aventine,* and *Titan*. The alien metropolis was kilometers wide and breathtaking in its elegance. It was packed with slender towers, sloping and curved structures that evoked waves and aquatic themes, and sky bridges that, from a distance, looked like gossamer filaments.

Behind him, the Riding Club was much less busy than usual. Most of the ship's crew was on duty or on a much-needed rest cycle, as repairs overlapped with preparations for the imminent confrontation with the Borg armada. Tensions were high. La Forge knew that he ought to be in main engineering, supervising the dozens of major projects currently under way, but he was confident that Taurik had matters well in hand.

The scent of fresh prune juice and the thump of deliberate footfalls alerted him to Worf's approach, and he looked for the Klingon first officer's reflection in the window. Worf had approached from directly behind La Forge and had revealed himself only with his last few steps. La Forge continued to face forward as Worf settled to a halt on his left.

"I guess you've spoken to the captain," La Forge said.

"I have." Worf sipped his prune juice.

La Forge looked at his drink. "Am I under arrest?"

"No," Worf said. "You are not."

He didn't elaborate, which worried La Forge.

"So what happens next?"

"The captain has rescinded his order."

That caught La Forge off-guard. He turned and looked at Worf. "Rescinded? Because of what I said?"

"Yes," Worf said, staring straight ahead into space.

"And he sent you down here to tell me that?"

"No. I came of my own accord. To thank you."

Recoiling in mild surprise, La Forge asked, "For what?"

"For saying what I should have said," Worf replied. "I feel as you do. Making such a weapon is a risk, and it would be an insult to Data's sacrifice." He clenched his jaw and huffed angrily. "I did not wish to confront the captain. But I should have." He turned his head and met La Forge's stare. "It takes courage to challenge authority on a matter of principle. What you did—for yourself and Data—was an act of great honor."

La Forge bowed his head and said, "Thank you." He looked up and out at the Caeliar city-ship. "Amazing, isn't it?"

"It is . . . large," Worf said.

"When I first saw it, I'd thought about asking the captain permission for a visit," La Forge said. "Just to see what makes it tick, y'know? And then I wondered what Data would think of it . . . and suddenly, I didn't want to go anymore. Not because the city wasn't interesting, but because I knew that every time I saw something new, I'd want to turn and tell Data about it—and then I'd have to remember he's gone."

Worf regarded the Caeliar metropolis with a somber look. "I understand," he said. "I, too, often wish that Data were still alive. Usually in the morning, when Spot wishes to be fed."

La Forge chuckled, recalling Worf's pained expression when he'd learned that Data's last will and testament had named the Klingon as the guardian of his pet. "How's the cat doing?"

"Spot is well—and his claws are sharp," Worf said with a prideful gleam. Then he softened his expression and clasped La Forge's shoulder in a friendly grip. "Data is gone, and it is not wrong for us to mourn him. But we must not cling too tightly to the past. We are still alive, Geordi, and we have each other. Perhaps that will be enough."

Nodding, La Forge said, "It's everything, Worf. Thanks."

Worf dipped his chin and removed his hand from La Forge's shoulder. The silence between them was calm and comfortable, and La Forge felt no need to disturb it. It was enough to stand next to his old friend, watching the stars and waiting to see what the future would bring.

# 27

One scan after another yielded nothing but good news.

"It's truly remarkable, Captain," Dr. Ree said to Riker, who stood with him in *Titan*'s sickbay, on the other side of the biobed, holding Troi's hand. Gesturing toward the vital-signs monitor above her head, the reptilian physician continued, "All of Deanna's readings are optimal, across the board. There's no sign of damage in the uterine wall and no abnormalities in the fetus."

Troi reclined on the biobed, her face beaming with joy as she looked at Riker. "She's okay, Will," Troi said. "Our daughter is okay." Tears rolled from her eyes.

Riker, still reeling from the revelation of his wife's recovery, asked Ree, "This is the Caeliar's work?"

"Yes, sir. And I've only told you part of the good news." He called up a new screen of information on the overhead display. "In addition to healing Deanna and her child, the Caeliar saw fit to restore all of her unreleased ova as well. Which means that if the two of you so desire, there's no reason you couldn't have more than one child."

Riker asked, "What about the risk of miscarriage?"

"I'm happy to report that's no longer an issue," Ree said. "Your complications were genetic in nature, and the Caeliar have amended that—quite ably, I might add. They've also rejuvenated much of Deanna's internal physiology."

It was Troi's turn to react with surprise. She sat up quickly as she said, "Rejuvenated?"

"Yes, my dear counselor," Ree said. "Inyx reversed much of the age-related deterioration in your tissues and organs. If one were to judge your age based solely on an internal scan, you would register as a woman of thirty, in the prime of your life."

A giddy smile brightened her face as she looked at Riker and said, "I guess that explains why I feel so amazing."

"Guess so," Riker said, mirroring her happiness. He looked at Ree and asked with intense interest, "How did they do it? Genetic therapy? Nanosurgery?"

Ree cocked his head sideways and tasted the air with a flick of his tongue. "I have absolutely no idea," he said. "Deanna's treatment was performed in secret. If I seem impressed by Inyx's amazing results, I'm positively stunned by the fact that he left no discernible trace of how he did it." He switched off the biobed, and the overhead screen went dark. "If you want, I can keep running tests to see if I can uncover his methods, but I doubt I'll find anything."

"Don't bother," Riker said, helping Troi to a sitting position on the edge of the bed. "We've had enough tests."

"I quite agree," Ree said, empathizing with the suffering Riker and Troi had endured over the past several months, from the invasive rigors of fertility therapy to the heartbreak of a miscarriage and the close call of a second failed pregnancy. "My prescription for the two of you is simply this: Go spend some time alone, and assuming the universe doesn't come to a fiery end tomorrow, come back next month for a routine prenatal exam—with an emphasis on *routine*."

"Thank you, Doctor," Troi said, wrapping her arm around Riker's waist. "For everything—including biting me."

"You're welcome," Ree said.

Riker did a double-take. "He *bit* you?"

"Let's go," Troi said, cajoling Riker gently as she pulled him out of sickbay. "I'll tell you all about it . . . in private."

Will Riker's relief was so profound, the burden that had been lifted so ponderous, that he felt breathless, as if he'd gone from the pit of the sea to the peak of a mountaintop.

His *Imzadi* was home and healed.

Their child was safe.

The future was theirs again, something to look forward to instead of fear. They'd stepped to the precipice, faced the fathomless darkness, and come back whole.

He and Deanna stood in the main room of their quarters on *Titan* and held each other. The fragrance of her hair, the warmth of her body, and her empathic radiance of well-being combined in his senses to mean one thing: *home.*

She hugged him with greater vigor and pressed her face to his chest. "You don't need to say it," she said, reacting to his unspoken, still-forming thoughts and confirming for him that their telepathic bond was as strong as it had ever been.

"Yes, I do," he said. "You know I do." He kissed the top of her head. "I'm so sorry I left you. I didn't want to."

"I know," she said, reaching up to stroke his cheek.

"Please forgive me," he said.

Deanna pressed her palms softly on his cheeks and pulled his face to hers. She planted a delicate kiss on his lips and another on the tip of his nose. "I forgive you," she said. "It was a terrible choice. I'm sorry you had to make it."

Clasping her hands in his own, he felt the sincerity of her forgiveness and the intensity of her elation. Lost in a giddy haze, he asked, "Are you hungry?"

"Not at all," she said, shaking her head and smiling.

"Neither am I," he said, and they laughed for a moment. It was goofy laughter, like an unmotivated overflow of joy.

In a blink, Deanna's mood turned bittersweet, and tears welled in her eyes. "Thank you," she said.

"For . . . ?"

"For supporting me when we argued with Dr. Ree a few days ago. I know you disagreed with my decision, for all the right reasons, but in sickbay, you always took my side. You trusted me."

"I *believed* in you," he said, looking with wonder at the amazing woman who had deigned to spend her life with him. "And, as always, my faith in you has been richly rewarded."

She relaxed back into his arms, and he was glad to support her weight. It had been months since they'd felt this close, this in tune with each other, and he found it deeply gratifying to feel wanted—and *needed*—again.

"After everything," Deanna said, "I still can't believe it's finally happening for us. A family, Will. Children. We can even have more than one if we want."

"If I didn't know it was thanks to science, I'd call it a miracle," he replied.

Deanna reacted with a sigh and a look of concerned dismay. "Now all we have to fear is the Borg," she said. Riker tried to think of some way to defuse her anxiety, but he was at a loss, because he knew she was right. She continued, "We're so close, Will. So close to living the life we've always wanted, and now we're hours away from the biggest confrontation with the Borg we've ever seen. We've fought so hard for this child, for us, for a second chance. I can't stand the thought of seeing it taken away." She implored him as much with her gaze as with her words, "Please tell me we have a plan, Will. *Please.*"

"I know Captain Hernandez does," he said. "And Jean-Luc might be cooking up one of his own. So, yes, there is a plan."

"Okay, so *they* have plans," she said. "What about *us*? What are *we* going to do?"

Riker shrugged, glib humor his defense of last resort. "The same thing we always do," he said. "The impossible."

Ranul Keru found Torvig—with guidance from *Titan*'s main computer—in a remote, hard-to-reach forward compartment located just above the main deflector dish. The young Choblik engineer stood on a narrow catwalk and gazed through a broad sliver of a viewport. He turned his ovine head in Keru's direction as the tall, brawny Trill approached him. Light from the surrounding machinery glinted off Torvig's metallic eyes and cybernetic enhancements. For once, the normally loquacious young ensign remained silent and resumed staring out into space.

The security chief stepped carefully across the grid-grated cat-walk, mindful of its low guardrails and the precipitous drop into the workings of the deflector dish. Shuffling along for the last few steps, he sidled up to Torvig and asked, "Hiding?"

"I desired an isolated place in which to think."

"Your quarters aren't private?"

"I've not yet earned enough seniority to receive private ac-commodations," Torvig said. "Since my return, Ensign Worvan has asked me one hundred thirty-four questions about what I observed during our incarceration in Axion. He's been most *per-sistent* in his efforts."

Keru tilted his head. "Gallamites are like that." He looked out the narrow gap to see the majestic lines and mass of Axion, shin-ing against the sprawl of the cosmos. "Is something bothering you, Vig? You seem . . . out of sorts."

"I'm unaware of any direct irritation to my person."

"No, I mean, are you experiencing anxiety about something?"

Torvig shifted his weight back and forth, from one foot to the other, and his mechanical hands clenched the railing in front of him. "Is it true that the Borg armada has reversed course and is on its way here?"

"Yes," Keru said.

"Then my answer is yes. I'm feeling anxiety."

"It could be worse," Keru said, heaving a disappointed sigh. "While we were in Axion, a lot of people from here and the *En-terprise* and the *Aventine* boarded a Borg scout ship and fought in close-quarters combat. We lost Rriarr, Hutchinson, Tane, Doron, and about half a dozen other really good people. And sh'Aqabaa might live through surgery, or she might not." It was a bitter sting for Keru that he had been denied the chance to fight the Borg face-to-face. Even after so many years, he would have found such violence deeply cathartic for his beloved's death at their hands. Now, facing much less forgiving odds, he doubted he would have such an opportunity again.

He looked at Torvig and realized the squat, short ensign was quaking. "Calm down, Vig," he said. "Officers don't shiver."

"I apologize, Ranul," Torvig said. "I'm having trouble remain-ing objective about our circumstances. Until now, I'd considered the Borg as a phenomenon, or as an abstraction of accessories and behavioral subroutines for a holodeck program. Now that I'm about to face them, I realize that I'm not ready."

Keru squatted next to Torvig and patted the Choblik's armored back. "You'll be fine, Vig. Nothing to be scared of."

"At the risk of sounding insubordinate, I disagree," Torvig said. "Do you recall my tests of the crew? The ones I used to verify a link between my crewmates' anxious behaviors toward me and their feelings about the Borg?"

Rolling his eyes, Keru said, "How could I forget?"

"I now have a greater understanding of one part of that equation," Torvig said. "Now I'm afraid of the Borg, too. It was a mistake for me to compare their cybernetics with those of the Choblik. The Great Builders' technology was a boon to my people—it gave us individuality and sentience. The Borg's technology takes away those things. It debases its members." He let go of the railing and lifted his bionic hands in front of his face, flexing them open and shut. "I imagine my mechanical elements betraying me, and it frightens me. That's what it would be to become one of the Borg." Looking plaintively at Keru, he added, "Don't let them do that to me, Ranul."

Keru reached out and clutched Torvig's bionic hand, thumb to thumb, flesh to metal, and he looked his friend in the eye. "I won't let it happen, Vig. To either of us. You have my word."


Most of the beds in the *Aventine*'s sickbay were still full when Captain Dax walked in, and Dr. Tarses and his medical staff looked wrung out by a day of gruesome surgeries. She caught his eye with a wave and waited while he walked over to her.

"Thanks for coming," he said.

Up close to Tarses, Dax saw that the young doctor's hair was matted with sweat, and his eyes were red from exhaustion. She nodded and said, "Where is she?"

Tarses took a few steps and motioned with a tilt of his head for Dax to follow him. She walked with him past one row of biobeds, and then past a triage center, into a recovery ward. All of the beds in this compartment were occupied as well. Near the far end of the ward was the person Dax had come to talk to. She reached out to Tarses and tugged his sleeve. "I'll take it from here," she said, and he acknowledged the dismissal with a polite nod and let her continue past him.

Dax approached the problem patient without hesitation and

placed herself at the foot of the bed. "What's this I hear about you not wanting to return to duty?"

Lonnoc Kedair stirred from her torpid, dead-eyed languor to meet Dax's accusing stare. "It's not about what I want," the Takaran woman said. "It's about what I deserve."

"If I could, I'd give you a month's liberty," Dax said. "I read Simon's report. You got mangled pretty bad on that Borg ship. Unfortunately, we have about four thousand more of them on their way here, and I need my security chief back at her post." She frowned as Kedair turned her head and averted her eyes. "In case I wasn't clear, I'm talking about you."

"You were clear," Kedair said. "I wasn't. I'm not saying I deserve time off. I'm saying I deserve to be in the brig."

*Just what I didn't need,* Dax fumed behind a blank expression. *Something to make my day a little more interesting.* "Care to elaborate, Lieutenant?"

Kedair seemed unable to look Dax in the eye. The security chief shut her eyes, massaged her green, scaly forehead, and combed her fingers through her wiry black hair. "On the Borg ship," she began, and then she paused. After a grim sigh, she continued, "I made a mistake, Captain."

"Stay here. I'll convene a firing squad," Dax quipped.

"Curious choice of words," Kedair said. "Because that's basically what I did." Looking up, she added, "I caused at least three friendly-fire deaths during the attack, sir. Maybe more."

Dax stepped to the side of Kedair's bed and moved closer to her, so that they could speak more discreetly. "What happened, Lonnoc? Specifically, I mean."

"I was looking out across that big empty space in the middle of the ship," Kedair said, her eyes turned away while she searched her memory for details. "I thought I saw an ambush closing in on one of our teams. It was so dark, and everybody was wearing black, and with TR-116s in their hands, at a distance, they looked like Borg with arm attachments." Dax nodded for her to go on. "With the dampeners, we didn't have any comms, so I fired a warning shot at the team that was—that I *thought* was being ambushed. I signaled them to turn and intercept." Kedair closed her eyes, and her jaw tensed.

Wary of pushing too hard, Dax asked, "What happened next?"

"The first team took cover and waited for their targets to close to optimal firing distance. Then they—they lit 'em up." She shook her head. "A few seconds later, the squad leader called cease-fire, and they popped off a few gel flares. That was when I saw what had happened." She bowed her head into her hands for a few seconds, then she straightened and added, "Lieutenant sh'Aqabaa's still in critical condition. The rest of her squad from *Titan* is dead."

The rest of Kedair's actions on the Borg scout ship after the boarding op were starting to make sense to Dax. "Is that why you volunteered to stay behind when the Borg Queen attacked? To try and make up for your mistake?"

"I did that because it was my duty, and because it was the right tactical choice," Kedair said defensively. "Please don't psycho-analyze me, Captain. I can always go see Counselor Hyatt if I'm in the mood for that."

"I think Susan might echo my diagnosis," Dax said. "But you're right, it's not my job to give you therapy. It's my job to give you some perspective and put you back at your post."

"You ought to put me out an airlock," Kedair grumped.

Sharpening her tone, Dax said, "That's *enough*, Lieutenant. Listen to what I'm telling you. You did not pull the trigger on Lieutenant sh'Aqabaa and her team. It's not your fault."

"How can you say that? I flagged my own people as a target. I gave the order to fire. How can it possibly *not* be my fault?"

"It's called the 'fog of war,'" Dax said. "You go into sensory overload. Everything happens so fast, you can't process it. Mis-takes happen." She sighed as she confronted painful memories from her years on the *Destiny* and on Deep Space 9. "I saw it a lot during the Dominion War. It had nothing to do with how well trained someone was or the quality of their character. In combat, you have no time to think. Information gets scrambled. You're surrounded by chaos, and you try to do the best you can—but no one's perfect."

Kedair's eyes narrowed. "Sounds like an excuse," she said. "And not a very good one, either. I don't want to make excuses, Captain. I should have verified the target before I told my people to fire."

"I've read a lot of reports from squad leaders who were on that ship," Dax said. "I doubt you really had the time to check every target. No one did. Under the circumstances, I'd say your actions were entirely reasonable."

Angrier, Kedair replied, "I was sloppy. I lost track of where my people were. It was my job to know."

Vexed by Kedair's toxic brew of self-pity and self-loathing, Dax leaned forward and took hold of the security chief's collar. "I'm trying to be patient, Lonnoc, but you're not making this easy. Stop feeling sorry for yourself. This is war. It gets bloody. People die. Deal with it." With a shove, she released Kedair and continued, "The team on the other level could have fired gel flares first, just to see who they were shooting, but they didn't. That was their call, not yours.

"Add up the facts. You had no communications, in the dark, in hostile territory, while under attack, and you made an honest mistake. You want to blame yourself? Go ahead. Wail and gnash your teeth and cry yourself to sleep at night—I don't give a damn. There was no criminal negligence here and no criminal intent—in other words, absolutely no basis for a court-martial.

"So I'm giving you a direct order, Lieutenant: Get your ass out of that bed, and report to your post on the bridge. We're less than ten hours from facing off with a quarter-billion Borg drones in more than four thousand cubes, and I don't plan on letting you goldbrick your way through it. Understood?"

Kedair stared at Dax in shock, her eyes wide, her jaw slack, her back pressed as deeply into her pillows as she had been able to retreat in the face of Dax's harangue. The Takaran woman blinked, composed herself, and sat up. She swung her legs over the side of the bed and stood up, facing Dax.

In a level, dignified voice, she said, "It's a damned good thing you switched to the command track, Captain. Because if this was you as a counselor, you suck at it."

"*That* is called insubordination, Lieutenant. And if you keep it up, it *will* get you a court-martial."

The security chief perked up. "Good to know. Now, at least I have something to shoot for."

Axion was windless and silent beneath the endless night of deep space. Erika Hernandez drifted alone through the motionless air that surrounded the city-ship inside its invisible force field.

Darkness and starlight were reflected to perfection on the brilliant façades of the metropolis, which gleamed with its own inner light. Hernandez felt the awareness of the millions of Caeliar who dwelled in the city. Now conscious of her bond with the gestalt, they shied from her in subtle ways. They would never deny another mind in their communion, but many of them radiated discomfort at the discovery that it now included a non-Caeliar.

As meticulous as the Caeliar kept their city, to Hernandez, it still felt less antiseptic than either of the Starfleet vessels she'd visited in the past several hours. Inside the sheltering embrace of the city, she caught the fragrance of green plants—grass and trees, bushes, flowers—and the rich scent of fertile earth. Water still danced in the fountains.

None of that distracted her from her search.

Inyx had left the Quorum hall before she'd finished her proposal to the *tanwa-seynorral*. As soon as he'd gone, he'd started masking his thoughts from the gestalt, withdrawing from contact. *Apparently, the Caeliar appreciate privacy on a personal level as well as a cultural one,* Hernandez realized. Nonetheless, she suspected that she knew where he would be.

She was correct.

She descended without a sound, her posture relaxed, legs crossed at the ankles, arms at her sides. Air displaced by her passage tousled her mane of dark hair and fluttered the fabric of her Starfleet uniform. For the sake of nostalgia, she alighted on the glossy black water of the reflecting pool by the petrified tree. Inyx stood beneath the tree's bare boughs, in whose ragged shadows he seemed to have partially vanished.

Without causing so much as a ripple, Hernandez walked calmly across the pool to the tree's small island at the far end. She bounded onto the isle with her last step and landed with balletic grace in front of Inyx.

Feigning boredom, he said, "I wondered how long it would take you to master that trick."

"Not long," she said. "Less than eight hundred years." She cocked a teasing eyebrow. "Told you I was a fast learner."

"About some things," he said.

She ambled past him and made a slow circle of the tree, letting her hand play across its glassy, obsidian surface. "I've never seen you in such a hurry to leave the Quorum hall," she said. "Did my proposal bother you that much?"

"I made my objections to the gestalt," he said, and then he

added, with an extra degree of sarcasm, "But of course, you know that, since you are, apparently, completely attuned to the gestalt and can share in it whenever you please."

She took his rebuke in stride, because she had already sensed his pride in her accomplishment. "I'm sorry I lied to you, Inyx," she said. "But your people aren't the only ones who value privacy."

He made a derogatory huffing noise inside his air sacs, which puffed up around his shoulders. "There is a difference, Erika, between privacy and secrets—and between secrets and deceptions." His ire dissipated. "What's done is past. I'm more concerned about your next potentially fatal mistake."

"I know it's a risk, but I think it's worth taking," she said. "And the Quorum agrees with me."

"By a narrow margin," Inyx replied.

"I'm certain it will work," she said.

"Certainty is not the same thing as infallibility," he said. "If you're wrong, or if you've underestimated the Borg's capacity for adaptation, you might be condemning this galaxy and many others to aeons of oppression."

"If I'm wrong—if I fail—I'm counting on you to persuade the Quorum to honor the spirit of our agreement and protect the galaxy from the Borg."

He said with grim regret, "I can't promise that, Erika."

"Promise me that you'll try," she said.

With a small bow from his waist, he said, "You have my solemn pledge. I *will* try." Melancholy seeped into his voice. "I wish it didn't have to be you taking this risk."

"Well, it's not like anyone else is in a position to do it," she said. "You sure can't, and neither can those starship crews." She shook her head. "Believe me, if there was another way, I'd take it."

"If you do not wish to make such a sacrifice, why go?"

"Because my people need me, Inyx. They need me to step up and do something no one else can. And all those people trapped in the Collective need me even more than the Federation does. I failed a lot of people when I let the Romulans get the drop on me and destroy my convoy. I led my crew into captivity, and then I failed to control them, and millions of *your* people died. All these centuries, I've been living with those failures, with no way to atone for any of them. Now, I might have that chance."

Inyx passed a long moment in somber reflection.

"The consequences of failure seem clear enough," he said. "But what would be the price of success? If your plan goes as intended, what will become of *you*, Erika? Will you ever come back to Axion? Will I ever see you again?"

Unable to hold back the tears welling in her eyes, she replied, "I don't know."

"Then perhaps you've finally received your wish," he said, with a tenor of defeat. "You'll finally be free of Axion . . . forever."

She placed herself directly in front of him. "Maybe," she said. "But that doesn't mean I'm happy about it."

With both hands, she reached up and gently pulled Inyx's ever-frowning visage down to hers. "I probably won't get a chance to do this later."

She kissed his high, leathery forehead with tender affection. "Good-bye, Inyx."

# 28

"Whatever Captain Hernandez is planning, it involves the Borg, and that means it has the potential to go horribly wrong."

Picard stood at the head of the table in the *Enterprise*'s observation lounge and watched the seated Captains Riker and Dax nod at what he had just said. At his invitation, they had beamed over to meet with him in private aboard the *Enterprise,* so that they could confer without risking the interception of their conversation by the Borg—or by the Caeliar.

Exasperated, Dax replied, "You want a contingency plan for what to do *after* we're surrounded by more than four thousand Borg cubes?"

"Better than not having one," Riker said, scratching pensively at his salt-and-pepper-bearded chin.

Dax blinked, conceding the point, and replied, "For that matter, we'll need one even if she succeeds. I mean, have we even thought about how we're supposed to repatriate a quarter-billion ex-Borg from across the galaxy?"

"We're getting ahead of ourselves," Picard said. "Frankly, as powerful as the Caeliar seem to be, I doubt they—or any other entity, short of the single-letter variety who shall not be named—can effect such a change by force."

"There's another scenario to consider," Riker said. "What if they succeed but only temporarily? The Borg Collective is based on adaptation. Even if she frees all the drones from the Collective's control, who's to say it'll be a permanent shift?"

Nodding, Picard said, "Those are all valid concerns. In success or in failure, Captain Hernandez's proposal—what little we know of it—will present us with staggering logistical and tactical crises. In just over eight hours, the first wave of the Borg armada will reach us. Whatever backup plan we intend to prepare, it needs to be ready by then."

Riker leaned forward and folded his hands together. "If this turns into a shooting match, I think the Caeliar can take care of themselves," he said.

"Against these odds?" asked Dax.

"That I don't know," Riker said. "But if the fight turns against them, the Caeliar can open a subspace tunnel and slip away. Which doesn't help us but would keep the Omega Molecule generator out of the Borg's hands."

Dax frowned. "Captain Picard made a good point the last time we talked with Captain Hernandez. A team of twenty-second-century MACOs outflanked the Caeliar and destroyed one of their cities. That gives me the impression that strategy and tactics aren't the Caeliar's forte. What if the Borg get the better of them? What if they can't escape to safe ground?"

"Then we have a problem," Riker said.

"More than a problem, Will," Picard said. "A disaster." Resting his hands on the headrest of his chair, he continued, "If Hernandez fails to disband the Collective, our top priority must be to prevent the Borg from assimilating anything of the Caeliar. If that means abetting their escape, so be it. But if the only way to keep their city-ship from the Borg is to destroy it, then we need to be prepared to take that step."

Dax keyed in some commands on the tabletop interface at her seat. She called up a map of Axion on the wall companel behind Riker. "This is based on scans and observations made by Captain Riker's away team while they were in Axion," she said. "It shows the approximate position of the Omega Molecule generator. That's what powers the Caeliar's civilization, and it's probably our best chance of destroying them if we have to. If we can destabilize the generator when the armada's on top of us, we could vaporize them instantly."

"Along with the rest of the galaxy," Riker said. "We'd also end warp flight in most of the local group. Not exactly what I'd call a plan for victory."

Arms out, palms up, Dax said, "If you know another way to destroy Axion and the Borg at the same time, let's hear it."

He rolled his eyes and shrugged. "Well, we know the Caeliar can modify their subspace passages for time travel."

"Tell me you're not serious," Dax said. "What do you plan to do? Go back in time, find the origin of the Borg, and wipe them out before they ever existed?"

"Why not?" Riker said. "They tried to do it to us."

"And look what that got them," Dax said.

Picard raised his voice. "Captains, *please*." He waited for Dax and Riker to calm down and acknowledge him. "We need to consider every alternative at this stage, no matter what the ethical or broader tactical consid—"

"*Bridge to Captain Picard,*" Worf said over the comm.

"Go ahead, Commander."

"*We are detecting extreme levels of local subspace disruption,*" Worf said. "*And we are being hailed by Axion.*"

"Red Alert, Mister Worf. I'm on my way. Picard out." As the channel clicked off, he added to Dax and Riker, "Captains, will you join me on the bridge, please?" Picard was already stepping through the door to the bridge by the time Dax and Riker had risen from their seats. He had no idea what fresh calamity was unfolding, but he had a sinking feeling that, as with so many events of late, it would be one for which he had no plan.

Riker hurried onto the bridge of the *Enterprise* several seconds behind Captain Picard, who was met at the trio of command chairs by Commander Worf. Picard and Worf conferred in tense whispers as Riker and Dax moved past them, down to the center of the bridge. Then came Picard's authoritative baritone: "Commander Kadohata, put Captain Hernandez on-screen."

Kadohata tapped a sequence of commands into the ops

console, and the main viewer blinked from an image of Axion to the youthful beauty of Erika Hernandez.

Beside her was an alien with a bony, skeletal body and an enormous, bulbous head fronted by a stretched, frowning visage. Riker looked at the being's pearlescent sea-green eyes, its skin of mottled purple and gray, and the tentacle-shaped ribbed air sacs draped over its shoulders, and he realized that its head reminded him vaguely of an octopus.

*"Hello, Captains,"* Hernandez said. *"I'm glad I found you together, as this concerns all of you."*

Picard stepped forward, passing between Dax and Riker to place himself at the forefront of the conversation. "Captain Hernandez," he said, "have the Caeliar agreed to help us?"

*"Yes,"* she said. *"After a fashion."*

Suspicious, questioning looks passed between the captains on the *Enterprise* bridge. Turning back toward the main viewer, Picard asked, "Would you care to be more precise, Captain?"

*"First, I should apologize to all of you and your crews for misleading you, but I give you my word that I believed it was in everyone's best interest for me to do so."*

Holding up one hand, Picard cut in, "*Misleading* us? About what, Captain?"

*"It would take too long to explain,"* she said. *"Besides, you'll see for yourselves soon enough. All I can say is that old habits die hard, if at all, and if I learned anything living with the Caeliar, it was how to play my cards close."* She looked at Riker and then at Dax as she continued, *"Will, Ezri, thanks for treating me like part of your crews. It was nice to feel like I was home again, back in Starfleet. I knew I'd missed it, but until today, I hadn't realized just how much."*

"Captain," Picard said, "what's going to happen?"

*"I honestly don't know for certain,"* Hernandez said. *"No matter how this plays out, you and I probably won't see each other again. If I and the Caeliar fail, then we're all about to have a very bad day. And if we succeed, then something new awaits us—all of us."* She smiled. *"Wish us luck."*

Riker eyed Picard's profile. The elder captain was standing slackjawed and at a loss for words as he watched Hernandez close her eyes and lift one hand in front of her, fingers spread wide, as if she were reaching for some unseen object.

Just as Riker was about to ask Picard what was wrong, Inyx

spoke and snared everyone's attention with his mellifluous baritone. *"Captains, for your own safety, I recommend you move your vessels to within one kilometer of Axion—immediately."*

Picard still seemed frozen, so from the aft deck of the bridge, Worf called out, "Helm, put us alongside Axion, distance eight hundred fifty meters. Commander Kadohata, relay those orders to *Titan* and the *Aventine*."

Kadohata and Lieutenant Weinrib gave overlapping replies of "Aye, sir" as they carried out Worf's orders.

On the main viewer, Hernandez's raised hand began to glow. A nimbus of light formed around it, growing so bright that it shone through her fingers, making them blaze red like hot coals. Her face was the very portrait of serenity. She opened her eyes, which burned with an inner fire, and she said, *"It's time."*

A hush fell over the bridge.

Captain Picard tensed with a sharp intake of breath.

Proximity alerts shrilled from multiple consoles.

"Massive energy surge from the Caeliar city," called out Lieutenant Choudhury at tactical.

"Subspace tunnels," added Lieutenant Dina Elfiki, who was racing to keep up with the rush of data on her console. "Thousands of them, opening in a spherical distribution around Axion." The attractive, chestnut-haired science officer added, "The city is definitely controlling them, Captain."

"Incoming vessels," Choudhury announced.

Worf replied, "Shields up!"

Riker wished that he was on the bridge of his own ship at that moment, but he was also grateful that his crew at least had Vale, Tuvok, and Keru back aboard to lead them in his absence. On the viewscreen, Erika Hernandez maintained a steady countenance.

Choudhury looked at Worf. "Borg cubes are emerging from the subspace tunnels, sir—thousands of them. The entire armada."

"Split screen," Worf said. Kadohata adjusted the main viewer to show two images: Hernandez and Inyx on the right and, on the left, the arriving Borg armada surrounding Axion and blotting out the stars with their sheer numbers.

Dax sounded as if she simply couldn't believe what she was seeing. "The Caeliar brought the Borg here sooner? Why?"

Riker shrugged, equally dumbfounded.

Then he looked at Picard, who nodded slowly, as if with a

dawning comprehension. Riker sensed that something unspoken was transpiring between Picard and Hernandez.

Finally, Picard said to Hernandez, "You're not disbanding the Collective . . . are you, Captain?"

*"No,"* Hernandez said. *"We're assimilating them."*

A two-meter-tall oval of mirror-perfect quicksilver took shape behind Hernandez, who turned and stepped through it without so much as a ripple. Then the oval faded into vapor, sublimated into nonexistence, leaving only Inyx on the screen.

Riker snapped, "What's going on? Where'd she go?"

"To the source," Picard muttered.

Glaring at Inyx, Riker said, "Show me where she is!"

*"As you wish,"* Inyx said.

The Caeliar's image dissolved to that of a view from deep inside a massive Borg vessel. A haphazard, slapdash collage of metal, tubes, wires, ducts, and random machinery filled the screen, all of it illuminated through its narrow gaps by a sickly viridian light. The point of view roved through the dark, industrial-looking labyrinth until it found open space and arrowed down toward the vessel's core. Passing like a phantom through solid matter, the image speared its way into the central plexus, to the most elaborate Borg vinculum Riker had ever seen.

In the bowels of that biomechanoid horror, Erika Hernandez walked without fear toward an advancing phalanx of Borg drones. Behind them, atop a dais festooned with regeneration pods and a plethora of bizarre devices, stood the Borg Queen, commanding her foot soldiers forward to intercept her rival.

"No!" Riker shouted. "You have to stop her! She doesn't know what she's doing!"

Inyx replied, *"I assure you, Captain, Erika knows exactly what she is doing. And I would have stopped her if I could."*

Riker watched, horrified, as the drones set upon Hernandez in a savage pack—and impaled her with assimilation tubules.

# 29

Hernandez fell into the arms of the drones and gave herself up, surrendering to their violations. Viselike hands seized her arms and ripped every loose fold of her clothing. Assimilation tubules extended from the drones' knuckles and pierced Hernandez's flesh, each puncture as sharp as a serpent's bite.

A cold pain coursed through her, surged in her blood, and clouded her thoughts. There was no fury in the drones as they smothered her, only the brutal, simple efficiency of machines subjugating flesh and bone.

Beyond the one-sided melee, the Borg Queen stood on her dais and regarded Hernandez's fall with haughty dispassion.

The voice of the Collective flooded Hernandez's mind like seawater pouring into a sinking ship, and her thoughts drowned in the aggressive swell of psionic noise. Panic bubbled up from her subconscious. For a moment, she wished she had prevented the drones from injecting her. It would have been within her power to turn them back, to wrest them from the will of the Borg Queen, but instead she had let them strike unopposed—because that was the plan and had been from the start.

A black fog of oblivion enfolded her.

*This is the only way,* she told herself. *The only path.*

None of the Caeliar could do this for her. Hernandez knew that only she could serve as the gestalt's bridge to the Borg. The Caeliar, with their bodies of catoms, were immune to assimilation; the Borg's nanoscopic organelles needed at least some trace amounts of organic matter to invade and transform as part of the assimilation process. In the body of a Caeliar, the organelles would find only other nanomachines—all of which would be far more advanced and powerful than the organelles and utterly impervious to them.

It would have been equally futile for any member of the Starfleet crews to volunteer for Hernandez's mission. Without the Caeliar catoms that infused her body, and which had altered her genetic structure, another organic being would be unable to survive the assimilation process while acting as a conduit for the focused energies of the gestalt.

*Only I can do this,* Hernandez reminded herself. *I have to hang on. Can't give up . . . not yet.*

The icewater in her veins turned to fire as assimilation organelles and Caeliar catoms waged war for possession of her body. Needles of pain stabbed through her eyes, and a burning sensation pricked its way down her back.

Every inch of her was consumed with excruciating torments.

Two deafening voices raged inside her head: the soulless roar of the Collective and the hauntingly beautiful chorus of the gestalt.

As the Collective became more aware of the gestalt through its bond with Hernandez, the singular intelligence behind the Borg launched a mind-breaking assault on her psyche. Unlike the first time the Borg had assailed her, however, Hernandez wasn't alone. Reinforced by the shared consciousness of the Caeliar, she dispelled the Borg's demoralizing revisions of her memories. Its lies broke like waves against an unyielding seawall.

She felt the Caeliar gestalt reassert its primacy in her mind and body, and then it landed its own first blow against the Collective, dredging up fragments of an ancient memory—bitter cold and empty darkness, loneliness and despair, fading strength and dwindling numbers. And, above all, *hunger.*

Paroxysms of rage shook the Collective, and Hernandez knew, intuitively, that the Borg armada was firing en masse at Axion, unleashing every bit of destructive power it could marshal. All of the Collective's hatred and aggression was erupting, and the Caeliar had become its sole focus. As the bombardment hammered Axion's shields, however, there wasn't a glimmer of distress or even concern in the gestalt. At best, the Caeliar reacted to the fusillade with equal parts curiosity and pity.

*So much sorrow and anger,* opined the gestalt. *Such a desperate yearning . . . but it doesn't know what it seeks, so it consumes everything and is never satisfied.*

A surge of strength and comfort from the gestalt flowed through Hernandez, and the chaos of its struggle with the Borg gave way to a sudden peace and clarity.

Then the Caeliar projected their will through her fragile form and usurped control of the Borg Collective.


The Caeliar gestalt beheld its savage reflection.

The Collective looked back, hostile and bewildered, like a wild thing that had never seen a mirror nor caught sight of itself in still waters.

Inyx perceived the shape of the Collective and was shocked at how it could be both so familiar and so alien. Two great minds, the Collective and the gestalt, had shared a past until their paths had diverged. The Borg had been forced down a road of deprivation and darkness, while the Caeliar, despite being wounded, had been afforded the luxury of a more benign destiny. Now their journeys, separated by time and space, had converged.

A roar of voices spoke the will of the Borg.

*You will be assimilated. Your diversity and technology will be adapted to service us. Resistance is futile.*

The gestalt was overwhelmed with pity for the primitive and autocratic posturing of the Collective. Like a child that had never been disciplined, it laid claim to all it surveyed, seized everything within reach in rapacious flurries of action, and never once questioned if it had the right to do so.

Brute force was the Collective's tactic. The drones that surrounded Axion outnumbered the Caeliar population five to one. Across the galaxy, there were trillions of drones, in tens of thousands of star systems, on innumerable cubes and vessels. Had the Collective's conflict with the Caeliar been one of simple numbers, there would have been no contest.

*How tragic,* Inyx mused openly in the gestalt. *It doesn't understand at all.*

Ordemo Nordal replied, *All it sees is power to be taken.*

Edrin, the architect, asked, *Do we know who it is?*

*It's time we found out,* said Ordemo.

The *tanwa-seynorral* focused the gestalt's attention on breaking through the noise of the Collective, penetrating to the true essence of the Borg, exposing its prime mover, revealing the mind at its foundation and the voice behind its Queen.

Wrapping herself in the shelter of a hundred million hijacked minds, the Borg Queen sought refuge from the scalpel-like inquisition of the Caeliar. With patience and precision, the gestalt evaded the crude latticework of enslaved minds and found the Queen lurking in the dark heart of it all. Then it pushed past even her, in search of the truth.

Cut off from the Collective's core essence, the Borg Queen stumbled in confusion—deposed, disoriented, directionless.

Locked in the core of every Borg nanoprobe was the key to the Borg's ethereal shared consciousness, an invisible medium that spanned great swaths of the galaxy. Unseen, it was never heard directly except through the Queen. Its presence was always felt by every drone, and every sentient mind it pressed into service amplified its power.

At first, it seemed less a personality than a collection of appetites. It was fear and hatred and hunger, and beneath even those primal urges lurked a deeper wound, the impetus for its insatiable appetites: an inconsolable loneliness.

It had no memories of its own, no name beyond *Borg*, but as the gestalt took its full measure, it was recognized by one and all for what and who it truly was.

*Sedín,* said Inyx, baring his grief for what had become of his confidante and beloved companion of several aeons. Sedín had been brilliant, imaginative, and ambitious. To see her debased into a violent scavenger was both horrifying and heartbreaking. Even worse was contemplating the atrocities she had wrought on other sentient beings. Those were crimes beyond atonement.

Once, she had been a Caeliar scientist and poet. All that remained of her now was a tormented fragment of consciousness, a suffering with no name and no connection to its own greatness. Inyx imagined that Sedín, in a moment of weakness, had been unable to let herself disincorporate. She had clung too fiercely to life, lingering even after her faculties of reason had faded, rendering her little more than a sophisticated machine bent on feeding its own ravenous energy needs and perpetuating its own existence.

Taking the initiative, Inyx projected comforting impulses to Sedín, quieting her rage. Then he counseled her, *It's time to let go, Sedín. Let yourself rest. Let the light fade.*

She fought. Rage and fury pulsed through the Collective. Driven by fear and habit, Sedín lashed out, to no effect.

Inyx calmed Sedín's psychic rampage with a dulcet tone, a harmonizing thoughtwave of love. The Collective fell silent.

He reached out across space and found Erika, teetering on the edge between resistance and surrender, and bolstered her with the will of the gestalt. *Balance has been achieved,* he told her. *The next step is yours.*


Hernandez's mind was clear as she got up from the deck inside the vinculum. The pack of drones that surrounded her retreated in confusion as she looked past them and met the panicked gaze of the Borg Queen, and they parted before her as she walked forward to speak to Sedín through the deposed monarch.

"Can't you see what you've done here, Sedín?" she said. The

drones all were watching her, and through her bond with the gestalt—and the gestalt's new link to the Collective—Hernandez realized that everything she did and said here would be known by every Borg drone throughout the Milky Way.

Ascending the steps of the Queen's dais, she continued, "Did you forget everything you stood for? Nonviolence, pacifism, the Great Work . . . did they all lose their meaning for you?" As she reached the top of the dais, the Borg Queen stumbled backward and collapsed before her. Hernandez felt the Queen's dismay and discerned its cause: She was unable to make sense of what was happening. The nature of the Caeliar had caught the Collective by surprise; despite having believed they could assimilate nigh-omnipotent beings, the Borg had met their betters.

Standing over the fallen Queen, Hernandez understood that the Borg's figurehead was powerless now; she had become little more than another, glorified drone.

Hernandez turned away from her, shut her eyes, and extended her senses within the Borg vessel, throughout its armada, and then, with the power of the Caeliar gestalt, across the entirety of the Collective—all of which was one mind, one damaged sentience craving peace but not knowing how to find it. She lifted her hand, fingers parted wide, as a somatic cue to focus and direct the power of the Caeliar.

"Sedín, have mercy on all these souls you've stolen. You've held them all long enough, and you've done enough damage—to them, to the galaxy, and to yourself. This has to end." She quelled Sedín's fear and let the gestalt begin to place the wounded Caeliar sentience fully under control. "We have to lift this cruel veil from your victims' eyes," she continued. As the gestalt wrested the last vestiges of control from Sedín, the Collective dissolved, leaving behind trillions of minds still bound to one another by a shred of shared awareness.

She spoke now to the drones. "Awaken . . . and know yourselves."


Across the galaxy, a trillion drones reeled at the sudden absence of the Collective, as if an invisible hand had released its throttling grip on their throats and let them all breathe for the first time in six thousand years.

In unison, they inhaled and tasted freedom. Their numerical

designations were stripped away, leaving some with nothing—
and giving others back their names.

Clarity brought awareness . . . and then came bitter memories.
Staggering multitudes of liberated psyches remained inextricably
linked, their thoughts exposed and crowded in on one another,
and the result was pandemonium.

A billion minds panicked without the Collective's guidance,
and a billion more laughed in triumph at the fall of their oppres-
sor. Tens of billions emotionally imploded and filled the shared
mindspace with their plangent wails of grief. Searing tides of
rage swelled and swept like a force of nature through the emancipated drones. What one felt, all felt, all at once.

The entire Borg civilization was in chaos. In the span of a
single breath, it had descended into madness.

Hernandez couldn't breathe. She was only one woman, one
mind, one spark of consciousness trying to stand against a tsunami of sorrow and terror.

She could hear the psychic voice of every drone calling out for
succor, the doleful cries of those who had awakened to find their
lives shattered beyond recognition, the misdirected fury of those
who had tasted revenge and hungered for more.

A flood-crush of feelings and memories pummeled the gates of
her mind. Souls masculine, feminine, neuter, and wholly alien
to her all turned toward the light, the radiance of the Caeliar and
their Omega Molecule generator, and they all saw Hernandez as
the conduit to those long-sought perfections.

*I can't finish this without your help,* she told the gestalt. *We've
come this far. Take the final step.*

The gestalt struggled to cope with the onslaught of negative
emotions from the freed Borg drones. Such cacophony offended
their precious harmony of mind, and all that Hernandez could
do was hope that they would rise to the challenge it presented.
Then came Inyx's reply. *We're ready, Erika.*

Strength surged in her chest like a river breaking through a
dam. She felt Axion's generator increase its output by orders of
magnitude, and suddenly the overmatched gestalt had assumed
control. Its energy flowed within her and empowered her, and
through her it found the Borg.

Hernandez gave the power a purpose. She shaped it, molded it, directed it. She spread it across the galaxy, to every last drone, on every cube, in every complex, on every assimilated world. In every corner of the galaxy that had been darkened by the scourge of the Borg, Hernandez opened the way.

Her body rose from the deck and ascended quickly toward the high ceiling above the vinculum. *Freedom,* she thought, and the core of the Borg cube obeyed her. The massive supports and exterior structures of the vinculum peeled away and opened like a steel flower in bloom, revealing the great hollow core of the Borg Queen's domain. Her catoms burning brightly with the light of the Caeliar, Hernandez soared into the great emptiness above.

*Open your eyes,* she told her new brothers and sisters in the gestalt. *See the future. It's here. Its time has come.*

Jean-Luc Picard had never broken down like this. Not when Robert and René had died, not when he'd gone home after being liberated from the Borg for the first time, not when Gul Madred had nearly shattered him beyond recovery.

He collapsed onto his knees, unable to stand against the storm of emotions that raged against him. All thoughts of pride were forgotten now. He had no sense of the other people on the bridge of the *Enterprise*. In the final moments before he had been felled by the psionic barrage, Riker and Worf had moved to his sides to shield him from the crew's sight.

*It doesn't matter,* he realized, submerging into the ocean of his hopelessness. *The center didn't hold. It's all falling apart. There's nothing we can do.*

Doubts and fears dragged him deeper into his own bottomless despair. How could he ever have hoped to fight the Borg? He was only one man, mortal and weak, and the Borg were a force of nature. He'd failed to challenge them in System J-25, when he first encountered them. He'd underestimated them a second time and had ended up facilitating the slaughter of his own people at Wolf 359. If not for Data, he'd have been beaten by the Borg Queen. Arrogant enough to think he could fool them long enough to infiltrate one of their ships, he had tried to impersonate Locutus, only to succumb to assimilation *again.*

*I'm a failure,* he berated himself. *I might have lived out my life in peace, but I had to tempt fate by starting a family. I've doomed us all.*

Heavy sobs wracked his chest. He cried into his palms until his ribs hurt and his eyes burned and mucus filled his sinuses.

And across the galaxy, a trillion drones wept with Locutus.


A quarter-billion voices were screaming at Deanna Troi.

She pitched forward to the deck of *Titan's* bridge, and Christine Vale was at her side in an instant. "What's wrong, Deanna?" Vale asked. Troi wanted to reply, but she could barely breathe through the avalanche of wild emotion smothering her.

Vale snapped out orders. "Tuvok, she needs you! Rager, we need a medic. Keru, tell Ree to check on all psi-sensitive personnel immediately."

The world around Troi seemed to fade behind a wall of anguished keening and wordless, angry roars of noise. It was all coming from the Borg, but they had none of the focused malice or icy detachment that had marked their previous encounters with the Federation. There was only tragic lamentation and sullen fury, emotional aftershocks of a shattered culture of slavery.

Then a comforting thought broke through the bedlam, and Troi became aware of warm fingertips against her temple and cheek. *My mind to your mind,* Tuvok projected, easily surmounting her crumbled psychic barriers. *My strength becomes your strength. My calm becomes your calm. Our thoughts are fusing. Our memories are merging. We are united. We are one.*

She opened her eyes and saw *Titan's* bridge clearly. Everyone, it seemed, was watching her and Tuvok, who hovered on the edge of her vision, though he was foremost in her thoughts. Troi still sensed the mental turbulence of the millions of distressed souls in the Borg armada who were crying out for help, but the mind-meld with Tuvok had given her the strength to restore her telepathic barriers and recover her composure. She saw in Tuvok's mind that the meld had proved fortuitous for him as well; his own control also had faltered from the shock.

Inside the meld, he asked, *Are you all right, Counselor?*

*Yes, Tuvok. Thank you.*

The crew's attention was pulled away from Troi and Tuvok as Keru pointed at the main viewer and shouted, "Look!"

On the center screen, the Caeliar metropolis of Axion began to shine with an unearthly glow. It grew brighter in a rapid flash, like a star building up to a supernova, yet Troi found something about its penetrating white radiance comforting.

What she saw next was more than just a turning point in history. It was the end of an era and the dawn of another.

It was a moment too incredible to be coincidence.

It was a moment of destiny.

A trillion pairs of eyes bore witness.

It was a vision, a phantasm sprung fully formed from the void, a revelation of what had been and what was to come. The former Queen was no more, laid low, made common, deposed. In her place had risen a hue and cry of inconsolable sorrow.

A billion mothers awoke from the Collective's iron bondage to find their children riven from them. Billions of children opened their eyes to find their parents gone forever, along with worlds they could barely remember. Spouses, lovers, friends, and comrades sought one another through the gestalt and found few of their numbers still living. Billions of souls were alone.

There were no rich or poor. No one was famous, powerful, or privileged. There were simply those who had awakened. Liberated from the cold grip of the machine, they searched for the keys to their lost identities. Then they found them, and the gestalt sang with a trillion names reclaimed from the fog, revealed by the blaze of light piercing the gloom.

Every mind touched by the gestalt looked to the source.

Where once a dark tyrant had reigned, a bright and dazzling queen now rose like the dawn, bringing illumination and comfort. Unfettered by the bonds of gravity, she soared freely, bursting with light, a splendor among shadows, exorcising six thousand years of night in a single moment of ineffable beauty.

The harsh chord of the Collective yielded to the harmony of the gestalt. Then there was no more pain, no more rancor, and no more sorrow, for those things had passed away, leaving only the possibilities of the present and the promises of the future.

A living death was conquered, and for a trillion souls who had dwelled in night, it would never again hold dominion.

*We are the Caeliar.*

* * *

Riker kneeled beside Captain Picard and kept one hand on his friend's back and the other in a firm but gentle grip on his arm. Captain Dax was on the other side of the *Enterprise*'s captain, in a pose that mirrored Riker's. It was Riker's suspicion that Dax was just as uncertain as he was about how to react to Captain Picard's inconsolable emotional collapse.

Picard was on all fours, doubled over, face almost touching the carpeting of the bridge, hyperventilating and sobbing. Then he stopped with a sharp intake of air, and he clawed at the deck for several seconds before bunching his hands into fists under his chin. His body quaked as if he'd just come in from the cold.

As desperately as Riker wanted to defend Picard's pride by concealing this display from the rest of the bridge crew, he knew that it would be even more damaging for them to see their captain carried off the bridge. In any event, this wasn't Riker's ship, and it wasn't his call to make, it was Worf's. Until the XO said otherwise, Picard would remain where he was.

Choudhury looked up from the tactical console and pointed at the main viewer as she shouted, "Something's happening!"

Axion had flared like a supernova, flooding the screen with light and all but bleaching the solid spherical formation of Borg hulls of their details. Then the armada of Borg ships—every cube, probe, and sphere—cracked open and bled light. Intense white radiance poured from every fractured vessel. In a flash, the *Enterprise* went from being huddled in a pit of starless metal darkness to dwelling in a heart of pure light.

As Riker, Dax, and the bridge crew watched, the multitude of imposing black ships imploded. Vast sections of every ship were sucked inward, and delicate spines of brilliant, gleaming metal jutted out from their cores, reaching in every direction. Within seconds, the Borg vessels had all become incandescent spheres surrounded by dense formations of long spikes. Squinting against the ships' blinding glare, Riker mused that they looked like massive sea urchins cast from flawless silver.

Picard's breathing steadied, and he looked up through tearstained eyes, first at Dax and then at Riker. In a knowing whisper, he said, "Everything's changed."

Then he turned his gaze to the image on the main screen. He stared in wonder, taking it all in . . . and then, ever so slowly and by infinitely cautious degrees, Picard cracked a smile.

"Everything's changed," he repeated.

And then he laughed. Not like someone amused by a joke or given over to the mirth of madness; he let out the triumphant, joyous gales of a man tasting freedom after living in chains.

Riker threw an amused, wary look at Dax.

She shrugged. "As long as he's happy," she said.

Of the fifty million Caeliar bonded through the gestalt, only Inyx was willing to do the unthinkable. He dissolved the last of Sedín's corrupted essence, condemning the last of her residual charge into the gestalt at large and returning her, in a poetic and somewhat entropic fashion, to the home she had unknowingly sought for six millennia, with trillions of innocent beings yoked to her unconscious purpose.

*It is finished,* Inyx declared, overcome with shame for his deed, sorrow for his friend, and relief for the end of her pain.

The gestalt empathically echoed his agonies, and from Ordemo Nordal, he felt the blessing of absolution. *There was no other way,* Ordemo said. *It was too late to save her.*

Then it was time to open themselves to the sentient minds they had set free, which they welcomed into the gestalt. It was a decision motivated partly by mercy; after all that Sedín's victims had endured, in light of all they had lost, the Quorum concurred that the gestalt had an obligation to alleviate their suffering and offer them a safe haven, a new beginning.

A more honest accounting of the situation demanded that the Caeliar admit the truth, however: They needed the emancipated drones as much as the drones needed them.

Hernandez had persuaded the gestalt to aid her by appealing to its own sense of self-interest. Standing before them only a short time earlier, she had argued her point with passion.

"Your obsession with privacy is killing you," she'd said. "You made these catom bodies of yours, and you figured you'd live forever in your invulnerable cities, on your invisible planet. You never thought about what would happen if you had to procreate. It never occurred to you that your whole world could get shot out from under you and take ninety-eight percent of your people with it. Well, it did. And the law of averages says this won't be the last time something bad happens to you.

"How many more losses can you take and still be a civilization? What if another accident happens? Or a new, stronger enemy finds you? The Cataclysm nearly *exterminated* you. Haven't you ever stopped to consider that all your efforts on the Great Work will be lost if you die out?

"If you want to explore the universe, you'll need strength, and the best place to find that is in numbers. I don't know if there's any way for you to get back the ability to reproduce, but it's not too late for you to learn how to share. You need to bring non-Caeliar into the gestalt. You need to teach others about the Great Work—before it's too late."

Her proclamation had provoked a schism in the Quorum and sent shockwaves of indignation through the gestalt. The debate had been swift and bitter, but in the end, it had fallen to Ordemo Nordal to persuade the majority that Hernandez was right. It was time to expand the gestalt or accept that it was doomed only to diminish from this moment forward. The Quorum and the gestalt had to choose between evolution and extinction.

In the end, it proved not so difficult a choice, after all.

As the gestalt embraced the freed and bewildered drones in its protection, Inyx appreciated at last how right Hernandez had been. The Caeliar had granted to the Borg all it had sought for millennia: nearly unlimited power, a step closer to perfection, and the secrets of Particle 010. In return, the legions of drones who flocked into the warm sanctuary of the gestalt had given the Caeliar what they had most desperately needed: strength, adaptability, and diversity. In one grand gesture, the Caeliar had become a polyglot society with an immense capacity for incorporating new ideas, new technologies, and new species.

For the Borg, it was the end of aeons of futile searching.

For the Caeliar, it was the end of an age of stagnation.

The lost children had come home. The gestalt felt whole.

*Now the Great Work can continue,* Inyx announced, initiating the newest members of Caeliar society to its ongoing mission. *More important,* he added, *now the Great Work can evolve.*

\* \* \*

Jean-Luc Picard was on his feet again. He felt taller than he had in ages. So many emotions were whirling in his mind that he couldn't name them all. Relief and joy were at the forefront of his thoughts, with wonder and gratitude close behind.

The aft turbolift door opened, and Beverly stepped out. She hurried straight to his side. "Worf called me," she said.

She reached up, as if to touch his arm in a gesture of polite and dignified comfort.

Too full of life to settle for that, he embraced her, pulled her close, and pressed his face into the tender space between her neck and shoulder. He reveled in the sweet scent of her hair, the pliant warmth of her body, the gift of her every breath, the miracle of their child—their *son*—growing within her.

At first, she seemed caught by surprise, and he understood why. Picard had never been one for public displays of affection, especially not in front of his crew. He no longer cared about that. She was his love, the one he had waited for, the one he had almost let slip away because he had been too timid to follow his heart, too cautious to indulge in hope.

He was done being careful. More than fifty years earlier, it had taken a Nausicaan's blade through his heart to teach him that lesson the first time. It had taken a trip to the edge of annihilation to remind him that life was not only far too short, but also far too beautiful and far too precious to enjoy alone.

"I'm all right, Beverly," he whispered. "We all are." He pulled back just far enough to kiss her forehead and then her vibrant red lips. Parting from her, he looked around the bridge and saw a dozen faces bright with mildly embarrassed smiles. He brightened his countenance to match and said, "Carry on."

Riker and Dax stepped forward to pat his shoulders. Just as Riker was about to say something, he was interrupted by Lieutenant Choudhury. "Captain," she said to Picard. "Incoming hail, sir. It's Captain Hernandez."

"On-screen," Picard said, stepping forward behind the conn and operations consoles.

Erika Hernandez's girlish features and enormous, unruly mane of sable hair appeared on the main viewer. "*Will, Ezri, Jean-Luc, I just wanted to speak to you one last time before we go, to tell you that I'm okay—and to say good-bye.*"

"Before 'we' go?" Picard said, echoing her. "You mean you and the Caeliar?"

A new understanding gave Hernandez an aura of calm. *"You don't need to speak of us as separate entities anymore,"* she said. *"I am one of the Caeliar now. In fact, I have been for a long time; I just hadn't been able to really accept it until now."*

Riker stepped forward on Picard's left and asked, "Erika, what's happened to the Borg?"

*"There are no more Borg,"* Hernandez said. *"Not here, or in the Delta Quadrant, or anywhere else, for that matter. There are only Caeliar."* Her beatific mien gave way to a broad smile. *"And if you'll excuse us, we have a new mission to begin."*

Dax edged forward and said, "What mission?"

*"To find and protect cultures of peace and nonviolence—so that perhaps someday in the distant future, the meek really can inherit the universe."*

"Good luck," Riker said.

*"You, too,"* Hernandez said, and then the signal ended.

The screen switched back to the view of magnificently glowing, urchin-like Caeliar vessels huddled around the miniature star of Axion. Then, though Picard wouldn't have thought it possible, all of the ships and the Caeliar metropolis flared even more brightly, scrambling the main viewer image into a distorted crackle of white noise. Less than a second later, the light had vanished—and so had Axion and its brilliant new armada.

On the screen, tiny and alone in the cold majesty of the cosmos, were *Titan* and the *Aventine*. The rest was silence.

Worf relaxed his shoulders a bit and said to Choudhury, "Cancel Red Alert."

Whoops of jubilation erupted from the other officers around the bridge. Picard and Riker clasped each other's forearm and slapped each other's shoulders. "We did it," Riker said.

"No," Picard said. "Erika did it. We just lived through it." He smiled. "And that's good enough for me."

He and Riker let each other go, and Riker turned to help Dax coax Worf into joining the celebration. Picard fell back into Crusher's arms and treasured the moment. There was a lightness in his spirit, an exuberance and an optimism he hadn't felt since the earliest days of his command of the *Enterprise*-D.

It took him a moment to put a name to this sublime feeling.

*I'm free,* he realized. *I'm free.*

\* \* \*

Admirals Akaar and Batanides were pressed against the situation monitors in the Monet Room and surrounded by a clutch of junior officers, all of whom were scrambling to confirm the latest reports from the *Enterprise, Titan,* and the *Aventine.*

If the subspace messages from the three starships were true, it would be nothing less than a miracle. It would be one of the most stunning reversals in the history of the Federation.

President Bacco knew she ought to be waiting on the admirals' report with undivided attention, but she was focused on a different spectacle. She and the other civilians in the room had gathered in a tight huddle in front of the painting *Bridge over a Pool of Water Lilies.*

Tucked in a fetal curl on the floor beneath the painting was Seven of Nine.

The statuesque blonde was normally so intimidating—Jas Abrik had described her with the less forgiving adjective "castrating"—that it shocked Bacco to see her like this.

Only minutes earlier, Seven had been conferring with the admirals and analyzing the reaction of the Borg armada to its sudden dislocation across vast reaches of space. Then, before anyone had realized anything was wrong, Seven had staggered away from the situation consoles, dazed and trembling. Seconds later, she had collapsed to the floor and folded in on herself.

Most of the people in the room had reacted by backing away from Seven, as if she might be transforming back into a drone bent on assimilating or assassinating them all.

Bacco had dashed from her chair toward the fallen woman, only to be forcibly intercepted by her senior protection agent.

"Ma'am, you should stay back," Wexler had said.

"Stay close, Steve, but get your hands off me."

Wexler let go of Bacco's arms and backed off. "Sorry, Madam President." She'd continued past him to Seven's side, and he had fallen in right behind her. His presence had seemed to reassure the others, who had slowly regrouped in a clutch around Seven.

Now Seven lay on her left side, with her arms wrapped around her head, unable or unwilling to respond to the gentle queries from Bacco and the others.

Piñiero asked Seven, "Can you hear us?"

No answer.

"I think she's hyperventilating," Abrik said.

Secretary Iliop said, "Maybe she's having a seizure."

Agent Kistler joined the huddle. "A doctor's coming."

Press liaison Kant Jorel asked, "Should we take her pulse?"

Piñiero threw a glare at him. "Are *you* a doctor now?"

Abrik cut in, "I wouldn't touch her if I were you. Last time we checked, those Borg implants of hers still work."

"Oh, for crying out loud," Bacco grumbled. "Move." She reached a hand toward Seven but paused as Akaar called to her.

"Madam President," the gray-haired admiral said, his voice loud and bright with the promise of good news. "The all-clear signals have been verified, and Captain Picard has confirmed that the Borg threat is over."

Piñiero asked with naked cynicism, "For how long?"

"Forever," Akaar said. "Captain Picard reports that the Borg . . . no longer exist."

Wide-eyed, Abrik stammered, "H—how?"

"The captain assures me it is 'a long story,' which he will explain fully in his report."

"He damned well better," Bacco said. "Because that's a story I want to hear." The sound of the secured door opening prompted her to look over her shoulder. One of the Palais's on-call doctors and a pair of medical technicians hurried inside, and Agent Kistler waved them over toward Seven.

"All right, everyone," said Agent Wexler. "Move back, please. Let the medical team through. Thank you."

Even as the others retreated to make room for the medics, Bacco stayed by Seven's side. The stricken woman was whimpering and sobbing into her shirtsleeves.

The doctor, a young Efrosian man who sported a haircut and a goatee that were trimmed much shorter than was customary in his culture, kneeled beside Bacco. "Madam President, we can take it from here," he said, opening his satchel of surgical tools.

"Just give me a moment," Bacco said. She reached out and placed her hand lightly on Seven's shoulder. Leaning down, she whispered in as soft and soothing a voice as she could muster, "Seven, it's Nan. Are you all right? Can you hear me, Seven?"

Bacco waited, her hand resting with a feather touch on Seven's shoulder. Then she felt a stirring, a hint of motion.

Seven's breathing slowed but remained erratic. In gradual motions, she lowered her arms, pushed herself from the floor, and rolled onto her back. As her face and left hand came into view, Bacco gasped.

The Borg implants were gone. A tiny mass of fine, silvery powder lay on the floor where Seven had rested her head, and a glittering residue clung to her left hand and temple.

"Seven," Bacco said, stunned. "Are you all right?"

With her beauty no longer blemished by the biomechanical scars of the Borg, Seven looked up at Nanietta Bacco with the tear-streaked face of an innocent.

"My name is Annika."

# 30

Rubble and dust crunched under Martok's boots and cane as he struggled to the summit of a great mound of shattered stone and steel, which only that morning had been the Great Hall.

He ignored the bolts of pain shooting up his broken leg. It had been crudely set and splinted with long, inflexible strips of metal salvaged from a ruptured bulkhead on the *Sword of Kahless*. His flagship's sickbay and all of its medical personnel had been killed during the calamitous battle against the Borg hours earlier. Without any of the advanced surgical tools that could repair his fractured femur, he had been forced to settle for a more old-fashioned treatment of his wound.

At the peak of the smoldering mound of debris, he steadied himself and kept his weight on his good leg. Pivoting in a slow circle, he drank in the devastation around him. The First City was a husk of its former self. Only the scorched, denuded skeletons of a few prominent architectural landmarks were still recognizable. Where once the city's main boulevard, the *wo'leng*, had cut like a scar from the Great Hall to the smooth-flowing waters of the *qIJbIQ*, its second great river, significant portions of the broad thoroughfare had been erased by chaotic smears of smoking wreckage and crashed transport vessels.

Thick clouds of charcoal gray and deep crimson blanketed the sky. A sharp, acrid bite of toxic smoke was heavy in the air, and the profusion of airborne dust left the inside of Martok's mouth dry and tasting of chalk. It reminded him of historical accounts of Qo'noS in the years immediately following the Praxis disaster, which had pushed the Klingon homeworld to the brink of environmental collapse. This was a catastrophe almost on par with that one. Seven major cities on Qo'noS had been destroyed before the Borg cubes had, inexplicably, withdrawn on reciprocal courses, back toward the Azure Nebula.

Councillors Kopek, Qolka, and Tovoj had died with the home guard fleet and a force of their allies defending Qo'noS. Councillors Grevaq, Krozek, and Korvog had died with Martok's fleet. Most of the other members of the High Council were at that moment missing in action, and Martok had no idea which of them would turn up alive or dead.

For the moment, Martok alone was the High Council, and the temptation to wield unitary power was taxing his will; the call of ambition was powerful, and it was all he could do to remind himself that succumbing to it was what had fatally undermined his predecessor, Chancellor Gowron.

*I will not make that mistake,* he vowed. *I will not be that man. That will not be my legacy.*

He limped across the ruins to stand with General Goluk.

"Do we have casualty reports yet, General?"

"Only preliminary numbers, my lord," Goluk said, poking at the portable computer in his hand.

Martok scowled to mask a sharp jolt of pain from his leg. "Tell me," he rasped.

"Sixteen million dead in the First City. Another seven million in Quin'lat, eleven million in Tolar'tu. Based on rough estimates from Krennla, An'quat, T'chariv, and Novat, we believe their combined death tolls will exceed forty-three million."

A dour grunt concealed Martok's dismay. "So, seventy-seven million worldwide?"

"Yes, my lord. Though, as I said, that's just an estimate."

Nodding, Martok looked away and let his eyes roam across the vista of death and destruction. Despite the solemnity and tragedy of the moment, he permitted himself a sardonic chortle.

Goluk asked, "Is something amusing, Chancellor?"

"This is the second time since I became chancellor that the Great Hall's been leveled," Martok said. "I could be wrong, but I think I might be the only chancellor who can make that claim." He stabbed the rubble with his cane, and bitter laughter welled up from his throat. Shaking his head, he continued, "Do you know what irritates me most?" He glanced at Goluk and then looked at the shattered stone under their feet. "I'd finally learned my way around this maze, and now I have to start over again."

Both men laughed, though Martok knew neither of them had any mirth in his heart. Though the Borg had been routed, to call this a victory would at best be an exaggeration.

The day was theirs, but no songs would be sung.

President Nanietta Bacco closed her eyes and drew a long breath to calm her frazzled nerves and steady her shaking hands. She waited until the pounding of her heart slowed by even the slightest degree, and she nodded to her press liaison, Kant Jorel, and her chief of staff, Esperanza Piñiero. "I'm ready."

Piñiero said to Agents Wexler and Kistler, "Let's go."

The two presidential bodyguards stepped forward and were the first ones through the door at the end of the hallway. A deep susurrus of echoing conversations filled the air. Bacco walked with her shoulders back and her chin up, leading her entourage into the main chamber of the Federation Council, which occupied the entire first floor of the Palais de la Concorde.

Her eyes adjusted to the dimmer lighting in the chamber and to the glare of the spotlight pointed at the lectern on the podium along the south wall. Every seat in every row on both the east and west sides of the chamber was filled, including those in the supplemental rows. The visitors' gallery was packed to capacity, and a row of security personnel held back a standing-room-only crowd of Palais staff and VIP guests along the north side of the speakers' floor.

Bacco wondered if the intensity of interest demonstrated by the staff, diplomats, councillors, and guests was any indicator of the public's interest in the address she had come to deliver. *I guess I'm about to find out,* she decided.

She moved to the lectern at the front of the podium and waited while the Council's leaders called for quiet. A constellation of small red lights snapped on in the shadows on the opposite side of the room, informing her that live subspace feeds of her address were being transmitted throughout known space.

From her right, Piñiero gave her the ready signal.

Speaking to the half-shadowed faces in the gallery and the focused stares of the councillors, Bacco intoned in her most stately voice, "Members of the Federation Council, foreign ambassadors, honored guests, and citizens of the Federation . . . this day has been a long time in coming."

As the glowing text of her speech crawled up a holographic prompter situated just off-center in front of the lectern, Bacco continued almost from memory, delivering the first address in decades that she'd composed without the aid of her chief speechwriter, Fred MacDougan, and his staff, who were all still light-years away from Earth, caught up in postevacuation chaos.

"It is my pleasure and my honor to be able to bring you good news," she said. "The Borg threat is over.

"The officers and enlisted crews of three starships have done what so much of our marshaled might could not. A joint effort by the *Starships Enterprise, Titan,* and *Aventine* has turned the tide this day, bringing an end not just to the Borg invasion of our space but to the tyranny and oppression of the Borg throughout the galaxy."

Spontaneous, powerful applause and cheering erupted from the gallery and the councillors' tiers. Bacco basked in the roar of approval for a few seconds, and then she motioned for silence. Gradually, the room settled, and she continued.

"In keeping with the finest traditions of Starfleet, these three crews accomplished this not through violence, not through some brute force of arms, but with compassion. This war has been brought to an end not by bloodshed but by an act of mercy.

"They took a chance on the better angels of their natures, reached out to a new ally, and transformed the Borg Collective into something benign, perhaps even noble. I am informed that across the Milky Way, trillions of drones have been liberated, their free will restored."

As quickly as she had earned the room's praise, now she felt its condemnation. Bitter whispers traveled among the councillors, and disapproving noises hissed in the gallery.

"This outcome might feel inadequate to those among us who want revenge on the Borg. I understand, I assure you. There is no minimizing the scope of the tragedy we have endured. According to even our most conservative estimates, more than sixty-three billion citizens of the Federation, the Klingon Empire, the

Romulan Star Empire, and the Imperial Romulan State were slaughtered by the Borg during this invasion."

She paused to compose herself, and she swallowed to relieve the dryness in her mouth and throat. "Sixty-three billion lives cut short," she said. "The mind boggles at the scope of it. Such a horrific crime against life seems to demand payback, in the form of a proportional response. But we must move beyond hatred and vengeance. The Borg Collective no longer exists, and we must remember that those who carried out its atrocities were victims themselves, slaves taken from their own worlds and their own families. Now the force that controlled them has been disbanded, and its emancipated drones have vanished to points unknown. There is, quite simply, no one left to blame."

A deep and thoughtful silence hung over the chamber, and Bacco took it as a positive sign as she pressed on.

"Let us instead remember those whose actions have earned our trust and our gratitude. Our staunch allies, the Klingons, stood with us in our hour of need and inspired us with their fearlessness. We witnessed great acts of gallant bravery and sacrifice by starship crews from the Imperial Romulan State and the Talarian Republic. The warbird *Verithrax* sacrificed itself in the defense of Ardana, and the Talarian third fleet was all but destroyed holding the line at Aldebaran, halting the Borg's advance in that sector. These heroic gestures must never be forgotten." Murmurs of concurrence filled the room.

Bacco found it difficult to read the next portion of her address, but she had no choice. The truth had to be faced.

"It is unfortunate," she continued, "that at a time when we should be rejoicing in our victory, we must mourn losses so tragic. It's natural, at a time such as this, for us to think of ourselves. We had not yet completely recovered from the Dominion War, and now dozens of worlds—including Deneva, Coridan, Risa, Regulus, Korvat, and Ramatis—lay in ruins. Dozens more, including Qo'noS, Vulcan, Andor, and Tellar, suffered devastating attacks. And we must remember that the Borg did not discriminate between us and our unaligned neighbors. They inflicted widespread damage on Nausicaa, Yridia, and Barolia. It is all but impossible to quantify the true scope of this calamity, to calculate the unestimated sum of sentient pain.

"In the aftermath of such a monumental catastrophe, the

prospect of rebuilding appears daunting. Some might say it's impossible to recover from such a disaster. I say it is not only possible, it is *essential*. We will rise anew. We will rebuild these worlds, and we will heal these wounds. We will reach out not only to our own wounded people but to those of our allies and our neighbors and even to those who have called themselves our rivals and our enemies."

Polite applause interrupted her, and she accepted it with a humble nod of thanks and acknowledgment. Then she lifted her voice and declared, "We will not shrink from the challenge of raising back up what the Borg have knocked down. We will honor the sacrifices of all those who fought and died to defend us, by committing ourselves to repairing the damage that's been done and creating a future that they would have been proud of.

"We will also rebuild Starfleet, to guarantee that all we have gained, with so much suffering and sacrifice, shall be preserved and defended."

This time, the clapping and cheering from the gallery were thunderous. Emboldened, she spoke more strongly, punching her words through the clamor.

"More important, though Starfleet is needed for recovery and reconstruction and to render aid, we will renew our commitment to its mission of peaceful exploration, diplomatic outreach, and open scientific inquiry. The *Luna*-class starships will continue— and, in *Titan*'s case, resume—their missions far beyond our borders: seeking out new worlds, new civilizations, and new life-forms and offering, to those that are ready, our hand in friendship.

"There are those who might doubt our ability to do all of these things at once. To them, I would say, don't underestimate the United Federation of Planets. Just because we have suffered the brunt of the injuries in this conflict, do not assume that we are weak or vulnerable. Don't mistake optimism for foolishness or compassion for weakness.

"With patience and courage, this can become a time of hope. As long as we remain united, we will emerge from these dark and hideous days into a brighter tomorrow, and we will do so stronger, wiser, and safer than we were before. Together, we can become the future that we seek and build the galaxy we want to live in. It will not come about quickly or easily. But until it does, never flinch, never weary, and never despair.

"Thank you, and good night."

Bacco stepped back from the lectern as the chamber shook with deafening applause. Shading her eyes with one hand, she saw that the councillors and the visitors in the gallery all were standing as they delivered their roaring ovation. She waved to both tiers of councillors, then to the far end of the room, before Piñiero and Wexler coaxed her to leave the podium and follow them out of the Council Chamber.

Her entourage, including security adviser Jas Abrik, fell into step around her as they moved to the exit and quick-stepped into the hallway beyond.

Only once they were through the door did Bacco realize that the corridor was now lined with members of the press. Questions were shouted at her from both sides, the words overlapping into a muddy wash of sound. Jorel and Piñiero repeatedly hollered back, "No comment! No questions, please!"

At the far end of the hallway, Wexler and Kistler ushered Bacco and her senior advisers into a secure turbolift, then stepped in after them, placing themselves directly in front of the doors as they closed, muffling and then erasing the hubbub of pestering press run amok.

Bacco sighed heavily. "Thank God that's over."

Kant Jorel replied, "It went well, Madam President."

"Yes, Jorel, I know. I was there."

Rebuked, he bowed his chin. "Yes, ma'am."

"It was a wonderful speech, ma'am," Piñiero said.

"It was all right," Bacco replied. "If Fred and his people had been here to polish it, it would've been great." She threw a pointed look at Abrik. "Whose idea was it to put them *all* on the transport to Tyberius? Was it Iliop? I'll throttle him."

He replied, "No idea, ma'am, but I thought the Churchill homage at the end was a nice touch."

"Absolutely," Piñiero agreed. "It's what people needed to hear."

Frowning, Bacco replied, "It's what *I* needed to hear." The pressure of the past month, far from being lifted, only seemed to weigh heavier on her shoulders. "The Borg are gone, but now everything else is up for grabs."

Abrik tilted his head sideways. "There's certainly the potential for a period of instability."

She looked at the middle-aged Trill as if all his spots had just fallen off. "Instability? When there's a water shortage on Draylax, that's cause for instability. We've got a dead zone for a hundred light-years in every direction around the Azure Nebula. More than forty percent of Starfleet's been *destroyed*. Sixty-three billion people are *dead*. Deneva's been wiped out, and our economy's about to implode. We're long past unstable. When the shock of all this wears off, I think we'll look back on the last sixteen years with longing and envy."

The turbolift doors opened onto the top floor, and the group stepped from the lift into the lobby outside Bacco's office. Wexler and Kistler entered the presidential office first. They stepped clear of the doorway to let Bacco, Abrik, Jorel, and Piñiero file in, and then the two agents faded into the woodwork, as always.

Bacco stepped behind her desk and looked out the panoramic window at the nighttime cityscape of Paris. She was filled with a sense of foreboding, a feeling that there was always some new evil lurking in the darkness. "It's a whole new ball game," she said. "But we have no idea who's playing—or what the rules are."

Piñiero replied with a shrug, "That's what keeps the job interesting, ma'am."

# EPILOGUE

Mourners moved in slow packs, their steps leaving crisp prints in the fine-ground regolith of pulverized stone and flesh. Tuvok noticed that the graphite-colored powder stuck to everything—his boots, his pants, his wife's shoes, the hem of her jacket, the tips of her close-cropped hair.

He had seen Deneva's lush Summer Islands years earlier, when they had boasted pristine white beaches, dazzling cities, and a thriving culture of visual arts and live music. It had been a vibrant, stimulating, and prosperous place.

When his youngest son, Elieth, had told him and T'Pel of his intention to take up residence there, it had seemed an unlikely locale for such a serious young Vulcan man. Then, after Elieth had moved, he had revealed his ulterior motive: He had gone to Deneva to persuade Ione Kitain, a daughter of the Fourth House of Betazed, to become his bride. At the time, T'Pel had decried Elieth's actions as "illogical." Tuvok suspected that his wife had used the term as a euphemism for "disappointing."

Elieth and Ione had wed while Tuvok was presumed lost with the rest of *Voyager*'s crew, and over the next few years, T'Pel had learned to accept her new, non-Vulcan daughter-in-law. Ione's sophisticated telepathic skills had helped matters along, but what had finally earned T'Pel's respect and acceptance was the great contentment and peace of mind Ione seemed to bring to Elieth, whose logic had long felt troubled during his youth.

Squatting low to the ground, Tuvok scooped up a palmful of gray-brown dust, which had the consistency of greasy flour. It clung to his skin even as he tried to clap it off.

T'Pel looked away, past the distant clusters of roving kith and kin to the dead. "Why did we come here, husband? Starfleet told us nothing survived in the Summer Islands and that there would be no remains or relics to recover."

"I wished to see this for myself," he said, rubbing his hands clean on the front of his trousers. He stood straight. In every direction, the Summer Islands lay like flat smears barely raised from the ocean, which now was stained brown and black.

Mastering the turmoil of his thoughts had become taxing for Tuvok. Despite the psionic therapy he had done with Counselor Troi to fortify his psychic control and telepathic defenses, which had been compromised by years of neurological trauma, he felt overwhelmed. Primitive emotions threatened to crack his dispassionate veneer. Rage and grief, despair and denial—they were black clouds blotting out the light of reason.

Resolved not to embarrass himself or T'Pel or to disgrace the memory of his slain youngest son, Tuvok stood firm against the darkest tides of his *katra,* even as he feared drowning in them, submerging into madness and never surfacing again.

"We should return to *Titan* now," T'Pel said.

"No," Tuvok said. "I am not ready yet."

T'Pel was confounded by his reply. "There is nothing else for us to find or do here. Staying longer serves no purpose."

"I do not wish to explain myself, T'Pel. I will remain here while I reflect on what has happened. I would prefer that you stay with me, but if you wish to depart, I will not stop you."

In pairs and trios or in small groups, people both young and old, male and female, and pilgrims of all species milled in stunned shock across the level stretch of total desolation. Tuvok watched them all seek in vain for something that was no longer to be found, for tangible artifacts of loved ones now gone.

An empty hush of wind off the sea roared in Tuvok's ears, and the breeze kicked up clouds of foul-smelling, choking dust.

When it died down and the heavy cloud started to settle, T'Pel said, "If you are pondering the details of our son's death, I would urge you to consider that most likely, it was swift and entailed only fleeting pain."

"The specifics of his demise are not important," Tuvok said. "I question his decision not to escape with Ione when it might still have been possible."

"Elieth was committed to law enforcement and to the service of others," T'Pel said, as if she were telling Tuvok something that he didn't already know. "If he and Ione stayed behind after the final transports left, he must have thought their choice to be the one that was most logical."

Tuvok's sea of troubled emotions swelled and threatened to swallow him whole. He grappled with a surge of irrational fury provoked by T'Pel's remark. His fists clenched white-knuckle tight, and his face hardened with bitter anger.

"I can see no logic in this, T'Pel. My son is dead."

Dark clouds were pulled taut across the leaden skies of Deneva. The ash-covered peaks of the Sibiran Range were obscured by tin-dull mists, and a diffuse light cast a dim gray pall over the desolate hills and plains that spread south from the mountains.

Worf tried not to inhale too deeply. The entire planet had a dusty, smoky odor, like a lingering tang of burnt hair. During his approach from orbit, via shuttle with Jasminder Choudhury, he had seen no traces of green on the planet's surface. Until they had pierced the bottom of the cloud cover, in fact, they had barely seen the surface at all. All but the most extreme polar latitudes of Deneva were encircled by rings of ash, dust, and smoke—the airborne residue of its vaporized cities.

He stood on the scorched plain and watched myriad shuttles and small ships descend from the death-polluted sky and seek out remote places to set down. Hundreds of thousands of people had come to Deneva in the past few days, since the travel interdiction had been lifted. The Federation had quarantined its surface until Starfleet had verified that visitors and returning denizens would face no lingering threats, either from the Borg or from radiation and other toxins. According to a message he had received that morning from his son, Alexander, conditions were much the same on Qo'noS and many worlds of the Klingon Empire.

A few meters away from him, Jasminder kneeled and scanned a patch of soil with her tricorder. She switched off the device. "Close enough," she said, standing up as a gust of warm air pelted them both with sand.

Worf squinted against the stinging breeze. "Are you sure?"

"The whole planet's a cinder," she said. "One patch of dirt will serve as well as another. We should get started."

They walked together to the back of their borrowed shuttle from the *Enterprise* and opened its rear hatch. Most of the passenger compartment had been filled with tools, supplies, and their one piece of precious cargo. Jasminder grabbed two shovels and handed one to Worf. "Thank you for coming with me."

"I am honored . . . and moved . . . that you invited me."

She favored him with a small, bittersweet smile, and then they stepped out of the shuttle and returned to the spot she'd selected. This, she'd told him during the flight down, was where her family home had stood, before the Borg had erased it from existence. They circled the spot she'd marked until they stood on either side of it, facing each other.

"Ready?" she asked.

"Yes."

Shovel tips were pressed into the dry, blackened soil and driven deep with pushes from their heels. The parched skin of the planet cracked and broke as Worf and Jasminder pulled on the shovels' handles. The two officers lifted thick clumps of dirt and heaved them to one side. They dug at the hard ground for a few minutes, until they had excavated a pit three-quarters of a meter deep and half a meter wide.

Setting aside the shovels, they returned to the shuttle and retrieved more supplies. Jasminder brought a large, clumsy-heavy pouch of chemicals, and Worf hefted a small drum of water onto his shoulder. They methodically emptied both into the hole.

Worf waited behind while she returned to the shuttle for the last and most crucial element.

She returned carrying in one hand a diminutive twig—Worf thought it hardly deserved to be called even a sapling, let alone a tree. He waited while she lowered it into the soaked and fertilized hole they'd prepared, and he held it upright and steady while she shoveled the dirt back in around its linen-wrapped roots. She tamped down the dirt with her boots, and then she piled more on top, until at last she had crafted a gently sloping round island around the skinny oak's wrist-thick trunk.

By the time Jasminder had finished, tears were flowing from her eyes, but she herself was quiet. She took a few backward steps, setting herself at a remove to survey her handiwork.

Worf stood beside her and said nothing. Across the blood-hallowed ground, the wind whispered its benedictions.

Jasminder wiped the tears from her face with the back of her hand, without once taking her eyes off the tree.

"It's so . . ." Grief robbed her of words. He reached out and rested his arm across her shoulders. She huddled beside him, under his embrace, and then she started over. "It's so *tiny*."

With a firm yet gentle clasp of her shoulder, he pulled her close and said, "It is a beginning."

Xin Ra-Havreii stood at the forefront of a throng gathered at the broad, starboard-facing windows in *Titan*'s arboretum. Much of the ship's crew had departed two weeks earlier for extended shore leave, after it had limped home to the Utopia Planitia yards above Mars for repairs and upgrades—all to be made under Ra-Havreii's expert supervision.

The Efrosian chief engineer stroked one long droop of his ivory-white mustache and speculated that his absent shipmates would regret not having been aboard to see that day's event with their own eyes.

*Sometimes videos do history no justice,* he mused.

A majority of the personnel who had packed into the high-ceilinged compartment to take advantage of its unobstructed view were not regular *Titan* personnel but technicians, mechanics, and engineers assigned to the Utopia Planitia facility. Among them, Ra-Havreii recognized many former friends and colleagues of his, from his days working there as a project director and starship designer. He hadn't spoken to many of them since the accident years earlier aboard the *Luna,* and he felt no desire to do so now. For their part, they seemed content to ignore him as well.

A whiff of delicate perfume stood out from the scents of flowers and green plants, and it turned Ra-Havreii's head. Standing behind his left shoulder was Lieutenant Commander Melora Pazlar, once more outfitted in her powered armature. Ra-Havreii smiled at her. "Good morning, Melora," he said.

"Good morning, Xin. Room for one more up front?"

The young Catullan man standing on Ra-Havreii's left glanced at Pazlar and then at the chief engineer, who furrowed his snowy brows and growled, "Make a hole, Crewman."

"Aye, sir," said the Catullan, as he nudged the rest of the line down a few steps to free up room for Pazlar.

She inched forward and pressed in close beside Ra-Havreii. "Thanks, Xin."

"My pleasure," he said. Looking around at the crush of spectators, he added, "I thought you hated crowds."

"I do," she said. "But I hate missing out even more."

Over the soft murmuring of the crowd, someone at the aft end of the compartment shouted, "Here they come!" Everyone leaned toward the windows and craned their necks, straining to see past everyone else, to bear witness to history.

Pazlar and Ra-Havreii shifted their weight and stood at matching angles while staring out at the stars, awaiting the main attraction. Facing aft, the blond Elaysian woman had her back to Ra-Havreii, who savored the fragrance of her hair.

"It's too bad they had to shut down my holopresence network while making repairs," she said over her shoulder, making eye contact as she noticed how close their faces were.

He nodded. "Yes, it's a shame. But the interruption is only temporary. Oh! Did I tell you about the new asymmetric interaction mode I created for it?"

"No, I don't think you did."

"You're going to love it," he said with unabashed pride in his work. "It lets your holographic avatar inflict amplified physical damage on real opponents while preventing any harmful effects from being transmitted back to you. It could prove very useful if *Titan* ever gets boarded again."

She smiled at him. "I have a theory about the holopresence system, you know."

"Really?" His eyebrows climbed up his forehead. "Do tell."

"I think it's proof you're in love with me."

Affecting a nonchalant air, he replied, "Ridiculous." Noting the amused glimmer in her gaze, he added with some hesitation, "I mean . . . love is, um, such a strong word, and we hardly—that is, we . . ."

"Simmer down, Commander," Pazlar said. "It's not the least appealing idea I've heard lately. And some of your past conquests have assured me that you know how to be gentle." Another teasing look. "Which is important for a gal like me."

"Well, obviously," he said. Tamping down his surging excitement, he decided to handle the matter with delicacy. "I find your invitation almost irresistible," he began.

She sounded insulted. "Almost?"

"Nigh irresistible," he corrected himself. "But before I surrender to my passions—and yours—it's absolutely vital that I be completely honest with you."

"About what?"

"Well, about me," he said. "I am deeply attracted to you, Melora, and in ways that I haven't felt about someone in a long time. But I'm afraid it's simply not in my nature to be, well, *monogamous.*"

She snickered, and then she laughed. "Who's asking?" Shaking her head, she turned aft and added softly, "Let's just see how our first date goes, okay?"

The more he learned about her, the more he adored her.

"Okay," he said. "Sounds like a plan."

Shining brighter than the stars, a white point grew larger as it neared the Utopia Planitia orbital shipyard. Edges resolved into forms and then into two distinct shapes linked by a glowing beam. At the forefront, a *Sabre*-class starship. Towed behind it, and held together by who knew what kind of high-tech legerdemain, was a twenty-second-century *NX*-class starship, its hull and nacelles scarred but still together.

An announcement over the intraship comm echoed from the overhead speakers. *"Attention, all* Titan *personnel,"* said Commander Vale. *"Muster starboard for passing honors."*

Outside, the *Sabre*-class vessel adjusted its course to glide past overhead, giving Ra-Havreii and the other spectators a perfect view of the registry on the ventral side of its primary hull: *U.S.S. da Vinci* NCC 81623. With precision and grace, its tractor beam guided its ward, the *Columbia* NX-02, past *Titan* to safety inside a docking slip.

Ra-Havreii didn't feel foolish or embarrassed to have tears brimming in his eyes while he watched the *Columbia*'s long-overdue homecoming, because everyone else in the arboretum did, too. With a solemn nod of salute to the old vessel, he whispered, "Welcome home, old girl."

The personal transport pod had barely settled to the ground near Vicenzo Farrenga's home in Lakeside on Cestus III when his five-year-old daughter, Aoki, was out the pod's side hatch and sprinting for the front door of their house.

He called after her, "Sweetie, wait for Daddy!"

The sable-haired little girl stopped on the snaking path of organically shaped paving stones that led away from the landing area. Vicenzo and his cousin, Frederico—more commonly known as Fred—pulled themselves out of the vehicle with the stiffness of men tasting their first years of early middle age.

"If you want to take the twins, I'll grab your bags," Fred said, using his handheld control to open the rear hatch.

"That'd be great, thanks," Vicenzo said.

He released the magnetic locks that held in place the horizontal bar of his infants' tandem safety seat. Then he lifted them out one at a time—Colin first and then Sylvana—and guided them into a double-pouch baby sling that enabled him to carry both children at once, one against his chest and the other on his back, while keeping his hands free.

As he straightened under the weight of his heavier-by-the-day scions, he saw that Fred had finished unloading the luggage and apparently was pondering which pieces to take inside first. "Don't hurt yourself," he said to his cousin. "Start with Aoki's bags—she mostly has pajamas and stuffed animals."

"Right," said Fred, who stacked Aoki's smaller flowered bags on top of a large one with wheels, extended the bottom bag's towing handle, and pulled it behind him as he followed Vicenzo toward the broad, immaculate A-frame cedar house.

Vicenzo breathed in the cool early morning air and admired the view of Pike's Lake surrounded by mostly undisturbed forest. Sunlight sparkled on the water, and a breeze brought him scents of wood smoke and pine.

His was one of few homes that had been built around the lake. One of the most attractive features of this piece of property, in his opinion, was that none of the houses around the lake had a view of another. Each was sequestered in a nook of the shoreline and sheltered by the forest.

He checked and confirmed that his two canoes and one row-boat were still tied to the small dock behind his house. The lawn furniture didn't appear to have been pilfered during his absence, and that much more was once again right in his world. He'd just spent seventeen days making an arduous, impromptu round-trip journey with his children, who had pestered him with an endless barrage of questions. There had been no way to tell them that they had, in fact, been running for their lives from the Borg, because Mommy had said to leave Federation space.

Even after President Bacco's startling address, when it had become clear that the Borg threat was over, getting home hadn't been easy. By then, he and the children had reached Pacifica, along with several million other hastily displaced refugees. It had taken six days to get there, then five days to book passage on another transport back to Cestus III. And, as he'd feared, he'd been deprived of communications every step of the way, up to and including the moment he and the kids had landed.

Fortunately, Fred had never even considered being evacuated from Cestus III and had been home with nothing better to do, as usual. After a gentle browbeating, he had agreed to come pick up Vicenzo and his brood from the starport in Johnson City.

Trudging up the walk to the house, Vicenzo winced as both twins began crying at once. In front of him, Aoki hopped with manic energy after barely plodding along behind him for two weeks. She cut the air with a shrill plea: "Faster, Daddy!"

"Hold your horses, Pumpkin," he said.

*It's good to be back at the house,* he thought with relief. *It'll be nice to sleep in my own bed. And eat my own cooking.*

As he approached the front door, it swung open ahead of him, and he stopped in midstride.

His breath caught with hope and surprise.

Aoki spun around toward the house and shrieked, "Mommy!" She ran at a full gallop into Miranda Kadohata's wide and waiting arms. Miranda scooped the girl off her feet, kissed her, and spun her around and around as they laughed with glee.

Vicenzo desperately wanted to sprint to his wife, but he didn't want to risk shaking the twins, so he trotted in a funny way that minimized the bouncing of his hurried steps.

Miranda turned, perched Aoki on her sundress-clad hip, and held the girl steady with her right arm; she used her left to embrace Vicenzo and the babies. She felt amazing in his arms, and she smelled even better. He had missed every inch of her.

"Welcome back, love," she said, her eyes gleaming with grateful tears. She kissed the top of Colin's head, and then she touched her fingertips to Sylvana's sparsely covered scalp and massaged it, in a peculiar flexing gesture that Vicenzo had nicknamed the hand spider. Within moments, both twins had stopped crying. She smiled at Vicenzo. "It's good to be home."

He kissed her again. "It is now."

\* \* \*

"A toast," Picard said, standing up from the table and raising his champagne glass. He waited for his dining companions to lift their own flutes, and he continued, "May our friendships, like fine wine, only improve with time's advance, and may we always be blessed with old wine, old friends, and young cares. Cheers."

"Hear! Hear!" replied Will Riker, who saluted Picard with his glass and then took a sip, cuing the other guests to drink.

Picard returned to his chair beside Beverly, who sat on his left. Riker occupied the other seat beside her, and past him was Deanna Troi. An empty chair separated Troi from Ezri Dax.

"What an amazing dinner," Dax said, gathering another spoonful of chocolate mousse. "Thank you for inviting me."

"Every new commanding officer deserves to be treated at least once to a meal in the Captains' Lounge," Picard said with a collegial smile. "Not only is the cuisine exquisite, but the view is spectacular."

His comment turned everyone's eyes to the vista beyond the restaurant's concave wraparound wall of flawless transparent aluminum. Set against a perfect black curtain of star-flecked space was the majestic, looming curve of Mars's southern hemisphere.

The real focus of attention, however, was the newly arrived vessel in the docking slip below the VIP guests' table. The *Columbia* NX-02 was being swarmed over and doted on by a small army of engineers, mechanics, and technicians, who had begun the task of restoring the ship so that it could return under its own power to Earth orbit, completing the ill-fated journey it had started more than two centuries earlier.

Riker sighed with admiration of the vintage starship. "They really knew how to make 'em back then, didn't they?"

Dax replied with mock injured pride, "I think they make 'em just fine now, thank you very much."

"It is amazing, though," Troi said. "To think of how much of history was shaped by the fate of that one ship."

"Like the butterfly effect," Beverly interjected. "One decision today can spell life or death for a billion people a hundred years from now. You just never know."

"True," Riker replied. "Maybe the universe is more like the subatomic realm than we normally think—full of invisible effects and unseen consequences." He looked at Picard. "What do you think, Jean-Luc?"

"I think perhaps you've all had enough champagne," he said, trying to hold a stern poker face and failing as a smile cracked through his mask of propriety. It felt good to laugh and be the man he'd hidden from view for so many years. He felt as if he had come home to himself at long last.

His friends chortled good-naturedly with him, and then Riker said, "Seriously, though, what do you think?"

Picard permitted himself a moment of introspection. Until recently, he had dreaded such self-reflection, because his inner life had been haunted by the shadow of the Borg. Now, granted a measure of peace and solitude, he thought about the sensations and impressions that had lingered after the Caeliar's transformation of the Collective. He sipped his demitasse of espresso and appraised his newly altered worldview.

"I think that we're all echoes of a greater consciousness," he said. "Cells of awareness in a scheme we can't understand. At least, not yet."

Beverly seemed taken aback by his answer. Leaning toward him, she rested her hand on his forearm and said, "Is that really what you believe, Jean-Luc?"

He arched one eyebrow. "I hesitate to call it a *belief*," he said. "Let's just say it's an *idea* that I'm entertaining."

"Pretty big idea," Riker said, flashing his trademark smile behind his close-cut salt-and-pepper beard.

Picard shrugged. "Why think small? Thinking is free."

Dax folded her napkin and set it on the table. "Sorry to eat and run, but I have to get back to the *Aventine* by 1900. We're expecting new orders from Starfleet Command."

As she got up, Picard and Riker stood as well. Smoothing the front of his tunic, Picard said with genuine optimism, "An exploration mission, perhaps?"

"Not likely, I'm afraid," Dax said. "I spoke to Admiral Nechayev before I came to dinner. She told me the *Aventine*'ll be needed to help coordinate rescue and recovery efforts inside the Federation for at least the next few months." She frowned. "Seems like a waste of a perfectly good slipstream drive, if you ask me. Now that it's fully online, I was hoping we'd get to visit a new galaxy or something."

Riker gently chided her, "A *new* one? Do you mind if we finish exploring *this* one first?"

"Don't be silly, William," Dax teased, standing on tiptoes to plant a chaste kiss on his cheek. "That's what Starfleet has *you* for." The sweetness of her smile took the sting out of her jibe. To Picard, she said, "Captain, it's been a pleasure and an honor. I hope our paths get to cross again someday."

"I'm certain they will," Picard said. With a nod at the table, he added, "But next time, you're buying dinner."

"You're on," the diminutive Trill captain said. Then she turned, said her farewells with Beverly and Troi, and left the restaurant in quick strides, without a backward glance. By the time she had finished her exit, Troi and Beverly had risen from the table to stand with Riker and Picard.

"She's something else," Beverly said, with a combination of admiration and exasperation.

"Yes," Troi said. "She's exceptionally sure of herself."

Picard and Riker traded amused glances, and Picard said to the two women, "She can't help it—she's a Dax."

Crusher poked Picard's chest. "And I'm a Howard woman."

"And I'm a daughter of the Fifth House, heiress to the Sacred Chalice of Rixx and the Holy Rings of Betazed," Troi said. After a horrified pause, she added, "And I'm turning into my mother."

"God, I hope not," Riker muttered.

"What was that?" Troi snapped.

"Nothing."

"Mm-hmm."

Sensing that it might be a good time to change the subject, Picard said, "Does *Titan* have its new orders yet?"

"Nope," Riker said. "We're moving to McKinley Station tomorrow at 0800 for some upgrades and refits. We'll find out what's next once we're done with repairs." He shook his head and after a rueful sigh, added, "I do love a surprise."

"Listen to you two," Beverly said to the men. She and Troi looked irked with them as she continued, "You talk like the biggest things in your lives are light-years away."

Troi added, "Did you forget your new assignments already?"

Knowing glances of mock dread passed between the two men.

"Parenthood . . . ," Riker began.

". . . the final frontier," Picard finished.

Beverly pretended to ignore them as she asked Troi, "Have you two picked out a name yet?"

"No," Troi said. "You?"

Beverly shook her head. "Not yet. It's been a matter of some . . . contention."

"I know the feeling," Troi said, wrinkling her brow in frustration at her husband, who rolled his eyes.

"We should go," Riker said. He reached forward and shook hands with Picard. Before the elder captain could speak, Riker added, "Don't tell me to be careful."

"I wouldn't dream of it," Picard said. "Be bold."

"That sounds like the Captain Picard I know." He let go of Picard's hand, slapped his shoulder, and added more softly, "Good to have you back." He and Troi bade Beverly farewell, and Picard saw them off with the hopeful valediction, "*Au revoir.*"

Then he and Beverly were alone in the Captains' Lounge, which had been closed for his private event. Sometimes being a famous savior of the Federation had its perquisites.

Beverly took his hand, and they stood together, staring in wonder at the austere majesty of the universe. A grim chapter of his life now felt closed, and a new, brighter chapter was about to begin. Old debts had been settled, and old promises had been kept. His obligations to the past were fulfilled, and for the first time in decades, he was free to contemplate the future.

Wistfully, Beverly asked, "What will you do in a universe without the Borg, Jean-Luc?"

He didn't answer right away. It was not a glib question.

Squeezing her hand in his firm but gentle grip, he met her reflected gaze in the window and said, "I'll hope that our son is born healthy. . . . I'll hope that we can be good parents. . . . I'll hope that he can grow up in a galaxy of peace."

He regarded his own reflection with a smile.

"I'll hope."

*Terminat hora diem, terminat auctor opus.*

# APPENDIX I
## 2156

### Featured Crew Members

*Columbia* NX-02

**Captain Erika Hernandez**
(human female) commanding officer

**Commander Veronica Fletcher**
(human female) executive officer

**Lieutenant Commander Kalil el-Rashad**
(human male), second officer/science officer

**Lieutenant Karl Graylock**
(human male) chief engineer

**Lieutenant Johanna Metzger**
(human female) chief medical officer

**Lieutenant Kiona Thayer**
(human female) senior weapons officer

**Ensign Sidra Valerian**
(human female) communications officer

**Major Stephen Foyle**
(human male) MACO commander

**Lieutenant Vincenzo Yacavino**
(human male) MACO second-in-command

**Sergeant Gage Pembleton**
(human male) MACO first sergeant

# APPENDIX II
# STARDATE 58100
# (early February 2381)

### Featured Crew Members

#### *U.S.S. Enterprise* NCC-1701-E

**Captain Jean-Luc Picard**
(human male) commanding officer

**Commander Worf**
(Klingon male) executive officer

**Commander Miranda Kadohata**
(human female) second officer/operations officer

**Commander Geordi La Forge**
(human male) chief engineer

**Commander Beverly Crusher**
(human female) chief medical officer

**Lieutenant Hegol Den**
(Bajoran male) senior counselor

**Lieutenant Jasminder Choudhury**
(human female) chief of security

**Lieutenant Dina Elfiki**
(human female) senior science officer

**Lieutenant T'Ryssa Chen**
(Vulcan-human female) contact specialist

#### *U.S.S. Titan* NCC-80102

**Captain William T. Riker**
(human male) commanding officer

**Commander Christine Vale**
(human female) executive officer

**Commander Tuvok**
(Vulcan male) second officer/tactical officer

**Commander Deanna Troi**
(Betazoid-human female) diplomatic officer/senior counselor

**Commander Xin Ra-Havreii**
(Efrosian male) chief engineer

**Lieutenant Commander Shenti Yisec Eres Ree**
(Pahkwa-thanh male) chief medical officer

**Lieutenant Commander Ranul Keru**
(Trill male) chief of security

**Lieutenant Commander Melora Pazlar**
(Elaysian female) senior science officer

**Lieutenant Pral glasch Haaj**
(Tellarite male) counselor

**Lieutenant Huilan Sen'kara**
(Sti'ach male) counselor

**Ensign Torvig Bu-kar-nguv**
(Choblik male) engineer

## U.S.S. Aventine NCC-82602

**Captain Ezri Dax**
(Trill female) commanding officer

**Commander Samaritan Bowers**
(human male) executive officer

**Lieutenant Commander Gruhn Helkara**
(Zakdorn male) second officer/senior science officer

**Lieutenant Lonnoc Kedair**
(Takaran female) chief of security

**Lieutenant Simon Tarses**
(human-Romulan male) chief medical officer

**Lieutenant Mikaela Leishman**
(human female) chief engineer

**Lieutenant Oliana Mirren**
(human female) senior operations officer

# ACKNOWLEDGMENTS

A trilogy is a large and complex undertaking, one that I knew from the outset would be greater in its scope and more demanding in its execution than any of my previous projects. I am, therefore, grateful for the support and encouragement of Kara, my lovely and patient wife, who was so good to me, and so understanding, as I spent most of my nights for more than fifteen months secluded behind closed doors writing this trilogy. Kara, my love, it would have been unbearable without you.

As for where all this started, I guess we can thank (or blame) artist Pierre Drolet, whose painting of the crashed *Columbia* NX-02 in the book *Ships of the Line* planted the seed of this idea in the minds of my esteemed editors, Marco Palmieri and Margaret Clark.

Margaret and Marco, I thank you for tolerating my bouts of uncertainty, my moments of dudgeon while I received your eminently reasonable story notes, and my adolescent practical jokes as we neared the finish line. ("All work and no play makes Mack a dull boy.") I couldn't have done this without you both.

Geddy Lee, thank you for taking an hour of your time to talk with a stranger, and for sharing your lovely anecdote about French vineyards, and the way that vines are like people, in that adversity adds depth and complexity to their characters. I hope you will forgive me for making use of it in this tale, and that you will approve of the manner in which it was applied.

Keith R.A. DeCandido, Kirsten Beyer, and Christopher L. Bennett, thank you one and all for going above and beyond the call of duty to help me vet all three books of this trilogy. My thanks also go out to Michael A. Martin and Andy Mangels, who graciously tweaked their *Star Trek Enterprise* novel *Kobayashi Maru* to track with situations I had established, and for suggesting that Doctor Ree ought to bite Counselor Troi. Nice idea, gents!

Heartfelt thanks also are due to authors Geoffrey Thorne and Kirsten Beyer, for their moments of sage advice. And, if I'm being honest, I really ought to thank google.com, dictionary.com, thesaurus.com, Memory Alpha and Memory Beta (the *Star Trek* wiki reference sites), and WikiPedia. How did people write novels without the Internet?

# ACKNOWLEDGMENTS

To revive an old tradition of mine, I wish to thank the composers who helped create the numerous original film and TV scores that serve as my link to my muse while I write. Many of my favorite moments throughout the trilogy were coaxed from my imagination by the music of Bear McCreary (*Battlestar Galactica*), Tyler Bates (*300*), Alan Silvestri (*Beowulf*), Javier Navarette (*Pan's Labyrinth*), Thomas Newman (*The Shawshank Redemption*), Hans Zimmer (the *Pirates of the Caribbean* scores), and Dario Marianelli (*V for Vendetta*).

Penultimately, I need to thank author Robert Metzger for having made me aware of the concept of catoms, in an article he wrote for the *SFWA Bulletin*. Astute readers might have wondered if the character of Doctor Johanna Metzger in *Gods of Night* and *Mere Mortals* was named in his honor; she was.

Lastly, I'd like to extend my heartfelt thanks to those few, special people in Lynchburg, Tennessee, who do what they do so well, so that I can do what I do at all.

# ABOUT THE AUTHOR

DAVID MACK is the national bestselling author of more than twenty novels and novellas, including *Wildfire, Harbinger, Reap the Whirlwind, Precipice, Road of Bones, Promises Broken,* and the *Star Trek Destiny* trilogy: *Gods of Night, Mere Mortals,* and *Lost Souls.* He developed the *Star Trek Vanguard* series concept with editor Marco Palmieri. His first work of original fiction is the critically acclaimed supernatural thriller *The Calling.*

In addition to novels, Mack's writing credits span several media, including television (for episodes of *Star Trek: Deep Space Nine*), film, short fiction, magazines, newspapers, comic books, computer games, radio, and the Internet.

His upcoming works include the new *Vanguard* novel *Storming Heaven,* and a *Star Trek* trilogy scheduled for late 2012. He resides in New York City with his wife, Kara.

Visit his website, www.davidmack.pro/, and follow him on Twitter @DavidAlanMack and on Facebook at www.facebook .com/david.alan.mack.